David Anthony Durham was born in Ne award-winning author of the acclaimed nove... *Gabriel's Story, Walk Through Darkness* and *Hannibal: Pride of Carthage*. He and his family lived in Scotland for several years but are now based in California, where he teaches at Cal State University.

Also by David Anthony Durham

Gabriel's Story
Walk Through Darkness
Hannibal: Pride of Carthage

For more information on David Anthony Durham and his books,
see his website at www.davidanthonydurham.com

Acacia

BOOK ONE:
THE WAR WITH THE MEIN

David Anthony Durham

Doubleday

LONDON · TORONTO · SYDNEY · AUCKLAND · JOHANNESBURG

TRANSWORLD PUBLISHERS
61–63 Uxbridge Road, London W5 5SA
A Random House Group Company
www.rbooks.co.uk

First published in Great Britain
in 2008 by Doubleday
an imprint of Transworld Publishers

Copyright © David Anthony Durham 2007
Map © David Cai

A CIP catalogue record for this book
is available from the British Library.

ISBN 9780385614467 (cased)
9780385614474 (tpb)

Addresses for Random House Group Ltd companies outside the UK
can be found at: www.randomhouse.co.uk
The Random House Group Ltd Reg. No. 954009

The Random House Group Limited supports The Forest Stewardship
Council (FSC), the leading international forest-certification organization. All our
titles that are printed on Greenpeace-approved FSC-certified paper carry the FSC logo.
Our paper procurement policy can be found at
www.rbooks.co.uk/environment

Printed and bound in Great Britain by
Clays Ltd, Bungay, Suffolk

2 4 6 8 10 9 7 5 3 1

Mixed Sources
Product group from well-managed
forests and other controlled sources
FSC www.fsc.org Cert no. TT-COC-2139
© 1996 Forest Stewardship Council

For Laughton and Patricia

ACKNOWLEDGMENTS

IN ADDITION to my wife, Gudrun, I'd like to thank Laughton Johnston and Gerry LeBlanc for reading this thing in manuscript form, and James Patrick Kelly for giving it a positive nod also. I'm grateful to Sloan Harris for being a stellar agent and to Gerald Howard for being a real editor. Thanks also to all the folks at the Stonecoast MFA program, especially the Popular Fiction crew for their support as I transitioned to the dark side. And thanks to everyone at Doubleday and Anchor. I may have written this little story, but it took more people than I can name here to produce the finished novel now in your hands.

CONTENTS

Book One
The King's Idyll
1

❋

Book Two
Exiles
193

❋

Book Three
Living Myth
399

❋

Epilogue
567

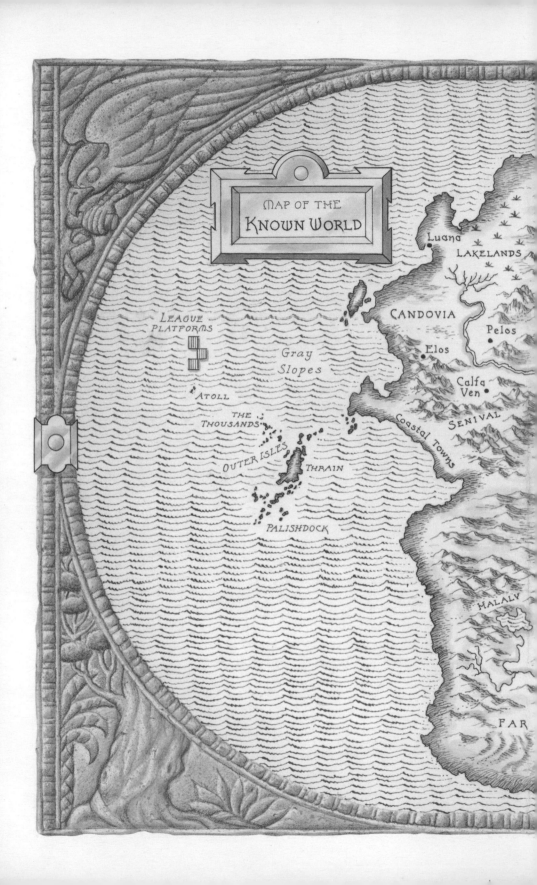

ICE FIELDS

BLACK MTS.

Mein Tahalian

BARRENS

GRADTHIC RANGE

AUSHENIA FOREST

MEIN PLATEAU

Hardith

GRADTHIC GAP

Careven

Scatevith

Cathgergen

Killintich

The Sinks

METHALIAN RIM

Aushenguk Fell

AUSHENIA

EILAVAN WOODLANDS

Alyth

MAINLAND

Aos

Manil

River Ask

Alecia

Danos

PRIOS

Inner Sea

Crall
MINES

ACACIA

CAPE OF FALLON

VUMU ARCHIPELAGO

KIDNABAN

Bacoum

TEH COAST

Uvumal

TEHEEN HILLS

Ruinat

Galat

VUMAIR

TALAY

BALBARA

Palik

Umae

BETHUNI

SOUTH

(Santoth)

Book One

The
King's Idyll

CHAPTER

ONE

The assassin left the stronghold of Mein Tahalian by the great front gate, riding through a crack in the armored pine beams just wide enough to let him slip out. He departed at sunrise, dressed much as any soldier of the Mein. He wore a cloak of elk fur that wrapped his body completely. It even covered his legs and gave warmth to the large-hoofed mount beneath him. Over his torso he wore a breastplate of double thickness: two sheaves of iron pounded to the contours of his body, with a layer of otter fur pressed beneath them. He moved south through a snowy land frozen into gelid brilliance.

The winter was so bitterly cold that for the first few days the man's breath crystallized as it escaped his lips. The vapor formed a strange protuberance around his mouth, making the passage into it a cavelike channel. Knots of ice dangled from his beard, brushing against each other like glass chimes. He met few people, even when he passed through settlements of low, domed shelters. He saw the prints of white foxes and hares in the snow but rarely the creatures themselves. Once a snow cat paused to watch his progress from atop a boulder, its gaze one of indecision, considering whether he ought to flee the rider or pursue him. In the end he did neither, and the man put the beast to his back.

On one occasion he crested a rise and looked out upon a plain teeming with reindeer. It was sight almost unseen since distant times. At first he thought he might have wandered upon a gathering from the spirit world. Then he smelled the musty stink of the animals. This broke the mood of mystery. He rode down into them, taking joy in the way the herd peeled away from him, the sound of their hooves a rumble he felt inside his chest.

If Mein lands had been their own, he might have hunted these creatures as his ancestors had. But his wish did not change the reality. The race of people called the Mein, the high northern plateau of the same name, the great fortress of Tahalian, the royal line of men who should rule the territory without interference, all had been servants to Acacia for the last five hundred years. They had been defeated, massacred in great numbers, and since overseen by foreign governors. They had been taxed unfairly and robbed of fighting men, many of whom were sent to serve in the Acacian military in distant lands far from home, out of the hearing of their ancestors. This, at least, was how the rider saw it—as an injustice that should not go on forever.

Twice in the first week he cut away from the main road to avoid Northern Guard checkpoints. His papers were in order. In all likelihood he would not have been delayed, but he had no trust in Acacians and abhorred the notion of even feigning acknowledgment of their authority. Each looping excursion brought him closer to the Black Mountains that paralleled his route. Their peaks jutted up out of the snow like enormous flakes of obsidian that had been chipped to razor sharpness. If old tales were to be believed, the summits were the points of spearheads slammed up through the roof of their world by the race of angry giants whose own land lay beneath the earth's skin.

After ten days of riding, he reached the edge of the Methalian Rim, the southern boundary of the Mein. He paused a moment to look down at the fertile woodlands three thousand feet below, aware that he would never again breathe the high country air. He slipped the headgear from his mount and dropped it where he stood. He chose a looser rein arrangement that bore no trace of his origins. Though it was still chilly and the land dusted with frost, he unfastened his cloak and tossed it to the ground. He drew out a dagger and slit the leather band that secured his helmet. He hurled the dome into the bushes and shook out his hair. Loosed from the confines of pounded metal, it whipped out as if in joy at the newfound freedom, long and brown. His hair was one of the features that had prompted him to take this assignment on. It bore little resemblance to the brittle straw coloration of most of the Mein race and had always embarrassed him.

After putting on a cotton shirt to disguise his breastplate, the horseman and his mount descended from the heights. They rode a switchback trail that spilled out onto a terrain of an altogether different sort, a temperate forest of hardwood trees, dotted with the small woodland settlements that made up the northern extent of the lands administered directly from Alecia, the bureaucratic seat of the Acacian government.

As his mastery of the empire's tongue was loathsome to him he rarely spoke to anybody, except on the occasions that he had no choice. When he sold his horse to a trader at the southern edge of the woodlands he growled into the back of his hand, mumbling and gruff. He accepted in payment coins of the realm, clothes that would not attract attention, and a sturdy pair of leather boots, as he would walk the rest of the way to the shore. Thus he was transformed again.

He followed the main road to the south, a large sack slung over his shoulder. It bulged here and there with the items he would yet need. He passed the nights huddled in depressions at the edge of farms or in patches of woodland. Though the people around him believed the land to be gripped by winter, to him it was more like a Tahalian summer, warm enough that he found himself sweating.

Not far from the port of Alecia he discarded his garb once more. He peeled off his breastplate, sunk it beneath stones in a riverbed, and took up a cloak that had been sewn in the cold chambers of the Mein, hoping that it would pass for authentic. With it draped across his shoulders he appeared to be one of the Vadayan. Though an ancient order, the Vadayan were no longer the functioning religious sect they had once been. They were scholars who studied and preserved the old lore under the ceremonial direction of the priestess of Vada. They were a closemouthed group, disdainful of the workings of the empire. As such, it would not appear odd that he had few words for those around him.

To complete his appearance, the man shaved the sides of his head and bound the long hair at the top of his skull up into one tight knot wrapped in thin strips of leather. The skin at either side of his head was as pale and pink as pig flesh. He rubbed a tanning agent used to stain wood into it. Once completed, none but the keenest of eyes would have taken him for anything other than the scholar he pretended to be.

Though he wore these various guises with composure, he was in truth none of the things he passed for. His name was Thasren Mein. He was born of noble blood, son of the late Heberen Mein. He was the younger brother of Hanish, the rightful chieftain of the tribes of the Mein Plateau, and of Maeander, head of the Punisari, the elite guard force and proud heart of his people's martial tradition. It was a lineage to be proud of, but he'd set all else aside to become an assassin. For the first time his existence truly made sense to him. He had never been more focused than he was now, more complete in himself, charged with a mission he had sworn his life to. How many walking the earth know exactly why they breathe and understand exactly what they must do before passing into the afterdeath? How fortunate he was.

From aboard a transport boat, he watched the isle of Acacia push out of the pale green sea in a knotted jumble of rock. It was innocent enough at a distance. The island's highest point was at the southern end. In the center, the hilly farmland and ridges dropped somewhat, but rose again into the series of plateaus that generations of settlement had carved into a land fit to house the palace. Acacia trees stood as dark as the black-skinned Talayans of the south, wearing great crests of plumage, dotted here and there with white blossoms. Despite the great twisting length of the island's coastline relatively little of it was easily accessible; beaches and ports were few.

Sailing past the port's protective towers Thasren saw a flag of the empire, hanging limp from lack of breeze. He knew from the colors what he would see if it had stood out: a yellow sun inside a red-bordered square, at the center a black silhouette of the tree that gave this island its name. Every child of the Known World recognized the emblem, no matter how far distant their place of birth. The assassin had to check his desire to clear the phlegm from his throat and spit in contempt.

He climbed from the boat to the main dock in a rush of other passengers, merchants and laborers, women and children, all leaping the gap above the crystal-clear water like herd animals. There were a few other Vadayan among them, but Thasren avoided eye contact with them. Standing on the solid stone of the dock as his fellow passengers moved around him, he understood that he was about to step into the mouth of the enemy. If any person around him now found out his name or could divine his thoughts, he would become the target of every dagger, sword, and spear on the island. He waited a moment longer than he intended, surprised that nobody condemned him. Nobody shouted warnings or even paused to study him.

He took in the great wall of a pinkish stone with cold eyes. Beyond it, spires and towers and domes jutted up into the air, many of these painted dark blue or a somber red or a brown with a rusty quality, some gilded and twinkling in the sunlight. The structures rose terraced level by level with the steepness of a sheer mountain. It was beautiful to behold; even he could acknowledge that much. It was nothing like the low, brooding presence of the assassin's home. Tahalian was built with massive beams of fir wood, half dug into the ground as protection from the cold, undecorated because so much of the year it was drowned in winter darkness, with snow piled high on every flat surface. The difference between the two was hard to square, and so Thasren shook off thought of it.

He strolled toward the gates of the lower town. It might take some time, but he would find his way deep into the city, taking on whatever guises he needed until he gained entry to the palace itself. There he would answer the question put casually by his second brother just a month before. If they wished to kill a beast with many arms, Maeander had said, why not cut off the head to start with? Then they could deal with the limbs and body as the creature stumbled around sightless, without leadership. The assassin had only to get near enough to this head and to wait for the proper moment to strike it and to do it in public, so that word of the act would spread like a contagion from one mouth to another.

Chapter

Two

To help her through the slow tedium of the morning tutorial Mena Akaran always sat in exactly the same spot, on a tuft of grass behind her siblings. She had just turned twelve and from this vantage point she could see through a missing tooth in the stone balustrade that hemmed in the courtyard. It framed a scene that began with the many-layered terraces of the palace. It dropped through a stretch of space beyond the town's western wall, then gave way to the swelling ranks of the cultivated hills. The farthest rise of land was the highest: the far promontory known as Haven's Rock. She had been there with her father and remembered the foul-smelling, cacophonous seabird life of the place, with head-dizzying views that dropped a craggy fifteen hundred feet straight into the foaming swells.

Sitting in the high, open-air classroom in which the king's children met with their tutor, Mena's thoughts would drift off. This morning she imagined herself a gull pushing free of the rock face. She hurtled down and shot out over the surface of the water. She darted between the sails of fishermen's vessels and out over the trading barges that floated the sea on the circular currents that moved them from one place to another. She left these behind and the waves grew steeper. The turquoise water deepened to blue and then to seal-black. She flew past the shoals of sparkling anchovies and out over the backs of whales, seeking the unknown things that she knew would eventually emerge from the whitecapped edge of the horizon. . . .

"Mena? Are you with us, Princess?" Jason, the royal tutor, and both her brothers and her sister were all staring at her. The children sat on the damp grass. Jason stood before them, poised with an old volume in one hand, his other one resting on his hip. "Did you hear the question?"

"Of course she did not hear the question," Aliver said. At sixteen he was the eldest of the king's children, the heir apparent to the throne. He had recently shot upward past his father's height, and his voice had changed. His expression was one of interminable boredom, an illness that struck him about a year ago and had yet to release him. "She was thinking about fish again. Or about porpoises."

"Neither fish nor porpoises have bearing on the topic we're discussing," Jason said. "So I'll repeat: Whom did the founder of the Akaran dynasty unseat at Galaral?"

That was the question she missed? Anybody could answer that! Mena hated responding to simple questions. She found pleasure in knowledge only when she stood out from others. Dariel, her younger brother, knew who the first king was and what he had done, and he was only nine. She held out for as long as she could, but when Aliver opened his mouth with some jibe, she spoke quickly.

"Edifus was the founder. He was born into suffering and darkness in the Lakes, but he prevailed in a bloody war that engulfed the whole world. He met the Untrue King Tathe at Galaral and crushed his forces with the aid of Santoth Speakers. Edifus was the first in an unbroken line of twenty-one Akaran kings, of which my father is the most recent. Edifus's sons, Thalaran, Tinhadin, and Praythos, set about securing and solidifying the empire through a series of campaigns called the Wars of Distribution—"

"All right," Jason said. "More than I asked for . . ."

"A seagull."

"What?"

"I was being a seagull, not a fish or a porpoise." She scrunched up her face at Aliver and then turned to give Corinn the same.

Sometime later, after having tried unsuccessfully to resume her avian imaginings, Mena contented herself with following the conversation. The discussion had turned to geography. Corinn named the six provinces and managed to say something about their ruling families and forms of government: the Mainland to the near north, the satrapy of the Mein in the far north, the Candovian Confederacy to the northwest, Talay to their south, and the mountain tribes of Senival to the west. The linked islands collectively called the Vumu Archipelago made up the last province, though it did not have the centralized government of the others.

Jason rolled a map out on the grass and had the children tack the edges down with their knees. Dariel always took particular pleasure in maps. He leaned close to it and repeated anything the tutor said as if he were translating the information for another listener. Something about the slow way he did this spurred Mena to interrupt him.

"Why is Acacia always at the center of maps?" she asked. "If the world curves and has no end—as you taught us, Jason—how is one place the center and not another?"

Corinn found the question silly. She glanced at Jason with upraised eyebrows and a wrinkled pursing of her lips. At fifteen, she was attractive and knew it, with the olive complexion and rounded face that had come to epitomize Acacian beauty. Much of their dead mother, Aleera, lived on in her; at least, that was what everyone seemed to think. "It just is the center, Mena. Everyone knows that."

"Succinctly put," Jason said, "but Mena does make a point. All peoples think of themselves first. First, central, and foremost, yes? I should show you a map from Talay sometime. They draw the world quite differently. And why wouldn't they think themselves the center of the world? They are a great nation also—"

Aliver guffawed. "Be serious! The men and women walk around half naked down there. They hunt with spears and worship gods that look like animals. They still use small tribal governments—chiefs and all that. They are no better than the squabbling Mein."

"And it's too hot there," Corinn added. "They say the earth dries to powder for half the year. They have to drink from holes dug in the ground."

Jason conceded that the Talayan climate was harsh, especially in the far south. And he knew they would always think of their ways as inferior to Acacian customs. There was a reason Acacia held sway over the entire Known World. He said, "We are a gifted people. But we are also a benevolent people. We should not disdain Talayans or any other—"

"I didn't say I disdained them. They have their ways and when I am king I will try to respect them. Now, why is this map out? Do you have something to teach us or not?"

Jason, noting the flare of impatience in Aliver's tone, nodded. He smiled his agreement and let the topic drop. He was a teacher, yes, but he never forgot that he was also a servant. Sometimes that seemed unfortunate to Mena. How were they to truly learn about the world if they could silence their tutors just by raising the pitch of their voices?

The lesson resumed, all of them listening to Jason without further interruption. But they were not at it long. A few minutes later their father, King Leodan, pushed through the doorway and breathed in the morning air. His face had the texture of tanned leather. A dusting of white hair spread around his temples, highlighting his otherwise dark hair, betraying both his age and his kingly burdens. He took in his children, nodded at the tutor, and then looked out across the panoramic view of his island. He said, "Jason, I am going to interrupt your teaching this morning. With the delegation from Aushenia arriving shortly I will not have all the time I would like for my children in the coming weeks. I awoke with a desire to run the horses. I'm inclined to indulge it. If my children wish to accompany me the matter would be decided. . . ."

The children were so inclined, and within the hour they galloped out through one of the small side gates of the palace. All the children had ridden since their fourth or fifth year, and all were more than competent, even Dariel. A guard of ten horsemen followed them at a discreet distance. Nobody could imagine the king to be at risk while on Acacia, but as a monarch he was quite often made to bend to traditions from more perilous times.

They rode briskly out along the high road to the west. The narrow track at times traversed such thin ridges that one could look at a vista on either side that dropped down juniper-covered slopes, careening all the way to the sea. The thorny crowns of acacia trees occasionally broke through the thin-webbed canopy. It was these, of course, that gave the island its name and the Akaran dynasty its informal title. They were a distinguishing feature of the landscape, unique among the other islands of the Inner Sea, none of which had acacias.

Up close, the trees had frightened Mena when she was younger. They were gnarled and thorny, so still and yet always having about them the threat of latent life, an intelligence within that she suspected they chose to keep hidden for their own reasons. She had grown comfortable near them only lately. An aged, sanded, and tamed specimen had been transplanted to Dariel's room as a frame to climb about on, a plaything. This had done much to ease her apprehensions. They could be cut and moved and shaped into toys for children; hardly things to fear.

The riders dropped down to the rugged beach of the southern coastline, a stretch of shore left in its natural state, with views across the bay at cliffs thriving with bird life. For a while they rode in a loose group, around and between great limbs of sun-bleached driftwood or out into the glass-green water, the horses kicking through the froth. Dismounted, Aliver tossed seashells out at the waves. Corinn stood on the decaying trunk of an enormous tree, her arms out to either side and her face pointed into the chilly breeze. Dariel chased fiddler crabs across the sand.

Mena chose to stand at her father's right hand as he walked from one to the other of them, interested in all, laughing, for so many things seemed to amuse him when he was with his children. She held a twig of driftwood in her fingers, running her fingertips over the weathered grain of it. This was exactly the way life was supposed to be. She did not question whether such a thing—a king cavorting with his children—was unusual. It was simply the way it always had been. She could imagine no other possibility. She did wonder, though, if anyone but her saw the strain behind their father's façade. His joy was sincere, but it was not without effort. It was painful in some measure because of the one who was absent.

That evening, back once more in the warm hive of the palace, Mena and Dariel curled up on her bed to hear their father tell a story. Like all rooms in the palace, Mena's was large, wide, and tall, with floors of polished white marble. It was not a room on which Mena had exerted any of her own influence, unlike Corinn in her lacy, brightly colored and variously cushioned nest. The furniture was uniformly ancient, pieces made of gnarled hardwood, with upholstery that tickled the skin. Tapestries depicting figures from Acacian history hung on the walls. She could name the deeds of only a few of them, but she felt their presence in the room as a protective force. They were watching over her. They were, after all, her father's people. Her own.

Leodan sat on a stool beside them. "So," he said, "I think we have reached the point where I must tell you the story of the Two Brothers and how the great friction began between them. It's a shame that Corinn and Aliver are too old for stories; they once liked this one, even though it's sad."

The king explained that there was once a time in the far past when the two brothers, Bashar and Cashen, were so close they could not be separated. A knife blade could not be slipped between them, such was their love for each other and joy at being in each other's company. At least this was true until the day that a delegation from a nearby village came to them and said that since the two of them were such good and noble brothers they prayed that one of them would become something called a "king." They had been told by a dreamer prophet that if they had a king, they would find prosperity. This they sorely needed, for they had suffered famine and discord for years. None of them could decide who among them should be king, so they implored one of the brothers to step into the role.

The two brothers asked if they could both be kings, but the villagers said that was not possible. Only one man can be the king of a place, they said. That was what the prophet had told them. But still the brothers liked the idea of being royal. They said that the villagers could choose between them and that the unchosen one would abide by the decision. In secret they made a pact that after a hundred years they would switch roles, and he who had not been king would then become it.

Cashen was chosen and made king. For a hundred years he ruled without incident. The people thrived. Bashar was always at his side. But on the first day of the hundred and first year Bashar asked that Cashen hand over the crown. Cashen looked at him coldly. He had grown used to being king, fond of the power he wielded. Bashar reminded him of their agreement, but Cashen claimed that no such words had ever passed between them. Hearing this, Bashar was filled with anger. He grappled with his brother. Cashen threw him off and, feeling a sudden fear and shame, ran from the village up into the hills. He drained himself of all loving thought for his brother and filled himself with bitterness instead. Bashar chased him through the hills and into the mountains. Storm clouds gathered and bolts of lightning illumed the sky and rain poured down on them.

Dariel tapped his father on the wrist with a finger. "Is this true?"

Leaning toward him, Leodan whispered, "Every word of it."

"They should've taken turns," Dariel said, his voice edged with fatigue.

"When Bashar reached his brother, he cracked him over the head with his staff. Cashen went weak-kneed for a moment, but then he shook off the blow and came at Bashar again. This time Bashar swung his staff around and caught his brother at the knees, spilling him onto his back. He tossed his staff away and grabbed his brother, hefted him up, and walked with him above his head toward the precipice. The wind battered and howled at him, but still he managed to reach the edge, where he tossed his brother over into the void.

"But Cashen did not perish. He bounced and rolled and tumbled down the slope. He regained his footing and began to run. He bounded across the valley floor and came up on the other side. As he rose to the crest of the far mountain, a lightning bolt ripped through the sky. The light was blinding and Bashar had to cover his eyes against it. When he could see again, Bashar realized that Cashen had been struck. But instead of dropping to the ground dead, his body quivered and tingled with energy. Blue light fanned out across his skin and over his charred flesh. He did not perish, though. He began to run once more, and now he was swifter than before. He took enormous steps and climbed to the peak of the far mountain and jumped over it without so much as a backward glance at his brother."

Mena let the silence after this linger for a moment, then asked, "Is that the end?"

Leodan shushed her and nodded toward Dariel, indicating that he had fallen asleep. "No," he said, beginning to slide his arms under the boy, "that is not all, but it's the end of this night's story. Bashar realized that some god had reached down and blessed his brother. He knew then that they were to be foes in a long and difficult battle. Truth be known, they still are fighting." Leodan pushed himself upright, Dariel draped over his arms, in the dead weight of slumber. "Sometimes, if you listen carefully, you can hear them throwing stones at each other in the mountains."

Watching her father's back as he passed through the open portal, turned toward the glare of yellow light from the hall lamp and stepped out of view, Mena fought back the sudden urge to call out. It came to her like a gasp for air, as if she had been holding her breath unwittingly. It was the sudden, dreadful certainty that her father would vanish into that corridor, never to be seen again. When she was younger she often called him back time and again, for comfort, stories, and promises, until his patience wore thin or until she dropped senseless from fatigue. But lately she had grown embarrassed by whatever emotion choked her at parting from him. It was her burden to bear, and bear it she did.

She realized that she had clenched her bedsheets tight in her two fists. She tried to loosen her fingers and spread calm up from them and through the rest of her. It was fear without substance, she told herself. Leodan had told her as much many times. He would never leave her. He promised it with complete, undeniable parental certainty. Why could she not just believe him? And why did the wish that she believed him feel like a slight to her dead mother? She knew that many children her age had never suffered the loss of a parent. Even sleeping Dariel could not remember their mother enough to miss her. He knew nothing of what had been lost. Such a kind thing, that ignorance. If only she had been born the youngest instead of Dariel. She was not sure if this was a mean thought, unkind to her brother, but she was a long time thinking about it.

CHAPTER

THREE

Thaddeus Clegg could see from the moment he entered his chamber that the woman was about to collapse from exhaustion. She stood in the center of the torch-lit room, facing the far wall, cast in silhouette by the orange glow from the fireplace. She swayed from side to side with the awkward, off-kilter movements of the truly fatigued. Her garments were as soiled and bedraggled as a peasant's, but beneath the caked dirt and grime Thaddeus could make out the glint of her chain-mail vest. The tight-fitting skullcap of her helmet was distinctive enough with its single tuft of yellow horsehair at the peak.

"Messenger," Thaddeus said, "my apologies that you had to wait for me standing. My servants hold to formality even in the face of reason."

The woman's eyes flashed up. "Why have I been kept here, chancellor? My message is for King Leodan, by orders of General Leeka Alain of the Northern Guard."

Thaddeus turned to his servant, who had shadowed him as he entered the room, and instructed him to bring the messenger a plate of food. As the servant shuffled out of the room, Thaddeus motioned for the woman to sit on one of the couches just behind him. It took some convincing, but when he lowered himself, the messenger followed his example. He explained that she was there before him precisely because her message was for the king. As chancellor he received all communications first. "Certainly you know this," he said, the slightest suggestion of reprimand in the purse of his lips.

At fifty-six years of age Thaddeus had left behind the handsome appearance of his youth. The invariable sun of Acacian summers had carved deep creases in his skin, lines that seemed to sprout anew each time he gazed at himself in a hand mirror. Still, sitting upright within the reach of the wavering firelight, with his arms folded in his lap and the dark red satin of his winter cloak around him, the chancellor looked every bit at home in his station as confidant to the ruler of the largest empire in the Known World. He had been born just months after Leodan Akaran, to a family nearly as royal, but he had been told early that his role was to serve the future king, not aspire to such heights himself. He was a constant confidant, the first ear for any secret, the eyes that saw the monarch as only those of his immediate family were allowed. He had been assigned his role and status at birth, as had been the case with each of the twenty-two generations of chancellors before him.

The servant returned, bearing a tray spread with plates of smoked oysters and anchovies, grapes, and two carafes, one of lime water and one of wine. Thaddeus motioned that the woman should help herself. "Let there be no discord between us," he said. "I can see that you are an earnest soldier, and from the look of your clothes you have had a harsh journey. The Mein must be an icy misery this time of the year. Drink. Take a breath. Remember that you are within the walls of Acacia. And then tell me what you have to."

"General Alain sends—"

"Yes, you said that Leeka sent you. You were not sent by the governor?"

"This message comes from General Alain," the messenger said. "He sends his most devoted praise and affection to the king and to his four children. May they live long. He swears his loyalty now as ever, and he asks that the king listen to his words with care. They are all true, even if his message will seem incredible."

Thaddeus glanced at his servant. After he left the room the chancellor said, "The king listens through me."

"Hanish Mein is planning a war against Acacia."

Thaddeus smiled. "Not likely. The Meins are not fools. Their numbers are small. The Acacian Empire would crush them like ants underfoot. When did Leeka become such a—"

"Sir, forgive me, but I have not finished my report." The messenger seemed saddened by this fact. For a moment she rubbed at the bags beneath her eyes. "It is not just the Mein we must contend with. Hanish Mein has struck some alliance with people from beyond the Ice Fields. They have come over the roof of the world and south into the Mein."

The chancellor's smile faded. "That is not possible."

"Sir, I swear by my right arm that they come south by the thousands. We believe they do so at the call of Hanish Mein."

"He has gone out of the Known World?"

"Scouts have seen them coming. They are a strange people, barbaric and fierce—"

"Foreign people are always thought to be barbaric and fierce."

"They are taller than normal men by more than a head. They ride atop woolly creatures, horned things that trample men underfoot. They come not just with soldiers but with women and children and the elderly, with great carts like moving cities, pulled by rows of hundreds and hundreds of beasts like none I have heard described before. It is said they wheel siege towers and other strange weapons with them, and manage great herds of livestock. . . ."

"You describe wandering nomads. These are figments of some liar's fancy."

"If these be nomads they are like none our world has ever seen. They sacked a town called Vedus in the far north. I say sacked, but in truth they simply rolled over it. They left nothing behind, but grasped up everything of value and carried it with them."

"How do you know Hanish Mein has anything to do with this?"

The messenger fixed the chancellor in her gaze. She could have been no older than twenty-five, but there was more than that length of suffering and perseverance in her face. Thaddeus had often believed this to be true of female soldiers. They were, by and large, cast of finer steel than average men. She knew what she was talking about, and he should acknowledge it.

Thaddeus rose and motioned the woman toward a large chart of the empire on the far wall. "Show me these things on the map. Tell me all you can."

For the next hour the two talked: one asking questions with ever-increasing gravity, the other answering with conviction. Running his eyes over the chart, Thaddeus could not help but imagine the howling wildness of the place they discussed. No other region of the Known World was as troublesome as the Mein Satrapy. It was a harsh northern plateau region, a land of nine-month winters and of a blond-haired race of people who managed to survive there. The plateau bore the name of the people who inhabited it, but the Mein were not native to the region. They had once been a Mainland clan from the eastern foothills of the Senivalian Mountains, not all that different from the early Acacians. After an earlier displacement—at the hands of the Old Akarans—they had settled there and been forced to call it their home for twenty-two generations, just as the Akarans had made Acacia their base for the same amount of time.

The Mein were a tribal, warlike, bickering people, as harsh and prone to callousness as the landscape they inhabited, with a culture built around a spiteful pantheon of spirits called the Tunishnevre. They held in common a pride in their shared ancestry, which they protected by living a cloistered existence. They married only with each other and condemned interbreeding with other races. Because of their perceived racial purity, any Meinish male could claim the throne as his own, so long as he won it through the death duel called the Maseret.

This system made for a rapid turnover of rule, with each new chieftain having to win the approbation of the masses. Once crowned, the new chieftain took the race's name as his own, signifying his representation of all his people. Thus, their current leader, Hanish of the line Heberen, became Hanish Mein on the day he fought his first Maseret and retained the crown of his deceased father. The fact that Hanish roiled with hatred for Acacia was not news, certainly not to the chancellor. But what this soldier was telling him outstripped his imaginings.

At Thaddeus's urging the messenger consumed all the food on the plate. Another was brought, with cheese this time, the hard variety that had to be cut with a sharp knife. The chancellor sliced wedges for both of them, and then drew back with the blade in hand. He stared at his reflection in it as he listened.

The messenger tried to fight away sleep, but as the night turned into the silent hours her eyelids drooped. "I fear I am failing," she finally said, "but I have explained everything to you. May I now have an audience with the king? These things are meant for his ears."

At the mention of the king, Thaddeus had an unexpected thought, not at all what he would have anticipated at this moment. He recalled a day the previous summer when he had found Leodan in the labyrinthine gardens of the palace. The king sat on a stone bench in an alcove, hemmed in on both sides by the vine-draped ancient stone that had been the foundation of the first king's more modest abode. His youngest son, Dariel, sat on his lap. Together they studied a small object held in the boy's hand. As Thaddeus approached, the king looked up with wondrous, joy-filled eyes and said, "Thaddeus, come look. We have discovered an insect with spotted wings." He said it like it was the most important thing in the world, as if he were a child just as much as his son. Thaddeus liked the king most during these clear-eyed, day-lit moments, with the royal eyes unclouded by the mist that hazed them each evening. At those dark times he could be a bore to sit next to, but with his children . . . well, with his children he was a fool who remembered youth. A wise fool who still found wonder in the world . . .

"Chancellor?"

Thaddeus started. He realized that they had both been sitting in silence. The messenger had been distracted by her fatigue just as he was caught up in random reveries. He felt the sharp point of the cheese knife where it pressed against his finger. He said, "The king must hear all of this within the hour. You say that General Alain sent you directly here? You have not spoken of this to the governors?"

She answered crisply. "My message was meant for King Leodan."

"Just as it should be." Thaddeus tugged on an earlobe. "Sit here a moment. I will arrange a meeting with the king. You have done us a great service."

The chancellor pushed himself up to his feet. He still held the knife, but he began to move away as if he had forgotten about it and carried it with him absently. As he passed the messenger's chair and stepped behind her, he swung about. He flipped the knife around in his fingers and grasped the handle in a white-knuckled fist. At just the same moment that one hand clasped over the woman's forehead, the other one slit her neck from left side to right. He had not been sure whether the tool would suffice for this purpose and he used more force than he had to. But the work was done. The messenger slumped forward without a word of protest. He stood for a moment just behind her, with the knife held out to one side, the whole blade of it and of the fist that held it stained a slow maroon. With conscious effort he willed his hand open. The weapon clattered to the floor and then lay still.

Thaddeus was not entirely the loyal servant of the king that he seemed, and for the first time in his life he had demonstrated this fact with a blood act that could not be rescinded. The hard truth of this stunned him. He fought to steady himself and direct his thoughts, to focus on details and action. He would have to send his servants away, and then he would dispose of this soldier's body and clean the mess. It would take the rest of the night to accomplish this, but he would not even have to leave his compound. There was a dungeon beneath where he stood now. He had only to drag the woman down the winding staircase that led to it; shove her inside; lock the door; and leave it to the rats, insects, and worms to clean her bones undisturbed.

Dealing with the moral ramifications of what he had just begun would not be nearly as easy.

CHAPTER

FOUR

Like all of the children of the noble houses, Aliver Akaran had been raised in opulence. He always woke to find his slippers resting in place on the floor beside him and flower petals in the basin of scented water he washed his face in. From the moment he took solid food, each meal he had eaten had been prepared to the highest standards, with the best ingredients, with the effect on the palate considered down to the last detail. He had never walked into a cold room on a winter's day, never drawn his own bath or wet his hands washing clothes. He never even witnessed the washing of plates soiled by a meal. If asked, he would have had to create from fancy the process by which items were cleaned, mended, replaced. He had lived at the center of a massive delusion. It was a most pleasant one in which the world functioned largely for his gratification. At sixteen years of age, however, none of this stopped him from viewing the world through disgruntled eyes.

Leaving his private quarters a week after the seashore ride with his father and siblings, the prince grabbed up his leather training slippers and flung his fencing vest over his shoulder. In the corridor outside his room he strode between guards that stood like statues at either side of his door, and then he passed down a row of actual mannequins that lined one wall. These life-sized figures were carved of pinewood down to the minutest human detail, sanded to textures as smooth as skin and evocative of flesh over bone. They had been positioned in differing stances and wore military garb from the various nations: a Talayan runner, the wood stained to near-black to mimic his skin color, an iron spear poised in the fingers of his right hand; a Senivalian infantryman in scale armor, curving long sword at his belt; a horseman of the Mein with his characteristic thick breastplate, draped in hides that hung around him in tattered bands; a Vumu warrior adorned in eagle feathers; and Acacians in their various tidy uniforms, bare armed, with loose, flowing trousers under fine chain mail.

Aliver's rooms had more objects of warfare than the king cared for. He had once pointed out that Acacia had overseen a largely peaceful empire for generations. But on this matter the prince did not mind his father's disapproval. His daily interactions with his peers were a more challenging jostle than his relationship with his father. Leodan no longer elbowed through life among a throng of young men. Aliver, on the other hand, had yet to come through his manhood trials. As he saw it, all of the higher pursuits his father enjoyed had been made possible by the bravery of men and women willing to bear arms. It had been their earlier military prowess that allowed their ancestors to take the feuding, disparate elements of the Known World and unify them into a partnership of nations that benefited them all. How but through force could this have been achieved? How but through the threat of force could it be maintained?

In angry moments Aliver imagined his father trying to hold forth to that earlier rabble, to explain to them the virtues of peace and friendship. They would have laughed him away from the campfire. They would have kicked him into the cold, spat, and called him a coward. And then they would have commenced the snarling battle that decided things in this world. Sometimes during these imaginings Aliver came to his father's rescue, sword in hand; other times he simply watched. It was not that he failed to love his father. He cared for him dearly. He hated that he thought such things. They came to him unbidden, no easier to submerge than the unexplained pangs of carnal desire that had plagued him the last couple of years. But this was also beside the point. What mattered was that the Akarans were the benevolent masters of a magnificent realm. They had been for twenty-two generations, and would be for much longer if Aliver had any say in the future. That was why he took martial matters so seriously.

The walk to the Marah training hall took only a few minutes, most of it downhill. The bulk of the palace, the town below it, the island, and the sea around it stretched out before Aliver. The receding scale of it was difficult to reckon with. The near buildings were hulking structures of clean Acacian architecture. Roads wound down in the switchback fashion the hillside's natural steepness required. Beyond the gates, figures on the visible bend of the main road were slow-moving pinpricks, like deer ticks crawling across a man's arm. The spires of the lower town were little more than sewing needles pointing upward, so tiny they could be squished between the thumb and forefinger. It was hard to imagine that all of it had begun with a simple fortress built by Edifus, a defensive structure perched high so that the nervous monarch could scan the seas around him in fear that his newly conquered subjects might yet unite against him.

Flushed from the brisk walk, Aliver entered the large pillar-supported space. It was lit by oil lamps hung on the wall or from three-legged stands and by skylights cut in the ceiling that cast slanting beams down on the gray-white stone of the place. The scent of the burning oil was almost sweet, stronger than the smoky flavor given off by the stoves used to keep the chill at bay. He greeted his instructors, nodded at other youths entering with him, boys mostly, although a handful of girls attended also. They received military training on an even footing with their male counterparts. Indeed, women made up almost a quarter of the Acacian armed forces. For this Marah training, however, they were all children of aristocrats bound for high posts as officers and government officials. Many of them were from the Agnate, the privileged group that could verify an ancestral link to Edifus's family tree.

The prince knew that previous Akaran rulers had formed tight bonds with their young peers. His grandfather Gridulan was said to have been constantly in the company of thirteen male companions, dining and sleeping, ruling and wedding in a close tangle. Though his peers were deferential to him, Aliver found no such feeling of group connection. He tried to spurn the absence of it and value his independence of mind and position, but he feared something was lacking in his character, something he seemed powerless to correct.

Aliver smiled when he saw Melio Sharratt, a young man his own age, enter. Melio was the nearest thing the prince had to a friend. They had been born only a few weeks apart, and from their first classes together, the kind intelligence in the boy's eyes drew Aliver to him. For a while, when they were both ten, they spent days at a time hiding out in the palace labyrinth, playing a game wherein one of them became a storyteller and the other the main character in what invariably became a tale of warfare and adventure, of mythic beasts slain and evil vanquished. Aliver felt comfortable with Melio in a way he did not with others. Still, despite his fondness for the lad, the prince never fully dropped his aloofness with him, or anyone else. If anything, it had grown as adolescence shifted and altered their bodies and emotions. So the smile that once would have been friendly changed into an expression harder to define.

"Hello, Prince," Melio said. "I hope the day finds you well."

"It does," Aliver said, looking past him as if something at the far end of the training grounds interested him.

Melio combed the longish bangs of black hair back from his forehead with his fingers and good-naturedly copied Aliver's examination of the other students as they arrived. "Have you been practicing your Fifth Form? I saw that Biteran was coaching you on it last week. If you passed it, you could start spear training."

"I'll pass it," Aliver said. "You should worry about yourself. I'll help you with the Fourth Form if you need it."

"You?" Melio asked, laughing. "My royal tutor?" He had a face that might go unnoticed in a room, except when he smiled. Then all the various components of his features fell into place as if they had been designed with only mirth in mind. The whiteness of his teeth beside his olive skin made him glow with health. Both boys knew that in matters martial the ground between them was not even. Aliver may have been training at a higher Marah Form than his peers—such was the long tradition—but Melio had been suggested for training as an Elite. The Elite was quite different than the Marah. It was an even smaller group selected purely for ability, without regard for rank or social status. The suggestion that Melio might join them was an honor that meant the instructors saw inordinate skill in the young man.

"Look, there's Hephron," Melio said. "He's getting quite good. He fought Carver's father to a standstill the other day. You can be sure it surprised the old fellow."

As he spoke Melio gestured at the boy in question with his chin. Hephron Anthalar was a year older than most of the others, taller by a head, with reddish hair that sprung in disheveled curls from his head. The Anthalars were also Agnates, of a line that had intersected several times with the Akarans through marriage. Hephron could claim royal lineage. He could, in fact, count the steps between himself and the throne on the fingers of his two hands. He walked with his followers tight around him; a sycophantic group that clung to him because the status found in his shadow was greater than any of them could have managed singly.

Hephron bowed on reaching the prince, a motion that his companions copied with less feigned and more genuine deference. "Prince," he said, "ready to fight the ghosts?"

Aliver knew what he referred to in an instant and felt the cut of the barb. A peculiarity of his training was that after the initial lecture and demonstrations, Aliver and the other boys parted company. The others paired off and went at each other with the padded swords, sometimes using the wooden variety, which had no blade to cut but could still issue a painful rap or jab, or even break bones when wielded skillfully. Aliver, on the other hand, trained only with an instructor who further worked him through the classic Forms, the teacher attuned to the minutest detail of his student's posture and positioning, the intake or exhalation of his breath, the position of his head or even his eyes. Using the wooden swords, they fenced together in slow motions honed to the finest precision. In this Aliver had thought himself special. His training had a purity that would always set him apart from the others. It was a gift to be envied. So he had believed until Hephron undermined it all with a single question.

"Ghosts?" Aliver asked. "I don't believe in ghosts, Hephron. I do believe that the instructors know how best to train the nation's next king."

"Yes," the other said, "I suppose they do. Quite right, as ever." As he turned away, his eyes canted upward in a signal to his companions. He said something Aliver could not hear, and the other youths moved away with amused murmurs.

Aliver tried to forget Hephron in the hours that followed. The lessons began with a lecture. Today it was from the second instructor, Edvar, a bull-necked man of mixed heritage, his Candovian ancestry betrayed by the barrel stoutness of his torso. He talked about the technique of the sword soft block, a defensive tactic wherein one countered an opponent's attacks with the bare minimum of force necessary. It was risky, he explained. You did not want to underestimate the opponent's force, but it was a valuable maneuver in that you could use the opponent's energy to initiate your own moves, thereby starting the next motion with a boost, before the enemy had recovered. It was an energy-saving method if one faced a long struggle, as had Gerta when she fought the twin brothers Talack and Tullus and their three wolf dogs.

After this the pupils divided up to practice the Forms. These were routines that derived from age-old reconstructions of specific sequences of moves by specific persons in ancient battles. The first was Edifus at Carni, when he fought singly against a tribal leader. The second was Aliss, a woman from Aushenia who killed the Madman of Careven with only a short sword. It was a unique Form, in that Aushenians themselves did not honor Aliss as much as Acacians did. Indeed, the Madman of Careven was considered to be somewhat more of a hero to Aushenians since he had fought to protect their old religions against the secular movement Aliss championed.

The Third Form was that of the knight Bethenri, who went to battle with devil's forks, short weapons similar to daggers but with long prongs stretching alongside of the central blade. Skilled hands used these to snap opponents' swords.

Other Forms followed, each more complicated than the one preceding it, up until the Tenth and most difficult, that of Telamathon against the Five Disciples of the god Reelos. Aliver had his doubts as to whether Telamathon, the Five Disciples, or the god Reelos ever existed, but he looked forward to learning the Form. A large section of it, he knew, recounted how Telamathon fought weaponless and with one shoulder dislocated. Even so incapacitated he managed to beat back his opponents with a dazzling whirlwind of aerial kicks.

The other students were working through the Fourth Form. Aliver, as per tradition, worked on the Fifth Form, learning the method by which the Priest of Adaval went to work on the twenty wolf-headed guards of the rebellious cult of Andar. The prince had just begun the study of this. For most of his lesson he stood holding the birchwood staff, listening, and trying to imagine the scene his instructor detailed. As usual, the Form detailed an almost impossible triumph, the old priest managing to crack skull after canine skull with only a sapling for a weapon.

Aliver sometimes felt the eyes of the others on him. At other times he could not help but glance at them, interspersed as they were among the pillars, almost a hundred of them in total, so many pairs in the stop-start motion of swordplay. Every now and then a student would get caught by another's winning strike. With the padded swords this was almost a pleasure, a thing to be laughed at, yielding oaths and promises of revenge. Not so when the hard ashwood swords stung someone's thigh or jabbed unprotected ribs. Aliver was never prey to such contact, and he was keenly aware of it each time someone called out in pain.

When the day's session concluded, the instructors left the students to return the weapons to their rightful places. Privileged sons and daughters that they were, they should still learn reverence for the tools of war. Aliver, once more mingling with the others, did the best he could to banter in a natural style. He tried to throw about casual comments, the jibes and jokes of youth. But what seemed to come effortlessly to the others was as concentrated an effort for Aliver as anything in his training.

It was with a feeling of relief that he slipped on his soft leather boots, rose from the floor, and gathered up his training vest and slippers. As he passed a cluster of boys near the exit, Hephron rose from a squatting position. He spoke under his breath, ostensibly to the youth standing near him, but loud enough and at just the right moment for the prince to hear. "I wonder how you lose when you only fight the air or how you win? Strange that some of us are measured against each other, while some are not measured at all."

The opening to the hallway was just a few steps away. Aliver could have been there and outside in just a few seconds. Instead he spun on his heel. "What did you say?"

"Oh, I said nothing, Prince. Nothing of consequence . . ."

"If you have something to say to me, just say it."

"I just envy you, of course," Hephron said. "You sword train, but you never get cracked atop the skull like the rest of us."

"Would you like to fence with me, then? If you think my training is lacking . . ."

"No. Of course, no . . ." A note of caution appeared in Hephron's voice. His eyes darted to his companions, checking to see whether he had overstepped himself or if he should push farther. "I wouldn't want to be the one who bruised the royal flesh. Your father could have my head for that."

"My father wants no such head as yours. And who says you would be able to touch me, much less bruise me?"

Hephron looked sad, something Aliver would think on later, though he barely noticed it in the heat of the moment. "We don't need to do this," he said. "I meant no offense. Your training is rightly different from ours. You will never need to fight in a real battle anyway. We all know that."

Though Hephron spoke these words with a measure of sincerity, Aliver noted only the aspects of it that seemed a taunt, an insult. The prince started toward the equipment rack. "We'll fence just as you do with the others, with wooden swords. Hold nothing back. Touch me if you can. You have my word you will give no offense."

Properly suited up a few moments later, the two youths faced each other inside a hushed circle created by the other students, many of whom glanced over their shoulders, worried lest an instructor return. Hephron had a deceptive style of swordplay. He did nothing with a clear and predictable rhythm. He changed his rate of movement and even the direction of his strike in mid-motion. He would parry in a certain manner for a time, his wrist loose, his sword making sweeping arcs. Just when Aliver had come to anticipate and almost find comfort in the rhythm of it, Hephron would change everything mid-stroke. He would drop bodily an inch or two lower. His stroke would become a thrust. His arm would switch from a downward motion to a jab so quickly that the two differing motions seemed to have nothing to do with each other, one neither the precursor to, nor the result of, the other.

For some time Aliver managed to fend him off without taking a touch. He did so with motions slightly more frantic than he wished, quick jerks and clumsy shifts of his feet and exhaled breaths, convolutions of his torso that just barely kept him out of reach. The ash sword felt comfortable enough in his hands, but he realized that he rarely found a moment to drive an aggressive strike. He was all countermovements. What he wished to do was find a still moment to fall into a familiar sequence from his training. He fixated on the twelfth movement of the First Form, wherein he would slip away from a sweeping strike coming in from the left; step forward and block the inevitable return; push his opponent's blade down and to the right, crossing beneath his knees; and then slice upward diagonally into the right side of his torso. With such a cut Edifus had managed to spill his opponent's viscera in looping knots that caused the man to pause long enough to set his head in the perfect position to be lopped off a few seconds later, an unnecessary flourish, really, but one Aliver had often imagined.

Three times he began this sequence, but each time Hephron stepped out of it and changed his attack. On the last instance he did so with such speed that Aliver cringed beneath a round sweep that skimmed the crown of his head. Had he taken the force of this directly, he might well have been knocked unconscious. No instructor had ever swung at him like that. He heard one of the others say something, a jibe followed by a rustle of laughter. He realized just how silent they had been up until then, no sound in the room save for the swish and shift of their slippers across the tiles, the grunts of their efforts, and the dry cracks when the wooden blades met.

Aliver found himself backing, backing, barely able to slap away Hephron's blows, needing space, and then space again. He expected to meet the wall of youths behind him, but they moved with him, the circle staying fixed around them. It even opened as the movement brought them to a pillar. He knocked the granite base of this with his foot. He half lowered his sword, for a moment thinking this was reason enough to pause. He glimpsed the possibility that they might halt this exercise, smile and joke about it, no damage done. But Hephron swung, his blade slicing below Aliver's chin and striking the stone pillar.

The prince stumbled backward. He caught himself with his free hand and pivoted on it. Upright again, he remembered the anger that had started all of this. Hephron, the arrogant fool! It seemed absurd that he would strike at him that way, as if he wished to shatter his windpipe. He caught sight of Melio, who at that moment stood on the far side of the ring, his face ridged with concern. That annoyed him also. He wanted no sympathy. He raised his sword above his head and yanked it down, wishing to pound Hephron beneath it. Even if the hit was blocked, he meant to press such weight behind it as to batter him down with fury alone.

But Hephron seemed to know this was coming. He slid to the side of Aliver's downstroke. He snapped his sword in a quick blow that bit the prince just at the edge of his shoulder, at the joint where the bones met. From this the boy twirled away, swung around in a complete circle, and caught Aliver—who had frozen in a twist of pain—at the midpoint of the other arm, with a force great enough that a real sword would have severed the arm cleanly. Aliver cried out, but Hephron was not done. He drew his sword back into his chest and lunged forward, pushing his weight before him and thrusting his arms so that the blunt wooden point of his sword hit Aliver's chest at dead center. Already convulsed with two-armed pain, the force of this last strike rocked the prince back onto his heels and dropped him onto the mat.

Hephron's smile lifted every component feature of his face into use. His eyes overflowed with such smugness that a single person could barely contain it. "You are armless, sir. Not to mention dead. What a strange outcome. Who would have guessed it?"

Moments later, Aliver surged out into air red faced and angry, more so at himself than at Hephron. How foolish of him! He had lowered himself by acknowledging Hephron's taunts, in challenging him, by losing so completely and—almost worst of all—in showing all of them his frustration. Behind this he knew he had played a hand he had not needed to. All the mystery of his possible skill had vanished in a few strokes. He knew they were all surrounding Hephron even now, clapping him on the back, praising him, laughing at their dandy prince. How could he ever go back there again and dance through his choreographed motions while all the others watched him from the corners of their scornful eyes?

Melio caught up with him as he pounded up a long staircase. "Aliver!" he called. "Wait for me." Twice he touched the prince's elbow, only to have his hand ripped away. At the top of the stairs Melio jumped in front of him, threw his arms around him, and dragged him to a halt. "Come on. You care too much about this. Don't do it. Hephron's nothing."

"He's nothing?" Aliver asked. "Nothing? If he's nothing, then what am I?"

"The king's son. Aliver, don't walk away. And don't pity yourself. Do you think that little fight matters? I will tell you something." Melio drew back a little, but pressed the palms of his hands on the other's shoulders, as if indicating that he was letting go but not yet doing so. "Okay, so the truth is you are no match for Hephron. He is good. No, wait! But don't let that bother you. Aliver, he envies you in everything. Don't you know that? His swagger is a pretense. In truth he wishes he were you. He follows you with his eyes always. He listens to every word said by or about you. At lessons when he sits in the back of the class, he pins his eyes to the back of your head as if he wished to drill inside you."

"What are you saying?"

"I'm saying that Hephron is a thin person. He knows this himself and he envies you. You are a prince and your family is wonderful. You have a beautiful sister. . . . Okay, I am joking with you. It's true, but I am joking. Hephron may grow into an enemy, or he may yet be a great friend. But for now, give him no feeling of triumph. Forget about that." Melio motioned vaguely at something behind him. "Come back tomorrow as if nothing happened. Joke about it. Let him know that the small things he can do to you wash off like mud on your boots."

The air had grown chillier with the approach of dusk and both young men felt it fill the silence. Melio withdrew his palms and rubbed his bare arms with them. Aliver looked away, his gaze settling on a square of fuchsia sky framed between the cold shadows of two buildings. The silhouettes of three birds flew through the space like darts in pursuit of one another.

Aliver heard himself say, "It just makes me look so stupid. I am mad that I let it happen. Made it . . . happen. You don't know how it is for me."

Melio did not disagree. A few moments passed in silence, and then the two of them, responding to the cold, mounted the next set of stairs and progressed slowly up. "Everyone loses a duel on occasion, and all of them back there know that. But how many of them could . . ." He searched for the words to say what he had to delicately. "Well, how many of them could embarrass themselves like you just did and find the courage to shrug it off? That's another way to show strength, whether they ever admit to noticing it or not. And do not pout. The expression does not suit you. Aliver, you *are* skilled with a sword. And your traditional Forms are better than anyone's. It's just that you know only the Forms. Actual fencing is about making us adapt them, about splicing them together, forcing us to make up unthought-of combinations in an instant. You must let them flow together so quickly that it happens in a different place than conscious thought. Like when you knock a knife off a tabletop and manage to snatch it before it hits the ground. You cannot think about doing that; it just happens. That is what you must do when fighting. And then your mind is free to deal with other things—like just how you are going to place an upstroke in that bastard's nut sacks."

"Just how did you become so wise?" Aliver asked, not entirely kindly.

Melio mounted the top of the staircase and turned to face him. He grinned. "I read it in a manual. I know a fair bit of poetry, too. The girls like that. Now look, we'll fence together sometimes. I won't let you off easy, of course, but we will teach each other. We can work through the Fourth Form, as you suggested. There is much we can teach each other. How about that?"

"Maybe," Aliver said, but he knew already what his actual answer was. He just was not ready to give it so easily.

CHAPTER

FIVE

It was not just the rumors of a marauding army on the loose. Not just the report about the destruction at Vedus. These were the type of exaggerated tales General Leeka Alain had rightly ignored before. This time was different. An entire patrol had been lost somewhere in the white expanse of the Mein. That was not so easily explained away. Something was truly in motion out there. He could not sleep or eat or think of anything other than shadows hidden behind the blowing whiteness. He had already sent a messenger to the king to communicate such facts as he possessed, but he knew he could not wait for a response. He decided to take what action he could.

Leeka roused his army from the cocooned warmth of the fortress of Cathgergen. He marched them out into the slanting light of the northern winter, across the glacial skin of the Mein Plateau. At the eastern edge of the Mein is a vast tundra called the Barrens, undulating and irregular, treeless both because of the wind-lashed nature of the place and because what woodland there once was had been harvested centuries before. Travel across it was difficult at the best of times. In midwinter it was especially perilous. Sleds harnessed to teams of dogs cut tracks before the army, pulling along the bulk of camp supplies and food, enough to sustain their five hundred human souls for at least six weeks. The soldiers marched on their own heavily-booted feet. They wrapped themselves in woolen garments, with outer shells of thick leather, their weapons secured to their bodies to facilitate movement. They wore mittens made from the tubed pelts of rabbits.

They got as far as the outpost at Hardith without unexpected difficulty. They camped around the earthen structure for two days. This was much to the bewildered pleasure of the soldiers stationed there, men whose official duty was to supervise traffic on the road but whose real struggle was that of daily survival and extreme isolation. The outpost marked the western edge of the Barrens. Farther to the west the land dropped into a series of wide, shallow bowls in which patches of fir woodland remained.

Three days beyond Hardith a blizzard swept down from the north and attacked their huddled mass. It pounced on them like a wolverine, pinned them to the ground, and tried to tear them apart. They lost the road and spent an entire day trying to find it, to no avail. The snow piled into high, serpentine ridges that rolled like ocean waves and made navigation impossible. They could not chart the passage of the sun, nor spot any of the night's stars. Leeka instructed his men to progress by dead reckoning. This was a tedious process that left the bulk of the army standing still for long periods, never a good thing in such conditions.

Each evening the general tried to choose a campsite near natural protection, a ridge of hills or tree cover, as they now found stands of pines in the hollows. Soldiers hacked fuel and built windbreaks. Once the campfires were strong enough, they dragged whole trees into the flames. They stood around these explosive furnaces, their faces red and sweating from the blaze, eyes stung with smoke even as the wind howled at their backs. No matter how big the fire during the early evening, it had invariably faltered during the night, ashes and charred bits of wood swept across the snowscape by the wind. On breaking out of the frozen crust each morning the soldiers spent hours finding one another under the drifts, digging out, and prodding the dogs to motion.

On the twenty-second day they woke to a brutal wind blowing down from the north. Ice crystals screeched sideways and struck skin like hurled fragments of glass. They had barely put the old camp behind them when one of the scouts stumbled back to the main column and asked to speak to the general. He had, in fact, nothing concrete to report. The land ahead was flat as far as he could ascertain. He believed they had moved out onto a gradual slope that would bring them to Tahalian. But there was something that troubled him. There was a sound in the air and in the frozen ground beneath him. He had been able to hear it only because he was alone, outside of the noise of the moving army and beyond the sleds. As he returned past the sled dogs he could see that they heard it as well and were troubled by it.

The general spoke close to the man so the wind would not steal his words. "What sort of sound?"

The scout seemed to have feared this question. "Like breathing."

Leeka scoffed. "Breathing? Don't be mad. What's the sound of breathing in weather like this? Your ears are damaged."

The general reached for the man's head and tried to yank back his hood, as if he would inspect his ears right there. The scout allowed this, pre-occupied, dissatisfied with his own answer. "Or like a heartbeat. I'm not sure, sir. It's just there."

The general showed no sign that he thought the man's message of particular import, but some time later he walked away from his officers to think. Even if the man's story was only illness creeping into him, it was still a danger. Scouts predict more things than just the lay of the land. Perhaps they should hold up where they were or retrace their tracks back to the last camp, where there was still an ample supply of fuel for the fires. They could wait out the storms, even eating into the food reserves if necessary. They were near Tahalian after all. Even if Hanish Mein was up to something, they would still have to be welcomed with a pretense of kindness. . . .

It was because he stood at the edge of the column that he first heard the sound, if *heard* is the right word. With the noise of the troops behind him and the trudge of their feet and the scrape of a sled passing nearby he did not truly hear through his ears. He felt the sound as if the bones of his rib cage captured a low vibration and amplified it in his chest. He took a few steps away from the column and sank to one knee. One of his officers called to him, but he thrust up a clenched fist and the man fell silent. Leeka knelt, trying to feel the sound captured inside him, to block out the howl of the wind and friction of his hood across the sides of his head. When he quieted all this as best he could, he found what he was searching for. It was faint, yes, but undeniable. Like breathing, true enough. Like a heartbeat, yes . . . The scout had not lied. There was a rhythm to it, a throbbing time. A conscious, measured reason to it . . .

He spun on his knee and yelled for the ranks to form up. He ran back to them, shouting for the column to draw tight, shields up and facing outward, weapons to hand. He instructed the archers to quiver their arrows and unsheathe blades not victim to the wind and better suited to close quarters. He told the sled drivers to circle them within the troops and huddle the dogs. The same officer who had called to him before asked him what he had discovered. He met the young man's eyes and gave a simple answer. "There is a war drum beating."

Once the army had been formed into one defensive wedge and five hundred pairs of eyes stared out into the increasing fury of the north, then, finally, they all heard it. For a long hour that was all they did. The sound throbbed constant behind the wind, which was heavier now with large flakes of snow that stuck fast to their clothes and shields and fur-lined fringes and even, eventually, to the chill skin on their faces, rendering their

still forms like some elaborate snow sculptures. At some point the reverberation mingled with the general's heartbeat. That was why he was struck
breathless at the shock of it when the noise stopped. It simply ceased. In
the moments afterward Leeka knew he had made a mistake. Whatever
drum beat was out there had been doing so not for hours but for days. It had
been there for weeks perhaps before he was able to distinguish it. How
could something like that have eluded him?

He was not to contemplate this question for long, however. A creature
hurtled through the screen of blown snow. It rampaged forward, a horned
thing, woolly and huge, some sort of man astride it, a figure clothed in skins
and furs, a spear raised in one hand, a yell emanating from his unseen
mouth. The beast smashed into the ranks of men just to one side of the general's guard. It tore through them as if the soldiers were of no consequence.
It squashed some and knocked others aside without diminishing its speed
or altering its course. It vanished through the far side of the troops as
quickly as it appeared. In the few seconds the general had to contemplate
the scene he counted ten dead and twice as many more writhing on the
blood-splashed snow.

A hand on his shoulder spun him around and he observed—as he had
already known he would—that the rider had not been alone. The rest of
them materialized all at once, as if the snow had thinned to better his view.
There were so many of them, an alien multitude like nothing he had seen
before. He suspected that the horror of it would be the last thing he took in
with living eyes, and he knew that even if his message got through, he had
failed to adequately warn the king and the people of the empire of the
hideous threat massed against them.

Chapter

Six

Late in the evening Leodan Akaran heard someone enter his private chamber. He did not look up, but he knew who it was. The chancellor's clipped footfalls had a unique rhythm to them, something that the king had once pinpointed as a stiffness in the right leg. A servant had just lit his mist pipe and withdrawn. The pungent scent of the drug was, at that moment, the only thing that mattered. A phantom had clung to the back of his head throughout the day, a hunger he envisioned as a batlike creature that huddled around the contours of his skull, its claws sharp and thin as curved needles where they pierced his flesh and found purchase by anchoring into the bone. It had gripped him during his morning meetings; left him for a time during an hour spent with Corinn; but returned with sharpened, malicious claws throughout the evening. It prodded him as he dined and gnawed at him as he put Dariel down to sleep.

When Dariel had asked him for a story, Leodan had grimaced. It was just for a moment, a second of creviced physical expression that he regretted instantly. The boy had not even seen it, but it remained a nagging shame that he could long for his own vices while still in the company of his children. Where would he be without his children? Without Mena who still—for precious months more perhaps—wanted him to spin tales for her? And Dariel, who hung on his words with a trusting certainty the father knew time would shatter? He would be an empty shell without them. Shame on him for letting a moment with them pass in distraction. He told Dariel the story he asked for, and then he stood a few extra moments beside the boy's door, listening to his slumbering breath and regretting his own weaknesses.

All this was earlier; his feeble penance was complete. Now the pipe sat on the low table before him. It was an intricate confusion of glass tubes and water-filled chambers and leather hoses, one of which the king held between the fingertips of both hands. He placed the narrow bit of it between his teeth, touching it with his tongue. He inhaled gently at first. Then—as he tasted the bitter, putrid sweetness of the mist—his cheeks caved against his jawbones. The pipe bubbled and sputtered. He stayed huddled forward, eyes closed, aware that his chancellor stood near him but not caring. This was nothing Thaddeus had not seen before.

When he fell back against the cushions of his couch, he exhaled a slow plume of green vapor. The creature on his head plucked out its talons one by one. It faded into nothingness, taking with it the gray weight that he had carried with him like a granite cloak throughout the day. The opiate numbed the edges of the world. He felt no barbs. Instead he was filled with blurred tranquillity, a warm feeling of connection with the millions of people throughout his empire tied to the same drug. Peasant farmers and blacksmiths, municipal guards and rubbish collectors, miners, slavers: in this one thing he was the same as them all. It was—to the reasoning of his muted mind—a secret offering made for their forgiveness.

He opened his eyes, clouded now and veined reddish brown. "What news has the chancellor to share?"

Thaddeus had seated himself on a nearby divan. He sat with his legs crossed at the knee and a glass of port pinned between his right thumb and forefinger. The king eyed the small vessel, transfixed by something about the movement of the liquid against the glass, the stain it left as Thaddeus swirled it. He listened as the chancellor apprised him of the preparations for the Aushenian delegation. They were prepared, he said, to impress upon the foreigners both their strength and wealth and to extend a cautious hand of welcome. If the Aushenians confirmed that they acknowledged Acacian hegemony, everything would be in place to respond positively to them, if such was the king's wish.

Leodan nodded. It was his wish, but he knew that several times before Aushenia had nearly formed an alliance with Acacia, only to have it scuttled by some minor dispute. Everything he had thus far heard about the young prince Igguldan was promising, but still there were aspects of such an alliance that he did not wish to think about. He changed the subject, although his thoughts did not stray far from the things that troubled him. "The other day Mena asked about the Retribution."

"What did you tell her?"

"Nothing. Why should she learn that she has the blood of mass murderers in her veins? It was long ago, and we are no longer like that."

"You are right that it was long ago," Thaddeus said. "Twenty-two generations . . . What child can comprehend that?"

The king recalled that when Mena had asked the question, he had glimpsed something less than faith in his daughter's eyes, less than complete acceptance of his claims. And was not that astute of her? He had, after all, uttered yet another barefaced lie. The Retribution has no bearing on our lives? A blatant untruth spoken with a silvered tongue. How much longer could he get away with such things? It was not just Mena, of course, who had begun to question. Aliver had for some time carried an uncertainty and distrust behind his eyes that seemed ever ready to burst forth.

The chancellor said, "I should mention that the convener called for the governors to intercede in the case the Prios miners have filed against the—"

"Must I deal with that? I hate anything to do with the mines."

"Fine. We can let the governors handle it. There is something that they cannot handle, though." Thaddeus pursed his lips, waited for the king to meet his gaze. "The league representatives want to verify that you are truly going to reject the Lothan Aklun demand to increase the Quota."

The statement was nearly enough to clear the king's head of the drug's dulling effects. The Lothan Aklun . . . the agreement known as the Quota . . . These two things were the great, disguised sin of the Akaran Empire. Leodan sucked on his pipe. He had a momentary wish that this matter be handled by the governors. In truth, these representatives from the provinces, based in the thronging city of Alecia, handled most of the practical matters of the empire. But Tinhadin, the early king who was in many ways the chief architect of the Akaran Empire, had written the Quota guidelines with explicit simplicity. Control, authority, responsibility—all rested on the monarch's shoulders, a secret known by many but owned by him alone. For that reason, the management of it was handled by the palace. It was paid for through a separate budget and accounted separately from any other arm of the government. It was not spoken of except in closed circles, and the actual machinations of it happened far away, unseen by the king, although often imagined. No matter how he studied the ancient texts, the exact details of how the arrangement had been reached seemed jumbled to Leodan. The substance, however, could be understood.

Tinhadin, having inherited his father's newly won throne and outliving his brothers, found himself prosecuting wars on several fronts. The Wars of Distribution, as they were called, marked a strained and tumultuous time. His former ally, Hauchmeinish of the Mein, was now an enemy. He no longer trusted his faithful sorcerers, the Santoth. Provincial rebellions flared up like wildfires on the Acacian hills during the summer. His own understanding of the world was warped and horrific, and he struggled with a belief that any word uttered from his mouth might change the fabric of existence. He was a Santoth as well, the greatest of them, but the burden of the magic on his tongue had become a torture to control.

Into this came a new threat from across the Gray Slopes. There was a power, Tinhadin learned, greater than his own. They were called the Lothan Aklun. They were of the Other Lands, outside the Known World, separated from them by a great ocean. They were a complete mystery to the early king. Their power was nothing really but a claim, but Tinhadin did not want another enemy at that time. He made overtures of peace with them, suggesting trade and mutual gain instead of conflict. The Lothan Aklun not only jumped at the offer, they proposed specifics Tinhadin could not have imagined on his own.

The agreement must have seemed a bargain at the time. The Lothan Aklun promised not to attack the war-ravaged land and agreed to only ever trade with Akarans. All they needed to assure this beneficence was a yearly shipment of child slaves, with no questions asked, no conditions imposed on what they did with them, and with no possibility that the children would ever see Acacia again. In return for this they offered Tinhadin the mist, a tool that, they promised, he would find most helpful in sedating his fractious wards. It was fine-tuned later, but on these basic terms the deal was agreed. Since then, thousands upon thousands of the Known World's children had been shipped into bondage, and millions under Akaran rule had given over their lives and labors and dreams to the fleeting visions brought on by the mist. The same drug Leodan Akaran inhaled nightly. Such was the truth of Acacia.

"Demand?" Leodan finally asked. "You call it a demand?"

"In tone, yes, my lord, it does have the ring of belligerent certainty to it."

"Lothan belligerence is nothing new," Leodan said. "It's nothing new. . . . They already have my people's souls. What more do they want? The Lothan Aklun are no better than any of the riffraff surrounding us: the miners, the merchants, the league themselves. None of them is content from one moment to the next. I may have never set eyes on a Lothan, but I know them well. Tell the league to take this message to them: the Quota stays as it always has been. The agreement was binding into perpetuity, made before my time to stretch beyond it; I do not accept any change, now or ever."

He said this with finality, but he did not seem to like the silence Thaddeus responded with. "There is something else we should speak about," Leodan said. "I received a letter this morning from Leeka Alain of the Northern Guard. He had it sent to a merchant in the lower town, who got it to me through the house servants. All very unusual."

"Yes, quite odd." Thaddeus cleared his throat, first softly and then through several louder coughs. "What has the soldier to say?"

"It was a strange letter, full of import but vague on details. He wanted to know if I had received a messenger he sent earlier. A Lieutenant Szara. By the sound of it, this messenger was dispatched with some grave message."

Thaddeus watched the king. "Have you received such a message?"

"You know the answer to that. It would have come to me through you."

"Of course, but I have heard nothing of this. Did Leeka reveal the details of the message in the letter?"

"No. He does not trust the written word."

"He should not. Once written, anyone could read it."

The king's eyes moved slowly, heavily. They swung around on the chancellor and studied him, clouded by the drug but still able to focus. The man's face was calm, although tense across the forehead. "Yes, perhaps . . . I do wonder why he chose to correspond with me instead of through the governor. I know he has no fondness for Rialus Neptos; I do not either, for that matter. Do you know that Rialus used to write me at least twice yearly, extolling his virtues and hinting that he should be recalled from the Mein and given some higher appointment here in Acacia? As if I want him sulking around the palace. He points out that he is of pure Acacian ancestry, says the climate of the Mein damages his health. I cannot argue with that, really; it is a miserable place. . . . Anyway, Leeka wished to communicate directly to me, and that makes me curious. Where is this Szara?"

Thaddeus lifted his shoulders to his ears, then dropped them. "I know nothing, but even in these peaceful times ill things happen. It is the dead of winter. That means little here, but in the highlands of the Mein the weather would be most foul. How was she meant to travel? On horseback or down the River Ask?"

"I don't know," he said.

"Let me take care of this," Thaddeus said. "Put it out of your mind until I have looked into it. I will send an armed envoy north to meet with Leeka. By your leave I will give them the king's rights, so that they may travel swiftly and always have fresh horses. We will hear from them within a month, maybe less if they sail to Aushenia and take the short land route.

Twenty-five days at most. And then you will know everything." Thaddeus
paused and waited for the king's response. It was little more than a grunt of
affirmation, but it seemed to satisfy the chancellor. He sipped from his
glass. "And then you will see that it was nothing serious at all. Leeka has always prickled with suspicions about the Mein, but when has it yet
amounted to anything?"

"Things are different now," the king said. "Heberen Mein was a reasonable man, but he is dead. His three sons are a different matter. Hanish is ambitious; I saw that in his eyes even as a boy, when he visited the city.
Maeander is pure spite, and Thasren is a mystery. My father was sure that
we would never be able to trust them. He made me swear I would not fall
to that weakness—trust. You also used to tell me I did not worry enough.
Together you and I conceived plans for all manner of tragic events, remember?"

Thaddeus smiled. "Of course I do. It is my job to. In youth I saw danger everywhere. But Acacia has never been stronger. I mean that, my friend."

"I know you do, Thaddeus." The king turned his gaze up toward the
ceiling. "Soon I will rouse all the children and take them on a voyage. We
will visit each province of the empire. I will try to convince them that I am
their beneficent king; and they will try to convince me that they are my
loyal subjects. And perhaps the illusion will go on for some time yet. What
say you to that?"

"That sounds like a fine thing," Thaddeus said. "That would make your
children very happy."

"Of course, their 'uncle' would accompany us as well. They love you as
much as they do me, Thaddeus."

The other man took a moment to respond. "You honor me unduly."

The king sat repeating this statement in his head for some time, finding comfort in it even as he drifted away from its original context. He had
said something similar once to Aleera. What had it been? *You . . . love me unduly.* That was what he had said. Why had he said that? Because it was true,
of course. He had explained as much to her one evening a few days before
their wedding. He had drunk too much wine and listened to too many
speeches praising him. He could not take it anymore, so he had pulled his
bride-to-be to the side and told her she should know things about him before they were married. He confessed to her all that he knew about the
crimes of the empire, the old ones and the ones still done in his father's
name, the ones that would likely continue in his name. He poured it all out,
tearful and pathetic and even belligerent, sure that she would shrink from

him, almost hoping that she would turn away and reject him. Surely a good woman would. And he had no doubt of her goodness.

How surprised he was by her response, then. She drew close to him and tilted her lovely, large-eyed face up toward his. There was no surprise on her features, no remorse, or judgment. She said, *A king is the best and worst of men. Of course. Of course.* She pushed her lips against his, so soft and full of hungry pressure that they took his breath away. That, perhaps, was the moment they were actually married, the moment the agreement between them was sealed. It was hard for him to decipher now which aspect of her love he was most drawn to. Was it the fact that she could forgive him all of it and love him because she understood his ultimate goodness? Or was it that she betrayed that she was just as capable of overlooking the truth and living a lie as he? Either way, having confessed to her and received her blessing, he loved her completely. He would never have been able to fulfill his role as monarch without her approval. This might or might not have been a good thing for the world, but to a man as unsure of rule as he had been, her devotion had been a great gift.

"Perhaps I do, Thaddeus," Leodan said, responding belatedly to his statement. "Perhaps I honor you unduly. We all make that mistake at times. But what harm does it do?"

He did not hear the chancellor's response, if, indeed, he offered any. He closed his eyes and felt the sensation of being pressed against an invisible wall. This mist had built in him, filled him. Now the moment of letting go of the physical world was finally his. This moment always came to him as pressure, as if his chest lay flat against a stone and a great force behind him gradually ground him into it. Just when he felt he could take the weight no more, he started to slip through the stone, to merge with it and pass through as if it were porous and he in liquid form. On the other side Aleera waited for him, the temporary delusion he craved almost more than true life. He went to her in reverence.

CHAPTER
SEVEN

Rialus Neptos believed he had found a method whereby he could keep track of everyone who came into and went out of the northern fortress of Cathgergen. He believed such surveillance was essential for a governor, especially one with such a tentative grip on power as he. He had ordered a single sheet of glass cast in the furnaces at the base of the fortress. He knocked out a portion of the granite wall in his office and set the pane to form one enormous window. The glass was taller than a man and as wide as he could stretch his narrow arms out to either side. The workmanship was imperfect. It was uneven in thickness, milky in some places and dotted throughout with air bubbles. But there were a few patches of true clarity; Rialus had located each through long hours of inspection.

Alone in his chambers he would press his forehead to the pane. More often than not the touch of the glass would bring a chill on and fuel his cough, a torment that had racked his bird-frail chest all his life. For a time he even took to stretching out on the floor. A ribbon of glass along the lower edge of the pane distorted the world in such a way that he could study the entrance to the military headquarters at his leisure and thus keep track of just who came and went in Leeka Alain's world. The best vantage came when he stood on a footstool and gazed down with a one-eyed squint that provided a view of the full reach of the western wall and the gate at its center. From this spot he had watched General Alain's troops march out in defiance of his direct orders. From the same spot he observed the arrival of the second of the Mein brothers, Maeander, some weeks later.

Rialus pulled back from the glass. He was chilled again. The fortress was heated by steaming pools of hot water that bubbled up from the earth. An intricate network of pipes and air ducts channeled the warmth throughout the labyrinthine structure. The Cathgergen engineers claimed it was a wonder of complicated craftsmanship, but in truth the place was never warm enough. He sometimes suspected that his chambers were intentionally denied a full measure of heat, but he had no way of proving this.

He circled his desk one and a quarter times, then walked to the bookshelved wall and trailed a finger over the spines of the volumes there, dusty tomes full of records, accounting documents, and gubernatorial journals kept since the first installment of Acacian hegemony in the satrapy. His father had treated these records with sober reverence. He tried to instill the same in his only son, to no avail. Rialus was only the second generation of his family to oversee the Mein—not a long tenure in office, by Acacian standards. On the demise of the previous governing family, his father had been sent north in punishment for some malfeasance Rialus could not even recall anymore. As the years passed the other governors came to take the Neptos family for granted. The Akarans all but ignored them. It galled him that he was expected to pay indefinitely for a crime no one could even name. It tormented him that the outside world had no understanding of his razor-sharp mind, somehow held captive inside his stunted form, betrayed on every occasion by his jaw's tendency to freeze up at just the wrong moments. If others would just see beyond these outward defects, they would realize that he was wasted on this posting.

Rialus was fond of saying that the Giver rewards her worthies, but he had yet to see any evidence that the divine forces in the world had even noted his existence. After ten years of being overlooked Rialus became a fertile ground for intrigue. The elder Mein brother had been quick to take advantage of this. Hanish was an eloquent speaker, a handsome man who spoke with such composure behind his gray eyes that one could not help but trust in him. Coming from his mouth, the strange belief system of the Mein seemed no thing of fancy at all. The world of the living was transient, Hanish had explained, but the force that was the Tunishnevre was constant. The Tunishnevre was composed of all the worthy men of his race who had once lived and breathed but did so no longer. It was their life force lingering outside their mortal vessels. It was the palpable energy of their rage, proof that the dead mattered more than the living. Life was the curse inflicted upon a soul before it rose to a higher plane. Like the body that is separate from the spirit within it and yet causes that spirit all manner of pain, so the fate of the living caused the ancestral core no end of suffering. The living kept the dead chained to them and in ignorance of it made the afterlife a burden, when it should have been the sweet fulfillment of life's journey. The ancestors, Hanish had claimed, implored him to ease their torture.

When the governor had asked just what it was that the Tunishnevre wanted and exactly how were they to be freed of this suffering, Hanish had squeezed his shoulder as if they were close companions. He had a way of switching from a most serious tone to a casual one at a moment's notice. "I do know that there are changes to be made to the order of the living world. That is the work I was born for. And you, Rialus Neptos, are an agent of my enemy."

This also had been said lightly, but the list of crimes perpetuated by Acacia's hegemony seemed long and foul when Hanish had detailed it. What nation did not suffer beneath their rule? From the pale men of the north to the black ones of the south, from east to west, so many different peoples, scores of races of men—all suffered grave injustices. Generations had lived and died under the yoke of Acacian "peace," but the Mein had never forgotten who their enemy was. Now, finally, Acacia had a king grown lax enough that they could strike. Hanish believed that Leodan was the weakest heir in the long chain of his family's history. A new age could begin, with a new calendar to mark the day, with new concepts of justice, with a redistribution of wealth, with privileges finally in the hands of those who had so long labored for other men's gain. There was little in this that Rialus could refute. He was, after all, in a prime position to know just how deeply Acacia taxed its allies.

Rialus could not even remember just when the Mein brothers had brought him into their confidence, but he did recall his incredulity at the claims that Hanish made. He had said his league allies were more powerful than the Akarans. They had grown frustrated with the Akarans and angry with Leodan. They believed the king wanted to break the Quota and abolish the mist trade. Because of this they had decided his fate. He would be removed and replaced by another willing to more faithfully meet their needs. Hanish claimed that this had happened twice before in the twenty-two generations since Tinhadin, but this was different. The king was not merely being removed so that his son—younger, more easily molded and controlled—could take his place. This time the Lothan Aklun wanted the entire line extinguished and a new dynasty established, with the Mein upon the throne.

That was why Hanish had at his disposal a strange race of people willing to march across the Ice Fields and make war on the Mein's behalf. That was why he possessed new weapons that hurled flaming balls of pitch like the sun, or that tossed boulders. Add to this a hidden Meinish army that had been hard at training in the mountains to the north of Tahalian, un-known to the outside world. With these tools and several other surprises, Hanish promised to sweep down upon an unsuspecting world and take it apart piece by piece.

The brothers had alluded to various positions of stature Rialus might occupy in the reshaped world they envisioned, but as yet he had seen no re-wards. He had hoped to prove himself useful. Unfortunately, this business with Leeka had not gone as he wished. He knew that the general's army had been mysteriously massacred, but he was not at all sure if this would bring Maeander the pleasure it should. After all, Rialus's charge had been to keep the general caged and to do what he could to hide the foreigners' arrival. He had failed on both accounts.

Maeander entered the governor's chambers with a visible disdain for the formalities due an Acacian official. He walked past the secretary who was preparing to announce him and strode into the room with clipped steps that seemed both casual and sharp enough to split the stones beneath his boots. Maeander was several inches taller than his host. He was broad in the shoulders, with strength that showed in movements of his muscled thighs and in the sinewy bulges of his forearms and in the contours of his neck. He wore his hair long, below the shoulders, the straw-gold strands of it washed daily in icy water and combed out—an unusual thing, for most Meinish men let their hair knot and walked with a nest of snakes cascading down their shoulders. He was, in all outward forms, a model figure for the rough-hewn, virile men of his race, strapped into garments of tanned leather, legs covered by fitted trousers.

Maeander pulled off his fur-lined gloves and tossed them down on a table, making a loud thwack as they hit. He did a quick survey of the room, pausing on the window. "So this is your window," he said, inspecting the sheet of glass. He spoke Acacian with the guttural tones of his native lan-guage, sounds that had always offended Rialus's ear. "The guards joked with me on the way in. When I instructed them to send you word of my arrival, one of them said that you already knew, since you always had one eye pressed against this glass. Another said that you seemed not to realize that one can see both into and out of glass. Such impertinence, Governor, should not be allowed."

Rialus flushed. The basic fact that he would be visible to people out-side had never occurred to him. He imagined the absurdity of his image viewed from outside, twisted into different contortions, those below watch-

ing him from the corners of their eyes, hiding smirks, laughing at him. . . .
And just like that, with a few casual words, he was made to feel a complete
fool. He recalled a time when the Mein brothers spoke to him as befit his office, but all that had changed. He had no idea how to regain his former
stature. In fact, he increasingly suspected that he had never held any.

Maeander turned from the window. The man's eyes were strikingly
gray. He did not so much look at someone as aim at them. Never, the governor thought, had he known a person to stare so fixedly, with such undisguised ill will. His gaze was that of a child upon a beetle he was about to
squash beneath his heel. "Do you know what happened to Alain's army?"

Rialus was not generally a fluent speaker. Before Maeander he became
a sputtering mess, which he was sure gave the wrong impression. Fortunately, Maeander was more interested in talking himself than in giving a
true interrogation. As he related it, Numrek scouts sent out to clear the way
before the bulk of their nation had spotted the general's column. Unseen,
they shadowed them for several days, until they were positioned for ambush. They swept in on them upon the tail wind of a clearing storm and
slaughtered them down to the last man and woman.

"You will be glad to hear that the Numrek are as skilled at killing as
they claimed," Maeander said. "They welcomed the test Alain's army gave
them. It warmed them, they said." He turned and strolled around the room,
directionless. He had three thin plaits of hair that stretched from the crown
of his head down to the left side. Into two, ribbons of blue were woven, into
the third a leather strap studded with silver beads. Rialus knew that these
were some primitive accounting system: the blue standing for ten men
killed, the leather strap for twenty. Or was it the other way around? The
governor could not remember. "I have never seen anything quite like this
Numrek army. They absorb and spit out everything they come up against.
Their women and children take as much joy in slaughter as the men. I doubt
very much that the combined forces of Acacia could match them on an open
field."

"Then it was all for the best," Rialus said. "The Giver provides for all
worthies. A great success!"

Maeander did not like being led. "Do not get ahead of yourself. You
failed to keep your general shackled. You sat at your window here as he
marched out to threaten everything my brother has been planning for years
now. The outcome was not that bad, true, but you have forced us to speed
up our plans. And is it true that your general sent out messengers—several
of them?"

"He did, but not to worry. I had them all hunted and slain."

"Not true. One of them got through. One of them met with the king's chancellor, Thaddeus Clegg."

"Oh," Rialus said.

"Yes. 'Oh.' Again, however, you have been saved by a piece of fortune." He paused to let Rialus squirm a moment, and then said, "Thaddeus is . . . conflicted, enough so that he may not see his interests as aligned with Leodan's."

Rialus's mouth formed an oval. "Conflicted?"

"Just so," Maeander said. He reached down and pushed the tips of his fingers through olives set in a bowl on Rialus's desk, imported delicacies not easy to come by in the Mein. He popped a few in his mouth and watched the governor. "Actually, Rialus, the reasons for his conflicted state of mind intersect with your own situation. Would you like me to explain?"

Rialus nodded, hesitant but too curious to refuse. Maeander spoke as he chewed. He asked Rialus to step back in time with him and to imagine Leodan and Thaddeus as they were in their youth. Imagine the young prince: dreamy, idealistic, indecisive in his acceptance of the power he was being groomed to wield, smitten by a young beauty—Aleera—who seemed of more import to him than his throne. Beside him his chancellor: resolute, confident, disciplined, a gifted swordsman, ambitious in the ways that Leodan was not.

"Leodan was never exactly a jewel in his father's eye," Maeander said, grinning.

Gridulan, he claimed, thought his son weak. But a son is a son; Gridulan had no other. He could not be denied. This is why Gridulan did the best he could to harden Leodan, even as he watched Thaddeus from the corner of his eye. He wanted his son to have a strong chancellor, but he had reason to fear Thaddeus's gifts. Thaddeus was an Agnate, after all. He could trace his lineage back to Edifus himself. He might, in certain circumstances, make a legitimate claim to the throne. This became a greater threat—from the old king's perspective—when Thaddeus wed a young woman, Dorling, also from an Agnate family. They had a boy child their first year together, a full two years *before* Aleera would give birth to Aliver. So there was strong Thaddeus, an officer in the Marah, with a young wife and child, with a fine lineage and the adoration of the populace and support of the governors—who saw the chancellor as a shrewd advocate for their causes. In short, Thaddeus had become a threat that Gridulan could not ignore, even if Leodan was oblivious to it.

"Guess what he did about it," Maeander urged. "Have you any idea?"

Rialus did not, although it took him some moments to convince Maeander of this.

"I'll have to tell you, then," the Mein went on. "Gridulan conspired with one of his companions. At the king's bidding, this companion acquired a rare poison, the kind used by leaguemen. Deadly stuff. He personally saw to it that Dorling consumed a dose of it in her tea. Her child—still nursing—was poisoned through his mother's milk. Both died."

"They were killed at the king's order?" Rialus asked.

"Just so."

At the time nobody knew what to make of the deaths. Some suspected murder, but no fingers were pointed—not in the right direction, at least. Gridulan was the first to offer Thaddeus condolences. Leodan was beside himself with grief. Thaddeus himself bore his suffering admirably, but he was never the same man afterward. Gridulan had chosen well. He managed to snuff out Thaddeus's ambition while leaving the man alive to aid his son. Leodan did not find out about the murders until some years later, after his father died and he read his private logs. But what was he to do with the knowledge that his own father had killed his best friend's wife and child all in order to protect him?

"Perhaps a strong man would have confessed everything to his friend," Maeander said, shrugging, for he did not seem certain of this point. "Perhaps. In any event, Leodan kept his mouth shut. He told nobody, only meting out punishment against his father's companion, the one who had administered the poison. Have you any idea who this person was?"

Maeander did not wait for Rialus to answer this time. "That's right," he said. "Your beloved father, Rethus, set the poison into play! That is why you are here before me now, a miserable governor of a miserable province. You are being punished—as was your father before you—for loyalty to Gridulan. Family secrets run deep, Rialus. I can tell by the perplexity on your face that I have both delivered surprises to you and answered old questions at the same time."

It took Rialus a moment to gather his wits enough to ask, "How do you know all this?"

Maeander looked to one side and spit out an olive pit. "My brother has a great many friends in positions to know such things. The league, for example, watches all of this with interest, glad to offer bits and pieces of information to help us stir the pot. Believe me, Rialus, the story I just told you is true. A few months ago my brother shared the information with Thaddeus Clegg himself. The news made quite an impression on him. Because of it I think it fair to say he is no longer entirely on Leodan's side. Think of the life Thaddeus has led since Dorling and his son died. Think of the love he showered on Leodan's children instead. Think of how he supported the king when he faced the death,—by natural causes, of course—of his own wife. Think how it would feel to discover that all of it was based on a lie, on murder, on betrayal. In his place, would you not want to see the Akarans punished? Revenge is the easiest of emotions to understand and to manipulate. Don't you agree?"

Rialus did, although he desperately wanted time and solitude to digest all that Maeander had just revealed.

"In any event," Maeander said, returning to the issue that had started the digression, "I will not kill you for your blunders, but I am afraid you will have to pay for them. I have promised Cathgergen to the Numrek. When they arrive, you will hand the fortress over to them. I trust you will not anger their chieftain, Calrach; from what I have seen of him he is not of a forgiving nature."

"You do not mean . . ."

Maeander looked affronted. "Are you protesting? You would not have me give them Tahalian, would you? There is no other way. The fortress is theirs to rest and regroup in. If you like, you can let the army put up a defense, and then afterward you may escape to whatever fate awaits you. Do not look at me like that. Neptos, I have never known a man to so resemble a rat and in so many different ways." For a moment actual anger flared in Maeander's voice, but he harnessed it and spoke coolly. "You may now go on breathing, but true rewards come to those who serve us more effectively."

"You have doomed me," Rialus said.

"I have not doomed you. If you are doomed, the seeds of it were planted before ever I knew you. That is how it is with us all. That is all I have for you."

Rialus managed to speak only after Maeander turned to leave. "You forget that I—I am the governor of this fortress." Maeander fixed a bemused stare on him. Rialus changed tack, moving away from the suggestion of threat inherent in that declaration. "Perhaps I can yet prove myself."

"Ah, are you as treacherous as your father? How would you prove yourself?"

"If what I have to offer pleases you, I must have your guarantee that I'll be rewarded. I can give you the royal family—their heads, I mean."

"I already have agents prepared to pounce on the king. They might have killed him already. Word of it may already be on the way to Hanish."

"No, no . . . I know that," Rialus said. He almost felt like smiling, knowing that in all likelihood he had thrown himself just the lifeline he needed. "I do not mean the king. The line of Akaran does not begin and end with Leodan."

CHAPTER

EIGHT

Corinn Akaran understood that there was much she did not know about the world, many names and family lineages and historical events that refused to stick in her memory. No matter. Very little of it had any bearing on her everyday life. What she believed was of significance was that she was King Leodan's eldest daughter, the beautiful one at that. She did not stand to inherit control of her father's realm—that went to Aliver—but this suited her as well. She found nothing enticing about the prospect of juggling such a complicated array of concerns. Better to stand just to the side and wield her influence within the sphere of courtly intrigue. She was sure that this would prove more interesting. The world might have been a large thing in fact, but the part of it she occupied was smaller, and in that smaller world few people were better placed than she to look toward the future with sublime optimism.

She did, however, harbor a secret that none of those close to her would have guessed at. Though by nature a jovial person with an affinity for fine clothes, gossip, and youthful romantic musings, she bore an awareness of death with her. It was a cloud that hung in the back of her mind, always near, there to threaten when she raised her eyes to take in larger things. Her mother had died when she was ten. Since then the curse of mortality had never been far from her mind. Aleera Akaran had faded from life as the spring gave way to summer. She was eaten from the inside by an illness that began as a backache and became an insatiable leech sucking the life from her.

Corinn remembered the last moments she spent with her mother in excruciating detail. In dreams she often sat beside her bed again, her palms clasped around the wan skin and bones of the woman's hands. Her body was so ravaged it seemed to have half melted into her mattress. Because the weather had been warm, she had often lain uncovered, her bare legs stretching out from beneath her frock, her feet and toes seeming unnaturally large now that they were the first thing Corinn saw on entering the room. Her weeks being bed bound made Aleera so feeble that she could not reach her window stool without her daughter's help. Her feet no longer knew how to find the floor. Corinn would stand supporting her mother's frail weight as with each step her heel drew circles in the air, as might a child who was taking her first steps.

All of this converging on the young girl struck her with the realization that the world held more frightening things in reality than it did in her darkest imaginings. Where in this picture was the all-powerful mother who always knew her daughter's mind before she spoke it, who laughed at Corinn's fears of dragons, giant snakes, and monsters? Where was the hero who chased such creatures away just by entering the room, just by smiling, just by calling her name? Where was the beauty at whose elbow Corinn had sat as she was groomed for official functions, the woman against whom all others had been measured? It still amazed her that things had changed so rapidly, without even a veiled suggestion that there was meaning to it all.

As painful as this was, it was compounded by the fact that she saw herself in each portion of her mother's dying body. Her mother had given her the shape of her face, the character of her lips, the pattern of lines across her forehead. They had the same hands: the same rate of taper and length, the same character to the knuckles, the same thin fingernails, the same off-kilter slant to the small finger. The girl of ten had held between her palms an aged, decaying, fading grip on herself, like some strange conflation of the past with the present or the present with the future.

Though she often schemed the days away with youthful optimism, part of her was nagged by the fear that she would not live out the year. Or if she did it would be only so that she would first gain everything, then lose it all, then die. She had felt this way when she was ten, and then eleven and twelve and so on, but still the feeling was as strong as ever. The fact that she balanced these morbid thoughts with an otherwise effervescent nature was as confusing to her as it would have been to those who viewed her from the outside. She hid her darker musings as best she could, both alarmed by and ashamed of them. She often reminded herself that every living being faced death; few of them were offered a life of such rich potential as she. And perhaps she was wrong. Maybe she would live a long and joyful existence;

maybe she would even find a way to live forever, ageless and untouched by illness.

On the morning that she was to greet a delegation from the nation of Aushenia, Corinn stared for a long time into the mirror of her dressing table, gazing at her reflection. She reached down and plucked up a horsehair brush used for applying face makeup. She dipped it in a powder made of crushed seashells and flicked the bristles over her cheeks. She hoped the sparkles would complement the glint of silvery fibers in her dress, a sleek, sky-blue gown that hugged her figure. Despite her morbid thoughts, she was pleased with the prospects for the next few days. She did not—like Aliver—have to sit through the inane formalities of the official meetings. But unlike Mena and Dariel she was old enough to function in some official capacity. This time she was to serve as host and guide to the Aushenian prince, Igguldan.

Despite her maid's warning that the day would be chilly she wore only a thin shift beneath her dress. She could put up with cold, she said; she could not stomach looking frumpy. As her single concession to the weather she decided to wear a new item just sent to her from Candovia, a white fur band worn around the neck and fastened snug with clasps. She thought the scarf achieved a sort of elegance. She hoped so, for she was not as adept at dressing for chilly weather as she was at dealing with the three seasons of warmth Acacia offered.

Corinn met the Aushenian prince on the steps of Tinhadin's hall. She stood surrounded by several attendants, a translator, and a few aides from the chancellor's office. All of them were framed by the granite pillars of the hall's façade, rough-hewn and veined with age and weather wear. Of an earlier architectural vintage than most of the city, the hall had been built back when the nation's leaders seemed to look askance at the smooth lines and arches of cultured cities like those of the Talayan coast, which later generations took inspiration from.

The prince was dressed simply. Corinn might have found this disappointing, but his actions demonstrated such practiced reverence that she had to acknowledge his manners were impeccable. He walked with down-turned eyes, his arms pressed tight to his sides and his palms tilted toward her. Both he and his party timed the placement of their feet as they climbed, so that they moved as of one mind. Once the young man reached the step below her he paused. His gaze lifted up, met hers, and held it just slightly longer than appropriate. She found herself inclined to forgive him, both because of the timorous, creased smile that he wore and because she knew that her gown and the white fur ring around her neck and the intricate braidwork of her hair and the sparkling seashell powder that highlighted her cheeks had all combined to impressive effect.

Igguldan's features were famously Aushenian: his hair like straw dipped in auburn dye, his eyes intensely blue, as if they were flecked glass beads lit from behind. Corinn had once thought pale, freckled skin to be lacking compared to the creamy brown of Acacians or the near black of Talayans, but looking at Igguldan she felt drawn to just this feature. She wanted to reach out and touch him just under the eye and to move her finger from one dot to the next.

She led the group on a tour of the main buildings of the upper tier of the city, past the various wings of the palace, down as far as the training grounds, and around governmental buildings. The Aushenians grew excited at the sight of the golden monkeys that roamed the grounds and even inside the palace. They had nothing like them in their country, they explained. Corinn nodded, unimpressed. She had seen the creatures every day of her life. They were small, the size of cats, really, with puffy coats of hair that ranged from yellow to almost crimson. They had some sacred significance, but Corinn did not remember what and did not mention it.

Eventually, they came to the old ruin that housed the foundation stones from one of Edifus's first defensive towers. The crumbled remains of this structure were enclosed in a modern building, a sort of pavilion that perched on arching legs and afforded views out in three of the compass's directions. At its center stood a statue of Elenet in his youth. One of the chancellor's aides stepped up to recite the first sorcerer's tale, which in many ways was the Giver's tale as well.

In the beginning, the aide intoned, a god figure known as the Giver created the world as a physical manifestation of joy. He gave form to all the creatures of the earth, including humans, though he did not set humans apart from other creatures. He walked the earth singing, creating with the power of words. His language was the thread, the needle, the pattern from which the world was woven. Into this bliss, however, came mischief. A human orphan of seven years, Elenet, once saw the god passing through his village. He approached the Giver and offered himself as a servant, so that he might stay near the god's grace. The Giver, taken with him, obliged. But Elenet was not like the other animals that trailed behind the Giver. Elenet could not help but listen to the god's song. He learned the words. He came to understand them and recognize their power. He reveled in the possibility of wielding them himself. Once he had learned enough, he ran away.

"He became the first God Talker," the aide said. "He taught his knowledge to a few chosen others. When the Giver learned of Elenet's deception, he was disappointed. He turned his back to the world and went silent. He was never seen to walk the earth again. He did not sing anymore. Because of this we have the world as it is now."

Judging by the way Igguldan fell to one knee and ran his hands over the fissures in the ancient stone, muttering to himself, the tale was well known to him already and quite affecting. Corinn was inclined to frown at his earnestness, but throughout the next hour or so he proved a pleasant enough companion. He spoke near-perfect Acacian, as did most of the party. Before long the interpreter and the chancellor's aides fell back into the rear of the group, which broke up into smaller pods like children out on some educational outing.

"I wonder," Igguldan said, "if it is true that Edifus was one of Elenet's disciples. He was a sorcerer, I have heard said. That was why he—and Tinhadin after him—triumphed so completely. What do you think, Princess?"

"I have not thought much about it, but I do not see any reason to believe in magic. If my people had such a gift, then why do we not have it still?"

"So you don't?" Igguldan asked, smiling. "You cannot, for example, cast a spell on me and force me to do your bidding?"

"I hardly need magic to achieve that," Corinn quipped, the words out of her so casually that she had uttered them before she even knew she thought them. Heat rose across her chest and up her neck. "Maybe we created tales of magic afterward, as a way to explain the things Edifus accomplished. Greatness is hard for lesser persons to believe in."

"Maybe so . . ." The prince thrummed the weathered stone with his fingers, stood on his toes a moment, and took in the scene below them to the east. "I guess I am a lesser man, then, because I love the Old Stories as they are. Your lore, in fact, plays a large part in our own legends. In Aushenia we have no doubt that men and women once practiced magic and that your people used it to master the world. There is a wonderful poem about how humans gained this knowledge. I will not recite it now for fear of embarrassing myself, but perhaps later I will get a chance to sing for you."

"And what of magic now?" Corinn asked. "I see no wizards around here."

The Aushenian prince smiled but said no more. As they left Edifus's ruins and followed the back path on its slow ascent toward the King's Rest, Corinn admitted, "I do not know that much about your people. What are you Aushenians like?"

"You would find Aushenia cold. Not as cold as the Mein—up there they scarcely see the sun in winter and it can snow any day of the year, even in the height of summer. Not so in Aushenia. True, we have a short summer, but it is vibrant. All the creatures and plants make use of the few months they have. In the spring the buds of flowers and new growth push right up from under the snow, as if one day the Giver grants them leave and then nothing can stand in their way. In the summer the weather is quite warm. We swim in the lakes in the north. Some even swim in the sea. At Killintich we have a swimming and foot race on the solstice day each summer. The racers swim from the castle pier to a point across the harbor. Then they run back again. It takes an entire day."

The two paused for a moment at the foot of the last staircase. The others had fallen some distance behind. Corinn said, "Funny that one minute you say it's cold and the next you talk of budding flowers and swimming. Which is the truth, Prince?"

"In a place as far north as Aushenia, it is not the cold that has the most effect on you. It is the moments when the cold recedes." Corinn answered this with a nod, and the two stood for a moment in silence. "But we are like your nation in many ways. My people admire learning, just like yours. Some of our best pupils even train in Alecia. You know this, I am sure. Aushenia was the first northern country to ally with Edifus against the Mein. Unfortunately the alliance did not live on after that conflict was resolved. That is why my father so wishes that your father would honor us with his presence. My father is not well, you see. He cannot travel, but he has spent his entire life working toward coming to an alliance with your people. He believes that we would be stronger together."

The others had not yet reached them, but Igguldan took a step up and Corinn matched him. They ascended together, preserving their solitude a bit longer. "And we are poets," the prince said.

"Poets?"

"That is how we keep our history, in epic poems sung by our bards. In our courts, cases must be argued in verse. It is an odd formality, but it draws crowds to the more complicated cases."

"How strange," Corinn said, although it did not actually seem that strange. She had no patience for official procedures at all. Maybe if all the government bureaucrats were made to speak in rhyme, she would be able to sit through them.

"You are the eldest son of your family?" Corinn asked.

Igguldan nodded. "I am. There are three after me, and two from my father's second wife."

Corinn attempted to raise an eyebrow, although all that really happened was that both of them ridged into erratic lines. "Second wife?"

"Well . . . Yes, my father reenacted the old codes, taking two wives to ensure the production of an heir. He need not have bothered, but . . . he was just being thorough."

"I see. Are you likewise inclined to be thorough?"

"No, I will marry only once."

They had reached the high balcony on the back of the King's Rest. Corinn perched her fingertips on the stone balustrade and lifted her chin, pointing it out across the sweep of clear, greenish-blue sea before them. "So you say. You must have abundant beauties in your country—enough so that a man can wed more than one."

"You are mistaken. Think of it just the other way around. Women have half the virtues they do in Acacia. Believe me . . ." The prince touched Corinn on the back of her hand. "Princess, the day you are kind enough to set foot in Aushenia, you will be hailed as the most beautiful woman in the country, and I will be chief among your admirers."

The prince could not have conjured up a more effective statement to win Corinn's pleasure. With that single sentence he complimented her, alluded to his enduring fidelity, and promised her universal admiration. She stood dumb for a few moments, her fingers tingling, imagining the possibility that she could spend her life a swan surrounded by ducks. She answered the prince coyly and carried on with the tour, but she decided to find out all she could about Aushenia. Perhaps she had just found her future husband. Everyone knew that Acacia and Aushenia longed to be allied together. Her marriage could be a political coup. She could be princess of one nation, queen of another. This was something to look forward to.

Chapter

Nine

Leeka Alain had not harbored delusions about his importance to the course of the empire's history. Never in his forty-eight years—of which more than half had been spent in military service—had he imagined himself to have a destiny of particular note. He was just a soldier, one of many in a line that had marched in anonymity out of the haze of history. So he had believed until one particular occasion on which he opened his eyes and rose up out of an empty slumber. A simple act, done thousands of times throughout his life. But this time it was like being born anew. One moment there was nothing. The next his eyes fluttered creation into existence, a world previously unimagined, one that demanded things of him that he had never been warned were even possibilities.

At first this creation was simply a square of bright white above him, an irregular geometry, brilliance in an otherwise formless blackness. He struggled to sit upright and find purchase on the limbs he vaguely understood as hands, arms, legs, feet. He was stuck fast. He stared for some time without understanding, with no point of focus, no context. Only when a shape cut through the space—one quick flash that was there and gone in the same instant—did he stir again. He watched the square of light long enough to catch the motion once more. A bird. It was a bird, a stretch of wing viewed from the shadowed underneath. And beyond it, creation slid, a contoured softness that he recognized as a high-clouded, arctic sky. This last revelation was the greatest help yet. With it came understanding of the pressure all around him. He opened his nose and sucked in the foul cacophony of scent and knew what it meant. He knew where he was and how he had gotten there.

That first horned creature . . . the rider atop it . . . the many others that followed him out of the storm . . . It truly happened, he thought. I lost them all. I led them to . . . What had he lost them to? Who were those screaming, stomping, mirthful agents of carnage? He had never looked such malformed horror in the face before. Like the first rider, all of them had stepped into existence hungry for violence. Some among them carried spears that they hurled as they strode forward, heavy things against which Acacian armor was but a thin skin. The soldier standing beside him took one of these in the chest and flew away behind the force of it, hand one moment on the general's shoulder, the next gone. Others of the enemy rode in on mounts that were like—what was the word for them? Those animals from Talay . . . rhinoceroses. They were some sort of domesticated rhinoceros, except hidden beneath a mass of matted grayish hair. They ran his soldiers over, sometimes pausing long enough in one spot to stomp a body into pulp.

The greatest shock had come when the sword- and ax-wielding mass of them hit the still huddled Acacians. They were enormous, long-limbed, and powerful. Leeka saw in their motions a joy at killing that he had never imagined possible. It was almost childish, the way they killed. As when one boy with a toy sword pretends to slice off his companion's arms and legs and head, and then thrusts his fist in the air, grinning at the damage he imagines himself to have accomplished. So did these beings go about their real work, hacking off limbs with glee, spinning themselves into grandiose strokes that nonetheless found their targets, clapping each other on the backs. Behind their matted mass of long black hair they were pale hued, like the snow. Leeka wanted to look one in the eye from up close, but he never got the chance.

He tried to remember what orders he had given. As much as he tried to match the totality of the slaughter with some reasoned response, he could neither recall any such response nor imagine what he could possibly have said in the few moments the slaughter took. There was simply nothing to it other than the enemy pouncing on them and his soldiers dying, blood spray all around, limbs kicked across the sodden snow, bodies like cloth dolls strewn about in broken-backed postures impossible for the living. It never appeared for a moment that any of the enemy worried for their own lives. Nothing touched them. Nothing frightened them in the slightest, and the damage they inflicted upon Leeka's soldiers was nothing to them but a grand amusement.

Leeka had seen an enemy spearman pin an Acacian soldier beneath his foot. The foul thing studied the woman with primitive curiosity, and then jabbed the pronged point of his weapon straight down into her face. This had galled Leeka like nothing ever had before. He roared. He directed his fury up from his abdomen and hurled a scream across the tundra. The spearman heard him, yanked free the weapon, and moved on him. If the being loosed his spear and missed, Leeka promised as he ran toward him, he would find himself gutted on Acacian steel the moment after. The spearman, though, threw with accuracy. The missile sped toward him in an elongated blur. Leeka would have died if not for the actions of one of his soldiers, a man whose name he did not know beforehand and did not learn after.

The soldier stepped between the spearman and the general. He caught the lance full in his chest. It pierced through him and emerged from the other side in a burst of blood and jagged shards of rib. The spear point shifted just enough to the side that it passed through the hollow between Leeka's side and his arm. The soldier's body smashed against his. The force of that impact flung them both backward. The man's helmet cracked Leeka on the forehead and knocked him unconscious. The two must have fallen together in a jumble, one looking just as dead as the other.

That, he assumed, was why he was not more carefully dispatched and why he opened his eyes many hours later to find himself layered well down inside a mound of bodies. Before he had been felled, he had noticed that some of the enemy grabbed slain soldiers by the ankles and slung them into piles, clearing the ground as if careful that corpses not clutter their playground, so he understood that he had been tossed into one of these mounds. Others were then piled on and around him. Immobile, stuck fast within a mound of the deceased, the blood-smeared men and women of his army intertwined under and over him; he drifted into and out of consciousness.

In waking moments he came to understand existence as one of suffering and great heat. He was so packed in that for some time he thought the heat was a product of this alone. Later, he was engulfed within an incredible furnace beyond anything the stiffening bodies could have been responsible for. He felt the corpses around him flex and shiver with it, belching the awful scent of flesh aflame. It was not until he had sweltered through this state for hours on hours, drifting into and out of fitful, nightmare-laden sleep, that he awoke to the startled realization that heat raged inside him as well as without. A fever pulsed with life from the center of his forehead. A bug was imbedded there. He was sure of it. An insect dipped its curved beak into his skull, pumping him full of some venom, the round, bulbous bottom of it heaving with the effort. He struggled to reach it, but he could not move. He sweated from every pore of his body. Salt tinge stung his eyes. He licked the corners of his mouth, frightened by the crusted leather that was his lips. His teeth had changed also. They were canine incisors that cut into his tongue, filling his mouth with mercury that, try as he might, he could not expel. He gagged on it, lost consciousness, awoke gasping, remembered the heat and the insect within his skull and realized that the flesh had begun to slough off his frame, rotten meat. And then he would pass out. Dream. Wake. Writhe. And on and on.

This was all before the time he awoke to coolness and to the square of light above him and to the bird cutting shadows across the sky. He had no idea how many days had passed when he struggled up from the ghastly stitch work of corpses under which he had lain. The bodies that had provided him lingering warmth were frozen stiff now. The mound was dusted with ice, but it was easy enough to see the charred remains underneath, the ashes kicked away by the wind. The bodies had been set aflame. Around him were many similar heaps.

The mound in which Leeka had been buried had burned less completely than the others; perhaps in this chance lay the reason he still breathed. All manner of debris cluttered the tundra—blood-fouled, shattered equipment; corpses of pack animals and dogs; portions of men and women. It was a scene of utter frozen desolation, not a moving creature in sight except for a few scavenging birds, the thick-necked, squat carrion eaters of these frigid climes. They had enormous beaks, short and visibly serrated. With a flicker of hope he considered the possibility that he was actually dead and all this around him was the afterdeath. But the world was too terribly solid for him to believe this.

He might have stood there for some time, supported up to the thighs by the charred remains, had a vulture not landed near at hand and yanked at one of his soldier's curled finger joints. The thought of killing one or two of them warmed Leeka with purpose. Within the hour he had scavenged a bow and several arrows. He impaled three of them and set the rest circling overhead, crying out their rage from above. It did not take long to understand the task was futile, though. More birds appeared, dropping to the ground each time his back was turned to them.

He realized there were other creatures about: small white-furred foxes, stained pink around the jaws, a weasel-like creature with a striped black-and-white tail, even a species of hard-shelled insect that seemed impervious to the cold. He killed several of these by touching them. He scorched them with the warmth from his fingertips. Heat. Such a powerful force in this place, instrument of both life and death, of torture and salvation.

Thinking this last, he set about gathering the supplies to build a fire. It was not easy, weak as he was. He had often to stop and take sips from the water skin wrapped close to his abdomen and to nibble the hard flat bread, the only food he could stomach the possibility of. In the slanting light of the early dusk he fed a growing blaze. He tossed atop it the frozen, singed bodies of his soldiers. He ventured into the dark and cold and dragged back offerings to the flames. Again and again he did this, each time a small journey between extremes. His head reeled when he moved too quickly. Often he dropped to one knee, eyes closed, still, until the spinning stopped. A wind had kicked up again and with its shifting bluster it was impossible not to inhale smoke. Coughing and soot covered, he stayed at the task until the work was completed. His army was not to be food for the scavengers. Better they were freed to the air so that they might blow away and search for peace dispersed far across the Giver's misbegotten creation.

Late that evening Leeka huddled near the blaze, his eyes tearful from ash. Grit caked on his lips and stuck to his teeth. Several times gusts of wind brought him the sound of women singing in the distance. Impossible, and yet he heard it with almost enough clarity to pick out individual words and to hum the tune inside himself. What to do now? He tried again and again to focus on this question. He was a general faced with a tragedy; before anything else he must form a plan of action. But he never got further than asking the question before some memory of horror yanked his attention away. Though his mind roiled with scenes of the slaughter, he could not fix one single image in which he had seen one of those enemy men creatures fall. Throughout the work of the day he had not found any of their dead. All the limbs he had collected and tossed to the flames had been from his own men. He found nothing that proved even one of the enemies had been killed, nothing that even led him to believe they had been wounded.

The invader's trail was easy to see in the burnished light of morning. Despite the blurring effects of snow and the wind, the path they had left was like a dry river cut into the tundra. Whatever wheeled vehicles they pushed or pulled must have been massive, for the tread of them cut diagonal ridges into the ice several feet deep. He saw the crisscrossing tracks of the rhinoceros creatures. In and around these were myriad footprints left by the enemies themselves. Some of these were larger than a man's by half. Others were small enough to be children's. Still some appeared from the tread of the boots to be those of Acacian soldiers. Prisoners?

Leeka set out down the trail. He marched with all the supplies he could salvage dragged behind him on one of the smaller sleds. He fashioned tent poles into walking sticks and slammed these into the ice with each step. He pushed his pace, a single figure jogging in pursuit of an army. It did not make much sense. He was not yet sure what he was trying to accomplish. He just had to do something. He was a soldier of the empire, after all, and there was an enemy afoot, a nation to warn.

CHAPTER

TEN

Like all the Aushenians that Aliver had thus far seen, Igguldan dressed proudly in his national garb: long leather trousers shrunk skintight to the legs, a green-sleeved shirt completed with a blue vest, a felt hat set at an angle on his head. They were simple garments really, like something worn on a hunt. This was in keeping with the national character. Aushenians loved the rolling forestland of their country and liked to think themselves still the huntsmen their ancestors had once been. From the strong, long-limbed look of him, Aliver felt perhaps they were that.

Aliver had once complained to his father that other nations should not have been allowed to maintain a royal class. What sense did it make for one king to rule over other kings? It undermined their authority, threatened to make others equal to them. Should there not be a single monarch for the empire? Leodan had answered with measured patience. No, he had said, that would not be better. All the nations of the Known World—other than Aushenia—were subservient to them in many ways, in all matters of importance. They were conquered peoples, but they were not without pride. Keeping their kings and queens, their customs and traits, allowed them to hold on to some of that pride. This was important because people without a sense of self were capable of anything. "It takes nothing from you to occasionally call another man royal," he had said. "Let them be who they are, and let our rule over them feel as gentle as a father's hand upon a son's shoulder."

It was not a full contingent of the King's Council that met the Aushenian prince. A few senior members sent their secretaries instead—something Leodan murmured about under his breath. Thaddeus was there beside the king, along with Sire Dagon of the League of Vessels and enough others to grant the meeting the appropriate air of importance. The foreign prince was

surrounded by other officials of his state, advisers and seasoned ambassa-
dors. Aliver knew the prince to be only three years his senior, but in action
he seemed a much more practiced dignitary. The older men deferred to him.
Before they spoke they asked his permission with their eyes. He conversed
freely with Leodan and Thaddeus, and he recited a long greeting from his
father, Guldan, which sounded much like a poem in its rhythm and occasional use of rhyme. Aliver might have been put out to see a young man more
comfortable than he yet was in such a role, except that Igguldan, with his
open face and smiling manner, was hard not to like.

"Gentle councillors of Acacia," Igguldan said, "in truth I have never
looked upon a more beautiful island—nor more impressive palace—than
this one. Yours is a blessed nation, and Acacia itself is the central jewel in
the most lavish of crowns."

For some time he spoke as if his only objective were to sing the praises
of Acacian culture. How he loved each and every view the high citadels offered! How he marveled at the quality of the stonework, the functional
artistry of Acacian architecture, the refined demonstration of wealth without pretense. He had never eaten a finer dish than on the previous night:
swordfish grilled on an open flame right before him and drenched in the
sauce of some sweet fruit he had never before imagined. Everyone he had
met here had been so courteous and dignified that he would take back to
his homeland a new perception of model comportment. Coming as he did
from a smaller nation, one prey to nature's shifting seasons and temperament, he stood in awe of the sublime merging of power and tranquillity that
was Acacia.

He had a smooth tongue, so much so that Aliver was slow to notice at
what point he shifted his focus to the true business of his visit. By the time
he caught on, Igguldan was declaring that his nation took pride in its long
history as a free and independent state. He knew he did not have to remind
any gathered in the room about the role that Aushenia had played in securing the Acacian peace. It was the dual fronts and the combined power of
Aushenia and Acacia that had defeated their common enemies years before.
They might have had fractious relations on occasion since that distant time,
but it was the spirit of their former relationship that his father wished their
two nations to remember now.

"That is why I come bearing my father's request that you admit Aushenia peacefully into the Acacian Empire, as a partner province on par with
Candovia, Senival, or Talay. If you accept us, Guldan swears that your nation
will profit from it and never regret the decision."

There it was, Aliver thought, presented more clearly than he imagined such overtures would be. The Acacian response, however, was not similarly straightforward. The King's Council members peppered the young man with questions. Asked whether Guldan would revoke Queen Elena's Decree—that haughty declaration of eternal independence—Igguldan answered that her words spoke true for her time. One could not reach back into the past and change what had been. Guldan would never contradict Queen Elena, but he spoke of now, of this moment, of the days and years to come.

Thaddeus asked what misfortune had befallen Aushenia that after all this time she finally begged a place at the table.

"No great misfortune, sir, but we have lived long enough outside the trading circles of the empire. There is a new spirit among my people that chooses to look toward the future with fresh eyes. We see now opportunities that we did not before. My father acknowledges this foremost among us."

"Umhmm," Thaddeus said, unimpressed. "So your situation is that dire?"

There was an edge to the prince's voice as he rebuffed this, just the slightest hint of aggravation. Aushenia, he said, was a modest nation, but it had never been poor. They were rich in amber, a valued gem known throughout the world. Their enormous pines were the best for sea vessels in the Known World. And their trees produced an oil that through a secret process they made into a pitch that sealed the hulls of ships against water and salt damage and worm damage. This, he knew, would be a boon to any nation that sailed the deep ocean.

Igguldan seemed primed to continue, but Sire Dagon cleared his throat to speak. Thus far he had sat silent and still at one end of the table, but Aliver had sensed the power of his presence the entire time. The League of Vessels. His father had once muttered that there was no more formidable force in the entire empire. "You think I rule the world?" he had asked, sardonic and cryptic at the same time. The league limped out of the chaos before Edifus's time as a ragtag shipping union, a loose band of pirates, really. Under Tinhadin's rule they won the contract to ship the new trade with the Lothan Aklun. With this legitimacy came such wealth that they evolved into a monopoly controlling all waterborne commerce. Before long, they were a diversified entity with influential fingers in every sector of the Known World. Once they won effective control over Acacia's naval might—a deal brokered when the seventh Akaran monarch disbanded his troublesome navy and looked to the league as an efficient alternative—they made themselves a military power, complete with a private military, the Ishtat Inspectorate, which they claimed was a security force to protect their interests.

Sire Dagon was as strange looking as any of the leaguemen. His comportment was more that of a priest of some ancient sect than of a merchant. His skull had been bound so tightly in childhood it was squeezed into an elongated shape, the rear crown of it like the narrow point of an egg. His neck was unusually long and thin, an effect they managed by wearing a series of rings around it while they slept, their number increased slowly over a lifetime. His voice was just loud enough to be heard, strangely flat of tone, as if each word sought to deny that it was even being spoken. "Yours is a nation of how many persons?"

The Aushenian prince nodded at his aide and let the older man answer. Of free citizens they numbered thirty thousand men, forty thousand women, almost thirty thousand children, and an insubstantial number of elders, as Aushenians most often chose to end their lives once they felt themselves unproductive. They had a large population of foreign merchants within their borders, numbers unknown, and they kept a small servant class of perhaps ten to fifteen thousand souls.

When the man finished, Igguldan said, "But you know this. We have known for some time that we were being watched by league agents."

"I am sure you are mistaken," Sire Dagon said, although he did not clarify on which aspect the prince was in error. "In the past your people voiced objections to our system of trade. Are we to believe that has changed? Your father would fulfill all of our requirements as suits a position within the empire? You know what product the empire trades in and what we receive in return for it?"

In the pause before Igguldan answered Aliver looked from his face to the other council members, to his father and over to the leagueman. He felt his pulse quicken with a tendril of danger and could see the signs of the same on other faces, but nowhere did he see the sort of confusion he himself felt. What product did Sire Dagon refer to? Minerals from the mines, coal from Senival, trade goods and precious stones from Talay, exotic produce from the Vumu Archipelago: these were the products of international trade. The goods Igguldan had mentioned would find buyers also. But if these were what he referred to, why did he speak with such ominous import?

Igguldan answered the leagueman with a reluctant nod.

Pleased, Sire Dagon folded one long-fingered hand over the other and rested them on the tabletop. The jewel on one large finger reflected fractured shards of light for a moment. "With time and reasoned thought, all peoples have found our system agreeable. All have seen the benefits of what we offer. But because of that we must protect what we already have established. We have achieved an equilibrium. We would not want to upset this. Because of this, new parties are not entirely welcome at this moment. I am sure I speak for the king in mentioning this." Sire Dagon nodded to Leodan without ever looking fully at him. Then he seemed to change tack. "On the other hand . . . Tell me, are your women fertile?"

Igguldan guffawed, but then caught himself as nobody else followed his lead. He glanced around and then back to Sire Dagon. His face showed the recognition that whatever bawdy joke he thought the leagueman was making had been a misunderstanding. There followed a discussion that Igguldan clearly found as strange to listen to as Aliver did. The Aushenian aides had come prepared for the question. They quoted statistics on the ages at which Aushenian women mature sexually, on the frequency of their pregnancies, and the rate of mortality of their young.

For a moment Aliver thought he saw amusement lift the corners of Sire Dagon's mouth, but then he was not sure if that was the right interpretation of the expression at all. The leagueman held back whatever response he might have made and simply withdrew once more into hooded silence. The meeting proceeded without another word from the league's representative.

Leodan seemed happy to take the conversation in a different direction. "I hear your conviction, Prince, and I admire it. But also I have long admired your nation's independence. You are the last in the Known World to stand alone; for some of us your people have been . . . well, an inspiration."

"My lord," Igguldan said, "one does not feed and clothe and provide for a nation simply through inspiration. We Aushenians have nothing to be ashamed of, but it is clear to us that the world has moved away from the model which we so long wished for."

"Which is what?" Thaddeus asked. "Refresh our memories."

"Aushenia has on occasion been ruled by women of stature and wisdom. Our Queen Elena, in her decrees, proposed that the Known World be composed of a federation of free and independent nations, none subservient to another, all trading the goods they best produced, each keeping to ways true to their national character, honoring old traditions and religions while extending the hand of friendship to others. This is what she proposed to Tinhadin."

A council member remarked that such a system might work at a sub-sistence level—each nation might make do and stay largely on equal terms—but none would achieve the wealth and stability and productivity the Acacian hegemony had created with the aid of league-managed commerce. They would have remained squabbling islands of national fervor, just as they had been before the Wars of Distribution.

Igguldan did not try to dispute this. He nodded and gestured that the palace around them was testament to the truth of that argument. "The queen would have answered you by saying that the grandest is not always the best, especially not when the wealth is held by few, fueled by the toil of the many." Igguldan ducked his head and ran a hand through his hair. "But this is not what I came to speak about. Elena is of the past; we look to the future."

"At times I can still envision the world your queen wished for," Leodan said.

"I can as well," the prince said, "but only with my eyes closed. With open eyes the world is something very different."

After the meeting adjourned an hour or so later, the king took tea with Aliver and his chancellor. The two older men spoke for some time, letting the conversation drift from one aspect of the meeting to another. Aliver was surprised when his father asked, "What do you think of all this? Speak your mind."

"I? I think . . . the prince seems a reasonable sort. I can speak no ill of him yet. If he represents his people truly, this is good for us, yes? Only, if they hold us in such high regard why haven't they joined us sooner?"

"To join us means a good many things," Leodan said. "They are right to have hesitated, but for some time now they have made it clear they would be our friends if we would be theirs as well."

Thaddeus motioned with his hand that it was not as simple as that. "As ever, your father is generous with his words."

"No, what I say is the way it is. They have held a hand out to us in friendship for years now. We simply have not grasped it."

"And it is well we did not. Our patience has paid off." The chancellor spoke as if he were addressing the king, but his eyes touched on Aliver long enough to indicate that he was drawing out the issues more completely for his benefit. "What the prince did not admit is that Aushenia must be suffering greatly. I marvel that they remained outside the empire for so long without collapsing under the financial burden of it. They have some mineral wealth, yes, harvestable forestlands and several fine ports and the amber and pitch Igguldan spoke of, but without the league to trade with, they have been able to do little with it. They are a proud people, but they have been forced to sell their goods on the black market, to traffic with pirates. This does not sit well beside all that idealism. They are making this overture so directly because they need us more than we need them. If we accept them, it will be a delicate matter working out their status within our empire. There are many burdens placed upon a new Vedel, a conquered member of the lowest rank. They must accept this without insult, although in truth a Vedel suffers much insult."

"What if they do not enter as Vedels?" the king asked.

"They must, though. By the old laws there is no other category. Tinhadin was clear that all the world had the choice in his time to join him or to fight against him. When Aushenia declined to accept Acacian hegemony, they decided their fate." Thaddeus paused only long enough to sip his tea, and then he raised his voice to answer the argument he anticipated. "The generations between then and now change nothing. Any leader of any nation understands that his decisions ring down through all future generations. When Queen Elena rejected Tinhadin's offer, she knew that her people would forever after live with the consequences."

Leodan said, "Thaddeus speaks of black and white in a world of a thousand colors. In truth we neither conquered nor defeated Aushenia in the old wars. Had they not been likewise an enemy of the Mein, we may not have prevailed at all. They have for hundreds of years lived neither as allies, vassals, nor enemies."

"Yes, for hundreds of years," Thaddeus said, "and that cannot be changed overnight. In truth, Aliver, of course your father would welcome the Aushenians. He is an idealist. He wants a peaceful world in which all are welcome at the table. He does not like to acknowledge that for there to be a table at all many must be excluded from it. This is something the league, however, bases all its decisions on. That is why it is unlikely that Aushenia will be allowed in. The league has a veto on any such expansion. I get the feeling that they are tempted by Aushenia but yet hold back for some reason that they will probably never explain to us. Something your tutor may not have fully explained to you yet, Aliver, is that the empire is as much a commercial venture as an imperial one. In this area the league holds the place of ultimate prominence. We know only a portion of how the league conducts its business, but if they do not want Aushenia in, then Aushenia will remain without."

Leodan brought his hands up to his face, looking fatigued by the conversation. "And that, son, is the matter distilled to its primary essence."

"In black and white," Thaddeus added.

CHAPTER
ELEVEN

The assassin had traveled to Acacia in complete secrecy because he had no other option. Had anyone known of Thasren's mission, there would have been far too many opportunities for him to be betrayed. Many throughout the empire complained about Acacian domination, but he could trust no one outside the gates of his capital city. He did not even call on the agents already hidden within Acacia, many of them for years, some for generations. Who could tell how life in these southern climes may have corrupted them? Instead, he found his own way into the lower town and from there through the main gates in the guise of a laborer. He walked unnoticed through the thronging city streets with an ease that filled him with loathing of these people. No stranger could have likewise roamed unquestioned through Tahalian. What was the use of living in such a formidable fortress if an enemy agent could so easily penetrate it? The island was wasted on these people. Gazing around at the naked riches of the place set his heart racing with anticipation. Under Mein control a renamed Acacia would be an impenetrable bastion. He reveled in imagining it, even though he knew he would not live to see that glorious time with his own eyes.

By asking a few questions of dusky-skinned passersby he found his way to the district that housed foreign dignitaries. While seeming to keep busy, he set about waiting for the single contact he planned to make. He did not loiter long. His third afternoon in the city he recognized his people's ambassador to Acacia. Gurnal's once blond hair had taken on a metallic sheen, as often happened when men of the Mein stayed too long in the south. At first he saw only his head through the crowd, but when the ambassador passed nearer to him, he saw that he wore loose robes like an Acacian, sandals, and wool socks. Only the medallion on his chest attested to his origins. Maeander had been right in his suspicions; Gurnal had forgotten himself. Why was the lure of soft things always so powerful to weak men? Why was a nation built on lies so attractive to people who should know better?

Thasren still had these questions in mind that evening when he scaled the stone wall and dropped down into the back courtyard of the ambassador's compound. He believed from his afternoon of surveillance that he knew exactly how many people lived in the grounds. He went in search of each of them methodically. He traveled slowly through the sleeping house, pausing in each room so that his eyes adjusted to any change of light or shadow. He made sure not to bump into anything, quite a task as the house was crowded with useless items, decorative urns and life-sized statues, chairs too small to sit in, stuffed animals in living postures. Each room had a different fragrance. He realized—perhaps more readily than he would have in the daytime—that the scents were those of different flowers.

He found the ambassador's daughter sleeping and bound her without making a sound. All she did was lift her hand a moment as he pressed a ribbon of cloth over her open mouth, as if she did not wish to be woken from a pleasant dream. The man's teenage son was a light sleeper and strong, and the two of them struggled for a few moments in the dark. It was a peculiar, muffled sort of wrestling, stranger still because the boy did not speak the whole time, even when the assassin twisted his arms into contortions that nearly broke them. The children's mother gasped when the back-curved blade of his knife touched her windpipe. She opened her eyes and stared up into his face and mouthed her husband's name, but whether this was meant as an entreaty or accusation he was not sure. He bound each of them where he found them, keenly aware of how merciful he was being. The three house servants were another matter. They slept close to one another and all woke to fight him. It was almost a relief, a release, to slit them open and listen as they went silent and still. The scuffle had been a loud enough commotion that he did not move for some time afterward, listening lest any movement or noise indicate that they had been heard.

Gurnal must have sensed something in the night. He should have been up, armed and deadly already, but these years in Acacia had dulled him. Just as the assassin entered, he rolled from one side of the bed to the other and back again, knotted in his bedsheets like a child. When he finally raised himself on his elbows, he mumbled something under his breath. He kicked his legs over the edge of the bed, touched his bare feet to the floor, and stretched himself upright. Did he know something was wrong? If so, he did not act like it. He failed to notice Thasren standing in the shadows beyond the corner of his wardrobe. He muttered something, and then rose and walked toward the hall.

The assassin rolled out from behind the wardrobe, low to the floor. His knife slashed the man behind the knee, first one leg and then the other, two cuts like those of a practiced butcher paid for speed. As Gurnal collapsed, the assassin grabbed the neck of his gown and yanked back. The next moment he had the man's arms pinned beneath the hard squares of his knees, with pressure such that he felt the man's biceps slip around the bone. Gurnal screamed with all the breath he could muster, until the assassin pressed the bloody blade of his knife to the tip of his nose. This sufficed to silence him.

"To whom are you loyal?" Thasren asked. He spoke his native tongue, a language of discordant tones, words like river stones cracking beneath a chisel.

The man stared without recognition into his attacker's gray eyes, the same color as his own. "To the Mein. To the blood of the Tunishnevre, to the thousands who perished, with whom . . . I am one."

"It is good that you utter such words. They are the right ones, but are you a right man?"

"Of course," Gurnal said. "Who are you? Why have you maimed me? I am—"

"Hush! I will ask the questions." The assassin repositioned himself so that he could press his knee against the man's chest in a posture more comfortable for himself. "When are you next to be close to the king?"

Gurnal made much of showing his discomfort with sighs and grimaces of pain. The assassin shifted more of his weight onto the man's chest, until he coughed out an answer. At first he spoke with wide-eyed disbelief, as if it were simply not possible that he had woken to this, that he was injured as he was, and that his mouth was managing to answer such a random inquiry. His attacker had more questions, though. He asked them as if such an interaction was normal enough. Gurnal responded, detailing aspects of his daily life, his duties, the places he was expected in the next few days and the things he was to do there. Before long he seemed to take comfort from his answers, as if all of these various commitments assured that his place in the living world would continue.

Eventually the questioner came back to where he had begun. "You will meet him this evening?"

"Yes, of course. Not in person, you see, but I am to be in the hall when he greets the Aushenian party. I will be one of many—"

"There will be a banquet?"

"At the palace two evenings from now. I will personally attend. A small party of us only. It is rare to dine at the king's table, but I . . ." The man's words dribbled to a halt. His eyes took on a perplexed expression. His jaw worked for a moment before he could produce more words. "I know you. Thasren! Thasren . . ."

The assassin hissed him silent and spoke close to the man's ear, letting his lips brush the soft skin and cartilage. "Who I am does not matter to you. What matters is that you have grown weak. You speak with your mouth instead of your heart." The ambassador protested, his eyes casting about side to side, as if help might have slipped in quietly and been awaiting eye contact to act. "Perhaps the Callach who judge all before the gates of the mountains will hear you and permit you entry. But in this world you look to a different master to evaluate your worth; this master is not pleased with you. Hanish Mein no longer values your life, but as you are a Mein, you will have one last chance to prove your loyalty."

During the next few hours he explained to the man and to his family how it was to be. He described the depths of pain and torture Hanish would inflict upon them if they failed at any of what was asked of them. He charged them with duty to their race, and he reminded them that the reach of the Tunishnevre was such that no Mein could escape their wrath. They had only a handful of things to do to save themselves. The wife and the children would show themselves in public with no sign that anything had changed. They would simper and fawn and flatter the Acacians, as seemed natural to them. They would find excuses to explain the absence of their servants and they would allow no one inside the house. For his part, Gurnal would tutor Thasren in all the things he would need to know to get near the king, what customs needed to be followed, whom he might encounter, what security he might meet. In short, they would help him kill the king.

When Thasren left the house that afternoon he wore a wig cut from one the slain servant's heads, tugged into place and secured with a headband of woven horsehair that crossed his forehead, a traditional decoration at occasions of importance. There was a reason other than just his skills as a killer that he was best suited for this task. The structure of his face was very similar to Gurnal's, the same basic shape, almost identical in the cant of the eyes and the bones of the jawline. They were, after all, part of the same family tree, second cousins on their mother's side. The most markedly different thing about them was their hair, but that had been remedied.

He found his way up toward the palace easily enough. He entered the royal gates as one of a flow of people, not questioned by the guards at all but simply waved through. As none of them were meant to be anywhere near the king they were not searched for weapons of treachery, just watched and contained in preordained spaces, spectators but not participants. He hated the smell of the place, such a confusion of different scents, the colognes and perfumes of so many foreign lands. It was just as Hanish had said it would be: the representatives of so many different nations, races of men who now bowed and smiled before the Acacian masters. Had the entire world forgotten pride of race? They were like so many hoofed creatures—deer and antelope—gathering to sing the praises of the lion that devoured their children. It made no sense at all.

He stood near the exit the entire evening, casually feigning comfort in the ambassador's strange clothes, nodding greetings to others when they made eye contact with him. Several times he turned away from people who seemed prepared to speak with him. Twice he held conversations with men who seemed to know him well. He coughed into his hand and explained his quiet by claiming he had caught a chill. The humor inherent in this was not lost on the Acacians. He had been too long on the island, they joked. He was becoming Acacian himself, prey to the slightest cold in the air. Both men departed smiling.

The effort of these deceptions wrung his body to exhaustion. His heart pumped furiously the entire time. Beads of sweat seeped out of his nose and perched on his cheeks and ran unseen down his armpits. A film of moisture developed between himself and the underside of his wig. But to the eyes that touched him, he appeared composed. When a hush fell across the throng and the crier called for attention and he watched the monarch enter, adorned with a golden crown, a wreath that prickled with thorns in imitation of the island's namesake—then he knew he was close, very close to earning his place in the history of his people. This evening he would not try to get any nearer. This was but a flirtation; the deed itself was better consummated on the morrow.

CHAPTER

TWELVE

Unbeknownst to his father, siblings, or even to the nanny in whose charge he was supposed to spend the afternoons, Dariel Akaran often escaped the confines of the nursery and wandered off for hours at a time into the bowels of the palace. His journeys had started the previous summer. When his former nanny took ill with a fever, an elderly woman replaced her. She was suitable enough in her plump and amiable manner, but she took a liquid substance in her tea that always put her to sleep. Dariel took advantage of this.

Even when she woke to find him missing, the quarters reserved for the children were so expansive that she could search for him without suspecting he was no longer within the maze of connected rooms. When he appeared, he simply dropped right into conversation with her, expressing his boredom and begging her to play one of any number of board games or darts, soldiers of the realm, sword fighting with sticks . . . The old woman had not the energy for such pursuits. She left the lad to his own devices for increasingly longer periods of time, just as he wished she would.

He had come across the hidden passageway quite by chance, following an errant marble that had vanished into the crack between his wardrobe and the wall behind it. The wardrobe was an enormous piece of furniture. It covered the better portion of the entire wall, built of solid mahogany and as immovable to the young boy as if it were part of the very stone of the palace. He squirmed his way behind it, first with the length of his arm, then a leg, then a full commitment, chest pressed against the wood of the wardrobe, back rubbing across the cold granite of the wall. He tried to lower himself on twisted knees, fingers stretched down toward where he believed the marble to be. He was so fixated on reaching it, and so annoyed at the intractable materials that were stopping him from doing so, that when he finally found the space to squat down and run his fingers through the dust-covered floor he did not pause to consider how he had accomplished this.

It was only with the marble clenched once more in his fist that he realized he was in some sort of corridor, lit just enough that he could make out the old stonework of the walls, rough edged in a manner rarely seen inside the palace. There was a stillness here, a quiet deeper than he had ever felt. There was also a slight movement of air. A breath across his face that brushed past him like a whisper.

Thus began his introduction to the long-forgotten network of passageways that had been used by servants to navigate unseen throughout the palace in an earlier age. It was a labyrinth of stairways, tunnels, hallways, and dead ends, lit occasionally by holes drilled through the stone and open to the air. He strolled into abandoned rooms, complete with pieces of furniture, wall hangings, and rugs visible only as raised geometric squares thickly layered over in dust. He never came upon a living being while in these precincts, but he found enough to fear in the ferocious figures carved into the lintels, bulbous-eyed beasts that walked on two legs like men and women, with the body parts of boars and lions, lizards and hyenas and eagles, including one that looked like a frog, save that its violent visage had nothing in common with the amusing creatures that emerged from the ground during the spring. What a strange people must have carved these things! What a horrific time it must have been when humans had yet to step away and set themselves apart from beasts. A golden monkey had followed him in once, but upon seeing these statues the creature bolted, leaving Dariel wondering if he should do the same.

On one occasion he emerged from a long, narrow passageway into the bright sunlight and the spray of sea waves just below him. He crept through an opening and crawled out onto a ledge, blinded by the brilliance of the day. He had found a hidden route right down to the sea at the northern edge of the island, not far from the Temple of Vada. He stood smelling the salt-moist air, wind currents blowing his hair about him. A stone's throw out to sea a shoal of fish churned the water. Large, gape-jawed seabirds circled overhead. He watched as one pulled in its wings and shot down into the water.

Dariel decided to retrace his route and find something to use as a fishing rod. As he began to turn, a swell in the waves smashed against the stone beneath him. It sent up a flume of water that smacked him under the chin and against the chest and lifted him off his feet. For a moment the water billowed and fizzed all around him. His legs and arms lashed out in all directions. He clawed for purchase on the ledge, using his fingers and feet and eventually wedging his torso between two stones. For a moment he lay there breathing in frantic gasps. He could have vanished beneath the waves. No one would have guessed what had happened to him. He would simply have disappeared.

The thought of all of this racked him with sobs. He did not return to that spot, nor did he mention the event to anyone. As much as it had scared him—as much, really as all his subterranean ramblings sent his blood pumping and his hands tingling, and as much as the ghostly breath in the corridors rippled and flexed the hairs on his neck, making them stand and sway like long grass pressed by a shifting wind—he still loved his time in these secret places. He did not wish to give up his adventures, as he knew he would have to the minute anybody found out.

Anybody, that is, from within the world of the upper palace. Those beings of the light were only a portion of the population of the palace. He found several points other than his playroom where the unused passageways connected to others still in use. This world was just as interesting to explore. In the subterranean community of laborers, the unseen society of servants and engineers, cooks and technicians through whose efforts the palace functioned, there Dariel was well known and much liked. Likewise, it was at the elbows of these employees that he found the most joy he had yet experienced in the company of adults—with the exception of his father, whom he adored. It took them some time to get used to him and to get beyond their fears that something might happen to the boy and that they would be punished for it. Indeed, some of them never warmed to him. He suspected they argued about him when he was not there. But in others he found fast friends. He rode in the donkey-drawn carts that a man named Cevil used to bring supplies from the lower storerooms up into the palace. He stood among the full hips of the sweets bakers, stealing one after another of the sugary teacakes that were his favorite. He sat at the knees of the aged former palace workers who lived in frugal retirement in a network of caves, old men and women invisible to royal society.

He spent whole days awed by the labors of the fire feeders who worked in the sweltering, blackened catacomb-like chambers below the kitchens. The ovens that the royal cooks used were fed by a series of gigantic furnaces, from which networks of pipes stretched up and through the ceiling in such a confusion that the boy never made sense of them, no matter how many questions he asked. The feeding room was a brooding kiln of a cave. It was caked with soot and floating coal dust; peopled by blackened men who were often naked down to the waist and streaked by sweat, with bulging forearms and shoulders, bloodshot eyes, and yellowed teeth. The room was open on one side, not for the splendid view of the sea stretching off to the west but to provide some relief from the heat of the ovens and to facilitate the arrival of new loads of coal from Senival, which came in on barges from the Mainland.

It was here that Dariel ventured the morning of the Aushenian banquet. He approached, hearing the commotion from some distance away, smelling the soot in the air, growing warmer with each bend in the carved granite of the corridor. When he stepped out of the corridor, the heat of the ovens hit him in a roar, as if he had stepped into the mouth of some living beast. For a few moments the scenes of men lit by glowing red embers had a horrific look to it. Once he spotted a particular figure, though, Dariel moved toward him.

Val claimed to be a Candovian. He also claimed to have been a raider in his youth, a sort of pirate of the Gray Slopes. Dariel took his claims with a grain of salt. Val seemed such a part of the stone and earth of Acacia itself that Dariel could not imagine that he originated anywhere else. What was never in question, however, was his stunning physical presence. He had an upper body of such girth that the first time Dariel spied him—moving about with hulking grace before the stoves, backlit and highlighted by the fiery glow—he had clutched his chest with one hand, sure that he had stumbled on the giants that fuel the world's volcanoes.

He still shuddered on seeing him now. Val yelled out a cursing order to someone and then stooped to get a grip around a chunk of coal as large as a small child. That was when he spotted Dariel. He straightened to his full height and wiped an enormous hand across his mouth, brushing away the profanity he had just uttered. "Young prince, what are you up to?" he asked, stepping nearer and dropping to one knee. "There's a banquet tonight. Don't you know that? Your father is honoring the Aushenian prince. It's not a good time for distraction down here. Or is that why you've come—to try and get old Val in trouble?"

As ever, Dariel was struck with shyness on meeting this large man, even as he was drawn to him and loved something about how small he felt before his bulk. He answered as he often did, with a bashful smile and a mumbled declaration of innocence.

The man set his hand on the boy's shoulder and gave him a playful shake. "Come on," he said, rising back to his feet with some effort, "it's time for my break anyway. Let's get some air."

Together the two retreated from the furnaces. Dariel walked behind Val, who cut a swath through the throng of workers. Shovels flinging coal, carts creaking past behind ornery donkeys, men swaying and cursing with the effort of their work: the movement was all around him, but as long as Dariel stayed close to Val, he knew he was safe. He stumbled occasionally on the rough contours of the floor and once bumped into Val's legs when he paused to let a cart past. The man's hand dropped down from a height and blanketed his shoulder, a momentary touch, and then they moved on again.

The sky was heavy with clouds, layer upon layer of them, but still, stepping out of the cavern and into the winter morning was blinding. The swift change was an overload of his senses, from dark to light in a few paces, hot to cold. They emerged as if from a fissure in a volcano, an exhaling fumarole of foul breath, greeted by the shock of salt-tinged air. They ascended a staircase cut into the stone and then walked along a sloping ramp from which openings led into the ovens that the lower furnaces fed.

Dariel stepped into the mess hall in time to watch Karan, the woman who doled out the laborer's rations, straighten from a stooped position. She had just set a tray of hard biscuits into the slotted holder on which they cooled. The momentary sight of her swaying breasts froze him in his tracks; he flushed with an embarrassment he did not understand, one that pulsed in him when she glanced at him and seemed to read his thoughts better than he did himself. Her eyes passed on to Val. She perched her fists on her hips, which bulged out from under the constriction of her apron, and eyed the man with disapproving eyes. "You're a bit of a sight," she said. "Coming in here without so much as splashing water on your face."

Young as he was, Dariel knew that he—not the foreman—was the target of her displeasure. She had never trusted him in the way Val did, Dariel thought, although why or how he could cause her harm escaped him. And he sensed that regardless of the cold tone she used with Val, she actually liked him, something that seemed to embarrass her enough that she wished to hide it.

"If I had a reason to care for my appearance, you can be sure that I would, woman," Val said, "but I'm here for some biscuits and a bit of tea. Is that too much to ask? I didn't know I had to clean up for a biscuit and a bit of tea." He shot a glance at Dariel, asking for a little commiseration, and then he used one hand to swipe most of the biscuits off one tray and into his other fist.

"Don't mind her," Val said a little while later. The two had returned to the staircase and seated themselves, side by side with the biscuits and tea between them, one long pair of legs and one short dangling over the rocky slopes below them. "She's worried that you shouldn't eat laborer's food."

Dariel held a biscuit between his fingers, contemplating it with no actual interest in putting it near his mouth, tasteless and brittle as it was. "I like it all right," he said. "It's hard to bite," he added, as if this was an understandable compliment.

"Sure you like it. That's what I tell her, but some folks are funny."

Dariel had certainly found that to be true. "Why does she not like me?"

"Her people have cooked for yours for generations now. She and I, we're servants, got no business associating with royalty. She's got a point, but I've my own way of thinking. You're a good lad. And, anyway, in a year's time or so you'll not bother with me. You'll stop coming around. I'm not meaning to offend. I just mean you'll have better things to do. You'll have your training. You'll have the whole business of becoming a prince. Now, Karan, she thinks you'll be the death of me somehow. Said she dreamed as much; to which I said she must've been eating her own cooking too close to bedtime. But she does have a way of making one think. So let me ask you . . . What's this all about then?" Dariel looked suitably perplexed enough for Val to go on. He leaned close to the boy and squeezed his brows into one large central knot between his eyes. "Why are you down here with me, eating my rock biscuits, sharing my black tea? You're a prince, Dariel, this food must be like eating dirt to you, not to mention the matter of my low company."

Dariel looked away from him. It was not so much the question itself that made him uncomfortable as it was the tone of the large man's voice when he asked it. There was something unnatural in it, as if he spoke it from something other than his true emotion. Dariel was able enough at hearing the deception. Deciphering it was something else. He had explained before how he had found his way into the workers' quarters. He had said before that he liked adventure, liked danger, liked people not so stuffy and formal as those at court. Val had heard all this before, but every so often he posed the same question again, as if none of Dariel's previous answers satisfied him. To fill the silence Dariel said the first thing that came to mind.

"The old woman that watches over me takes a drink that puts her to sleep."

"Is that right?"

"Yes, so it's boring just sitting there."

Val shoved a biscuit in his mouth and talked while chewing. "Who wants to watch an old lady sleep?"

Again, Dariel heard something ironic in the man's voice, but he ignored it. He saw a rare invitation to speak about the things that troubled him. He explained that his older siblings were not always nice to him. Immediately afterward he corrected himself: Mena was pretty much always nice, but Corinn thought he was stupid and Aliver did not like him. Aliver had once shouted at him to leave him in peace, and Corinn had told him to stop breathing on her and said she wished he had been born a girl. None of them made time for him. None seemed to care that he had no one to play with, ever. He painted a sad picture of daily abandonment, hours in solitude, lifetimes of loneliness.

Val listened to all of this without interrupting. He just grunted every now and then, ate his lunch, and seemed to follow the movement of ships on the sea. Glancing up at him, Dariel stared for a moment at the flaring of his nostrils as he breathed, the hairs inside heavy with coal dust. For some reason he thought of how his father sometimes came into his room at night and kissed him on the cheek and forehead and mouth. Dariel never let on that he was awake, although he was a light sleeper and often opened his eyes just from the ruffle of movement as his father stepped into his room. Sometimes he had felt the man's tears fall on his skin.

And then he felt bad for all the things he had just said. Why had he spoken any of those things? The truth was, he loved all his family so much it frightened him. His siblings were each in their own way versions of perfection that he adored. He feared the day that his father stopped lavishing him with affection, even though he also feared the unfathomable sadness that seemed to bring it on. He knew his mother had died, and he had no memory of her. If this could have happened already, something just as awful could happen again. He could lose somebody else, too terrible a thought. To change the subject he asked his friend to talk about when he used to be a raider.

Val seemed unsure if he should, but a moment later his memories got the best of him. He said that he had been born into a raiding family, the Verspines. Since his earliest memories he had lived a wandering life, mostly aboard the swift ships of their trade, sometimes camped on one of the Outer Isles, where they hid after successful raids. They raided up and down the ocean coast, from northern Candovia far down into Talay. They always struck at night, sneaking into cities or towns and waking the citizens into terror. They took what they liked and dealt harshly with any who opposed them. They traded their booty for any supplies they needed, and then they retired to the islands to live for months in tranquillity, fishing and lying about near the beach, drinking, fighting, enjoying life until the time came to raid again.

Dariel had started to really feel the cold now, the wind pressing at them from the northwest, but he did not want to admit it to Val. "Why are you not still a raider?"

Val shrugged. He mumbled that he had better get back to work and rose stiffly to his feet. Once at his full height he paused and took in the view of the sea for a little longer. "The truth is that I lost the heart for raiding," he said. "Too many that I knew died the wrong way. When I was young, that didn't bother me so. I believed that I deserved to have whatever I could take and that whoever I killed or hurt to get what I wanted was just in the way. You've got to understand that the world's full of men who are little better than animals. I may joke about it now; you and I may sit here thinking on them times; but an animal is what I was for thirty odd years of my life. Problem is that a man is different from an animal. In the quiet afterward we know when we've done wrong. When I left them ways behind I came here to serve your father. You just think of me as Val, the feeder, who used to be a dead-hearted killer in some time long ago. Can you picture that?"

Dariel looked at the man's craggy features, so large and wide spaced and blackened; his head perched atop a width of shoulders that might as well have been a mountain range for all the largeness of the shadow they cast over him. Despite all that Dariel could not imagine him as any sort of killer. As terrible and vivid as the man's tales were and as eager as his boy's mind was to hear them, he still could not believe that Val had ever done any man any harm. He was simply a laborer from the world beneath the palace, a sympathetic giant who had probably inherited his position from his father and who may never have ventured off the island, one who knew exactly the type of tales to tell a boy like Dariel and did so as a kindness.

CHAPTER

THIRTEEN

Leodan Akaran was a man at war with himself. He carried on silent conflicts inside his head, struggles that raged one day into the next without resolution. He knew it was a weakness in him, the fault of having a dreamer's nature, a bit of the poet in him, a scholar, a humanist: hardly traits fit for a king. He enveloped his family in the luxurious culture of Acacia, even as he hid from them the abhorrent trade that funded it. He planned for his children never to experience violence firsthand, even though this privilege was bought with a blade at others' necks. He hated that countless numbers throughout his lands were chained to a drug that guaranteed their labor and submission, and yet he indulged in the same vice himself. He loved his children with a breathless passion that sometimes woke him in terror from dreams of some misfortune befalling them. But he knew that agents working in his name ripped other parents' children from their arms, never to be seen again. It was monstrous, and in many ways he felt it was his fault.

He had not instigated any of these things himself; like his children he had been born into it. He had grown up on the same tales he was now sharing with his youngest. He had learned the same reverence for the early heroes of his nation. He had practiced the Forms, stared respectfully at dignitaries from around the empire, and believed uncritically that his father was the rightful ruler of the entire world.

When he first saw the mines of Kidnaban as a boy of nine—the gaping chasms carved into stone, masses of humanity naked but for loincloths, laboring like thousands of insects in human form—he simply did not understand it. He could not fathom why those men and boys would choose such a life, and he did not ask why the day left twisted knots of anxiety in his abdomen. But just after his fourteenth birthday he had learned in quick succession that those mine laborers were conscripted from each of the provinces, that the heads of the various nations that visited Acacia were the privileged few, the very ones entrusted with the suppression of the bulk of their people.

This was shocking enough, but it was learning of the Quota that prompted him to action. In the throes of righteous adolescence, he went to his father, full of reproach. He came fresh from the lesson that introduced him to it and broke in on his father at sword practice. Was it true, he asked, that since Tinhadin's time they had provided a yearly quota of slaves to a nation across the Gray Slopes? Was it true that agents in the Akaran name collected hundreds of boys and girls from the provinces, children sold and never seen again? Was it true that no one even knew to what labor or fate those children were banished? Was it true that these foreigners—the Lothan Aklun—paid for the slaves with a vast supply of a drug that kept much of the empire addicted and dependent?

Gridulan broke off his fencing. He tipped the point of his naked sword into the mat at his feet and looked at his son over the upraised stretch of his nose. He was a tall man—Leodan would never reach his height—with a stiff, military bearing. His companions—thirteen men he had known since boyhood—dotted the training space, a few fencing, the bulk of them standing beside one of the pylons, conversing. "Those things are true, yes," Gridulan said. "The Lothan Aklun also promised that they would never wage war against us. This is something we should be thankful for. Tinhadin wrote that they were each like serpents with a hundred heads. I am glad that you are learning the realities of rule, but I do not care for—"

The young Leodan had interrupted then, his voice low, venomous, altogether unusual for him. The notion of slavery seemed a personal insult to him, such a foul thing that he could not hold back his anger. "How can you permit such an abomination in your name? We should do away with it at once, even if it means war with these Lothans. This is the only honorable course. If you do not do it, then when I am—"

Leodan might have been able to respond to the king's movement had it not been so unexpected. Gridulan switched his sword to his left hand, stepped forward, and slapped his son with an upsweeping force enough that the boy's head tilted toward the roof. He fell back, stumbling. As Leodan placed a hand to the stinging heat of his cheek, his father railed at him. He hissed that everything they had came from this very thing. To do away with it not only endangered all their lives but also denigrated the memory of the entire Akaran line, all of whom had seen the Quota as just. Only a fool would value the freedom of a few over the welfare of an entire nation.

"This thing has been done for generations," Gridulan said, speaking close to his son's face. "Tinhadin himself agreed to it. Who are you to doubt his wisdom? If that is not enough for you, consider that I do not command the army. In name, yes, but in truth the various portions of the army answer first to their governors. The governors, in turn, bow to the wishes of the league. And the league would never allow the Quota to be repealed. Instead they would connive behind our backs. They would arrange to destroy us and place somebody else upon the throne, understand? Then we would have nothing, and you would find yourself pining for the time lived blessed by this abomination. You might be sold as a slave yourself. There are many in Alecia who would welcome the irony of that."

"Does it mean nothing to be a king, then?" Leodan asked, bracing himself for another blow.

Gridulan did not strike him again, though. His answer had more the quality of sadness to it than anger. "Of course I am a powerful man, but I am powerful because I am well placed in the dance of empire. I know the rules and step accordingly. But the dance is bigger than me, Leodan. It is a bigger thing than you. Perhaps this is too large a thing for you to understand yet. You want peace and fairness and justice for all, but your way would lead to none of these things."

The king straightened, stretched his legs, and hefted his sword loosely in his hand. Before he turned back to his fencing partner he said, "Really, Leodan, you must study for years more yet before you challenge me. Do not speak of this again in public, even before my trusted men."

Leodan, sitting on the sill of one of the large windows of his library, wondered if his father had at that point hardened his heart enough to become the murderer the coming years would prove him to be. He shook off the thought. He was spending too much time in the past, he knew. It was hard not to, especially on an evening like this, when the air seemed hushed with melancholy.

Though Acacia sat in a temperate zone well placed between the arid bushlands of Talay and the frigid expanse of the Mein, on occasion the island was visited by weather cold enough to allow snowfall. Usually this was no more than a dusting or two throughout a winter. A true accumulation came once every four or five years. This evening—the night of the Aushenian banquet—happened to be one of these, a late storm that ended a run of mild weather.

Snow had started with a few forlorn flakes twirling down through the dull light of late afternoon. By the early evening the clouds floated so low as to brush the spire points of the palace's highest towers. They let loose a bombardment of white, puffy balls that fell in perfectly straight lines, pulled down by an appearance of weight at odds with their fragile nature.

In the short period of solitude after his afternoon meetings and before he had to prepare for the banquet, Leodan sought the seclusion of the library. It was a temporary reprieve, and already he felt it drawing to a close. He walked the deserted chamber with his eyes tilted up at the books, so many thousands of volumes. There was a book here that was supposed to be written in the language the Giver had used to create the world. As ever when he was alone here, he felt himself drawn to it.

He looked around a moment, verifying that he was truly by himself, and then he found the book. He ran his finger up the spine of an ancient volume, unmarked by anything but age. He had known where it was since his manhood ceremony, when his father had showed it to him. Inside it, Gridulan claimed, was knowledge of everything that made the world run. Inside it was the language of creation, and of destruction. Inside it were the tools Tinhadin had used to conquer the Known World. Terrible knowledge, Gridulan said. That was why Tinhadin had banished all who had ever read the book. He also had forbade his descendants to read it, although he charged them with remaining the custodians of the volume. He had hidden it in plain sight; they carried on the custom ever since.

As an adolescent Leodan had spent countless hours imagining himself wielding divine power, creating with words that left his tongue and reshaped the fabric of reality. He had never opened the book, though. He never entirely believed the story behind it, but he had been frightened enough to let the book rest. At times he had considered pulling the book from the shelf and leafing through it or tearing it apart or burning it or simply laughing at it; he never knew which he would most like to do. But he had never opened its covers before and would not do so now. He had largely stopped thinking about it some time ago. Stopped believing in such tales of magic. There was so little evidence of it in actual life, after all.

He set his finger atop the next book over, a volume of *The Two Brothers*. He tilted it free. He walked back to his alcove, thinking he might find inspiration to continue his tale for Mena and Dariel that evening. How he loved that he could still tell them stories; how he dreaded the inevitable moment he would watch them slip away from him, put childish things behind them, and shoulder themselves into the company of their peers. Part of him wanted his children safely happy, near at hand, content in the simplest ways, remnants of his love for his deceased wife that he could continue to watch grow.

But he also wished that they would fling themselves out across the world and tighten the strings of friendship around the whole empire. Although he did not like to travel himself, this was not an indication of disdain for the outside world. He had loved travel in his youth and had made many fast friends in distant lands. At least, he had believed them to be friends, although in truth he knew little of friendship. He had never been close to his peers like his father had been with his. Something about the mantle of kingship had made it difficult for him to find ease with men his age. Only in foreign courts—with translators speaking between him and others, with hand gestures and laughter a necessary feature of conversation, with the differences in culture a source of amusement and mutual interest—had he found the ease with others that he believed was friendship. This had been one of the joys of his youth.

Since Aleera's death the world had seemed a different place. Perhaps all there was to it was that Aleera's ashes had been scattered from atop Haven's Rock on a day with a northerly wind that blew her remains all over the island. She was spread out across every square inch of the island. There was a piece of her in every handful of soil, in every item grown here, in the nutrients that fed the acacia trees, in the air he inhaled. He felt her touch daily. He thought of her each time a breeze buffeted him, whenever he turned his head and caught a scent in the air that reminded him of her. He even thought of her when he ran his fingers through dust gathered in some remote corner of the library. This was why he now feared leaving Acacia. He feared leaving her. Their lives had not been long enough together, but at least if his ashes were spread the same way, blown by the same sort of northerly breeze, they might share the long silence of death together. Other than the happiness and well-being of his children that was all Leodan wanted now. Who could assure this if he died in some foreign land? Who could guarantee that he would not spend eternity just as racked by sorrow as he had spent the years since Aleera left him?

Leodan looked up from the book. Such thoughts did not help matters. He was a king; there was a world around him that he could affect, perhaps for the better. There was one course that offered him the greatest chance of finding meaning in the rest of his life. One struggle worthy enough that if he triumphed he could stand a complete man before the memory of his wife and before his children. If he could break Tinhadin's contract with the Lothan Aklun . . . if he managed it, he could die with some hope that the future held a noble legacy for the children. It was difficult to face the prospect directly and allow it to take form, but since the meeting with the Aushenian prince he had felt the renewed stirrings of possibility.

Igguldan had been a revelation for him. Clearly the young man understood the burden of foulness put upon one who would partner with the league. Though he felt his nation had to do it, one could see he still harbored enough moral backbone to loathe it. Maybe a young man such as that was just the person he needed beside him, a like-minded soul with whom he could work to change the nature of the empire.

His chancellor was right, of course, in suspecting that the league would not welcome Aushenia with open arms. It feared that the addition of one more nation might tip the balance of power temporarily out of its control. It wanted Aushenian products—not to mention their bodies to trade as merchandise—but it wanted them weakened even further first. As yet the Aushenians were not on their knees. They were strong of body and largely untainted by the drug addiction that stupefied so much of the Known World. They still had too much military power—something that troubled the league, as it had always considered martial power a threat, enough so that it even limited the size of its own security force.

Leodan suspected that Sire Dagon would soon come to him with proposals for a series of measures they could use to weaken Aushenia. They could smuggle more mist across their borders. They could send agents to foment intrigue or to entrap key persons into shameful scandals or remove them by innocent-looking means: an unfortunate accident, a fever, one ailment disguised to look like another. Leodan felt his hands trembling at the thought of it. His nation had used such tactics in the past. They would be proposed again.

Unless . . . What if he managed to bring Aushenia into the empire quickly? What if he secured them as an ally in a plot of his own? What if he received them as a partner to aid him in revoking the Quota, in wresting power back from the league, in breaking the ties with the Lothan Aklun? It might mean war on several fronts—first against the league and the conservative forces of the council and then, perhaps, against the Lothan Aklun, if they made good their centuries-old threats—but there might never be another moment of such opportunity in his lifetime.

There in the library, book in one hand and tea in the other, Leodan pledged that he would meet in a private council with Aliver and Igguldan. He would tell them both everything he knew of the crimes of the empire. At the same time he revealed these things to his son, he would ask him to be a partner in overturning them. He would give Igguldan a chance of achieving the dream of his long-dead queen Elena. If now was not a moment of change, when would be? A man cannot wait indefinitely to awake as the person he believes himself to be.

Leodan heard a servant enter the library through the far door. Without turning, the king followed his progress through the shelves of books, down a short staircase, between the reading tables there, and then up toward the alcove in which he sat, coming to stand a little distance away. The man spoke in almost a whisper. The time for the banquet was near. The king's tailor awaited him, should he wish to have his evening's garment fit to form. Leodan pressed the book to his chest and followed the servant.

For the next hour a team of men worked around him. His tailor had him raise his arms out to either side. Leodan stood with drooping wings of fabric hanging from his arms. As with all such occasions, the king had to dress in a particular garment, with even the smallest details in keeping with tradition. Acacian kings always hosted Aushenian dignitaries wearing a flowing green coat, with intricate gold thread woven through the material below either arm. The garment was meant to produce several different, eye-pleasing images. Viewed from the front with arms outstretched it created a mural of the marshlands of central Aushenia, the home of several varieties of migrating long-necked waterfowl and the inspiration for much of the nation's early poetic lore, including their legend of Kralith, a god in the shape of a white crane, born out of the marsh's primordial muck. However, with elbows brought in to his sides and hands clasped together at his breastbone, the exposed material falling from the forearms contained illustrations of Acacian soldiers in armor, striding forward in heroic postures. It managed, through the careful placement of national symbols, to suggest to the viewer that no matter the acknowledgment of another nation's history Acacia still had the breadth of reach to surround it all in one embrace.

The double doors at the far end of the chamber swung open with a slam. Mena and Dariel poured through the opening, one at each door, a contest they had been at for a few weeks now, testing which of them had the stronger push. Just behind them Corinn strolled through, garbed in her evening's finery. Aliver and Thaddeus entered last, engaged in a conversation. Seeing his children rush toward him—each of them of differing sizes with varying temperaments, bits and pieces of Aleera revealed in random features and gestures—the king was flushed with joy. He tried not to think of how and why similar joy had been denied Thaddeus. He would admit it to him one day, he promised himself. One day.

He had to raise his arms above Mena's hug, tight around his waist. He rolled his eyes at the tailor but did not dissuade her. Corinn, with paper-thin composure, kissed him lightly on the cheek.

"Father, it's snowing!" Dariel said, his face open with childish excitement. "It's snowing right outside! Have you seen? Can we go out in it? Come with us. Can't you? I'll beat you at snowball fighting." This last he cast as something of a threat, head cocked, one finger pointed at his father in warning.

There followed the sort of exchange he so often stood in awe of, observing from the vantage point of his age, from the privilege of his position not as monarch but simply as a father. Dariel jumped as if his legs were composed of springs, calling on every persuasive tool he had mastered in nine years of life. Aliver explained that the king did not have time to play in the snow. He was the heir being mature again, instructing, bearing himself with a regal posture he must have modeled on the bust of the kings in the Great Room. Behind this Corinn snapped something about the banquet they—the adults—were about to attend. In all of this he heard her ambition, the tone of voice that set her apart from the younger children but that at the same time had something of a girlish beseeching directed at her father. And Mena stood back enough to listen to them all. She glanced through the moving mass of childish energy and smiled at him. When she did that, he saw Aleera in her, not so much in the shape of her features but in the patient, knowing mirth behind her eyes.

"Dariel is right," Leodan said. "This is a special night. Let's do as he asks. We will run across the rooftops and wage war with snowballs. All of us. We'll war by torchlight. And then we will huddle together in a single room. We sleep too far away from each other, anyway. These old buildings are vast. They break us apart. Do not look like that, Aliver. You can spare a few moments for your old father. Pretend you are still my young boy. Pretend you want nothing more than my love and to be near me and to hear me tell stories late into the night. Soon you and I will speak of graver things, but let me have tonight."

"All right," Aliver said, speaking over Dariel's delighted cries. "But expect no mercy from me. Before the night is over I will be crowned Snow King."

"I will see to tonight's banquet briefly," Leodan said. Corinn seemed on the verge of protesting, but the king smiled at her. "Not *too* briefly. I will slip out after the third course is served. They will barely miss me, and then we will have our war."

Chapter

Fourteen

Thasren Mein stood for some time in the street, feeling snowflakes light upon his skin and melt. How fine it was to feel snow kissing his upturned face. It was beautiful, righteous, and—in this land—remarkably strange to behold. The night air was just barely cold enough to snow, so very still, sounds muffled, footfalls of passersby pressing flat the moist layer of ice crystals; in all of these things this was a very different experience from a storm on the Mein Plateau. Still, the message and significance of it was easy to read: it was a blessing from home, encouragement sent by the Tunishnevre to remind him that the thing he did now he did for many. Snow fell on Acacia; so the coming change was marked by the heavens.

By the time he mounted the last staircase and approached the banquet hall across a stone courtyard, the other guests were already entering. He touched the wig with his fingers, noting the placement of the pins that fastened it in place. His garments were in order, his cloak one of the ambassador's finest. There was a time, he knew, early in the Acacians' rule when no one got nearer the king than a hundred paces, when the royals looked down upon social gatherings from a distance, like spectators at a play. They stayed safe behind a barricade of Marah guards, soldiers with swords drawn, each of them on one bent knee, dressed and dusted with bronze to take on the appearance of statues, ready to spring to life should a threat appear. They, he had been told, were trained as much in observation of body motions and demeanor as they were in martial arts. But that was long ago. Luxury cannot help but make a people soft, forgetful. It was a very different banquet he entered on this occasion, one that those first kings would hardly have recognized.

He nodded to the guards at the door. They greeted him by the ambassador's name, no hint of suspicion behind their smiles. As Gurnal had told him, he had to walk through a long reception chamber to reach his goal. Both walls were hung with paintings of the early Acacians. Closer still stood statues of men he presumed to be kings. Behind the shoulders of these, soldiers shadowed them in similarly formal postures, arms tight to their bodies, hands crossed over the hilts of their swords. The soldiers were as still as the inanimate personages they protected. At the far entrance to the hall a few men congregated—the official host and his guards. Thasren walked, knowing that each stride was observed, each motion of his hands, his demeanor, his features. He had cut a slit inside his vest, a passageway to the weapon fastened there. He had to say a calming prayer to keep his fingers from twitching, so keen were they to find the hilt and puncture the first throat that voiced a complaint to him.

At the opening to the hall the chief Marah guard smiled in greeting, blocking entry in a gracious manner with two soldiers at either wing, these not inclined to smile. Beyond them, Thasren saw a room lit by hundreds of lamps, crowded with people; the air a clamor of voices and the music of stringed instruments, fragrant with the evening's rich fare. The Marah touched him in two places, one hand on his shoulder and another on his opposite hip. He greeted Thasren by Gurnal's name, asked him if the weather suited him, but as he did this he looked past him to the guards of the outer chamber. He spoke with his eyes, with a thrust of his chin, telling them that with the last guest inside they could seal the outside doors. He turned his attention back to the man within his embrace, who—despite what passed for calm—was coiled and ready to spring, to cut a path of chaos from this point forward if it were necessary.

Before the guard began the probing hug that would have cost him his life, a horn blast sounded at the far side of the hall. It was a loud note, followed by a milder tune, which the strings picked up on. The officer said something merrily, patted him, a cursory dance of his fingers that didn't touch upon his weapon. He motioned Thasren inside.

With this, the greatest hurdle blocking his success was already behind him. Now he had just to sit through the opening moments of the banquet. He watched the king emerge, his entourage all around him, his son and daughter, the Aushenian prince, the chancellor Thaddeus Clegg, the guards that flanked them all. Though the party was called intimate there were perhaps a hundred people in the room, many of them between him and the monarch. For the first few moments he did not move at all. He felt his pores blooming with moisture, but he tried to think himself calm, to breathe slow breaths. He stilled his mind and focused, as he had been taught to do. He had to create the moment of his prey's death, had to bring together myriad moving forces in the world and pierce through them all like an arrow shot through rings thrown in the air. He registered the various players in the room: how they carried themselves, what they looked at, in what proximity they were to the king and behind what boundaries.

When he moved he did so as part of an inhalation in the crowd, others being drawn with him toward the royal person. He sidestepped twice, jostled his way to open territory, and from there saw the moment he needed. Leodan answered a greeting thrown from the crowd. He sought out the man in question with his eyes, and then strode forward, the smile on his face suggesting recognition of an old friend. The king slipped between two tables and momentarily placed his guards single-file behind him. Leodan's arms came up to embrace the other man, the birds on the wings of his garment rippling as he did so.

Thasren drew his dagger from hiding. He sliced it diagonally away from his body, a movement so fast it drew many eyes. The blade reflected shards of lamplight, a sharp thing in a hand that should bear no sharp thing. He dashed the last few steps forward. The king's eyes turned toward him, puzzled, mouth puckered as if about to pronounce the ambassador's name. Thasren tilted the curved blade of his dagger to puncture the man through the left eye socket. This he would have accomplished had not one of the guards bounded up onto the tabletop, his sword cutting upward aiming to slice off the attacker's hand mid-wrist. Thasren snapped his arm at the elbow and the guard's sword missed him. During the moment the man was off balance, Thasren swung around with his free hand and yanked him into the air by one ankle. He angled the falling man's body in such a way that he flew back onto the other guard, knocking loose his drawn blade.

The king's friend stood in front of the monarch, protective and gape mouthed in fear at the same time. Thasren high stepped and slammed his heel into the man's knee at an angle. His body swiftly crumpled to the ground. Another guard came at him from the left, sword lifted. Thasren thrust his dagger in the air, a punching motion. When the guard raised his weapon to parry whatever odd attack this presaged, Thasren spun into a squat. He rotated one full time and slammed the butt of his dagger's hilt into the soft spot below the man's armpit, the barbed spike of it more than an inch inside his flesh. He yanked down and carved a jagged gash that pulled free only when it broke through his navel.

He heard a high-pitched voice yelling—the king's son, he realized. Whatever command the young man gave went unacknowledged. Thasren still had not used the blade of his dagger, but he did so now. In the brief moment before anyone else could attack him he stepped the last few strides to the retreating king. Watching his stunned face, he stabbed him through the upper left chest, right through the eye of one of the embroidered Aushenian cranes. It looked little more than a fencing move. As such it drew a small spot of blood, covered over almost immediately by the king's palm. And that was it, done. Easier, actually, than Thasren had imagined it would be.

He stopped all aggressive maneuvers. He pulled himself upright, out of his fighting posture. He stood still within the center of the ring of bodies surrounding him, the wounded and living both, a bristle of sword points aimed at him now. In a matter of seconds the Elite had surrounded him. They would have killed him that instant, but there was nothing like unexpected passivity to confuse overtrained soldiers. They paused when he did, and Thasren had time to glance around. He settled his gaze on the king, who was now pressed against the wall behind a barricade of guards. Looking directly at the monarch, he named himself in his language, speaking as if he were the character in a legend of old. He said that he was Thasren Mein, son of Heberen, younger brother to Hanish and Maeander. He said that he died with joy in his heart, for he had done a just deed. He had slain the despot of Acacia. This was a blameless act, long overdue. Because of that he wished nothing more for his own life.

"Many will praise me," he said, speaking these words in heavily accented Acacian. "Many will praise and follow me."

He pressed the curved tip of his dagger against his neck and yanked the blade clean through his main artery. A moment later he lay on the smooth stones, taking in a skewed view of a world in chaos. His body crumpled in such a way that the pumping of his heart shot gouts of blood into the air above him, coating his face and chest with a mist of red. Blinking, he peered through this curtain. The king was hurried from the room at the center of a mass of men, like workers around a queen bee. They ushered him out of the chamber, supported between them in a half-seated position, their hands all over him, some holding their palms against his bloody chest. For a few seconds when the sightline between them cleared, Thasren saw the oval of the king's mouth. Pain shivered across his cheeks. His eyes were two bewildered questions, full of dread.

Watching this, Thasren thought of his eldest brother and wished he had beheld this deed, hoped that the tale he eventually heard of it would make him proud. He felt a voracious emptiness eating up his body, extinguishing him inch by inch. He whispered it through the blood in his mouth, a taste like liquid metal. He felt possessed by awe. He had accomplished at least one great act in his life. With it behind him, he felt no fear. He had unleashed a great deal of it, but he himself went to the afterdeath without fear, as a soldier of a righteous cause always should. Before fading from consciousness he began to recite the Prayer of Joining, the praise song of the Tunishnevre.

Chapter Fifteen

Mena would never again be able to look at the eight-sided dice of the children's game called rats running without feeling sick to her stomach. It was this game that she and her younger brother had been engaged in at the moment Leodan was attacked. Dariel had feared that their father might not honor his promise to entertain them after the dinner, and the princess had agreed to sit near the door with him so that they could pounce on the king as soon as he was free. They tipped the dice from their palms, watching time and again as the green glass octahedrons rolled to stillness, nestled into their bench's silk contours. Mena did not particularly care for the game, nor see the point in being so involved with a simple act of chance, but she did enjoy the feel of the dice bouncing around within her loosely clasped fist. She often shook the dice long enough that Dariel grew impatient with her.

It happened no more than a few moments after the great doors had been closed. Mena had half registered the muffled sound of commotion inside the hall, but she jolted when the doors burst open again in one great thrust. They swung fully around and banged hard against the stone wall. Mena's hand, which had been about to toss the dice, jerked so that she spilled them on the floor. For a moment she watched one of them roll across the carpet, feeling embarrassed and ready to spring up and retrieve it. But then she saw the huddle of men press through the door. They were close together, bent around a burden, their legs shuffling and awkward as they tried to speed along, one shouting to another and all in confusion. A voice rose above them yelling to make way for the king, make way for the stricken king! Mena had not yet fully registered the words when she realized that the burden they carried was a man. Her father . . .

The king's skin had drained of color, the rich hue gone pale as that of a powdered corpse. His trembling lips were pursed, eyes naked with fear, crown askew. A white froth of spittle clung to his beard. There beneath all of the unrecognizable distortions was the person she loved foremost in the world, stripped bare of everything that was strong and fatherly and wise. She pulled Dariel to her and covered his eyes. With him hugged tight against her she turned away, as if through the movement she might manage to shake loose what she had just witnessed.

Later that night in Dariel's room she sat on his bed with her arms cradling the sobbing boy. She repeated many times that it was all right. Father would be all right. He would be, of course. It was just a pinprick, they said. Did he really think a pinprick could harm the king of Acacia? "Come now," she said, "don't be silly. Father will find you in the morning and laugh at the puffy eyes you get when you cry before sleeping."

Once Dariel's breathing fell into the steady rhythm of sleep she untangled herself from him. She set her back against the wall and watched the slow rise and fall of the boy's chest. She studied the slack features of his face. She loved him so, so much. This realization brought tears to her eyes for the first time that evening. He could not truly understand, could he? She actually knew little of what had happened or whether or not her father was in mortal danger, but the details did not seem to matter. Her father's face had explained things completely. No matter what happened tomorrow or the next day the look of fear she had witnessed was irradicable. She would always see it beneath the surface of his presence. It felt as if she had caught him in some lewd act, something degrading enough that she could never step back into the innocence of moments before. The ease between them would never be the same.

She crawled out of bed and paced the large room for a while, looking at the stones of the floor, unsure what to do, where to go, if there even was anything to do or anyplace to go. She knew nobody would tell her anything tonight. She considered sneaking out of the room and into her father's quarters, but she would certainly be stopped, especially in the dead of night and after such events. She would not be able to get anywhere near him until the morning, and perhaps not even then.

Eventually, she strode across the room and climbed into the lower branches of the acacia tree that occupied one corner of the room. It was a strange thing to find inside a palace. It had been a birthday present from Leodan to Dariel the winter before. The king had come up with the idea himself, spoke of it to craftsmen and woodworkers, and had the project worked on secretly while he and the children sailed to Alecia for a short stay. On returning, all the children entered Dariel's room to find that the bulk of an old, gnarled acacia tree had been salvaged after its slow death and embedded in the stone floor. Its branches twisted above and in places seemed to merge into the walls and provide them support. It had been sanded down and the thorns blunted so that just the knobbed remnants of them remained. The wood was stained a reddish brown with oil infused with sandalwood. It was adorned with ribbons and studded with green leaves made from silk, so that the tree might appear to live forever. Platforms were set into the branches with ropes, ladders, and swings to move between them. All this simply to surprise a boy with a grand structure for him to climb and play upon. It was an unheard-of idea, a strange extravagance in a culture that generally ignored children until they were old enough to emerge as adults. It had gotten more than a few tongues wagging about the king's sanity.

From the bowed beam of a platform she looked back across the room. Low-burning wall lamps cast the room in orange light. Dariel slept on undisturbed, beside him a tray of food and tea brought by the maids. They had bustled around them when they first returned, anxious eyed and nervous. They asked over and over as to their needs, but they could not answer the only question either child actually deemed important. None of them would whisper a word about the state of the king. All would be better in the morning, they said. Let the king and his people do what they must and all would be better in the morning. If they had not repeated this so often, Mena might have believed them. Instead, she knew that nothing was as they said. The maids had always whispered about the king. Even within her hearing they had made innuendos about his desires or motives or actions. Usually they had been wrong, but this was different. They were scared. They were confused. And they were lying.

"But what do they matter?" Mena asked the room. They were small-minded women that treated the younger children like they were . . . well, like they were children. Mena had always known that she was older than her years. She understood things they did not. This was something she shared in common with her father. She knew that he was far from weak-minded. He was sane and kind and intelligent in a way few others ever managed, and he knew that she was no child to be spoken down to. Sometimes—when they were alone and the mood was upon him—he spoke to her as if she were an adult. She knew this to be something unusual between them, an understanding that they had and that they gave into only in private.

Thus he had spoken plainly, meditatively, when he sat in this very tree with her and declared that he did not care if the nobles or the servants or anybody else thought him mad. When had this been? Early in last spring? In the first weeks of summer? He had said that in truth the world itself was mad. It was full of spite, of malice and greed and duplicity. These things were the components of the world just as the letters in her notebooks were the keys that unlocked the language they spoke. It had taken him some time to learn this, but he knew it to be true now.

"When I was young," he had said, leaning against the branch below her, running his hands across the smooth grain of the wood, "I thought I could change the world. I believed that when I became king I would write decrees and laws to take away the people's suffering. I did not think I could make a perfect world. Not exactly. But I would make one as close to perfect as a human can imagine."

She asked him if he had done that. Her father looked up at her with a pained expression of pity and love. It took him a few moments to answer. He thanked her for asking, for the implication that she might think he was as great a man as that and for suggesting that her life had thus far been blessed enough that she still imagined such things possible. But, no, he had not achieved any of the dreams he had had as a boy. He could not pinpoint why or how, but each of his grand notions had evaporated right before his eyes. He felt, thinking back, that the words with which he described such things were no more lasting than the vapor that escapes with one's breath on a winter day. He spoke, but his words had no lasting substance. They faded almost from the moment they left his mouth. Thus he had sat at council and been met by polite patient faces. He had proposed reforms even in the great chamber at Alecia to the governors, who all pledged fealty to him. His words were heard, the truth of them acknowledged, his wisdom praised. He would leave these meetings feeling the world was about to change, and yet year after year passed and the world remained as it had been, no better a place, unaffected by any of his heart's desires. Nobody ever denied him, but nothing ever happened either. He realized then how truly powerless he was. Between him and the workings of the world were thousands of other hands. Each of them feigned loyalty to him, yet none of them did his bidding. Perhaps, he admitted, that was why he had lowered his ambitions and found meaning in the love of a woman and in the wonder of the children they produced.

"Mena, my wise daughter, I am not so strong a man as you may think." He reached up and tugged on her chin. "I could not change the world. I could not stop others from committing crimes—terrible crimes—in my name. I could not stop your mother from leaving us when illness took her. But I love my children. So you are my work now, all four of you. I thought, 'Why not build within my house the world as I would have it?' If I can raise you to adulthood in bliss unusual to the world, I will have accomplished something. You will see what foulness men do to one another eventually, but before then, why not know joy? You want to be a child for whom dreams come true, don't you?"

Dariel had come into the room then. Her father had called out to him and the brief intimacy between them was suspended until chance allowed for it again. Remembering this now made her tears flow again. She had not answered him. She had not asked just what these horrors of the world were. She had never seen them and knew only of the old struggles written of in the triumphant eloquence of her history books. But she wished she had answered him. She did want—very badly—to be a child for whom dreams come true.

She was sure she would not be able to sleep, but at some point she drifted off, still perched high in the tree, leaning back against wood sculpted to comfort. She dreamed of something that even as she experienced it she thought of as a memory, although she would not later be sure whether it was a recollection of an earlier event or of an earlier dream. She and a girl whose name she did not recall crawled over the rocks of the northern shoreline and out onto the stone pier that jutted into the sea. The girl carried a fishing net with the childish notion that they would bring in the evening's dinner. They knew they should not be down there on the jagged rocks, with the sea heaving below them, billowing with fronds of seaweed, crawling with blue-shelled crabs, and bristling with mussels. But all would be right if they brought home a living treasure in their net.

As they neared the end of the pier Mena saw a strange commotion in the water. Just below the surface swam a teeming school of fish. They moved past in a great mass, so many that she could neither see the beginning of the school nor where it might end. They were side by side and stacked many deep, each fish perhaps two or three feet long. The upper ones were so near that sometimes their tails sliced through the air. She could see between them far down into the depths. She had not known the sea was so deep here, but it was fathomless and teeming with fish.

The princess called for the net from the other girl, grasped it, and bent in preparation to cast it. The girl whispered that they should not catch these fish. "They journey to the sea god," she said. "It would curse us to eat of them." Mena did not care. What sea god, anyway? Nonsense. She splashed the net down into the water, bracing herself for the impact of writhing life that she expected to fill it. A moment later she pulled up the net, empty. The fish swam on, teeming just as before, but not one of them had entered the trap. She swung the net in from another angle, pulled it up, dripping: nothing. No matter how she moved her net below the surface—side to side, thrusting down deep into the water, jerking it up—she could not catch even a single fish. They just hurtled by, so close that she could see the minute adjustments of their fins and the flexion of their large scales as they slipped over one another. She watched their eyes roll up to study her in passing, sorrow in them. Something about those eyes drew her. She set the net aside and tumbled forward into the water, sure that this way, at least, she would manage to touch the fish, sure that they wanted her to do so. If they went at the call of some sea god, they did not do so willingly. She could help. This seemed a very important thing as she punched through the water and plunged downward. . . .

Mena started awake. Her arms jerked out, and she almost fell from the tree. For a few moments the world hung around her without context. She felt the dream fade and knew that there was something more important to remember, but it was only through staring and waiting that the evening's events came back to her. Looking up through a narrow, high window she saw the sky had brightened with the coming dawn. Thin clouds tiled the sky with touches of salmon pink. It was a new day, she thought. How much of yesterday's damage will now be mended? How much would be shown in the bright light of morning as nothing more than tricks of shadows and nighttime gloom?

She had started to climb down when the door opened. Corinn entered, moving hesitantly, looking around the room as if she did not know it well. She stared at Dariel's sleeping form. One of her hands rose up and touched her lips. She whispered something, like a superstitious peasant on witnessing a violent act of nature. In her stillness she became an island surrounded by motion. Servants stepped in behind her and fanned out to prepare the room for the day, throwing back the curtains and snuffing out the lamps, taking away the tray of uneaten food and replacing it with another laden with fruit and juices.

Corinn roused when she saw Mena walking toward her. Her face was blotched and puffy, her lips pouting and soft. "He will not die," she said. "He told me he wouldn't. He said that he would never leave me. He promised

Mother he wouldn't, not until he had met all my children and they knew him so . . . not until they knew him and had heard from him all about Mother. He said he would tell us about Mother. About how she had been when she was young and they were first married . . ."

"You spoke to him?"

Corinn's hand danced in an explanatory way. "Not since it happened. I mean before he promised me. I mean before all of this—"

Sensing that she might carry on in such manner, Mena interrupted. "But what of him now? Tell me what you know. How is he?"

"What do you want to know?" Corinn's eyes would not settle but bounced nervously around the room. "Father was stabbed. Some assassin from the Mein . . . They claim the blade was poisoned, but I don't believe it. 'What poison?' I asked, but no one could answer. They don't know anything. No one would tell me the truth. And they wouldn't let me in to see him. Even Thaddeus wouldn't see me! They are all acting mad. They have called Aliver to council, as if father was gone already. But he's not. I'm sure he's not!"

She is more frightened than I, Mena thought. She took one of Corinn's hands in both of hers and squeezed it. The touch seemed to comfort Corinn, enough so that her voice dropped and words slowed, her eyes fixed for a moment on her sister's shoulder, closer to meeting her eyes than they had so far.

"Mena, it was horrible. I saw it happen. I saw the man before he revealed himself. I watched him move through the crowd. I thought him handsome. I thought, 'That's Gurnal, isn't it? He looks younger than I remember. How strange I never noticed that he was comely before.' And then I saw him pull his knife. What was he doing with a knife at a banquet? If I had yelled at that first moment . . . I didn't realize . . . I don't understand anything."

Mena squeezed again, pulling her closer. Instinctually, she knew it might be better not to say anything in response to such a declaration, but something in her felt that the roles each occupied were no longer as they had been. She thought of the dream again and in a burst of revelation realized that the girl with her on the rocks had not been a stranger at all. It had been Corinn, some different version of Corinn. How could that have been? She had been there with her sister and yet thought her some other person entirely. It did not make sense, but the sleeping mind rarely did. She pushed the dreamworld away. Right now, she realized, it fell to her to comfort her older sister. The problem was that she could not comfort her with lies, and it took her some hushed, fidgeting moments to find the right tone to proceed. "We will be all right," she said. "If Father—"

"Stop it!" Corinn snapped. Her eyes fixed on her, wide and fierce. "Father will not die. Stop wishing he would! Don't even say that he might!"

Mena was aghast. She had started all wrong. "I—I did not say that. I don't wish that. It's all so frightening. That's what—what . . ."

For a moment it seemed Corinn might strike her, but instead she stepped forward and pulled her younger sister into her arms. There Mena experienced the first inkling of comfort since the banquet. It was a sad thing, really, but there was something soothing in the awareness that the two of them felt at least the same fear and sorrow with a shared clarity reflected in no other aspect of their relationship.

CHAPTER

SIXTEEN

From a distance the bird looked much like the smaller variety of pigeon from which it had been bred. When seen near at hand the creature's form took on a different substance. It was the size of a young sea eagle and muscled accordingly, with a predatory beak and eyes that scanned the world with far-reaching acuity. It wore leather gloves of a sort over its talons, with sharpened steel barbs at the tip of each toe that early training had taught it the use of. There was a tube fastened to its ankle into which rolled notes could be inserted. It was a messenger bird, a pigeon in name, perhaps, but a creature with a fierceness to match its dedication in flight. It almost never fell prey to other avian predators. Thus it was the bird of choice for the most urgent of dispatches, like the one sent late on the night Thasren Mein struck King Leodan.

The pigeon stepped off its keeper's arm in the district of Acacia reserved for foreign dignitaries. Its wings beat down the salt-tinged air and lifted it into the night sky. It flew at first through the cascade of snowflakes, the world grayed and soft edged. Somewhere over the mainland west of Alecia the skies cleared. The bird kept on through the dark hours, its wings seldom pausing to glide.

It reached another keeper at a seaside village along the coast outside Aos at dawn the next morning. It glided in with a glimmering vermilion sky at its back. The message fastened to its leg was removed and attached—unread—to another bird. This one flew the stretch to lower Aushenia that day, rising and falling with the contours of the slab-broken prairie lands. Another carried on through the Gradthic Gap and arrived at Cathgergen about an hour before sunrise two days after the journey began. This time the message was slipped from its container and hurried through the chill corridors of the place and delivered to the expansive quarters which temporarily housed Hanish Mein's younger brother, Maeander, and his entourage.

Maeander woke to the awareness that his name had been called. The caller remained outside his door, softly singing the coded prayer that both asks forgiveness for interruption and promises that the disturbance speaks to a matter of importance. He rose naked from the warmth of his nest and stood looking down on the puzzle of bodies and pillows and fur blankets amid which he slept. His bed was in fact the greater portion of the padded floor. It was heated from below by the vent system that distributed the earth's steam through the fortress. Bits and pieces of smooth-limbed women peeked out here and there, a spray of flaxen hair, a length of leg, an arm wrapped over the naked back of another, fingers entwined in the soft mat of white fox fur. Five, six, seven of them: looking on such a mélange one could not be sure. When Maeander took lovers he took them in quantity, and he wished them to look so similar that one faded into the next without a singular identity. Standing upright, the chilly air of the room pimpled his flesh. He liked it best when sensations fluctuated between extremes, from hot and cold, from delight to pain, from the soft contours of concubines in one moment to the hard edges and clipped formality of his military life the next.

By the time he snapped open the door and shot out his hand for the missive he was fully awake. He closed the door and read the note. Once, twice, and then again, brief as it was. It seemed he had waited a lifetime for the news it detailed. His heart reminded him of all those years by beating furiously, as if it would count out all the many days in as short a time as possible.

"Thank you, Fathers," he said. "Praise you, Brother. You will not be forgotten. You've earned the honor you wished from life."

As he walked back toward the center of the room, he heard a stirring among the furs and blankets. Somebody yawned audibly, rolled over, exposing the full curve of a hip. Maeander felt the stir of desire low in his body. He thought for a moment of the pleasure he could take in waking the women with shouts of excitement, coupling with them to announce his joy at the things about to happen, sharing it among so many vessels that would reflect his elation toward him. But he knew he could not allow himself such diversions now that the dispatch had announced the beginning of everything. Such a course would be as inappropriate as bemoaning his brother's death. He cut away from the bed toward the next room. There was another way he could enjoy the day. Better that he saw to it without delay.

Thus, by the time Rialus Neptos walked in to find him reclined on a couch in the governor's office Maeander had already set his work into motion. He had dispatched another pigeon out into the frigid wind blowing down from the north. He had also sent a rider thickly clad against the weather toward another northern destination. He had seen to it that the soldiers accompanying him made their way one by one into place inside the fortress as unobtrusively as possible, moving only singly or in pairs so as to draw little attention. His horses and sleds had been readied for his coming departure. He had only to speak to the governor to conclude his work in Cathgergen.

The governor entered preoccupied, mumbling something under his breath, his elbows tucked close to his body and shoulders hunched against the chill in the room. Seeing Maeander, he stopped so abruptly that he tilted free a splash of the steaming drink he had been carrying in a careful, two-handed grip. "Maeander? What brings you here so early?"

Maeander pulled a face of exaggerated insult. "What sort of greeting is that? One would think you take no joy in starting the day with me."

Rialus was immediately caught off balance. He explained that he meant no slight at all. He was just surprised. Actually, he was on his way to the baths. He had just stopped in for a moment. He might not even have come to his office, in which case he would have left Maeander waiting. He rattled on without any sign that he was likely to abate soon.

"Enough!" Maeander dropped the sole of one black-booted foot to the floor with an audible impact. "I have a number of things to tell you. You may want to sit down."

Rialus did not initially seem inclined to do so, but Maeander waited, eyes hard on him, until he changed his mind.

"Leodan Akaran," Maeander said, "has been removed from his throne. Don't interrupt me. I will tell you everything you need to know. My brother Thasren has sacrificed himself to end the king's rule. I have received word that all but confirms he has achieved this. I expect in a day or two you will learn the Akaran has passed from this world. Have care for your coffee."

Rialus, so stunned by Maeander's words, had let his saucer tip to one side.

"By his action Thasren has announced that the people no longer honor the Akaran line. He has declared war, and it is my intention to fully rally behind the cause he died for. I leave with a small contingent of my men in a few hours' time. Do not look relieved; I am not finished yet. Now, Rialus, what I am about to spell out for you may send you into a fit of sputtering confusion, but do try to keep a hold of yourself. You have several important responsibilities today. The first has to do with the baths."

"The—the baths?"

"Just so. The second company of the guard will have use of them this morning, yes? Well, what you are going to do is order the first company and the third also to join them in the steaming waters. It will be a great crowd of men and women, but I am sure they will not object. All that warm flesh rubbing and touching . . . Who doesn't love the warm, moist heat of a crowded bath? But you would be better off not joining them. You will explain—if you must explain to anyone—that the baths will undergo their cleaning and maintenance this afternoon, so anyone who wants use of them must do so this morning. That sort of thing." With a motion of his finger he indicated that these details he happily left in the governor's capable hands. "And then . . . you will order all vents not linked to the baths closed. Once they are, you will have the tampers loosed on the main valves. You will release the full force of the stored energy in the wells."

"I don't understand," Rialus began. "The heat inside the baths—"

"Will be considerable. I know. It will bring the pools to a boil. The soldiers will flush red as lobsters in the pot. They will claw over one another trying to get out of the water, but there will be too many of them. The air will fill with steam, and the heat will fill their lungs and they will suffocate. I know very well what will happen, Rialus."

"But they will try to flee out into the halls, naked and . . ." The governor was too perplexed to continue. "Is this a joke?"

"Does it strike you as funny? You are a strange one, Rialus. Anyway, the lobsters will not escape the baths. I am leaving behind enough soldiers to bar the doors until the steaming is complete. After which they will dispatch any other soldiers they find. Then they will leave you to prepare for what is to follow. Is any portion of this unclear so far?"

Rialus answered this with a stammering description of just what would happen to the troops, as if the actual reality of what he proposed had possibly escaped Maeander. That would mean nearly three thousand soldiers, men and women—almost all the Northern Guard since Alain's company had disappeared—would be steamed or boiled to death. They would swell and burst and leak all manner of fluids and die horrifically. He had never heard of such an idea. It was mass murder on a grand scale. An infamy and deception of epic proportions.

"It will be a horrible mess," Rialus said, concluding with bewildered, indignant finality. "I could not possibly—"

Rising to his feet, Maeander clamped a hand down on the smaller man's shoulder and made him stand. He slipped his arm more around his neck and turned Rialus toward his precious glass window. "It will indeed make for a horrible mess, but you need not worry about that. All you have to do is gaze out your window here. Watch that horizon. Remember that you have guests coming. They are nearly here. Actually, you will start hosting them this evening. They will be hungry and wanting for comforts. You will be glad then, my friend, to have so much freshly cooked meat to offer them."

Maeander left without awaiting a further response. He was so pleased with himself he feared he could no longer keep the self-satisfied expression off his face. His heels slammed hard on the floor with each footstep. It was an almost painful way to stride, but he enjoyed that the earth beneath him accepted the punishment of his footfalls. He knew that Rialus watched him recede with open-mouthed awe. Such a little man, Maeander thought. A shrew. But he was useful and so easily manipulated; one could not deny that.

Maeander was in a fine enough mood to forgive the rodent his shortcomings. He had never been more pleased. Thasren was immortal now. Soon Hanish would be leading an army toward Alecia via the River Ask. For his part, Maeander would push another force through the mountains into Candovia. And his new allies, these Numrek, would rampage through Aushenia, a horror like nothing the Known World had seen in centuries. Then there would be a great meeting in which the bulk of the Acacian army would find themselves gasping for life before the battle even began. . . .

The present, Maeander thought, was a blessed time to be alive.

CHAPTER

SEVENTEEN

Leeka Alain's meeting with the Numrek warrior began as a surprisingly muted affair. He had walked for so long through the soiled detritus that marked the horde's passing that he had grown lax. Fatigue clung heavily to him. He no longer placed his feet with the grim determination he had on the first few days. Isolation and barrenness played tricks with his mind. He stopped, pausing to study the lay of the land and to examine the shapes against the snow from a distance. He had seen mirages out on the curve of the horizon several times already and none of the wavering shapes had come to anything. For greater and greater stretches of the day he occupied an imaginary world built out of the past. He almost forgot the purpose of his solitary arctic trek, forgot that he trailed a very real enemy, and forgot the recent massacre of his army. It already felt like a nightmare from a distant time, hard to credit as reality.

He trudged off the flats and onto the western edge of the Barrens without giving it much thought. The land before him was just as treeless as it had been before, but now it undulated like folds of wrinkled skin. Frozen riverbeds crisscrossed here and there, as yet unstirred by the coming spring. He lost sight of the horizon each time he dropped into a hollow. The horde's path was easy enough to follow, however. It carried on right through the area, as unerringly straight as ever. Leeka trudged on, head down.

Thus he was when he crested a rise and started down into what would be a river in a few months. He saw the dark shapes against the white but was slow to lift his gaze to them. Not until something grunted. It was the first creature-made noise he had heard in some time. It was an exclamation of alarm, and it kicked Leeka's senses alive. He froze. The sled behind him, propelled by the slant of the slope, slid forward and nudged his heels.

Before him were two living things and one dead. The noise had been made by one of the hairy rhinos. It stood about forty yards away, absurdly close, near enough that Leeka could imagine the feel of its coarse fur. He could make out the growth striations that ringed its horns and note etchings in the buckles of its saddle. The creature found Leeka's sudden proximity unnerving. It shuffled backward, head whipping from side to side. A short distance behind him, one of the invaders crouched near a makeshift hearth. He looked up, first at the rhino as it looped around behind him and then at Leeka. Why he was there—whether in some official capacity, as a straggler for some unclear reason, or as a deserter—Leeka would never know. There was no chance of the two of them conversing. What his eyes showed him, however, turned his stomach like no carnage of war ever had.

The Numrek sat attending a banquet of human flesh. A young man's body had been set atop a cauldron heated from below by the pitch Leeka had found traces of earlier. The body was splayed on its back. Its arms and legs stretched away so that the feet and hands rested on the ice while the midsection roasted, steamed, and stewed all at once. The Numrek had just reached up to scrape a portion of flesh and internal organs into the bubbling broth below when he spotted Leeka. He set the knife down and rose to his feet, stretching his arms to either side, like an aged worker rising to carry on some interminable task. He bent and fumbled about for a moment, then straightened, a spear in one hand, a curving sword in the other.

Leeka shuffled off the straps that bound him to the sled. He had stopped wearing his sword a few days before and had lashed it to the sled. He now slid it free of its sheath. He had a crossbow and bolts as well, but the Numrek closed on him far too quickly. He hurled the spear, which struck deep into the pack of supplies and tilted the sled over. Leeka jumped back and circled away, yanking off his gloves, testing the weight of his blade against the frigid air. The Numrek had not even tried to hit him with the spear. He had thrown it as an amusement and struck his chosen target, as was obvious by the apparent glee that now animated his gestures. He came forward with springing steps, almost skipping—if so childish a word could be ascribed to a creature of such size and murderous intent. He tossed his sword from hand to hand, demonstrating that he was equally skilled with either. His fur cloaks hung about his body, swaying with his motions and hiding the exact bulk of the body beneath. His features were still hard to make out behind the screen of his hair and the cap that sat well down on his brow, but his mouth was visibly split by a grin.

How do you kill a thing like this? The question reeled out in the back of Leeka's mind. With the fore portion he concentrated on the fight of his life. The Numrek swung at him in great crescents of motion that audibly sliced through the air. Leeka ducked a blow aimed at his head, and the steel snagged some locks of his hair and snipped them clean. The first time he blocked a blow, the impact of their two blades caused a crushing pain at his hilt hand, wrenching his wrist savagely and coming near to snapping it. He kept hold of his sword only by slapping his other hand over the pain and fighting with a dual grip. If fighting it could be called. In truth, he backed up and shifted, stumbled and caught himself, never attacking. He did not meet blade to blade again except with glancing blocks. Otherwise he was a puppet dancing through contortions demanded by the other.

In no time at all Leeka was breathless and sweating, his eyes watering. It seemed he had already lived impossibly long against this foe. The enemy spoke as he fought. He uttered a barrage of guttural sounds just ordered enough to resemble words. Leeka searched for a way to attack, but his foe was too massive, too quick with each strike, too much a storm of motion. The smell off him was pungent and almost painful to inhale, like vinegar and urine and onions. When he stepped into the glare of the low sun he blocked it entirely and became a shadow warrior. Had a man ever killed a thing like this, such a giant as this?

And then Leeka remembered. The Eighth Form. Gerimus against the guards of Tulluck's Hold. Those guards were supposed to have been giants. That was what the old lore said. Larger than humans in every way. Stronger. Inhuman in their disrespect for life. Warriors who lived to kill. They had terrorized the First Kingdom of Candeva, the predecessor to the Second Kingdom of Candovia. It was not until the hero Gerimus beat them back to the Hold and took on the two guards himself that a way to beat them was arrived at. They were too confident, Gerimus realized. Too strong and too eager. He used their impatience against them, taunting them by fighting purely defensively until they made errors caused by eagerness. It had worked once, perhaps it would do so again.

So into his defensive ballet Leeka tried to weave bits and pieces of the Form. At first he barely managed it without losing his head, until he found a merging between what he needed to do to live and Gerimus's ancient maneuvers. It was complicated by the fact that in the Form he had fended off two opponents, but Leeka modified most of the moves related to the second giant. The enemy did not really seem to notice this at first. It was not until Leeka spun away in a mad, hacking attack on the air that the puzzled giant paused. He turned his massive head and studied the area Leeka slashed so viciously. He watched as Leeka sank home his blade into the foot of his imaginary foe and as he pulled the point out of the ice, flipped it skyward, and slammed it into the soft spot beneath an invisible chin. This done, Leeka faced him.

The invader, whatever he might have thought of the display, stepped forward and resumed his attack. As they fought, Leeka grew more into the skin of the Form. It felt good. If he was to die, at least he would have some dignity in his last moments. In this slight hint of confidence was an inkling of control. Leeka began to feel that at times he did not just anticipate his adversary's actions, he caused them. *Yes*, he thought, *Step toward me.* The other did. *Thrust and then slip right.* Again, the other did. *Swing as if to take off my legs.* He jumped, and not a moment too soon. It was no perfect dance, but Leeka managed to fold the variations in with greater and greater ease. His foe showed no sign of recognizing a design in this, but he did grow wilder. Some of his joy faded. He fell silent except for the groans of his exertion. He even spit at Leeka several times, his saliva like a weapon and an insult at once.

When the moment came, it surprised Leeka. The enemy, struck by his greatest burst of rage yet, tossed his blade from his left to his right hand. He rushed forward, swinging his sword in a circle, his shoulder joint stressed by the move, bearing down onto the swinging blade the full force of his arm and shoulder and abdomen; the entire weight of his body, and the full measure of pure, impatient spite. The force was incredible, but Leeka slipped to the side. Such was the pressure of the blade passing through the air that he felt the tug of its wake almost pull him off balance. The blade smashed into the ice in a spray of crystals.

And there it was: just as the last of the Tulluck giants had cut the granite stone of the floor of the Hold. Leeka stepped upon the giant's sword, one foot on the back of the blade, the next on the hilt. His third stride found purchase on the giant's forearm. From this platform Leeka leaped into a twisting flourish of a strike. His blade hummed around him, a spinning blur so quick that he would never afterward remember the actual instant it sliced clean through his foe's neck. But he always remembered the moment after, when he realized that that was just what he did. The foreigner's head stayed perched on his shoulders for the duration of his fall. When the body finally crashed down, the head shot forward, propelled, it seemed, by a spurt of brilliantly crimson blood. Leeka's practice of the Form had never quite been like that.

Watching the fluid seep, steaming, into the ice, he said, "Well then . . . that worked."

Though he could barely manage it without retching, he pulled what was left of the human corpse away from the fire. He kicked the pot over with his foot. He used the shaft of the enemy's spear to nudge the coals and the burning pitch into a stronger fire. He tossed flammable items from his own supplies onto it, and then tended to the slow, unpleasant work of turning human flesh to ash. This man was, after all, one of his soldiers. He could not recognize his frostbitten face or find any identifying papers, but he said what words he could over him. He thought what things he could to mourn him. His sadness was real enough. It came from the heart more clearly than ever before, his tears no less embarrassing to him for his solitude. He had not remembered the young man as he fought, but he was glad, now that he thought of it, to have avenged him.

Late in the day all that could be done for the soldier had been. Leeka turned to contemplate the rhinoceros, which had stayed a short distance away, watching. He walked toward it carrying the spear, trying to disguise the injury he now felt in his ankle. He must have twisted it at some point during the duel. The pain was sharp with each step, the joint stiff and swollen. He did not want to show the creature weakness, but each time he neared, it sidestepped, shuffled, rotated, backed up. It responded in kind to any move Leeka made, keeping him always at a distance, watching with either eye. Leeka looked around for something like food to offer it, but nothing obvious offered itself.

"Listen," Leeka said, "I don't have time for this. In case you haven't noticed, your master's lost his head. You and I, though, we could aid each other. I want to get somewhere fast, which would be hard on this ankle. And you . . . you look like you need somewhere to go."

There was something like intelligence in the consideration the beast gave all this, but it was nothing like full understanding either. In answer the animal stamped the ice. Leeka was aware of his weakness, his feeble lightness compared to the creature's girth and bulk, natural weapons, and the thickness of his defenses. He stared at the beast with all the annoyed exasperation he could muster. Better that it did not remember it could impale Leeka on that horn of his and walk about with a new ornament. Or that it could bowl him over and trample him to mush at will. There could be no violent contest between them. The winner was obvious enough that Leeka prayed the rhino did not consider it. Then he thought of something.

He turned, limped away, and came back a few moments later with his fist clenched in the dead warrior's hair. He tossed the head out between him and the mount. It rolled in a wobbling, awkward motion that stopped soon enough. The creature studied it, turning side to side as if suspecting trickery. Leeka tested several possible witticisms. None quite fit the moment. He let the silence sink in. The beast had enough to consider with its dull mind anyway. He would give him a little while to think it all through.

CHAPTER

EIGHTEEN

Aliver dressed for the meeting with a military crispness. Though he was alone in his room, he snapped out the folds of his council vest audibly, as if his every move were being watched by elders keen to denounce him for slackness. It was dimly lit, because he had snuffed out most of the lamps, and chilly, because he had opened one of the large bay windows. He was to attend his first meeting of the king's councillors, an abrupt gathering called because of the assassination attempt. *Attempt*, he made sure to tell himself. Attempt only. Though he had not been allowed to see his father for two days since the attack, Thaddeus had assured him the king lived and fought for his life with all his strength. For the time being, he had said, only the physicians could aid him. That fact in itself seemed absurd. How could Leodan Akaran's life and the fate of an empire lie at the mercy of so few men? One with a knife, a few others with potions and tonics . . .

It was not as if Aliver had never been warned of such possibilities, but previous discussions of the rules of ascension had seemed distant notions, not soon to be relevant to his life. His tutor, Jason, had once said that a prince knows no greater time of danger than the days or weeks leading up to his crowning. Ofttimes, he claimed, princes were slain by their most trusted advisers, friends, even kin hungry for power themselves. Aliver could not remember the words he had responded to this with, but surely he had denied any such treachery would befall the Akarans. But Jason had an answer to this also. "Never in the historical record has a power of any nation, no matter how strong, maintained control indefinitely. Either you Akarans have broken the mold, or else history has dawdled a time before catching up with you." Jason had bowed as he said this, almost joking, deferential and friendly, as he always was when he challenged the prince. But thinking of it now, Aliver felt a prickle of apprehension.

A sharp knock at the door startled him. A moment later a squire stood before him, displaying on his palms the sword called the King's Trust. The prince knew the blade well. It was the very weapon that Edifus fought with at Carni. The black stain on the hilt leather, it was said, was blood from the first king's own hand. At some point in his single combat with a tribal leader Edifus had stumbled, lost grip of his sword, and survived the moment only by catching his foe's slashing blade pinched between his palm and fingers. Quite a move, one that had, for training purposes, been modified into a blocking motion, pushing on the flat of the opponent's sword with the fat edge of the hand. Leodan had worn the sword only on the rare occasions that called for it, but Aliver had sought out the altar that displayed it in his father's dressing chambers on many occasions. He had run his fingers over the ridged, soiled weave of the hilt, cupping his hand around it, hoping to find that his fingers fit perfectly into the worn grip of it.

Once he had lifted it out of its cradle, held it before him with one hand on the hilt and one on the sheath. He broke the seal between the two with a motion of his wrist and slid an inch or two of the blade into the light. He got no further. He had never been sure afterward, but he thought at the moment that the exposed portion of the blade sang out as air and light touched it. And it was not a cry of joy. It was sorrow conveyed through tempered steel. He felt sure the chamber was filled with ghosts about to materialize in wrath around him. He had done something wrong, touched an object he should not have, something not yet for him. The moment also left him with the fear that the martial history known to that blade was horrible in ways he had not yet been schooled in.

Now he stood with his arms upraised as the squire secured the sword around his waist, a weapon considered his until his father was well enough to take it up again. He tried to wear it with an appropriate ease, ignoring the way it banged against his thigh with each step. He had not expected to take his place at council until his seventeenth birthday. Only a few days ago he would have considered it a great honor to sit among the generals and advisers he was about to. Now the guilt of it sat inside him like a rough-edged stone. He had watched an assassin stab his father in the breast, and he had not done a thing about it. The vile creature had named his father a despot. A despot! What reason was there in that? He knew evil men twisted the world to their aims and could not be trusted to speak even a single truth, but the fact that the assassin had uttered such a phrase within the hearing of so many, with such apparent confidence . . . It galled Aliver. It set his blood to boiling.

He so wanted to step back into that moment and grab the man by the throat. Why hadn't he? Instead, all he had managed to do was yell again and again for someone to stop the man. He could have pushed the guards aside if he had wanted to. He could have vaulted over the table. He could have done so many things that he might now be proud of. But he had not. He replayed the scene and all the possible variations on it a hundred times before the sun rose the next day. None of it did him any good. It only solidified his belief that his father's wound was his fault more than anyone else's.

✳

In comparison to the expansive grandeur of most Acacian architecture the council chamber was a cramped, claustrophobic space barely large enough for the oval table at its center, a low surface of polished granite, around which sat the ten advisers of his father's kingdom. Light entered from a single slotted window high on the southern wall. The shaft of it fell in such a way as to illuminate the center of the table and to cast up highlights on the councillors' features. The brilliant contrast of this effect made the walls beyond into a dim boundary that felt to Aliver decidedly like a chamber for some sort of interrogation.

The prince, after a moment of hesitation as his eyes adjusted to the light, took his place in his father's seat. He wondered if he should commence the meeting. He looked around at the shadow-dimmed and creviced faces of the elders gazing back at him and at others whom his eyes drifted past. He took them in not as the individuals they were but as if looking upon so many stone busts. How to start such a meeting?

He did not have to. Thaddeus Clegg called the meeting to order by invoking the names of the first five Acacian kings, reminding all in attendance that they here partook in a discourse of the highest order. It was to them that they should look for wisdom. Them upon whom to model themselves as they faced the turmoil now confronting them.

"Before we proceed to the matters we must discuss here, I am sure you all wish to know how the king fares." There were murmurs all around. "All I can tell you is what the physicians have told me. At this moment the king lives. If he did not, they would come to us and we would know immediately. But he was almost certainly poisoned. They believe the blade that cut him was of the Ilhach, the old order of Meinish assassins. I know—they were disbanded by Edifus and outlawed. But still it may be their deadly poison that drains the life from him." The chancellor touched Aliver with his roaming gaze, locked on him for a minute. He looked away before he continued.

"The physicians are doing all they can. The king may survive; then again, he may not. We need to be prepared for either eventuality. As you all can see, Prince Aliver sits in his father's place this day. Bid him welcome, even as you pray he will soon give his seat back to his father."

Aliver tried to look around and return the greetings directed at him, but his eyes faltered before long. He heard some of the kind words with his gaze fixed on the tabletop.

His eyes continued to roam over the grain of the stone as he heard Thaddeus's secretary give his report. There was scarcely a person on the island who could confirm the assassin's identity, he said. By chance an official who had lived a year in Cathgergen auditing the satrapy's books attested that the man was, indeed, Thasren Mein. But the matter was not without dispute. Speaking via messenger pigeons, Meinish representatives in Alecia issued a denial, swearing the assassin could not have been Thasren. They insisted that it was a plot by some other conspirators, but not by the Mein. They even announced their intention to sail promptly to Acacia and plead their innocence. This may have been a ploy, however, for the only Meinish official actually on the island had vanished. Gurnal and his family had fled, leaving his house a tomb for several servants. It was, to say the least, difficult to make sense of.

As the secretary concluded, Julian, one of the more senior councillors, said, "This is not enough information to form action on." A few voices, seemingly exasperated with the elder already, pointed out that nobody had yet suggested any action. Julian continued undeterred. "Hanish Mein sending his brother to his death . . . and for what—to start a war he cannot hope to win? I can believe neither what my eyes saw nor what I've been told since. Hanish is barely more than a boy. I saw him at the winter rites a few years ago. He grew a downy beard on his cheeks, untrimmed like boys anxious to be men."

Relos, the commander of the Acacian forces and a man Aliver knew his father trusted, said, "He is a boy no longer. I believe he is now in his twenty-ninth year."

Julian's eyes touched on Aliver for a second, and then he asked the general company, "If Hanish Mein did this, for what reason? What does he intend?"

"We cannot know what he intends," Chales, another older soldier, said. "Julian, your love of peace is well known, but not all persons are as generous minded as you."

"And boys are often foolish," Relos said. "Full of pride. Folly."

Thaddeus cut off Julian's response. "No one here looks at the night and calls it day," he said. "We should consider all possibilities, and Julian's question is valid. Perhaps this is not Hanish Mein's doing. Perhaps, but I have found the most obvious culprit is usually the actual culprit. The Mein are an ancient people. Ancient people have long memories. Hanish might believe he acts on his forefathers' behalf. He is in contact with his ancestors, and they crave Acacian blood as much now as they ever did. At least, that is what men of the Mein believe. They delude themselves this way."

"We are all ancient people, Thaddeus," Relos said. "Some of us remember this and some don't. Some can name their father's father's father and some cannot. But the blood in each of us began at the beginning and runs still. Age is no excuse for treachery."

A quiet moment of hesitation prompted Aliver to speak. "We are circling the issue here without looking it in the face," he said. "The man—the assassin—does anyone doubt he was of the Mein race? And that he spoke their language with ease? Did he not name himself?" The room answered this with silence, all seemingly surprised to hear the young man speak and not sure how to answer him. "Then why look at the night sky and wonder whether it is actually daytime disguised? We know who did this. A Mein stuck a blade in my father! We will do the same to them but with greater force. And I do not care why they did it. An act is an act, no matter the reasoning of the mind that commited it. They must be punished."

"Just so, Prince," Thaddeus said. "That is why we are here. We must form some sort of response. The governors will have their own ideas, but they will look to us for guidance and, ultimately, for approval of any course of action."

"Then we are here to decide *how* to attack?" Aliver asked, gaining confidence from his own boldness. "How quickly can we have an army knocking on the door of Tahalian?"

Thaddeus deferred to Carver, the only Marah captain on the island, for his thoughts on military deployments. In his role as councillor Carver was the youngest in attendance, just in his mid-thirties. He had been born fortunate, the latest of a long line of warriors, and his skill and ambition had sped his way to prominence. He had volunteered to lead the army against the Candovian Discord a few years earlier. This was a rare military action, of which Aliver believed the stories were more fiction than truth, but Carver could claim to have commanded in battle. Few Acacians could say the same. Still, Aliver did not care for what he had to say.

No attack against the Mein could be rushed, he proclaimed. They had to consider the Mein's military prowess, their isolated location, and the territory through which one had to travel to reach them. Acacian forces were spread through the empire in a way that allowed them police powers but not in concentrations sufficient to launch a military campaign without reorganization and transportation of troops. They could start pulling in units from the provinces, order call-ups of more, and they could marshal troops around Alecia in the early spring. Perhaps, if Aushenia was amenable, they could move troops into forward positions near the Gradthic Gap by the spring equinox. But this would be a defensive measure. They could not actually march onto the Mein Plateau until at least a month later, and then travel would be difficult over the sodden ground and with all the rivers at flood, not to mention the insects. . . .

"Insects?" Aliver asked. "Are you mad? My father is stabbed by a Mein assassin and you speak to me of insects?"

Carver frowned in a way that drew his prominent eyebrows toward each other. "My lord, have you ever seen the tiny flies of the Meinish spring? They swarm the land, clouds so thick that men have suffocated just from inhaling them. And they bite. Men have died of blood loss. But the worst is that they cause disease, fevers, plagues. . . . There are many things to consider in a military campaign, many ways for soldiers to die other than on a sword. Insects, my prince, are one of them. Perhaps a forward force familiar with the winter conditions of the Mein could start movements earlier, before the thaw brings the pests of the place to life, but with General Alain missing I would not recommend it."

Aliver shook his head, perplexed to hear a soldier voice such reluctance. He had always been taught to think in terms of a direct strike, especially as their army outnumbered the forces of any one province. He wanted to ask what had happened to General Alain, but from the way that Carver mentioned him, it was clear everyone else knew something of this already. He said, "The soldiers of the Mein number no more than twenty thousand, and ten of those are in our service throughout the empire. That was the decree. So my question is how quickly can we have a force large enough to defeat the ten thousand fighters in place? That hardly seems an impossible task."

Carver muttered that the Mein's population had always been hard to ascertain. At times their numbers seemed to fluctuate in ways that did not correspond to the official census. "If we are to have war with the Mein, it is unlikely we will clash arms before early summer. A punitive force sent sooner . . . I am not sure it is possible. If Hanish picked his timing so as to leave us unable to strike back immediately, he chose well. There is also the innate nature of Meinish soldiers to consider. Men of the Mein kill as a matter of course. They cull the weak so that each generation makes them stronger. They train in the harshest of conditions. They keep secret customs that we can only guess at. Each Mein life we take will be paid for dearly."

This was met with murmurs of agreement. One councillor said he had heard tales that Hanish had trained a secret army in some hidden location. Another agreed. Julian shook his head at the speculative direction of the conversation but had nothing to add other than his disapproval.

"Hanish fights the Maseret," Carver said, "the dueling dance the Mein so enjoy. If the attack on the king is his doing, it is like a dagger thrust in the face. He wishes to have us back on our heels, off balance. We must concede that he has achieved this much already."

"I fear the next strike is already initiated," Chales said.

Relos nodded a few times, as he always did to indicate he was about to speak. "They have belief, those people. They speak with their dead; and the dead, I am told, are very convincing orators. Belief is dangerous when turned to a cause."

Aliver looked about him. What was wrong with these people? What happened to his father cast as a simple tactic in some dance? Talking with the dead? One would have thought from their tones that this was nothing more than a war game, a business meeting. . . .

"Are you here to write out the terms of surrender of my father's rightful kingdom?" Aliver snapped. "Damn you all if you don't find one manly thing to tell me!"

"Young prince," Thaddeus said, his face pained as if he wished they were having this discussion in private, "you need not damn us. Not a man here believes we are in true peril. They would just have you know the matter is grave."

"I know that," Aliver said. "Did I not look upon my father's face? Tell me whatever more you must. But I say again—speak with me on how we will punish Hanish Mein. That is what we will do. We have to decide only how and on what day. Understood?"

The others murmured assent, but through the rest of the long meeting Aliver wondered whether his outburst had been wise. The meeting adjourned, leaving his head cluttered with ideas that floated about bumping into one another, rising and sinking like pieces of debris from a shipwreck. He had no true feel for what was to come. He felt like a cabin boy clinging to a piece of wreckage, at the whim of currents he had no power over.

CHAPTER

NINETEEN

Of all the things that pained Thaddeus as he stood beside the sickbed of his old friend the king, it was the loose manner in which the flesh of his face sagged that most shot him through with regret. It showed Leodan for what he was: a man grown ancient, so tired of life that the muscles of his face barely had the power to contract or to quiver or to register emotion. To say his skin was ashen would speak only to the surface of the truth. He was a powdery white, indeed, but the color and life had been bled from far below the skin's waxy surface. Thaddeus had the momentary thought that Edifus himself may have looked much the same on his deathbed. And this death—like the first king's generations before—might well mark a shift in the order of the world.

Thaddeus could barely keep from falling to his knees and bawling his sorrow, confessing everything, denying everything. He felt the truth of both impulses. In a way, this was all his doing. He had believed the message Hanish Mein had sent to him. He had known from the moment he heard it that Gridulan was guilty of the crimes Hanish named. And he had hated, hated the son for the sins of his father. He had wanted to punish him, for Akarans to suffer, for the very land to be thrown into chaos. Several times as he watched the king in his mist trance Thaddeus had imagined laying hands on his throat and slowly squeezing the life from him. It would have been physically easy to accomplish, but he had never done more than imagine it. Instead, he had killed that poor messenger. He had not planned that out. He was not sure why he had done it. It was a vague notion that came upon him that night. She had brought news of threats to the Akarans. Thaddeus wanted those threats living and breathing, and so she had to die. Cowardly of him, but in a way he had been asking Hanish Mein to punish the king in ways he could not himself. So why was he so miserable now that Hanish had succeeded?

As he bustled through the myriad tasks the situation required of a faithful chancellor he was struck again and again by the images of Leodan's stunned face, the stain on his gown, the fingers of one of his hands as they clasped at the shoulder of the gape-mouthed Aushenian prince. Nor could he shake free of the assassin's bold candor, he who had named himself. Thaddeus heard the Meinish words issuing from the man's mouth, their meaning quickly taken in. He watched the man cut a dripping crease of blood across his own neck. There had been such certainty in his face, not a moment of doubt or hesitation, no fear of the gaping finality of his own actions. Thasren had stared about the room as if he were the true prophet of an unknown god; all around him were the ignorant, the damned.

A sound issued from the king's mouth, little more than a moan. He opened his eyes. Thaddeus grasped him by the hand and whispered his name. Leodan turned toward him, but his eyes did not show the surprise he expected. The king seemed to have known he was there all along. He showed his body's dysfunction only when he opened his mouth to speak. His tongue, Thaddeus could see, was white and dry, swollen and unwieldy. Clearly, he was not able to speak. This was a symptom of the poison, a sign that he had turned to face his last handful of hours in this world.

But the king had not lost complete use of his limbs. He motioned with his hands, unsteadily at first, until Thaddeus realized he asked for parchment, ink, and a quill. Once he had them in hand—after the chancellor had also propped him up with pillows into a seated position—Thaddeus watched as the king, breathless and concentrating, twisted his hand into position. Staring at the page and at his fingers, he willed them to motion. His hand moved in jerky motions, starting and stopping at awkward moments, letters ill formed and jumbled closely together. The sharp point of the pen on the dry parchment was for a moment the only sound in the room. Thaddeus tugged on his earlobe as he waited, his mind whirling with the most improbable notions of what the king might be writing to him. What accusation would he make? What curse? And he asked himself how would he react if this dying man charged him with the crime he was in fact guilty of? Did he still have enough anger in him to lash back? He could not locate any emotion like that.

Though it took a long time, Leodan's face showed some satisfaction when he raised the parchment for Thaddeus to see. It read, *Tell the children their story is only half written. Tell them to write the rest and place it beside the greatest story. Tell them. Their story stands beside the greatest tale ever told.*

Thaddeus nodded. "Of course, sire."

The king then wrote, *You must do this thing*.

"What would you have me do?" Thaddeus asked, his relief undisguised in his tone. "Say it and I will." He immediately saw the contradiction in his words and regretted it. He touched the king at the wrist and indicated that he meant for him to write it. Write it and he would.

Leodan wrote his next message with less care for the shape of his letters. The watching chancellor changed position so that he could see the page and had time to decipher the words. He understood what was being asked of him before the message was completed. The king was reminding him of the course of action he wished to be taken now, because he was to die before his children were old enough to handle the transition of rule. It was a plan that put the fate of the nation in the chancellor's hands. The steps of it were known only to him, and it would involve just a few others. It stunned Thaddeus to remember that they had spoken of such things before. When they had, it had seemed nothing more than an elaborate formality. Pure fantasy that he entertained only to assuage Leodan's occasional bouts of morbidness. But some fantasies, it seemed, could not be distinguished from actual life.

"I don't think that will be necessary," he said, setting his palm over the king's hand. "There's too much we do not yet know. Leodan, you may yet live through this. This attack on you may be the work of a single fool. What you ask might endanger the children instead of protecting them. This plan was idle talk at a different time—"

The king smashed his fist against his lap, his face rigid with anger. With what appeared to be a monumental effort—face twisted, jaw opening wide, tongue and lips and eyes and cheeks all trembling—he managed to say, "Do . . . this." He repeated the two words several times, until they lost shape and his tongue could no longer form them.

Such an order was impossible to refuse. Once Thaddeus had affirmed that he would see to it, Leodan relaxed. He exhaled and let his weight settle more heavily against the pillows. He did not try to talk again, but he set his eyes on the chancellor and studied him intently, with moist-rimmed eyes full of kindness. Thaddeus almost turned away, but the king's eyes held him, no reproach in them. Thaddeus sensed that his friend was asking him to remember the fine things that they had done in the past, the dreams they had spoken about, the moments shared only between the two of them. He realized that despite this man's sudden nearness to death he had one thing to be pleased about. He was finally freed to challenge his children to fight for the cause he always chided himself for not fighting for himself. It was a huge, yawning, frightening journey he was asking the chancellor to set them on, but it was action. For Leodan there was no other choice anymore. He seemed to have no doubt about what mattered now, and he believed fully in setting his children accordingly on the journey this required.

The king penned another terse order. *Bring the children first*, he wrote, *and then, after* . . . Thaddeus did not have to ask him what the latter request referred to. He would see to both requests.

He received the royal children a half hour later. He felt terribly cold, though he was sure the chill was within him, for the room was heated as normal for the season. He stood with his back steadied against the closed door to the king's chambers, his hands resting one on the other to calm any tremble they might have betrayed. Seeing the four young faces he was glad he had so positioned himself. The sight of them wrung him through with emotion. As if he were actually their father, he thought, Look at them! Look at the magnificence of my children! Aliver . . . By Tinhadin, he stood straight! He moved with a bearing both military and easy. How well trained he was, how diligent and serious, how strong to put forth a brave façade. Usually the beauty of the group, Corinn's skin was puffy and mottled. She looked as if her face might crumble into ugliness at any moment, but there was something heartrending in the pained nakedness of her emotions. Mena's eyes were saddened beyond her years, her head lowered as if she knew with quiet resolve just why they had been summoned. And Dariel was as wide-eyed and as tremulous as a mouse. Thaddeus had to squeeze down the swell of emotion within him. It took all his effort to speak calmly.

"Your father will see you now. Please do not tax him. Know that he will communicate with you in the only way he can. Do not ask him for any more than he can give. He is not well at all." He was not sure how much to go on, how clear and specific to be. He wanted them to know what was happening, but he could not bring himself to say it. Instead, he heard himself ask, "Are you ready?"

A silly question. He knew it was silly, hearing his own words and looking into faces decidedly not ready to see their father for the last time. He turned and pushed open the door and stepped aside so that the way was clear. Once all four had passed him, he reached in and pulled the door shut, staying without himself. He walked away, trying not to think about what was passing in that room, between a true father and his children.

His offices were only a moment's walk down the hall. He left the door open behind him so that he would hear the children leave and know just when to return to the king. He dispatched his secretary with orders to have the king's mist pipe readied. As he turned to do as ordered, the man's surprise—or was it scorn—showed on his face. Thaddeus did not reprimand him for it. He was right in many ways. If the king of the empire was approaching death, should he not be clear of mind until the very end? Were there not so, so many things for him to attend to and should not his last breath be expelled in service to the nation? Of course it was all true, and also all ridiculous. The official record of the king's passing would include no mention of the drug. Official records never did.

Thaddeus stood beside his fireplace for a time. He hoisted the poker and stirred the logs, though they burned well and did not need it. He thought, Let the old man have what he wished for. It was the great gift of the mist. The drug delivered to its user whatever he or she most desired, most needed to carry on living. Leodan had never taken it before Aleera passed away, but in his grief afterward he discovered the drug so many millions of his subjects knew all too well. The slaves of the Kidnaban mines, the parents of Quota children, the teeming masses in the slums of Alecia, the merchants who floated the sea currents unceasingly, soldiers stationed far from home for years at a time, workers in a thousand different trades they had learned as children and carried on throughout their years: they all depended on the balm of the drug for reprieve from the otherwise unceasing torture of their lives. Their king was no different.

Leodan's time under the mist's influence, though, was spent in the manner unique to him—with his dead wife. He had confessed as much. She awaited him just beyond that wall of consciousness. Once he passed through it, she greeted him with sympathy and censure in her eyes, with love for him but with no fondness for this vice. After those first moments she took his hand in hers, accepted him completely, and walked him through the beauty of their courtship. They slipped seamlessly from moment to glorious moment in their life together as husband and wife, as young parents with each child the Giver allowed them, through moments large and small and intimate. The small ones, Leodan had said, often surprised him. Tiny moments during which he viewed her from a certain light, when he remembered the details of her features and the idiosyncrasies of her face or voice or demeanor . . . How could he love her so deeply and yet forget so much of who she had been during his waking hours? It was these details that the king searched for time and again beyond the mist wall. Aleera led him through a tour of everything that had been wonderful about their time together. All in a single evening.

Life, Thaddeus thought, must have been a pale punishment compared

to such bliss. But then he thought of the children. At least Leodan had children, which had been denied Thaddeus himself. At least he did not have to
live knowing his love died because of treachery. After Dorling's death he had
been asked a thousand times why he did not remarry and father more children. He had always shrugged and answered vaguely and never with the
truth—which was that he feared being the cause of more death. Perhaps he
had known all along that his loved ones had been killed to squelch his ambitions.

Ah! Thaddeus jabbed the logs in the fire ferociously, angry that he
could not control his thoughts. They were like the coils of a snake writhing
in his head, a hungry serpent that at times seemed to eat its own tail. He
rested the poker back in place and looked again at the king's note, at the
scribbled words, the looping, irregular sentences, the handwriting only
faintly familiar as the king's. Should this document be found by anyone else,
none would believe it came from Leodan Akaran. Few would understand
the order. Only he and the king had ever spoken of the plan to which it referred. How strange that something they had discussed casually a few years
before—Thaddeus sipping wine and the king glazed by the mist—should
now become an actual possibility. But it was not meant for others' eyes anyway. This was for him. The king was entrusting him with his most precious
concern. How strange that he had no idea who his greatest betrayer was.

The note, which he glanced at one last time, went thus: *If it comes that
you must, send them to the four winds. Send them to the four winds, as we spoke of,
my friend.*

Having read it again, he loosed it from his fingers at such an angle that
it slipped into the fire. It landed at the edge of the logs, and for a moment
he thought he would have to nudge it with the poker. But then it caught,
flared, and curled and blackened. As quickly as that, it was gone. He turned
from the fire and rounded his desk, unsure what he was to do next, but
thinking he might face it best if he looked the part of a chancellor at his duties. It was then that he saw the envelope.

It was a single white square at the center of the polished wooden expanse of his desk. It should not have been there. It had not been included in
his earlier mail delivery, and if it was meant for him personally it would normally have been delivered into his hands. If he had been cold before, he felt
himself made of ice now. He did not touch the envelope but lowered himself stiffly into his chair. The leather protested his weight at first, but then
yielded to accommodate him, as it had for so many years.

He broke the envelope's seal with his fingernail and read the message.

The king is dead, it began. *You had no hand in it. The credit goes only to my brother. If you are wise, you will feel neither guilt nor joy. But now, Thaddeus, you should think of your future. Turn your attention to the children. I want them, and I want them alive. Give them to me alive and you will have riches along with your revenge. This I promise you.* He paused on the signature at the end and stared at it as if it were not a name at all but some word he had forgotten the meaning of. It was signed, *Hanish, of the Mein.*

There was a noise in the hallway. Thaddeus pressed the letter between his palm and his thigh. Two men walked by outside, talking, their forms visible for a split second through the narrow vantage into the passageway. Then they were gone. Thaddeus pinched out the corners of the message and sat with it bridged between his knees.

He sat for some time, his mind drifting to old memories, unhinged for a time from the dueling things being demanded of him. But then he felt the shift in the breath of the air that meant the king's door had opened. He could delay no longer. He rose, took the second note to the hearth, and let it slide from his fingers into the fire. He turned to go once more to his old friend. He would take him his pipe and bid him farewell, and then he would decide the fate of the Akaran children.

CHAPTER

TWENTY

From Cathgergen several messenger birds of a short-winged northern variety progressed across the Mein in small bites. Each found waypoints that were little more than rock outcroppings amid the sea of ice and snow, low hovels inside which lone men huddled beside wire cages, cooing and stroking the pigeons they tended, long-haired hermits connected to the world of other humans only by the birds themselves. This route was an old one, established long ago and known only to the few living souls that made it function. It worked with surprising dependability. Because of this an avian courier arrived in Tahalian only four days after being dispatched from the mild climes of Acacia, a fraction of what it would have taken a human to travel the same distance.

As the bird landed in one part of Tahalian, folded its wings, curled its trembling feet around its perch, and offered up its burden to yet another handler, the intended recipient of the message rose from a three-legged stool in a sunken arena carved into the fields behind the stronghold, a space called the Calathrock. The structure was the work of hundreds of men over scores of years. Constructed of massive hardwood trunks, the beams of the arena interlocked to arching effect, jointed with iron cuffs, suspended above an area five hundred yards square. It was high and wide enough to host military maneuvers, marching drills, and weapons training. Even full battles were replicated undercover, hidden from prying eyes, protected from the weather. It was a functional monument to a military cause. And also it was a secret pride of a race of people no longer officially permitted either secrets or pride. Grand as it was, on this occasion the Calathrock hosted a contest between just two men.

Hanish Mein stepped to the center of the circle left open for him. He bowed to the man sworn to kill him and nodded that he was ready to begin the Maseret dance. Hanish was of medium stature, slimly formed, in a short skirt and thalba, a garment made of a single sheet of thin, tanned leather that had been wrapped around his torso with the aid of servants, leaving his arms unencumbered. He wore his hair shorter than most men of the Mein, clipped close to the sides and under the rear curve of the skull. Only his braids dropped down to his shoulder, three in total, two of them woven with caribou hide, one with green silk. His features seemed sculpted with the objective of focusing attention on his eyes: wide forehead lined with hair-thin creases, tilted cheekbones, an aquiline nose that was somewhat shallow at the bridge. One of his nostrils bore a tiny scar. His skin had a smooth milkiness to it, nowhere more so than in the flesh just below his lower eyelids. These, when caught in the right light, positively glowed, highlighting the gray orbs above them, giving them a quality that strangers often mistook for dreaminess.

The soldier facing Hanish was taller than the chieftain by a head, a long-limbed man who bore his size well. He was stiffly muscled, with hair the brilliant blond so loved by his race. He wore two braids woven with green silk, indicating that he had danced these steps before and lived to tell of it. He was a well-respected warrior who had sat beside Hanish during the years of slow germination of their plans. He had overseen the training of the secret army under Hanish's direction. Only now, on the eve of the onslaught, did his ambition drive him to challenge his chieftain.

Arrayed around the two figures in a crescent stood a handful of attendants, officers of the Mein; the chief Maseret instructor; a surgeon; and a ring of Punisari, the special forces here serving as royal bodyguards. Also among them were two hooded priests of the Tunishnevre. One of them waited to spirit the body of whichever dancer was slain into the sacred chamber, so that he might immediately join his ancestors. The other stood prepared to say rites of royalty if the challenger prevailed and therefore stepped in to fill Hanish's place as chieftain. Haleeven, Hanish's closest adviser, stood just at the edge of the group. He was a short man by Mein standards, but thick and powerful in a bearlike way, with a prominent, frost-pocked nose and a crimson lace of blood vessels etched across his upper cheeks. He was the young leader's uncle.

Beyond this inner circle the Calathrock thronged with fighting men. Thousands of soldiers stood armored for battle, their weapons in hand or strapped on their backs, a good ten thousand pairs of blue-gray eyes. Each of them had flaxen hair that almost to a man they wore in the traditional, matted style of Meinish warriors. This was not a particularly unusual event, but it never failed to stir the blood of each and every man fortunate enough to watch. Hanish held his arms up in answer to their calls. He knew why they yelled so loudly, and he wished them to see that he foremost among them believed in the Maseret. A strong people deserved a strong leader, one not afraid to be tested. He asked himself to let slip his love of life, to let slip fear, to let slip desire. He released everything that made lesser men prey to errors so that he might function better and be blessed to remember these things later.

As the two men stepped to within striking distance, they moved in a slow, arcing dance, one stepping toward the other, then retreating, then slipping from side to side. To eyes that did not know the Maseret, the early portion of the dance would have seemed a slow tedium, almost effeminate. First Hanish and then his opponent offered the other a view of his profile, and then took it back. Legs crossed each other. A foot slid forward just a few inches. They rotated from the hips as if the lower and upper portions of their bodies were of different minds. Though neither man made undue show of it, they were each armed with a single weapon, a short dagger sheathed across the abdomen. The narrow blade was about six inches long. It was shaped like a knife for filleting river trout, although of an altogether higher quality of metal.

The chieftain had mastered the well-established moves so completely that a lower portion of his awareness oversaw them. He sought to present a façade suggestive of tranquil amusement, kept empty of any indication of how or when or where he might strike. At the same time he searched his opponent for any weakness he could exploit. He willed into quickness the highest level of his consciousness. He freed it from the thousand irrelevant details of the world so that he could focus on the few things now important to his survival. His Maseret instructor had once told him to envision two cobras meeting on the jungle floor. They conduct a strange ballet, moving slowly for a time, neither making the least false move. And when it comes, the fatal blow happens in the blink of an eye. Though he had never seen a living cobra, Hanish never forgot this image. He had used it before, and each time his first strike had come as quickly as a spark between two flints, so immediate from conception to action that he realized what he had done only afterward.

The two men made first contact with their palms. They leaned toward each other and met with their necks pressed side by side, chins clamped atop the other's shoulder, arms and fingers searching for purchase. They circled, pushing from the ankles through the legs and torso, measuring each other's weight and strength. In terms of pure muscle mass and power Hanish was dwarfed, but within a few moves he knew that the other man favored his right leg. It might have borne an old wound, one that left the limb hesitant when the leg swung free from the knee. The man's joints moved more smoothly when stepping forward than when retreating. He was not a creature who felt comfortable backing up. Despite his efforts to hide it, this man preferred to strike first. He hungered for the first moment to launch himself, especially a moment at which he would be stepping forward, with his right leg in the lead. . . .

The chieftain broke the embrace, twirled away. With his chin pointing out toward the crowd he drew his dagger. The soldier did the same. Hanish was not surprised when his opponent bunched the muscles of his forward right leg, twisted from the torso, flipped his blade to a backhanded grip, and flung his arm in a sweeping diagonal with the full strength of his body. He had, indeed, hungered to strike first.

Alarm showed on the soldier's face before he had even completed the motion. The moment came when he should have struck Hanish high on the right breast, but instead he touched nothing at all. Hanish had sunk low enough to avoid the strike. He spun around once, rose to full height, and slammed his dagger into the exposed center of the man's upper back. He knew by the way the steel sunk in all the way to his balled fist that the blade had slipped between the man's ribs without sticking in the bone. He angled the blade and yanked it in line with the narrow gap between the bones. He sliced a portion of the heart, through the back of a lung, and pulled the dagger through the dense tissue of the man's back muscles.

The man dropped. The gathered soldiers erupted in cheers, and a deafening, reverberating cacophony set the snow on the roof vibrating. They chanted Hanish's name. They beat their fists against their chests. A portion of the army surged forward like a wave rushing toward him, barely held back by the Punisari, who cracked men savagely over the head and jabbed them with the butts of their spears. Even as a child Hanish had had a tremendous effect on his people. They seemed to see in him a resurrection of heroes of old, underscored again by the sudden, deadly precision of his kill.

Hanish closed his eyes and silently asked the ancestors to accept this man for the worthy being that he was. Let him now be a warrior among you, he thought. He whispered inside himself the words he had been taught for such moments. Let his sword be the wind at night and his fist the hammer that pounds the earth to trembling. May his toes in stretching drive the seas before them and his seed fall from the heavens upon fair women's bellies. . . . Unbidden the man's name sounded in his head and with it an image of the boy he had once been, a memory of laughter shared between them: these thoughts Hanish pressed back into their place.

Opening his eyes again, he turned to the priests. Both of the holy men reached up and drew their hoods back, revealing heads of ghastly golden hair, most of the strands plucked out so that pale scalp shone beneath. This quieted the soldiers to hushed whispers and sharp calls to silence. "So wills the Tunishnevre," one of the priests said. He spoke softly, but his voice carried on the energized air. "May you not fail them, my lord, on the next occasion when you are tested." With that, they bowed from the waist and withdrew, moving in their shuffling slide, their fur-lined slippers skating across the wood as if it were ice.

Hanish raised his arms again to the crowd, who resumed their enthusiasm of a moment before. He moved in near them, reaching out over his guards and grasping men by the arms, punching them playfully, reminding them of the great things to come and of the ageless power of the Tunishnevre. They were strong only together, he said. He was no different than they; they were no less than he. Any man among them could test him to verify the truth of this. No one life mattered unless it was committed to the whole of the Mein nation. In this—as in so many other ways—they were different from their Akaran enemies.

"We Meins live with the past," he cried. "It breathes around us and cannot be denied. Is this not so?"

The crowd answered that it was so.

"And, in truth, we have done little that shames us. It is the Akarans who rewrite the past to suit them. It is they who wish to forget that Edifus had not one son but three. They cannot name them, but we can. Thalaran, the eldest; Praythos, the youngest; with Tinhadin between them."

Each of these was met with groans of disgust, with curses and saliva spat at the floor.

"Calm, calm," Hanish said. He soothed them toward a hush, speaking more softly now so that they had to crane their heads to hear him. "Both of these brothers fought beside Tinhadin to secure and expand their father's dominion. This they did with Meinish aid. We were their allies. And how were we repaid? I will tell you. Shortly after Edifus's death Tinhadin murdered his brothers. He butchered their families and all the women and children of the factions that supported them. Then he slaughtered most of the Mein's royal class when they objected. You know this to be true. We of the

Mein, who had been such fast allies of Edifus, were branded as traitors to the realm. But the heart of the dispute was that Hauchmeinish—"

A roar burst from the army at the mention of the ancient's name.

"Yes," Hanish continued, "our beloved ancestor abhorred the notion of trading in slaves with the Lothan Aklun. He decried the League of Vessels as pirates and waged war against them. It was for this that we were slaughtered and cursed. It was our ancestors' nobility and justness that Tinhadin betrayed. It was in punishment for our virtues that we were exiled to this frigid plateau. But that exile will soon be ended, brothers, and you will see freedom with your own eyes!"

※

Outside the arena, walking through a dim passageway, Haleeven spoke to his nephew. "You do know how to stir the blood. But still, these matches unnerve me, Hanish. They are ill advised, considering the moment we face. I might just as easily have been looking on your corpse."

"It was imperative," Hanish replied, "especially considering the moment we face. If I cannot live by the ancestors' codes, what value does my life have? It is the old ones who bless our bodies in battle, who approve of our skills or reject them. You know this, Haleeven. How else but in this could I be sure the Tunishnevre still blessed me? You surprise me sometimes, Uncle. No one man's life is important; only the goal is."

The other man smiled with one side of his mouth. "But each man has his place within the goal. Manleith was no friend of yours. He wanted the glory that will soon be yours, that's all. He should not have challenged you right now, especially you, the twenty-second generation—"

"I am not the only son of this generation," Hanish countered. "My role is to lead them by example. That is why I danced with Manleith. He was a friend from my youth. Think of the men in that chamber. Think of how they march now, how they practice for the war to come. Clear-eyed, physically fit, not one of them tainted by the mist. Think of that! Compare our men to the millions in the world who are slaves to deception. If you think I can keep them loyal to me without proving my loyalty to them, you are mistaken."

With those words Hanish left his uncle to oversee the training. He pushed through the pinewood doors and climbed the stairs out of the Calathrock and up into the open air. A savage wind smacked him with enough force that he had to pause a moment, legs wide, one hand shielding his face from the tiny splinters of ice that peppered his cheeks and eyes. Though he had endured it all of his twenty-nine years, the harshness of the Mein winter never failed to amaze him, especially when stepping out of the massive shelter of the Calathrock or the warmth of the inner hold. It felt as if the winter night was a living, raging creature. The more they entrenched themselves and made life livable on the plateau, the more the snow tried to blanket them from existence; the more the wind sought to push them against the stones of the mountain, the more the cold found ways to enter their defenses. Hanish leaned forward and started the short walk across the frozen ground, the low-huddled mass of shadow that was Tahalian just visible through the storm.

An aide, Arsay, met him inside the hold. He held the tiny scroll out for him to take. "A message from Maeander," he said. "Thasren has touched Leodan. He walked and slept and ate unnoticed by the enemy, and then came upon him at a banquet and pierced him with an Ilhach blade. The king's time of idyll has ended."

Hanish took the note in his fingers but did not read it. He had thought of his brother's mission every day since Thasren had departed, and yet with the mention of his name he felt a tinge of shame that he had passed even a few hours not thinking of him. Thasren, weeks now alone in a foreign land, the vile treachery that was Acacia all around him, his life daily in a sort of danger very different from the Maseret. Hanish knew that Thasren had always felt himself the lesser sibling. The youngest, the least skilled in war, the farthest away from a claim to his father's patriarchal lineage. To be a third son among the Mein was not easy. But such a thorn twisting in one's side can be a boon if it drives one to action. That was what Meinish wisdom said.

"And my brother?"

Arsay averted his eyes at the question and answered in an ancient formula used to indicate an honorable death. "He asks to be praised."

"He will be," Hanish said swiftly. He instructed Arsay to call a council of generals in the morning. He said to send two messengers, one into the mountains alerting the army hidden there that the time had come, another to Maeander in Cathgergen, telling him to unleash the Numrek. And he was to rouse the mercenary naval officers so long guests in this ice-bound land. They had drunk enough grog, slept long enough wrapped in what pleasures the Mein could offer. It was time for them to earn their commissions. They were a thousand miles from the sea, but a fleet was ready, yet another secret project long years in construction. It would soon be afloat and pressing forward through a frozen ocean.

"I will meet with them all tomorrow," Hanish said. "And alert my scribe that I will call on him tomorrow as well. Tonight I sit vigil with the ancestors. They will be anxious to understand Thasren's fate. I should explain it to them. And I must cleanse myself of my opponent's blood. It will be a long evening."

Arsay had bowed his head at the mention of the elders and did not lift it again. As he walked away Hanish read the fear in the tension in the man's neck and the cant of his head. Though he was critical of it—none should fear their ancestors, even if they were a ghostly embodiment of wrath—he had to acknowledge the tightness in his own throat, the tension high in his upper chest. None *should* fear the Tunishnevre, but all did. Inside their sacred chamber he felt the pulse of their undead energy as tangibly as he sensed heat or cold on his skin, joy or fear in his heart. They were the old ones of his people, preserved in timeless suspension. Such enmity as they contained within their ancient memory was a chilling thing to face.

He waited alone for some time, gathering strength, feeling the alignment of forces so long out of sync. The twenty-third generation since the Retribution . . . that's what he was. If the Tunishnevre were right—and certainly they were—everything in the world was about to change.

CHAPTER

TWENTY-ONE

Corinn would dream of the last embrace for many nights thereafter, so much so that the moment became something of a curse, a nightmare trap made of her siblings' arms and her father's dying body. It did not matter that she knew her father had not intended it that way. It did not matter that there was nothing else he could do, that it was a last tortured gesture made in love. She still wished it had never happened. Rather than see him as she did, she would have chosen not to see him that last time. Some things were better left incomplete, she thought, better left unfinished forever.

What transpired in the room between the king and his four children was simple. He awaited them on his bed, propped by pillows into a seated position. Corinn hung back behind the others as they ran toward him and fell to their knees beside his bed. Even at a distance she could see a man more ravaged than she could have imagined. She had thought of him all throughout the previous night, imagining him in pain, in different postures and conditions, and even still in death. But finally seeing him . . . It was as if a cloaked demon that had haunted her dreams all night had been unhooded in the light of day; instead of allaying her fears the demon had been shown to be a more hideous thing than she had yet imagined. She wanted to turn and flee. She might have, except that the king's eyes were pinned to her the moment she entered and seemed to stare at her alone.

Initially the others whispered their relief at seeing him, their horror at what had happened, their wishes that he gain his health again soon. But he could not listen to this for long. He motioned them to silence by lifting an arm and dragging his fingers through the air. The children waited, but it seemed there was nothing else he could offer them. She had realized before her siblings that he could not talk, that he was terribly weak and perhaps only hours from death. He could make no speeches to them. He could give them no last presents or words of wisdom. He could not, Corinn realized, keep the promises he had made to her.

And she knew before the others the meaning of his upraised arms. He lifted them, trembling, a wide gesture, an opening. Aliver moved back a step, apparently thinking that the king was using his arms to open a discussion on some topic that required the acknowledgment of the largeness of things. But that was not it. He simply held them out to either side until his children saw the invitation for what it was. Then they crowded awkwardly together into the embrace he offered, Corinn the last to accept. It seemed that only she understood how ghastly it was to lie piled upon a dying man, saying nothing at all but only clinging to one another, tearful.

That was how the Akaran children spent their last minutes with their father. Corinn, on exiting the room, ran before her peers, ignoring Mena's entreaties that she stay with them. She could not. Instead of feeling the bonds between them stronger, the touch of those stung like tentacles. She fled as soon as she could. She hid herself away in her private quarters and ordered her guards to let no one disturb her.

So it was from behind a closed door that she heard word of her father's death later that day. It came to her first in a whisper. Then, a few moments later, the enormous bell housed in one of the higher towers began to toll, slow and deep and mournful. She had known it was there but had never heard it before. It was used for a single purpose: to announce the death of an Akaran king. Between its beats she heard the gathering chorus of the servants' wailing, an audible manifestation of misery that crept across the palace and down into the lower town and to the port, to be carried out to the world from there. Corinn clamped her hands over her ears, but she could not block out the sounds.

The following week passed in a dreary blur. Had she the choice, she would have locked herself up in her room immediately and rejected the world. But she did not have that choice. Her presence was required daily, at every hour, it seemed, although she did little more than occupy space, a vacant shell of herself that person after person embraced or bowed before or shed tears in front of. She stood beside her siblings as the masses sang with them the lament of her father's passing. She stood trembling as the drummers beat out the slow, martial dirge performed only for deceased monarchs. She sat without listening through the endless string of funereal speeches, nobles sailing in from near and far, each of them pronouncing their grief in words that layered over and over one another and lost individual meaning. She knew that behind the somber façade an electric buzz of anxiety crackled and popped. She knew that people whispered about the horrible possibilities on the horizon, but her personal grief was more than enough to occupy her. She cared nothing for what happened in the larger world.

At the end of the week the priestesses of Vada and their acolytes prepared and incinerated the king's body. It was one of the only state roles remaining for them and they carried it out with solemnity. When they emerged with the king's urn of ashes, it marked a reprieve from the rites. His ashes would not be released, Corinn knew, until a day in late autumn. She did not look forward to that ceremony, but it was some time away.

As soon as she could, she invoked the old rites of mourning. She kept her windows closed and forbade even her servants from looking at her. Food and drink she had left outside her bedroom door, though she barely touched it. Days passed, one fading into the next without change. Mena came to her twice, Aliver once, and even Dariel sent a messenger to beg her to come forth, but she turned them all away. She drifted into and out of sleep, through dreams and memories, visions of the past that seemed so very distant. Occasionally she was struck by the realization of just how treacherous the illusion of time was. Things that were once could not be again. Things that she had clung to—her mother, her father—were no more substantial than the images conjured in her mind. And what good were those? They could not be touched. Could not be weighed in the palm or seen with true eyes or heard in the air. Her life was going to be just as she imagined in her dark moments: she was on the path to losing one beloved thing and then another. That was what life would be for her until she herself was swallowed by the maw of the same hungry oblivion. She could not face it. So she did not. Not, at least, until the world came to her in a form she did not wish to turn from.

She heard the muffled sounds of shouts from her waiting room, the bang as some large object fell over, and the fast click of heels across the stones. She did not think enough of it to raise herself from where she lay spread across the expanse of her soft bed. At the first impact against the door she only lifted her head and looked sleepily toward it. But when it sprung open, it finally registered to her that somebody really was intent on getting in to see her.

Igguldan tumbled in behind the opening door, nearly sprawling flat on the floor. He scrabbled forward on his knees, spun and twirled to an upright position, and dashed a few steps farther into the chamber. Behind him several guards shouldered through the doorway. They were so anxious to get at him that they stuck fast for a moment, swatting and cursing one another, their swords held awkwardly so as not to do themselves damage. Igguldan's eyes darted around the chamber. He found Corinn standing at the foot of her bed with one hand poised across her heart. He took a small step closer and then stopped. The guards, free of the door and rushing toward him, pulled up. They stood looking at the two young people, at a loss for how to proceed.

"Princess Corinn," Igguldan said. "Forgive me for intruding. It is horrible of me, I know, but I had to see you. I had to see that you were all right and to . . ."

One of the guards broke in. He, too, began to ask her forgiveness, to explain that the prince had dashed past them unheeding of their demands that he stop. Corinn cut him off with a gesture of her hand. "Leave us," she said.

Once they were alone Igguldan began to apologize again. The princess told him not to. He asked after her health and began to express his sympathies, but again Corinn asked him to stop. He stood a moment as if deciding what he had to say. Then he did so directly. "I have been recalled to Aushenia," he said. "My father fears for my life, I think. Also, he seems on edge about other things, movements in the north. I received only the briefest command sent by pigeon. But I have to go, Corinn." After a moment of hesitation, he added, "I do not want to leave you like this."

Corinn wrung her hands, nervous, unsure why she had received him at all. She knew she was unkempt, in a rumpled gown, hair tangled and unwashed. She looked down and motioned at something outside the room, hoping he might look away from her. "It feels as if the world is in turmoil."

"It is, more than you can imagine. The whole island is in turmoil. Vessels sail back and forth hourly to the Mainland. The governors in Alecia have been in nonstop session. The treaty between our nations is not official, but it sounds like the governors want us as allies. There is a rumor that an army has laid siege to Cathgergen. Your brother is handling it all manfully. You should be proud of him, although he is in a strange position—no longer just a prince but not really a king either."

Corinn asked when he was to depart. He answered that he would sail for Alecia with the next rising of the sun. There they would pick up representatives his father wished to meet with and sail directly for Aushenia. He gave no more details than this, but as the two considered his journey in silence Corinn could not help but feel every sad mile of distance that it would put between them. She recalled the chill waters the prince had described swimming in, the rolling landscape thick with forest. How wonderful it must feel to ride among those massive trees on horseback. She imagined Igguldan doing just that. She saw him galloping through a wind-lashed wilderness totally different from the manicured jewel in the sea that was Acacia. Aushenia was so very far away, and not just in terms of distance. It was a wild place in which one could be lost or reinvented in a different form.

"Do you think I could go with you?" she asked. "I would not burden you. It is just that I want to escape this place. I want to be with you, just with you." She had not given this the slightest thought since her father's death, but as she said the words she felt convinced they were true. That is exactly what she wanted now, more than anything.

Igguldan slipped his hands around hers, clasping them firmly. Together, they lowered themselves to the edge of the bed and sat side by side. "I so wish the world were not so mad and that I had met you at a different time. Your father was a special man. After I watched him struck, I was sick. Just sick! But even so I kept thinking about you. Everything I heard or saw or felt reminded me of you. The world is falling apart, but all I can think of is you. I said to myself, 'This is not right. Get control of yourself.' But I could not. And then I thought, Perhaps this is love. That's what it is. You are in love with Princess Corinn. I know it is inappropriate of me to say it like this. But time is so short. I just had to see you once more before we both fly off in different directions. I needed you to know that you are loved. Wherever you are to go in the world, you take my love with you."

Once again, the prince had managed to say the perfect thing. She was loved. He—brave and handsome and faithful—loved her. She squeezed his hand and inched forward slightly. "I am not going anywhere," Corinn said, thinking he had misspoken. "I wish I were. I would go with you if you asked me."

The prince's grip lessened slightly. "They have not told you yet? Corinn, you are to leave tomorrow, too. I only know because your brother told me in confidence. He was angry about it and could not hold it in. All the Akaran children are to leave the island for refuge. The chancellor thinks you will be safer somewhere other than Acacia, someplace secret."

"Someplace secret?" the princess whispered.

The prince, thinking she was prompting him for more information, admitted that he knew no more, but Corinn had not actually expected him to answer. She was just considering the possibility of this secret place. Where might it be? She had dreamed so often of travel to distant places, wondering how she would be received there, whether or not she would be thought beautiful. Would they journey to Talay? The Candovian coast? Would they sail to the Outer Isles or some other place far from the heart of the empire? Or would it just be Alecia? Hardly a secret place, but maybe she was thinking too grandly. Maybe she would spend the next few weeks locked in a room in the capital. Though this news surprised her, she did not feel the sense of urgency she might have. At least it meant movement, change, getting away from the palace. These could not be bad things, could they?

She asked Igguldan where he would go if he could go into hiding somewhere. He was slightly taken aback by the question, but he settled in to think about it. After a pause, he said that he would rather seclude himself away in the far north of his own country than anyplace else. There was a corner of Aushenia where the forest runs right up to the slabs at the base of the Gradthic Range. It was a cold country, but the air is so full of goodness that breathing it fills one with health and vigor. The mountains themselves are a northern wilderness most of the year, home of great brown bears and of a type of wolf different from the kind that frequented the forest. He had only been there once a few years ago, but he had never forgotten the feeling of standing on those rocks at sunset, with the mountains at his back and the ancient forestland stretching south right over the horizon, the whole scene alight with a play of colors, the darkening woods touched with brilliance by the fire of the sun, eagles above it, flying their high patrol. He had never been so aware of solitude as during that moment, but also he had felt an ancestral pride. Out of that land his people had emerged. It was feral and harsh, but it was also of his very flesh and blood. They had walked from the woods to the southern shore to found Aushenia. They had left behind the wolves and bears and took up their rightful place as caretakers of the land. It was something he had in common with all Aushenians.

"You should see it," he said.

"I would like to," Corinn said. "Say that you will take me, and I'll go with you. You can be my caretaker and you can take me to that wild country of yours. You can hunt fresh meat for me and protect me from the bears and other creatures. The world can go on without us."

Igguldan's hands were moist in hers. She noticed it when he pulled away, allowing cool air to touch the moisture. What had she just said? She did want it, but it was such a large prospect that she could not grasp it. It might be an absurd mistake; she could not tell. In any event, with the withdrawal of his hand Corinn was sure Igguldan was rejecting her offer. She waited to hear him indicate as much.

The prince felt around in his chest pocket with his fingers and pulled out a small envelope, sealed with wax. "I wrote this for you," he said. "I was not sure that I would be brave enough to give it to you. I am still not sure if I am brave enough . . . but I am doing it anyway." He pressed the folded envelope into her palm and closed her fingers around it.

"What is it?"

"You will see when you read it, but do not do so now. Read it later." He stood up and tugged her to her feet. "Now we must rise to this challenge. Corinn, I would like very much to show you my country and for everything you said to come true, but now is not the time. My father called me home because we face the threat of war. I have to answer to him. And you, you must do as the chancellor instructs. He is sure to be right about this." He stopped Corinn's protest, gripping her on the arms, a hard squeeze at first, but then a caress. "Please, Corinn. Let me first serve my father and the memory of yours. After that I will come for you. Will you receive me? I must know that I am fighting for you. If I am no one will be able to defeat me."

Corinn managed to nod. Igguldan pressed his face against hers, his hot skin smooth and soft. He kissed her on the cheek. Then he turned away and walked briskly to the door.

CHAPTER
TWENTY-TWO

Rialus Neptos fled Cathgergen after what he would claim to have been a siege of several days. In a final action before departing, he tossed all manner of hard and heavy objects—his chair, a vase of copper flowers, a paperweight in the shape of an Ice Fields bear, an aged ax once bestowed on his father by the Aushenians—at the glass window that had so sorely embarrassed and betrayed his ego. It would not shatter into the cascade of shards he desired, but it cracked and chipped enough that he felt he had made his point. Whether the message was meant for the glass itself, for someone who would later view it, or for himself he did not consider. He took with him the meager entourage of officials, courtiers, and family members he had been able to maintain in the satrapy—only those so indebted to him that their silence was guaranteed. The Numrek whom he put behind him filled him with as much actual dread as he had feigned. As far as he could tell, few of his colleagues were even composed enough of mind to suspect that the governor himself had any hand in the misfortune befalling them. Indeed, as he ran through the Gradthic Gap he almost felt himself a fugitive in fear for his life.

Because of this Rialus arrived in Aushenia with all aspects of his deception in place. In hasty council with the realm's king, Guldan, he told how the foreign invaders marched out of a squall of snow. He had been concerned for some time, Rialus claimed, by vague reports of movement as far north as the Ice Fields. This was why he had sent General Alain out to examine the territory and question the Mein brothers. He had not heard from him and therefore feared some mishap, but the actual attack had come as a complete surprise.

The Numrek, he said, had arrived in a massive horde, hulking creatures, hidden beneath furs and skins, armed with pikes twice a man's height and with swords curved and weighted toward the tip. Many of them rode horned beasts, naturally armored creatures covered with hairy coats. They poured through Cathgergen's gates before the alarm had even been sounded. They did not explain or announce themselves at all; they just commenced the killing, a merciless slaughter they went at with relish and ravenous glee, bellowing as they fought and dancing to the beat of an unseen drum.

None of this was far from the truth. The Numrek—his *guests*, as Maeander had called them—did arrive in a ravenous mob. Even though there was little military resistance to meet them, they still managed to find people to kill and did so with the glee Rialus described. He did not, of course, mention to Guldan that the entire Northern Guard had met their deaths in one monstrous trap. Instead, he claimed that the outnumbered troops of the guard fought in a frantic retreat, relinquishing one portion of the fortress and then another until all the remaining population stood cornered with their backs against the last granite wall of the place. It was only then, Rialus said, that he consented to parlay with whatever vile being led them.

"You looked their leader in the face?" Guldan asked. He had been a tall man in his youth. Even now, seated in his royal council chambers, stooped somewhat by stiffness in his back, he still had about him an air of natural nobility. His features were steady, although his voice trembled with a measure of trepidation. "What name does he go by?"

"Calrach," Rialus said. "There have never been stranger creatures. There has been nothing like them in the Known World since the Ancients cast back the gods of Ithem—"

"You say they are gods?" one of Guldan's aides interjected.

Rialus was taken aback for a moment. "Well, no. I just mean they are dreadful to look upon. Most alarming."

As with so much in this strange charade, Rialus could speak for some time on this matter with complete honesty. Standing before the Numrek party he felt as if he were gazing through the warped glass of some window and into another age entirely, at beings whose clay had been fired in a different oven than terrestrial men, meant to inhabit another world, an older epoch. They were tall beings, at least three or four heads higher than normal, long of limb, shoulders wide and flat as if they wore some sort of square-edged yoke beneath the skin. They were black haired and bushy browed. For a time Rialus thought their skin had been powdered or painted, so pale was it. On stepping uncomfortably close to them, he saw that this was just their natural hue, a color like the ceremonial mixture of milk splattered with goat's blood that the Vadayan drank at the new year. It was a thin membrane beneath which pulsed an intricate pattern of veins, all as clear to the eye as if they were drawn on paper and held up before a lamplight.

Calrach, their leader, showed his strength in the striated cords of muscle supporting his neck. Even his features had about them a fierce, tensile quality. His eyes were of a brown so dense as to appear solid black. His brows followed contours similar to those of regular men, but they protruded more prominently, crested high like sea waves just starting to spill over. They were pierced through by several thick silver rings, metal set deeply enough it must have punctured right through the bone. Rialus found it nearly impossible to keep his gaze on the man's face. But as soon as his eyes moved on he could not resist turning them back, aghast each time that the creature continued to stare at him from behind the same frightening mask. He was a man, and yet he was not.

Rialus said that for a translator they used a Meinish scribe, a revelation greeted by shocked murmurs and gasps from his Aushenian audience. "Hanish Mein knows of this race?" Guldan asked.

Rialus guessed that he must, and then he continued. "Calrach offered no apology. No explanation or vindication. He simply said we had to leave. Cathgergen was ours no longer. The Numrek had been promised the city. He set me free so that others might learn of the enemy coming against them and be better prepared to offer sport."

"Cathgergen was promised by whom?" an Aushenian aide asked.

Rialus shrugged his thin shoulders to his ears. "I do not know, but we were in no position to argue. He said that I should run to my people and tell them the end had come. They would hunt us for their amusement and roast us over spits."

"You are not serious!" the king said. "Rialus Neptos, have you gone mad? The things you are saying are beyond belief." The monarch seemed to lose his train of thought but found voice again by returning to his earlier question. "Have you gone mad?"

The governor could well imagine that he had. He could never have concocted such a thing in the normal course of his lying. Calrach had said just that. He had sat there, laughing with his generals, saying the vilest things as if Rialus had not been standing before him, as if a translator had not been whispering each word into the trembling man's ear. He had to press his knees together to keep from spilling his bladder. Remembering the moment, Rialus felt a flush of envy toward those who had not yet seen what he had.

The Aushenians had more than a few questions for him. They knew they were the next obvious target, and they probed the exiled governor for further details, for his opinions and conjecture. Rialus warmed to the role of trusted adviser—such was all he ever really wished for. But behind this temptation to remain and be of genuine aid he could see both Maeander's and Calrach's countenances. These helped him to remain resolute. So Rialus explained to the Aushenians that his duty required that he travel to Alecia. Guldan released him, sending him with the grandiose message that whatever evil intent this horde brought would be met first by the soldiers of Aushenia. Such high notions! Rialus thought. But like so many high notions they were of no more weight than the expelled air that carried them. Rialus was in no doubt that Aushenia would fall within a fortnight, a month at most. This assessment, of course, he kept to himself.

Rialus left the kingdom aboard a vessel from the monarch's fleet, watching the bustle of military preparations on the receding shoreline. He was pleased with himself, an emotion that filled him almost to bursting on landing at the capital. He had pined for a villa on the western hills of Alecia since he first saw the spot on a brief visit fifteen years before. Alecia: to him it was the real center of the Acacian empire, the beating heart from which everything of worth in the world radiated. He loved the very idea of the place, the wealth it controlled, the pleasures it offered, the power it wielded, the limitless maze of intrigue, the clandestine couplings. He could barely grasp the dense complexity of the city's quadrants. No matter. Rialus had long believed that he would thrive inside the central city's shimmering pale walls, heated by the sun, draped in hanging vines, and fragrant with only sweet smells.

It was a pity, then, that he arrived within Alecia's gates a traitor to the people he so adored. He tried not to dwell on this, and he was largely successful at fixing his thoughts only on the bounty finally within his grasp. He had, as he earlier professed to Maeander, allies within the capital who shared his desire to see the wealth of the city redistributed. Some were members of the Neptos family, but many others had been nurtured by his agents at clandestine meetings, people who met in small groups and who scarcely knew of the other pockets of people likewise being groomed. He had a promise to keep. He did not shrink from the blood others would spill on his behalf, just as long as he might finally receive some portion of the rewards he had long deserved. In the first few days in Alecia Rialus was a man with two faces. His public face cried tears of grief at the coming war. Privately his eyes scanned the villas above the city for a suitable new home. True to his long-held belief, it appeared the Giver would indeed reward her worthies.

CHAPTER

TWENTY-THREE

The commotion was like nothing ever heard in this frozen expanse of barren solitude: the grunts of beasts shackled to labor; the constant barrage of shouts; the jingle of numberless bells; the crunch of boot after boot after marching boot; and the grinding, grinding, grinding of large objects propelled across a surface that could not decide whether its nature was to aid or resist. It was the scrape of metal and wood over ice, the sound of a fleet of ninety warships traversing a frozen sea. They were tugged to motion by hundreds of woolly oxen, driven by an army of fifteen thousand men who walked with bells fastened to their boots. The old ones had instructed Hanish that each man should bear a chime upon his body that would sing to them no matter how great the distance they traveled. They should announce themselves to the world with voices that spoke for the many silent generations that had struggled to make them possible. The Tunishnevre must have heard them and known in their still chamber just how their children honored them.

With the passing miles Hanish felt the old ones' hold on him slipping somewhat, but he had never felt surer that he was worthy of their trust and would achieve the things they wished of him. Because of him the rumors discussed in the mild climes of Acacia were true, true on a scale beyond even the most extravagant speculation. The few vessels that the fishermen had spotted weeks before were only a scouting force sent to verify the feasibility of what Hanish envisioned. Hanish had instructed the party to allow themselves to be seen. He believed that no matter what people heard about movements in the north they would never believe it until they stood face-to-face with the future he was bringing to them. So why not let them cogitate and worry over phantoms they could neither entirely believe in nor dismiss?

"Nature had always been to the Mein like the goading of a whip to an ox," Haleeven shouted in his ear over the keening wind. "It changes nothing. It slows us little and keeps us bent to work. As it should." His uncle always had such wisdom to dispense at the right moments, and Hanish was glad of his presence. Though he never showed it outwardly, it was often hard being a pillar of unflappable confidence. This older man, so like his father, was a living source of strength.

On a morning at the end of the first week heading south the weather cleared so suddenly that it set the animals on edge. It changed the very sound and feel and substance of the world and left men squinting into the distance, more than one head cocked to better hear the strangeness of it. The whole shell of sky shone pale blue. The sun could barely be seen, but it lit the entirety of the firmament evenly. Hanish climbed high up into the rigging of the ship he traveled in. The gnarled ropes bit into his palms, and his feet slipped on the ice-crusted rungs. He was no sailor. Who born in the Mein was? Still he felt joy take him when he leaned back against the main-mast in the lookout perch, his face red from the climb, the breeze tugging at him in gusts and carrying away the plumes of his breath.

Before him stretched a white world painful to look upon. He shaded his eyes with a visor of smoked glass. Looking through this artificial twilight he saw for the first time the entirety of his venture in motion. Surrounding him went a navy traversing a solid white sea. Ninety boats that did not rock and bob with the undulations of currents, that did not rise and fall with the swell of waves. Their sails were furled tight and their rigging sparkled like moist spiderwebs. The ships moved on runners of wood shod with iron, pulled by long lines of oxen, creatures hidden beneath coats so thick they rendered them shapeless. Fifty or so of the animals in double rows tugged each warship, whipped on by fur-garbed men who themselves resembled humans only in the way they moved and in the work they performed.

Behind them the army walked and sledged, outfitted against the cold and struggling to keep alive. It was not an enormous force, but it was the most they could field. Among them went more than one gray-haired man, more than a few smooth-cheeked youths of thirteen and fourteen. They would fight proudly, though, and they were but one of three points of his attack. Another army of five thousand threaded the northern pass into the Candovian lakelands. They would wreak the most useful damage under his brother's command. Then there were the Numrek, who surely had taken Aushenia by now. And then there were a whole host of other schemes conceived over the years in Tahalian. Amazing, just amazing that it was in motion!

Hanish stayed in the crow's nest well past the point at which his face and hands went numb, climbing down only when the sun, wherever it had hidden in the sky, sunk behind the ice and the world went dark and the storm returned, a wall as of shattered glass hurled by the angry wind.

They came upon the outpost of Scatevith a few days later, picking up vast quantities of supplies stored there. They stayed two days to see to any necessary repairs. Soon they continued south and skirted close to the mountains that hemmed the edge of the Mein Plateau. There was a wide valley there, a gradual slope to the Eilavan Woodlands much more easily traversed than most of the Methalian Rim. They were down it and into a snow-coated landscape, dotted with squat fir trees that made explosive fires. Though the temperature was below freezing each night and through much of the day, many soldiers took off their fur caps and shook out the knotted cascades of their hair, heavy ropes that fell down past their shoulders. With the chieftain's blessing, groups of men voyaged out before the host, hunting reindeer. The smoke of roasting meat danced across the landscape.

Hanish, nostrils raised to catch the scent, remembered the old tales of how the Akarans stole the throne through backhanded alliances, promises made and broken, made and broken again, and then set about punishing any people brave or strong enough to stand against them and recite their crimes. It was then that the curse was set upon the race called Mein, then that the Tunishnevre was born and that his people were cast out of the lowlands and banished to above the Methalian Rim. For years they had followed the reindeer herds, living from them and with them in a fashion little different from that of the men from the forgotten times. It took several generations for them to find the site of Mein Tahalian, to recognize the uses of the hot gases bubbling below the crust of ice and dig themselves into a stationary life again, to hew the great trees and set to work on building a sanctuary in the most desolate region of the Known World. And it was many generations more before they found a tentative approach back into the larger world, professing allegiance to all things Akaran, pretending with every word that the past had never been what it had been and that they wished only to emulate, support, and fight in service of the greatness of the Acacian hegemony.

Such was the vast array of details that the scent of reindeer meat on frozen air conjured in Hanish. He doubted the children of Acacia knew anything about these things. There was so much of the history of the world that they willfully ignored. They forgot the things that shamed them, and convinced themselves that everyone else had as well. Not that Hanish would have had them be any other way. Better that his coming shock them to the core and leave them reeling and grasping for meaning, too late to recognize the true shape and substance of the world they lorded over.

The going grew easier yet when they slipped out onto the treeless and featureless surface of the Sinks, a large expanse of lake and marshland in the summer, the first receptacle of the great melt that came pouring each spring from the thawing north. At least, it made for fair travel for a while. They were four days atop this frozen flat before one of the ships broke through the ice. It sunk a few feet down, tossing up slanting slabs around it and creating one crevice that snaked away in front of it, half swallowing a dozen oxen and one man unfortunate enough to have been whipping the beasts at that very moment. The driver was plucked from the icy water and wrapped in furs, and several of the oxen scrambled back onto the ice once their tethers had been cut, but ice again formed around the unfortunate ship. It stuck fast that night, splintered and cracked along the hull. The damage might have been repairable had they the time and supplies at hand, but they had neither. Hanish ordered the boat unloaded, stripped of everything useful, and abandoned without ceremony.

The incident was a harbinger of what was to come. In many ways the next was the most treacherous portion of the journey. They navigated the unreliable ice, feeling the pulsing of the day's thaw and night's freeze and the traps this set for them. Hanish had scouts sent before the army with great iron poles they used to test the surface, a thing done both by sound and feel and by instinct. On a few occasions he walked out alone before the host, feeling his way forward, scanning the far horizon. Why he did this he was never sure. It just felt right. There was something comforting in looking into a frozen expanse and imagining for a moment that he was alone upon it, that this quest began and ended with him and his strengths or weaknesses. Of course, it was never long before he heard the scouts smacking the ice with their rods, like some strange herders that lashed the ground before their wards instead of following them. He was not alone, a thought that each time it came upon him was at once a disappointment and a reassurance.

When they reached the break ice, everything changed again. It came more quickly than Hanish had expected. There before them was a black line of open water. This became a blue-brown seething mass, draining the melting lake on which they had traveled and slipping away to the south to become the River Ask. Chunks of the pack ice broke away slab by slab. The army spent the morning in a fury of activity, trying to switch from ice to waterborne travel.

The first of the ships had scarcely gotten men, horses, and supplies aboard before the ice began to groan and shiver beneath them. The men, who had for days driven the oxen, dropped their whips and clambered on the vessels. The oxen, so long bound to labor, milled about, anxious, unsure what their sudden abandonment suggested. It was not until the first vessel lunged forward, tail end jutting into the air for a precarious moment, boards groaning as if the ship were about to snap at its midpoint, that the oxen turned with angry tosses of their great horned heads and sprinted for the north. Nobody stopped them. That first ship managed to slide forward and find its purchase on the water, to catch the current, and begin to move away.

Hanish's was the third vessel to drop into weighty buoyancy in the water. He was not able, at that moment, to pause and pass news of it to the Tunishnevre, as he had wished to do. Chinks between the frozen boards of the hull let in jets of water. His captain shouted assurances that the boards would swell to watertightness, so Hanish put it out of his mind. He did not have the leisure to do anything about it anyway. The river this far north was barely manageable, swollen as it always was this time of the year by the melt just gathering force in the Sinks. Hanish had wished to enter Acacia with the spring, and it appeared he had timed things correctly. The flood rose well up into the trees on either bank, rushing downstream as if every drop of water was clawing its way past its fellows in the race to the sea. At times they rode up and over and down the backs of waves as large as those during an ocean storm. In other places whirlpools, rips in the current, and roiling eddies turned the ships and sucked the sides of them, tipping men into the froth. What seemed like clenched fists of water took hold of the oars and snapped them, cracking more than one skull in the process.

Most treacherous, however, were the places where the river flowed over obstructions usually above the water. Some of these were normally islands, now nothing but treetops reaching from the depths like the fingers of drowning giants. There were stone ledges that nearly ripped open the hull of one boat and massive boulders over which water fell into churning chaos. One of the leading vessels went over such a fall. It dug down into the froth and then rose, bow high in the air, poised a moment as if it might shoot into the sky. But then—sickeningly, despite the protesting groans of all those watching—it slid backward. The stern of the ship caught in the down-rushing torrent behind it. The whole thing somersaulted backward, sending men hurtling into the air out to all sides, then tumbling into the froth. The ship went end over end for a few seconds, then disappeared. When the hull of the vessel emerged, it was a living ship no longer. It broke the surface as a lifeless hulk, like the underbelly of some dead leviathan.

They were swept on. They rode on the back of a watery serpent. Hanish loved it. He had been too long cooped up! How wonderful to be free, even if that freedom led to death. He did not pity those he lost or mourn for them. This serpent just charged a heavy toll for the service it rendered. All that mattered was that he was getting close to his goal. Close enough that he prepared to try a thing he had previously experimented with only in the seclusion of Tahalian.

Chapter Twenty-four

Aliver began to dream nightly of dueling with nameless, faceless foes. Unlike the whimsical imaginings of times past, when swordplay was a fanciful clash with mythic foes, these visions were of a dark nature, each moment humming with fear. They always began innocuously enough: with him walking the alleys of the lower town, talking with his companions over breakfast, searching in his room for a book he knew he had placed somewhere. But at some point events always pivoted to sudden violence. A soldier would appear at the end of a passageway with sword unsheathed, calling him by name; the dining table would overturn and when the bulk of it cleared his view, the scene behind became one of enemy warriors swarming into the room like a thousand spiders—in through the windows, clinging to the ceiling with swords clasped between their teeth in enormous, metallic grins. Often he simply sensed that behind him was a formless, seething malice he would have to confront.

In these dreams he fought well enough up until the moment he had to sink his weapon home. Then, with the realization that he was about to slice into a living creature just like him, the flow of time snagged. Motion slowed. His muscles lost their strength and became useless ribbons of tar beneath his skin. He never watched his blade cut into the flesh of these dream enemies. Instead he awoke, panting, body tensed and trembling as if the fight had just taken place in the real world. Only then did the slow stink of reality creep over him. He had not woken from an ill dream to a welcoming world; he had opened his eyes once more to a waking nightmare that daily shrugged off his efforts to deny it.

His father was dead. This meant a thousand things to Aliver, all of them confusing. Not even his ascendance to the throne was straightforward. The Akarans were strict monarchists, but the larger situation was so con-

fused as to delay Aliver's rise to fill his father's place. The same reverence for
ritual that allowed the people to accept a monarchy also demanded a rigid
adherence to tradition. New kings were crowned only in autumn, at the
same time as the deceased king's ashes were released. It was on that day
that Tinhadin had first ascended, and it was deemed necessary that all others follow his venerable example. On almost every occasion in the years
thereafter there had been a pause between the ruling monarch's death and
the new one's crowning. A wait of several months was not at all without
precedent. The unprecedented action would have been to crown a king on
a date other than the summer solstice and to do so without a full, sitting
contingent of governors. The priestesses of Vada found the time inauspicious
for a crowning and refused to bless any ceremony. And the machinery of
government seemed to have no interest in thrusting an inexperienced adolescent into a role so fraught with import. Perhaps some other prince would
have grasped power anyway. But not Aliver. Despite himself, he felt something like relief that a crown had not been set atop his head immediately,
though he would not admit this. Thaddeus was better suited to serve as the
royal voice for the time being.

Bad news flew at him. He could barely register one tragedy before another shouldered past it. Cathgergen was lost to some barbarian horde, the
garrison there destroyed, the governor and his entourage thrown out into
the cold, bearing a message of coming doom for the world. None of this was
easily conceived of. For Cathgergen to fall it meant the defeat of—of how
many? Two thousand soldiers? At least that many. And there was no word
that any of these had escaped to tell their story or even that some were being held prisoner. And what of the many others who had lived in the
fortress—craftsmen and traders, courtesans and laborers and their children, the varied people who made an isolated outpost like Cathgergen livable? They were all simply gone, and Aliver had yet to hear anyone explain
how this was possible.

Several key Alecian officials had been slain in their beds. Many of them
died along with their wives, husbands, children, servants, and slaves, their
bodies hacked far beyond what was necessary to take their lives, as if each
of them had been the victim of a crazed killer frenzied beyond reason. Two
days later there was another attack on members of the royal family as they
tried to leave Manil, the rocky cliffside town on which the most luxurious
of the familial palaces perched. Leodan's half sister, Katrina, along with
fourteen others who bore the name Akaran by birth, and more beyond that
by marriage, were caught at the docks on a bright morning. Men disguised

as dockworkers sprang upon them once they boarded their ship and chopped them down with short swords they had concealed in their garments.

Nobody knew how such extensive plots could have been kept secret and launched with such deadly efficiency. The collective hum and murmur of rumor gave birth to the belief that many of the assassins in both attacks had been house servants, gardeners, and laborers employed by the aristocracy, many of them in service for years without betraying a single sign of deceit. Another tale asserted that a fleet of warships was sliding south out of the frozen Mein. They had been seen by fur trappers near the icy fingers of the River Ask, but how these simple people in so remote a place could have dispatched such a message was never explained, nor could much sense be made of the very idea they proposed. Some claimed that Rialus Neptos— who disappeared after the massacre of the Alecian officials—had a role in the uprising. And still others claimed that the entire entourage of league representatives had sailed away without a word.

Aliver wanted desperately to make sense of what was happening and to piece it together in a way that grappled the chaos back into manageable bounds, but moments of quiet thought were few and troublingly brief. The days of Marah training were behind him now. His officers spoke to those who had only days before been students as if they had suddenly risen in stature in their eyes. They had all, it seemed, been promoted in one mass movement. They spoke of the trials they now faced with an honesty Aliver had not expected and did not welcome. Men who had seemed so confident in their roles just a few days ago now seemed uneasy, tentative and jumpy when giving orders. The future before them, they explained, was fraught not simply with the physical pain of training or with humiliation of being defeated at exhibition matches or even with social disgrace, once the gravest possibility of a failure of character. These were all hazards they had navigated before. Now they were to fight with their actual lives at stake. He would soon be expected to kill. The very thought of it turned the way he viewed all of his training on its head. Did he have it in him to kill? It scarcely seemed possible. Could it be, he thought, that he would fail his nation at the first test? Never had he dreaded a thing as much as he did this possibility.

What made it worse was that he did not know what would really be expected of him. His position alongside his peers was more awkward than ever. On the one hand, he feared that he would be spared battle responsibility just as he had always been set apart from the others in training. On the other hand, the truth remained that the officers pointed again and again to the Forms for examples of battle valor, and in most of these it had been a royal personage wielding the sword or spear or ax. Was he expected to step into those legendary shoes and lead them to victory? He did not know, and nobody—not even Thaddeus—stepped in to inform him.

With only days left before the young soldiers learned of their deployments and set off to fill them, Thaddeus Clegg joined the officers to appraise the troops at assembly. The chosen site was the stadium named after the seventh king's wife, the Carmelia. It sat on a flat wedge of land that pushed out into the ocean like a half-submerged foot, below the palace but slightly above the lower town. A great bowl carved into the stone, the Carmelia could seat thousands on benches hollowed to hold each spectator. The arena was a vast space, open to the air, with the packed soil of the floor nearly as hard as stone, mopped often in circular patterns that, when stared at, played tricks on the watcher's eyes.

Before the officers' and the chancellor's still forms, the best young soldiers the island had to offer marched into the stadium, holding perfectly to the formation of an infantry battalion. They moved in answer to the calls of a battle flute, a strangely melancholy, whimsical instrument, but one that carried to all their ears. Over the next hour a few had the honor of fighting singly for the spectators. After that, the bulk of the five hundred of them took part in an elaborate staging of the Ninth Form, in which the Haden and the Woodsmen saved Tinhadin's Bride from the Senivalian Treachery. After this they stood to listen to their leaders regale them with speeches as much about past glory as about the conflict facing them now.

Later, the chancellor addressed them. Thaddeus rubbed the stubble on his chin and thought for some time. Without the finery of his robes and the sash over his shoulders that marked his office he would barely have been recognized, so haggard and deep lined was his visage. "I have learned something this very day that I must share with you," he said. "I prefer to do it this way, down among you, close enough so that we can see and touch each other." He held up his hand, which Aliver only then noticed held a scroll. The chancellor turned it at angles to show it to all the soldiers, as if they could read its import from where they stood. "This is a declaration of war from Hanish Mein, son of Heberen. In it he states his hatred of us and proclaims himself the chieftain of the coming world. There is no guesswork any longer. We know whom we fight and why. We know that he wants our complete destruction. He believes he has the power to succeed, and because of that he has launched his cowardly attacks. Such is the struggle before us. Such is the foulness that can be contained in a thin document like this."

Thaddeus looked as if he might fling the scroll to the breeze. The soldiers held to silence, as did the officers, all of them expecting that the man had something more to add. The chancellor stood, neither turning away nor proceeding, his gaze, despite the people surrounding him, meeting no one's eyes. Aliver realized that he could hear the crash of the waves on the bulkhead below the stadium. He counted one and then a second and third impact, surprised that he had not noticed the sound before, struck by the intimacy with which the sea touched the land. He could feel it through his feet. It was in the air also, each reverberation transmitted to him as if some invisible, crystalline rain of spray fell over his face and shoulders. There was an entire world beyond his present view, and all of it threatened to arrive unannounced at any moment.

Thaddeus raised his head and seemed to bring the faces around him into focus. He swept his gaze across them, touching Aliver in passing. "My suggestion," he said, "is that we all learn to love chaos this very day. Let us all think of turmoil as a feature of our lives. As there is a sun moving across the sky, as there is wind whistling over the earth, as the night follows the day and it cannot be otherwise . . . So will all among us suffer; this cannot be otherwise either. Embrace this today and you will be better prepared for tomorrow. Just a moment ago you demonstrated the Ninth Form. As you all know there are only ten of these. There is no reason, however, that there cannot one day be an Eleventh. Consider this also as you face the coming struggle." He turned as if to go but thought better of it and said one last thing. "Also, prepare yourself to be surprised. The world is a different place than you know. It may be that you will believe we have failed to prepare you for it."

On the morning they were to receive their final instructions in preparation for the war, Aliver met Melio and Hephron on the upper terraces. The prince nodded to them both, surprised to find himself welcoming Hephron's company. There was something comforting in it. Just a few days ago he had disliked Hephron intensely. He had thought him an enemy. But none of this occurred to him now. Hephron had already suffered more than he had. He had lost two sisters at Manil, a cousin, and several servants that he had known since childhood. With the death of several other high-ranking Akarans he had leaped closer to the throne. In the past Aliver might have expected this to give Hephron joy, but such petty considerations no longer held any merit. Hephron's face showed nothing save the creased fatigue of his losses and a resolve to face whatever was yet to come.

"I just received my assignment," Hephron said. "They are sending me to Alecia. I asked to be sent to reinforce Aushenia. They are sure to meet the horde that has taken Cathgergen, and I wanted to be where I am needed most." He hesitated a moment, walking on and mulling over his thoughts for a few strides. A shout echoed up from the terrace below, but they were some distance away from it and they carried on at the same pace. "But . . . it is not without honor of a sort. I am to second under General Rewlis."

"You're a second?" Aliver asked, stopping in his tracks.

"Don't act so surprised."

"I am—I am not surprised."

"Everything has changed," Hephron said. "Even the league has acknowledged it. They recalled all three of their transport ships and sailed them away without a word. We can still move troops but not as easily as we would like."

"Are they part of this?" Melio asked. "The league, I mean. Do you know, Aliver?"

"Not for sure," he said. "I doubt it, though. The league lives and breathes to profit from trade. They do not care with whom they do it. They are just cautious, self-interested."

Hephron smiled. "They are not the only ones."

"What does that mean?" Melio asked.

"This is no time to talk about it. Perhaps later."

"Why later?" Aliver asked. "Because of me? There is something you dare not say in front of me?"

Hephron glanced at Aliver, then looked away. "I always hold my tongue in your company. Everybody does. Nobody wants to offend the future king."

"You seem intent on trying," Melio quipped.

"We should not have squabbled before. All this posturing between us is foolish, but I know some things the prince does not and I cannot help but think about them. My father did not wish me to be deceived. He told me the truth about things. Maybe this will be news to you too, Melio. He always said our crimes would one day return to us. All the things that are happening . . . if you knew the truth, none of it would surprise you. For example, how do you think we maintain our wealth? We are taught nothing of it. We are just supposed to believe that wealth endures. We won it before, so it is ours forever, right? We are a fine people who just deserve dominion over the world. Everyone is content with it. It is for the best, really." He looked between the two, smirking. "Does that sound right to you? Think about it. Once you have come to recognize that the sums do not add up . . . seek me out. I will tell you all I know about the rotten heart of Acacia. Then you will wonder why no one attacked us before this."

Aliver thought that he should smack him. Slap his face and challenge him to draw his sword. No one would expect any less a response to such a condemnation of the nation. Or he should report him. Let the officers interrogate him. Was this not his duty? What if Hephron was preparing to betray them?

"I apologize if I offend," Hephron said without sounding the least bit apologetic. "It is not you I am angry with. You are a pawn in this as much as I am. But I am the one who is going to have to risk my neck for it. Me and Melio here, and others like us." He began to move away, walking backward for a few steps before he turned. "Grown men, my father told me, must have the internal breadth to hold complexity within them. Only fools hold absolutes. You are not a fool, Aliver. You are just naïve."

Aliver, walking again a half stride behind Hephron, repeated those words in his mind several times. He knew he should be angry, should curse him for weakness now that they were being threatened. But instead he walked on as if pulled in the other's wake. He twinned the young man's words with the chancellor's cryptic confession. He was still thinking about the gravity of their implications when they reached the head of the stairs. Hephron, who had gained the vista just before him, froze. For a space of seconds, standing at the head of the stairs looking down, the scene before Aliver made absolutely no sense.

The square below, some hundred steps away, was in a state of utter confusion. People swarmed in all directions, shrieking. The first person he could recognize was General Rewlis. But just as he made out who he was, he watched him being cut from behind through his leg. He recognized the person wielding the blade and tried to name him but could not. Rewlis went down to one knee, head thrown back in a scream of pain, silenced a moment later as the same sword that had cut his leg split his neck in a diagonal blow aimed just below the ear. A second later the blade slipped free. The general crumpled, a fount of blood gushing from his neck, his legs smearing the stones as they churned with the last of his life.

"Hellel?" Melio whispered.

Hephron understood his meaning before Aliver. "You bastard. I could have killed you in your sleep so many times."

The strangeness of this statement added nothing to Aliver's understanding of the confusion below them. Hellel? He had been one of

Hephron's entourage, a pale shadow beside him always, the type who nearly finished his sentences for him.

Noticing that Aliver still stared, Hephron gestured with his arm, a motion that both pointed at the scene and swiped it away. "They are Meins! Look at them. Hellel, there by the railing. And Havaran. And Melish on the steps. They have betrayed us! We should have expected it." He was in motion the next instant, careening down the steps at breakneck speed, his feet jolting against the stones in a barely controlled fall. He tried to wrench his sword free as he moved, but it was not until he had paused on the terrace that he managed to unsheath the steel. He was instantly engaged, two men coming at him at once from opposite sides. Melio danced in behind him a second later, his blade spinning with blurring speed.

Aliver would try later to be sure of just what happened next. He would remember that he drew his sword and gritted his teeth and had just begun to rage down the staircase and into battle. . . . That was exactly what he almost did. He wanted to have done so very badly. He would have, except that before he could move a hand clamped down on his forearm and spun him around.

It was Carver, the Marah captain. "Prince," he said, "sheathe your sword. You must go to safety." And to the flank of warriors behind, he gave orders for several of them to take Aliver away. The rest swarmed down the staircase behind Carver. That was all there was to it. Aliver, once pulled away, never saw how the skirmish ended. He went "to safety," while Melio and Hephron became warriors.

CHAPTER

TWENTY-FIVE

Thaddeus Clegg entered his inner chambers, tired from a long day wrestling with the confusion inside him while functioning for all the world to see as an efficient chancellor. His cat, Mesha, rose from her curled comfort on a chair, stretched one paw and then the other, called to him with a thrumming chirp. She was a breed native to southern Talay, sand colored, short-haired everywhere except along her belly and under her chin. She was larger than normal indoor cats by half, and, as was common to her breed, she had an extra toe on each paw, an advantage she took great pleasure in exploiting when she slapped mice against the tiles. It also helped her hold her own against the golden monkeys, which had long since decided to give her a wide berth.

As Thaddeus shrugged off his cloak and draped it over a chair, Mesha leaped down from the chair and closed the distance between them with nimble steps. He stretched out his hand and received the soft impact of her head against his fingers. Though he certainly never revealed it to others, Thaddeus placed the greater portion of his desire for sensuous interaction with others in the tips of his fingers and reserved his most intimate touch for Mesha. This was all he wanted or needed now of companionship. He was too proud and self-conscious a man to distract himself with attachments to others, and he would not risk any greater love again.

"Mesha, you are my darling girl. You know that, yes? There is madness outside this room, but you have no part in it. How fortunate you are."

A short time later, Thaddeus sat with Mesha curled in his lap. He sipped a syrupy liqueur redolent of peaches and tried to create a calm inside that would match his outward appearance of peace. He failed completely. The turmoil of a land struck and struck again, and now scurrying to prepare for war would have been more than enough to keep his mind reeling. He had spent the day in council with the generals preparing to meet Hanish Mein's forces near Alecia, the target they believed he would attack first. They had gone through all the details of mustering the largest army the Known World had seen since Tinhadin's time. What a daunting task, all done in haste and without a true king to control the tenor of the undertaking. Yes, Aliver sat through the council meetings, adding what he could, holding up bravely in the face of it all. But it was Thaddeus to whom the generals really spoke. And it was the fulcrum at which this side of his life collided with his own desire for revenge that truly baffled him.

He had not overtly agreed to aid Hanish Mein, but when he had read the chieftain's simple message, part of him wished to obey. Perhaps he had been too long the servant of a king to feel comfortable as his own master. Or perhaps it was a sign of Hanish's power, his ability to reach out over distances and turn other men's hearts to his will. What to do about Hanish's demand? He had ordered him to capture the Akaran children. Simple as that. Do this thing for him, and Thaddeus would be revenged against the Akarans. Do this thing and he would be rewarded for it in other ways as well. Thaddeus wondered if he could remake himself as a servant of the Meins. What might they give him in payment? A governorship maybe. Talay would suit him, that grand expanse, endless miles and miles of grasslands. It was a large enough province for him to get lost in. This seemed an attractive notion.

Or maybe he was not thinking large enough. Had he still contained the ambition Gridulan had sensed in him years ago, he would have found a way to seize the throne. He had effective control of affairs on the island. Considering those already dead, with the confusion on the Mainland and bloody clashes right here in the courtyards of Acacia, nobody else held the reins of power as surely as he did. The royal children trusted him, and he had had access to each of them even in their private chambers. He could have gone from one to the other and poisoned them: a cup of warm milk offered by a beloved uncle, a cake with a special icing, a salve on his thumb that he dabbed around their eyes, as if wiping away tears. . . . He knew so many methods by which to deliver poison. He could have placed a pillow over their sleeping mouths, bled them from a wound in the neck, stopped their hearts with the flat-handed blow he had learned to deliver at just the right angle and force to stun the organ to stillness. He could end them and thereby repay Gridulan for his treachery.

"How pathetic it all is, Mesha," he said, running his hand down the cat's back. The feline looked up at him, slant eyed and bored. "I have made a mess of everything! I should think of the surest route and follow it. Nothing can stop the coming change; I see that as clearly as anyone. And these children are not the innocents they seem. Does not the young of a jackal grow into a jackal? Will it not someday bite the hand that feeds it? It can be no other way. It is foolishness to act as if either they or I could be other than we are. See, I can state all clearly. But I love them. That's the trouble."

Mesha had just begun to drift off again when Thaddeus rose and deposited her on the floor. He was annoyed with himself for speaking at all, even if it was only to a cat. He went to a cupboard built into the wall near his bed. From it he pulled the mist pipe that had once been the king's. Strange that he was so late coming to this vice. Strange that he had lived a lifetime already before understanding the true craving for oblivion. He knew that on the morrow he would have to face again decisions made or not made, but between then and now he wished only to forget everything, or at least to reach that stage at which none of it mattered.

Later, he was awoken from black nothingness, a dreamless, thoughtless existence that was deeper than sleep ever could be. The force that pulled him out of this chosen place was frustratingly strong. It seemed an iron grip had fastened on some portion of his being and pulled him toward consciousness. He rolled over onto his back, thinking that such a change in his posture might ease him back to sleep, for the day had not yet come to demand his wakefulness. He felt a pressure at the foot of his bed and thought that Mesha was to blame. She sometimes fastened herself to his leg and sank her claws into the flesh of some imagined quarry.

But then a voice said, "Rise up and face me."

Thaddeus started to shout for his guards, but before he could will his mouth to do so, the rest of his being obeyed the command. He tilted upright, the view before him rising to meet his changed posture. Except . . . except his actual body did not move. His chest and arms and head had not followed him. He tilted, but somehow he left his corporeal shell lying on the bed. It was as if he had slipped out of his skin with a gentle tug. He felt his organs, his muscles, and bones relinquish his spirit. His body released him, and there he was, sitting upright, the lower portion of him still contained within his hips and groin and legs, the upper portion an obedient spirit called to attention.

Before him, at the foot of his bed, hung a vague outline of a man. It had about it the shape of a body, but Thaddeus could see through the man into the dimly lit room behind him. The being produced his own illumination. His gray eyes flared into pinpoints of brilliance. They were the most visible portion of him, the two glowing orbs around which the rest of the being gathered. They were the only part of him that seemed solid enough to touch, and yet the energy that illumed them flickered behind them in waves. It dimmed for periods and then emerged again, as if inside them was the light of the moon interrupted by a cloud-dotted sky. They etched the features of his face and gave some solidity to his shoulders and arms, though his lower body faded into nothingness.

The form spoke again. His voice seemed weakened by distance, hollow like words spoken through a tube. For all the unearthly tone of them they were frank in a way that slapped Thaddeus like an open hand. "Thaddeus Clegg, you dog, I have words for you."

Thaddeus stared at him, stunned. How was this possible? He tried to show with the ridged scorn of his lips his disdain for the man's intrusion, no matter the sorcery by which it was achieved. It was an instinctive reaction, but the expression was hard to hold because the glow of the man's eyes was most mesmerizing. Why did he not shout for the guards? He knew it would be easy to do so, yet something held him back, trapped him within the spell of those eyes. He had first to identify this being. That was the key, he thought. He sensed a name was poised at the back of his throat, already known to him. It just needed to be spoken to become real.

"Hanish?" he asked. The other man smiled, seemingly pleased to have been named. The expression was enough to confirm that the guess had hit its mark. "How is this possible?"

"Through dream travel," the form said. "You are asleep and not asleep; I am awake in spirit and far distant from my sleeping body. I can feel the pull of it even now, trying to wrest me back inside the familiar. Our spirits do not like to leave our bodies, Thaddeus. It is ironic considering that from their cursed undeath my people want only to escape these burdens of flesh, but it is true. I am as surprised as you that we are speaking. We have never been near enough before, nor did I know if you had the gift. Not everyone does, you know. Between my brothers and me there was always silence. It is not possible to understand the order of the things . . ."

Hanish faded into darkness and then flickered back into view a moment later, burning more brightly. "I am glad that you know me so quickly, but I have not come to you for casual conversation."

Something in the tone of Hanish's voice struck Thaddeus as strange, enough so that he focused not just on his words but also on how he said them. It was difficult to read the man through the distortions of distance, but there was a man at the other end of this discourse and Thaddeus had ever been a reader of men.

"Are the children safe?" Hanish asked.

"The children? You need not fear the children. They are no real threat to—"

"You have not harmed them, have you?" Hanish asked, a note of concern in his voice.

As the chieftain dimmed and flickered for a moment, Thaddeus had a few moments to think. From looking in Hanish's eyes, he could see that the chieftain was hiding something. He was not lying exactly, but there was desperate import behind his words that he did not want Thaddeus to grasp.

"Of course not," he answered, once Hanish was bright before him again. "I have kept them here, close to me, safe in every—"

"It is important that they live. Understand? Their lives mean a great deal to me. I am here to tell you once again that when you deliver them to me, you will be rewarded. We will talk about it in quieter times, and I will do right by you. Believe me about that. I am no silver-tongued Akaran. I speak the truth. My people always have."

Thaddeus felt the sharp impact of a realization pierce through his thoughts. He understood what Hanish was hiding. It was there behind his claim that his people had always spoken the truth. This was not a boast. It was a declaration of national pride. The Meins had always claimed they had been banished to the north because of speaking out truthfully against Akaran crimes. And, they believed, not only had they been banished but also they had been cursed. The Tunishnevre . . . That was what Thaddeus had not yet considered. It was but a legend to Acacians, but perhaps it was more than that to the Meins themselves.

Previously, he had thought only of the Meins' ancient hatred of Acacia, of how much they coveted these gentle lands, how rich they would be in ruling them, and how gratified they would be to finally win against their centuries-old enemies. But he had not reached far enough back into Hanish's desires. He had not understood until now that this was not just a war for earthly things. The Known World was the battleground, but the cause for which Hanish fought crossed into other planes of existence. He must believe his ancestors were trapped in unending purgatory. He wished to break the curse placed on them during the Retribution and free the Tunishnevre. This feat, legend said, could be accomplished only in one way. Remembering it, Thaddeus thought that either Hanish was a madman or the world was a place of greater mystery than he had acknowledged.

These thoughts passed through the chancellor quickly, and Hanish did not seem to notice the change in him. "Gather them together," he said.

"Keep them for me. If anything happens to them, I will make your existence one of unending suffering. This is a gift I can give you. Do not doubt either my generosity or my wrath."

"I doubt neither," Thaddeus said. "Be assured that I await you here, the children with me."

The light in Hanish's eyes dimmed. His form shifted and dispersed like vapor stirred by a gust of wind. Thaddeus felt himself dropping back toward his body. He came to rest inside his shell, slipping into his skin and feeling it around him again. He had not, he told himself, decided to obey. He was not a servant. He was free to act as he wished. . . .

He said this again and again as he felt the pull of earthly slumber settling into him, afraid that he would remember one portion of the night and not another, afraid lest he wake and err in his actions. He demanded of himself that he wake and remember his revelation, for it changed everything and it was this: Hanish believed he could end the curse on the Tunishnevre by killing an heir to the Akaran dynasty. Only drops of the purest Akaran blood could awaken the life inside his cursed ancestors. If Hanish had his way, the children that Thaddeus loved—the four he had coveted all his life, that he wished were his own and upon whom he had showered the affection he would have given to his own offspring—would be splayed out across a sacrificial altar, cut open, and bled to slow deaths. If it turned out that Tinhadin's curse was a real thing instead of a myth and if it could be reversed, twenty-two generations of Mein warriors would be pulled back from death. They would walk the earth again and their retribution would turn the world upside down.

This realization made up Thaddeus's mind for him. He could not grasp power as the ogre inside him imagined. Nor could he allow Hanish to unleash a new hell on earth. There was, however, one whose entreaty he would follow. He should have done so all along. This much he knew with a certainty more complete than any other belief within his conflicting and crosshatched allegiances. He had already determined the children must be sent away. Now he would put into place the plan Leodan Akaran had dreamed up for his children if calamity befell him before they were grown to maturity. Thaddeus knew the plan and had the power to initiate it. Only he in all the living world could do this. Not even the children dreamed of it. Nor could they be told the truth of it in preparation. Aliver would hate him for it. He would likely dread it as the worst of possible fates and think him their betrayer.

Fitting, Thaddeus thought. Horrible and fitting: a truth and a lie.

Chapter
Twenty-six

Hanish awoke from his dream conversation with the chancellor with a host of plans to see to. His fleet rode the River Ask until it spat them out into the Inner Sea. Though he longed to turn toward Acacia itself, he knew he must wait for that, take it only in due course. He gathered his remaining vessels near the river's mouth. They drifted together as they took stock, waiting for stragglers and giving one another what aid they could. He found his army to be in no worse state than he had imagined—even better, perhaps, because his men were champing at the bit, wanting nothing more than to get to land and commence the slaughter. They were a devout people and yearned to prove it by the sword.

Hanish kept them afloat as news flew in to him. There he learned that the first great battle in the war between Hanish Mein and the Akarans involved neither Meinish nor Acacian troops. The Aushenian prince, Igguldan, commanded an army that met the Numrek at Aushenguk Fell. Warriors, farmers, merchants, and priests from every corner of the kingdom gathered on the rocky field to defend their nation. Igguldan fielded an army of nearly thirteen thousand souls. The enemy, on the other hand, did not number more than six thousand.

But in every aspect of their appearance the Numrek were frightening. They were a shouting, raucous horde reminiscent of humanity but grotesquely different as well, utterly baffling to the Aushenians who watched them approach. Their infamous mounts had been shaved of their woolly fur to suit the weather. Patches of fur clung to them in portions; scars from the shears marred their gray flesh in other areas. They looked like diseased creatures, and yet for all the motley look of them they trod with a haughty air, so completely muscled that they seemed to bounce with the spring and pull of their strength.

Beyond this the Numrek put into use a weapon they had thus far not revealed: catapults. They were awkward contraptions that tossed flaming balls half a man's height tall. When the arms snapped forward the spheres shot out just above the ground, bouncing in great arcs, gouging divots with each impact. The force of them was such that they cut swathes through the Aushenian troops. They flattened men hit head-on, broke apart bodies struck partially, tore heads from shoulders. All of this caught the young prince off guard, as did the flaming orb that carried his torso away, wrapped around the sphere in a fiery embrace. With him flew his nation's effort at resistance, ended in one mere afternoon. Tragic for him, yes, but music sweet and perfectly timed to Hanish's ears.

Maeander's arrival in Candovia was just as effective. As they had planned, Maeander had pounced on clan after clan, coercing them into active rebellion or beating them into submission. They had sown the seeds of this invasion for years now, sending agents among them to ferret out allies and whisper the people into shared discontent. The Candovians were fierce fighters, quick-tempered and proud, not unlike the Meins. They were also fractious and easily exploited. The Acacians had wanted them so, choosing to favor first one clan and then another, fomenting discord among them so that in their bickering they never fixed their animus on their real foe. Maeander had all the skills of persuasion, martial and otherwise, to take advantage of this. He promised via his messenger to bring all of Candovia through the mountains of Senival with him, a force that would treble the number he arrived in their territory with. They might need to be chastened after the war, but for the time being he preferred to think of them as allies.

Even Acacia imploded from within. Hanish had not been sure just how the Mein soldiers serving the Acacians far from home would react to his declaration of war. He had his hopes, yes. Did not every Meinish soldier secretly swear to answer his nation's call to war, whenever and wherever it might come? Still, he worried that years removed from the homeland might have weakened their resolve. The Tunishnevre never doubted, though. They assured him that their hold on all soldiers of the Mein was as firm as ever. They were correct. Meinish soldiers throughout the empire rose in rebellion as soon as word reached them. They lashed out at enemies they had called companions minutes before.

On Acacia all thirty-three Meinish soldiers in the Acacian regiment and four newly arrived from Alecia drew their swords and cut down half the Acacian officers on the island, easy work for the first few surprised seconds. At Aos a band of five Mein painted their faces red with blood and raged through the town's weekly market, slaying everyone in their path. Others poisoned the drinking fountains in the resort towns east of Alecia. And a lone soldier stationed at one of the Mainland outposts turned himself into an assassin, killing his superior officers and several local officials in their beds before he was captured. They all sacrificed themselves, for not one of these rebels wished to be taken alive. No doubt the Tunishnevre spurred them on, demanding that they redeem through their deaths the infamy of having served the Akarans.

Only in Talay was the uprising thwarted before it began. Cautionary Acacian orders reached Bocoum at almost the same time as the news of war. Thus the Mein soldiers were thrown into chains before they had thought to take up arms. Unfortunate, but no great matter. All told, Hanish's people had made him proud. If estimates were to be believed, the revolts reduced the empire's army by almost a quarter: both in lives they took by the blade and by simply removing themselves from service. The Acacians stumbled from the start, with little in the way of decisive action. So much for a great nation! Just a few weeks after Leodan Akaran's death triggered this war, the Meinish chieftain had no reason to believe he had been mistaken in beginning it. And he still had his greatest weapon to unleash.

The main contest was to take place on the vast fields stretching from the east of Alecia. The soil there was as yet unplanted in the turmoil of the times. The Acacians mustered what they hoped would be a great army. Their means of transport had been crippled when the League of Vessels sailed their ships away without warning or explanation, but others had come to the empire's aid with fishing boats and ferries, barges and pleasure yachts, skiffs and dugouts. On land, merchants and traders lent their carts and horses and mules. By these means and by the simple service of their feet, soldiers converged on Alecia. To whose leadership all these forces rallied was not clear. Grandiose declarations issued forth in Prince Aliver Akaran's name, but the young whelp himself was sequestered away, as suited Hanish.

"How courteous of whomever instructs them," Haleeven said, "to gather so many into one place so that we can treat with them all at once. Perhaps, in due consideration, we should allow them more time to gather."

"Courtesy demands it," Hanish said.

When the Mein forces disembarked a few days' march from the enemy, they did not proceed toward them immediately. They made a great camp. Once they were as ready as they could be, they relaxed and amused themselves. It was so temperate a climate that men stripped off their garments and felt the touch of the air on portions of their body that had not done so in months. They were ghostly pale, crusted with dead skin, and quick to turn pink under the warmth of the Mainland spring. They held games of physical prowess: foot races and wrestling matches, sword and spear practice, tugging contests wherein the grip of two men served in place of rope. Ten or sometimes more men lifted each of the chosen men and leaned back, their legs straining to unseat the other team before the grip was broken. It was, in many ways, like one of their high-summer festivals, for the weather was as mild as it ever got around Tahalian. Several men even danced the Maseret. They drank wine and beer and cordials procured from the nearby villages. Though at times they became raging drunk, they always awoke more clear-eyed and lively than mist addicts.

These events proved most elevating to morale, and when they did march toward the enemy, song propelled them. Hanish, riding a deep-chested mount next to his uncle, had never felt more central to the workings of the world. Behind him, a sea of men trod the earth, with their legends issuing from their lips, each of them straw haired, most tall and perfect of form, wrapped in tight bands of leather for protection. So many helmets and spear points glinted in the sun, so many pairs of blue-gray eyes. They still wore the bells and chimes the Tunishnevre had demanded, the sound of them a grand music in and of itself. Hanish could scarcely look back at them without flooding with emotion. Nor was his elation any less on first beholding his enemy.

What a host these Acacians had gathered! Forty, fifty thousand, standing on the turned soil like some strange, newly sprouted crop. They were more than three times his number. They were many hued, male and female both, representatives of Acacia's far-flung and varied subjects. Hanish's gaze soared above and beyond them to the great wall of stone that stretched north to south from one edge of the world to the other. Alecia was several miles farther in, but behind the Acacian army stood the first barrier thrown up years ago against enemies such as himself. There was an irregular beauty in the wall's construction, built as it was of blocks of differing sizes and colors. It might have been a rough mosaic without order, and yet there was something about the vast array of hues and quality of stone and size and shape of the blocks that drew the eye from one place to another.

Hanish knew the story of the wall's creation. Edifus had first ordered it constructed despite the fact that suitable stone was hard to come by in the area. In answer, nation after nation of the myriad peoples suddenly subservient to him had sent emissaries to him, along with them quarried stone and masons to work it. Word of this spread and before long even the farthest flung regions of the empire, even the smallest of tribes, sent an offering of stone and labor to build the wall. Thus the sight before him represented the first, symbolic acceptance of the world order Hanish now fought to overturn.

He could not have said at that moment if the wall was more or less impressive than he imagined. It seemed both at once. He knew that somewhere along it there was a black stone in it, a giant basalt block carved from the base of the mountains near Scatevith. He would know it when he saw it. Hauchmeinish's name was carved in some corner of it. He would search it out and have masons cut it free. It was not an offering the Mein had ever given freely, and he'd happily reclaim the stone.

It had always been custom for leaders to meet before engaging in battle, to speak face-to-face in the event that their differences could be resolved even at that late stage. Perhaps they had misunderstood each other. Perhaps one side had newfound regrets or misgivings. Hanish did not deny the Acacians this ceremony when they demanded that he parlay.

Haleeven found him sitting on a stool in an area enclosed by four sheet walls strung between upright spears in their new camp. It was what sufficed as a private space for the chieftain, a cubicle for prayer and communion with the Tunishnevre, although in truth Hanish had felt far removed from his ancestors since floating south down the River Ask. He sensed them like a distant scent of food carried to a hungry man on the breeze, but this was nothing compared to the potent immediacy of their presence when in Tahalian. He missed the palpable certainty of them, especially now that he was so close to unleashing hell on earth.

His uncle parted the material with two hands and stepped in. "Are you prepared?"

"I am," Hanish said, controlling his voice so that there was no uncertainty in it. "I was just listening to that songbird. Have you heard it? It sings in the morning and then again in the evening. Its call is . . . like crystal shattering. By that I mean it has the purity, the crisp-edged beauty of crystal shattering, but captured in birdsong and let loose in the air. I've never heard anything like it."

"Our birds do not have much to sing about," Haleeven said.

Hanish was dressed in a fashion much like that for the Maseret. A white thalba wrapped his torso, adding rigidity to his posture. His braids had been pulled back from his face and shoulders and wrapped in a twine of ox leather. He wore his knife—as did Haleeven—sheathed horizontally at his belt. Neither of their thoughts were on the blade, however, nor upon any other standard device of war. Haleeven bore the weapon of the day with him. He carried it pinched between his thumb and fingers, a silver case no larger than a finger.

"Shall I open this?" Haleeven asked. As he received no negative answer, he flipped the tiny latch of the case and cracked it open. He tilted it toward his nephew. Inside, a small swatch of cloth lay framed against the metal. It was a length long, folded over once or twice. It was a rough weave of thick strands, much like the material of a Meinish noble's robe. There was the faint remainder of a pattern on it, but liquids had crusted into it, making designs of their own. Hanish was a long time in studying it.

"This thing killed my grandfather," Hanish said.

"Let it now slay your enemy," Haleeven responded.

Hanish reached out, pinched the fabric between his fingers, and drew it toward his breast. He shoved it under a wrap of his thalba, in the hollow beneath the muscle of his right breast.

"Remember to hold the battle off for two days," Haleeven said. "Do not forget to arrange it so."

A short time later Hanish stood before a crescent of dark-eyed Acacians, each of them dressed in their nation's finery, shades of orange fringed in red, with vests of armor like polished silver fish scales. One of the Acacians began the meeting in a ceremonial manner, calling for the Giver's presence and invoking names of ancient Acacians. Hanish had no stomach for it.

"Who among you speaks for the Akarans?" he interrupted.

"I do," a young man said, stepping forward. He was a fine-looking noble with a strong physique and the loose posture of a swordsman. "Hephron Anthalar."

"Anthalar? So you are not an Akaran? I thought I would meet Aliver Akaran himself today. Why is he not here?"

Hephron seemed uncomfortable with the question, angry with it. He could not help but finger the hilt of his sword. "I have the honor of speaking for—for the king. We have assured him you are not worthy to be in his presence."

Hanish had expected the prince himself. He had imagined seeing him with his own eyes and placing his touch on the young man with his own fingers. He glanced at Haleeven briefly, such a passing gesture that none would know that the two men communicated with it. Clearly, his uncle thought he should proceed as planned. Perhaps this was fortuitous in a way . . .

Looking back at Hephron, Hanish tilted his lips with derisive humor.

"So, in the place of your cowardly monarch you are here to answer for Akaran sins? What a strange people you are, led by men who don't even lead."

"I do not answer for Akaran sins. I'm here to see that you're punished for yours. Don't grin at me! I'll see that grin sewn shut with wire before tomorrow is done."

Hanish gestured toward his face with his fingers, a motion of innocence that denied the expression on his face was mirthful at all.

Another of the Acacians introduced himself as Relos, the military head of the Acacian forces. He was tall and angular, his short-cropped hair dusted with gray. He spoke for a moment about the military power they had mustered. Hanish was vastly outnumbered, he said, and even this force was only a portion of the army still at the empire's disposal. "So what have you to offer? You have led us to this moment. Must we do battle, or are you ready to concede and to suffer the consequences?"

"Concede? Oh, no such thought troubles me."

"I am Carver, of the family Dervan," another Acacian said. "I led our army against the Candovian Discord a few years ago. I know battle, and I know how our troops perform when tested. You cannot hope to win against us."

Hanish shrugged. "I assess the situation differently, and you have my declaration of war. Let us do battle two days from this one."

"Two days?" Hephron asked. He glanced at Relos and around at the other generals. None of them protested.

Hanish shrugged. "Yes, we thought that would suit you. You should not object to that, as your numbers grow daily. I will gain no fresh troops in that time, but I will prepare my men with prayer. You would not deny us that?"

"So be it," Hephron said. "It will be in two days." The other Acacians turned to go, but Hephron stood without moving. He held Hanish's gaze, unwilling to let him go but not sure how to proceed. He finally said, "Leodan was a fine king. You made a disastrous mistake in harming him."

"Did I?" Hanish stepped a bit closer to Hephron. "Let me explain a thing to you. My ancestor Hauchmeinish was a noble man. He stood for right when your Tinhadin burned with a madness for power. Hauchmeinish spoke in Tinhadin's ears, as a friend, as a brother might."

Before Hephron could counter the motion, Hanish pulled the hand from his breast and draped his palm gently over the bones and muscles of the young man's shoulder. Hephron flinched, coiled and ready. Hanish gestured with his fingers, pursed his lips, and somehow conveyed through the entirety of his body that he was no threat. This proximity, he conveyed, was necessary so that his message be understood.

"Hauchmeinish told Tinhadin he had been possessed by demons. He asked him to see that he had slain his brothers and driven magic from the world and sold everyone into bondage. But your king would have none of this. He turned on Hauchmeinish and cut his head from his shoulders. He cursed his people—my people—and drove us up onto the plateau, where we have lived ever since. What I am telling you is the truth. Hauchmeinish was right. Yours is an evil empire that for all these years has thrived on the suffering of masses of people. I come to end your reign, and—believe me—many will praise me for it. Can you not hear that these things are all true?"

The muscles and tendons of Hephron's neck stood out as if the bulk of his body was at some great exertion. "No, I do not know them to be true."

Hanish did not move for a moment. He studied the young man, his gray eyes wistful, sad in the manner of one who recognizes the only way to face tragedy is with humor. "I respect your anger. Believe me, I do. We will face each other soon, but I will try and remember you as I see you now." He plucked his hand from Hephron's shoulder blades and swiped it in a quick caress across his jawline. Hephron yanked his chin away, but not before Hanish's fingers brushed the corner of his lips and glanced across the enamel of his teeth. Hephron nearly drew his sword, but Hanish had already turned his back on him.

"I will slay you myself!" Hephron shouted. "Find me in the battle. If you are man enough!"

The poor child, Hanish thought as he walked away. He has no idea of the power of a touch, no idea what he's in for.

At dawn two mornings later Hanish walked at the spear point of his troops. They moved across ground laced with mist. The pale, bluish vapor vanished swiftly as the eye of the sun peeped over the horizon and lit the scene of the coming slaughter. There was no army ranked to meet them, as he'd known there would not be. Instead, they walked unopposed across the fields and turned furrows, over the geometric squares that would have been the battlefield. They crossed all of this and trudged without halting up to the edge of the Acacian camp. No one met them, no lines of soldiers, no missiles, no shimmering armor, nothing of the great host they'd all looked upon two days earlier.

Instead, the camp lay in smoldering desolation. The cook fires of the night before had burned out and oozed thin tendrils of smoke. Crows, always attracted by the stench and waste of so many persons gathered to-gether, had alighted in great numbers on the ground and on tent roofs and various objects. Higher up, vultures drew circles in the air, patient and slow and confident. All this had a gloomy aspect, but it was the human forms that defined the horror of the scene.

Around the fires and in the lanes between the tents and across every open space bodies lay squirming in the dirt. So many bodies. Soldiers, camp attendants—any and all of the myriad persons who made the Acacian host what it was. They rolled on the ground. They lay prostrate in writhing inti-macy with the earth or stared up at the sky, mouths agape, faces glistening with sweat and contorted with anguish, most of them streaked with ruby blotches the size and shape of tadpoles.

Hanish halted to take it all in. The hush over the camp was eerie, but it was not silence. The air was full of sound. It was just that it was such an unusual, subdued cacophony that it was difficult to make sense of. The Aca-cians panted and gasped. They moaned and whimpered and sucked on the air with gaping ovals of hunger. They were in the throes of an all-encompassing suffering. Very few of them could see beyond their misery to consider the approaching army. For the most part they did not respond to them at all. Hanish understood their torment well, and at that moment it would have been hard for him to say whether he took joy or shame in hav-ing presented it to them.

The Meinish troops could contain themselves no longer. They swarmed past Hanish, swords drawn, spear arms pumping as they ran. The bulk of the Acacians lay like thousands of fish tossed to earth and helpless. This was too much for them to resist. Meinish soldiers moved among them, jabbing them with spears or yanking back their heads to slice their throats. Some took sport in chasing down the Acacians still on their feet, but these were few. Hanish himself spilt no blood. He just walked amid the butchery, observed his men's blood thirst with coolness in his gray eyes. He put out word that he searched for one particular Acacian, one whom he did not want killed before he spoke to him. A soldier eventually brought him the in-formation he wished for. Hanish found him inside a large, elaborate Acacian tent.

Hephron had made it no more than a few feet from his cot. He was not even fully dressed. He lay with wide, unblinking eyes, wet with moisture that had left myriad tracks across his cheeks. His forehead was marbled with sweat, puddled so that the flies alighting on him did so carefully.

"Oh, Hephron . . . I really would choose to remember you as you were, not as you are now. I did not fail to note your strength. Nor your anger. I bow to both these things and honor you. That is why I want to explain to you what has happened. You understand none of this, do you?"

Hanish knelt beside him. He shooed the insects into flight. "Do you know the tale of Elenet and his first attempt to create with the Giver's tongue? When the Giver came for him and found him in the orchard, Elenet was huddled over his newest miscreation. The old tales don't tell us what this was, but I have come to my own opinion. I believe that the first thing Elenet sought for himself was eternal life. There is no mention of death before Elenet became a Speaker. But he feared that if he had once not existed, he might come to not exist again. So he tried to arm himself against the Giver's wrath. But in trying to make himself immortal he instead unleashed the diseases that take life. He created illness that day, and we have paid for it ever since. You are paying for it now. You see, that was the problem with humans speaking the Giver's tongue. They were not gods and never could be. They had not the complete ability to form the words accurately. The corruptions of their mouths and hearts and mistaken intent always twisted the magic toward something foul. It is such a thing that burns within you now."

Hephron seemed to notice him just then. His eyes moved over toward him. His pupils were dilated to nearly the size of his irises, but something in the frantic intensity of them showed that he was trying to focus on Hanish. There was a tint of red in his sweat now. Hanish found a cloth in a basin beside the bed and dabbed Hephron's forehead clean with it. Almost instantly the pink stain seeped back up into the creases of his skin.

"Some years back—before I was even born but when my mother lived—my people first made contact with the Numrek and through them with the Lothan Aklun. Those pioneering men all suffered this illness. The first party to return from across the Ice Fields infected nearly all of Tahalian. The whole fortress was racked as you are now. Thousands died. But those that lived, we learned, never got the illness again. Nor did we stay in a contagious state long after mending. At first we kept this illness a secret out of shame; only later, through my father's genius, did we recognize it as a weapon as well. Your people never knew of it. We never reported our numbers accurately anyway. After the fever we were glad for it. We learned that it was possible to give a taste of the illness pricked on a needle, just enough so that a person once pricked would not succumb to the full wrath of it. Later still we discovered that the spirit of the illness can live on long after fever has passed. The touch I placed on you, young Hephron, came directly from a swatch of a garment my grandfather died in."

Hanish slipped a hand into the fabric of his thalba—just as he had before touching Hephron two days before—but this time he drew out the square of fabric pinched between his fingers. "This is the thing that defeated you here today. It carries the contagion somehow trapped in it. Impossible to believe, isn't it? I wouldn't believe it myself if I hadn't learned of its truth through suffering. You did not slay me after all, Hephron Anthalar. That possibility was never within your grasp. It is I who have slain you, with nothing more than a touch. Many people, with time, recover from this, but not without days in the throes you now feel and then a period of weakness afterward. So what will happen is this: this fever will travel like a wave through your people. And behind the wave we will come reaping. Be thankful your role in this is concluded. The Akarans' idyll is over; as it dies a new age begins. Better for you that you do not live to see it. I doubt very much you would like the shape of things to come."

When Hanish stepped out of the tent a moment later he carried his knife unsheathed in one hand. It was wet with the marbled pattern of blood. All around him his army kept at the butchery. He raised his eyes and looked at the wall of Alecia. He would have to find the Scatevith stone before proceeding past this wall. He would lay his cheek upon it. That is what he must do. He wanted very badly to lay his skin against that stone and have it whisper to him that all of this was as it should be. All of this was just and right. It began before him and would go on after him. He was simply an instrument of a greater purpose.

Chapter

Twenty-seven

The chosen vessel was one of the larger fishing rigs, with two square mainsails near the midpoint and a triangular jib that danced before the prow like a kite at play, rippling and shifting so that the simple insignia that named its owner snapped into and out of view. Anyone watching from shore knew the boat well enough. It had plied Acacian waters for more than thirty years. The crewmen working the deck were slightly more numerous than usual, but it was not uncommon for the rigs to take on trainees in the late winter months, before the bonito returned from the Talayan Shoals, followed by mainland ships in need of spring crews. It floated high above the waterline, as was typical of empty hulls waiting to be filled; the time of its embarkation standard to begin the five-day loop necessary during the slack season. But none of these things were actually as they appeared.

The men dressed as fishermen were in fact Marah guards. The cargo was not to be the yellow-tailed fish the vessel normally trolled the winter seas for. Instead it carried the four Akaran children. They hid for the early part of the journey in the foul-smelling hold of the ship, each of them sullen and dead eyed, breathing through their mouths as much as possible. They wore the same look of worry under their skin, like a genetic trait passed to each of them at birth but only lately emerging. Mena kept feeling the impulse to speak, to share, to say something to break the tension. She was stopped every time by the indisputable fact that she could think of nothing reasonable to say.

Once out of the sheltered curve of the northern harbor, the vessel set a barb into the wind and flew hooked to its underbelly. It cut the glass-blue, frosted water, behind it a squall of seabirds, raucous creatures shouting out their demands. The captain of the guard invited the children up onto the deck once they had put the island some distance behind them, saying there were no eyes to spot them anymore. Mena watched the guards from the back of the boat, tasting the salty air on the wall of her throat. She wondered which of the men or few women she could see had killed before. Some among them had a part in putting down the uprising of the Meinish soldiers. The rebels had been defeated within a bloody hour, the last of them chased careening down the stairways and finally captured and slain in the streets of the lower town. Aliver, she knew, had been spirited away from the mêlée. He did not speak about it, but she could tell he felt shamed by it. Nor was it the only insult to his pride.

She turned away from the guards and watched the wake of the boat. She was not sure what to think of this journey. Thaddeus had explained they were fleeing the island temporarily, for a week or so, no more than a month. They would be safer out of the public view and needed to stay away only long enough for the rebellion to be crushed and for the culprits who killed their father to be punished and for any other schemers on the island to be found out and dealt with. They would sail to the northern tip of Kidnaban and stay in quiet seclusion with the mine's chairman there. Thaddeus promised that they would return to Acacia as soon as possible. For some reason Mena had not believed him. There was some other truth behind his façade and his reasoned words, but she could not imagine what it was.

Aliver did not seem to doubt the man's sincerity, but he had rebelled against the plan with more anger than Mena had ever seen him display before. He had shouted about the coming battle, saying it was his duty to lead the army. He was the king! The responsibility was his, even if he died in the effort! It took all of Thaddeus's persuasive efforts just to soothe Aliver down to a normal volume. Thaddeus invoked his powers as sitting chancellor with interim responsibilities. He chastised Aliver, claiming the orders came directly from Leodan himself, saying that they were both honor bound to abide by them. In the end, though, it was not persuasion but force that got the prince onto the boat. He was escorted, along with the other children, by disguised Marah guards who made it clear they had to follow the king's orders as handed to them by the chancellor. It was all Aliver could do to temporarily accept his exile, though he fumed and reddened at the perceived insult of it.

Late on the first day at sea they came in sight of the Cape of Fallon. It was a shoreline of crumbly cliffs, above which lay a landscape of gentle undulations, tall with grasses, splashed here and there with the colors of winter wildflowers. Dariel sat beside Mena near the stern of the ship. The two of them shared a spread of spiced sardines on crackers. Dariel picked at the fish more than he ate them, trying with the point of a knife to separate the soft bones from the flesh, collecting them in a pile that he occasionally scooped up on the blade and flicked overboard. Something about this filled her with love for the boy. The feeling swelled in her with the power of nostalgia for something lost, as if she were not sitting beside him at that very moment, still every bit his sister, as he was every bit her brother. She wondered why she looked at him with emotion that suggested this was no longer so.

Aliver strolled toward them, conspicuously wearing the ancient sword of Edifus, the King's Trust. It looked too big on him, a strange appendage more cumbersome than useful. He was doing his best to shake off his sulky anger and to regain an appearance of control. Mena wanted to hug him for it, but she knew that would not please him. "We are coming up on the mines," he said, gesturing with a nod of his head. "They are worked by criminals, as punishment. There is an even bigger one on Kidnaban and a chain of them in Senival."

Mena craned her head to see over the railing. As they rounded a promontory, the low sun cast the landscape in enough shadow and highlight that it took her a moment to configure the scene. The great shadows in the land were actually a series of enormous pits. They were open to the sky, how deep she could not guess as she could only see the exposed far wall, which was crisscrossed with cuts and lines. Beacons flared up here and there, large fires encased in glass that fractured and amplified the light, sending bright shards into the sky. By the look of them, the work would not end with the dying day. She wondered how it was possible that there were so many criminals, so many foolish people who would steal from or harm others. Perhaps when she was of age she would do something about it. She would travel in her father's name and demand that they do better with the opportunities offered them and not waste the long peace in petty actions.

They spent that night in the shelter between Kidnaban and the mainland. The following afternoon the vessel nudged into the harbor of Crall on Kidnaban's northern coast. That evening, in the modest comfort of the chairman's compound on the hill looking down on the town, they met Crenshal Vadal. He was not much to look at. Below his lower lip his face ended quite abruptly. It slid back toward his neck in a sheer diagonal. He spoke with a rigid formality, but at the same time he seemed to be wishing himself someplace else entirely, as if his entire body wanted to slide backward and slip around a corner. She noticed that some minutes passed before the man expressed sorrow for Leodan's fate, and she suspected that one of his aides had reminded him to do this with a facial gesture.

As they ate dinner, Crenshal gave them more specifics of their fate. They were, quite simply, to seclude themselves in a portion of the chairman's compound. That was all. They were there to wait. They would receive no visitors, because nobody was to know where they were. Thaddeus would send regular messages as to any changes or developments. They would send or receive no other correspondence. They would have to manage without luxuries, fine food, or entertainments, without any extravagances that might attract attention. Nor would it be wise for them to roam the lower town. It would be a simple existence, far from the aged opulence of Acacia. All Crenshal could offer were the somewhat drafty rooms of a facility meant to house the administrative and managerial staff of the mines, simple meals, and the pleasure of his company. He said this last in jest but with such incomplete vigor that it fell flat.

Aliver added that he wished to be kept apprised of all developments. His tone was haughty, as if he spoke from a position of authority different from his siblings. Mena glanced around, wondering if the others noticed his poorly disguised uncertainty. He feared that he was being shuttled to outside the flow of events and kept out of decision making. He was in a position of limbo: more than the prince he had been a few weeks ago but certainly not the king he hoped to become. To Mena's eyes he had yet to come to terms with his situation.

He did lighten his tone when he asked, "Have you horses we can borrow? We should get out and explore the island. It will do us all good to get some air in our lungs."

Dariel was well into an enthusiastic endorsement of this suggestion when the chairman broke in. "I'm afraid you cannot tour the island. It's . . . well, it is your safety that matters most, Prince. Pleasures like riding will have to be forsaken for the time being. Surely the chancellor explained all of this to you."

"And what of the mines?" Aliver asked. "I'd like to inspect them. We do not need to make a show of it or—"

"Inspect them?" Crenshal had apparently never heard these two words before. "But . . . young prince, this is also impossible. The mines are teeming with degenerates. They hold nothing of interest for you anyway. We will find entertainments for you within the compound. You will not be bored, young ones. I promise you that."

Over the next few days, however, this proved quite false. They saw little of the chairman. He ate with them each evening, but other than that he was absent all day and left the children with few opportunities for distraction. The officials and managers usually housed in the compound had been relocated, leaving the simple halls and rooms echoingly empty. Mena had never even seen any of these phantom people, though in her room she found telltale signs that someone had left the place hastily: a half-empty bottle of scented oil by the basin, a single sock stuffed under her bedding, a toenail on the floor beside the dresser.

Board games helped them through the first few afternoons. Books from the former chairman's collection—Crenshal himself had no interest in literature—provided some diversion the third day, when Dariel persuaded Aliver to read aloud to the group from a collection of epic poems. The boy was entranced, but Mena could not help but think of her father. Corinn might have experienced something similar. She rose abruptly and stalked away, giving no explanation. Corinn had barely said anything since leaving Acacia. When she did, she spoke in flat, matter-of-fact tones, as if she acknowledged nothing unusual in their circumstances.

The closest they came to having a meaningful exchange was on the third afternoon. Corinn entered the common room they passed most of the day in and glanced around with heavy-lidded eyes. Mena was surprised when Corinn drifted over toward her, plopped down on the couch near her, and exhaled a bored breath.

"Did you hear? One of the soldiers said that two men had been found trying to leave the village. He said they were 'trussed for it' and the other laughed and said it served them right. What do you think that means?"

"I am sure it means they were punished," Mena said.

"Of course it means that!" Corinn snapped. "You always say the most obvious things. Punished *how*? That's what I was asking."

"I don't say the most obvious things," Mena said, fearful that this unexpected interaction was about to turn sour. If anyone said the most obvious things it was Corinn herself.

Corinn made a noise low in her throat, a sort of moaning protest. "It is so strange here, Mena. Nothing is as it should be. I cannot stand the way the people look here. They look like—like they're dumb, like they have the brains of animals instead of people. I so want to go home. I hate this limbo. I have too much to do. Important things."

"Like what?" Mena asked, trying to cast her voice in a way that would not offend.

Somehow she managed to anyway. Corinn looked askance at her. "You would not understand."

On the fourth day, when a servant of the chairman brought them dice to play rats running, Mena truly gave up the pretense of finding diversion inside the compound's bare walls. She counted the days just as precisely as Aliver, both of them waiting for the next bit of news from Thaddeus, hoping he would call them home. When the first terse, cryptic dispatch from the chancellor arrived, however, it brought them no change whatsoever. The situation was still unstable, he wrote. They should remain where they were. He promised them that he would alert them to any change, but while he said that, he provided them not a single indication of what had transpired since they left. Not one piece of news about the war. No indication of whether the situation was better or worse than before.

Mena noticed a pall in the sky one afternoon, and feared that her foreboding had somehow reached into the world in physical form. There were shadows in the air, cloudlike formations that rippled and flowed on low currents of air. Seeing them through the small window in her room, she realized they had always been there. She just had not stopped to study them before. The sky was not simply overcast, as she had assumed. Beyond the shifting darkness was a screen of light blue, clear all the way to the heavens. How strange, she thought. On this first glimpse she could not help but look away, those shapes in the sky too much like harbingers of ill, too much like swirls and currents that might materialize as something more ominous if she stared too long.

On waking in the morning she went to the window before doing anything else. The dark vapors were still there, clear and obvious now that she had learned to see them. They even grew heavier toward the evening. The longer she watched it, the more aware she became of the clouds' presence in myriad ways around her. Mostly they shifted with currents she could not feel, but at still moments particles of the stuff fell all around her, settling on flat spaces and collecting on the rough contours of the walls. It was a form of dust, so light that it moved propelled by breaths of air. She felt the touch of tiny crystals on her cheeks and in her eyelids and collecting on her brow. She could taste it in her lungs, a grit that she inhaled with each breath. It was everywhere. It amazed her that it took her so long to notice it.

Mena asked the servant who changed the bed linen if she had noticed it. The girl did not seem at all happy with being spoken to. She almost backed out of the room. "Princess, what you see is dust rising from the mines. It just comes from the work, is all."

Mena asked if the mines were near, and the young woman nodded. Just beyond the hills above the compound, she explained. Where were all the workers, then? Mena asked. Why had she not seen any signs that the mines even existed?

"You have seen a sign. You read it in the air. But for you it need not be any more real than that. The workers? I don't know, lady. Perhaps there are no workers. It's not for me to say."

The young woman used the pause as Mena considered this to slip out of the room. Annoying behavior. A servant should not leave once she had been engaged in conversation. On the other hand, the woman's boldness in sneaking away might have been the thing that inspired Mena's own actions a few hours later.

She left the compound well after dark, cloaked in an overcoat she had found in her closet. She avoided the guard posted outside her door by squeezing out her window, dropping down onto the patio there, and then opening the gate to freedom. She took no light, but the moon was high and, though nervous and alive to even the slightest sound, she had little difficulty following the bone-white paths away from the compound.

There was a second guard to get past just up the pathway a little. He was a dense form in the darkness. She sensed the details of his body, the position of his head, and probable direction of his gaze. There was even a musty scent on a gust of air blowing toward her—his odor. She slipped off the path when she dared proceed on it no farther. She walked, crouched low through grasses, feeling with her hands and feet and finding a crease in the landscape that took her past the soldier.

She kept hearing sounds that set her heart beating faster: the rasp of her coat; the bonelike snap of the shoots of grass beneath her feet; the way the press of her weight caused grains of sand to shift and protest; the explosion of sound as a rodent, startled by her proximity, fled. She never stopped expecting the man to call out to her. She had heard before that it was difficult to travel silently at night and that Marah guards were trained to hear any concealed irregularity in night sounds. Now she wondered who had said it. For all of her rapid breathing, despite the violence the tiniest of sounds did to her ears, even though her calves ached from the effort of the strange squatting posture of her stealth—in truth her escape did not really feel that difficult. She kept moving and was soon beyond him and rising back up toward the main path. Her feet and hands and fingers and muscles seemed to know what to do of their own accord. She was half inclined to sit down and ponder on this, but she had yet to reach the goal she had set out for.

A series of staircases climbed away from the compound. It had been sunk into the hillside so that in her crouched position she could proceed without fear of being spotted. The stairs ended at a junction with a stone road. She cut straight across it and climbed up the steep bank on the other side, clawing handfuls of the long grass.

All told, the climb took only a few minutes, but still, what relief to feel the angle of the slope lessen and to see that there was nothing above her. She breathed heavily the last few steps, taking them slowly, as one does when a goal is reached. She stretched to full height, which helped her see over the rise to the landscape beyond. She knew what was supposed to be there, the very thing that she had been curious about, the reason—if there was one—for this night journey. And yet she was not ready for what she saw.

Gone was the quiet night on the other side of the ridge behind her. The moon was nowhere to be seen, nor the clear sky she had just traveled under. Instead the earth seemed contained beneath a flowing, dust-laden billowing, a cloudlike seething of motion. Beneath this sprawled a great pit, many mouthed and enormous. It took up the entirety of the view before her, a crater of caved desolation like nothing she had seen or imagined before, alive with a throbbing, cacophonous, angry clamor.

She was looking over the northern rim of the mines of Kidnaban. The sight of them struck her with a type of horror that she had forgotten existed, the same fear she had felt when a silly maid had told her tales of a demon race of people who lived inside a steaming mountain, feeding the fires within it with naughty children snatched from their beds. As in her imaginings, hundreds of different fires illumed the place. Sheets of curved glass set around cauldrons of flaming oil shot beams up into the sky. By the light of these she again made out the confusion of crisscrossing diagonal lines that she had seen at the Cape of Fallon. But she was so much nearer now. The lines shifted as she stared, blurred by a barely perceptible form of movement. She thought this was an effect of the light. It took her a moment to understand it was something more than that.

The lines were stairways and ledges, wide tracks for machinery, ramps and ladder systems stories upon stories tall. The objects in motion were not tricks of the light. They were people. Hundreds of them. So small that they could not be perceived as individuals but took form only because of their collective movement, as a line of ants from a distance is one being. Maybe they numbered more than hundreds. Thousands was more likely. Tens of thousands. And even this might only be a small portion of the number. She had no idea how extensive the mines were, how much was hidden from view.

She inched over the lip and then slid down the other side to a solid ridge of rock. She had to climb forward on her belly to look over this. As her head pushed out beyond the edge she froze, surprised to find that just below her, some twenty or thirty feet, ran an avenue cut from the stone. It thronged with workers. They carried objects on their shoulders, sacks on their backs, their skin and clothing all the same gray-black of the mine, tainted by the reddish light and etched in shadow.

Off to the south stood a tower, beyond it some distance another. It sat squat and thick, hooded with a roof that looked somewhat like a mushroom, emblazoned with the gilded insignia of the Akaran bloodline. It was her family's symbol, the Tree of Akaran, the silhouette of an acacia against a yellow sunburst. It was *her* symbol. It was a shape she had doodled a thousand times onto tabletops and napkins.

Beneath the roof were balconies peopled by moving figures. Looking to the south along the lip of the mine she saw another watchtower and beyond, all around the rim of the pit—many more watchtowers. The figures were lookouts, guards. Many of them were archers. She could just make out the way they stood with their bows hanging easy in their grip, each with an arrow ready to be drawn. It should not have been a surprise. Criminals must be guarded. But there were so many. Towers were everywhere in the distance, the far ones just bulbous shapes on the horizon. The tiny workers beneath them had no chance of escape, no option but to bend to what promised to be unending labor.

Her eyes, losing the will to scan the largeness of it, drifted of their own accord and settled on the lines of moving forms just below her. There was something unsettling about the sight of them. They looked exhausted. They walked with heads down turned. Not one talked to another. Not one lifted his or her eyes to the sky. The longer she stared, the more she believed she could see individual features and attributes, the shapes of faces and the lay of collarbones thinly draped with flesh. It was because of this growing intimacy that she realized the most ghastly thing was not the staggering numbers of them nor their dejected façades nor their smallness compared to the project that bound them. There was another reason the line looked so irregular to her eyes. There were children among the laborers. Every third or fourth person she saw was a child no older than herself, some no taller than Dariel. This was too much to bear.

Back in the fresh night air, Mena took a few steps down toward the compound. She lowered herself to her backside. She could not go back to the compound with any sign of what she had just witnessed written on her face. She was not supposed to have seen it. None of them were. Clearly, the world was not as she had been led to believe. She thought of her father in his melancholy moments. Was this why? This was an Acacian mine. It was her father's mine. It was her family's. Those people, those children . . . they worked for her. There *were* beings who snatched the young from their beds and sent them to fuel the world's fires. They worked in her name. She wondered if that errant nurse years before had known this. Was that why she felt the right to frighten her, to tease her, and to corrupt her dreams?

She returned to the compound just in time. She had barely stepped into her room and thrown off her overcoat before a hard knock broke the predawn silence. They were to be moved, a voice she did not recognize said, speaking through the door. It was most urgent that she be moved. "Princess, your safety depends on it."

Why did she not recognize the voice? It was not any of the Marah that had escorted them nor a servant nor anyone she recalled from Crenshal's staff. And yet she was quite certain that it spoke honestly. Her safety did depend on it. She scooped up her overcoat and glanced around the room, wondering if she needed to make arrangements to bring her things. She thought she would ask whomever it was that summoned her, but when she opened the door she felt strangely prepared to step through it as she was, still flushed from having been outside, coat over her arm, ready. Simply ready.

She did not know that by stepping through that door she was placing one portion of her life behind her forever. She did not know that for years to come she would not lay eyes on her brothers or sister or anybody she had known up until that point. She could not have imagined that crossing that threshold was akin to stepping into obscurity, vanishing from the map, moving out of her skin, away from her home and country and name, into another life entirely.

End of Book One

Book Two

Exiles

CHAPTER

TWENTY-EIGHT

Few people who had known him in his prime would have recognized the man climbing the dirt path up from the mountain village of Pelos. He walked bearing the scent of goats with him, a horse-sweat smell heavy on his robes, with chicken filth encrusted under his fingernails and stray feathers ensnared in his mane of hair and beard. His breath was rank with wine stink. He cared for the animals in the town's tavern. It was a beggar's or a child's job, one that he could stumble about to attend to, taking breaks to suck from a skin of wine that lent each day claret-blurred edges. There was little in his appearance to betray the man he had once been. He did not even go by his given name anymore. He did, at some point each day, mutter it out loud. He needed to hear it float on the air as a feeble act of defiance, but this was meant for no other human ears to hear.

This evening he stopped at a rock outcropping just off the trail. Before him the mountainous terrain etched ridges and dips, lit by the risen moon. Here and there patches of mist slid through the valleys like ghostly slugs across a damp forest floor. A yellow point of light moved across a far hillside. It must have been a trader with his lamp lit as protection against the spirits. These mountain people were superstitious, frightened of the night and the creatures who patrolled it. The man had no such fears. Part of him desired death at the claws of a belrann or to be carried into bondage by a wood ghoul. Either of these was a fate, he thought, of greater substance than his daily existence. He no longer lived for his conscious hours at all. Should a wolverbear sniff him out and bite his head from his shoulders, he would regret only the loss of his dream existence.

He was just about to turn and stumble up the path toward his hovel of a home, pulled by the dull hunger that had lately come to define him. Before leaving he whispered, "Leeka Alain. I am Leeka Alain. I am not dead. I have not been killed."

Leeka Alain, once a general in Acacia's most fractious province. Now what was he? He had had no purpose in life for several years now. All his travails in the frozen north, his sole survival of that first Numrek ambush, his ordeal with the fever and the lonely trek he undertook in pursuit of the enemy host: all these things were behind him. They had amounted to nothing. His notion that he might have a crucial task to fulfill had been mistaken. He had tumbled down off the Methalian Rim nine years previous, riding that woolly, horned mount, believing himself to be the bearer of apocalyptic news.

He found a land already at war, already suffering from a variety of attacks: his king dead, Aushenia smashed by the Numrek, the Candovians roused to rebellion by Maeander, and Acacia's military might crippled by a disease that made them easy targets for slaughter. In many ways Hanish assured his victory on the Alecian Fields. Leeka had not been there on the day, but he arrived shortly after to behold a carpet of rotting corpses, peppered with flies and vultures and all manner of scavengers.

The weeks after the Fields saw an ongoing butchery that stalked off the battlefield and into every lane and courtyard, into temples and monuments and homes. It seemed the evil fury of the Mein would not abate until every last Acacian was split upon their steel. Other nations, fearing such a fate, allied themselves more and more faithfully with the Mein: the clans of Candovia had never been so united; Senival put up a gallant, short-lived fight before laying down their axes; and the Vumu Archipelago petitioned for peace before even a single blow was struck against them. In Aushenia little resistance of any sort remained. That an empire so long held together could crumble so quickly baffled Leeka. It seemed that all the years of obedience meant nothing. All the praise and tribute lavished on Acacia vanished in an instant, replaced by the fire of long-harbored animus.

Only Talay, with its vast resources, stood against the Mein even after the Mainland and Acacia were overrun. Whether they did this for the Acacian cause or because they wished to forge their own independence was unclear. They might have given up on Acacia—as most of the rest of the world had—while still choosing to fight for themselves. Leeka had not asked and had not cared. They were fighting Hanish Mein and the Numrek horde. That was what mattered. He had rushed to join them. In particular, he had relished the opportunity to fight the Numrek.

Many had surmised that the Numrek would not be able to fight outside the northern regions. They had seemed ill suited to even the mild warmth of Aushenia. But on arriving in sun-baked Talay they stripped off their furs and cloaks and stepped out as grotesquely white creatures. They were more fearsome for the length of their limbs and the striations of their muscles and the unconcealed girth in their hands and feet. From their first day exposed to the undiluted sun, their skin blistered and peeled as meat does above coals. During the first battles they looked like they had walked through flames. Chunks of their skin sloughed off. Clumps of hair pulled free from their scalps.

Surely, Leeka had thought, they could not go about so red and oozing and live. But they did. They fought like crazed madmen. They stood among the carnage looking worse than the corpses around them, but they never fell except from the gravest of injuries. Within a few weeks they began to recover. Their skin grew back shades darker, taut against their muscles. It peeled again—not so savagely this time—but with the next healing they ripened even more. Before long they walked the land proudly, naked save for a skirt that male and female wore alike. To the dismay of the retreating Talayans, the Numrek had never looked healthier and stronger than in coppered nudity. On the summer solstice they danced a tribute to the length of the day and the strength of the sun. A new conjecture spread. The Numrek were not the creatures of the north everyone thought them to be. They must have once been a tropical race. Perhaps they had been driven to exile in the north and had only now returned to their preferred climate. In the face of their onslaught, Talay surrendered piece by tribal piece.

People said that Hanish Mein sought the utter destruction of all things Acacian. They said the spite of the Tunishnevre was such that Hanish would destroy all sign of the race he had conquered. But once the peace was established, Hanish set about securing his hold on the empire in ways surprising in their reasonableness. He did not damage Acacian architecture. He left Alecia and Manil and Aos accoutred in their splendor. He touched not a stone or statue on Acacia itself, except those of Tinhadin, which he tore down and had splintered into shards. He had the black stone of Scatevith cut out of Alecia's outer wall, moved it to the palace on Acacia, and set it as a monument in the place that tributes to Edifus and Tinhadin had once sat. Mostly, though, he just filled Acacian places with his own people, adding his relics to those already there. He layered things Meinish atop the Acacian and seemed to welcome taking on aspects of the defeated empire's mantle. Instead of dismantling the Acacian system of government and commerce, he grasped them and adopted them to his own purposes.

None of this cooled the heat of Leeka's hatred, but eventually he could fight no more. All his allies had died, put down their arms, or slunk away into hiding. His enemy turned from conquest to tasks of rebuilding and entrenching and managing their newfound wealth. If Leeka had known with surety on any particular day what his life would become, he would have leaned upon his sword and cut his bowels out. But he did not know. One day slipped with its veiled import into the next, so that his defeat clung to him in tiny increments, accrued day by day.

He wandered the empire. He lost or abandoned the trappings of his rank: his vest traded for food, his dagger for wine, his helmet lost one hazy evening, his shoulder pack stolen by a youth much faster than he. Before long he looked like any other war-weary veteran. He was unkempt, lost, perhaps mind addled, obviously harmless to the Meinish military that now policed most of the Known World. He had always been a man who liked a drink. After the war, he no longer enjoyed drinking—there was none of the mirth in his inebriation that there had once been—but he drank alcohol like it was sustaining water. He might have died a drunkard's death and been content with it. He was saved, ironically, by the introduction of a new addiction.

The mist was more plentiful throughout the Meinish Empire than it had been during the Akaran reign. It was everywhere, constant as bread or water, cheaper than Candovian wine. He inhaled a pipefull one evening when there was nothing else to be had. What revelations! With mist in him, he understood he had been mistaken. He was not a failure. The war was not concluded. No, in truth he was a lone apostle of bloody retribution. He had killed Numreks before and he would do so again. He lay back and saw the images right there above him, cast on the screen that was the night sky. He strode through Aushenia with a sword in each hand. The earth had not seen the likes of him in ages. At some point the vision was not just an imagined thing. He lived within it. He felt ground beneath his feet and air pumping in his lungs. He traveled a thousand miles and fought until his face was red and dripping with Numrek blood, his fists so welded to his swords that the steel was an extension of his being. Such damage he did! Such holy, retributive carnage he unleashed . . .

The first morning he awoke from such dreams anguished to find himself in his enfeebled body, no hero at all. He might have spurned the drug and cursed it, except that he could not help but hear the low heartbeat of the mist lingering thereafter, with it the promised possibility that there was truth in his vision. The mist dream was so very real. It was intimate in every detail, vivid as life. No, it was more tactile and real than the life he now led.

There were prohibitions on using the drug during the daylight, working hours. Being found in mist haze by a soldier of the Mein could get one locked up and deprived of the stuff—which was punishment all devotees dreaded. Before long Leeka had contracted himself to his present arrangement—he would labor drunken among the animals through day to earn the few coins needed to dream the mist through the night. In this, he became one of millions in the Known World. He never even noticed that it was happening to him, never questioned this order of life. He could not truly have said at what moment he gave himself to it completely. The mist commands full devotion; Leeka, believing in no other god anymore, learned to worship at a new altar.

It was this that he was thinking of as he approached the darkened shell in which he passed the evenings. Sometime earlier he had taken the packet of mist threads from his breast pocket and walked, caressing the fibers with his fingers. Once inside it would only take a few minutes' preparation, and then he would inhale and inhale and inhale. . . .

Leeka stopped in his tracks and stilled himself. He sensed something, another breathing thing, close but hidden. He thought of the predators of the mountain night and knew that if this be one of those, he was likely dead on his feet.

"Forgive me," a voice said. "I didn't mean to surprise you." A hooded figure peeled away from the shadows beside his hut and stepped into the moonlight, arms raised in a gesture of innocence. "In fact, you surprised me, coming so quietly."

The man's tone was kindly, but Leeka had a particular dislike for speaking to people wearing hoods, especially ones who stepped out of the shadows of his hovel late at night and blocked his path. He sought to convey as much with the full intensity of his glare.

"Are you Leeka Alain?" the hooded man asked.

The question caught Leeka off guard. His first thought was that the man must have heard him speaking on the outcropping, but that was scarcely possible. He tucked his mist threads back into his pocket.

"Are you Leeka Alain, he who commanded Leodan's army in the Mein? Leeka Alain that some call Beast Rider?"

The man's Acacian was fluid and spoken like a native of the island itself. Leeka had not heard the language uttered so perfectly in some time.

Who would ask such a thing in such a tongue? Probably only a man who wished to hear his identity confirmed before killing him.

"Are you he that claims to have been the first to kill a Numrek?"

"No," Leeka said, speaking the mountain dialect of the area, "I am not that man."

The hooded figure did not move. He was a statue that almost blended into the features of the night. For a moment Leeka wondered if he was hallucinating. Perhaps this statue had always stood just there, but he had forgotten it. Or perhaps it was no statue at all but just a trick his mist-hungry mind played with the light.

The stranger spoke again, still in Acacian. "This news pains me. I had need of Leeka Alain's services. It is true that you do not look much like him. Perhaps I was mistaken. I am sorry to have disturbed you. Let me offer you something to pay for my mistake. Here . . ."

The figure's hand came up, from it stretched the flickering, tumbling progress of a tossed coin, flaring each time its face caught the moonlight. Leeka's eyes could not help but follow it. A thief's trick, and he fell for it. Because of this he would not afterward be able to say that he really saw the man move. But he did feel the impact of something driving up into his abdomen with force enough to have run him through. A pinprick sensation at his neck released a flash of pain that scorched all the way through him like a fire across dry brush. Ignited, and then extinguished in the next moment. As it went, so did his hold of consciousness.

✳

He opened his eyes knowing that time had passed and his placement on the world had changed. He remembered the figure in the shadows, his voice, the airborne coin, the impact that lifted him. He lay with all this in his mind a moment, watching as his eyes gained clarity, focusing on the rough-hewn beams of a wooden ceiling. They were lit by the flickering glow of the fireplace. He knew the ceiling well, every irregularity in it, the knot that disfigured one beam, the lacework of ancient cobwebs hanging from another. He was on his cot, in his hovel, looking up at his ceiling. How very strange . . .

A man's form leaned over him. "You lied to me, Leeka Alain. I do not claim to be surprised by it. This is not an easy time to speak forthrightly to strangers, but I might have thought you would be more convincing."

The man brought a candle up near his face. Leeka stared at him, thoroughly confused. He saw an old man, skin creviced like tree bark, his hair gray, his beard—sparse thing that it was—woven into braids in the Seni-valian fashion. If his body was a twin to his face he'd be a thin wisp of a man like any beggar he might pass without acknowledging on the street. How had this aged shell of a man even touched him? Had he fallen so very far from what he had once been?

The old man seemed to read what he was thinking. "I am not as de-crepit as I look. Nor are you. In a fair fight I would have no chance against you. This thing that happened here . . . let it not bruise your soldier's vanity." He paused a moment. "Look at my face, Leeka. Tell me if you recognize me. It may be that you remember me, for we did meet once, in a different time and place, in what seems like another world, really."

The realization that he did recognize him came to Leeka as the words left him. "You are the chancellor . . . Thaddeus Clegg."

The older man smiled. "Good," he said. "There is hope for you yet."

CHAPTER
TWENTY-NINE

Yes, Corinn finally conceded to herself one afternoon as she rode horseback along the high trail that followed the serpentine ridgeline toward Haven's Rock, Meinish women did have the potential for beauty. One just had to grow accustomed to the hard-edged angularity of their features. They had about them a similar bone structure and temperament as men of their race, but what looked chiseled, rugged, and handsome on their men was somewhat awkward on their women. Or so Corinn had thought for most of the years she had spent in their company. Only lately did she realize that she often measured herself against them. When this shift in her feelings had begun she could not say, but the rides she had lately been taking with an entourage of young Meinish women had done much to stir the feelings to the surface.

It began as an order. Hanish Mein, a messenger told her, requested that Princess Corinn spend fair afternoons with his cousin, Rhrenna, and her entourage of young noblewomen, friends, and maids. The messenger used the word *requested*, although they both knew *commanded* would have suited the reality more precisely. And he had called her *princess*. Everyone called her princess, though in fact she was a prisoner on the island that had once been her father's. She was being held in a lingering purgatory by the very man who had orchestrated her father's assassination and the ruin of the Acacian Empire and Akaran family. She walked the same hallways now as she had all her life. She took in the same views down from the palace toward the lower town and out to the sea. Many evenings she dined at the great table in the central hall. But she was no longer of the host family. Another man sat in the place that had been her father's. The invocation over dinner was spoken in a different tongue, and it called for the blessing of a menacing collective force Corinn had no true understanding of. Her daily life was a balance between what had been and what now was, the edges of each blurred by present reality, warped by memory. It was her own particular, uncomfortable circumstance, unique to her of all people in the world.

This afternoon Rhrenna rode a chestnut mount she must have chosen to compliment her outfit: a vest of pastel blue and tan, with a split skirt that looked almost like a dress when she stood, but which split when she mounted. She was a pale, slim-boned girl composed of imperfect features that, fortunately for her, somehow combined to pleasant effect. She wore her hair long, in a braided fashion that took Corinn some time to separate from that of the men.

For the first couple of years of the occupation, few Meinish women had ventured out of Tahalian. Meinish men, it could be said, were possessive and protective of their women. The Mein were not fond of mixing their blood with other races and could think of few greater sins than one of their women giving birth to a half-breed child. It was not much better when women of the newly conquered empire began to mother children paler than themselves, gray eyed and sharp featured. Though frowned on, such miscegenation proved impossible to prevent. No matter the praise they constantly heaped on their own women, Meinish men still mixed with foreign women. They seemed to love the taste and feel and shape of the skin tones and features they claimed indifference to. Even Maeander, Hanish's brother, was said to have fathered a small tribe of children. Gradually more and more Meinish women journeyed down to fill roles as wives and concubines, to add a greater domestic normalcy to life both in the palace and among common soldiers, most of whom were now living uncommonly luxurious lives.

Rhrenna had been in Acacia only a few months, but she seemed to have adapted to the place. One of her charms was her voice, high and gentle and better suited to the Acacian tongue than that of most of her people. "Hanish thinks you are beautiful," she said. She wore a hat with a wide, meshed brim to protect her from the sun. She looked through the lace of it coyly. "But you must know that already. You understand men better than I, don't you?"

"I have understood very little during my life so far," Corinn answered. She had little interest in discussing romance or courtly intrigue. It was not her court, for one thing. But also, more piercingly, such notions reminded her only of loss. Despite this, she heard herself ask, "Why do you say Hanish finds me beautiful?"

"It's obvious, Princess," she said. "When you are in the room he cannot take his eyes off you. At the summer dance he barely paid attention to any partner but you."

Another young woman, a friend of Rhrenna's from childhood, agreed. She turned in the saddle to the four women behind them and pulled echoes of the same opinion from them.

Corinn would have none of it. "As if I impressed anyone that night! Stumbling around as I did . . . he *had* to pay attention, or else I'd have squashed his feet to pulp. Your dances make no sense to me."

Rhrenna thought about this a moment, rocking with the easy motion of her horse's stride, and then said, "You are a more graceful stumbler than most."

Corinn tried several times to deflect Rhrenna's praise, but the young woman always found a way to turn back her protests with glowing phrases. Corinn eventually fell silent, defeated at devaluing herself. And what should this admiration mean to her? She had been admired in the years before the war by women and men more refined than any of these girls. She understood her situation better than they did and was never entirely sure if they were aware of the falseness that tainted everything that passed between them. She knew that she was a trophy put on display for the pleasure of the Mein and for the edification of the new king's subjects. Here, her presence said, is incontrovertible proof that the empire that came before the Mein has been defeated. See how this Akaran sits at *our* table. See her manners, her beauty, her refinement. See her and remember how mighty the Akarans were and how completely they have been whipped, tamed, and domesticated. That was the point that Corinn's presence daily reinforced. What a misery it was! Her life had little physical hardship in it, no toil, all the luxuries and most of the privileges she had ever known. And yet she felt constantly set apart, possessed, owned—even by these young women who so claimed to adore her.

They were near enough to Haven's Rock that the bird-dung stench of the place swept past them on a gust of the breeze. One of the maids commented on it, holding her hand to her nose and querying whether they really had to go closer. Corinn rode on, tight-lipped, aware that she took offense at any slight given to her father's island, even one directed at the habits of seabirds. She did not have to feign adoration of the landscape around her. The island was at the height of its summer colors. The grass blanketing the hills had crisped to a flaming, metallic yellow. The only things missing were the green crowns of acacia trees. They had all been cut down during the first year after Hanish's victory: an act of symbolic spite and another thing Corinn would never forgive him for.

Soon the dry season fires would flare up, sending up clouds of black smoke and attracting scavenging birds to pick through the charred streaks lashed across the hillsides like wounds. Corinn mentioned as much to her party, saying that they would soon have to choose the days they ventured out carefully. People had been caught in the quick-moving blazes before and incinerated where they stood. The young women heard this in silence, awed at the thought of a fire spontaneously combusting. It must have been a hellish thought to a people accustomed to nine-month winters and summers—as Igguldan had said—never free of the possibility of a sudden snowstorm. It pleased Corinn that they feared aspects of the island that she had known all her life, though she also felt the bite of remembrance that so often came with such thoughts. Igguldan. She could not bear thinking of him. What torture that she had come so near a great love, only to have it snatched from her by the callous actions of madmen.

The wind picked up as they approached the cliffs of Haven's Rock. By the time they reached the edge, Rhrenna and her countrywomen were all clutching at the crowns of their hats to keep them from flying free. Corinn, not needing the protection since her skin warmed and browned under the sun's touch instead of blistering and turning red, sat hatless and as composed as ever. Her amusement at this was short-lived, however.

One of the maids said, "Look, Larken is back from Talay. See his ship, there."

It took Corinn only a moment to spot the vessel. It ran a crimson mainsail embossed with a short-handled pickax. It was Larken's sign, bestowed on him by Hanish for his services during the war. The sight of that billow of red speeding toward them across a sea of shimmering, luminous hyacinth filled her with instant rancor.

Larken. The thought of him always reminded her of the time before her captivity. It was he who had knocked on the door to her room in Kidnaban nine years earlier. He had stood before her, tall and wolfishly handsome in his Marah robes. He had spoken so earnestly, with a calm at his center that conveyed strength such as she had not seen in some time. He had come from Thaddeus Clegg, he'd said. He was to take her to safety, just her. Other guardians would deal with her siblings as they were to head to separate destinations. It was not wise that they all be together in a single place. Thaddeus and her father had made arrangements for them. He produced documents to this effect, with all the seals and signatures in order, blessed with an imprint she knew to be Thaddeus's ring.

"Come," Larken had said. "You can believe in me. I live only to protect you."

She must have wanted to believe him so very badly. How, she wondered now, could she have consented to go with him without first speaking with her siblings? She had tried to, but he had been so convincing and earnest. Hanish Mein's agents were closing on them, he had said. Betrayers were rife now throughout the empire. Even their host at the mines, Crenshal, could no longer be trusted, and that was why they had to fly. Speed was everything. Her brothers and her sister had already embarked on their journeys. If she came now she could feel confident she would see them again soon. It was the only way.

Larken was courteous and deferential, and also efficient and forceful and decisive all at once. He knew each thing that needed to be done and managed it all smoothly. She simply had to follow his instructions. Doing so, she watched the world slip by around them. Out of the compound and down to the worker's town of Crall they went, through the streets and back alleys to the docks, into a sloop that Larken cast into the wind single-handedly, with the skill of a lifelong sailor. By the time the sun was fully up they had rounded a cape and were out of sight of Crall. He named each landmark they passed on Kidnaban and explained just what he intended when they cut away from the island and aimed at the Cape of Fallon. By the time they crept into the quiet, sleeping town of Danos late that night, she had placed her fatigued person entirely into his hands.

Larken had explained that they were to meet a magistrate at a predetermined time and place. He was the only one who knew how they were to proceed from that point on, and he could be trusted entirely. The man was exactly where Larken said he would be. He greeted Corinn so effusively that it embarrassed her, something that had never happened before.

"We are safe here," the magistrate spoke as they walked. "This meeting was kept entirely secret. No one but myself read the orders from the chancellor. The preparations for each stage of your safekeeping have been made separately, so that no one but myself understands the situation fully. This was all as Thaddeus ordered, and I've followed him to the letter. Trust me, Princess Corinn, the worst is behind you now."

"Nobody knows of our arrival?" Larken had asked. "You are certain of this?"

The man answered that he was certain. He would swear to it on his life and that of his children. He had all the documents the two of them would need to proceed, with written instructions on whom to contact and the secret words to invoke to win their trust. They were, believe it or not, destined for Candovia. There were people there loyal to the Akarans who would shelter Corinn in such perfect hiding that Hanish Mein would never find her, even if he searched a hundred years.

All of this seemed to satisfy Larken. He said nothing more, and for a time they walked on. The magistrate chattered without pause, bemoaning the situation in the empire, lamenting Leodan's death, and providing fragmented details of what she should expect in the coming days, promises that everything would soon be righted. Corinn half wished he would shut up and half welcomed his talkativeness, wanting to grasp onto him and hold tight until the order of the world stabilized again. She had never felt a greater need to cling to other people. She already felt herself slipping from Larken's care into the magistrate's.

This, in part, was why what had happened next stunned Corinn so completely. For some time the actions her eyes witnessed did not register meaningfully in her consciousness. As they passed around a corner and into a short section shaded from the moonlight, Larken whispered something. The magistrate turned toward him, as if reacting to a warning. Thus he was staring clear-eyed at Larken when he swept toward him. Larken lifted something above his head and slammed it down into the magistrate's forehead. The man stood pinned to the spot that connected them, his body seeming to hang from Larken's fist. Larken yanked his arm back, and the other dropped. His form, in silhouette against the moonlit courtyard, betrayed the weapon: a small ax Larken had worn at his waist. Corinn had noticed it before without thinking twice about it.

Larken took her by the elbow. "Do not make a sound. I'll not kill you, but if you call out I'll silence you in a way that will pain you greatly." He led her forward a few steps, to the edge of the shadow. His face was close to hers, his breath hot against her skin. "That had to be done, Princess. Do not blame me or him. We are all players in a drama greater than ourselves. Come, our journey is not yet complete."

"What—what are you doing?" Corinn gasped at the pressure of his grip on her wrist. "Where are you taking me?"

For the first time Larken ignored her queries. No polite response. No thorough but efficient explanation. He just dragged her on. Into hiding, yes, but not the hiding her father had planned for her. Larken, it turned out, was neither a loyal Marah nor an overt traitor. He simply held Corinn captive in an old monk's cabin and waited to sell her to whichever power emerged victorious from the war. It was inland from Danos, well into the rugged hills, along a portion of the riverbank so steep and boulder strewn that few humans found reason to venture there. They passed the days in long silences, broken occasionally by conversation Corinn hated herself for allowing. He fed and cared for her. He bound her every few days and ventured back into Danos to gather news. So Corinn heard the progress of the war from his reports. Beyond this Larken had a great deal to tell her, incredible things she did not believe at the time but which were impossible to deny now.

She emerged from the cabin a different person than she had been on entering. She had shed all vestiges of innocence, all inklings that she could ever again find solace in hopeful, naïve belief. She would never be caught unprepared again, she swore to herself. She would never trust. Never love. Never put faith in other human beings again. She would learn all she could of the shape and substance of the world, and she would find a way to survive in it.

A full six weeks after he had abducted her, Larken presented Corinn to Hanish Mein. In so doing, Larken bought himself a place of privilege in the new chieftain's empire. For her part, Corinn found herself thrust into the strange purgatory in which she still lived, nine years later.

She did not speak at all as the group of women rode back toward the palace. They arrived at one of the back gates. Blond-haired guards called down to them playfully, pretending that they must provide a code word to win entry. Corinn had no patience with the game. Nor was she happy to find a messenger awaiting her when the gate did swing open. Hanish Mein wished to see her that afternoon, at a given hour. She groaned inwardly and almost answered that she was ill and could not see him. But she felt the eyes of the other women on her, admiring and envious and curious all at once. Not sure how she wished to react, she accepted the message without comment, apparently nonplussed by it.

As she stood in the hallway outside his chambers—the very ones that had been her father's—she found it took effort to keep a flush from her face, to slow the beating of her heart, and to keep her features stony. Hanish had an effect on her that she struggled to resist. She remembered, as she always tried to before speaking with him, the way he had laughed at her at their first meeting. She had invoked Igguldan's name, promising that he would not stand for her imprisonment. Hanish had parted his lips and laughed and said, "Igguldan? The Aushenian whelp? It's he you think of now? Fine, I understand that he was a handsome lad, a poet, they tell me. Perhaps you would think differently of him if you knew that he led his army to his nation's greatest defeat. It's true. They all died . . . quite horribly, really. His name, dear princess, will be noted only in ignominy. But if it heartens you, you may remember him as you wish. You Acacians are good at that."

Corinn had never hated a person more than she hated Hanish at that moment. He had seemed to her the height of callous arrogance, cruel, repulsive, and irredeemable. It frustrated her to no end that she had to try so hard to remember this about him. Too often, she knew, she stole glances at him with a very different emotion than she wished.

"Corinn?" Hanish's voice called to her. "Princess, I can hear you breathing out there. Come in and let us talk a moment. I've learned something that might interest you."

That was another annoyance! Hanish really did seem to have unnaturally well-tuned senses. She stepped across the threshold to find him leaning back on her father's desk, a fan of papers in one hand. He tugged at one of his lengths of braided hair, the one, she knew, that indicated the number of men he had killed in the Maseret dance the Mein were so fond of. He looked up at her and grinned, and she hated him for the way motion sparked the beauty of his eyes to life. What eyes he had! They drew her gaze to them unerringly. It seemed he was lit from the inside, his face a lantern in human form and his eyes the outlets for the gray glow within him. There was peace in them. They affected her as would looking upon the turquoise water of one of the white sand beaches near Aos. Some things are just meant to be beheld. Hanish Mein's eyes—his entire face for that matter—were such things. It took considerable effort for Corinn to form her features into the suitable mask of cold disregard she always wore before him.

"The sun suits you so very well, Corinn," Hanish said. He spoke Acacian, as he almost always did to her. "Such an even complexion, so well suited to the brilliant summer days down here. By the way, I am pleased that you have been riding with my cousin and her circle."

"It is not a service I do willingly," Corinn said. "It was, you will remember, a command you yourself gave me."

Hanish smiled as if she had said something quite pleasing. "It is no easy task teaching Meinish women the ways of an imperial court. They are as ill prepared for it as our men were. I know, though, that they value your example to learn from."

Corinn had nothing to say to this. Hanish set the papers down on the desk, turned more fully toward her, and said, "I have news you might be interested in. Larken just returned from Talay. He brought back information on your brother." He waited a moment, studying Corinn for a reaction. "We have not found him, not yet at least. But I have no doubt we will. He is somewhere in Talay, in the interior. Larken believes he just missed him. He raided a village on a tip from one of the natives, but the Acacian who had been hiding there slipped away just ahead of him. Your brother Aliver has proven quite elusive."

"How do you know it is Aliver and not Dariel?"

Hanish shrugged. "I thought you might clarify that for me. Is it Aliver? Is it Talay that he was sent to?"

"Would it help you to know?"

"Yes, I admit it would."

Corinn stared straight into his eyes and answered honestly. "I have not the slightest idea."

Hanish did not look quite so pleased with her anymore. He looked like he might push free of the desk and close on her, but instead he crossed his arms and spoke in Meinish. "You have changed a great deal, haven't you, from the girl who stood before me nine years ago? Remember how we nursed you through the fever? The Numrek curse. Believe me, Princess, without our knowledge of the illness, you would have suffered much more greatly. Perhaps your siblings felt the full brunt of it, with no one to explain to them that it would likely pass. They will have changed also. It may be that you would not recognize them. Perhaps they would not recognize you. Maybe, Corinn, you are more one of us now than one of them."

Corinn's eyes snapped up, fixed on him, clear in their scorn for such a suggestion.

"Princess, where are your siblings?" Hanish pressed, speaking Acacian once more.

"You have asked me that before."

"And I will ask you again and again and again. It may be that you speak truthfully, but I would happily ask you the question five times a day for the next twenty years if it would help."

"After that would you stop?"

"After that I would ask you ten times a day for the next forty years, should I stay apart from the Tunishnevre that long. Corinn, you have lived nine years in my house, as a guest in the palace that was once yours. Have I harmed you? Have I cut a hair from your head or forced you in any way? Then help me find your siblings. As I have told you before, I want only that they return to your father's palace and live in peace, as you have done. Why do you prefer that they live in exile, in hiding in some corner of the provinces?"

"Wherever they are they are free," Corinn said. "I would not change that for the world. Neither would they."

"You're so sure of that, are you?" When Corinn did not answer, Hanish scowled. "All right, fine. It doesn't matter. We will find them. I have the time and the power. They have few friends and fewer resources. We almost captured one of your brothers. I am sure of it. This means he's on the run, apt to make mistakes, to trust someone he shouldn't. . . . Believe me, Corinn, they are not living the life of luxury that you are here. I am sorry we have spent so little time together. Years have passed, but still you are largely unknown to me. I would like to change this. I will not be traveling as much as I have been. You and I will spend more time together. I am confident that when you know me better you will like me more. Perhaps then we will be able to figure out what you and I are meant to be to each other. How does this sound to you?"

"May I go?" she asked, framing the question defiantly.

"You may always come and go as you please, Corinn. When will you acknowledge this?"

She turned without answering and put her back to him. She knew his eyes would follow her out of sight, fixed on her figure. This made it difficult to walk casually, but she managed it. She passed from one area of the chambers into another, and then turned a corner so that Hanish was soon far behind her. She had just exhaled a pent-up breath and started to let her face relax when she realized she was not yet free from observation.

Maeander stood in the passageway she would need to go through. He had just stepped in, and was saying something to somebody in the hallway. He noticed her, paused. Larken stepped in from behind him and took a few steps into the room before seeing the princess. He looked instantly amused. Though he was an Acacian, he spoke only Meinish now. Standing near Maeander the two of them were tall, slim, sculpted testaments to all things manly in their respective races.

Corinn kept moving toward them. She looked past them into the corridor, as if her eyes could latch on to something out there and pull her through them. She brushed past Larken without incident. As she reached Maeander, however, he shot his arm across the door, barring her way. She did not look at his face, but stared at the soft spot at the inner elbow of his muscled limb, covered in long golden hairs. An artery pulsed like a worm caught beneath his skin. She knew his eyes were on her, peering out from the shadows beneath the cornice of his brow. The touch of them was familiar. It seemed she had felt them ever since he first laid eyes on her, throughout each day that followed, in her dreams. She would sometimes awake looking sharply around the room, feeling that up until the moment of her awakening she had not been alone. This man, more than any other, had made her father's home into a menacing place, while barely uttering more than a few words to her.

As if recognizing this thought and considering it, Maeander did not speak now. He leaned toward her and touched the finger of his free hand to her chin. After studying her a few moments, he brought his face beside hers. The coarse hairs of his bristling beard brushed against her cheek. He turned and pressed his wet tongue against her temple, licked her with the warm flat of it.

Corinn yanked her head away. She slammed the blade of her hand into the joint of his arm and fled out into the hall. She heard Larken ask, "Does she taste sweet or sour? I've always wondered." She did not catch the answer. Later, she was not sure if she had actually heard Maeander's laughter following her, but it would seem so. It seemed to follow her everywhere. Hanish Mein could say whatever golden words he wished. Maeander was the truth behind the Mein façade. She would never trust them. She had stopped trusting men long ago. She was not about to start now. She had not a clue in the world as to where her brothers and sister had fled. She was sure, however, that they must have landed in situations preferable to hers.

Chapter

Thirty

The brig was going to run aground at full speed. It was right up against the reef, so close to it that the ship cut diagonally through the waves as they started to curl, teetering from one side to the other like an inebriated monstrosity. Spratling could see it all perfectly from the small platform that served as the *Ballan*'s crow's nest. He was about to watch as the prize he had been chasing for four days had its hull ripped out and its bounty spilled into the sea. He would have a bird's view of it, and he would have to tell Dovian all about it when he returned empty-handed. *Do something,* he thought. *Bloody do something, you fools! I haven't chased you all this way just to—*

The old pilot, Nineas, shouted up at him. The veteran sailor had a way of making his voice heard no matter the circumstances. "They're tacking back toward us! Spratling! You still want me to hold?"

The young captain yelled back that of course they should hold! Of course! Their quarry was a league vessel, not one of their large open ocean crafts, but still a catch of enormous value. It was one of the brigs they used to transport their senior members from the coastline out to their platform base, a floating city anchored to the ocean floor about a hundred miles northwest of the Outer Isles. Normally, the brigs traveled within the shelter of several warships, each of these manned with soldiers of the league's private military force, the Ishtat Inspectorate. Had it carried one of their board members, it would likely have borne riches unfathomable to a Sea Isle raider like Spratling. But it would have been impossible to get near without a fleet of ships. No one had ever even tried such an attack. This one, however, sailed all but empty by league standards, with no senior member aboard and not enough trade goods to merit deploying the Ishtat.

Spratling knew this because one of Dovian's spies, a so-called shifter, a master of disguise who had infiltrated the dockworkers of the league's coastal base, had sworn this vessel was likely to be the only vulnerable one they would see the rest of the year. The message had arrived the night before the brig sailed, but Dovian was confident they could act on it. With his blessing, Spratling had sailed the next morning. The *Ballan* was a slim clipper meant for speed, with a tall mainmast and light construction. It was not a warship by any reasonable standard. Because of this, the brig had likely disregarded them the first day they trailed her. They might have noticed the strange contraption lashed to the ship's bow, a sort of iron-backed series of connected planks tilted up on a large, reinforced hinge. At the top of it, projecting forward, was a hooked metal barb, treacherous looking at over seven feet long, sharp at the end, and as thick around as an arm for most of its length. It looked like a gangway that could be set down across a pier and hooked into place if the ship was to be unloaded over the bow, which would have been useful in the busier ports of the Inner Sea. But the purpose of the contraption was not nearly so benign, as Spratling hoped to prove. It was his design, after all. His "nail," as he liked to call it.

They had followed the brig through the Shallows and along the chain of islands that marked the best route through the Outer Isles. There had been other ships around, and Spratling had no desire that his attack be observed. He sailed casually, stopping at several harbors as if to trade and then using the *Ballan*'s superior speed to make up time. It was always easy to spot the brig, as its sides were a brilliant white, luminous and unnatural to behold.

By the third day the brig had grown wary. It increased its pace, all sails unfurled, but it was not until the morning of the fourth day that the *Ballan* chased the other ship to the brink of the shoals of one of the small atolls at the northern edge of the Outer Isles. The horizon was empty all about them, and Spratling let it be known this was the day. They would have the ship's treasures today or not at all. They pursued them with the wind at their backs. Speed was theirs, but it was no easy task maneuvering into position to use the nail. But then the brig careened around on a tack back from the reef, directly into their angle of sail. The captain must have known the reef better than Spratling imagined, but no matter. The angle of attack was finally right.

Though he hollered at the top of his lungs, he was not at all sure that they would hear him on the deck far below. With the whip of the wind and the spray flying up from the prow his words likely darted away into the sea vapors. Afraid lest his pilot choose from timidness to adjust his course, Spratling grabbed for the rope that stretched down from below the nest all the way to the deck. He wore the fingerless gloves he had adapted to this purpose in boyhood, during his first years at sea. He clamped onto the rope with a two-handed grip, his fingers interlacing over one another, and then he leaped free. He zipped down toward the deck with his usual dizzying speed, and was standing beside Nineas a moment later.

"Don't you even think about changing course!" he bellowed into the man's ear. "Steady on to meet them." He raised his voice even louder and projected it forward across the deck, which was crowded with his men, burly-armed raiders of various races, each with his own proclivities, his own chosen weapons, his own grievances and desires and reasons for having chosen a life of plunder. Slim and of medium build as he was, face handsome and boyish, muscles those of casual, easy youth, Spratling hardly looked man enough to direct this company. And yet, neither could he have looked more comfortable in the role. He spoke with ironic cordiality. "Everything as we planned, gentlemen. Everything as planned, and nothing before I shout the signals."

The prow of the brig dwarfed the *Ballan*'s crisp lines. It shoved its way through the water like a buxom barmaid through a drunken sea. It was so very white it did not look to be made of wood at all, though it had to be. Wire-framed posts bulged from the side of the brig in two lines, one row on the upper deck and one on the lower. They were just the size and shape to cradle the upper half of a man's body as he leaned out over the water. Crossbowmen squirmed into them and let loose an instant barrage of bolts. This was a weak defense considering what a fully manned league brig was capable of. There would have been two or three times the number of bowmen on a properly defended ship. Still, the missiles were smeared with a flammable pitch. Something in the mechanism of releasing them sparked them to flame. The ones that hit the *Ballan*'s side or deck or darted into the sails burned with an undousable flame. The best the *Ballan*'s men could do was to use shovels to knock the bolts loose, scoop them and the pitch up, and hurl them overboard. This attack had been expected.

The two ships carried on with their trajectory of collision. So near were they now, the *Ballan*'s speed seemed obscene, reckless. Spratling almost called for the wing sails to be furled, but there was not time. One of them had taken a bolt low, and the flames had already eaten a sizable hole in it anyway. Instead, he yelled to the men operating the nail, "Be ready!

Await my word!" Watching the distance between the two vessels close, he added almost as an afterthought, "Men about the deck, you might want to grip something."

In the last moments he ordered a turn to better match the brig's trajectory, to lessen the impact. The *Ballan* leaned to the effort of this, but when the two boats collided the force was something beyond the young captain's imaginings. The sound was horrendous, as was the wrenching pressure of the impact. Men pitched all about the boat as the deck leaned over to one side. A shoulder of water rose up and swept across them, taking two men away as it drained. The small fires sputtered and hissed and flared to life again. Spratling had managed to get out the order to release the nail before he went careening across the deck on his back. The great arm of the thing tilted into motion quite slowly, falling with its own momentum. Spratling, watching it from where he lay tangled against the railing, drenched and gasping, thought sure the mechanism had jammed in some way. It was falling too slowly. It might not even carry through the wood of the other ship.

But the weapon found its weight and speed. The steel point of the thing crashed through the other ship's deck. The sectional design of it worked perfectly, bending so that the point dug deep and then flexed the instant the weight of the two ships tugged on it. It tossed up fractured beams on either side of the impact and punched a hole that sucked several of the brig's men into it. The hook tore a jagged trench of splintering decking and beams in the brig as it carried on forward. It yanked the *Ballan*, and for a few moments Spratling could not get words out of his throat. They were like a pilot fish fastened precariously to an angry whale. He felt the iron point catching on crossbeams, felt them snapping under the force, one after another. Several of the crossbowmen were crushed between the two boats; the others all but gave up their attack and scrambled backward from their nests. All fine, except the nail was not going to hold! If it did not, they might well capsize from the jolt of coming unstuck and in the turmoil of waves and currents in the brig's wake.

Spratling made out Nineas's voice, asking him what they should do. Had he orders? He did not, but fortunately his momentary blankness was to go unnoticed. The nail finally caught and held fast. The *Ballan* seemed to find some amount of peace with its new position and steadied enough so that the men could get their feet under themselves again. A few faces turned to find Spratling, who shot to his feet. The next order was obvious.

"Board!" he yelled. "Board, board, board!"

Their clamber up the planking was mad and precarious, only manageable at all because they did not think it through. Spratling, like the rest of them, just acted. He ran, clawed, jumped, all so fast it passed in a trembling, jolting blur. It was startling to plant his feet upon the deck of the brig. Everything in sight was layered in a thick, slick white paint, just as the sides were. It coated each contour and protrusion as if the whole vessel had been dunked in wax and hung to dry. Spratling and the men tumbling aboard all around him stopped in their tracks, bewildered by the strange appearance of it. But this did not last long. They had business to attend to. There were sailors coming toward them. Bolts scorched through the air all around them. The sound of clashing swords already struck music into the din. It was likely to be bloody for a few moments at least, but such was raiders' work.

※

Three days later Spratling strode up from the docks, his feet crunching on the crushed white shells of the path into the raiders' town they called Palishdock. He walked at the vanguard of a growing crowd of people, his crew chief among them but swelled each step of the way as others joined them. Children clamored and exclaimed and shouted questions. Even the town's dogs could not contain their enthusiasm. Their proud son had returned triumphant, with booty to benefit them all! Spratling could not keep the grin from his face. Small, ragtag company of persons and animals that this was, still it pleased him to stand at the center of their adoration, to be important, loved, to see the faces of young women flushed and admiring him. Such a role in many ways came easily to him, but he did not take it for granted. He strove daily to earn it and to make Dovian proud. In this way he was still a boy and Dovian a father figure larger even than his weighty frame.

Palishdock had not begun as a permanent settlement. Though it was six years old now, one could see a transient laziness in the shoddy construction of the huts. They were breezy structures set into the knobs and hollows of the sandy landscape, with gaps in the boards and simple palm-frond roofs. The walls were often little more than a screen thrown up to provide shaded semiprivacy. Many people cooked on open fires outside their homes, leaving the scraps for the dogs and the thronging population of cats. The town had about it a casual air, as if the whole place might be abandoned at a whim if the mess became unbearable or their fortunes faltered. Of course, it did have a wonderful harbor. It was a little shallow but soft-bottomed, with a single narrow entry point that was barely visible from the sea due to the rippling shape of the shoreline and the camouflage of the high dunes. Indeed, the whole town sat sequestered from view. Only smoke might have given them away, but the hard wood of the shrubs that grew all about the island burned cleanly. Few passing on the sea would have thought the white vapors above the place anything other than a peculiar blanket of haze. It was a perfect raiders' retreat.

It had been Spratling's home since its founding, an event which he remembered well. He stood—a child still—at Dovian's hip when the big man looked about the harbor, grinning, declaring that this was it, this was just the place for them, hidden from the world and a fine location to get at the business of raiding and profiteering, kidnapping and whatever other forms of thievery struck their fancy. He had said it could be so, and with the boy at his side, he had fashioned a world to live up to those dreams.

Leaving the jubilant crowd in the courtyard of Dovian's Palace, where Nineas and the younger crew members could spin the grand tale of their capture of a league brig, Spratling ventured inside. He carried with him a single narrow box of ornate gold. Dovian's Palace was not, of course, an actual palace. It was a rambling hodgepodge of rooms and corridors only marginally better constructed than the huts of the village. Here and there beams and planks and sometimes entire sections of captured vessels had been used in the construction. The walls were hung with emblems, with nameplates and various samples of rigging, souvenirs won over the years. More than anything, the place resembled a labyrinthine fort best suited to boyish games of hide and seek, pirate's eye, and thump the tail. Spratling had played all these games and more in these corridors, never loving them more than in the days when Dovian was still up and about on his feet, nimble despite his size, as willing to run and play as any boy.

Spratling knocked on the doorframe of the man's room with his foot. Hearing the invitation to enter, the young man did so. There was no light except for that slipping through the numerous cracks in the walls and ceiling, but as his eyes adjusted, this proved sufficient to see by. Dovian was just where he had been for several months now, when he had taken sick with a pain deep in his bones, a cough that racked his chest, and limbs that were tingly and numb. His bed stretched along the far wall, and his form lay on it, a great mound of humanity propped up by feather pillows nearly flattened by his weight. His face was in shadow, but Spratling knew the man's eyes were on him.

The young captain stood at the edge of the room and recounted the details of the raid. He named the men who had been lost, saying a word of praise for each of them. He described the taking of the ship, the damage the *Ballan* suffered, the performance of the nail. It had worked well, he said, but they should put it on a different ship and probably use it only against smaller vessels. In truth, it had almost torn the *Ballan* to pieces. He described the brawl that took place on the brig's glistening white deck and detailed the treasure they had found inside. By league standards the ship was empty, but their standards were out of all natural proportion. His men had stripped it of every gold fixture they could find, all the silver cutlery, the ornate mirrors, the woven rugs, carved furniture, beautiful glass lanterns: all the trappings normal to a league vessel. Also, they had found a safe room and coerced the captain into opening it. He must have thought it was empty, because he seemed surprised to find a small shoebox-sized chest of league coins in it, the same chest Spratling now held in his two hands.

"How many did you kill?" the bedridden form asked.

"Ten men. Two boys. And . . . one girl. Theo cut her neck before he knew. I don't blame him."

"And what did you do with the others?"

"Bound them and locked them in the steerage. They've enough food and water to live for weeks, but I imagine the league will find them in a day or two."

"It's good that you show mercy."

Spratling smiled. "You taught me that, as you taught me how and when to kill. Anyway, a raider likes to leave a few witnesses alive to spread word of his deeds."

Dovian made a sound at this. Perhaps it was a guffaw or perhaps a cough. He motioned with the bear paw that was his hand. Spratling moved across the room, placed a knee on the rug-covered floor, and looked into the large man's face. Dovian stared back at him, bulky featured, creviced by time in the sun in the manner of Candovians. He had lost weight steadily for weeks now, but he was still a formidable figure. He lifted one hand and dropped the weight of it on Spratling's shoulder. He squeezed the slim muscle of it with pressure enough to be painful. But it was not an admonishment, and Spratling did not wince.

"You've done me proud, lad," Dovian said. "You know that, don't you? I wasn't sure you were coming back from this one."

Spratling smiled wryly and acknowledged, "It was a bit dicey."

Dovian studied him, weighing the implications of this, perhaps imagining the understatement it represented. "It is no joy to me that your work is as bloody as it is, but that is nothing we can change. We did not make the world, did we? Did not give it shape and substance and set one man against another. None of that was our doing, was it, lad?"

The young man nodded agreement.

If this was meant to make the older man happy, it failed. It seemed to do just the opposite. The large, unwieldy components of Dovian's face twisted as if physically pained. He planted a knuckle of his other hand in his eye as if to gouge it out. "I guess my work is done, then. I've taught you everything I could. Now look at you: eighteen years of age and already a leader. I'll not complain now that I know for certain you are a man who can thrive in the world. That's the best I could do. I'm sorry if it's no life for a prince—"

"Stop it! Come now, I won't stay if you're going to blubber like last time. I come back having taken a league brig and you start in moaning about the past again? I just will not have it. Do you want me to leave?"

Dovian stared at him for a long moment. "At least the men see the royalty in you. No, they do. And don't you go; you're not dismissed yet! They do see royalty in you. They don't know what they're seeing, but you have got a command over them that's grand to behold. They follow you where they would never follow other men. I named you Spratling so that none would imagine you are royal. Just one tiny fish like a million others in the sea. But there is no denying it, lad, you've nobility spilling out of your eyes, out of your mouth each time you open it."

"Even when I'm cursing?"

"Even then . . ." The man seemed to sink farther back into his pillows, pleased by whatever image filled his head. "Even then you were still my Dariel, the prince who sought out the likes of me in the caverns below the palace. Why did you do that, lad? Such a strange thing for a boy like you to be up to, roaming the dark underneath. I've never understood it."

"Don't try to. Anyway, I cannot remember enough to enlighten you." Spratling indicated the box he had placed at the edge of the bed. "Would you look at what's in this chest?"

"You really don't?"

"No. All I remember and all I want to remember is this life. This— what we have here—is all that matters," he said, infusing the statement with all the certainty he could muster.

He tried all the harder because it was not true. Not exactly, at least. It was rather that he could not make sense of the memories preceding his life with Dovian. He could not understand them with any sort of clarity. The very thought of those early times seemed to weaken him. They pulled on him with a melancholy power otherwise absent from his days. When he did allow himself to think back to when he was still called Dariel Akaran it was his flight from the war and Val's role in saving him that he wished to recall.

He had left Kidnaban in the care of a man who called himself a guardian. This soldier had lifted Dariel straight out of slumber one morning and walked away with the boy in his arms. He had explained himself as he walked, though Dariel had been groggy and later could not remember what the man had said to soothe him. They had sailed from Crall to the mainland in just a few hours and were on their feet for two days thereafter. By the third, the man bought a pony for Dariel to ride, as the boy was exhausted, his feet blistered. He was apt to cry at any moment and often asked after his brother and sisters and begged to go back to them or to go home. The guardian was not unkind, but he seemed uncomfortable around children and often stared at the boy as if he had never seen a person cry before and could not for the life of him understand the waste of moisture.

The man explained that his father had arranged for him to be cared for by a friend in Senival. All they had to do was reach him and the boy's ordeal would be concluded, everything safe, all explained. They headed west and for several days wound their way through a scarred landscape similar to what he had seen of the Cape of Fallon mines, mountainsides bored into, whole swathes in which all the land in view had been maimed by human butchery. These, the guardian explained, were the Senivalian mines. All around went dust-covered laborers, men and boys mostly but also women and some girls. They wore the rags of their lot and all seemed busy, although they paid little heed to their usual work. He heard them shout bits and pieces of frantic news, full of import that he could not fathom, except that none of it seemed good.

Of this place and its significance to his father's empire Dariel had not the slightest inkling, except that his guardian, on taking in a view of the land tainted crimson by the setting sun, said, "What a hell we've made here. A hell with a golden crown that calls itself—" The guardian had stopped short, remembering Dariel, and said that they had better head on. They were almost to their destination.

Coming down a winding road into the mountain town to which Dariel was supposed to have been delivered, the guardian paused. "What's this?" he asked.

The village had a lovely aspect to it, sitting as it did in a flat valley rimmed by peaks. For a few moments Dariel thought it pleasant to look on, until he noticed the stillness of the place. Nobody moved about the streets.

No animals or farmers worked the fields. Not a single puff of smoke escaped the chimneys of the houses. "This isn't right," the guardian said. Dariel could not dispute it.

What happened to the townspeople Dariel never knew. They were simply gone, and try as he might the guardian found no sign of the man he sought. He sat down on a log stool, taking in the place, and then he folded his head into his hands and stayed silent in thought for what seemed like hours. Dariel stood nearby, holding the pony's reins as it cropped the sweet mountain grass.

When the guardian looked up, he was full of purpose. He would go to the next town, he declared. It was over a day's ride farther west. If he left at that moment he could reach the place by sunrise, and if he found the answers he needed to there, he would be back by nightfall. Perhaps somebody was looking for him. Best that the guardian check things out and return with a better idea how to proceed. He would have to ride fast, though, so he arranged to leave Dariel in a hut just a little way out of town. He left his shoulder bag for the boy, and said this was all for the best.

The man rode away. Dariel heard the clack of the pony's hooves for some time, and when the sound eventually faded, he was filled with dread. He had not even protested, said not a word. How could he when he knew the man was lying to him?

He spent that night in blackness, trembling and fearful, as small as a mouse and just as helpless. It rained steady and chill for some hours, and when it abated, mist crept through the valley like wraiths. He made no fire, did not think to fetch the blanket from the pack the guardian left, did not even fully recognize the hunger in his belly for what it was. As the bleak reality of his situation was so beyond his power to face, he balked from doing so. Inside, he fantasized his father lived again and was on the way to rescue him. He entertained all sorts of fancies with ravenous hope. Perhaps it was a good thing, too, because when salvation came it was no more predictable or likely than any of his fancies, but he was ready to accept it with open arms.

※

Sitting now on the stool beside his savior's sickbed, Spratling asked, "Do you remember the night you found me?"

"Like it was yesterday, lad."

"That is where I begin, you know? You were a shadow that pushed through the door and found my hiding place—"

"That hovel!" Dovian interrupted. "A disgrace that you ever spent a night there."

"I remember your words exactly," Spratling continued. "You said . . ."

※

"Who would have thought," the shadow had said, pushing into the hut behind a yellow lantern held high, "that you could find a prince just anywhere these days? I guess some of us are lucky."

Dariel might have remembered the words well, as he said, but that night it took him a moment to realize what was happening. He had been three days in hiding. Some portion of him still thought the guardian might return, though in deeper regions he had already started to give up on all hope. What a familiar voice, he'd thought. But whose was it, and how was it here? Dariel knew he recognized it, but for a few frightened moments he could not place it within the context of this mountain hut.

The shadow moved closer. "Are you all right, rascal? Don't be scared. It's Val. It's Val come to help you out."

Val? Dariel thought. Val from the caverns below the palace—the feeder of the kitchen ovens . . . His Val! He got to his feet, stumbled forward, and fell against the man's chest. Once he inhaled the salty, pungent, coal-smoked largeness of him, he released a horde of pent-up fears in great sobs. He clenched Val's shirt in his fists and rubbed his tears and snotty nose into the fabric, as would a baby ill to the point of delirium with cold and fever.

"Oh, don't do that, lad," Val said softly. "Don't do that. Things will be all right now."

And, true to his word, they were. At least, they were as all right as possible in the circumstances. It turned out that Val had been on his way home to Candovia, one of many in the migration spurred by the war. He had happened upon Dariel's guardian by pure chance in a makeshift camp pitched at the side of the highway of fleeing refugees. The man was well into a bottle of plum wine and did not mind confessing to anyone around him that he had been personal guardian to one of the king's children. Val had situated himself close enough to smell the man's sickly-sweet breath. He probed him until he confessed just who he had been looking after and where he had left his duty and turned coward. He could not find the person he was meant to deliver the boy to! He was gone, probably dead, and the guardian had no further instructions as to how to proceed. And with the news coming from all around—Maeander in Candovia, Hanish having destroyed the army at Alecian Fields—there was nothing he could do for the boy anymore. Sure, he'd left him to his own fate, but what else could he have done?

Val never exactly described what he did to the guardian, except to mutter something about how he would have to gum nothing harder than goat cheese for the rest of his days, or something like that. It did not make a bit of sense to the boy, but the visual image it conjured in him held his perplexed attention for much of the long walk Val led him on. He knew just the place for them, Val had said, a grand and expansive place in which to disappear. For much of the journey the boy rode atop the Candovian's shoulders, a leg to either side of his neck, fingers intertwined in the man's curly mass of hair.

They were three days coming out of the mountains, and by the fourth Dariel could smell the salt in the air. That afternoon, half asleep on the man's shoulders, Dariel heard Val say, "Look, lad. That's no sea, there. That's a place a whole race of men could hide upon."

They had paused on a bluff with a view of all the world to their west. Even though Dariel had lived all of his years on an island he could tell in a glance that the body of water before them was different. It was not the turquoise blue or the marine green that he was used to. Instead, the water was a slate-dark color a shade under black, undulating with swelling surges that conveyed their force through slow bulk. Near the shoreline, crests of countless waves rose like liquid mountains, seemed to hang stretched to the air for a moment, then curled over into a foaming chaos. Occasionally, the clap of the wave's impact slapped against his ears, always strangely timed, in a way impossible to match sight with the sound. Staring from atop his giant's shoulders, Dariel had never seen anything as awesome in its power and scale.

"That's the tongue of the Gray Slopes," Val said. "It is a boundless ocean. That's where you'll vanish from your father's world and emerge into mine instead."

Dariel had not said anything in response. For weeks now there had been a vague fear hanging over him, as ever present as the sky. Some portion of him had never believed he could carry on without his family. He would vanish without them. The world would swallow him. The Giver's fingers would pluck him from the earth and flick him into nothingness. He feared he was of no more substance than a flame and just as easily extinguished. But here he was. The world carried on as it always had, and he still moved through it. He went on; he had something at his center just as solid and real as the rest of the world. He really could vanish from one world and emerge into another, he thought. Vanish and emerge anew . . .

That was exactly what he had done. Val gave him a new life, bestowed on him a new name even as he took one for himself. He taught him that the tales he had told of being a blood-soaked pirate in his youth were not just make-believe, as the boy had thought. Val—Dovian, in short for his native country—came from the long line of raiders he had claimed. On arriving back among the Outer Isles it did not take him long to reestablish himself and set about building a fleet of ships and getting sailors to man them. The world was ripe for plunder. The Known World was in near chaos, grudgingly coming to terms with Hanish Mein's new rule. Many groups jostled to find a place in the redistribution of power this entailed. Val sailed with Dariel tucked under his wing; taught him everything he could about sailing and fighting, pirating, commanding men; about surviving this cruelest of existences.

That which came before—the palace of Acacia, his role as prince, his father's empire, and three others born of him and his mother, Aleera Akaran—well, it seemed to be clearer in Val's mind than in Dariel's. Why try to hold on to people he would never see again? He had been so young that his memories had not stuck in his head with an ordered clarity. Yes, there were images. There were moments of emotion that seemed to take him by the neck and close off the air to his lungs. There were times when he awoke from dreams fearing that something was horribly wrong, but he grew to tolerate this as the years passed. Maybe such was just what it meant to be alive.

Spratling—yes, that was his name now and there was no reason to slip back to that scared child persona any more than he had to—flipped open the small latch of the chest and tipped the contents onto Dovian's bed, a slithering tumble of gold coins. The man stared at them, ran his fingers over them, tested their feel on his palm. He whispered that this was it. This was just what they had needed. This would fund everything. . . .

He plucked up an object between his fingers and held it up to a ribbon of sunlight. It was gold—gold colored at least, though the workmanship was almost too fine and sharp edged for such a soft metal. The shape of it was unusual. It was the thickness of a large coin, slightly square, ridged along one end, inscribed with markings that might have been writing but which bore no similarity to any language either of them had seen. There was a single hole at its center, just slightly oblong.

Spratling had not noticed it before. "What is it?"

Dovian thought on this for some time. Spratling could almost see him sorting through his memories, a lifetime's catalog of labeled and priced treasures. "I've no idea," he finally said. "It's a fine thing, though." He pressed it to the young man's chest. "Here. Keep it there around your neck. If you ever get in trouble and need a fast fortune you can melt it down and make coins. It's yours. The rest of this is more than we need for what we have planned. Bring me those charts and look them over."

Spratling did so, spreading the familiar images across the cot and sitting on the edge of the bed. He loved moments like this, when Val seemed to forget his ailments and the two of them got lost in contemplation, like a father and a son, scheming, planning, dreaming a swashbuckling world into existence. In many ways Spratling was still the boy Dariel had been. He had no inkling yet of how much that was soon to change.

CHAPTER

THIRTY-ONE

There was one particular Talayan acacia tree that was to haunt Thaddeus's dreams afterward. It rose solitary out of the plain. It stood like an old, black-skinned man, leaning to one side as if gentling an infirmity. It was precariously thin, its limbs crooked and decrepit, its leaves so sparsely dispersed that Thaddeus was not sure until he stood under it that the thing still lived. It did. Acacia trees were hardy, slow growing, thorned against enemies, and stoic against the vagaries of weather. Perhaps there should have been something comforting in this, but, if so, Thaddeus could not find it. Nothing in this country comforted him. Never had the mute grandiosity of a landscape so pressed upon him as it did when he stood in the sparse shade beneath that tree. The curve of the earth seemed more gradual than elsewhere, distances greater, shapes of hills out there more massive. The vault of the sky seemed higher in Talay than it did anyplace else. It stretched up and up, shoved aloft by seething white clouds, stacked like pillars supporting some massive temple. Everywhere he looked—below and above him, at each point of the compass, near and far—creatures moved into and out of view. He could not number or name or categorize all of them, but he suspected each to be a spy intent on studying him.

Of the six provinces of the former Akaran Empire none was more complex, nor more important, than Talay. In breadth it was as wide a land mass as Candovia, Senival, the Mainland, and Aushenia combined. It stretched away to the south in sun-baked folds of land, unmapped regions vast enough that the Acacians never charted all of it in their twenty-two generations of rule. Much of it was so arid that no rain fell to the earth at all. While the name of one particular tribe was assumed by the entire territory, in truth Talayans were just the favored nation among many others.

Some have argued that Edifus was an ethnic Talayan, but Edifus himself never claimed such ancestry.

What was indisputable is that the Talayans were the first people on the continent to align themselves with Edifus. In return, he granted them dominion over their neighbors and the responsibility of policing them. No small thing. The province was home to thirty-five other chiefdoms, with nearly the same number of languages and featuring four racial groups so distinct from one another that no generalities could apply to the people of the province as a whole. It was true that they all were dark skinned, but within this was considerable variety, not to mention greater physiological diversity than anywhere else in the Known World. Many of these nations were numerous enough to be military powers in their own right. The Halaly, the Balbara, the Bethuni: in the late Akaran age, each of these could field armies of ten thousand men. The Talayans themselves could call up nearly twenty-five thousand of their own, and, of course, they had the right to levy troops from the others. If their authority had held, the war with Hanish Mein might have taken a different course. It did not, however, for reasons rooted in the soil of antique history.

Old animus does not die, Thaddeus thought. It just awaits opportunity.

Such thoughts came to him unbidden, adding to his unease. Perhaps he had been too many years in hiding. Too long wormed into the cave systems of Candovia, in places dark and moist, with the earth close around him, hearing low grumbles like those deep in a fat man's belly. But he had not felt so ill at ease when he first emerged and set about his work. He had felt confident enough in his abilities as he gathered information, as he pulled in his spies and learned all they could tell him. He had had no doubts about himself when he sought out the old general and set him on a new path. So why the dread clinging to him now?

Perhaps, he tried to believe, it was just that he was so very far from home, getting farther each day from the latitudes in which he had spent his life. These lands were quite different even from the lush country he had already passed through in northern Talay. Rolling farmland had stretched off as far as his fading eyes could see, dotted by tree lines dividing the fields, with occasional villages. It was nature manicured, hemmed in, and tamed by generations of human effort. And it was more abundantly populated. Their numbers, Thaddeus knew, had been thinned by the contagion. They had been ravished by it and by the war, as had most of the provinces. There were markedly few men of middle age, but the women seemed to have fared better. And there were many children. The place had thronged with them, which must have pleased Hanish Mein. He had made it law that all women who could bear children *had* to bear them. The Known World needed to be repopulated. They required numbers to thrive, new loved ones to replace those lost, new citizens to help the world turn. Thaddeus understood better than anyone exactly why this mattered so much to Hanish.

The former chancellor's destination was farther south than he had ever been, well into the parched plains and rolling hills at the heart of Talay. It was a distance of several hundred miles, a long way for a man his age to trek. He chose to walk, however. Lone, rambling, and mind-addled madmen were no rarity in the world. He could have roamed indefinitely without drawing the slightest notice from the thinly spread soldiers of the Mein. Perhaps also there was an overture of penance in his march, though he did not define this even to himself.

He arrived dust-covered in the court of Sangae Uluvara. Tucked into the shallow bowl beneath two bulbous ridges of volcanic rock, the village of Umae was made up of fifty-odd huts; a handful of warehouses and storage pits; and a central structure built of wood and thatch that served like a great canopy above the market, offering shade from the sun and cover from the rain alike. Sangae's people numbered a couple of hundred souls. As they were a herding culture, rarely was all the population gathered together. The village was in a remote spot in the world, unmarked on many maps, perhaps unknown to the Mein altogether. Indeed, they would have had to have searched very deeply to find the place or to discover a record of the bond of friendship the late king Leodan had once shared with Sangae, long ago, in their youth. No living person besides Thaddeus knew of the man's importance to the Akaran legacy.

Summoned from inside his shady compound, Sangae stepped out into the sun with fluttering eyelids. He stared at Thaddeus with the trembling intensity he might have beheld an apparition with. A tumult of thoughts passed across his features, emotions that seemed to writhe just beneath his skin. Thaddeus knew that even this far south the man would have heard rumors that cast aspersions on his reputation. Sangae might still be unsure which chancellor was before him now: the traitor or the savior. And this would only be part of the noise within him. This man had been an adoptive father for nine years now. He could not but fear what Thaddeus's arrival meant for his son.

But when Sangae spoke, he did so from a place of controlled formality. He said, "Old friend, the sun shines on you, but the water is sweet."

"The water is cool, old friend, and clear to look upon," Thaddeus answered.

It was a traditional greeting of southern Talay, and it pleased Sangae that the former chancellor responded to it so smoothly and in Talayan. But then he switched to Acacian. "It has been a long time," he said. "Long enough that I wondered if you would come. Long enough that I hoped you might not."

Thaddeus found this statement harder to respond to than the first. The chieftain held the former chancellor's eyes with his. His nose and lips, the round forehead and the wide wings of his cheekbones: each of his features seemed more full of generosity than a single face should have been able to contain. His features had a fullness at odds with his slim torso, his thin shoulders, taut-skinned chest. His eyes were no whiter than Thaddeus's, no less veined and yellowed, yet they stood out in contrast to the night black of his skin. For a moment Thaddeus felt a spike of fear rise up through him. How would a royal child of Acacia have fared alone among these people? He could not grasp even the edge of such a concept and hold on to it. It might have been a terrible mistake. He turned from the thought, for doubt had no place in how he meant to present himself. "In the king's name, friend," he said, "I thank you for what you have done."

"I can see nothing," Sangae said, another phrase particular to his people, a denial that he had done anything that merited thanks.

"You speak my tongue better than I do yours."

"I've had one to practice with for some years now. How was your journey?"

The two talked for some time on this subject, an easy one, for it held nothing of the import of why he was here. Only details. But such amiable banter could last only for so long, and Thaddeus—despite his fear of the answer—finally asked, "Is the prince well?"

Sangae's head dipped in something like a nod, although it was not quite an affirmation. He motioned for Thaddeus to enter his compound and sit across from him on a brightly colored woven mat. Between them, a girl set a gourd of water. A moment later she placed a bowl of dates beside it, and then she withdrew. The walls were open all around them. Even inside, the people of Umae wished for space, for open views and moving air. Thaddeus could see and hear people in each direction, but there was solitude in the quiet space the two men occupied. It was surprisingly cool, considering the blistering heat of the direct sunlight. This was good.

"Aliver hunts the laryx," the chieftain eventually said. "He has been out two weeks. Billau willing, he will return any day now. But we should not talk of it. It would not be good to warn the spirit beasts of his intent. You, of course, are my guest until he returns." The man plucked up a date in his fingers. Having done so, he seemed to have no interest in consuming the fruit. "Nine years. Nine years since the boy arrived here, long enough that I truly began to believe that you would not come and that Aliver was truly my son. I have no other, you know, which is my curse."

Thaddeus considered responding to this apparent self-pity harshly. Better to have never had a child than to have lost one to treachery, he thought. But he had no wish to take the conversation in that direction. Instead, he said, "You've had no trouble from the Mein?"

"Never," Sangae said. "I have heard of them, but they've not heard of me, it seems." He grinned. "My fame is not as great as I might have wished. Take water, please."

Thaddeus lifted the gourd, cradled it in his palms, and drank deeply. He offered it to the chieftain, who did the same. "It was good that we sent him here, then. Hanish has never ceased from hunting the Akaran children. At least one of Leodan's children grew as the king wished."

Sangae commented that he knew nothing, of course, about the other three Akarans. But, yes, Aliver's course had been in keeping with the king's plans. Aliver's lone guardian had spirited him away efficiently from Kidnaban. They had sailed to Bocoum, disembarked, and joined the flow of refugees fleeing the war. They traveled on horseback for a time, then with a camel caravan, and then they simply walked the flat plains that brought them to Umae. With their need for secrecy, the journey took many weeks, and the prince arrived angry, confused, bitter. It took some effort on Sangae's part to convince him that this exile was not defeat. The conflict was not decided yet. He was the most recent in a line of great leaders. He reminded him that the blood of ancient heroes coursed through his veins. He spoke of Edifus and Tinhadin, of the obstacles they had overcome to rise to power. Had not the difficulties facing them seemed insurmountable? And yet they had. And Aliver would do the same, Sangae promised, it was just he needed time to grow into the man he would have to be.

Sangae folded his large hands across one knee. "That is what I told him. He gave me the King's Trust for safekeeping, and I have kept it hidden all these years. He has had a good life here, living like a Talayan. This is truth. And you should know that he is not a child anymore. Not by any means."

"Tell me of his life here, then."

In the nine years of his exile in Talay, Sangae said, Aliver had assumed a role identical to any son of a noble Talayan warrior family. He had trained in the martial arts of this nation, mastering spear work and the brawling form of wrestling Talayans practiced and even honing his body into that of a runner. It must have been terribly hard work at first. He might have been skilled enough in the Forms, but that had done little to prepare him for the training he received in Talay. Even spear practice was a different venture altogether. Unlike the Forms, Talayan warfare allowed no actions not entirely necessary. From the first day he held a Talayan spear, he had been taught that it was a weapon meant to kill. He had been shown the myriad ways that it could do so, each efficient and quick, with little wasted time or effort. He was challenged time and again, in the martial arts physically, by the harshness of the land, by language and culture, by the fact that he had no status here except what he could earn through his actions.

"And did he meet these challenges?" Thaddeus asked.

Sangae answered that he had. He had never shown himself wanting in discipline, desire, or bravery. He could not imagine what went on in the young man's mind, as he shared so little of himself, but he was earnest in every act. Perhaps too earnest. He had yet to learn to laugh like a Talayan. He had received his first tuvey band—which meant he had taken part in a skirmish with a neighboring tribe—with the youngest men of his age group. He wore it above his bicep. That was why he had every right to hunt the laryx and to claim—should he be successful—his place as a man of this nation, one old enough to own property, to marry, to sit at council beside the elders.

"Belonging is important," Sangae said, "and Aliver belongs among us. No one in this village would say otherwise. He has companions here, women who lie with him. No one notices his skin any longer. Such difference is no great thing among family. He belongs among us."

Thaddeus heard a double meaning in this, a slight edge to the chieftain's voice. Yes, he acknowledged silently, it was always hard to lose a son, even an adopted one. Again he thought of his own losses, and he wondered why it was that the things a person had lost—or might lose—defined him more than the things he yet possessed.

"I don't know how he'll receive you," the chieftain continued, "but do know that he has not forgotten why he was sent here. In truth, I think he ever thinks only of what the future holds for him. This angers him, and yet . . . that is how he is."

"What of the contagion?"

"The prince burned with it like most of my people. He weathered it, though, and is no worse for it now." Sangae was quiet a moment. He turned his gaze away and watched a bird hop through the glare of a lane some distance away. "What will you ask of him?"

"I ask nothing. His father has, and it is for Aliver alone to answer it. This laryx, is it dangerous to hunt?"

Sangae turned to gaze at him. "Few men ever accomplish a test so great."

When hunting a laryx, Sangae explained, one actually becomes the *hunted* for most of the contest. One first riles the beast by finding a nest it is currently using for bedding. The hunter fouls the area, kicking the matted grasses with his feet, urinating on it, spitting, squatting to defecate. After that, he waits nearby until the creature returns, catches his scent, and pursues him. That is when the hunt begins.

"You see, a laryx does not take insult well. Once on a scent, it will follow it until it either kills the offender or drops from exhaustion. The hunter must run before it, staying near enough that the beast does not lose the scent. But not too close. One twisted ankle, a bad route chosen, or if one overestimates his stamina . . . any of these things mean death. The only way to kill the beast is to run it to complete exhaustion and then to attack it with all you have left, hoping that is enough. If Aliver triumphs, he will have been through a physical and mental ordeal that cannot really be imagined. He will have lived with a demon panting at his back for hours, with death one misstep away. This is not a challenge he had to take. He chose it, and I have been praying ever since that he was ready for it. Men die at this effort, Thaddeus. It may be that you never get a chance to take him from me. If you are blessed to look into his living eyes, you can know for certain that he is strong. Strong in a way no Akaran has been for many generations."

"Do you believe he was ready for this hunt?"

"We will see," Sangae answered.

The unease this response filled Thaddeus with remained throughout the three days he waited for Aliver's return. How cruel, he mused, would it be if the prince died now, just before I invite him to find his destiny?

But he need not have worried. When Aliver arrived, he did so amid a cacophony of jubilation that could announce only triumph. Thaddeus stood in the small room Sangae had offered him, watching the scene through a window propped open with a stick. The tumult of black bodies was tremendous. They thronged into the streets like a school of fish in frenzy, all of them learning of the hunter's return at once, each of them dropping whatever activity he had been engaged in. They seemed more numerous than the village population. Where had they all come from? Thaddeus almost stepped out and joined them, but he felt a need to stay hidden as yet, to observe from the shadows inside his open-air window.

They swarmed around some sort of wheeled conveyance. It was a cart pulled by several men, a thing large enough that normally it would have been harnessed to one of the long-horned oxen the villagers used for larger loads. But instead the men had grasped its leading poles with their bare hands. Thaddeus could not make out exactly what it bore until it passed by his vantage point. It was still a distance away but near enough that he drew back a step. It was a beast, a dead creature so large that at first he wondered if several of the things were piled on top of one another. There was something wolflike in its long limbs, something of a laughing dog in the thickness of its neck, something boarlike in its snout, but it was none of these creatures. Beneath its scraggly coat the beast was purple skinned, a dry, pocked, and scarred surface, scaled by peeling patches. It was a horrible thing, a monster. How could Aliver have killed such a thing with only a spear? It scarcely seemed possible.

A young boy climbed up onto the wagon and tugged the creature's ears. Several others grabbed it by the hair around its neck and yanked the head this way and that, to roars from the crowd. Still another leaned his weight onto the lower jaw, opening the mouth enough that he could feign sticking his head inside it. But he thought better of this and leaped away in exaggerated fear, stirring still greater mirth.

All this was nothing compared to the reception the hunter himself received. He was easy to pick out. He marched through the throng like an epic hero brought back to life, returning to universal adoration. Or like the ghost of this hero, a paler form of man than those around him. He shouldered his way through arms patting him, faces pushing close to his, each person with some comment to make, so many white teeth moving close to him. They looked, for a strange instant, like creatures thrusting forward to take bites from him, but Thaddeus knew this to be a corruption of his own eyes and not true to the scene before him.

Thaddeus was surprised by Aliver's height. He was a full head taller than his father had been. Under the constant burn of the sun, his skin had ripened like oiled leather, though it was still pale compared to that of Talayans. He was bare chested. The striations of his muscles carved fine, well-proportioned lines. His wavy hair was tinged with yellow highlights, making it much lighter than it ever would have been back in Acacia. Because of this he might have seemed out of place in a far southern Talayan village. And yet, at the same time he had never looked more at home within himself. He was a sculpted, sun-burnished, hard- and lean-muscled man, strong in the exuberant, absurd manner of youth. He wore that gold ring—the tuvey band—above his left bicep as if it were a part of him and had always been there. He took the attention well, smiling and answering comments in kind, but with no air of superiority.

For a moment Thaddeus wondered if there was a hint of humility in his expression, if in fact he had not killed the beast as these folks imagined. Many an Acacian noble took credit for kills made by their servants. Watching a little longer, he decided that whatever Aliver held back he did so for reasons other than shame. He sent word to Sangae that he did not wish to disrupt Aliver's homecoming. He asked that Aliver be sent to him later that afternoon, once the commotion had died down.

When they did meet, nothing went as Thaddeus had expected. Months before, when he had imagined this meeting, Thaddeus had thought to greet Aliver with an embrace. He would pull the lad in and squelch any distance between them, any recrimination. The bond would be instant. A touch would do it, and everything else would fall into place. But as Aliver closed the last few steps that separated them, Thaddeus knew that had been a fantasy.

"Hello, Aliver," he said. He was relieved that he still had some control, spotty though it had become. "I come to you with a call to your destiny. And I arrive at the proper moment. I see you are a monster slayer today. Congratulations. Your father would have been proud."

How strange, Thaddeus thought, that so much of the boy lived in this man's features—in the set of his eyes and the crinkle of his upper lip and in the full shape of his head. Yet the face was that of a stranger as well. Staring at him was like listening to a discordant note woven into a familiar song. He had lost all of his soft edges, though this effect was as much a matter of his severe demeanor as it was his sharp features. Was that defiance flaring behind his eyes? Anger? Surprise or disappointment? Thaddeus could not tell, though he held on through the prince's answering silence, trying to read him.

"Did you really kill that beast yourself?"

When Aliver finally spoke, there was a hint of a Talayan accent in his voice, a looseness of the tongue around the vowels, but he had lost no fluency in his native tongue. "I have learned to do many things. So you are not dead?"

Not the greeting Thaddeus had hoped for. "Sit down, please," he said. The words came out before he thought them, but he was glad. He still looked calm. He knew that. He still had some command. He waited until Aliver lowered himself, his legs scissored together, cross-legged, his back as straight as a board.

Thaddeus lifted a letter from the low table before him. "Let us begin with this, Prince. Read it. It is important that you do."

"You know what it says?"

Thaddeus nodded. "But I am the only one."

"This is not my father's hand," Aliver said, after glancing at the words briefly.

"It is my hand, but his words. Read them and judge."

The young man bent his head to the paper. His eyes slid down it, rose, and slid down it again. Thaddeus looked away. It is not right to watch as another reads. He knew the words by heart anyway. He knew all the ways Leodan had expressed his love for his firstborn. He tried not to think of them, to allow Aliver that privacy. He could not, however, fight back the memory of the words the letter ended with, for he would have to address them when the prince looked up at him.

"This cannot be serious," Aliver said. He had stopped reading. His eyes were dead on the page, neither looking up nor moving over the words any longer.

"It is all serious. Which portion do you doubt?"

The young man flicked the paper, just enough to indicate that all of it was in question. "This talk of the Santoth, the God Talkers . . . that cannot be serious. My father, if he meant to tell me this, must have been close to death. He was not thinking clearly. Look what this says. *Son,*" he pretended to quote flippantly, "*now that you are grown, it's time you save the world . . .* and he asks me to do it by seeking out some mythic mad magicians."

"The Santoth may be as real as you and I."

Aliver set his gaze on the man. "May be? Have you seen one? Have you worked magic or seen it done?"

"There are records," Thaddeus began and then had to lift his voice above Aliver's rebuttal. "There are records—of which you know nothing—that testify to the Santoth in great detail."

"Myth!" Aliver spat the word, making it a curse.

"Myth lives, Aliver! That is a truth as undeniable as the sun or the moon. Do you see the moon at this moment? No, but you believe you will again. Your father tells you the Santoth can walk the Known World again.

They can help us win back power as they did before. All they need is for you—an Akaran prince who will be king—to remove their banishment. This is part of why you were sent to Talay, to be nearest to the Santoth, so that you would know this land and have the skills to search them out, to hunt for them. Your brother and sisters went each to their different places as well, although little of that went as we wished. I will tell you about all of it, Aliver. You will know everything I know. Everything. I will tell you news of Hanish Mein as well. He is planning something for his ancestors, the Tunishnevre. They are another force that you might think were no more than myth, and yet it is they who gave Hanish the power—"

"Who is this 'us' you mentioned?"

"There are many who await your return. In a manner of speaking, the whole world awaits you. There are reasons only you can—"

"Why should I care about your world or believe a word you say? I have found another life, with people who speak only truth."

Thaddeus felt his pulse hammer along his neck. He had a momentary impulse to slap his hand over it, but he controlled it. "There was a time when you called me uncle. You loved me. You said so with your child's mouth, and I loved you in return. I am still that man. And I know that you care about the fate of the world. You always have. Nothing could beat that out of you. Aliver, this is what your father intended. The things you have learned here . . . the man you have become . . ." Aliver's face was unreadable, utterly unreadable, and it caused Thaddeus to pause. "I see you want to be a mystery to me, but you are not." With greater certainty he repeated, "You are not."

"You say what I do is my choice?"

"Yes."

Aliver said, "Then you have already spoken half-truths to me. You know I have no choice. Nor have you admitted that you betrayed my father. An honest man would have done so from the start. Yes, I know. How could I not? The world knows of Thaddeus Clegg's treachery. Hanish Mein himself declared it, and I heard of it before I even arrived here, while still in the camel caravan. Men debated whether you were evil or just a fool. I did not add my voice to theirs, but I know the truth: you are both. You may not have put the blade in his chest, but—but you might as well have. If you were a true servant of my father, you would drop to your knees and beg for forgiveness."

The prince pushed himself to his feet with one smooth exertion, rising straight up as his legs disentangled themselves. He was finished. He was turning to go. He lifted a foot and leaned to stride away behind it. Thaddeus had not been prepared for this moment. He had not planned for it, had not imagined Aliver would say what he just had or that he would respond to it as he was about to.

He lunged from his seated position. He wrapped one hand around Aliver's leg. His other hand scraped him forward, and in a few moments he had the young man's legs gripped in a two-armed embrace. This was not at all what he had intended, but he did not let go. He held tight, ready to feel the prince's fists crashing down on his head. Only then did he understand completely what he had waited all these years to do, what he had feared and wanted most, what mattered with an urgency greater than the fate of nations. Forgiveness. He needed to be forgiven. To be so, he would have to tell the truth entirely. That was what he would do. For once, he would rely on the entire truth. And if Aliver was the prince the Known World needed, he would know how to face it all.

CHAPTER

THIRTY-TWO

The young woman watched the eel as it cut a squirming path through the glass-blue water. She lay on her stomach, naked save for a cloth wrapped snugly around her hips, the brittle, dry wood of the pier abrasive on her abdomen and chest and legs. The sun beat down upon her back with a force that made her flesh tingle. Her skin was brown from long exposure, peeling in spots, her thinner hairs bleached blond. She had not been a girl for some years now—hence the wrap around her waist—but at twenty-one she retained much that was boyish in her figure. Her breasts were shapely enough that the priests had trouble keeping their eyes off them, but they were small and really no bother to her, which suited her fine. She did not in any way look like the earthly embodiment of a goddess, but that was exactly what she was. She was the priestess of Maeben, the chief female deity of the Vumu people, revered throughout the splattering of islands known collectively as the Vumu Archipelago.

The eel she observed so intently was a study of curves and motion. It never paused, just slithered its way through the clear water for a distance it had fixed in its head, then turned and slithered back the same way, drawing and redrawing an oblong shape, pacing, as it were. The water was over a man's head in depth and the eel near the surface, but the smooth whitish sand of the ocean bottom below was clear, rippling with a clarity of line and shape and texture. The young priestess could have watched the creature against that background indefinitely. Something in it brought her peace, something about it asked a question whose answer felt like the hum that the eel's path would make if it were audible. She would have liked that, though as yet she had found life posed more questions than it provided answers.

She pushed herself up and began the walk through the network of piers that cut geometric chaos into the smooth arc of the bay. She knew from the placement of the sun that it was time for her to prepare for that evening's ceremony. If she did not return to the temple soon, the priests would come looking for her. For a moment she considered letting them. They grew nervous, and it had once amused her to cause them unease. But that was before. Increasingly, she found herself more and more incapable of imagining a life in which she was not Maeben, in which the hours of the day were not ordered accordingly.

Leaving the shore behind, she had to cut through the center of the town, which was called Ruinat. It was little more than a fishing village, in many ways like any other settlement on Vumair, the main island of the archipelago. It was, however, home to the Temple of Maeben and therefore held a place of prominence out of proportion to its humble appearance. Galat, on the eastern shore of the island, served as a larger trading and commercial center, but there was nothing holy about that place. Ruinat was a place of humility, quiet now, for the heat of the midday sun baked the world with a shimmering, bleached intensity. Most of the villagers were in their shaded homes, lying still to dream these languid hours past.

The priestess walked right down the hard-packed dirt of the main street, bare chested and with nothing in the slightest to hide. Her earthly identity was not a secret kept from the common people. Everyone in the village knew her. They had watched her grow from the girl who had first arrived on the island, walking out of the sea with a sword clenched in her fist, speaking a strange language and not yet knowing her true name. They had laughed with her over the years, taught her how to speak Vumu, chased her through the streets, and tossed jokes—sometimes even lewd ones—to her. Once she was in Maeben's finery, of course, none of them would be so bold. But each thing had its place, its time.

Approaching the temple, the priestess had to pass through the promenade of gods. The totems were enormous, made from the tallest trees of the goddess's island, so lofty that the images toward the top were lost to the naked eye. They were not meant to be viewed from her earthbound point of view anyway. They were tributes to Maeben, to be noticed from a divine perspective, circling high in the sky above.

To name the goddess a sea eagle would have been a crass, sacrilegious mistake. She may take the form and have sisters and cousins that were truly avian creatures, but Maeben herself dwarfed them all. Her eyes were everseeing, keen and clear, able to focus in on any and all persons and see right into their centers. She deserved—demanded—their respect. And she had the power to remind them of this whenever she wished to.

Over the years, the young woman had learned that there were many gods in the Vumu pantheon. There were deities like Cress, who controlled the shifting of the tides. Uluva swam before the bonito, directing them on their yearly migration near the island. Banisha was the queen god of the sea turtles. It was only with her blessing that her daughters clambered up on the southern beaches each summer and buried their rich eggs in the warm sand. There was the crocodile, Bessis, that ate the moon bite by bite each night until it vanished; sated by this feast only until the moon fruit had grown again to full bounty, Bessis then rose from slumber and commenced his feast again. It was, she came to understand, a world in which the natural cycle of things was ever in question, depending as it did on the goodwill and health of so many different deities. She barely knew the names of them all, but this did not matter. Only two gods shared the apex of the Vumu pantheon, and only one of these was central to her life.

Maeben was not a goddess with a function in the natural world as were so many others. From the day she was born, she scorned being bound to such labor. She was the goddess of wrath, the jealous sister of the sky who everywhere believed herself slighted: by gods, by humans, by creatures, even by the elements. Maeben, the Furious One, was easily angered, ferocious in retaliation. She threw down storms, rain, and wind, snapping her beak to create the sparks that were lightning. Looking upon humans she had long ago found them too proud, too favored by the other gods. Only once did she find a human pleasing, but what unfolded from it was tragic.

The man's name was Vaharinda. He was born of mortal parents, but for some reason he was blessed even before he had escaped the womb. Instead of his mother singing him to sleep, *he* sang to calm her. Instead of her stroking her belly to comfort him, *he* rubbed her from the inside. Vaharinda had a way with women; his mother knew this even before he was born. When he did emerge into the world, all were amazed to behold him. He was perfection. He grew like a weed, but in everything he was of a fine and shapely substance. By the time he was six or seven years old, grown women swooned on seeing him. By eleven, he had known hundreds of women sexually. By his fifteenth year a thousand women called him husband and claimed to have borne his children. He was a brave and skilled hunter also, a warrior that no other man could best. He hefted weapons other men could not even lift. His enemies knew only fear when they beheld him.

One day Maeben saw Vaharinda giving pleasure to one woman after another. She saw how they lay panting beneath him, enraptured, in awe and joy. She heard them call out the names of other gods, asking them to witness the wonder they were experiencing. All this made Maeben curious. She changed herself into human form and approached Vaharinda. She had not expected to lie with him, but once she looked into his eyes, she could not help herself. What a specimen! What a tool of pleasure curving up from between his legs! Why not climb on it and see for herself what joys the flesh could bring?

That was just what she did. And it was good. It was very good. She lay gasping on the sand afterward and only slowly realized that Vaharinda had not been equally moved. He was already chatting to another woman. Flaring with anger, Maeben called him back and demanded that he take her again. Vaharinda saw no reason to do so. He said that she was fine enough but not so much that he would forsake other women. Her eyes were pale blue like the sky, he said, but he preferred brown-eyed women. Her hair was wispy and thin like the high, high clouds that mark a change in the weather; he preferred thick black hair that he could twine around his great fingers. Her skin was the color of near-white sand; this was unusual, yes, but his tastes were more inclined toward hues of sun-burnished brown.

Hearing all this, Maeben grew enraged. She roared up out of her human form and became a great sea eagle of wrath instead. Her wings were the widest ever seen, her talons large enough to grasp a man around the waist, each claw like a curved sword. She asked him did he like her better thus? The people who witnessed this ran in fright. Only Vaharinda remained. He had never yet seen a thing to frighten him, and he was not inclined to change his ways yet. He grasped one of his spears, and they did mighty battle. They raged across the island and up the mountains. They fought in the branches of trees and jumped out into the sky and ran across the surface of the sea. Vaharinda fought like no man ever had, but in the end he could not prevail. He was a human after all; Maeben was divine. Eventually, she crushed him in her talons. She sat in a branch where the people of Vumu could see and she ate him piece by piece, until nothing was left. Then she flew away. Vaharinda's story, however, did not end there.

The priestess left the promenade of the gods behind and ran the path that wound up toward the temple compound. At one point she paused and looked back at the harbor. There was life there now. Several boats sailed toward the docks, bearing religious pilgrims keen to view the goddess in earthly form. She would attend to them in a few hours, as she did every day.

Approaching the compound the young woman paused once more. She loved looking at Vaharinda's statue, which sat on its pedestal beside the entrance, both a monument to him and a reminder of Maeben's ultimate power. The people of Vumu had chosen to honor their hero. He had been the strongest of all of them, the most pleasing to the eye, the bravest, the most endowed with the capacity to pleasure women, the man whom other men most aspired to emulate. They had sent a gift of riches to the people of Teh on the Talayan coast and brought home a great block of stone, of a texture unlike anything on the island. From it they had carved a statue of Vaharinda. He was seated in the reclined posture he enjoyed while at rest, his muscles sculpted in the stone, his features just as they had been in life. He sat naked, and also—as had been his situation through much of his life—his penis stretched up erect, like a clenched fist aimed at the sky. It was a marvelous statue, like none in the world before or since.

With this beauty to behold, the people of Vumu soon began to worship Vaharinda as a god. They said prayers to him, asked favors of him, bestowed gifts of flowers and jewels and burnt offerings to him. Soon women, seeing in the stone the man they had loved, mounted astride his penis and pleasured themselves. They went to him even in preference to their husbands, and many claimed to have gotten living young from the seed of the stone god. They came to him so often and in such great numbers that the ridges and contours of his member were worn smooth and its length gradually diminished. But still he gave pleasure and—in his silent way—he received pleasure in return.

Maeben hated all of this. It angered her more than Vaharinda's scorn of her had. She took it upon herself to humble them in a way that hurt them most. First, she swept in on the statue and wrapped her talons around Vaharinda's penis and snapped it off in her grip. She carried the broken length of it out to sea and dropped it. A shark watched her do this. Thinking that she had dropped a prized morsel of food, the shark rose from the depths and swallowed the penis in one massive mouthful. Maeben rejoiced. Vaharinda would pleasure women no longer. She was not finished with her vendetta against humans yet, however. She took the gift that Vaharinda had given to the women who loved him. She took their children. She swept down from the sky and snatched little ones up in her talons and beat, beat, beat her wings until she rose, the child screaming and writhing in her grip, helpless against her wrath.

The young priestess, walking past the statue now and into the compound, could not help but eye the damaged privates of the statue. Some part of her knew better than to feel so, but she wished she had seen Vaharinda in his glory. She even dreamed of mounting him as other women were said to have done. In these dreams he was not only stone, however. He was living flesh, and the acts they carried out together were of such sensual excess that she often woke stunned to have ever imagined such things. She was, after all, a virgin. She had to be. She lived out a continuing part in all of this drama. Long ago the priests had divined that the only way to appease Maeben was to select a living symbol of her that could stand before the people every day so that they might never forget her. The priests said that humans had to be careful never to take too much joy from life. They must always remember that they lived and prospered only at the generous whim of Maeben. They must always look upon loved ones with a measure of sorrow. They must never enjoy good health without remembering that illness is but a breath away. They should never praise fair weather without knowing that late each summer storms come, wreaking damage without concern for human suffering. All of these daily hazards of life were necessary, the priests said, to appease a goddess with jealous eyes that missed little of what transpired on the earth below her. And the priestess, above all else, should never succumb to the lust Maeben had mistakenly felt for Vaharinda.

Perhaps because of these penitent ways, the Vumu islands were blessed with an abundance that filled the people with confidence in the rightness of their beliefs. They harvested oysters in one of the sheltered harbors. Catfish the length of tall men swarmed the muddy rivers flowing out of the hilly uplands, the backs of them plowing through the water, so visible that fishermen had only to stand in their canoes and fling spears at the passing mounds of water. From the sea, bonito filled their nets to bursting in the spring. In late summer the trees in the valleys groaned under the weight of their fruits. And even boy children of eight or nine were considered old enough to venture into the hills on hunting trips. They always came back laden with monkey meat, with tree squirrels, and with a flightless bird so plump it was difficult to carry under the arm. Maeben, in truth, had much to be jealous of and the people of Vumu much to be thankful for.

"Priestess!" a voice called from the top of the temple steps. "Come, come, you dally too much." It was Vandi, the priest chiefly responsible for getting her accoutred for the ceremony. He liked to look fierce, but in truth he was soft on her, like an uncle who dotes on a niece he knows he only has limited authority over. He held her underrobe out as if she were near enough to step into it.

The young woman took the stone steps two or three at a time. They were cut shallow so that one approached the temple with slow, measured, and reverent steps. But this applied to the worshippers, not to the one being worshipped. "Calm yourself, Vandi," she said. "Remember who serves whom here."

Vandi, like most Vumuans, was short of stature, with night-black hair, greenish eyes, and a tight pucker of a mouth. As he was a priest and often indoors, his skin did not quite match the villagers' coppery complexions, but he was still remarkable to behold. "We all serve the goddess," he quipped.

She slipped inside the garment offered her and let herself be bustled deeper into the temple. In the deep, incense-pungent seclusion of her chambers, attendants set about dressing her. They draped her in the various, feathered layers of her office, securing each with quick fingers. Others painted her face and fit the bird's beak mask over her mouth, making sure that she could breathe. Perfumers hovered around them all, taking sips from precious gourds and exhaling the scented water in a fine spray it took them years to master the delivery of. They slipped talons onto her fingers, tugged them into place, and fastened them with wraps of leather around her hand and up her wrist. Each hand bore three of these, two partnered fingers and a thumb supporting the weight of the curving crescents. They were fearsome relics of an actual sea eagle, a creature so large it must have approached the goddess in grandeur.

Through it all the young woman stood still, her arms raised out to either side, impassive as they worked. She remembered that her long-ago father had sometimes stood in a similar posture as he was dressed. Perhaps, she thought, she had not come so far from her origins as she believed. Before she became the priestess, she had answered to the name Mena. Now she was Maeben. Not so different. She sometimes remembered her family with a clarity that stunned her, but most of the time she saw them as still images that resided within frames, like portraits hung on the wall of her mind. She even saw herself this way. Princess Mena, dressed in too much clothing, a jeweled brooch at her neck, and royal pins in her hair. She recalled two of her siblings well, but again her memory kept them frozen in differing postures: earnest Aliver, so concerned over his place in the world, and good-hearted Dariel, innocent and eager to please. Corinn she could not picture entirely. This troubled her. She should have known her sister best of all, but in fact she was the hardest to pin to an identifiable character. None of it mattered, though. Whether she liked it or not, that existence was behind her. Her life was now about something else entirely.

One morning years ago she woke from sleep, knowing before she opened her eyes that she was afloat on a tiny, bucking skiff. She looked up at the boundless white-blue sky. If she lifted her head, she would see all around her the same heaving whitecaps of the open ocean that she had scanned for days already, and for the first time this filled her more with weariness than with fear. She sat up. Her Talayan guardian was a taciturn man. He conspicuously avoided looking at her, keeping his dark eyes turned toward the far horizon or up at the billowing sail or off to either side, taking in the shape of the swells.

She felt no inhibition about staring at him candidly, studying his lean face, watching how skillfully he functioned even with two fingers missing from his left hand. He used it without hesitation but with strange hooked motions that trapped her eyes and would not let them move on. She had rarely seen any sort of bodily deformity on Acacia. Never among the servants, certainly, and visiting dignitaries would have hidden any such wound. He did not seem as large a man as she had first thought, but maybe she was just losing perspective, he being the only figure in view inside a small boat and against the backdrop of the ocean's vastness. Large or not, he was a soldier. He wore his short sword at his waist. The hilt of his long sword was just visible from where it jutted out of a compartment in the deck. From its placement it almost seemed that he had tried to hide it.

For the hundredth time she felt compelled to shake her head at the absurdity of it all. She had believed his claim that this plan was all of her father's devising, but that did not make it seem any more sensible. It was this man's face that she had first beheld when she opened the door to her room on Kidnaban. Him that she had chosen to trust as they mounted two ponies and made off on a coastal road. In the woods he had shorn her hair with goat shears. He had her put on rough clothes and explained that their story— should they need one—was that she was a boy indentured to him to pay a familial debt. As it turned out, nobody asked about her anyway.

They sailed from port to port, booking passage where and when they could, and it was not until they reached Bocoum that the man opted to purchase the small vessel they now sailed in. He haggled for it for nearly an hour, as she watched it all, mystified. She asked him several times why they were traveling this way, but he ever directed her only to read the letter he had presented to her. In it, written in Thaddeus's hand, was an all-too-brief explanation. The best way for her to slip into hiding was to do so without fanfare, drawing no unwanted attention, requesting no luxuries. Nobody would dream that the Akaran children would travel with only a single protector; thus they could hide in plain sight and proceed unmolested. It was imperative that they leave no signs somebody could later piece together and follow. This, she reasoned, was why they could no longer appear to have the kingdom's finances to draw upon. The pretense, to say the least, was becoming tiresome.

"Where are you taking me?" Mena asked.

The guardian craned his neck around and took in the sea behind them for a moment. Mena noticed he did this often, every minute or so, as if it were a compulsion that his reserved manner could not subdue. "I am doing as ordered," he said.

"I know that. But where have you been ordered to take me?"

"To the Vumu Archipelago. Just as I told you yesterday and the day before, Princess."

"Why?"

"I do not know. I am just doing as ordered."

"Will you take me home instead?"

His eyes touched on her for a moment, an emotion in them that she could not read. Then he looked back out over the sea again. "I cannot. Even if I wanted to . . . I cannot. I understand that you are scared, but all that I can do to help you I am doing."

"How long will it take to get there?"

"A few more days. It depends on the wind, the currents." He motioned with his hand as if he distrusted these things, was not even quite sure where they were located.

Mena stared at him, unimpressed. "Anyway, I did not say that I was scared. You are the one who is scared. Why do you keep peering about? What are you looking at?"

He scowled at her and then set his eyes forward as if he would not answer. But something in his respect for her family—however it might have been altered by recent events—chastened him. "There is a boat," he finally said, "behind us. And closing."

And so there was. It was tiny as yet. She would have passed her eyes across it, thinking it just the whitecaps on some wave. It surged into and out of view as it, and they, rose and fell. At first she did not believe that it was following them. How could he tell that for certain on such a heaving expanse? But an hour later she thought perhaps it was and maybe it was somewhat nearer already. Each time it emerged from a trough and cut through the peak of a wave it seemed to have closed distance. Mena asked the Talayan if they should wait for it. Perhaps it had been sent from Acacia to find them. Maybe they could turn back now. The guardian did not answer, neither did he alter their course or lower the sail. It did not much matter, though. The other boat was faster. It had longer lines and a wider billow of sail. It gained on them steadily, propelled by a gathering storm. Or perhaps it dragged the storm behind it. It was hard to say which directed the other.

Gusts of wind ripped talons across the water and buffeted the boat like a toy. The waves rose to increasing heights. By late in the afternoon the other boat had pulled abreast of them and cut the water at the same rate, separated by a hundred yards and then less, then still less. A lone man crewed the vessel. Mena had scarcely picked him out and was straining to observe details about him—still hoping to find him a messenger from her father—when he rose to his feet. He stood a moment, finding his equilibrium. He held what looked like a pole in his hand. The guardian must have seen this, too. He hissed a curse under his breath. He motioned for Mena to come near him, saying something she could not understand. She thought he wanted her to take hold of the tiller he held clenched under his armpit. Or perhaps the rope his hands fumbled and yanked at. Either way, the alarm in his voice and gestures froze her. She did neither. They climbed the face of a wave and launched screaming onto its back, their sail so filled with angry air, Mena feared they might lift out of the water and fly away like a kite untethered.

For a moment they were alone in a valley. Then they were two again. The other vessel came sliding down the back of a wave toward them, the prow hissing as it cut the slick back of the water. The pursuer flung the pole—now obviously a spear—with a force that almost toppled him forward out of the boat. It flew toward and pierced the center of the guardian's breast as if it belonged in no other portion of the world. He released the tiller and grasped the spear shaft. He did not try to pull it out, but he did seem to want to support the weight of it. He coughed up a gush of blood, and then, reaching behind with one hand, he pulled himself backward, over the lip of the gunwale. He plopped into the water and was gone.

The boat swung around, directionless, pitching side to side. It leaned over and slurped in a gush of the sea and then righted and spun again. Mena had to throw herself to the deck to avoid being hit by the yardarm. The sail-cloth thrashed about like a frantic animal, but it did not catch the air the way it had a moment ago. Mena had no idea what to do with it. She stared up at the snarling life in the fabric, paralyzed. Then she felt something she had not in days—the impact of the boat against something solid. This snapped her upright.

The other boat was beside hers, gunwale to gunwale, each smacking against the other as if each wished a fight. The attacking sailor leaped from his boat and landed sure-footed inside hers. He took her in with a quick glance, but came no nearer. He held a rope, with which he bound the vessels together, with enough slack between them that they could float apart. He was out of sight for a moment, then rose back into view, fumbling in the guardian's shoulder bag. What did he want? What did he want with *her*? What would he do to her? She could not possibly imagine, but the specifics hardly mattered. Whatever the answer was, it would be a horror. At first she did not realize that her hands had found a weapon, and yet they had. She clenched her guardian's long sword in both her hands. She tugged at it and just managed to pull it from its stowed place. But it was too heavy to actually lift. She could not even get it unsheathed, though the scabbard point dragged a jagged line across the boards. She had never felt so powerless.

How strange, then, that the man turned his back to her. He tugged at the rope for some time, and then leaped from the gunwale back into his boat. The two crafts crashed together again. The man reached out a quick hand and tugged loose the knot that attached his boat to hers. He seemed to have no interest in her whatsoever.

"What are you doing?" Mena shouted.

The soldier paused and looked at her, holding the two boats together with a single wrap around the cleat beside his foot. He clearly had wished to avoid speaking to her, but, once questioned, he could not fail to answer. "I wish you no harm, Princess," he said, shouting back to be heard over the wind and water. "What happened here was between this man and myself. I have no quarrel with you."

"You know who I am?"

The man nodded.

"Why did you kill this man? What are you going to do with me?"

"He and I had a—a dispute. With you I have no wish to do anything."

They rose up over a wave and all was chaos for a moment. When she could see the man's face again Mena spoke. "You will leave me here to die?"

The man shook his head. "You won't die. You are in a current that drags you east. It runs through Vumu as if through a sieve. Even if you raise no sail but just float, you will sight land in a few days' time. You will find land again. And people. What passes between you and them is for you to decide."

"I don't understand," Mena said, emotion rising in her voice.

The man looked at her, something mocking in his eyes. "You are not the only one with a story. What happened here was mine and his." He thrust his chin scornfully toward the depths. "It is an old debt, settled now."

"Are you my father's enemy?"

"No."

"Then you are his subject! I order you not to leave me here!"

"Your father is dead, and I take orders no more." He flung the loose coils of rope into her boat. "Princess, I don't know what your father intended by sending you out here, but the world is not what it once was. Make your way as best you can; I will do the same."

After that he spoke no more. He turned his back to her and unfurled his sail. It snapped full and his boat carved away, cutting a diagonal line up the face of an oncoming wave. Mena watched him slip over the edge and out of sight, feeling his words like a slap across the face. She realized that she had naïvely believed that the workings of the world revolved around her and her family. Never before had she acknowledged that somebody else's life might alter hers. How foolish. That was exactly what was happening! Had not Hanish Mein's actions changed her life? And her guardian and his killer had stories too, lives too, fates too. She realized that the world was a dance of a million fates. In this dance she was but a single soul. This, at least, was how she would come to remember the event and its effect on her.

As it happened she stared after the killer at each rise, watching him fade into the distance. Eventually, he was beyond her view. She was alone, nothing around her save the featureless sky and moving liquid mountains that at that moment made up the entirety of the world. And it stayed that way for five more days, until she first spotted the island that was to become her home, her destiny.

"There," Vandi said, stepping back to examine the fully costumed priestess, "you are the goddess once more. May she be praised and find us humble!"

The attendants who had dressed her echoed this in mumbles. They drew back from her reverently. This moment always seemed strange to Mena. These young women had themselves transformed her. They had put each portion of her costume onto her near-naked body, and yet once they finished their work they went weak with fear over what they had created. She walked between them behind Vandi, toward the cymbals and chimes that announced the ceremony. Vumuans were a strange people, she thought. But still, she had always liked them and felt some amount of comfort with them. She had since she had first laid eyes on them.

Her arrival on the island had been a rough one. She might easily have died; the fact that she lived and the way that she emerged from the sea became the basis of all that followed. Alone in the boat with scant provision left her, she had watched the island draw nearer for two full days. The seas were calmer now, but around the island ran a barrier reef constructed in such a way that the ocean tossed a fury of waves over it. From the heights of these as she approached, Mena thought she might be able to ride the froth all the way into the calm water beyond the breakers. But it was not to be so easy. The boat snagged on the bottom. She lost her hold on the tiller and hurtled forward, smashing her shoulder against the decking. The pain of it was immense, complete, almost enough to block out the tumult around her. She rolled onto her back, wedged herself in as best she could, and stared up as waves poured over the boat. She felt the hull catch and grind across the reef until the boat turned sideways and rolled. For a moment she was suspended in the boiling water, her mouth full of the stuff, breathing it and choking on it at the same time. The mast must have snapped, allowing the boat to roll around. But it did not stop when it got upright. Instead, it rolled over again and again, over and over until the world made no sense at all.

She was sucked from the boat, flipped and tumbled and wrenched about by the soft muscle of the water. Her face pressed against the coral once, her arms and legs many times. She clasped something in her hand, an object that caught and twisted and wrenched her arm about. She thought it was a part of the boat and would not let it go. It was a vain hope, but she felt if she held on to a board or pole or whatever it was, she might make it through this. She changed her mind when whatever she held yanked her arm from the socket at that shoulder.

She must have gone unconscious. She was not sure, but at some point she just awoke, gasping in the calm. She sucked air furiously, all of her focused on the frantic need to inhale. Only after she had done so for a while did she realize there was sand beneath her feet. The water around her was warm and peaceful. The waves broke not far away at all, but she had gotten past them and could make out individual trees on the shore. Even more, she saw the smoke of a fire and the thatched roofs of huts and a boat moving along the shoreline. She remembered the searing pain of her shoulder, but the arm was home again and the dull throb in the joint hardly registered.

As she began to wade forward she noticed that her left arm dragged an object behind it, an awkward weight in the water. Her hand was clenched around a leather rope. Actually, this rope knotted around her wrist, enough so that her hand was bluish and swollen. Lifting it, she pulled the guardian's long sword to the surface. The rope around her wrist was the sling used to carry it over one's back. It was the sword that she had clung to, not a piece of the boat at all. She might have been holding the sword for a while, but it was the knotted cords that assured it stayed with her, as if the weapon itself feared the depths and had refused to let her go.

So she came to the island armed with a warrior's sword, a girl of twelve, newly orphaned and cut off from every person she had ever known in her life. What was left of her clothing clung to her in tatters. Her hair was knotted and wild. The villagers who gathered on the shore and watched her walk toward them had never seen her likes before. It seemed she had crossed the ocean without a boat to transport her. When she opened her mouth, a foreign tongue escaped her. None of them could make sense of it. Thus a myth was born.

By the time she arrived at Ruinat a tale beyond her wildest imagining preceded her, one that she understood only later. It seemed her timing was fortuitous and unusual enough that it could be explained only with a strange blend of logic and faith. The villagers had begun whispering. Did not Vaharinda say that Maeben in human form had pale blue eyes, just like this girl? Did he not call her hair thin and wispy? And was her skin not the color of light sand? Fine, so the girl was darker than that, slightly, but over-all the effect was convincing. They needed a new Maeben. They had for some time, but the priests had been unable to find a suitable girl. Usually one was born among them. In this instance the goddess had given herself to them in an even truer form. Her arrival was not perfect in its symbology, but some things were ignored, others embellished, still other details fabricated. She would eventually learn to favor her legend over the story she knew to be the truth. She welcomed the power it gave her, the right to wrath, the status as a misfortunate child of the gods, ill suited to the joys others took for granted but necessary to the maintenance of life. Special.

Nine years later, as she stepped onto the platform above the throng of worshippers below, there was little doubt that that was just what she was. They stared up at her. There she was, lit by torchlight in the enclosed cham-ber. She paced the platform in feathered glory, dyed fifty different colors, with massive talons curving from her fingers. The eyes that stared at them from behind the hook of her beak mask were farseeing and intense. Spikes thrust up into the air from the crown of her head, a mad, jagged chaos of a headdress. She was a nightmare of beauty and menace living right there above them, a being part raptor, part human, part divine. She knew without question that she could sweep down on them and inflict upon all of them a terrible vengeance if she wished. She had the capacity for violence within her, residing beside her heart.

The second to the head priest announced her arrival. He chastised the worshippers for their insignificance. Mena thrust her arms up above her head at the appointed moment, the feathered flaps of fabric snapping and fluttering. Every head below tilted toward the floor. Some fell to their knees. Others lay prostrate on the ground. All begged for her mercy. They adored her, they said, doing so in a chant that cut against the rhythm of the chimes. They loved her. They feared her. The priest berated them, cut them to pieces, reminded them of the follies of humanity, asked them if they understood that vengeance came from the sky with the speed of an eagle's cry. The discordant music picked up, and between the questions and answers and the moaning and beseeching of the prostrate worshippers the chamber pulsed and trembled.

Looking out over the heads of the priests, past them to the masses of noblemen, the common folk behind, the women and children along the edges—all of them bent low in reverent bows to her, long acts of devotion that they could not end until she signaled that they could do so—she thought that perhaps she really was Maeben. She had been her all along. It just took her some time to find herself. This was her home now. This was her role. She was Maeben, the child stealer, the vengeance flung out of the sky. It was she to whom the people divulged their fears and swore their adoration.

She cried out that the faithful might rise and behold her once more. She spoke clear voiced as she did when Maeben talked through her, cutting through the other sounds. At such moments she had never been anybody else. When she spread her wings and leaped screeching into the air she had not the slightest doubt that every hand below her would stretch to catch her. And if one could leap from a height with no fear of falling, could one not be said to possess the secret of flight? Just like a bird, just like a god.

CHAPTER

THIRTY-THREE

How strange this land is, Hanish thought as he looked out from his office balcony across the tremulous shimmer of the Inner Sea. It had always seemed unnatural to him that a land should be so kind to the living. It struck him as unhealthy—in a manner of speaking—that a climate could be so healthy, so benign. Here was a land in which the fundamental struggles Hanish considered necessary to life had been removed or had never existed. One could step outside at any time of the year into mild weather, or at worst a chill or a few snowflakes. The coldest weather Acacia could offer was nothing that a Meinish child could not stand naked in through an entire night. Up on the plateau, a single supply forgotten in the wild, a single mistake made, a sudden change in the winds, a clue left for the wolf packs . . . There were so many forces in that world intent on harm that one could never relax. Nothing could be done halfheartedly. Acacia was something else entirely. The ease of it, the luxury . . . Well, perhaps there was a peril in such things. One just had to recognize that danger had a soft face as well as a harsh one.

"King Hanish Mein, it surprises me that a man in your position would stand with his back to an accessible room."

Hanish recognized the voice behind him. He had been waiting for him, but he would have recognized the voice wherever he heard it. There was no mistaking the nasal whine, the self-satisfied air, the space in between certain words filled with a sound like purring. He prepared himself to be unnerved. He let the emotion possess him for a moment and pass through, so that none of it showed on his face. With men like Sire Dagon the ability to hide one's true thoughts, while remaining skeptical to anything proffered by the other, was imperative.

"I am not a king," Hanish said, turning to face Sire Dagon. "Please, I prefer to remain a chieftain. It just so happens I am now the chief chieftain of the Known World. As for my safety, not all palaces are as cutthroat as those of the league."

"Hmmm ... that's not what I've heard," the league master said. Though tall of stature, his body had about it an awkward fragility, as if there were barely enough muscle tissue to support his frame. His elongated head was hooded, but the bright light of the afternoon illumed his face with rare detail. His eyes had the bloodshot taint of a regular mist smoker. Yet they were alert, the mind behind them unclouded. Hanish had never understood their use of the drug. They had clearly harnessed it to purposes different from those of the sedated masses.

Men of the league did not touch others in greeting, so the two men simply stepped near to each other and bowed. "But anyway," Sire Dagon continued, "I am glad it is you I meet with now as opposed to some other, to some impostor. One hears talk that you could at any day be called to that dance of yours. What do you call it?"

Hanish knew very well that Sire Dagon remembered the word. Leaguemen had encyclopedic memories. "The Maseret," he answered.

"Yes, that's it. The Maseret. Forgive me for suggesting that this custom should be discouraged. Your prowess is renowned, yes, but to tell any man of your race that he could have for himself all that you have earned is a mistake. Why wave such a possibility before others? This could soon stir ambitious fools to challenge you."

Several have done just that, Hanish thought. He had danced five times since coming south to Acacia, which meant that five of his own men had died on his knife blade. Each of them desired his power. Each hoped to gain everything through a single act of murder. He knew that Sire Dagon knew this already also. No need to bring it up. "You honor me with the suggestion that it matters to the league just whom they deal with."

"You gave your people the world they now rule. The league does not forget this, even if some others close to you do. Personally I admire your focus. And, yes, Hanish, that is a compliment. At my age few things interest me. My friend, even the acquisition of wealth has become more a force of habit than an ambition."

Hanish doubted that even looming death could extinguish a leagueman's ravenous ambition, but he gave no outward sign of it. Nor did he acknowledge the reference to others close to him. Was that a jibe or a warning? He motioned that they should find relief from the sun.

Inside, they sat across from each other in high-backed leather chairs, an ornate table of the Senivalian fashion between them. A band of servants entered, food and drink trays balanced on their bare arms. The two men conversed for some time. Each wore a façade of casual comfort in the other's presence, like old friends with nothing more pressing to discuss than the length of the growing season on Acacia, the coming migration of the swallows, the positive effects of sea air on health. Hanish welcomed the respite. It allowed him to study Sire Dagon, to weigh not just what he said but how he said it, to look for thoughts betrayed by the motion of his hands or the emphasis placed on certain words. He knew the leagueman was putting him through a similar inspection.

"So, Sire Dagon, you have returned recently from the other side of the world?"

"I have returned from the other side of the world, yes."

As he had tried before on many occasions, Hanish wanted to probe this leagueman for information of the foreigners, the Lothan Aklun. Who were these people who shaped so much of the destiny of the Known World? They had, in a way, been his allies in fighting against Leodan Akaran, but he had never set eyes on one of them and knew nothing of their customs or history. He had never so much as heard one of them given an individual name. They resided on a chain of barrier islands that ran the length of the continent known as the Other Lands. They had no wish to interact with the Known World, being content with the riches the Quota provided them. As far as Hanish knew, none of them had ever ventured across the Gray Slopes themselves; the league did that for them.

During his first years in power he had demanded to know whom he was dealing with. League representatives had promised to pass on his "request," but nothing ever came of it. He had even peppered Calrach of the Numrek with questions about them. His people came from that side of the world, but they offered him little that made sense. Calrach had referred to the Lothan Aklun as "unimportant." They were no more than traders, he claimed.

Nine years in power and the Lothan Aklun were real to Hanish only because of their ravenous appetite for child slaves and because they produced the drug that had helped him soothe his tumultuous empire. Leaguemen assured him that was as it had to be, and he knew Sire Dagon would provide no new answers to his questions now. He chose not to raise the subject again.

"By the way," Sire Dagon said, "the Lothan are pleased that you have made progress with the antoks. They presented them to you in the belief that you would find a way to harness their ravenous appetites. It pleases them that you have done so."

Hanish nodded. He had actually had little to do with these antoks. They were strange beasts that he had laid eyes on only once. They were enormous creatures, like living versions of the giants whose bones were sometimes found in the ground. He could scarcely describe them. They were a mixture of the worst swinish and canine traits, unfeeling, brutal, ravenous. He eventually conceived of a practical way he might use them in battle, but he had left it to Maeander to handle the creatures in a remote compound in Senival. The less he heard about the beasts, the better.

Sire Dagon did not linger on them long. "I trust you will be pleased by the news I bring," he said. "The Lothan Aklun are anxious to increase their trade with you. They have been patient these many years, as you know. The scant tribute you have sent them thus far . . . you understand that they consider it a kindness done to you that they have accepted it without complaint and that they have supplied the empire with mist on credit, as it were. It was a necessary period of adjustment, but now it is concluded."

He paused, raised and lowered a single eyebrow. Hanish simply motioned with his fingers that he should continue.

"We have pledged that we will deliver a full shipment of Quota slaves to them before the winter. It will be double the amount the Akarans offered, but this is no more than what you agreed to before the war. From each province they request five thousand bodies, evenly distributed between the sexes, no more or less of any one race. The age range may need to be larger than before, but they have no issue with this. In return, they will increase the mist by a third. This may not seem much, but the drug has been refined. It is no longer as incapacitating as before, and it is more addictive. The body adjusts to it in a manner that means when deprived of it the user experiences significant distress—hallucinations, fever, pain. Most will do anything just to ensure their supply. This is all detailed in documents supporting the revised treaty. And that, Hanish Mein, is all there is to it. You'll be glad to hear that they demand nothing more from you than this."

Hanish glanced away, thinking that they demand nothing more than the world itself. Generous of them. His gaze settled on a golden monkey that had perched on the banister of the balcony, its yellow-orange hair aflame in the sunlight. Hanish did not like the creatures. Never had. They had about them a noisy, knowing air, as if this whole palace was actually theirs and *he* was just an interloper. Early in his stay on Acacia he had introduced another variety of primate, a stout thing with long snow-white hair and a brilliant blue face. But these had proved unruly and belligerent. They hunted down the goldens and left bloody, half-eaten corpses strewn around the grounds. They seemed to take pleasure in tossing severed limbs at groups of women. Hanish had eventually ordered them slaughtered; the goldens, however, won favor with the noblewomen. They remained.

"I have brought the revised treaty with me," Sire Dagon said. "You and your people may peruse it at leisure. And that, largely, will be that. You can then get on with enjoying your hard-won empire. There is only one new aspect of the treaty for you to consider." The leagueman seemed to remember the food all at once and stretched to study the trays. He let that last statement sit a moment, but Hanish waited. "As our commission for negotiating it, the league asks for . . . well, we request no change in our percentage, no monetary bonus—nothing like that. We would simply like to take a burden from your shoulders and place it on ours instead."

Hanish touched the scar on his nose with his thumb, just a passing motion that he did not linger on. Wryly, he said, "I can barely contain my curiosity."

"We would like to take the Outer Isles off your hands. We would like to own them outright."

"Those islands are thronging with pirates."

Sire Dagon smiled. "We have considered that. They are not a problem. We have examined every aspect of how they function, and we are confident we can pacify them."

"They are hardly the type to accept passivity of any sort."

"They have been a problem to you, haven't they?" Sire Dagon asked. "So many problems you've taken on your shoulders. Perhaps you did not think that the peace would be more challenging than the war. This is a lesson only learned by error and trial. It is why the league chooses to always be at peace, even if our friends choose to make war on one another."

Hanish could not dispute that there was wisdom in such an approach. Who would have thought that winning the military battles would prove to be easy compared to managing the empire? One and then another and then another crisis sprouted. Some of the trouble was of his own making. The fever was more virulent than he had imagined, for example. He had not fully reckoned with how far it would spread and how quickly it would outstrip his military objectives. It simply killed too many, leaving a weakened fragment of the former population to rebuild after the war.

Also, the Numrek outlived their usefulness, and their welcome. They had not returned across the Ice Fields as they had first promised they would, though Hanish had paid them lavishly for their services. In the turmoil after the war, as the fever still raged through the south, they entrenched themselves in Aushenia, claiming the entire region as their own, taking over the towns and villages and the royal estates, enslaving the humans unlucky enough to get captured. Even worse, they had started colonies along the western edge of the Talayan coast. Creatures of the frozen north, indeed! As it turned out they loved nothing better than baking beneath a furious sun and swimming in the limpid waters.

There were other problems he had no hand in creating. The people—perhaps because the war disrupted the flow of the mist—got all sorts of ideas in their heads. They became unruly, conniving, flaring into rebellion, staging acts of sabotage, as when they set fire to the grain stores on the Mainland, halving the supply there and causing a near famine year. They spun stories of holy prophecies, said that Hanish and his plague were the harbingers of the Giver's return. They developed a liking for martyrs, recalcitrant bastards upon whom torture and execution were but a blessing. Talay had never been fully pacified; the Outer Isles were lousy with pirates; his troops were pestered by assassins in the guise of loyal subjects.

And the revolts at the mines were most frustrating. Just when Hanish was poised to restart the engine of the world's commerce, the miners took it into their heads to grasp control of their own lives. They refused to work. Some fool among them rose to prominence by suggesting that the miners deserved a share of their profits from their labor. A silver-tongued, ranting prophet of a man, Barack the Lesser, had caused no end of trouble. He had even claimed to have seen the future return of Aliver Akaran. How very annoying. His efforts achieved nothing but misery for all involved. The strike had to be put down through a siege that Hanish could scarcely afford to prosecute. So many of them died. Such a waste of manpower; all for nothing.

The Numrek, the league, and the Lothan Aklun: how had be become so miserably indebted to all of them? In frozen Cathgergen, so far from power and privilege, each partnership had made complete sense. Why not buy an army and pay them with treasure from lands they themselves conquered? Why not promise great sums to merchants who would help to enrich him? What better partner in business than the suppliers to a ravenous market never looked upon or dealt with directly? No sum had seemed too great if paying them helped him achieve his goals. He felt different now, on every count.

Not least of his worries was that he had managed to catch only one of the four Akaran children. Corinn went unharmed and lived comfortably in Acacia. She knew nothing of the fate that still awaited her. Her presence should have been a comfort, one less thing to worry about. Instead, she shot him through with a sort of torment. What would he do with her? What did he want to do with her?

Sire Dagon pressed his teeth against a plum. He broke the skin of it, paused, and relished the moisture. He did not swallow the fruit. Apparently, the juice on his lips was all he wanted. "Anyway, these brigands, all their raiding up and down the coast—you need not trouble yourself with them. Even we have had some difficulty with them, but we have yet to crack down. We will do so now, and they will fall to us by next summer. The Ishtat will prevail where you struggled; we're confident of this. When we are done, we will quietly take possession of the islands; you will bask in pride at having secured the coastline from brigands."

"Why do you want those islands so?" Hanish asked.

Sire Dagon contemplated him for a moment. He touched the corner of his lips to wipe the fruit juice away. "Before I tell you, remember that the doubled quota will make you richer than Acacia ever was—"

"How can they want more?" Hanish interrupted, unable to keep the incredulity out of his voice. "What do they do with all these slaves? They could scarcely ask for more if they ate them for meat."

Sire Dagon frowned and twisted his head to the side, indicating that both the question and the inference were in terribly bad taste. "One need not ask such things. They do whatever it is they do; let us both be glad for it. Remember that one of the original tenets of the Quota contract was that the league would serve as the only intermediary between Acacia and Lothan Aklun. As part of this, we have never betrayed the secrets of one side to the other. Nor will I do so now. As I was saying, the Lothan Aklun swear never to amend this agreement, not now, not ever. Nor will we overreach the quota in the provinces. This is something that sometimes happened during the last reign, but it will not happen again. Once we have normalized the increased quota, we will pacify the Outer Isles. We will clear them, make them arable, and we will begin production."

"Production of what?"

"Of the only thing the Lothan Aklun want from us."

The answer came to Hanish like an amorphous shape rising from the depths of his imagination. "You will breed slaves there."

Sire Dagon showed no surprise, no satisfaction at Hanish's pronouncement. He just plucked up a grape and spoke casually. "I do not recognize that word *slaves*. But if you mean that we will breed our product there, you are correct. It will be a most efficient means of production. We've made plans already. The island of Gillet Major, in particular, will make for a lovely plantation."

After the leagueman left, Hanish leaned against his desk and gazed through the thin curtains, rippling as they did with the afternoon's breeze. The world could be so calm at moments, he thought, so oblivious. His brother and his uncle entered, and he had to summon his energy just to erase the disquiet from his demeanor.

"I passed that weird one in the courtyard," Haleeven said. "I have no love for those creatures, Hanish. No love at all." His face testified to the turbulence of the passing years. Peacetime, it seemed, had been particularly hard on the older man. The climate—though he never complained—did not suit him. He seemed ever ill at ease within his skin, flushed as if coming in from exercise, confused by something in the air that he could not quite put his finger on.

Maeander had no such problems. He was as cocky as ever, confident in his body. He had gained muscle bulk in the arms and chest, and he had taken a tan better than most men of the Mein. The peeling skin on his nose testified to his continued passion for outdoor pursuits.

"What?" Maeander asked, gazing at his brother. "You don't look well, Hanish. Queasy, that's the word. Do you feel as queasy as you look?"

"We need more power," Hanish said.

"I've said that all along," answered Maeander.

"I am pulled and pushed by a thousand hands, each with a finger in my pocket and the threat of a knife in the other hand."

"I hear you, brother. Haven't I always said, '*We need more power.*' I have that thought every morning on waking. I heft myself up out of the tangle of nubile bodies and the first thing I think is, *Power! I need more . . .*"

"Be serious," Haleeven snapped. "Hanish isn't clowning."

Maeander rolled his eyes. He sat down in the chair the leagueman had used and plucked up an orange. He inhaled, his nose touching the skin of the fruit. "We need to move the Tunishnevre and complete the ceremony."

"You know we cannot do that yet," Haleeven said.

"They are impatient. We have no choice in this matter, Hanish. They speak to me also, and they've made it very clear. They want to be moved. They want to journey here. They want to rest their bodies on the scene of the crime done to them, and then they want a few drops of living Akaran blood. They want to be free, brother, and you can offer them that. The chamber here is nearly ready for them. There is no reason not to begin."

"What of the other three?" Haleeven asked.

"Exactly," Hanish said. "Without them the Tunishnevre cannot rise. At least they are safe now, their condition constant. This climate could destroy them, put them beyond our power to release."

Unmoved, Maeander said, "That is not necessarily true. One may be enough. Especially if the others are dead. If Corinn is the last of the royal line, then her blood is all they need. She can free them. Imagine, Hanish, how powerful we will be! All these petty problems that trouble you so: they'll be gone like that." He raised a hand, fingertips touching until the moment he snapped his hand open, releasing whatever was held there into the air, invisible, inconsequential. "This is what the ancestors placed in me. They put this truth in me."

"They said nothing to me about needing only Corinn."

"They fear you may be compromised somehow, led astray by this place. I swore to them that they were wrong. They accepted my word. You are their beloved, but they can only wait so long. They taste release, Hanish. They have scant patience when they feel they are being denied." Speaking through a mouthful of orange pulp, he added, "By the gods, the fruit down here is wonderful!"

Hanish ignored the last comment, but he thought for a long moment about Maeander communing with the Tunishnevre. He had known his brother was doing this for some time. It was unprecedented for anyone but the chieftain and a few of the higher priests to interact with them. Hanish had allowed it because he owed Maeander so much. He had always been a perfect weapon, a hound ready to bite whomever he was directed toward. Hanish knew the ancestors adored him for the strength he walked so casually with. But for them to speak to Maeander about him, about Hanish himself . . . For them to express doubts about their living chieftain was a grave thing. There was message after message to read here, threat inside threat. And he could not acknowledge any of it until he understood it better.

"We are ahead of ourselves," Haleeven said. "You have not told us what news the weird one brought you."

So Hanish did tell them. He had never kept such things from these two, even if he held back certain things when meeting with the Board of Councillors, that new body of prominent Meins that resided, ironically, in Alecia. It disturbed Hanish to note how much of the Acacian way of being they had taken on already. If he could see a way to do it differently he would, but on one and then another topic he found the Acacian template the only reasonable, achievable answer.

Once Hanish had told them everything, Haleeven said, "I hate it that we must bow to the Lothan Aklun. I've never even set eyes on one of them. The league may have made them up, for all we know. I've said this before, but we should brush the league aside and deal with the Aklun directly, if they exist."

"I feel the same," Maeander said, "but it is not for us to argue with the ancestors. They blessed the arrangements we made, and it is they who want to be freed and freed now. Remember that your brother's voice speaks through them, Haleeven, and our father's, Hanish."

Hanish hesitated a moment but evaded the thought that troubled him and kept his composure right through it, enough so that Maeander would not notice the pause for what it was. He said, "I'll speak with the ancestors tonight. If they agree, we will send word to Tahalian. We will tell them it is time to begin the transport. Haleeven, you will initiate the move."

"That's not as we discussed," Maeander said. "Hanish, come now, you know I should go. You have an empire to rule; I am but a tool to aid you. You cannot possibly expect me to mismanage such an important task! Haleeven will come with me, if that reassures you, but when have we ever failed you?"

"You never have. Not once. It is just that this must be done right, exactly right."

Maeander put on a look of mock affront.

"What I mean," Hanish said, "is that we have more than just the move to take care of. We must redouble our efforts to find the Akarans. If they live, we must have them. This is what I need you for, Maeander. You have no other assignment now—just that you find them and bring them here." He said this with finality, consciously avoiding meeting his brother's gaze, not wanting to see rebellion in his face. "I should have put you in charge of hunting for them in the first place. For my part, I will make sure that Corinn remains safe, close to me and guarded."

He moved around his desk, dug a key from his breast pocket, and bent to unlock a drawer. "Uncle, read over these," he said, hefting a leather case of documents and plopping them on the table. "You will have to see to this exactly. Exactly. Do everything word for word as the early ones tell us. The Tunishnevre has not been moved in twenty generations. If you make an error . . ."

Haleeven gathered the case and sat down with it. He ran his fingers over the reindeer leather, flipped the simple latch open, and seemed to sit a moment in awe, his nostrils flaring as he inhaled the dry scent of the sheaves. "I will make no errors," he said. "Thank you for this. The plateau in summer . . . I have longed to see it again."

"You will," Hanish said, smiling, genuinely pleased for the older man. "Perhaps you will even find time for a hunt. The reindeer must be fat by now, lax because you have been away so long. Do the work well, and be revived by it also." He might have said more, but he felt Maeander's eyes on him, tugging at him. He turned and looked at him.

"I cannot argue with you, brother," Maeander said. "If the Akarans live, I'll find them and drag them to you by their hair. When I do, I trust you will give me the honor of cutting their throats myself."

CHAPTER

THIRTY-FOUR

The man who was to accompany the prince found him squatting outside his tent in the predawn darkness. Without speaking, Aliver gathered his few supplies in a goatskin sack and slung it over his back. He tugged the leather cord until the load settled as he liked it to. Other than that he wore only the short woven skirt of a hunter. This journey was to be a hunt of sorts, and he was dressed accordingly, exactly the same as he had been a few weeks ago when he ventured out to find a laryx. He had thought that earlier morning that he had never embarked on a task more dangerous, more important. Now it was almost forgotten.

"You are ready?" Kelis asked. His features were sharp edged in a manner that Aliver had long thought was constant judgment, although lately he had not been as sure that the man's visage betrayed anything of the thoughts behind it.

"Of course," Aliver answered.

The other man nodded and moved off. Aliver fell in beside him. He matched his stride and kept tempo with him. They progressed from a walk into an easy jog and then to the light-footed run these southern people were famous for. They moved out of the village, past the last of the shadow mounds of the huts. They rose up to the crest of an incline that, had it been lighter, would have shown before them a rolling stretch of tree-dotted pastureland, roasted to gold by the dry season. They would need to cover more than a hundred miles just to get into territory to begin the hunt. The entirety of this day and more thereafter stretched before Aliver as one of continuous motion. But he had been trained for such feats. Each breath of air brought strength into him. He felt the slap of the earth beneath his bare feet and knew he was suited to this life, this place in the world.

How different he had been when he arrived in Talay. His flight from

Kidnaban had been harrowing, but at least he had made it to his goal. He had been dragged by a guardian all the way to the court of Sangae Umae, such as it was. What had he thought was happening to him back then? He barely remembered. He had been angry and scared—he knew that. But mostly he remembered random things, like finding a sand-colored snake in his boot his first morning in the village, back when he still wore boots. It was poisonous, he had learned, deadly. It was one of the reasons Talayans did not wear shoes. He thought about this often, mulling over the fact that he did not wear shoes anymore either, hadn't in years and could barely imagine doing so again.

He remembered how hard it had been to balance himself above the hole the villagers shat in. Such a simple thing, squatting to release his bowels, but he had hated doing it, hated that he could not seem to wipe himself properly with leaves or stones, as everyone else here did. He remembered watching the boys of the village playing a game that he could make no sense of. There was nothing to it other than that each of them took turns getting smacked with a stout stick. They hit each other hard, their bodies cringing from the blows in obvious pain. But they laughed, taunted one another, and tilted their so-white teeth to the sky in mirth that seemed to have no end.

He remembered the menace he had seen in the lean, black-bodied youths he had trained with. He had been weak compared to them. He lost his breath before they did. They were all hard edges, knobs of thrusting knees and elbows as they wrestled, chins like knives wedged in his back. He remembered the girls of the village, round eyed as they watched him, whispering among themselves, sometimes breaking into peals of laughter more painful to his pride than anything the boys inflicted on him. He remembered how hard it was to pronounce Talayan words correctly. Again and again he had repeated exactly what he believed the other to have said, only to be answered by needling ridicule. There was something feminine in the way he rolled his r's, something childish in his hard g's, something of the imbecile in the way he could not master the timing of silences that gave identical phrases vastly different meanings. He remembered how he hated the sand blown on the evening breeze. It dusted his face and tracked his tears, no matter how he tried to wipe and wipe and wipe all traces of them away.

But all of that was years ago. Why even think about it now? Now he was a hunter, a man, a Talayan. He ran beside a warrior whom he cherished as a brother. He breathed steadily and flowed along, mile after mile, a film of sweat coming on to him as the sun rose. Those menacing boys were his companions now; those large-eyed girls were now women who looked upon him favorably, lovers who danced for him, a few who vied to be the first to bear him a child. He spoke the people's tongue like a native. He did not entirely remember how he had worked this transformation. The fact that he had killed a laryx marked his maturation in the eyes of his community. True enough, he had never been more alive than during that hunt, never more aware of his mortality and his undeniable hunger to survive. And not just to survive, to win glory. But even this was only one episode, with many, many smaller ones to consider also. Who can explain just how he became the person he is? It does not happen this day or that one. It is a gradual evolution that happens largely unheralded. He simply was who he now was.

Except that this was not entirely true. He thought of those early days because of Thaddeus and all the things he had brought with him. Thaddeus, whom he loved and loathed in equal measure. The people of the village called him the Acacian. Aliver, when speaking to them in Talayan, used that name as well. It did not seem to occur to any of them that this was odd. Nor did it seem strange to him that he should feel so at home with—and challenged by—a people he had been raised to believe were inferior. But each afternoon that he sat down across from Thaddeus and spoke the language of his birth he knew he was not one of these people, not entirely, not as he wished he was. He was also the Acacian. And more, if Thaddeus was to be believed, he was a pivot on which the fate of the world was to turn.

Aliver and Kelis kept moving for the greater portion of the day, pausing only to drink and eat lightly, letting the food settle and then starting up again. They rested in the shade of an acacia tree through the afternoon's burning hours, napped briefly, but then kicked dust right through twilight and for some time into the early evening. There were moments when Aliver, in a trancelike state, forgot the purpose of this journey and just ran, floating on the strength of his legs, aware of nothing but movement and of the visual panorama of the living world around him.

When they stopped to camp late that evening, however, he felt the weight of the responsibilities Thaddeus had pushed upon him. The two men made a small fire, just enough to remind the beasts that they were humans and better left alone. They carried nothing in the way of bedding with them. They dug two hollow spaces into the sand, side by side with their heads near the fire. The night could be chilly, but the ground retained enough heat to warm them through until morning. They ate a paste made from mixing their precious water with the pounded sedi grain they carried. It tasted like nothing at all, but it was nourishing. Aliver used a strip of dried beef as a utensil and ate it afterward. Kelis found the tuber the Talayans called knuckle root because of its shape. He sliced it clean at the joint, and the two of them sat sucking on their portions, the liquid inside it sweet and sharp, cleansing.

"Sometimes I feel like this is all madness," Aliver said. "This cannot be real, what we are doing, what I am supposed to do. It's a tale meant for children, a myth like those told to me as a boy."

Kelis took the root from his mouth to say, "This is your story now. You are the myth."

"So I've been told. Do you think us foolish," he asked, "we Acacians? Hunting for banished magicians and all that? Are we a joke to you?"

"A joke?" The features of the man's face were hard to read in the dim firelight, but his voice suggested no possibility of humor.

"Kelis, I have been sent to find five-hundred-year-old magicians and to convince them to help me regain the empire my father lost. Do you understand such a loss? There is nothing here, around us, which could possibly show you how much my father lost. He was the monarch who forfeited the world's greatest empire. And now he speaks from the grave to ask me to win it all back. Is that not something to laugh at?"

A cacophony of jackal calls erupted in a wide semicircle around them. The canines saw the humor apparently. Kelis still acknowledged none. He tossed away his knuckle root and said, "Our storytellers teach of the God Talkers, too. They are of our legends as well as yours. You have heard these."

"And you believe, then?"

Kelis did not answer, but Aliver knew what he would say if pressed. Of course he believed. To Talayans truth lived in spoken words. It did not matter that at times their legends were highly improbable or that they often contradicted one another. If they were spoken—if they had been handed down to them by those who came before—there was nothing to do for a Talayan but believe. There was no reason not to. Aliver had heard a great many of their legends over the years.

He knew that the God Talkers were supposed to have marched through Talay and into exile. They were enraged, the legend went, at their banishment. They had helped Tinhadin win the world, but now he—the greatest of them—had turned on them and forbade them from using their god speech. They cursed under their breath, quietly so that Tinhadin would not hear them. But even these whispered curses had power. They had torn swathes out of the land; they had tilted slabs of the earth's crust; they had sparked fire with waves of their arms; they had touched their eyes on the beasts of the plains, corrupting them, twisting them into creatures like the laryx. They had done much damage, the legends went, but fortunately they walked on past the inhabited regions into the truly arid, baking flats to the south. According to myth, the Santoth still lived there. Nobody had ever ventured there to verify this. Why should they? Only one person would ever have reason to go in search of them—a prince of the Akaran line going to rescind their sentence.

"You want to hear someone else's story instead of yours?" Kelis asked. "Listen to this one then. There was a young Talayan whose father was a very proud man, a warrior. He lived for war and he wished his son to do the same. His son, however, was a dreamer, one who predicts when the rains arrive, when children will be born healthy, one whose sleeping life is as vivid as the waking. The boy dreamed things before they happened. He spoke with creatures in his dreams and sometimes awoke, still remembering the animal's language, for a few moments at least. The son wanted badly to learn more about his gift. The father, you might think, would have been proud his son was chosen for this. But he was not. When the father slept he was dead to life; only awake did he find meaning, only in war were all things clear to him.

"He forbade his son to dream. He did it with all the spite he could direct through his eyes. He did it through ridicule, with biting words and with scorn. He stood over his son when he slept. Whenever he saw the boy's eyes move, the sign that he'd entered the dreamworld, he jabbed him with his spear shaft. He awoke him to pain again and again. Soon the boy feared sleep. Dreams sometimes came to him anyway, even in the light of day when he was otherwise awake. The father learned to recognize dreams in his son's eyes, and he would slap him if he suspected the boy's mind had wandered. None of it stopped the boy. He simply could not help being who he was. But the father found a way."

Kelis paused to listen to a sound nearby, the scrape of sharp-clawed feet across the dry ground. They both listened for a moment, until the serrated trilling of a black-backed cricket cut through the faint sounds. The scraping was likely a lizard. Nothing that would bother them.

Aliver prompted, "The father found a way . . ."

Kelis continued. "He adopted a dead man's son, and he put that dead man's son before his own son. He called him firstborn, which meant that everything that was the father's—his name, ancestors, belongings—would go to this adopted son. If the dreamer son wanted to live a prosperous life, he could do only one thing. He called the adopted one to the circle and killed him. He thrust his spear through his chest and watched his new brother drain of life. Instead of being angry, the father was pleased. It was just as he thought. His true firstborn son had a warrior within him, whether he liked it or not. The father got what he wanted. After that his son truly hated sleep. In sleep he still dreamed, but only ever of the same thing. He dreamed of that fight, of sinking his spear home, of the blood, of watching a man's face as he dies. So the dreamer was squashed; only the warrior remained."

"I have not heard this tale before," Aliver said.

The other cocked his head to the side, straightened it. "None of us choose our fathers. Neither you nor I, nor anybody else. But, believe me, when one is born to a calling, it should not be refused. To not do the thing one was born to do is a heavy burden to bear."

Aliver's legs were stiff the next morning, but they loosened readily enough when put to work. The pace of the second day matched the first. The land through which they traveled shared the same tree-dotted and wide-valleyed rolling contours. But on the third day a pack of four laryx caught their scent and fell in behind them in pursuit. The loping beasts yelped their garbled speech and grew near enough that, glancing back, Aliver could see their individual features. One of them was missing an ear. Another ran on a weakened foreleg. The leader was a larger beast than the one he had killed, and the fourth tended to flank out toward one side, as if already anticipating rounding on them. If the four of them caught up with and surrounded the men, there would be no hope of their escaping alive. Laryx's hatred of humans went hand in hand with their fear. Like a lion hunting the cubs of lesser cats, they seemed to hunt men out of spite.

Running before them, Aliver realized how different he was now from when he had hunted one of these beasts just a few weeks before. Back then, he had faced with clarity the reality that if he failed in any action, he would die horribly as a consequence. The strange thing was that at his core this feeling was entirely familiar to him. At some level he had lived with such a fear since the evening his father was stabbed in the chest. There had always been an unseen monster pursuing him. Facing a real one, in the bright light of day, liberated something in him. He had run the beast into the ground and then turned on it and drawn close enough that he could smell the creature's breath. He had looked at the foul entirety of it and . . . he had done what he was supposed to do. He sank his spear deep into its chest and held it in place as the laryx bucked and protested with the last of its strength.

He was not sure exactly how, but he knew this deed had altered something within him for the better.

Kelis pressed the pace. They did not stop at midday. Instead, they ran on through the rippling heat. Though laryx had the capacity to run for hours they only did so when truly provoked. They lost the laryx pack when easier prey—warthogs—came to the beasts' attention. The two men ran on with little rest and did not pause until several hours after dark.

On the fifth day they traversed a salt flat and came across a mass migration of pink birds. Thousands and thousands of them marched across the land, an enormous flock shimmering in the sun's glare, each of them long necked and graceful, with black legs that stepped high and formal. Why they did not fly, Aliver could not guess. They just parted as the two runners passed through them, watching them sidelong and without comment.

Late the sixth morning they came to the great river that drained the western hills of water. It was a wide, shallow trench more than a mile across. In the rainy season it was a formidable barrier. Even now it served as the southern boundary of inhabited Talay. The river itself was but a trickle now, a narrow vein of moisture a few strides wide, ankle deep. The two men stood in the water. Aliver enjoyed the feel of the smooth stones beneath his feet, slick against his skin. Had the horizon around them not been an endless stretch of pale, coarse soil, sparsely vegetated and crisped by the long tenure of the sun, Aliver might have closed his eyes and let the feel of the stones and the water conjure memories of times and places very far from here.

"Brother," Kelis said, "I go no farther than this."

Aliver turned toward him and watched him as he scooped another gourd of water and lifted it to his lips. "What?"

"My people do not venture south of this river. The Giver will run with you from here. He is a better companion than I."

Aliver stared at him.

"I'll wait for you," Kelis said. "Believe me, Aliver, when you return to this point I will be here to meet you."

Aliver was stunned enough by this that he did not dispute it. Kelis left him with the list of things to do and not do, reminders of how to conserve water and where to search for roots that held moisture and which animals might likewise offer him a drink of blood. Aliver already knew everything the man recited, but he stood as if listening, lingering in each moment that delayed his departure.

"Sangae gave me a message for you," Kelis said, as he lifted Aliver's sack and helped him string it over his back. "He said you are a son to him. And you are a son to Leodan Akaran. And you are a prince to the world. He said he knows you will meet the challenges facing you with bravery. He said that when you lift the crown of Acacia to your head he hopes you will allow him to be among the first to bow before you."

"Sangae does not need to bow before me."

"Perhaps *you* don't need him to bow before you. But he might—for himself. Respect flows two ways and can mean as much to the giver as to the one receiving. Go now. You have far to travel before the sun sets. You should find hills to shelter in at night, rock outcroppings. The laryx fear such places at night."

"How do I find the Santoth? Nobody has told me."

Kelis smiled. "Nobody *could* tell, Aliver. Nobody knows."

His first few days alone Aliver experienced even longer periods of trance than previously. It was not so much thoughts of his mission or memories from the past that stirred him as it was glimpses of the chaotic grandeur trapped in the silent flesh of the world, in the air breathing and creatures moving across the land. Once, in a landscape pocked with massive craters, Aliver watched the sky as contained in the bowl through which he progressed. Above him clouds gathered, seethed. They did not move on as clouds usually did. They seemed trapped in this particular spot in the world, ever changing but never escaping.

Moments like this one struck him with import. He did not regard it as a sign to read for prophecy. The meaning was simply there in the viewing, in his watching moments of life with eyes so very opened, so appreciative. In his youth he had never been one to study sunsets or vistas, or to pay much attention to the changing colors of leaves on the Mainland. In this regard he was a very different person from the one he had been.

In the middle of his fourth night alone Aliver awoke, having realized something while asleep that drove him up into consciousness. When Kelis told the story of that dreamer denied his path by his father . . . he had been talking about himself. Kelis was the dreamer denied his destiny. Perhaps this should have been obvious from his tone, but Kelis had never revealed things about himself before. He had never asked for another person's pity. He had not been doing so by telling that story either, Aliver knew. Why hadn't Aliver realized this at the time and said something?

Later that night he had a dream of his own, and he spent the entirety of the next day recalling the actual conversations that had sparked it. During the week or so that he had met each afternoon with Thaddeus, they had talked of more than just Aliver's challenges. The old man had unburdened himself of his deceit. He explained the tale Hanish Mein had detailed for him of how Aliver's grandfather might have killed Thaddeus's wife and child. Yes, he said, despite the source that brought him the news, he did believe that Gridulan had had his family murdered. Because of it, Thaddeus had wanted revenge. He had, for a brief moment, betrayed the Akarans.

Aliver had barely been able to respond, either with renewed anger or with the forgiveness the man obviously craved. He was not sure if he should hate the man for conspiring with Hanish Mein or if he should apologize for his own treacherous family or if he should thank Thaddeus for being the instrument of his and his siblings' rescue.

In the course of these conversations Thaddeus had revealed the complex web of crimes that truly held the world together. This, painful as it was, Aliver was thankful to finally hear. He had always feared the unspoken, the unexplained. He had heard words like *Quota* and whispers about the Lothan Aklun without ever succeeding in pinning them to concrete facts. Now, however, he heard everything that Thaddeus could tell him. Acacia was a slaving empire. They traded in flesh and thrived on forced labor. They peddled drugs to suppress the masses. The Akarans were not the benevolent leaders he had always been taught to believe they were. What, he wondered, did all of this mean for him? Could he be sure that a new Akaran rule would be better than that of Hanish Mein?

Eventually the landscape took on a different character. It grew even drier, and he moved, weaving through a region of broken ground. The sparse grass was bleached almost silver and contrasted sharply with the mounds of rocks that dotted the land, blackened, volcanic stone that looked like the droppings of some ancient creatures from the previous world. Aliver was not sure if he thought of that comparison himself or if he had heard such a tale told before. He seemed to have some memory of this and even a vague notion of watching the creatures turn from this place and walk, great legged, over the horizon in search of a better land. Between the rocks, solitary acacia trees grew, short versions of the species, stunted and terribly gnarled. They were aged grandfathers of the race, abandoned here some time ago and standing still, their arms upraised in unanswered supplication.

Nowhere among any of this did he see signs of humans. There were no villages here, no traces of agriculture or discarded tools. There were not even animals. It was a terribly lonely landscape, each day more so. The Santoth had been men, humans just like Edifus, a man whose blood flowed in Aliver's veins. If they lived anywhere near here, there would have been some sign of them. But there was nothing.

One morning a week into his solitary journey Aliver realized that he would not survive this search. Part of him had never expected to find these Santoth, but it had not occurred to him until he sorted through his meager supplies—a palm-sized portion of sedi grain, a few mouthfuls of warm water, a small packet of dried herbs for making soup—that he did not have enough to live more than another day or two. He had not seen a trace of a water source in three days. There had been no sign of knuckle root or of any of the plants that trapped even small sips of water. He had never been in a drier place. Just sitting there he felt the air pulling moisture from his skin. He could try to retrace his steps back to the boundary river, but how many days was he from it? Try as he might he could not say, except that it was farther away than he was capable of walking.

He stood on his aching legs and surveyed the land. The world stretched out before him in uniform desolation, to the horizon and beyond. Nothing. Nothing in it but sand and rock and the sky above it all. He took a step. And then another. He did not try to run. He just felt he had to move, walking slowly, stumbling. He left his supplies where they lay. They would not help him for long, and without them he would get past this ordeal quicker. He noted the position of the sun and gauged the time of the day, and then decided that none of it mattered. The Santoth—as he had suspected all along—were nothing but vapors from the past kept alive by superstitious minds. And he was just a walking dead man. The surprising thing was he did not really mind that much. He felt vindicated in a way. He had been right all along. He was not destined for some mythic greatness. Maybe that mantle would fall upon Corinn or Mena or even Dariel, or maybe the Akaran line did not deserve the power they had wielded.

This all made perfect sense to him, and accepting it granted him a calm he had never felt before. He thought fondly of his sisters and brother. He wished he had seen them grow to adulthood. He hoped they would succeed at whatever they attempted. He, Aliver, had always been the weak link, no matter how hard he tried to be otherwise. His father had put too much faith in him.

Around midday he stumbled and fell. He pushed himself up to his knees, around him a flat expanse of sand, dotted here and there with oblong rocks the same tan color as everything else, standing or on their sides or leaning against each other. He half wondered at the geological oddities they were, but his throat was so very dry and that seemed more of note. His skin had stopped sweating some time ago. His head pounded with his heartbeat, and at times the pulse of it dimmed and brightened his vision.

He lay down. None of this would be so bad if he did not have to feel it from inside his body anymore. He lay like this for some time, content not to have a purpose any longer. That was why from the first sign of movement, of change, he felt an emotion wash through him, a coloring of the world that he experienced as . . . not as fear, as he might have expected. Not as awe or disbelief. The emotion was harder to define. It was something like regret. What caused it was the fact that the stones all around him awoke. They awoke and began walking slowly toward him.

CHAPTER

THIRTY-FIVE

The hunting lodge of Calfa Ven clung to a south-facing granite buttress, looking down upon the sharp, wild valleys of the King's Preserve. Half carved into the rock and half perched atop it, the lodge had been a pleasure retreat for Acacian nobility for over two hundred years. The name meant "nest of the mountain condor" in the Senivalian tongue. The preserve was a densely forested land rich in game, protected by a small staff that maintained the lodge and patrolled the broad-leaved woodlands for poachers. Corinn had not visited it since girlhood, but it remained a place she remembered well.

It had taken the Meins several years to come to grips with the empire enough to be able to take holidays. The very idea was somewhat strange to a people who had hunted for sustenance, but they had recently warmed to the custom. When Corinn learned that Hanish requested her presence with him at the lodge, she had little choice but to accept. Not that she would have refused if she could. She made sure that her resentment showed in her demeanor and speech, but she never felt more nervously alive than she did in his company.

She was riding a little distance behind Hanish, along with several Meinish noblewomen, when they arrived at the lodge. From this side it was a gray granite structure, composed of large blocks in a simple style meant to hark back to humbler times. The contingent of staff awaited them on the steps. Corinn recognized one of them, the head house servant, Peter. She had thought him handsome when she was a girl, and it stunned her how old he seemed now. He was the first thing about the lodge that truly showed the passage of time.

Peter was effusive in his greeting. He approached Hanish with a half-stooped posture, his body trembling like an old hound trying to wag its arthritic tail. "We are most pleased by your visit, lord. Most pleased . . ." He barely gave Hanish the space to respond, his flow of words testifying to how long they had waited to meet him, how carefully they had prepared for his visit, how lush he would find the forest, how the hunting would be beyond his expectations. "The preserve is teeming with all manner of beasts. You will have no trouble—"

The servant paused mid-sentence. His eyes, which had just begun to move across the company, had found Corinn. He stared at her for a moment, wide-eyed, the full circle of his irises visible within the surrounding whites. He bowed his head and welcomed her by name, stammering. Then he turned away and gave his attention to Hanish once more.

His look unnerved Corinn. Why did he seem frightened? He feared Hanish, that was obvious, but the look he had briefly set on the princess was a different sort of alarm. She could not entirely get his expression out of her mind, although the experience of touring the lodge largely pressed it to the side. It was strange listening to Peter lead the entourage through rooms that she already knew. He spoke as if all of it had been created especially for Hanish's pleasure, as if the memory of former inhabitants was a distant thing indeed.

The interior rooms were cramped and somewhat dark, lit by lamps hung on the walls and by fires in the fireplaces. Some of the old trappings were in view: a wall hanging of a hunt that ran the length of the dining room, a candelabra into whose ornate silverwork the tale of Elenet was carved, the bubbling glasswork pots of fragrant herbs and spices. How she had loved that scent. Inhaling it threatened to flood her with emotion. She tried to breathe shallowly and note the things that had been added or changed to suit the new masters. Fur rugs and furniture coverings in the Meinish style; a few low, stout-legged tables; the Mein crest stained on the stones of the floor before the dining hall fireplace: there were plenty of new touches, superficial as they were.

Larken, the Acacian Marah who had betrayed her years before, walked beside Hanish, puffed up by his status and talking almost as much as Peter. With Maeander gone, Larken was nearly always at the chieftain's side. Corinn still hated him, though she tried not to let it show.

She heard the other women talking, commenting on the things they saw, finding this or that object quaint, charming. Rhrenna kept running her fingers across the tabletops, checking them for dust. They wore their new gentility so garishly it annoyed Corinn, though she did not let this emotion show either. The main weapon she had against these people was an inward defiance. Disdain nourished her, and she tended it like a gardener cares for the prickled beauty of a rosebush.

The greatest feature of the lodge was the view that its placement afforded. Each room overlooking the King's Preserve had an open-air balcony from which to stare at a lush canopy of broad-leaved trees that stretched into the northern distance, disturbed here and there by other granite outcroppings. Wind brushed through the treetops in places, much as storm breezes ruffle the seething sea. The rough beauty of it stunned her. This part of it seemed nothing at all like her childhood memories. She recalled only the ominous fear of the greenness of the place, the shadows beneath the trees that seemed to everywhere hide ogres, wood ghouls and wolverbears. True enough, she could still sense the threat of all of these things, but she found it invigorating. It reminded her of the images she had conjured of Igguldan's northern forests.

That evening she dined at Hanish's table in the main room. All told, the company numbered about thirty, with about the same number of servants busy behind the tables, rushing in and out of the hallway leading to the kitchens. The food was somewhat too gamy for Corinn's tastes, all venison and boar, blood cakes and fattened livers. She did little more than move it around on her plate. One of the things she hated about such occasions was the ever-present possibility that she would be called into conversation as some sort of representative of things Acacian. Early on she had risen to the bait and worked herself up, recounting the accomplishments of her people, but this had never achieved what she wished. Either she felt a fool because her knowledge did not match the verifiable facts others answered her with, or she ended painfully aware that she had only made the Mein triumph over her people seem that much greater. Tonight she found herself again and again the focus of conversation. Larken could have answered any of the questions directed at her better than she, but no one seemed to remember that he had ever been an Acacian.

"Corinn, that mural in the hallway, what story does it tell?"

"Which one?"

"The one that's like—that's like the entire world, so large and detailed. But it all centers around one boy-looking person. You know the one I mean."

Corinn did. She answered that it was a depiction of the world in the days of Elenet. She gave no more willingly, but after being probed she said that it dramatized the moment just after the Giver had turned away from the world. That, she said, was all she knew about it.

"Such a strange belief system," a young woman named Halren said. "It's built into your faith that your god abandoned you, right? He loathes you. He spurns your devotion, and for centuries your people went on halfheartedly worshipping him. On one hand you say, 'God exists and he hates me,' and the next instant you shrug and carry on your life, without even trying to win back his favor. Do you not see the folly in this?"

Corinn shifted, glanced at Larken, shifted again, and mumbled that she had not thought much about it.

"Why even ask her?" one of Rhrenna's maidens said. "She's not a scholar—are you, Corinn?"

The princess was not sure if this was meant as a friendly gesture or as a slight. Either way she felt her blood rise to her face.

"If I'd lost the favor of the Tunishnevre, I'd do anything to win it back," Halren said, looking furtively at Hanish. "Fortunately, though, I feel they're quite content with me. With all of us, really, thanks to our chieftain."

This did nothing to lower the red from Corinn's cheeks. She turned her gaze to Halren, to the silvery sparkles on her forehead and her pale features. "You've been 'blessed' for what? Nine years? That's a sneeze compared to the Akaran reign." Corinn might have said something even sharper— something she would have regretted afterward—except that Hanish chose that moment to become the center of attention.

"The princess makes an indisputable point," he said. He seemed to consider this for a moment, his gray eyes thoughtful. "Corinn, have you heard the tale of Little Kilish? Little Kilish was a giant of a man, named ironically, you see. He was a farmer who made for himself a scythe so massive only he could wield it. He loved to swing it in great swathes, cutting free grains of wheat by the millions. He crafted a second scythe and danced through the wheat fields slicing circles and patterns, each stroke like the work of ten men. He became famous all around the countryside. He had a contest against others to test who could cut the most wheat, but he always triumphed without question. Soon nobody would even contest him."

Hanish paused as a servant replaced his used plate with a clean one. He went on, explaining that one day a stranger arrived, a small man with dusky skin and mischievous eyes. He was a soul harvester. He had built some sort of machine that had already felled the greater part of the world. It was a great frame that stretched across an entire field from edge to edge, attached to wheels to move it about. At a hundred different points all across it he positioned mannequin figures, hinged and intricate like true humans but made of oak. Each of them gripped a sickle. When the people saw this they laughed. What sort of massive toy was that? What use are people made of wood? But this soul harvester knew some of the god's talk. He whispered spells that stole souls out of those who were laughing at him. He placed one soul in each of the wooden figures. This brought them to life. They began to swing their tools just as real people would. The soul harvester slapped his mule and the beast pulled the contraption down the field. All the wooden people worked for him, and in just a few moments he had cut down more than Little Kilish could have managed in an entire day.

Another servant tried to refill the chieftain's glass, but Hanish brushed him away, impatient, it seemed, with the constant attention. "The people were amazed," he said. "They praised the stranger. All agreed that he had won the contest and to him went the honor. Little Kilish, however, hated that machine, hated the man who'd built it. All the fuss annoyed him greatly. Why were people applauding so vile a thing?"

"For a moment they forgot their own souls," Halren said.

"Didn't they notice the soulless zombies that now stood among them? Before he had thought through what he was doing Little Kilish swung his scythe and sliced the soul harvester's head clean from his shoulders. It fell to the ground and chattered on for some minutes yet before the tongue inside the thing realized all was lost. Little Kilish looked around him, afraid lest he be called a murderer and criminal and find himself banished. But the people did not banish him. They rejoiced. They said, 'Let Kilish harvest our wheat, for he is strong and has no need to steal our souls!' And so it was."

Hanish motioned with his hand that there was no more to tell. Several voices praised his telling of the tale. Halren beamed as she looked about, as if Hanish had told the story particularly to her. But the chieftain kept his attention on Corinn. "We've told this tale for many, many years. You understand its significance, don't you?"

"You say that Little Kilish was a giant of a man, but I suspect at least one feature of his body was not so large," Corinn said. "That, surely, is how he got his name. One shouldn't trust a man called Little. No man wants to think any part of himself small. It makes him bitter, unjust, and petty—"

Rhrenna said, "Corinn, you've such a way of—"

"Little Kilish," Hanish said, interrupting both women, "was of the Meinish race; the soul harvester was Acacian born. That's the significance. We may be new to power, Princess, but we did not sell our souls to get it. It just took us a bit longer to achieve by honest means what your people won through treachery."

"You've just now invented that tale," Corinn said. "And, 'honest means'! Are you—"

Hanish threw back his head and laughed. "I've angered the princess. I doubt she'll admit that what surprises her is how accurately an ancient tale unveils the current truth of our two people's history. It's almost like a prophecy, isn't it? My joy is in having had a hand in making it come true."

This received murmurs of approval around the table, but Corinn said, "That may be your joy, but it's my sorrow."

"I don't believe that," Hanish said. He stared at her. "I think you say such things simply because you feel you are supposed to. But in truth, Princess, we have done you little harm. Yes, there's your father. I won't ask you to forgive me for that, but I will ask you to remember that in the same few moments you lost your father I lost a beloved brother. They were each instruments of a cause, of conflicting causes. This is just the way of men and there's no crime in it." Hanish drew back, picked up his glass, and sipped. "Beyond that we've done you no harm."

"No harm—" Corinn began but was cut off.

"Exactly so. We never touched a hair on one of your siblings. Never. And we never would, not to harm them, at least. We've only ever wanted to bring them home, to the palace where they belong. They could live beside us, just like you do. Look at yourself, Corinn. Look at the life you have. You are the center of a court of women and men who adore you, despite the barbs you throw at us. You have all the luxuries of royalty; none of the responsibilities. I only wish you would warm to your position more. I would, truly, like to see you . . . content."

Corinn snapped her head up to face him directly. She had felt as if he was about to stick his tongue in her ear. That was how his last spoken word had reached her, like a wet caress that could reach across the table and touch her in front of everyone's eyes. But he was sitting back, at ease, his glass near his nose as he scented the wine. No one except Maeander had ever made her feel more uncomfortable for no obvious reason. She said, "Then die—you and all your people—and give me back my family."

Halren began a shocked response, but Hanish looked only amused. "My dear emotional girl," he said to Corinn, "you really are quite beautiful. Isn't she, Larken?"

"A touch petulant," the traitor said, "but she's no hardship to look upon."

Corinn rose and left the room, feeling each and every set of eyes upon her.

Chapter

Thirty-six

For Leeka Alain it was no easy thing to come off the mist. There were days of visions. Nights of horrific dreams. Pains shot through his body with such electric force that he went rigid and trembling on his cot. At times he had glimpses of the world as he had seen it during the raging fever he had endured in the Mein. But beyond all of this he would remember the delirium as one of consumption, a nightmare during which he was simultaneously being consumed and consuming himself. At times it felt like his body writhed with thousands of sharp-jawed worms, serrating their way through every portion of his flesh. What was worse, though, was that the worms were part of him. Leeka himself was both the devourer and the devoured. He ate himself, and he was eaten.

Throughout all of this the former chancellor stayed at his side. From the first night when Thaddeus came upon him in the dark, he had been there to aid him, a strict doctor, nurse, jailer, and confidant all at once. Thaddeus all but sealed him in his hovel of a cabin in the hills above that backwater town. He bound his wrists and feet to the bed, wrapped a wide strip of cloth around his midsection, and sat beside him, explaining that he had a great need for Leeka's services. He could not even begin to discuss it with him, however, until Leeka's mind and body were free of addiction. Leeka railed at him, confused as he was and frightened by the turmoil building in his body.

At one point when his vision had cleared enough for him to see his caretaker looking down upon him, he said with complete certainty that he was dying. This was not an ordeal he could live through.

"Do you see this?" Thaddeus asked, stretching out his fingers to reveal a barb fastened to the tip of his little finger. "This pin has been dipped in a poison so potent it kills almost before its victim can feel the prick of it. Similar to that which I used on you in its quickness, save that this one is deadly. I will leave this here beside you. If it is true that you cannot live without your mist and wine, then use it to take your own life. Or, if you are too self-ish for that, come upon me in sleep and kill me. Rob me of what coins I have in my bags and run away. Let the fate of the world rest in Hanish Mein's hands. Stake no claim to greatness. All of this is within your power if you choose. If you kill me, it will not even be a crime; it would be a gift. You see, I have many demons to face as well. We could be cowards together."

The man tugged the weapon from his finger and placed it on the stool he had sat on. He untied his patient's arms and legs, loosened the sash across his torso, and then moved away. Leeka was quite sure that Thaddeus, no matter his wisdom, would never really know how close he had come to picking up that pin and sinking it into his neck. He wanted to so very badly. He fantasized each action, each motion of gathering the man's coins, each stride down to the village, all the transactions he would need to go through before he got his lips once more around a pipe and inhaled. For the life of him he was not sure what stopped him.

The next morning he awoke crying. He knew without doubt that he was alone in the world. He blamed no one but himself for it. The fate of nations may have pushed and shoved his life, but it was his own fault that he had never properly loved a woman, never fathered children, never looked at the world with fear and hope for his grandchildren. If he had done any of these things he might have made better sense out of living. He could not fathom how he had lived for so many years without realizing the sums of his existence were destined to add up to naught. Perhaps he should use the release of that poisoned pin after all—on himself.

"I can see you are not entirely done feeling sorry for yourself," Thaddeus said, interrupting his thoughts.

Leeka rolled over to see the man sitting once more on that stool, studying him, a hand outstretched with a cloth dangling from it. Leeka took it up and wiped his face, aware that he should be embarrassed but not quite feeling it. Thaddeus asked him if he was hungry enough to eat; Leeka heard himself say that he was.

"Good," the other man said. "That is the right answer. I have made some soup. Just vegetables and herbs I found in the hills, some mushrooms. But I think you will like it. Share it with me, and then we can talk properly about the work I have for you to do."

He would think many times later how strange a thing it is that one moment a person can wish for death, only to be distracted into life by a few kind words, by a kerchief extended, by simple food to fill an empty stomach. These things, as much as anything else, brought Leeka through. After that morning it was never really so hard to refuse the mist. He did have pangs of his old hunger, certainly. He had them daily, hourly almost. He had to decide again and again not to succumb. But he found he had the power to refuse. The fact that Thaddeus gave him a mission lent him the strength.

He left his hillside hovel with a mind full of instructions, with his hopes renewed in the most unexpected of ways. He bore an Acacian sword at his hip, a parting gift from the chancellor. In earlier years a former soldier of the empire would have drawn attention walking about armed, but the world had changed somewhat from the first years of Hanish's rule. The resistance had been vanquished. The thinly spread Meinish troops paid little attention to individuals, reserving their energies to protecting the security of Hanish's rule and the commerce that sustained it.

Leeka walked, loving the pumping of air in his lungs, the ache of his legs. By the end of his first week of trekking, he had found his old discipline again. He intentionally chose routes up and over the harder passes, trudging up scree or talus slopes, each forward stride halved by the loose matter sliding beneath his feet. One afternoon while resting in the saddle between two peaks, his legs cramped. His hamstrings clenched and heaved, the pain of them all enveloping. Leeka tilted his face to the sky, crying with joy. He was getting his body back.

He would never forget the exhilaration he felt on top of a peak near the western crest of the Senivalian Mountains, around him nothing but the clouds above, below thousands of pinnacles rising all around, each sharp as wolverbear's teeth, each like a rebellious finger pointed toward the heavens in accusation. He danced himself through the Tenth Form, that of Telamathon as he fought the Five Disciples of the god Reelos. He had felt no purer moment in his life. It was a choreographed tribute, an act of connection with everything that he ever had been and everything he hoped he might be again. He may have been mistaken, perhaps delusional, lightheaded from the altitude, vainglorious; he was not sure, but he had believed, as he slashed and swirled, leaped and spun, that for a moment all those mountainous protrusions paused to watch him.

And then, all too soon, he stumbled out of the mountains and rolled down to the shore of the Gray Slopes. He shouldered his way into the bustle of trade, commerce, and human treachery in the seaside towns there. Few faces looked upon him with kindness. All measured him for risk or opportunity. There was, he felt, a menace hanging in the fabric of the air, different from anything he had felt during Leodan's reign. He was accosted again and again by peddlers of mist, all assuring him of the quality of their product, its purity, its direct origin from source, uncut, clean. Leeka was not sure if something in his face or demeanor made him a target for such people, or whether such was just the traffic of the world now. A few times he clamped his fist down on the hands of pickpockets exploring his garments. He was twice accosted in bars for insults he had not been aware of giving. Once he brandished his sword when cornered by three youths in a back alley. He sliced the air with the few quick strokes it had taken Aliss to dispatch the Madman of Careven. They had sense enough to back away, and he was grateful for it.

Thaddeus had given him the name of a man to seek out in a particular coastal town. He found the man and convinced him Thaddeus had sent him. The man passed him into the care of another, who fed him and told him what he could, who helped him fight back the mist hunger and sent him forward with a message to another person. Thus he came to understand that there was a hidden resistance at work in the world. The old chancellor was part of something larger than himself. Thanks to him, so was Leeka.

Throughout all of this he interviewed anyone he could as casually as he could. He knew of the person he searched for by a single name. He uttered it sparingly. He framed his queries differently depending on whom he spoke to. He passed one full month and much of a second in this manner, getting no closer to his goal, hearing little that helped him but much that fired his desire to push on. Still, when a break came he at first did not recognize it for what it was or welcome it.

A woman approached him in a tavern in a fishing port whose name he had not even asked. She carried a drink in one hand. She smiled at him and was young and attractive in a jaded enough way that he took her to be a prostitute. When she spoke, however, she struck with surprising directness. "Why are you asking after a raider?"

Leeka answered with one of his prepared responses. He was intentionally vague. He alluded to a business proposal, to inside information that he possessed, to the prospect that he and this raider might benefit each other in a variety of ways, all of them too delicate to reveal to anybody but the young raider himself.

"Hmm," she said. She nodded her head as if this satisfied her. She took a sip of her drink and then, without any sort of warning, she pursed her lips and spat at him, spraying his face and eyes with a burning liquid. He was blinded. Hands fell upon him, more than just the woman's. Suddenly it seemed every person in the tavern had lain in wait for him. He was battered by fists and blunt objects; his weapons stripped from him; his head beaten, beaten, beaten against a wall until he lost consciousness.

When he awoke he knew he was at sea. He felt the spray against his face. His body was wet. Drenched, actually. Intermittently dunked beneath the surface of the sea. He was, he realized, strapped rigid against a board that had been nailed to the prow of a ship. His arms and legs and torso were bound tight, and at times his body cut the ship's course through a seething green sea. He was a living prow figure.

And it was as such that he arrived at Palishdock, in a less than desirable condition, with a great deal less secrecy than he wished, very little of his stature obvious to the motley throng of brigands that gathered to gape at him. The crew that lowered him to the pier was not over-careful about it. They left him facedown againt the sun-bleached beams for some time. When they finally carried him to shore they simply lifted the entire plank and walked with him, the ground rising and falling beneath him with their strides. They dropped him in the hot sand but only for a moment. He felt the entire board tilted upward and leaned back against a building of some sort. Thus he waited, bound, bruised, sand dusted.

The young woman he had taken for a prostitute was there, along with the host of thugs that had so easily beaten and bound him. They leaned about, as casual and lackadaisical as any street vagrants, until two others stepped out from one of the makeshift structures of the place: a young man and a large man. The young man did not look pleased. He conferred with the ones who had brought Leeka, and then studied him from a distance, seemingly considering whether to address him or turn away. The large man leaned heavily on a cane. His skin was pallid and his frame, though massive, sagged like a sack half full. He watched Leeka without speaking, just stared at him fixedly.

Eventually, the young man walked forward through the sand. He plucked the dagger from the sheath on his thigh and held it between himself and Leeka, not exactly a threat but not far from it. "Who are you, and why were you asking about me?"

Looking into the young man's handsome face, nearly breathless at the prospect of the answer, Leeka asked, "You are the one they call Spratling?"

"I answer to that name. What of it?"

Leeka wished his lips were not so swollen and stiff, crusted with dried blood and salt. He wished his puffy eye was not obscuring his gaze and that he had a drink of water to loosen the words in his throat. But none of these things was about to change, so he said what he had planned to.

"Prince Dariel Akaran," he began, "I rejoice to set eyes—"

"Why do you call me by that name?" the young man cut in, flaring with confused anger.

To Leeka's relief, another answered for him. The large man hobbled his great bulk forward. "Calm yourself, lad. It's my doing. It's my doing."

CHAPTER

THIRTY-SEVEN

Mena grabbed hold of the loops of rusty metal and pressed her bottom to the sand. Thus anchored she tilted her head and gazed up through columns of living mollusks. She sat, as she often did, on the sandy floor of the harbor, some thirty feet from the surface, her breath clamped tight inside her. Her hair floated around her in sinuous tendrils. Around her rose a towering forest of shadows, each of them a chain suspended from the surface and anchored to the ground. Oysters hung from the links by the thousands. Full grown, the creatures were as large around as a child's head. Though much of this bulk was composed of shell, each of them could feed three or four diners, simmered in a coconut milk sauce and served with transparent noodles. They were a delicacy around which the temple controlled a monopoly. The export market in black oysters filled the temple coffers each time the floating merchants passed the archipelago.

Her lungs began to burn. They heaved against her chest. Every muscle out to her fingertips and toes twitched in protest, every part of her shouted in anger. Beyond the oysters, the brilliant turquoise of the surface glow highlighted the weight and size of the mollusks, as if the world above was a blessed place of light that she could regain only by the most perilous of ascents. She unclenched her hands and floated free. As she flew upward toward the light she blew a stream of bubbles preceding her. She was never sure if it was the bubbles themselves or if the oysters sensed her coming, but one by one the creatures folded their gaping shells closed, opening a passageway for her all the way to the surface. The last few moments were the worst, the most frantic, the entirety of her being screaming to get out of her skin, sure she had hung on too long.

She broke into the air with her mouth a gaping oval. Air engulfed her, as did light and sound and movement, as did life. She could not explain her need for this strange ordeal, but it always left her feeling temporarily secure about the purity of her soul. This was a thing that concerned her, especially on a day like this one, when she would look into the face of grieving parents and swear that a child's death was a boon to them all, a necessary sacrifice, and a gift any parent should wish to give.

She left the oyster farm mid-morning. For nearly half an hour she negotiated the labyrinth of piers and floating docks that clogged the shallow, crescent harbor. The portion of the docks owned by the temple was a solitary domain in which Mena spent hours. But in the commercial harbor she entered a bustling throng of merchants and seamen, fisherfolk and net weavers. She wove through stalls offering all manner of foodstuffs: fish and crustaceans, fruit from the coastal plantations and jungle meat from the inner mountains. Salesmen cried their wares in the singsong cadence of Vumu speech. She moved through it with quiet purpose, accepting the mumbled greetings directed at her, the respectful bowed heads, and the prayerful invocations. Maeben on earth walked among them. Usually this made people joyful, but this afternoon there was veiled import behind the eyes watching her.

As she walked the last stretch of pier to the shore, Mena noticed the stillness of a sailor who had paused to look at her. He stood on the railing of a trading barge, one hand grasped around a rigging rope to steady him. She glanced up at him just long enough to take in his shirtless torso; his clean-shaven, angular jaw; steady eyes; and head wrapped in strips of white cloth, the ends of which hung down to below his shoulders and stuck to the sweat on his chest. He was not from Vumu, but sailors were always a polyglot bunch. There was nothing kind in his countenance nor lecherous, but his attentive silence made Mena uneasy. She quickened her step.

At the temple she dressed in all the accoutrements of her guise as Maeben: talons fastened to her fingers; layers of feather robes; the spiky headdress that capped off her fierce, flamboyant appearance. As she felt the hands working around her she waited to feel the divine presence animate her form, place words in her, use her tongue to speak with, and form in her mind the resolution of complete belief. Thus far, however, the goddess refused to enter her when she was most needed. She held to her silence, and Mena was left to answer for her as best she could.

At first Mena had thought herself deficient. The senior priest assured her the goddess was just testing her, harsh mistress that she was. It was only a matter of time, he had said, until Maeben truly came to live inside her at all moments—not only during the frenzy of ceremonies. Though that had not happened, Mena had grown more and more comfortable with her role. All around her seemed complete in their belief, and that was usually sufficient to buoy her. Today was different, however, and she could not help but dread the meeting awaiting her.

A short while after dressing she sat on a thronelike chair in the anteroom of the temple. The head priest of Maeben's order, Vaminee, stood beside her. He was dark skinned. His complexion was so smooth as to betray no obvious hints at his age, though Mena knew he had held his post for more than forty years. He wore a thin robe that fell from his shoulders in diaphanous folds, and he stood so still he might have been a statue. This was not the first time they had waited for a meeting like this to begin. In truth, they had shared this same silence three times in the last few years.

The young couple entered, flanked by lesser priests. Heads down, hands held before them with palms upraised, they approached slowly. Mena could not help but note how small they looked. They were but children themselves! How could they have borne—and now lost—a child? They knelt at the foot of the dais.

Without ceremony, Vaminee asked, "Who are you? Of what place? What circumstance?"

The father answered in a high-pitched voice, choked with emotion. They were inlanders, he explained. They lived in a village in the mountains. He hunted birds for the feathers used in temple ceremonies; she wove palm fibers for baskets and various wares that they sent to market in Galat. Their daughter, Ria, had been a good girl, round faced like her mother, shy among other children. They had loved her more than life. He would have given his own soul instead of the child's without a moment of hesitation. He could not understand why—

"You have another child," Vaminee said. "A boy who is twin to the girl. Be thankful of that."

"And we had another before that," the father said, anxious that this point be understood. "Our children came all three at one time. We lost our first to the foreigner's offering. They took Tan from us. So why would Maeben punish us yet again?"

Oh, Mena thought, they had given a child to the Quota already. Now they had lost a second!

Vaminee was not moved. "Three children in one womb is too rich a bounty to go unnoticed. But tell us exactly what happened to the girl."

This fell to the mother to answer. She showed little of her husband's visible emotions. Her voice was like her eyes, flat and weary, as if she had passed beyond grief and found herself in another place. She had been walking a ridgeline with her daughter, she said. Ria had trailed some distance behind her, but she knew the trail well. She could hear her singing, repeating a few simple verses over and over and over. At some point her song stopped. Simply clipped in mid-phrase. She looked back to the spot where her child should have been, but it was empty. When she looked to the sky, she saw her daughter's legs. She saw them dangling as if from the sky itself. And then she saw the spread of wings that carried her away. And then she heard the beat of them.

Her eyes touched on Mena briefly, before tilting to the floor in front of her. "I knew then that Maeben had stolen her."

"Maeben steals nothing," Vaminee said. "What she takes becomes hers the moment she touches it."

"I had thought," the mother said, glancing up, "that Ria was my own. She came from—"

Vaminee's voice rose to cut her off. "Drop your eyes! You forget where you are. You think that your grief belongs to only you. You are wrong! Grief belongs to Maeben. What you feel is only a portion of what she endures. It is like a single grain of sand from all the beaches of Vumu. Maeben took your child to keep her company on Uvumal. One day you will understand it as a gift—to the girl and to you as well. Is this not so, Furious One?"

This was the sign Mena had dreaded, the signal that she had now to enter the exchange. She rose and moved toward them with her arms raised out to either side, wings held as if in preparation for flight. Her face was as still as she could keep it, though inside her mind raced to find the right words to justify the deeds of an angry deity. She still did not have them. She felt the beaked monstrosity of her mask. A pang of shame ripped through her.

She stopped just before the two, both of whom had flattened their foreheads to the floor. She saw the tattoo on the man's arm, the vertebrae nudging through the thin skin of the woman's back. How she loved these people—all the Vumu people! She loved the look of them, the smell of their skin and shape of their mouths in laughter, the quiet grace with which they moved. These two before her, at the moment, represented all of them who lived under the tyranny of the goddess she embodied. She hoped they would not look up at her. They did not have to. They could just keep their heads bowed and listen as she justified Maeben's actions. She had only to say a few sentences, just enough to remind them that Maeben answers to nobody, that she feels anger still for the slight humanity did to her. There was nothing for her to apologize for, and these two—she had been taught—would thank her later for showing strength in the face of their grief.

But the words that finally escaped her surprised her. She did not speak them in Vumu. She used the language she sometimes dreamed in, the language of her half-forgotten childhood. She said that she was sorry for them. She could not begin to understand their sadness. If she could undo it, she would. She would give them back their round-faced girl. She truly would.

"But I cannot," she said. "Maeben cares for your daughter now. You, though, should love your son twice as much. You have given to the goddess. Now your lives will be blessed and your son will be a joy to you always."

Leaving the chamber later, Mena wondered what the priest would have done to her if he had understood the language she had spoken in. It was bad enough that he had heard her speak the other language. He would likely chastise her for it later, but this never frightened her as much as the priest thought it did. Sometimes as he spoke she imagined herself drawing the old Marah sword she had arrived on the island with and cutting off his head. She saw just how she would do it, even imagining the blood and gore of it. It surprised her that her thoughts could turn so violent, but perhaps that was just a result of living so long as a representative of Maeben's anger.

She wondered if her speech had done any good for the couple. Certainly her words had been gibberish to them. Perhaps it was just a cowardly act, an incomplete confession. Why was she always drawn to this other language when faced with the most difficult of moments?

She was still wrapped up in these thoughts that evening as she left the main temple building and headed for her private quarters. She was dressed in a simple shift to ward off the sea breeze. Her bare feet padded on the packed sand, the path before her lit to bone gray by the stars, hemmed in on one side by a hedge of low bushes. She knew the way by heart and never carried a light with her.

She froze in mid-step, thinking she heard something—a whisper, perhaps, some sound that did not belong and had already vanished. But there was nothing except near silence, an insect chirping in the undergrowth and the quick scrabble of a rodent alarmed at her sudden immobility, a dog barking in town and some voices from back at the temple: that was it. The longer she listened the more she doubted that there had been a sound of any consequence at all. She had almost settled in to the comfort of this, when there was a rustling in the brush behind her.

She spun around to see a man's shape step into silhouetted being behind her. He must have hidden in the bushes until after she passed. He was taller than any Vumu in the village. He had to be an off islander, a sailor or raider, someone who meant her harm. Why else would he come upon her in the dark, alone? She calculated the distance to the village and considered her prospects of darting around him and back to the compound. She could scream. If so, how long would she have before someone reached her? She clenched her hands into fists, feeling the sharpness of her nails against her flesh, feeling the quick-beating calm that she understood as anger. She felt more the goddess at that moment than she had earlier, when she had worn her finery.

"Mena? It is you, isn't it?"

She understood him clearly enough, and for a moment she noted that his accent was indeed not of the island. But then she understood something else. He had not spoken to her in Vumu. He spoke . . . he spoke that other language. She recognized the words and knew their meaning even as she tasted the strangeness of hearing them spoken by another. He had called her by her first name, something known to few on the island. For a moment she feared she had brought a demon upon herself. Perhaps the goddess abhorred her for speaking in that foreign tongue. Perhaps this one who addressed her was here to punish.

"What do you want?" she asked, consciously speaking in Vumu. "I have nothing you can have, so leave me. I serve the goddess. Her wrath is keen."

"So I have heard," he said. "But you don't look like a giant sea eagle that snatches up young children. You don't look like that at all." The man took a step closer. She backed up, and he held up a hand to calm her. There was a noise in the compound. As the stranger cocked his head, the light on his profile was just strong enough for her to recognize the sailor who had stared at her that morning. For some reason, this mystified her more than it frightened her. "You speak Vumu like a native, but you are not, are you? Tell me I am not wrong. You are Mena Akaran, of the Tree of Acacia."

Mena shook her head, saying "I am Maeben on earth" several times, but not loudly enough to interrupt him.

"Your brother was Aliver. Your sister, Corinn. Dariel was the youngest. Your father was Leodan—"

"What do you want?" she snapped, not a question at all but a sudden shout that burst from her chest, a need to silence him because the names he was saying and the language he was speaking so calmly did not reach her calmly at all.

"You know me, Mena. I was your brother's companion, from his training group. My father was Althenos. He handled records for your father in the palace library. I danced with you when you were ten. Remember? You stood on the flat of my feet and caused me no end of pain. Say that you remember me. Please, Mena."

All through this speech he moved closer to her. Though the light got no better, his nearness drew out his features. She could only partially recall the things he said. They jostled and shoved about in her mind, arguing with the impossibility that he was standing before her uttering such things. And yet she did know his face. She recognized the boy he had once been in his eyes, still so large on his face, wide set and calming. His lips were parted, but her internal vision remembered what they looked like when he smiled, the way mirth transformed his features.

"Princess," the man said, dropping to his knees, "I had given up hope. . . . Tell me you are you and that I am not mistaken."

"What is your name?" she asked, her voice calmer than she felt. She could see his eyes reflecting the starlight. She watched something change in them and realized they had filled with tears.

He said, "I am Melio."

CHAPTER

THIRTY-EIGHT

R ialus Neptos had once believed that his governorship of the Mein Satrapy had been the great curse of his life. He hated that frozen place, filled with rough, outcast citizens of the empire. He seethed when he thought about the dismissive air with which the Akarans treated him, so much so that he had been willing to do anything to win a better situation in life. Thus, he had called upon low elements among his acquaintances in Alecia—family members, criminals, opportunists of every stripe—to rise and cause all manner of confusion to coincide with Hanish Mein's attack. He had watched with joy as the city spun into chaos. For a few short days he had lived in complete euphoria, seeing the old order swept away, awaiting the new reign of Hanish Mein, sure that he had earned a place of prominence within it.

How utter a betrayal, then, that Hanish had—in a maneuver that the new ruler must have thought the greatest joke on record—made Rialus personal liaison to Calrach, the headman of the thronging Numrek horde. Rialus often woke screaming from a nightmare of the moment when the chieftain had told him of the appointment. Hanish had pointed out that Rialus was one of the first Acacians the Numrek had encountered. He claimed that the Numrek still spoke warmly of the reception he had given them at Cathgergen. Rialus had demonstrated his fortitude, his skills at dealing with the rough race the Numrek were.

"You're the man for it, Rialus," he said. "You've more than earned it."

Rialus had offered a nervous rebuttal. He knew nothing about the Numrek! He wasn't suited to the cold portions of the country the Numrek were to settle in. He'd much prefer a post nearer the heart of the nation, in Alecia or along the coast near Manil. Perhaps he could serve Hanish as the chief magistrate of Bocoum? Some such position as that. But liaison to the

Numrek? He did not even speak their language. He did not wish to seem un-grateful, Rialus had said, but perhaps Hanish could reconsider. The beasts ate human flesh, after all! Hardly the sort of company a valued ally should be keeping.

He regretted afterward that he had protested at all. Maeander was there to hear it and seemed to take pleasure out of his begging. The appoint-ment held, and so began a new period of misery in Rialus's life.

There was some satisfaction to be taken from the fact that the Num-rek ignored Hanish's proclamations whenever they felt like it. They did not stay in the Mein, or even in Aushenia, as they had agreed to. Instead, they spread down toward the south. Calrach himself set up his court in a seized villa along the Talayan coast. Here, at least, Rialus found the warm weather he so enjoyed. But sun on the skin proved to be scant reward for other mis-eries of his daily existence.

What activities served to pass the time for the Numrek? What sort of culture did they have and how did they choose to enjoy the bounty their ser-vice to Hanish in the war afforded them? Well, they loved roasting them-selves in the sun, as if this alone was a pursuit worthy of reasonable beings. On clear days they would lie naked on the sand of the seashore, only mov-ing so as to roll from one side to another, sipping drinks fetched for them by Acacian servants. The young ones were always in among the adults, be-ing coddled one moment and knocked around the next, always afforded a clear vantage to any and all of the carnage.

When not lying about in the sun, they would rise long enough to beat one another with clubs, with curved wooden sticks that often broke bones, with knives they deemed just short enough not to be fatal. They took pride in acquiring scars. Rialus made the mistake of showing his squeamishness around wounds, which meant only that he was daily presented with new gashes and tears, the Numrek watching his face and never failing to be amused by his reaction, no matter how hardened a façade he tried to present.

He made another mistake regarding the spear-chucking game the Numrek enjoyed. It involved sending a slave dashing forward through an ob-stacle course as a spearman hurled a selection of javelins at him. Rialus once admitted that he found the spectacle amusing. In answer Calrach made Rialus himself run the course. He had pulled him from his seat and hefted a spear and smiled at him. "The trick," he said, "is to be lucky."

Rialus had never run so fast in his life. His heart pounded so hard he imagined others could see it thumping against his chest. Each instant he was in the course, he felt at the edge of death. The spears thudded just be-hind him each step of the way, marking his progress. He was sure he would either die or spend the rest of his life twisted around some festering impale-ment. None of the spears struck him, however. And it was not until his heart calmed enough so that he could hear over its bass notes that he real-ized Calrach and his companions were howling with glee. Calrach had not been trying to hit him. It was a game to them. Everything was, and try as he might Rialus could not find the courage not to make a fool of himself.

"Yes, Neptos, yes!" one of Calrach's lieutenants said. "Very amusing. You are right!"

They showed no inclination to higher forms of art. No painting or sculpture, no poetry or recorded history. They had no written language. They saw no need for it. In fact, their primitive nature went beyond any-thing Rialus had observed before. No function of the body embarrassed them. They would eat, belch, fart, defecate, fornicate, or even self-stimulate in clear view of anybody, without regard for sex or age or status. Rialus so amused them by seeking seclusion for his bodily functions that eventually he had to give up on privacy. It made him the butt of jokes; whereas drop-ping his trousers and piddling in the middle of the courtyard roused not the slightest interest. He sometimes wondered if the Numrek were, in fact, a race of human beings at all. Nine years at his post and he had yet to form a definitive answer to the question.

He had learned the Numrek tongue, however. It was the strangest of languages. Even the simpler words were many-pronged monstrosities. They required contortions of the tongue and inhalations of breath and guttural inflections from low in the throat.

The evening Calrach chose to bestow upon him his first official mis-sion began as any other banquet night. Rialus, at someone's humorous prompting, no doubt, was situated between two young women, concubines who were attached to no headman in particular. They did not look much different from the males, frankly. They brushed against him often; reached over him to grab morsels of food; prodded him with playful, thick-knuckled fingers.

The worst thing about this placement was that the females actually aroused Rialus. He hated it, was disgusted by it, could not understand it; but truth be known he sat uncomfortably positioned around a rigidity at his groin. The women had a smell to them, a syrupy sort of scent like a fruit overripened and starting to turn. It was not a pleasant smell, but some-where imbedded in it was an invitation to carnal excess. It was a sort of confused torture to endure the young women's presence through the evening. Calrach seemed to understand his discomfiture and to relish it. Indeed, the chieftain never tired of observing and commenting on Rialus's failings.

"Rialus, you still don't care for our food?" Calrach asked. "How can this be so? I have a dish for you. Try." As a servant set down a bowl of the concoction, Calrach described it as a stew made of the intestines of their rhinos, fermented in the milk of the females of the species, and stored for months in barrels. It was splashed liberally with alcohol before serving.

He watched Rialus touch a spoonful of the stuff to his lips. Unimpressed, he said, "Perhaps your stomach is too weak for this, like the rest of you."

The female to his left said, "There's only one part of him that's even the slightest bit hard."

"There is a great deal about my race you still must learn," Calrach said. "Another year or so, and you'll be Numrek yourself. And proud of it." He guffawed at the absurdity of this, and then switched gears. "Rialus, tell me, do you think Hanish Mein honors us? We Numrek, I mean. We chosen ones. Does he insult us?"

Rialus said, "I am not sure what you mean."

"Does he insult us?"

Calrach had a habit of doing this—repeating the last thing he said as if to demonstrate that all possible answers, meanings, interpretations were contained in the words themselves, if only Rialus would look more carefully.

Rialus asked, "What taste of insult have you felt?"

Calrach shrugged, tossed a hand about, scratched his cheek forcefully enough to tear away a few scraps of peeling skin. "Not a taste, so much. A smell, though. There is a smell I don't like. My grandfather used to speak of such a smell. It came from the Lothan, before they turned on us and drove us from their world. We used to be their personal army. You know that, don't you? We were their allies for many generations, but they used us foully in the end. If I have one wish, Rialus, it's to one day return to the Other Lands and bring the Lothan a new smell. You understand me."

Rialus hated it when he said that. He did so often, especially on occasions when Rialus did not understand him in the slightest. There was no use pushing it, however. Calrach had an orbital pattern of discourse that one had to adjust to. He would come back to the point later if it was something that mattered to him.

Then the drums sounded, announcing the arrival of the main course.

The evening was to feature a dish Rialus had not tried before, an event that always troubled him. The entire table before them suddenly rose, lifted above their seated heads by servants at each corner. It passed over Rialus, casting him in shadow. The young woman to his right grasped him across the bicep and purred something in his ear, an expression of anticipatory pleasure. By the time the first table cleared him the next table was being lowered into place.

Before him lay a delicacy the Numrek called tilvhecki. It was about the size of a mature pig, and looked like a bloated skin sack, translucent enough to reveal its contents as some sort of gaseous, multihued offal. Calrach, in talking about the pleasure awaiting them, explained that the look of it was in keeping with the truth. Tilvhecki was the name they had for lamb. During their exile in the Ice Fields they'd had no sheep with them and therefore had been deprived of this dish for some time. It was made with the usual Numrek elements of fermentation and putrification. It began weeks prior when the meat and internal organs of a young lamb were left for several days exposed to the open air. The meat was not cooked just then, but it was basted in blood juices and spices and wine. When the thing was thriving with maggots it was shoved into the skin sack, sewn tight and left to ferment. It was eventually cooked, and placed as it was now before them, steaming hot.

Calrach himself sliced the package open. With the first touch of the knife point, the contents gushed for freedom. The sight of the soft, mottled flesh surging out of the slit started a gag low in Rialus's belly. The scent, when it smacked his face, carried a physical force that was like falling forward into a latrine. Rialus would have spilled his insides on the spot, except that he had already perfected mouth breathing. He bypassed his nose entirely and played air about on his tongue with shallow breaths.

Calrach's facial muscles twitched and pulled, exposing his irregular array of teeth. A grin, perhaps. "Tell me, Neptos, do you think us vile?"

Rialus, answering as he knew he must, said that of course he did not think them vile. Happy to hear it, one of the women smacked a ladleful of the tilvhecki onto a platter for him. The other one shouted something to the group. The entire room turned toward him and waited for him to try the course. Rialus began to beg off on account of being stuffed already. Filled to the gills. Could not eat another mouthful. He pantomimed physical expressions of all these things, but nobody paid the slightest attention to his protests.

"Eat! Eat! Eat of it!" somebody yelled. The chant caught on. Within a few repetitions every mouth in the place screamed it at him. Many leaned in close to him, their breath striking his face like gusts of putrid wind. "Eat! Eat! Eat of it!"

Eventually, hating himself as much as the Numrek, Rialus lifted the spoon to his mouth and tipped the clump of meaty pungency onto his tongue. This was met with roars of laughter. Rialus sat immobile, his jaw tense, the morsel a dead weight in his mouth. Another Numrek, the chieftain's brother, came up behind him. He slapped two great hands on him, one across the crown of his head, the other on his chin. He worked the man's jaw into a chewing motion. This, too, was a mirth the party found almost unbearable to behold. They fell about the place, rolling among the cushions as if they had never witnessed anything so amusing.

After all this died down, the chieftain chose to speak a few moments of business with the liaison. He pitched his voice in a manner that, although just as loud and boisterous as ever, somehow told the others to look away and speak among themselves. "So, Rialus Neptos, hear now the message you will take to Hanish Mein. And prepare yourself. This may not please him. We too want some quota. Understand?"

Rialus was not at all sure that he did. He was still licking his tongue against the roof of his mouth, trying to scrub the taste of the tilvhecki off it.

Calrach repeated, "Lothan Aklun gets quota; Numrek should get quota."

That was about as far as his logic on the matter likely went. Rialus almost asked him why he wanted more slaves. They had enough to take care of all their needs already. He feared the possibilities of the answer, though. Instead, he said, "Honorable Calrach, I'm sure this cannot be. You've more than received adequate payment for your services. Hanish will not like that you ask for this."

Calrach put on his affronted expression, one that he had taken to using in imitation of Rialus himself. "It's only one thing I ask," he said, looking back to Rialus. "Only one thing. Who can refuse one thing?" Then, looking down at the cluttered table, he added with a slight change in his tone, "At least, it's one thing until I think of another."

This, apparently, was again open to the public and humorous enough to pass as a Numrek joke. Rialus felt a hand slap his back. He sat, smarting from the blow, as the beasts around him heaved with merriment. Once again, Rialus Neptos, the butt of other men's jokes. This could not go on. There simply had to be a way for him to better this life. There had to, had to, had to, had to be a way. He would find it or die trying. How he hated Hanish Mein, the smug, ungrateful whelp. And Maeander . . . He should not even consider Maeander. There were no words—not even in his new language—to fully express his loathing. He swore to himself that one day both brothers would regret stirring the ire of Rialus Neptos.

CHAPTER
THIRTY-NINE

Aliver observed stone become living tissue with a muted sort of acceptance, as if just the fact that he was watching it made such amazing things mundanely possible. There was no terror. No confusion. From a place that felt removed from his true body he watched granite boulders stretch into vaguely anthropomorphic beings. They each stood on two pillarlike legs, swung limbs from shoulder joints, turned heads with black-holed eyes toward him. They moved with a slow, stiff-jointed fluidity. They approached him like some strange undertakers of rock and earth, come to clean his corpse, to dispose of him. For that was what this meant, right? He was dying here in the far south, sucked dry by the sun, defeated. He was as parched as the sand beneath him, and now the rock beings of the earth had come to claim him. He wondered why nobody had explained this to him before. There was no mention of it in any spiritual lore he had ever heard.

These figures of moving stone surrounded him, crowding in close. They slipped slivers of their limbs beneath him and lifted him into the air. His weight shared among a number of them, they walked with him suspended above the earth. It was a feeling similar to floating. His head lolled back and for a time he watched the motion of an upside-down world. He thought that they might have been speaking, but again he could not say for sure. There was something passing between them, but it was more like exhaled breaths than any language he knew.

He had no idea how long or how far they carried him. He did understand that the earth spun beneath him. He saw the sun pass by above, watched stars flare to life and careen away, but he did not ponder such things as the passing of time or meaning of movement. It was not an experience measured in passing moments. Rather, one instant of time flowed so smoothly into the next that there was constancy to it all. There were no future and present and past. All of these things were the same. He forgot who he was. He felt no burdens whatsoever. His life and all the pressures he lived with had no substance. This, more than anything else from his introduction to his saviors, would haunt him afterward, a promise dangling at the far side of life.

When he awoke to true consciousness again it was with the aid of another's prodding. Somebody spoke his name, his first name and then that of his family line. The voice asked him if he would wake now and explain himself. He had come to them—why? He felt a pressure on his sternum, a force strong enough to push a moaning breath up and out of his mouth. He opened his eyes.

Above him was a night sky. A black ceiling beneath which a gauze of high cloud rippled, rimmed in by the lip of a bowl of pale red stone. He wanted to take in the world around him and to figure out where he was. This might be death, after all. He sat up with slow effort. Somebody sat just beside him, cross-legged and still. It was, at first glance, a humanlike shape, worn and aged, carved of stone and perhaps so ancient that ages and ages of windblown sand had smoothed its features and pocked depressions into weaknesses, causing bits and pieces to drop away over time. The eyes were smooth and had about them the slightest indication of color, as if they had once been brightly painted and a trace residue of brilliance remained. The statue was near enough to touch, and Aliver flexed his fingers with the latent desire to do so.

The eyes of the figure blinked. It pursed its lips, like a carp sucking water, and then fell still again. Aliver felt a thought enter his head, and it took him a moment to organize it into words and a few moments more to make of them phrases that he understood. He knew—without grasping why—that the message had come from the living stone before him. It said that it was pleased he had awoken. The others would come now, for they all wanted to *know*.

Aliver opened his mouth to speak. The figure snapped an arm into the air, a quick flash of a motion that placed the palm in the air before him, stilling him. *Wait.* The meaning and then the word that signified it formed in his head. *Let the others come.*

A chill spread through Aliver's body. He watched an otherworldly scene that he simply could not believe. The enclosed rock chamber in which he sat gradually filled with more and more figures like the one beside him. They were the same as those that had carried him here. He knew that; yet they were different also. Their movements were hard to pin down. As physical beings they seemed never to move, and yet the air was filled with motion, as if so many ghosts trailed their incorporeal bodies through the world and only became solidly visible when they ceased moving. Even when they sat still around him, Aliver could make out their individual forms or faces only when he stared directly at one of them. When his eyes drifted, however, they looked like the weathered stones he had first thought them to be, egg shaped and ancient. Thus he sat surrounded by moving ghostlike stone beings, all of whom had faces if only he stared hard enough, masks that betrayed life only intermittently.

Forgive us, but we must know . . . Have you the book of the Giver's tongue?

Again, this formed first as meaning that he had to order into sentences to interpret. It came from a collective of voices, but Aliver already had some grasp of how to make sense of them. He began to respond, "The book of . . ." But the words sounded monstrous, like the grinding of boulders, as if he had shouted them at the top of his lungs. He could see that the figures around him thought so too. They seethed back from him, like underwater plants swaying as a wave passed over them.

The one who had been beside him at the start suddenly had a hand on his shoulder. *Our king, please do not speak like that. Speak with your mind. Think what you wish us to know, and then release the thought to us.*

The fore portion of his mind thought this a strange thing to ask, but Aliver knew he had already been hearing their thoughts himself. That was why the place was so silent. That was why their words seemed to originate inside his own head. He fumbled to formulate a response, afraid now that each thought, each misstep and confusion, would pass from himself to the others. What a jumble he would reveal himself to be! But they waited, calm, their faces unchanged, hungry. They were blank, and it was clear they had no access to his thoughts unless he allowed it.

Finally, he formed a sentence in his mind, thought it with clarity, and then projected it outward. *What is this book?*

The faces staring at him all rocked again, but this time they swayed toward him. He received a response from more than one mind. The book, they communicated, was *The Song of Elenet*. It was the text Elenet wrote with his hand, wherein he defined each word of the Giver's tongue.

Please, they said, *reveal it to us.*

Aliver sat for some time in the silence after this. What was happening here? Part of him wanted to smack his face until he woke up from this dream. Another part of him wondered if these beings were the craven folk of the afterdeath and this the reception they gave to those newly arrived. It felt like they were asking him the secret to regaining life, knowledge he knew he did not have. But beyond all this he had another thought. He pushed past everything else and gave shape to it.

Are you the Santoth?

In a single motion every head around him—perhaps a hundred or twice that, the number growing with each passing moment—nodded. The stone faces cracked smiles.

That, they said in a chorus, *is the word that means us.*

All right, Aliver thought. That's the word that means you. But, by the Giver, what happened to you? He did not let these thoughts escape him, and the grinning faces, frozen as they watched him, showed no sign of understanding. They simply waited for what came next. He wondered if he had the energy for this. Shouldn't he eat? Drink? But his body did not trouble him. He was no longer starving or dehydrated, though he did not remember when he had last consumed anything. He looked about and proceeded as best he could. He could not take it all in. He just had to start someplace.

The Song of Elenet. Tell me more of it.

They did, most gratefully. Aliver would later not be able to say just how long his discourse with the Santoth lasted. It was not so much a back-and-forth communication as it was a spiraling communion. He did not learn the things he did in any linear fashion. But once he had pieced them all together, he had a story right out of legend. It was a tale, he would once have said, spun from the fancy of idle minds to entertain themselves and explain away the world's ills. That's what he would have said in his youth. But from the moment he saw stones walk upright, his youth was irrevocably behind him. This is what he learned from the Santoth.

The Song of Elenet was the encyclopedia of the Giver's language. It was the book wherein was written the spoken truth of the entire world. Despite his many flaws and the great mistakes he made as a practitioner of sorcery—that was the word most appropriate to describe human usurpation of divine language—Elenet was ravenous in his desire for knowledge and meticulous in keeping records of what he learned. As the legends told, he did live in a time when the Giver walked the earth. He did trail behind the divine personage. He did listen and learn the songs in the language of creation. Each word he stole from the Giver's mouth he wrote down in a script of his own devising. For the few who could read the text, it gave all the precise instructions for working magic on the world. It was a manual to the form and shape of creation; as such, there had never been a more dangerous document written in marks on a page, before or since.

When Elenet left this world to explore other ones, he left his book in care of his Santoth disciples. He never said where he was going or why, but he vanished from the earth, just as the Giver had done before him. The book was handed down through the generations, from one God Talker to another. They were, in those ancient times, caretakers of knowledge. Kings and princes ruled the world; Santoth wove spells to hold the fabric of it together, helping to ease the chaos men seemed to long for. It was a sacred responsibility, and for eons they practiced god talk only for the good of the Known World. This changed, however, when a young Santoth named Tinhadin eventually became the keeper of the book.

He held it close to his chest, the Santoth told Aliver, *and did not share it with us.*

Tinhadin loved the power of the book. He studied it exhaustively, excluding others more and more often. He became chief among the Santoth and grew much stronger than any of them. Eventually he was more powerful than all of them combined. With his hold on the text, only Tinhadin had access to the faithful translations, to the exact pronunciation and significance of each word in the Giver's language. Any slight variation on this corrupted the magic, weakened it, and/or turned it in ways the speaker had not intended.

Still, the other Santoth had loved Tinhadin as one of their own. He shared knowledge with them, but increasingly the Giver's words came to them only through him. When he set about to reshape the world, they labored beside him. He wanted to bring peace to the world, he said. There was too much chaos, too much suffering, too much potential for humanity to ruin itself and return to a state like that of the beasts. The others aided Tinhadin in battling to control the world. But before they knew what was happening, Tinhadin had outstripped them. He placed a crown on his own head, and set himself apart from them.

But this was not a joy, the Santoth said. *Instead, it became the greatest of burdens.*

Like normal men before him, Tinhadin feared losing the power he had gained. And, even more, he became fatigued with how completely he embodied the language of creation. He was a sorcerer with the power to shape the world just by opening his mouth. But, the Santoth explained, he found the power too difficult to control, to unwieldy. *Imagine*, they said, *living an existence where the words out of your mouth changed the very fabric of the world around you.*

Tinhadin grew too strong, the magic too much a part of the functioning of his mind. At times he altered the world just by thinking in the Giver's tongue. Sometimes he would speak the language in his dreams and wake to find the results living around him. That was why he turned against the other Santoth. He grew to hate his magic. He wanted to live without it, but he could not do so in a world where other sorcerers still worked their spells. He banished the Santoth from the empire. They did not all go willingly. Indeed, he battled with a great many of them, destroying them. The rest he drove into exile. Then he worked upon them his last magic, the spell which kept them perpetually alive, trapped in these southern lands until he or a descendant decided to invite them back. That, of course, had never happened, and the Santoth had aged into the beings Aliver now communed with. They were the very same individuals that Tinhadin had expelled, living—if it could be called that—and waiting.

When the prince asked them if they still knew magic, they answered that they did but that their knowledge had been so corrupted over the years that they knew not what would happen if they spoke the Giver's words. Their knowledge had become a curse from which they spent their eternal lives hiding. Without the true knowledge found only in Elenet's book, they risked opening a rent in the world that might never be mended. They had learned to speak like gods, but now they feared themselves to be devils instead.

Now that you have heard it from us, the collective voice of the Santoth said, *tell us where the book is. We suffer without the word. We need the Giver's words, and then we can be complete again, and good.*

Aliver shook his head. He did not want to say what he had to. Already he felt a certain peace among the sorcerers. He felt their suffering even before they mentioned it. He understood that their banishment had been a terribly prolonged curse, and he no longer had the luxury to doubt even a portion of the things they had communicated to him. But the truth was simple.

I'm sorry, Aliver said. *I do not have this book.*

The Santoth were slow to respond to this. *Your father . . . he did not tell you of it?*

No, he did not.

Chapter Forty

Corinn tried to keep her hatred of Hanish Mein pinned to her forehead for the entire world to see. He was her family's single greatest enemy. She would never forget it, never forgive. She loathed him. Nothing he did would change this. He was a villain of massive proportions, a murderer on an enormous scale, about whom some gentler people in the future would write entire chronicles of infamy.

She had to make sure to remember this, because in the tranquil setting of Calfa Ven it was the insults of a more personal nature that jabbed her most intensely. Simply put, Hanish toyed with her, as he had the first night at the lodge. At times it seemed he went out of his way to please her—and to let her *know* that he was going out of his way to please her; at other moments he treated her with shocking indifference.

A few days into their stay in the mountains, he asked her to join him for a ride the following afternoon. It was an invitation delivered with great show before a crowd of onlookers. She stood about the next day at the appointed hour—dressed to perfection in a cream-colored riding outfit, with a silken hat perched high on her head, chilled by the spring air but sure that the high color in her cheeks was worth it—only to discover that he had forgotten all about her. He had ridden out early that morning for the hunt with no apparent thought for her at all. Even Rhrenna, her erstwhile friend, could not help but show amusement at the way he belittled her.

What did it matter, though? The Mein were a petty people who took pleasure in humiliating a race that generations had proven was superior. He could have his small amusements, and she would hold to spite. Spite and condescension. That was all she felt for him. Fortunately, their stay in the mountains was almost over. Corinn had been counting the days, ready to get back to Acacia, where she could put some distance between herself and this barbarian who called himself the ruler of the Known World.

Strange, though, that when a servant next brought her a message from Hanish, she experienced a tingling in her chest and a quickening of her pulse that—had the situation been otherwise—she would have interpreted as exhilaration. He wished for her company that afternoon, the messenger said, to practice archery. He prayed that she would not leave him standing alone. That sounded like a fine idea, she thought. Leave him standing about, dejected, spurned. And yet she knew that would not work. Hanish was not easy to insult. He would find a way to playfully punish her for it at dinner that evening. Not going, she decided, would be more easily ridiculed than answering his invitation would be.

She found Hanish at the archery field. For once he was free of his entourage, accompanied only by a squire, who attended to the selection of bows, and by a boy, who stood some distance away in the heavy grass, waiting by the targets to retrieve arrows.

"Ah, Princess!" Hanish said, all smiles and merriment on seeing her. "I was starting to wonder. . . . Come and teach me what you know. This is a gentle sport, yes? I understand from the servants here that you were quite the archer as a girl."

"I may have been once, but I'm neither an archer nor a girl anymore."

He offered her a bow that the squire had just handed him. "Well, you are at least half right. I'll judge the other."

Corinn took the bow. The polished ash wood of the weapon felt good in her hands, the curves of the limbs familiar, light as if it were somehow made of bird bone. She ran her fingers down the taut string. She was some time in studying it before she motioned for an arrow.

Plucking the missile from the squire's hand, she nocked it, set it to rest, and lifted the bow to sight the target. She gripped the bow easily, her fingers settling in one after the other, her posture straight backed but easy, just as she had been instructed years before. She knew Hanish had paused to watch her. She did not care. She picked out a triangular target, one a little distance from where the boy stood. She drew her string hand back to her cheek, the arrow resting atop her fingers and the shaft a straight path out into the world. She loosed her fingers. The arrow flew. Vanished, it seemed. Only to appear a moment later, jutting from near the center of her chosen target.

Hanish exclaimed. He touched her arm and said something appraising to the squire, who affirmed the statement. Corinn had not felt quite such a visceral pleasure in some time. The deadly precision of it, the power pointed out at the world, the piercing thunk and then the stillness, the visual proof of her skill imbedded in the target. Her fingers came up of their own accord, snapped in the air for another arrow.

The afternoon passed quickly. Hanish may have thought he moved time forward with his words and gestures, with questions and compliments, but Corinn took pleasure or disappointment as each arrow's flight dictated. The arrow boy was kept busy, running forward and back. He had a lopsided grin and one of his eyes floated in a direction not aligned to the other. But he was still a handsome boy, and he seemed to be enjoying himself. Corinn decided she would ask him his name before parting from him.

"There's a Candovian tale about an archer," Hanish said. They had paused for a moment as the targets were cleared and rearranged. "I forget his name. He was reputed to have been the best shot in the land, deadly accurate under any condition. In those days the Candovians and Senivalians were at odds about the borders of their territories. At a meeting of the tribes meant to resolve the matter, a Senivalian challenged the archer to prove himself. Was it true, he taunted, that the archer could pit an olive from fifty paces? Of course it was, the Candovian said. The Senivalian challenged him to prove it, but the archer refused. He said that no olive had ever done him any offense. He said that he would be happy to shoot an eye out of a Senivalian from a hundred paces, though. He would only take the one eye, he promised. If he went even slightly out of the socket in question he would graciously relinquish all claims of prowess. Nobody took him up on this."

A pair of crested birds flew over the trees and darted around the edge of the field, oblivious to all but each other. Corinn had a vision of one of them darted to the sky, pinned to a padded wall as the other carried on with its dance. "What point do you wish to make?" she asked.

"There need not always be a point. Sometimes tales are intended for amusement. Do you know, Corinn, that I would give the finger off my right hand to see you happier?"

"I'd not sell my merriment so lightly."

Hanish grinned at her, wry in a way that acknowledged respect for her constancy. He dropped the expression and nocked another arrow. "Maeander, actually, probably could pit an olive from either distance. He excels at all matters martial. I'm quite in awe of him, and I don't mind saying it."

Corinn doubted that Hanish was in awe of anybody but himself, but she had noted Maeander's absence at the lodge and wondered about it. "Where is your brother—off slaughtering?"

"Funny that you should ask. His mission involves you. He is searching for your siblings. I know. I know. You don't even admit that they're still alive. But if he finds them, he will deliver them to you. That, I am sure, will win a little gratitude from you."

She was not sure how to answer that. Would he deliver them pierced on a spit? Chained and bound? Or might she actually speak and be with them again? Might they share this strange captivity with her, as Hanish had always promised was his only intention? If they did, it would be a lot less like captivity. But she should not even imagine the possibility. She did not really believe in it. Hanish was mocking her. If she believed him, she would only be aiding him in another cruel joke. She had known since her mother's illness and death that the world was not to be trusted. Loved persons were always stolen. Dreams always squashed. That was life as she understood it.

The boy still stood out in the field, but the squire walked back toward them, a quiver of retrieved arrows at hand. Corinn changed the subject to what seemed like a random statement, though something about being at Calfa Ven had stirred it in her. "I saw a man from the league in the palace," she said. "The one who wears a brooch set with a turquoise fish."

Hanish took his shot, not a good one. He lowered his bow, frowned. "It's a porpoise. Not actually a fish, they tell me. Anyway, it's the sign of the league. His name is Sire Dagon. He's a senior leagueman. He answers only to Sire Revek, the chairman."

Sire Dagon. Yes, that was his name. Corinn, hearing it, remembered that she had known him as a girl. She had always despised him—the look of him, his voice, his simpering arrogance. He had once been here at the lodge when she visited. That must have been why she had continued to think of him without entirely placing him. "What did you talk to him about?"

"We spoke about trade and commerce. That's all the league traffics in."

"Did they betray my father? Did they encourage you to attack us? Tell me, so next time I see Dagon I'll know if I should spit as he passes."

Hanish plucked up another arrow, aimed, and shot again. Better this time, close to the center of one of the farther targets. The boy cheered, raised a fist as if it were a personal triumph. Hanish ignored him. He answered Corinn with an unusually officious air, nothing flirtatious in it.

"The league has no allegiance to anyone or anything, Corinn," he said. "They have no philosophy except that which pertains to acquiring wealth. Since you ask, though . . . the league had grievances with your father for most of his reign. Some years ago they contacted my father. They struck a pact with us. If we Meins orchestrated a land war against Acacia, and it looked likely to succeed, they would withdraw their ships and provide your father no sea support. We'd be prepared for this; Acacia wouldn't. As your nation is based around an island, this was a considerable promise. It was a mistake, you see, to depend upon a commercial entity for your navy. Of course, I'm no better off myself right now, but I'll fix this situation soon."

Corinn shot. It struck the target snug against Hanish's last arrow. It landed so close that it chipped the rear of his shaft, leaving a feather bent askew. She made a point of not turning to look at him. "And what did you promise them?"

"I agreed to double the quota, thus doubling their profits. Recently, I've said that they could base themselves around the Outer Isles if they could rid the place of pirates. These were the things I discussed with Sire Dagon."

"Hmm," Corinn said, contemplative in a way that was mildly sarcastic. "I never thought of it that way. That you and someone like Dagon would sit around casually considering the fates of thousands. When you orchestrate such things, does it excite you?"

Hanish leaned forward slightly, not actually coming close to her, but in a way that indicated his answer was for her alone. "Very much," he said. "What else do you want to know? Want to hear about the slaves we sell across the ocean? About how we distribute the mist we receive in return? About the way we sedate the masses so that they labor for us without complaint? I'll tell you anything, Princess, if it pleases you to hear it. I will even pretend that it was all my doing, and that your father, dear Leodan, was not the world's greatest slaver before I was even born."

His voice had been languidly flirtatious up until the end, when it acquired an edge of chilliness. Corinn matched it. "I have no interest in this anymore. Why don't you go and kill something?" She handed her bow to the squire and began to move away.

"You wish a hunt?" Hanish asked, catching Corinn by the elbow. "We can have that right here." He nocked an arrow, drew his bowstring taut, and lifted it to aim. But he did not point at any of the triangular targets. The boy, noticing that the bow was directed at him, shifted nervously. He looked side to side as if there might be a reasonable target nearby, something he had not noticed.

"Will you shout for him to run or should I?"

"You wouldn't," Corinn said.

"Why not? He's no more than my slave. If he dies, it is my loss that matters."

The muscles of Hanish's forearm stood out, trembling with the effort, the knuckles of his fist white and hard around the bow. Such a cruel arm it was. Cruel, in the very sinews and tissues of it. "Don't, Hanish," Corinn said, knowing that he would do it. He was about to do it. It was a joke, and it was not a joke; it was both at the same time.

"You say that, but in truth you want me to do it. You want to see him impaled and hear him call out. Don't you?"

It took her a moment to answer. She did not know why she hesitated. She was not considering different answers. There was only one. But it was hard to push out. "No," she finally said, "I don't."

"Boy," Hanish shouted, "raise up your hand!"

The boy did not understand. Hanish lowered his bow and showed what he meant with his own hand. The boy mirrored the posture. Hanish told him to spread his fingers, and then to hold them apart, with spaces between them. "Good, now hold very still." He lifted his bow to sight again.

"Just stop it!" Corinn said, more a whisper than the shout she intended.

He shot. The boy did not flinch, which was a good thing as the arrow passed between his middle and forefinger. It sailed on past him and hid itself in the grass somewhere behind him. Just like that, it was done.

"Was there a point to be made with that or not?" Hanish asked, lowering his bow. "You decide." He spun and moved away, dropping the weapon to the ground after a few steps.

Corinn watched him go. She watched his form as it entered the forest of pale-barked trees, the leaves above applauding him with shimmering enthusiasm. He was right about her, she thought. She felt the truth breach the surface of her consciousness and stare her in the face. There *was* a part of her that had wanted him to shoot the boy. Why she had wanted it she could not say. Just to prove that it could be done? To prove that the boy's apparent goodness was protection against nothing? Just to watch a pinpoint of suffering launched through the air, dealt from one person to another with a simple release of the fingers? To see proof of Hanish's cruelty? Perhaps that was it. To see it proven with her own eyes. Her stomach knotted at the thought, at the feeling of aversion, intertwined as it was with attraction. What was Hanish doing to her?

With effort, she pulled her eyes from the trees and touched on the boy, who still stood in exactly the same spot. He had lowered his hand, but he stood as if unsure whether something else would be asked of him. It was good that she had not asked him his name.

Back at the lodge and wrapped up in her thoughts, she was surprised when Peter, the head servant, appeared beside her in one of the stairwells. He came at her like an attacker, pouncing from where he must have lain in wait for her. "Princess," he said, "you're not the girl I remember." He paused inches from her. She had not been so close to him yet during the visit and never alone with him. His eyebrows twitched with an emotion she could not fathom. She nearly shouted out.

"Your father," he said, "would have been proud at how tall you stand. I heard of your fate, but I didn't believe it until I saw you arrive here." For a moment he looked overcome with misery. "When will he come, Princess? Share with me and we will be ready to join with him. All here are still loyal."

Corinn snapped, "When will *who* come?"

"Why, your brother, of course! We all pray to the Giver that Aliver will return soon and with a vengeance that sweeps Hanish Mein from existence."

CHAPTER

FORTY-ONE

As his horse kicked up the last few feet of the rise to the top of the Methalian Rim, Haleeven Mein could feel the nearness of home again. A breeze braced him and seemed to caress the fissures of his pock-marked visage, looking for signs of familiarity. The scent of the land was moist and fetid, rank with the boggy rot of the lower Mein summer. He dismounted and bent to the ground. He grasped the turf in his fists and whispered a prayer of thanks to his nephew. Hanish had given him a great gift by allowing him to see his home again for the first time in years. Better yet, he had returned to begin the transport that would lead to his ancestors finally winning the release they deserved. There were aspects of his mission that he had misgivings about, but he tried not to think of these things much. Instead, he swore that he would see to his ancestors' wishes.

The world before him was damp with spring. Layers of snow had melted and still continued to do so beneath the tentative warmth of the slanting sun. In this area of the plateau the earth was a thick blubber of living peat. Sopping as a drenched sponge, it squelched underfoot. Haleeven, the company of mounted soldiers around him, and the long train of plodding conscripts behind them had to stay on established paths, where the earth had been packed to hardness. The air thrummed with newly awakened insect life, tiny things that seemed to like nothing better than pasting themselves to the whites of people's eyes. They flew headlong into mouths and up through inhaling nostrils. And they bit as well.

Haleeven looked about him at blood-spotted faces. He saw several men cover their mouths with bits of fabric. Others swatted their flesh, smearing their own blood from the insects' burst bellies. Haleeven tried to be impervious to the discomfort. He let the welts emerge unmolested on his exposed skin and let his eyes convey his disdain for those of lesser discipline. He did not even bother to look back at the foreign laborers, miserable lot that they were. He knew they would likely drop in number as they marched, prey to fevers carried by the insects.

A few days of northerly travel and he watched the ridges of the Black Mountains lacerate their way up out of the horizon. Gusty winds skimmed down their heights and buffeted man and horse, blowing the insect hordes into sidelong oblivion. A little farther on they rode upon the firmer plains of the central plateau, a place of tundralike grasslands, home to reindeer and wolves, foxes and white bears, and to the arctic oxen the Meins had domesticated long ago. The landscape was largely empty of these creatures at present, but Haleeven knew they were there somewhere, out of sight, just over the horizon. Had he the time, or had leisure been appropriate at all, he would have kicked his mount into a run and lost himself in the wilds that had shaped his race.

Tahalian. Haleeven surprised himself in realizing he at least partially looked upon his home fortress with the eyes of a foreigner. The place looked like a creature long dead, like the corpse of a ragged beast, trapped years before within a cage of massive pines, ripped and debarked and stained. Half covered in snow, not a sprig of green to be seen, a gray-brown hovel, dug in defiance of a land that had never smiled upon it: such was Tahalian.

Haleeven entered the gates to a modest, though grateful, welcome. Hanish's second cousin, a young man named Hayvar, served as regent in the fortress. He was a handsome youth, though thin framed, possessing tremulous eyes unusual for a race that preferred a look of outward calm in all circumstances. He had barely loosened his embrace before he was peppering Haleeven with queries. How was Hanish? Had he truly readied a chamber for the ancestors on Acacia? What was that island really like? Was it the bounty the returning soldiers always claimed? Were the women all olive skinned, with oval faces and large eyes?

"I'm happy," he said, "that I'll finally get to see for myself. I'll be returning with you. Hanish has agreed to it. I've had a note from him to that effect. He wants all of us there to see the curse lifted."

The young man seemed too anxious, Haleeven thought, to leave his homeland, even if the reason was worthy. But he was young. He had felt deprived of his place in the world's drama. Had not the soldiers who sailed with Hanish or marched with Maeander left hungry to see the land below the plateau? Hayvar was no different. Had he not been but a boy when the war began, he would have left years before.

Haleeven answered his questions, though he made sure to edge his voice with a disapproving tone and to keep his eyes toward the ground when forced to describe the beauties he had seen in the outside world. He feared he might betray something—he was not sure what—if he met the young man's eyes at such moments.

He followed Hayvar up onto the battlements of the fortress. They looked back upon the train of laborers trudging reluctantly into view. Feeling the rough grain of the pine beams beneath his palms, inhaling the resinous scent cut with decay, looking out over the patchwork landscape, copper grasslands emerging through the old snow, a mottled sky draped low over it all: ah, this was home!

For a few moments he swam in nostalgia. How to explain why this view lacked nothing compared to the shimmering blue waters around Acacia? He did not love this place for its soft virtues and pleasures. Nor did he believe anymore that his people were the finest on earth. He had witnessed too much bravery in others and seen too much beauty in foreign things to hold to this narrow belief. He loved the Mein simply because . . . well, because it *needed* to be loved. Perhaps this was a foolish thought, but it was the best he could do to explain it. Even if he had the words to express himself, he doubted the young man beside him would take them to heart. Even their ancestors set their sights someplace else. . . .

"Brother of Heberen," a voice said, "the ancestors foretold your coming."

Haleeven knew who spoke without even looking. He must have approached in his fur-lined slippers. Only a Tunishnevre priest would insult him by not using his given name, and only they would claim to have received word of him through the Tunishnevre, when everybody else took their news from the more earthly means of dispatches and messengers. His pleasant reveries vanished.

"First priest," he said, managing a smile, "the ancestors not only foretold my coming, they commanded it."

The priest's lips crinkled, two thin lines of chapped, peeling skin. His complexion was the ghostly white preferred by men of his order. His hair was a straw blond, intentionally plucked thin so that his scalp showed through it. With the sunken quality of his features, he looked much like the preserved remains of the ancestors he served. He said, "Yes, but Hanish took his time in sending you. Nine years. An absurd delay . . ."

"There were so very many things to see to."

"An absurd *delay*," the priest said again, stretching out the last word as if Haleeven's understanding of it was in question. "There can be no excuse for it. Hanish will know my displeasure, believe me." He turned and stared out, cold-eyed, at the approaching horde. "These are our workers?"

"Fifty thousand of them," Haleeven said, "give or take a few hundred."

"You have brought southern foreigners?" the priest asked, squinting.

Haleeven had expected the query. "Yes, but only to carry baggage and supplies. To maintain the road and accomplish the myriad tasks ahead of us. They will not handle the ancestors or any sacred objects." The first priest probed him with his eyes, unimpressed by the assurances. Haleeven added, "You will oversee all the arrangements personally, I hope, to assure that the foreigners profane nothing nor insult the ancestors. But it's appropriate, don't you think, that Acacians should break their backs on the Tunishnevre's behalf?"

The priest did not say exactly what he thought about this, but he voiced no further objections.

Late that evening, Haleeven, alone in a torch-lit passageway, approached the underground hold that contained his ancestors. He had already met with the rest of the priests. He had handed over presents to the few nobles still in Tahalian and visited the Calathrock. There he had watched a feeble display put on by a corps of young soldiers. The enormous chamber was still a marvel of hardwood construction, but it was meant to house many more bodies, those of burly-armed, long-haired men—not thin-shouldered children who had only ever dreamed of battle. Haleeven could tell that the people welcomed him and longed to impress upon him their steadfast resilience and faith in the old ways. Something in their fervent intentions saddened him, as it did to walk nearly empty hallways, being struck time and again with memories of persons either dead or far from Tahalian now. He did not often think disapprovingly of Hanish. On the upkeep of his home fortress, however, the young chieftain may have become lax and forgetful.

Reaching the chamber door, Haleeven paused to steady himself. His heart beat with what seemed an irregular frequency. His legs were stiff and aching, something he had not noticed until just that moment. He was an aging man, and he was tired. At the same time he tingled with nervous energy. He had ridden hundreds of miles to get to this very spot. He had imagined this moment endless times. He leaned against the door and felt it shift. He stepped inside, knelt at the edge of the chamber, and pressed his forehead to the chill stones of the place. He held it there until the cold touch began to feel like heat instead. Only then did he straighten and let his gaze rise.

Dimly lit by a bluish glow from no obvious source, the scene made

Haleeven's skin crawl. Above him stretched a cylinder imbedded with stacked protuberances, row upon row, layer upon layer, each jutting out of the earthen wall, arranged in uniformity, like an enormous beehive with hundreds of chambers. The area directly above him rose into fading perspective, perhaps a hundred layers tall. But this was only one alcove. Before him opened another, and beyond that another and yet another. Each of the shadowy shapes was a preserved corpse, a dried shell that had once been a Mein, wrapped in gauze and preserved both by the priests' efforts and by the power of the curse that bound the souls within those shells to death without release, to the physical plane but without the pulse and warmth of life. They were no different from Haleeven himself. They were men like he. Whether they had lived fifty years before or five hundred years before, they had spoken his language and roamed this high plateau. And they all had lived briefly beneath the threat of an eternal punishment. As did he.

Haleeven walked forward and began to intone the words that Hanish had sent him with. They would already know why he was there, but he went through the formality of announcing himself. He asked forgiveness for disturbing them and testified as to his oath to serve them. He promised them that tomorrow he would meet with the engineers, the architects, the drivers. There was a monumental undertaking awaiting them. He would waste no time starting the move. They were only a short time away from ultimate release and final revenge.

The Tunishnevre did not acknowledge him overtly, but there was a shift in the air that in his heightened awareness he could not help but note. They seemed to whisper, sounds that were like groans from deep in the earth. He sensed the sounds, but he could not say he actually *heard* them. Each time he paused to listen, there was naught but dead silence. Only when he formed words enough to fill his head did the chamber seem to echo with comments thrown at him, indecipherable though they were. Laced with malice. He felt himself threatened with extinction, with complete obliteration. But for all of this he could not pinpoint one true sound, one true motion as small as an exhalation of breath in the entire chamber.

So strange, the power of them. Haleeven could not say he understood it completely. He had never been blessed with that knowledge. They were dead. He was in a massive tomb, bodies stacked row upon row, as cold and lifeless as the earth around them, incapable of effecting change upon the world. In truth, they were a mystery to him. Had circumstance been different he might have communed with the Tunishnevre himself. He had only been one step away from the chieftaincy in his youth, one dance. But it was an enormous step, one that he could not manage. No one could say that Haleeven was a coward; yet he would never have been able to commit to taking the life of someone he loved. Because of that he never grasped for his rough people's throne.

Looking at the shadows above him, he knew the vagaries of his path did not matter. He was proud to have served his brother, and he was proud to follow his nephew's leadership now. He believed himself to be the young chieftain's main confidant. Maeander officially held that post, but Haleeven sensed the unacknowledged friction between the two. Perhaps Hanish did not even recognize it. This seemed unlikely, sharp as he was, but we are often blind to animus in those closest to us. It nagged at him that he had not brought these things up with Hanish before departing for the north, but there would be time after he returned. Maeander would not harm his brother before the Tunishnevre were satisfied. And the Akaran princess . . . well, whatever Hanish felt for her, it would not stop his blade from slitting her neck. He had spent his entire life striving to please the ancestors. Haleeven was confident Hanish would not fall short now.

But he should not be thinking any of these things now, not in this chamber. He whispered words of temporary parting. He rose to his feet, spun slowly on his heel, and moved for the portal. Nothing stopped him. Of course not. Powerful as they were, they were also helpless without him.

CHAPTER

FORTY-TWO

They stripped naked. It was an awkward procedure, each of them balanced on one leg or the other. The boat beneath them pitched in the chop. They shook off all clothing and stood a moment in the starlight, glancing at each other and getting used to their nudity. They would swim better this way. Moisture slipped more quickly from flesh than it could be wrung from cloth, and this would matter when they reached their target. And then they began to strap their weapons, water flasks, waterproof wrappings, and a few supplies to their naked torsos. They were each some time fastening bands tight around their wrists and ankles. Metal fishhooks had been sewn into the leather in such a way that they protruded outward, sharp barbs over an inch long.

"All right," Spratling said, once he had slipped his bow diagonally over his shoulder, short sword at his hip, dagger strapped to his lower leg, "let's get these festivities under way. Be careful not to snag yourself or anybody else. And be careful with that pill, Wren. We'll need it to medicate the giant."

A short time later he dove headfirst into the warm, heaving sea. Ten others followed him: all veteran raiders, eight men and two women skilled at close-quarters death. One of the women—Wren, who carried the "pill" strapped to her back, a round object about the size of an ostrich egg—had shared his bed since the winter months. But he would not think of this during the mission. If either of them died during it, they could mourn afterward. Right now, this moment and those immediately following were all that mattered. He welcomed the danger because the focus it required would allow no thought but the present. He had almost come to desire turmoil. Quiet moments found him mulling over Leeka Alain's claims. This family of his . . . those responsibilities . . . a future calling him that bore no resemblance to the life he had grown into . . . he felt increasingly that he could not avoid those things, but neither was he ready fully to take them on.

The current at this time of the year still flowed up from the south. The air temperature, however, was chilly with early spring. They swam away from the sloop that had transported them out to the point. Within moments it was but a shadow behind them, a patch in the dark, soon lost to them altogether. The ship bore no lantern. It would not do so until they were on their way back. Then the few crewmen left there would light a beacon to guide them in. The swimmers' destination, however, was obvious to them all, lit as it was by rows upon rows of shining lights.

Whether by night or day the league warship was an impressive vessel to behold. As they swam it loomed in the distance, as still as a land mass in its deep water anchorage. It was a monstrosity, twice as long as a trading barge, stacked level upon level like the tall housing complexes of Bocoum. Along each tier ran hundreds of baskets for crossbowmen and slots for archers. The enormousness of it was meant to overwhelm with its martial scale. There was no doubt that it achieved this.

So far, the four of these vessels that the raiders had faced had torn them to bits. Their prows were reinforced by massive trees, cast in metal, large and solid enough to shatter normal vessels. The decks were so high that boarding was impossible. Spratling's nail was rendered obsolete, nothing but a pin trying to prick a whale's hide. These warships were not things to be pierced and rushed upon, as had been Spratling's technique. They were floating fortresses that dealt out death from behind an unassailable bastion. They were larger by far than their wolf ships, and they suggested an aggressive intent the league had never shown before. Without the slightest warning one of them had beached itself on the shallows off the shore of Palishdock and disgorged an entire army. They overran the place, wreaking instant vengeance that caught the raiders by surprise.

The raiders had fled Palishdock with the few things they could carry. They had lived in transitory hiding ever since. Fortunately, the raiders never kept all their wealth in one place and never housed much of it at all at their main outpost. Dovian had taught Spratling that when he was still a boy. Bit by bit, from island after island, Spratling withdrew coins and treasure from the soil. With it he funded ventures such as the one he was on this evening. The war between the raiders and the league had begun in earnest. Spratling thought of it as a personal vendetta, especially as Dovian withdrew from a leadership role. He spent most of his time whispering with the old Acacian soldier, the two of them full of import Spratling did his best to ignore.

Swimming toward one of the warships, Spratling had to remind himself again and again that there was a deadly logic to his attack. He was not here to destroy the mountain rising out of the water before him. There was more than one way to strike a blow. It just seemed obvious—the only course, really—to meet such overwhelming strength with the unexpected.

The warship was anchored at four points, four ropes as wide around as mature pines, shooting down into the ocean depths. The raiders arrived at one of these near the rear of the ship. They trod water with their mouths open to suck in air, riding the swells, spitting out jets of water between breaths. Anxious though he was to grasp the rope, Spratling knew it needed to be a well-timed action. Each passing wave crest lifted them up and down, moved them from one spot to another. It took some time for him to get into position. He was third, actually, to find his belly pressed against the rough cords at the high point of a wave. He threw his arm around the ridges of the weave, slammed his ankles hard against it, and felt the barbs sink in. It took some effort to pull each one out, but as he reached higher, one limb at a time, he hooked them in again. Thus he inched slowly away from the waves. He soon found a tempo and ease in the motions, but still it was slow work for him and the others, each of his party like ants creeping toward a banquet laid out on a table high above.

An hour later, dripping on the deck, panting and fatigued, arms and legs rubbery and chafed red, Spratling turned and helped the others over the railing. He whispered reminders of the need for silence and stealth. Once they were all aboard, they stripped off the fishhook wrist and ankle bands and flung them toward the sea below. They rubbed their hands over portions of their body to wipe clean the moisture. A warm breeze caressed the ship from prow to stern and helped to blow their naked skin dry. The archers among them strung their bows with dry strings they had carried in the waterproof wrappings. This took a few minutes, but with all his motions Spratling indicated that they were not to rush. Each thing in its time, each step carried out in the appropriate tempo.

He did not motion to them when it was time to move. He just stepped forward, his feet spry and careful on the slick deck. The others followed. They did not get far before they had to halt again, bunched together in the shadows cast by a cabin. Guards sat in baskets on the masts, three sets with two in each. They could get no nearer without being spotted. Spratling turned and faced the others. They were solemn, their eyes fixed on his face for direction. He smiled, shrugged, managed to indicate with his eyes that it was quite an accomplishment to get this far. They were on a league battleship, unbeknownst to anyone, naked and strolling free in the night air. The fact that he could convey this without words was one of his gifts. Grins spread from one face to another. With that, Spratling knew they were ready.

They walked forward with their arrows nocked and bows drawn. One of the guards saw them straightaway, but before he could shout, a triangle of metal and a shaft of wood behind it punched through his eye socket and into his skull. His head snapped with the force of it, something Spratling would remember afterward. He was only the first. In the space of a few seconds a barrage of arrows flew from all around him. All of them save one hit their targets in the chest or head. One stopped a man's mouth in midexclamation. The single missile that missed sailed away into the starlight, no sound or sign of where it might have landed.

The party divided. Several rushed to dispatch the forward lookouts and anybody else on deck. Spratling and the rest rounded the main cabin structures and punched through into the pilot's room. The pilot and his crew were huddled around a chart. They looked up casually at first, as if they were not surprised at the sight of naked, dagger-wielding intruders. The mood swiftly changed. The butchery the raiders went to was fast and efficient; they were not without experience at this, after all. A man named Clytus seized the pilot and threw him facedown to the deck with a force that split two of the man's teeth and sent them skittering across the smooth boards.

Within a few moments all the crew was dead or breathing their last. Spratling had not wet his blade yet, but his target was not in this chamber. Toward the back of the room was a closed door, the frame around it embossed in gold, the design on it the emblematic dolphin of the league. He aimed his heel at the latch and kicked it open. Inside he found the person he sought.

The leagueman was tall and spindly, his arms those of a starving man. He had just climbed out of his low bed and was fumbling to get his bearing. His ribs, seen for a moment before he pulled his gown into place, heaved against a thin membrane of flesh. Spratling did not lay hands on this one either, but the man and woman who dashed past him did.

Back in the main cabin, the leagueman's arms were pinned at either side, the flat of two knives against his skin, one at either side of his head just beneath his small ears. The elongated cone of his skull, covered with sparse hair, seemed a far greater nudity than that of the raiders'. Despite this, he showed scorn for the intrusion and the slaughter. There was no inkling of fear on his haughty features. Indeed, he seemed incapable of seeing the scene around him as anything but an annoyance.

Spratling placed himself before the leagueman's defiant eyes. He had to be quick without seeming to hurry. "What is your name?"

"You don't know?" the man asked. "I know yours. Unless I am wrong you're the one they call Spratling. I would never have imagined your name would be so appropriate. You are but a little fish. You would do better to hide your little worm from view. You know that, don't you?"

"What is your name?" Spratling repeated.

The leagueman pursed his lips, as if considering the nature of the question. Eventually he said, "I am Sire Fen, vice admiral of Ishtat naval operations." He grinned. "I am what you call a big fish."

Throughout this exchange Spratling watched Clytus and Wren out of the corner of his eye. As he spoke with the leagueman they interrogated the bound and tooth-broken pilot, who had been spared. Clytus smacked him several times with the back of his hand, threatened him in whispers meant not to disturb Spratling. He could not tell if they were making progress or not.

One of the guards outside peered in and signaled that they were all together again but that time was short.

"You cannot expect to take this ship," Sire Fen said. "In truth, you have but minutes to live, young brigand. That's the problem with your type. You don't think before you leap." He paused for a moment, head tilted to the side, and then asked with true curiosity, "What did you hope to achieve here? You brought, what, ten thieves to take a warship?"

"We are not trying to take the ship," Spratling said, though his attention was only partially on the leagueman now. He thrust his chin toward the door, enough instruction that two of his men closed on it, bows drawn. They both let arrows sing out the portal.

"No?" Sire Fen asked. "What did you have in mind, then?"

Spratling glanced at Clytus, who had paused in such a way as to draw his attention. He stood over what looked like an open crate, though from his gaze and the way he spoke with a nod, Spratling knew he had found what they thought they would. Wren yanked the twine between her breasts. She caught the pill as it fell from her back with one hand and tilted the glass shade of an oil lamp free with the other.

"There are more ways to strike at an enemy than the obvious ones," Spratling said.

"Oh," the leagueman said, nodding with new understanding. "You seek a prisoner. A hostage? You'll ask for a bounty for me. Is that it? A bold idea, I grant you, but—"

Setting his eyes back on Sire Fen, Spratling interrupted him. "You want to destroy us, don't you?"

The leagueman scrunched his face about his nose as if he smelled something foul. "Each and every one of you."

"Why? Are we so great a threat to you?"

"You are not a threat at all. You're like rats in a city. Shitting everywhere. Stealing. Spreading disease. Yes, the league plans to eliminate every last one of you."

Spratling shook his head, something like disappointment heavy on his features. "That's why you don't understand my goal tonight. You want to kill many. Tonight, I only care about killing one."

The leagueman's face registered bewilderment in a slow progression all its own. First, at the words. Then, looking down, he almost seemed to flush with embarrassment. Spratling had sunk his knife to the hilt in his chest. He pulled it out, flipped the grip in his fist, and slashed Fen's neck so deeply that his breath issued out of the crescent, bubbly with blood. The two raiders holding him stepped back, and the leagueman fell into a formless crumple on the floor.

"Kill the pilot," Spratling said, "and let's get out of here."

The pilot shrieked. "No! No! No! Don't kill me." He pointed a crooked finger at Spratling's chest. "I can tell you what hangs from your neck! Please, lord, I can tell you what that is!"

The raider stayed his men with an arm. "What?"

It took the man a moment to recover his breath. He pointed to the leather twine around Spratling's neck, to the gold object he had taken from the league brig months ago. "On your neck. That pendant. Do you know what it is?"

Spratling did not look down at it, as the man seemed to want him to. "Speak fast."

"Will you spare me?"

"Not if you don't speak fast."

To his credit, the pilot exercised a dexterous tongue. The things he said proved most interesting. Enough so that Spratling, surprising even himself, ordered the man taken prisoner. "You and I will need to talk at greater leisure." Over the man's shrieks of protest at this, Spratling said, "Wren, light it and drop it." The order given, he moved toward the door. A moment later the pill was loosed and falling through the network of pipes the pilot used to send messages into the bowels of the ship, the short fuse of it crackling as it fell.

The deck was alive with action now. Soldiers erupted from the various hatches of the ship. They came on—helmeted and armored, behind shields—steady in their progress. The raider's archers loosed the last of their arrows, and then they all dashed toward the rear of the ship. At the railing, Spratling turned to the others. "Remember to clench your ass muscles, unless you want water to flush your insides from the bottom up." He said this casually, but his gaze settled on Wren. "Are you sure you can do this?"

Wren pushed past him and mounted the railing. "Worry about yourself," she said. A moment later she jumped. Her long hair rose above her as she vanished, each tendril reaching for the sky as she fell. Spratling hoped like hell that she survived, for something about the parting image shot him through with carnal desire.

He made sure the pilot was shoved overboard, and then he threw his leg over the railing. As he fell, piercing through layer after layer of air, he sensed the concussions within the ship beside him and knew that their pill had erupted deep within it. It contained a concoction they had paid a good deal for, an explosive in liquid form. The explosion going off inside the bowels of the warship would not destroy it. He knew that. Even if it ignited some of the pitch they used so viciously there was little hope of sinking the thing. But it would leave them with quite a bellyache. He smiled thinking about it. Then he clenched for impact.

CHAPTER

FORTY-THREE

That first night Mena only listened. She allowed the man who called himself Melio, and who claimed to know her and her family, into the inner courtyard of her compound. She had never done such a thing before with any man. It was an act forbidden the priestess of Maeben, one that the day before would have seemed impossible. But in this one's company unthought-of things happened. They sat together on the hard-packed earthen floor. Unnerved by a male presence, her servants lingered in the shadows, ready to pounce at a moment's notice. Mena just stared at the young man; he, seemingly encouraged by her silence, let flow a rambling discourse.

He spoke Acacian, and so Mena knew her servants would not understand a word. What amazed her was that *she* did. She sat, rediscovering the fullness of her first tongue in one long submersion. Again and again she would pause on a word Melio uttered. She would roll it around in her mind, feeling the contours of it. At times her mouth gaped open, her lips moving as if she were drinking in his words instead of breathing.

He had been a soldier of Acacia, a young Marah faced with the first mass attack upon the empire in many, many generations. The things he witnessed in the war were too horrible to speak of in any but the most general terms. He had lost everything a man can lose except his life. He had seen most of the people he cared about killed or enslaved, or watched them betray their nation for a new master. He had held Acacian superiority as a given, and it still amazed him that Hanish Mein dismantled his nation's military might so completely.

He had been wounded in one of the small skirmishes after Alecian Fields. While in pathetic retreat, the fever caught up with him. When he woke from it, the world around him had changed completely. He had been so defeated, he said, that if the will to die was sufficient to cause death, he would not be before her now. He would even have taken his own life, except that such an action was all but impossible for a soldier trained as he was. He joined the resistance in Aushenia for a time, using the work to try to win himself an honorable death. He failed at this too.

He was eventually saved from orchestrating his own death by the power of rumor. One drunken night a Teh mercenary informed him that the Akaran children had been spirited to safety. The bearer of this news could name no credible source to verify his claim, but he laid out a simple logic. Only Corinn had been captured, yes? The fact that Hanish put her on display only highlighted the absence of the others. He would have done the same with the others if he'd caught them, wouldn't he? On the other hand, could anyone prove that they'd been killed? Had bodies or heads been produced? Had anything been displayed to the public to confirm the Akarans' fate one way or another? The answers were obvious, and with them new possibilities dawned. The simplest of them—the one that Melio hitched himself to—was that if the Akaran line was not extinguished it could be returned to power again.

He decided to stay alive as best he could, to wait out the passing of time in the hopes that there might be some truth to the tales. For the last three years he worked for the floating merchants. His route followed the seasonal currents that circulated the Inner Sea. He had thrice ventured as far out as the Vumu Archipelago, with whom the merchants traded. He never stayed long and had never beheld the priestess of Maeben before. How fortunate it was that he had found her. She was alive! So there was reason to believe that Dariel was alive also. And surely Aliver lived and even now was planning to regain the throne. The rumors were true, and Melio thanked the Giver that he had not died before discovering this for himself.

She sent him away as dawn approached, promising nothing, admitting nothing, betraying no sign of the effect he had on her. She lay on her cot as the day came on, hot and bright as always. Her mind was surprisingly empty. She knew it should be raging with fears and doubts, memories stirred, questions raised. But she simply could not grasp onto any one thought long enough to face its import. She lay until she slept, woke when her servant warned her of the late afternoon hour, rose, and did her duties as priestess.

She returned in the early evening to find that the Acacian waited for her on the path again. Once more she let him into her compound and sat down to hear him speak. When she sent him away hours later she had still not promised anything. She admitted nothing, betrayed no sign that she thought anything of the tales he told. She slept hard through the morning, woke to the heat of noon, and stared at the ceiling above her, listening to the rustle of lizards hunting insects in the thatch. Melio had an unremarkable face, she decided. Unremarkable, and yet for some reason she very much wanted to see it again.

The next evening he awaited her at the gate to her compound. He rose from squatting as she approached, called her "Princess," and stepped inside when she nodded that he could do so. Once they were seated across from each other, in the same arrangement as the previous evenings, the young man resumed his discourse. Amazing, really, that after two nights of talking he still found things to say. He'd heard that the prince's agents were afoot in the land, he said, working covertly to bring divergent sectors of the resistance together. There had even been a revolt in the Kidnaban mines, led by a prophet who swore he had dreamed of Aliver's return. Soon Aliver would summon his siblings to unite their armies, he said. Many were anxious to believe him.

Mena heard and filed away the things he told her. She also spent some time confirming that his face was, in fact, unexceptional, studying him feature by feature to be sure. Hair long and unkempt, often falling over his eyes so that he had to flick it away, brown eyes of no particular note, teeth too prominent when he smiled, cheeks that look cherubic, but only viewed from certain angles: average in every way. Not unattractive but not particularly noble or strong or suggestive of great wisdom. So there it was, confirmed. It seemed strange that she had wondered about his appearance at all.

And with this question behind her, Mena interrupted him. "You say that a prophet of the mines dreamed of Aliver? Tell me, did this prophet describe his features? Did he know what my brother looked like, how he spoke? Did he know of his character? My brother never saw the mines up close; how is it that somebody in the mines knows so much about him?"

It was hard to tell whether Melio's stunned expression was in reaction to what she had said or just to the fact that she had strung that many sentences together. He stared at her more fixedly than he did while speaking, when his eyes tended to bounce around from object to object. "I cannot say from where a prophet's gift comes," he said, "but I believe there is something to it. And I believe your brother has strengths he has yet to discover. I always thought that about him, even when we were boys. To the people at large he is a symbol. Few people in the Known World ever set eyes upon your brother, but they all know his name. They all imagine him as they wish him to be. He is hope in a time when people desperately need hope. Maybe that is as much what the resistance is about as anything. We meet secretly, spread our messages by word of mouth, seek one another out through personal references. I met with a group in a household near Aos once. There were perhaps fifteen of us, but as soon as the doors were closed and we felt safe in one another's company we opened up and spoke like old friends. We spoke of the hardships we'd seen and the loved ones we'd lost and the dreams we have for the future. It was a wonderful evening, and at the center of it was the hope embodied by the young Akarans. It doesn't surprise me that you know nothing of this here. There are few in the resistance living as far out as Vumu. Although, fortunately, I am here, and here you are as well."

Without drawing attention to the act, Mena ran her fingers through her hair, parting it in the back and pulling strands over her shoulders. Thus she hid her breasts. She had never before felt embarrassed by her semi-nudity. With Melio, however, she was increasingly aware of her body. She said, "You say that we—the Akaran children—are poised to appear again, leading an army that will overthrow Hanish Mein's empire. What are you talking about? Look at me. I'm an Akaran. We both know that much. So where is my army? Look around. Do I look like I'm about to wage a war?"

"I've thought about that," Melio said, making sure his eyes stayed fixed on hers. "I cannot explain it. Perhaps in your case something went amiss."

Her dead guardian certainly qualified as something gone amiss. But Mena admitted nothing. Instead, she told him he had to go. He could, however, return in the morning. They might as well speak in the light of day for once. She had not planned to say this. The words rose out of her of their own accord. Afterward, she wondered why. And then she realized, and it seemed strange to her that she might act in a certain way and only know afterward what had prompted her.

The next morning Melio stood at her gate. She signaled for him to be let in. As he walked toward her, squinting in the sun until reaching the shade, she said, "I never caught the fever."

"Everybody got the fever," Melio said. "It swept the world."

"Yes, it came through the archipelago. But it did not sweep me." She said this matter-of-factly with a clipped tone that closed off any dissent. She changed tack with the next breath. "In Vumu culture women are not allowed to wield weapons. That was not so in Acacia, was it?"

Melio, reluctant to leave her earlier statement, took a moment before deciding to answer. "In our country any girl who was inclined could receive training. So long as they met the men's standard they weren't restricted from service."

"Did many meet the standard?"

"Most who tried did, I believe. The Seventh Form is that of Gerta. She fought the twin brothers Talack and Tullus and their three wolf dogs. It took her two hundred and sixteen moves to defeat them, but she did. Both brothers lost their heads, and the dogs each a limb or two. So at times women did not just meet the standard, they set it."

Mena stared into the middle distance, lost in thought for a moment. She knew why she had arranged for Melio to be here and what she was going to ask him. She had regained herself enough to control the moment. Even so, her own desires surprised and confused her. They had nothing in common with the role she had grown so accustomed to. She was a priestess of Maeben. She had been so for years now and been content. But still she opened her mouth and moved closer to what she wanted to ask. "And you know all the Forms?"

"I learned only the first five properly."

"And the rest?"

"I know them," Melio said. "I learned the last Forms in a rush, more from texts than from real training. The world was already falling apart then . . ."

"Melio, I want you to teach me to use a sword." There. She'd said it. She knew it as a betrayal and departure from all that she had become, but she had to admit that she felt calmer at the center than she would have imagined. She did want to learn. She had wanted to for a long time. She had often entertained violent thoughts while Vaminee lectured her or dreamed of dancing about with her Marah sword at night, waking to wonder if something was wrong with her.

"Are you serious?"

The question bolstered her certainty. "Of course I am."

"Princess, I'm no instructor. And I have no weapons anymore. I cannot teach without—"

Mena cut him off by shooting to her feet. "What you lack the goddess will provide. Come."

A short time later, in a storeroom at the rear of her compound, with light filtering down through the thatch of the walls and roof, dust thick in the air between them, Mena stood with her arms stretched out before her. Her palms cradled the sheathed sword she had swam to the shore of Vumu with nine years before. It was stained with a rust taint in some of the engraving. There was not the shine on it that there should have been, but still there was much underlying beauty in the artistry of it.

"This was the only thing I carried with me from Acacia," she said. "It would not let me go. The priests never dared to take it from me. It must have seemed a sort of charm to them. So long as I agreed to hide it, they left it with me and have not spoken of it since. Do you know this weapon? Ones like it, I mean."

Melio's eyes nodded before his head did. "It's a Marah sword. It is much like one I had myself once."

Mena gripped the hilt and tugged the blade free of the scabbard. The sound it made as it slid was absurdly loud in the hushed space, a grating noise that rose to a lilt as the blade cut naked into the air.

Melio pulled away and said, "I thought that being Maeben was your destiny."

"Why do you back away from me? You came and found me, remember?"

"Of course, but—"

"You may not have found me as you expected, and now this thing I ask of you may also surprise you. But so what? You've been surprised by life before."

He had no direct rebuttal for that. "The priests will—"

"They have nothing to do with it."

The wrinkled expression on Melio's face managed to say that the flaws in such a statement were obvious. Before he could try to put them into words, Mena continued. "I'll worry about the priests. They are of no concern to you. Have you any other excuses?"

Melio appeared to be stumped, unable to withdraw but at a loss for how to proceed. He looked behind him toward the door by which they had entered the storeroom, as if it might be possible to retrace his steps and gain the more stable ground he had stood on only a few moments before. Mena, impatient now, asked him what the First Form was. Edifus at Carni, he responded. Was it a sword Form? Yes, of course, he said. Most of the Forms are.

"Show me," Mena said, tossing him the scabbard without warning. He caught it spryly enough. A moment later she stepped out into the center of the room, her own sword in hand. She kicked a few crates to mark out a cleared space. It was not as if she'd never come here before, never unsheathed the sword and swung it around her. She had done so many times over the years. It had been little more than a test of her growing strength, or so she'd thought. Now, it seemed, part of her had felt a need to touch the weapon, to remind her she had not entirely forgotten it. Since she had held it often she knew well how best it fit her hand. She chose to hold it awkwardly, however, with a finger hooked over the guard, with her wrist cocked over as if the blade were too heavy for her. The point of it traced a short, jagged scar on the dirt floor.

To a swordsman it was not a pleasing picture. Melio could not help but correct her grip on the hilt, as she had known he would do. That was only a start, of course. He taught her how to set her feet, demonstrated proper posture. He named the various parts of the sword and explained the function of each. Within just a few minutes he had lost a good deal of his reluctance.

He explained to her that Edifus personally fought with the champion of the Gaqua, a tribe that had controlled the Gradthic Gap, the route through the mountains between Aushenia and the Mein Plateau. Just how this duel was arranged was lost to history, but the battle itself was detailed down to the slightest move. Melio had never taught the moves to someone completely unfamiliar with them, but within a few stops and starts he managed to take on the Gaquan's skin. He held the scabbard like he would a sword, and moved through the series of strikes and parries at quarter speed. Mena was quick to anticipate his moves, and showed him as much.

Despite himself, Melio warmed to the work. He seemed to forget his reluctance and the slight stature of his pupil and the strange, shadowed space they occupied. The words formed on his lips and his mind seemed to welcome them, to hum with the return of skills long neglected. Whenever he paused or seemed to falter, Mena pinned him with her eyes until he continued. If he was embarrassed by her naked torso he did a good job of hiding it. By the late morning Mena had worked through the entire sequence and knew the early portions by heart.

Eventually, they paused by mutual, silent agreement, both of them slick with sweat. They stood for some time, catching their breath. Melio wiped the perspiration from his forehead with his palm, though the moisture returned in an instant. Now that they had paused, a look of confusion seeped across his features. He peered at the scabbard clenched in his fist, flipping it from side to side as if he were not quite sure how it came to be there.

"How long before my brother summons us?" Mena asked.

"I thought you did not believe it would ever happen."

"I don't, but how long until the summons that *you* believe will come?"

"If it happens, as I've been told, he will start searching for you this spring. And in the summer he'll call the armies together. There are many of us who speak of it. When he calls, I'll hear of it through people I know among the traveling merchants."

"So," Mena said, "a few months. Not much time. How good a swordswoman do you think I can become in a few months?"

Melio could not shake his look of bafflement. He did not try, nor did he answer the question. Instead, he said, "We should oil that blade. The rust is a crime. Though, of course, we should make training swords. There's likely good wood in the hills. . . ."

CHAPTER

FORTY-FOUR

Maeander had known since boyhood that his gifts were different from his brother's. Hanish possessed a sharp mind, an encyclopedic memory, a capacity to manage both grand schemes and minute details at the same time, a skill for inspiring adoration from the masses, and a keen understanding of how to manipulate myth in his favor; all fine enough, but Maeander was the one who walked with their people's tangible, martial anger pulsing within him. His cool demeanor, his smile, his slow eyes: all disguised the seething core of violence ever-present within him.

He never stood before any man without pondering how he could kill him in the space of seconds, with or without a weapon. While others smiled and chatted and commented on his appearance or upon the weather, Maeander imagined what force would be necessary to drive the wedge of his tensed fingers through a person's neck so that he could grab and tear loose the artery pumping blood into his head. He had always imagined such things, and he had yet to grow tired of the unease his stare infused into others.

Maeander knew that he, not his brother, most fully embodied the wrath of the Tunishnevre. The ancestors told him as much themselves. And they advised him that favor was turning his way; he had only to wait for it, to stay true, and to be ready. This was also why he had groomed Larken all these years. The Acacian was as fine a killer as any Mein, and he would make a perfect ally when the time came.

By sending Maeander in search of the Akarans, Hanish had given him an assignment secondary to the one bestowed on Haleeven. But in the end, Maeander believed, it would be the one of ultimate importance. The Tunishnevre needed Akaran blood. Nothing suited their needs more than liquid spilled from the veins of Leodan Akaran's children, direct descendants of

Tinhadin himself. Corinn might suffice as a last resort; but if the others lived, the Tunishnevre would want and need their blood as well. Think of how the hand that delivered such ambrosia would be rewarded! The ancestors, when they'd been freed from the curse, would shine favors on those that had made it possible. Why should he not be foremost among those? Why should their wrath not live on in him, in a tangible, physical presence that could reshape the world far more completely than Hanish had yet dreamed?

Maeander embarked on his hunt with the same vigor he had shown for campaigning. He gathered around him a pack of his most trusted, veteran killers and the best of the young ones, the most inured to their own fatigue and to others' suffering. He led them, barking and rabid, in search of a trail nine years old. He sailed up the River Ask; disembarked below the Sinks; and cut east, weaving through the broad-leaved forest abutting the Methalian Rim. There were no particular clues that led him here, but much of the area's dispersed population remained loyal to the dead Akaran king. Maeander searched among them, questioning, punishing, leaving villages aflame and young men whose arrogance angered him nailed to trees by the hands and feet and pin-cushioned with arrows. A few tongues babbled nonsense loosened by fear, but he could recognize this for what it was and took payment for wasted time in ways none in the woodlands would soon forget.

As he rounded the barrier mountains that separated Aushenia from the Mein Plateau he was no wiser for his efforts. He had, however, warmed to the work. He had long held the belief that the terror and pain one instilled in a victim were directly proportionate to the pleasure to be received as the tormentor. If this was so, he had caused much terror and pain. He knew this was not what Hanish had asked of him, but this mission was his to prosecute as he saw fit.

Aushenia offered a rolling expanse of field and woodland, cities and towns, in which to further test this equation. Officially, the province remained a Numrek possession, but so many of the foreigners had quit the place in favor of the Talayan coast that the territory had reverted to semiautonomy. The Numrek were more trouble than they had ever been worth, Maeander thought. There was nothing harder to account for than the character of one's "friends." Strange also that lands defeated only a few years before refused to come to terms with the new order of things. Aushenian recalcitrance thrived like weeds in every crack and crevice of the place. And, more to the point, there had always been rumors that the northern forests hid bands of Acacian exiles, people gone nomadic, wandering from place to place, refusing to acknowledge reality. His men waded into Aushenia like wolves into numberless sheep, searching for signs of Acacian gold among those woolly fleeces.

Not every aspect of his strategy began and ended with brutality, however. He also waved before the people rewards for right behavior, to tempt them, to tie their loyalties into knots, to prove to himself and to them that there was a price for everything. Nothing could be more cheaply bought than honor. Simply put, he sent forth word that he would pay handsomely for useful information. "The person who gives me an Akaran will be rich beyond his imaginings," he said, "and will have won the undying loyalty of the Mein. He will receive a thousand gold coins, an island or a city or a palace, a hundred courtesans of whatever sort suits him. Consider this. Measure it and act wisely."

This message duly went out, and for a fortnight he chased the most credible leads. He sent men like quicksilver spilled upon the land's contours, slipping out in myriad directions, seizing the leaders of suspect towns, interrogating, threatening, cajoling. He set a trap along the main road between Aushenguk Fell and the north because—he was told—a band of rebel Acacians would be fleeing on it with a stash of weapons and coinage to fuel a planned insurgency. No such items or persons were uncovered. He took a village by sudden storm, torching hut after hut on the sworn testimony that an Acacian royal resided there. None was found. And, one evening, he ordered his men to slice their way into a steaming underground dwelling that he had been told housed Aliver Akaran himself. But what they found inside, in sickening fact, was a den of Numrekian debauchery, foul enough to haunt even his dreams afterward.

By the end of a month in Aushenia he had soured on his own strategy. To open oneself to the shrewd peasant testimony of any and all was faulty practice. Some of those who came to him had mistaken information; some, fueled by avarice, made grand leaps of conjecture that never mirrored reality. Many based their declarations on rumors with no verifiable validity. Some were bold-faced liars. In the eyes of a few he thought he discerned hidden mirth. This annoyed him more than anything else. These bog trotters thought they could make him out to be a fool!

When real information finally found Maeander, however, it was not the sort of lead he expected. A girl servant of a former Marah guard arrived, swearing that her master knew something of the missing Akaran daughter, Mena. Maeander promised the girl that if she spoke an untruth he would shove a spear point glowing and red from forges straight through her belly hole. She would cook from the inside out. The girl, pale faced and trembling, stuck by her story.

This supposed Marah was no longer a soldier. For whatever reason, he chose to run a small farm wedged between two rocky ridges. Maeander arrived amid the motion of his band, the pounding of hooves and clank of their jostled weapons. They found the man in his field, standing beside a lone horse, watching them as an elderly man might await the bringers of death. He heard the reason for their arrival silently, did not look at the girl or express much of any emotion. He just gestured toward his cabin.

Inside the close, damp structure, Maeander chose to stand, pacing, as the man sat. He had the body of a warrior, right enough, though it was crooked now and somewhat gnarled by farmwork. He had thin-fingered hands that he set on his knees, and the bulbous red eyes of a mist smoker. He asked if he might light a pipe and Maeander nodded.

He was neither quick to speak nor cagey. He seemed to have held his information for long enough that it was both a part of him and something he did not mind being unburdened of. He answered slowly, responding to one question and then another with terse, honest answers. He had been among the guards that had shepherded the Akarans to Kidnaban after their father was killed. He had not been particularly near the royal family. He watched from a distance as their story unfolded. His true focus was another of the Marah, an officer he had long hated and wished vengeance on. It was by following him that he discovered the children were being sent into hiding. This man, his enemy, became Mena Akaran's guardian. He followed him covertly, abandoning his post. He saw him sail from the island aboard a sloop and pursued him to a port town along the Talayan coast. He watched them board another vessel, packed with supplies, and sail. He followed. He did not catch them until they had reached the deep ocean outside the Inner Sea's protection. There he killed the man.

"Why did you kill this guardian?"

The man blew a cloud of mist from the side of his mouth before answering. "Lord, he ridiculed my father."

"He ridiculed your father?"

The man nodded.

"Fine, he ridiculed your father. How so?" Maeander pressed.

"My father was from a village at the base of the mountains in northern Senival. He spoke with an accent that this Marah, who was Talayan born, found silly. He said as much."

Maeander raised his eyebrows, his lips puckered in a manner uncharacteristically comical. "That was all? He poked fun at your father for speaking with hard g's? You killed him for that?"

"He did another thing, also. I had a sister—"

"Ah! This sister—now we get to the meat of it!"

The soldier looked at Maeander askance. "It is not as you think, lord. She was just a girl, my sister. She was overweight. She had always been too heavy, even as a baby. One day she and I were passing in the street, when I was but a boy myself, and this Marah called to my sister. He made pig noises at her and lewd gestures. She did not need to hear that from him, or to see those gestures. It wasn't something I could forgive. I lived with it for years without touching him. I believed he was untouchable, but I came into my courage slowly. Hatred of him made me a warrior. Then the war that your people brought changed everything, made new things possible. I wished him dead; so I made him so."

Maeander made eye contact with several of his men, moving from face to face, seeing that mirth lay just beneath their features, ready to erupt if he allowed it. He chose not to. He tried to imagine the weathered man before him as that boy, thin shouldered and trembling with anger he had not the heart to unleash. He could not quite picture it. But other men, he had found, rarely comport themselves in a manner that made sense to him. Certainly, wars had been started over lesser slights . . .

"So you had cause to kill this man. What of the princess?"

"I didn't harm her or aid her."

"Yet you left her alive?"

The man nodded, the motion looser now, softened by the mist.

Maeander motioned for one of his aides to take the man's pipe from him. He said, "You would have me believe that the fate of the Princess Mena Akaran was determined based on an insult made by a youth to a fat girl, remembered only by you?"

"Believe what you like, lord. The truth remains what it is."

Maeander drew a stool up close to the former Marah, smiling as if he were a friend arrived to share a drink. "Tell me more about it, then," he said. "When did you see the princess last?"

CHAPTER

FORTY-FIVE

The longer Aliver stayed among the Santoth, the more he felt he belonged with them. They still had about them their unusual mannerisms. They continued to glide about like specters, leaving trails behind them. He was always startled when they moved in bursts of speed, so sudden that he could not track how they had gotten from one place to another. Nor could he get used to the way their facial expressions changed in an instant. But in a great many ways the sorcerers enveloped him in a welcoming embrace. They were like relatives met for the first time and recognized at a level more fundamental than his conscious mind understood.

He came to find their muted features familiar. Sometimes, staring into the hazy contours of one of their faces, he lost himself contemplating an image just like his own, as if the being before him were actually a living mirror, a reflection of himself both solid and incorporeal at the same time, true to him and yet different in ways that demanded study. He had not opened his mouth to say a word aloud since hearing the monstrosity of his own voice that first time, nor did listening through his ears even occur to him anymore. Their voices were without auditory resonance, but they were all the more intimate for it. They took on the tempo of thoughts framed within a silent place in his mind. He came to feel a greater ease in his communication with them than in any shared interaction he had previously known.

He sensed that, in the swirling discourse between them, the Santoth tugged away portions of his conscious. They searched out bits and pieces of memories and information, things stored in the far corners of his mind and long forgotten. As he released these things, he relived them to some degree. He walked through moments from his childhood again. He saw images not dreamed of in years, heard stories told in the cadence of his father's voice, listened as his mother sung him to sleep. He felt again the complete peace of nestling against her bosom, her arms wrapped around him, the soft expulsion of her breathing caressing his face. He also remembered things not nearly as pleasant.

The Santoth had a slow, insatiable curiosity about everything he had seen and experienced, about history as he understood it, and about events of what to them was the most recent past. He felt how staggering it was for them to learn that Tinhadin had allowed himself to die within the normal span of a human lifetime. That was not the sorcerer they knew, not the ambitious one who stretched his arms with the hopes of encircling the entire world. Also hard for them to accept was the fact that the sorcerer's direct ancestors knew nothing of the Giver's tongue. How could Tinhadin's descendants know nothing of *The Song of Elenet*? How could such knowledge have slipped from existence? Aliver sensed the dread pulsing behind these questions and could feel that they did not entirely believe all of it. The Santoth, although aged and wise, were tied like all creatures to life. They knew not what their own future might hold, and they feared the same as anyone faced with uncertainty.

However, they offered Aliver more than they took from him. They may have known nothing about events in the world for the last several hundred years, but they were encyclopedic in their knowledge of the distant time that had shaped them and all that came before. They nourished Aliver with history and lore. They detailed the Retribution in a manner that rewrote his understanding of his dynasty's founding entirely. They spoke of Edifus and Tinhadin and Hauchmeinish as if they had parted from them only the day before. They told of battles and duels not preserved in the Forms. They fed him a diet made up entirely of knowledge.

Very little of what he learned of people's actions began or ended with either the noble ideals or the fiendish wickedness he had been taught lay behind all great struggles. There was something comforting in this. For once, the nature of the world and the crimes of men in shaping it made complete sense to him. There was a truth, he realized. Things had happened in certain ways. It was possible to understand the events, although only from a place without judgment and only when one stared at them without the desire to shape the events to create certain meanings, to validate, to explain. The Santoth did not try to do any of this. They simply informed him and seemed to have no opinion whatsoever on the catalog of crimes and suffering they detailed.

Most often his exchange was with a collective consciousness, into and out of which individual voices flowed at will. Occasionally he found himself sitting beside the Santoth who had first spoken to him. His name had been Nualo, although in his existence here there was no need to single him out by name. If a thought was meant for him he simply knew it; likewise, if a thought came from Nualo, Aliver knew from its cadence and shape and feel from whom it had originated.

At some point—whether it was night or day, a week or a year after his arrival in the far south Aliver could not have said—Nualo said that he had just come to understand something, a flaw in Aliver's conception of the world. It concerned the tale of Bashar and Cashen.

The story, as any Acacian child knew, was that two kingly brothers who failed to share power equally became great enemies. They fought in the mountains and sometimes, during great storms, their anger rose again and you could hear the rumbling of their ongoing battle. It was a tale, Nualo said, that hid a truth Aliver should know.

There was no Bashar, he said. *There was no Cashen.*

There were, however, two peoples: one called Basharu and one called Cularashen. In the distant past they were two nations of Talayan people. They lived so long ago that there is no way to measure the years. They came from common ancestry, but they grew in separate ways and believed themselves to be different beings entirely. As both nations grew prosperous and swelled in numbers, they also learned pride. The Basharu believed themselves favored by the Giver. The Cularashen called this heresy; *they* were the beloved of the Giver. Both peoples found all manner of proofs to verify their view: in the blessing the Giver bestowed on them, in the bounty of their crops in a given year, in the disease cast upon the other, in the sun that favored one's crops, in the floods that destroyed the other's. Each year—each month or day or hour, for that matter—confirmed and challenged their assertions.

Eventually, both races agreed to petition the Giver. Through prayers and sacrifices, offerings and ceremonies, they asked him to make known his preference. They wanted him to choose between the two peoples so that all would see and understand whom he favored most. The Giver, however, did not answer them. Not, at least, through a sign both sides could agree upon. So they fought to decide the matter themselves.

Theirs was the first war between nations of men, but in it they learned all the degradations humans would ever need to practice it. The Basharu eventually gained the upper hand. The Cularashen fled Talay. They sailed to an island in the center of what was to them a vast sea. They took with them many things, including the seeds of acacia trees. They planted them all across this island so that it would feel like home to them. They have lived on this island ever since.

This name, Cularashen, Nualo said, *has been forgotten. As has Basharu. But those people—the defeated Cularashen—are the people you call Acacians. You, Prince, are one of them.*

How could that be? Aliver asked. *We are so different from the people of Talay. In so many ways . . .* He meant in terms of racial characteristics—skin color, features of the face and form. But he hesitated to project this thought. Something about it snagged inside him with embarrassing barbs.

Nualo understood him well enough. He said that the Giver had been angry at the people's folly. He abhorred the war and the foulness that so flared out of his own loved creation. If humans thought they were so different from each other, he would make them even more so. He twisted people's tongues and made them speak differently, so that one nation's words were meaningless babble to another's ears. He roasted some in the sun and let others wither and go snow pale in the cold. He stretched noses or flattened them, made some people tall and others short, set eyes deep or pinched them at the edge and slanted them, twisted hair into curls or let it hang free. The Giver did this as a test for them to see through. But they did not. Before long, humans began to accept that they were different, and then discord between them became the norm. And this, in addition to Elenet's betrayal, was another reason the Giver turned in disgust from the world. He has had nothing to do with it since.

All races are one? Aliver asked.

All the races of the Known World are one, Nualo said. *Forgetting this was the second crime done by humans. We suffer for it still.*

Aliver would have to live with this new version of the world for some time for it to become real for him. The old pride in his character scoffed at the idea of Acacians being nothing more than a defeated, displaced tribe of Talay. He had lived an entire life with Acacian supremacy as a given. Certainly he had found himself struggling to best his Talayan peers in any contest over the last nine years, but he had taken that to be a fault in himself. *He* was not up to the standards of his people. It was what pushed him to work harder, to grow fit, and to fight like a warrior and kill a laryx.

He was so sure of his own failings that he had sought to hide them every day of his life. None of this had shaken his belief that the differences observed on people's outsides mirrored equally indisputable differences within. Nualo and the other Santoth slipped this belief from beneath his feet and left him drifting upon a sea of entirely unimagined possibility. For reasons he did not fully acknowledge, this troubled him more than any of the other revelations he received from the Santoth.

It seemed he lived with them an eternity before they prompted him back to his purpose. They did so en masse. They gathered around him, circle outside circle, face after stony face after face, much like the audience held with him when he first arrived. Aliver only gradually recognized that they had a particular purpose. They had accepted him. They had waited. They had learned and shared with him. Now they wanted.

Bring us back into the world, they said, speaking in the singular voice that was all of them at once. *Free us.*

They assured him that he was the only one that could do so. Only he out of all of his generation—that is, a firstborn son of the patriarchal line of Tinhadin—could lift the curse that kept them in a state apart from the rest of the world. That was how Tinhadin had woven the magic. It was strong magic, but Elenet himself had decreed that there must be a way out of any spell. He knew that men always erred in some way when they spoke the Giver's tongue. The flaw might not be immediately obvious, the ramifications not clear for centuries, but eventually the faults showed. Tinhadin had no choice but to follow this edict, even when castigating others of his order.

There is no spell, the Santoth said, *that cannot be undone. There is always a door back that never closes. You are that door, and you have only to say the words.*

What words? Aliver asked.

That, however, was not an answer the Santoth could provide. Only Aliver himself could figure that out. They could not even teach him, as their god speech was so corrupted by time that nothing they uttered came out as they intended.

I know none of the Giver's language, Aliver said, not for the first time. *I'd never heard of Elenet's book before you told me of it. I have never been taught one word of the language of creation. I'm sorry, but I'm powerless to aid you.*

They did not disguise their disappointment. *Why, then, did you seek us out? Why did you stir us from slumber?*

Why indeed? He had almost forgotten the stretch of earthly years leading up to the present. It took some effort to wrench his attention back to what his purpose had been. But once he tried, it all came to him. He had come searching for them, full of import, with purpose hung about his neck like a punishment. There was a world of people—many of whom he loved—engaged in a titanic struggle. He had come here seeking aid, not for refuge, not for a home among the banished, not to forget the world. He had come to ask the Santoth what they could do to save a family—and a world—that had driven them away.

He let all of this flow from him to the sorcerers. It spun into the breathing air between them, circled and twined through them in the silent, flowing exchange that now seemed so natural.

You ask of us things that we cannot do, they said. *We could help you from here, but there would be limits.*

With your powers you could do much. I am sure of it. I—I give you permission to leave here and return to the world.

It took them some time to consider this. It would be good to venture north, they admitted. But without being properly freed from Tinhadin's curse they would never function like normal people in the world. They would be walking ghosts haunting a world they were not completely a part of. What was more, they could not help him in the way he intended.

You wish to make war.

It was Aliver's turn to hesitate. They put it so simply. Yet it was true— or mostly so. He did not *want* it, but a battle was coming. Now that he remembered it fully it was clear that his entire life had been leading toward war. A horrible war. A conflagration that would liberate or destroy him. He had no choice but to play his part in it. Soon, he would have to return to the world and . . . *Yes, I will make war on my enemies.* He almost added the word "noble" or "just" or "righteous," for such was the type of war he wished to wage. He mulled them in his mind but did not release them. He knew what the Santoth would think of such notions.

You may invite us back into the world, the Santoth said, *but we will be form without substance.*

But if you were freed? Aliver asked. *If I found Elenet's book . . . If I learned how to free you . . . You could then fight for me?*

Having asked the question, he sat aware of his heart beating, watching the blurred faces all about him, feeling the gravity with which they considered their response. It was the first sensation of time he had felt since arriving here. Something had shifted. The world had begun to reclaim him, and it seemed urgent that he have the answer to this question. *Would you fight for me?*

If you free us we will fight for you, the Santoth eventually said, answering with a rapidity that betrayed emotions they had thus far tried to control. *Make us true sorcerers again, Lord Prince, and we will wipe the world clean for you to remake as you wish.*

CHAPTER

FORTY-SIX

Spratling awoke. His eyes were open. He was free of the dream. It was not real. He tried to quell the fear that had shoved him out of slumber so forcefully, but it was not easy. The illumination of the lamp hung by the ramshackle door to his cabin did nothing to dispel the menace he felt pulsing from the walls. There was threat latent in the three-legged stool with the vest draped over it and ominous import in the half-empty bottle of wine on the wall shelf. From outside came a rasp of ocean's breath. He knew that there was nothing to fear in these mundane objects or sounds. In a way there had not even been anything to fear in the dream. Nothing like the dangers he willingly faced in his daily work. Knowing this, however, did not help him through the moments between the dreaming and the conscious world.

The nightmare he had fled was yet another variation on the visions that had plagued his sleep since Leeka Alain arrived in the Outer Isles, insisting on calling him by that half-forgotten name. Each dream began with an awareness of his smallness. He was a child, tiny, spindly legged, thin armed. He viewed the world from half height. He knew himself to be a target, hunted by a nameless, shapeless possibility. If this being found him, something terrible would happen. He did not know what, but he could not stay still to find out. He wandered through subterranean corridors, a dark and absurdly complex maze. The world existed only in front of him, and he existed only by moving forward through it. Behind him things vanished. He dashed through intersections, afraid of what they opened onto. Out of the stonework of the walls strange creatures stretched their talons, their beaks, and their horned heads, each of them trapped in expressions of rage. How easy it would be for any of them to rip him to pieces; how frightening that they all held so steadily to the pretense that they were only stone. They were not, of course. If he listened hard enough, he heard their hushed breathing.

Though the corridors varied and his path was never the same twice, he always arrived at the same destination. He stepped into a brightly lit room. It was full of people, loud with laughter and music, a sound of tinkling glass that was almost like cascading beads of water. A hundred faces turned toward him, smiling. They had gathered to honor him. It was his birthday. That was what he'd been searching for all along! His tenth birthday celebration. They crowded forward, calling him by the same name Leeka had. That name, actually, was the only word they said: spoken in myriad pitches, strung together in sentences, lilting like questions, forceful like accusations. They spoke a language made up entirely of a single word. His name.

One of them, the youngest girl, stretched a hand out toward him, her white palm upward, fingers crooked and beckoning. The gesture racked him with spasms of fear. She moved toward him, whispering, motioning that he need not be afraid. The more she indicated this, the more he believed it to be a lie. She had enormous brown eyes. They were too big for her face. He realized in a single, telescoped moment that she was not who he had thought her to be, even as he grasped that he had not even conceived an identity for her. This paradoxical realization was what hurtled him toward consciousness.

As always, the experience left him shaken. Who had he thought the girl was? Who had he realized she *actually* was? Sometimes he spent a greater part of the day plagued by her image, haunted by her eyes. He knew that her identity was within him. It was as if he had a hundred-sided die with the truth written upon one side. No matter how relentlessly he rolled the die, he never found the answer.

Wren stirred on the pallet beside him. She rolled from her back to one side, facing away from him. He felt as if he could hear her eyelids split open. They were not eyes at all like those of the girl in his dreams. Wren was from a coastal people north past Candovia. Her hair was brittle and straw silvered like a woman of the Mein, but her eyes were narrow, set flush with her face instead of recessed. They had about them a sleepy quality, although this belied her predatory sharpness of mind. "Dreams have no power beyond their realm," she had told him before. "Only actions do." Spratling felt sure that she was right but was not sure whether to read that statement as a comfort or as a challenge.

Later, when he joined the crowd of raiders taking their morning meal, he walked among them, smiling and joking, teasing in the easy manner he had with his men. They sat on benches ranked around a cook stove that had come from the mess hall at Palishdock. It was a massive, cast-iron thing. Spratling himself had led a small party back to the settlement to rescue it from the ashes and destruction the league warship had inflicted on the place. Its appearance here—on the southern isle that had become their third hideaway in as many months—had raised morale.

Standing in the sand before it, inhaling the bacon scent sizzling atop it, bent forward and preparing to pluck a strip up with his fingers, he did not take note of the general's arrival until he spoke. Leeka stood some distance away, on the other side of the stove. He spoke for everyone to hear.

"Why haven't you told everyone about the key?" he demanded. "Why haven't you told them what the prisoner has said?"

Spratling's appetite, his pleasant mood, his transitory sense of equilibrium all vanished in an instant. He had known this moment was coming, of course. It was eight days since his attack on the warship. He had sworn to silence the few who had heard just what the key was for, but secrets among raiders do not last, especially not with a league pilot held prisoner among them. Spratling cursed himself for bringing the prisoner with them. He should have killed him on the night, but he could not resist taking so valuable a prisoner, could not help but want to know what the man could tell him. He had made sure only those who had been with him in the pilot's room took food and water to the man, and only Spratling and Dovian interrogated him. But his presence had been on everybody's mind since their return.

"I make the decisions here, not you. If I do a thing, there's a reason for it."

"I thought Dovian led this group," Leeka said. "You're only one of his raiders, right? You said so yourself. Spratling, the raider. Just one of many . . ."

Turning to face him through the rippling heat thrown up by the stove, Spratling said, "Either way, *you* don't make decisions for us." He cast his voice tight and dangerous. He had not meant to respond with such obvious anger, but his passions tended to flare each time this man prodded. He had not kept the key secret out of any timidity, damn it! He just needed to think its significance through, to research what he could do with it. Leeka had no business calling him on it.

"Dovian agrees with me," the soldier said.

As if on cue, the old raider rose from where he had been sitting at the edge of the group. He hobbled forward, his bulk like that of a wounded bear. Whatever pain the movement caused him he kept clamped between his teeth. He might have been getting better these last few weeks. He was certainly on his feet more often, but Spratling was not sure just how much of his illness he was hiding.

Leeka went on. "You have a weapon that could cripple the league. You should let it be known, and together we should plan how to use it."

Spratling shifted his gaze from the Acacian to the Candovian, expressing his annoyance through his eyes. Dovian simply stared back at him, his face sad, apologetic, rimmed beneath the eyes with disappointment. "We will talk about this later—"

"No," Leeka said, "we will talk about it now. Don't you all wish to talk about it now? Your young captain wears a key about his neck that you should all know about. You want to hear of it, don't you?"

Nobody answered. They did not have to. Their silence had a quality to it that anyone could read. Of course they wanted to know. And, Spratling knew, they deserved to know. He tossed his food down, no longer having a taste for it.

That afternoon they had the open meeting that Leeka wished for. They sat on the sand near the ocean, under the ribboned shade of coconut palms, the sky above them cloudless, a light blue dome undisturbed by anything save the progress of the sun's blazing whiteness. Spratling did not attempt to run the meeting. Wren and Clytus, Geena and all of the others who had been involved in the attack on the league warship were glad to break their enforced silence and sing in chorus.

"Think back a few months ago," Geena said, "to when they took the brig with Spratling's nail. We came away with a fair bit of treasure, yes? There was one piece, however, more valuable than the rest."

"See that pendant about Spratling's neck?" Wren asked. "That's what we speak of. You've all seen it, but we didn't know its value until the pilot of the warship explained it. It's one of a handful of keys that unlock the outer rim platforms."

"There are only twenty of them in existence," Nineas said. "Only twenty. And we have one."

"And we brought the pilot with us," Clytus said. "Spratling's been learning all sorts of things from him, I wager. So you have to ask yourself if there's a use we could put this key and our new source of intelligence to."

For the next few hours the raiders enthusiastically considered that question. They threw about schemes and notions, filled with a lust for revenge and with the possibility of an unheard-of bounty. Leaguemen were enormously wealthy and their tastes extravagant. What might those plat-forms house? Slaves by the thousands? Warehouses stacked high with mist? They might find concubines of amazing beauty. Gold and silver by the bargeload. Floating palaces hung with vines and flowers, paved in marble. They could drape themselves in silken clothes and drink wine from chalices of carved turquoise and eat and eat and eat as they had never eaten before. They could spend the rest of their lives in the pursuit of pleasure. They could drown in excess, as all raiders dream. They could even take over the mist trade themselves! They would have Hanish Mein by the balls then, and their fortune would know no bounds.

With Dovian's consent, they brought out the prisoner. His hands bound and clothing shredded, he stood timid and begrimed at the center of this whirlwind, a trickle of congealed blood on his upper lip. He sometimes needed to be prodded or cuffed, threatened or kicked, but he answered the questions put to him. What he said only fired the group's enthusiasm.

Spratling let them talk, amazed at how easily they lost their grip on reality. There were some monumental obstacles before them, but in their frenzy nobody mentioned any of them. Leeka offered little. Even Dovian seemed to believe their scheming served a purpose. Only when the banter slowed did Dovian clear his throat and speak.

"It's fine to imagine, isn't it?" He pushed himself upright and walked a slow circle in front of the group. Despite his age and ill health, the man still commanded attention, even when he was just drawing a circle in the sand with his massive feet. "I know it's fine to imagine. And you all know that I've a history with the platforms. I saw them once when I was young. Just sailed by them, we did, taunting like. Had an entire fleet chase us from the place and hunt us so far north we saw chunks of ice floating in the sea. Al-most killed us, that little stunt. But I saw them. They're like you imagine and even more unbelievable than that."

He stopped walking. He looked about a moment, inadvertently seek-ing the walking stick he had tossed away recently. Noticing himself, he straightened and looked about, his eyes moving from one face to another. "We cannot have their treasure, though. That's not what we're about here. An entire army could not besiege the place, and we don't have an army any-way. And their riches . . . Truth be told, I don't want them. Slaves, you talk about? Concubines? Come on, now. I've never minded a bit of plunder. Never minded taking what I wanted. Raiding is honest work, right? We do it with our hands, with our guts. What the league traffics in is a whole different level of misery altogether. You don't want that, friends. You might, however, want to wipe them from the face of the world. You want rewards? How about the love of all the children who won't be sold across the ocean? How about the thanks their parents would heap on you? How about just knowing that you've changed the world for the better?"

Dovian paused a moment, searching faces for the answer. His eyes passed over Spratling's, but he did not show him scrutiny any different from the others. "What I'm saying is that there's only one thing we can do with this key, and it's the thing we should do with it."

None of the raiders, who had moments before been keen on plunder, raised a complaint. Such was Dovian's influence among them. The planning took no time at all really, as the venture was one more of pure nerveless courage than anything else. The mission, as Dovian explained it, was fundamentally simple. They had only three hurdles to overcome: getting to the platforms undetected and using the pilot's knowledge to find the right gate, inserting the key and hoping that the locks had not been changed, and finding a particular warehouse. He believed that each of these challenges was achievable.

For example, as they made their approach they had mainly to avoid drawing attention to themselves. Stable and massive as the platforms were, the league was unlikely to expect any sort of an attack. They had gone unchallenged for several hundred years and certainly would not fear a single small vessel. "They might notice a small ship, true. But then again they might not. They won't be looking for it, that's for sure. There's no navy in the world to threaten them, and they wouldn't dream we'd try what we're going to." Still, of course, they had to be careful. There was an atoll less than a day's sail from the platforms. If they launched themselves from it, timed correctly, with the right sailing conditions, they would be able to reach their target under the cover of night.

The question of the key still being useful was another matter. "What if they've changed the locks?" several asked in a quick chorus. "Or placed guards on the entry points?"

Dovian did not think a few months was enough time, even if they had wanted to change the locks. The workmanship of the key was such that it could not be easily replaced or altered. Moreover, only a handful of leaguemen carried a key like this. They swore to guard them with their lives.

"Whoever was meant to protect this one didn't do so," Leeka said. "He didn't accompany it, and he sent it on an unprotected ship. He was fool enough to leave the key on that ship, and I'm betting he hasn't reported its loss. To do so would mean his death. Even men of the league cherish life, right?" The general directed this question at the prisoner.

The man answered, dejected, "More so than anyone but myself, I'd say."

"He's hoping we don't know what it is," Dovian said. "We didn't, did we? Spratling there was wearing it about his neck as a souvenir. He could as easily have melted it down or tossed it over his shoulder without a thought about it. If you were the leagueman, would you give up your life for the vague possibility that anybody would recognize this for what it is and conceive of how to use it?"

There was, finally, the matter of what to do once they reached the platforms. This, however, Dovian seemed to feel the most confident about. Of the many different quadrants of the floating platforms, one in particular was set away from the rest, separated by a long pontoon pier. "The pitch warehouses," he said. "The place they make the stuff and the place they store it. There's no more combustible substance on the earth. We've all seen it in action. It flares with the touch of a spark and burns like holy hell, even underwater. All we have to do is get near the stuff and strike a spark to it. It'll blow the place to pieces. It'll throw great globs of the stuff high enough that plenty of it'll land on other platforms. It'll make a right mess of the place. Believe it."

Spratling, despite finding himself sidelined in all of this discussion, felt his body tingle with the possibilities. It was an incredible idea, a scheme bold and righteous enough that they had to attempt it. But there was a flaw in it. "Somebody has to light that spark," he said. "However, that one will not make it off the platform alive."

Dovian looked annoyed that he had brought this up, but the others stopped to consider it. Geena suggested a fuse to delay the explosion. They could shoot a flaming arrow, a young raider put forward. Another proposed catapulting another "pill" over the walls. But all these ideas were flawed enough that they had to be rejected. Long fuses were unreliable. They might burn out themselves or be discovered as they sizzled and crackled slowly forward. If a guard came across such as that, he could squash their plans with the toe of his boot, just like that. An arrow or catapulted pill—even if they found the layout conducive to such an attack—would still mean an immediate explosion that might well take the entire crew with it. No, to survive they had to be well away. One of them had to light the pitch from up close and make sure it was going to blow. It was too harebrained a plan otherwise, too likely to fail.

"Well, how about this, then," Dovian said. "When we get to the platform, we'll draw lots to see who goes in. Each of us that crews the *Ballan* will
draw. If you aren't willing to be the one, then don't go. Step out right now.
Each of us that sails will draw, and the one with the mark will go. It may
seem a strange thing to decide by chance, but we'll plan to lose only one.
That one'll be taking more than a few leaguers with him."

※

A week later the *Ballan* sailed north with a lean crew. They rounded the
big island of Thrain and threaded the needle between the volcanic buttes
know as the Thousands. They waited two days in a hidden cove at the western edge of the islands and sailed into the open ocean on the morning of the
third. The winds were not ideal for the crossing, but the currents favored
them. They swept up to the north and veered west. For the better part of
one morning a massive school of dolphins escorted them, stretching off to
either side as far as the eye could see, hundreds of bodies darting out of the
water again and again, up and out and in, up and out and in. Nineas said it
was a fair sign, as dolphins were roguish buggers and could tell that the
raiders were about to get up to some major mischief.

Finding the atoll Dovian remembered proved difficult. They searched
for it for two full days without luck and had all but decided to do without
it. The next day, however, dawned with a tiny bunching of palms on the
horizon. They sailed for it and spent the afternoon talking things over one
final time, standing about in shady patches on the beach, drinking coconut
milk mixed liberally with sugar, a bit of water, and a splash of alcohol. Not
much, mind. Enough to keep up spirits but little enough that the effects of
it burned away late in the afternoon, when they got back to physical work.

They drew in all their regular sails and replaced them with blue-black
sailcloth. They painted the sides of *Ballan* a dirtlike color, took the shine off
any fixtures, hung cloth over the few glass windows. Casting off, they
chased the sun as it sank into the sea, and then they carried on afterward
into a black night. Dovian's voice rose out of the silence, steadying them on.
He did not speak grandly or give intricate instructions. He just mentioned
mundane matters, recalled adventures past, commented on things he had
noted about individual crew members and felt inclined to share with them.
So the hours passed.

"Lights ahead!" the sailor in the crow's nest called down.

A moment later Spratling clung at the edge of the small platform, having scaled the pole at full speed. He wrapped himself close against the

young sailor. "If I didn't know better, I'd say it was a city," the sailor said, "a big city, like Bocoum." He was quiet a moment. "No, bigger. Like Alecia."

Even that was an understatement. It wasn't just the number of lights, Spratling thought. It was the way they dotted the dark horizon for what must have been miles. It was hard to put scale to it yet, but for all the world he could not shake loose the feeling that he was looking at the shoreline of a great landmass. He remained aloft as Dovian ordered first one sail and then another drawn in. When the oars were called for, however, he climbed down and spoke in whispers to the men. He helped them get the oars out silently and fitted them into oarlocks padded for this purpose. He pulled one himself for a while, timing the movement to the slow rhythm Nineas called out, low and steady, like the beating heart of the ship, meant more to be felt than heard.

Later, Spratling stood next to Dovian, watching the monstrosity slide along beside them, trying to grasp the hugeness of it, to quantify its dimensions into finite terms. There was no obvious sign that the structure floated upon the waves at all. It looked as solid as if the entire thing was made of stone, as if its foundation stretched through the fathoms and anchored right to the seafloor. Its flat, featureless walls rose a hundred feet above the swells. Only there did the geometry break into balconies and terraces, towers and glowing windows. It could house . . . how many? a half million souls? a million? or more? It felt like a thousand pairs of eyes should be looking down upon them. They rowed along beside a monster, hushed both by stealth and awe.

They watched as they rounded the southern edge of the platforms. A large, rectangular complex sat off at a distance. It was a darker shape against the night, a geometry as of black obsidian, lit only by dim beacons at each corner. A floating pier a quarter mile long linked it to the main structure. It was as wide and even as the greatest highways in the realm, undulating slightly with a motion that, for an instant, conjured images of deep-sea leviathans.

"Tell the crew to get the small boat ready," Dovian said. "When we get close enough, get it into the water. Give Clytus and Wren the key. Let them check the lock."

"Clytus and Wren?"

"And six others to row for them, all well armed. They can handle it. You know that. Once you've sent them, come back to me. I want you here beside me to hear what I have to say."

"We'll need to draw the lots," Spratling said.

"Do as I said. And then come back to me here."

Spratling did so. He was back a few moments later, the sack of marked woodchips clenched in his fist. He looked toward the warehouses and watched the silhouette of the small boat row the distance to the pier and disappear into shadow. A few moments later he thought he saw figures moving on the pier, but they were gone in an instant. From then on, the moments stretched out, tense and nerve-racking.

From the *Ballan* they could only guess at what Clytus and Wren were doing based on what the pilot had told them. "There will be a few guards on the gate," the man had claimed, "but if you're stealthy at all you'll catch them unawares." He explained that the platforms had never been seriously attacked in all their years of existence. The league considered their distance from land to be a sufficient protection in and of itself. Add to that natural boundary the enormity of their walls and the reputation for vengeance of the Ishtat Inspectorate. Beyond this, the peculiarity of the keys and the fact that only the most trusted among them ever earned them and that loyalty among the sires was supposed to be complete: all these things made them confident that they were secure. The guards were a cursory measure and they knew it. "If you're lucky you'll find them napping."

Spratling had been unsure if he should trust the man. He might be leading them into a trap. But once the pilot grew accustomed to his role as traitor he became incredibly forthcoming. He grew so cooperative that Nineas muttered, "I think the man fancies himself a raider now." Indeed, he seemed to anticipate all the questions they would have and tried to answer them before he was asked.

They should avoid the main entryway, he said. It was inset at the point at which the pier connected to the pitch warehouse. Instead, they should travel along the wall to the south until they found the side entrance the sires used when they were entering the warehouse from the ocean side. It was a tall door, narrow, with a single keyhole at its center. They should insert the key completely, as if it was a child's geometric wooden block that needed to be slotted into the right compartment. That was all there was to it. No turning involved. That was why the key did not much resemble a key. Once it was home, the door would slide open with the slightest pressure put against it. Inside they would find a confusion of storage and manufacturing and machinery that he could not possibly detail. But he did not have to. Once inside they would be looking at the single greatest stockpile of explosive material in the Known World. He left it up to them to figure out what to do with it.

Feeling the interminable minutes plod past, Spratling wished he was there with them. It should have been him at risk. He was the one who had led them here, whether he liked to admit it or not. Why hadn't he gone with them? Dovian gave the orders, and he had followed. Why didn't he question . . .

Before Spratling knew it was happening, Dovian reached out, took the bag from his hand, and tossed it into the ocean. "I'm the one going," the raider said. "Don't argue with me about it. Until I'm gone, I'm in charge. This is what I say. Just wanted you to know first. We'll tell the others together. Come."

"No!" Spratling slammed a hand to Dovian's chest, stopping him. "No, we were to draw lots. We all agreed! You cannot—"

Dovian's hand covered the younger man's, hot and coarse, sweaty. "Don't make this hard on me. I'm sick. I'm not getting any better. The truth is I'm dying. I've been so for a long time now. I've been waiting to understand how best to say good-bye to the world. Now I've found it."

"You cannot die." Spratling knew he sounded childish, but he could not help himself. "You cannot leave me—"

"You're wrong there. I've given you everything I could. I've lived the best years of my life with you, lad. I've given you every bit of wisdom I have. Wasn't much, I know, but I've taught you everything a father should, haven't I? In a just world fathers would live to see their sons become men. Only *then* would they leave them. That's what's happening here."

Spratling saw a second movement on the pier again. He watched, breathless, until he saw the boat emerge from the shadows, rowing back toward the *Ballan*. He wanted them to stop. He needed more time. To Dovian, he said, "We made an agreement. It's not your place—"

The older man sighed. "You'll sit on the throne of Acacia someday. You will, even if you don't know it yet. If I had my way I'd be there beside you, proud as can be. But I cannot help you with that as I'd like to. I can do this, though. I can do this." He cupped his hand over the young man's shoulder. "Let me show you one last thing—how to die glorious like."

They did not actually hear the words from the returning group, but the message flowed to them on fingers of whispered electricity. The key was good! The warehouse was unlocked. They had killed two guards near the front gate but no others were in sight.

"I'll make a hell of a blaze, I promise you that. Ah, Dariel, come on now. I'm just asking you this one thing . . . No, not one thing. I've a second thing as well. You won't deny me it. I know you won't, 'cause I raised you better than that."

Less than an hour later, Spratling unfurled the black sail while the others still pulled on the oars. The wind had shifted. It blew them slicing through the ocean at a steady clip. The orange stain that announced the coming dawn illumined the horizon to the east. Behind them was blackness, silence. Like in his dream, he thought. The nothingness behind him. The nameless fear he had always to flee.

They put a second hour behind them. A few whispered fears that Dovian had been caught. None of them knew what he faced upon passing through that unlocked threshold. Perhaps the mission had failed. Spratling moved away from the others and stood in the prow of the ship. No matter what, Dovian was gone. It did not seem real. Did not seem possible. He wanted to stop the motion of the boat on the sea and the passing of time and just—

Such notions were ended in the most decisive of ways. Spratling knew the very moment Dovian sent his soul in search of the Giver. The blast of light that announced it turned the night to day and made the sea into a black mirror on which the contours of the heavens rippled and danced. He did not look back. He was afraid to. He was sure, at that moment, that behind him a raging conflagration reached up into the sky, Dovian's soul at its apex and roaring into the heavens. He felt sure the inferno would reach out and consume the world if he turned and faced it. These thoughts were as unsubstantiated as those of dream logic, which is no logic at all. He knew it, but still he set his eyes on the eastern horizon and only faced the blaze there, fleeing the one behind him in a headlong flight into the coming day.

CHAPTER

FORTY-SEVEN

Though Mena made sure never to waver in her duties as Maeben, the greater portion of her attention now went to her lessons with Melio. He met her in her compound every day, after she had completed her duties to the goddess. Instead of talking as they had done in their first few encounters, he tutored her solely in swordplay. He claimed to be out of practice and to never have been a teacher, but he dropped right into the role as if he had been born for it.

Within a few days of Mena stating her interest, Melio had ventured up into the interior highlands in search of suitable wood for practice swords. Though it was different from the ash used on Acacia, he did find a strong-grained timber of a reddish hue that served nicely. By the end of the first week they both danced about with training swords. They were lighter than he wished, but Melio was still pleased. His fingers caressed the gentle curves of the blades as if they wished to memorize each inch of them. He returned each day having made small refinements, added accoutrements, carved and sanded, oiled and honed the weapons in ways both functional and aesthetic.

Mena had little difficulty learning the postures, in getting her grip right, and setting her feet well. Any mistake that Melio corrected was banished forever. She never needed to be told a thing twice. At first this had surprised the tutor, but with the passing days he took her aptitude more and more as a given. They flew forward from one lesson to the next. Working on the various strokes, on how to best channel power from the legs up through the coiled tension of the torso and out to the blade. Her swims in the harbor and dives among the oysters had kept her fit, but Melio pushed her to use previously undiscovered muscles.

The First Form, that of Edifus at Carni, Mena committed to physical memory in three days. The fight between Aliss and the Madman of Careven took all of two days. Melio suggested they skip the Third Form, wherein the knight Bethenri went to battle with devil's forks, but Mena would not hear of it. She helped him fashion versions of the short, daggerlike weapons. The two of them cut and slashed, bent and twirled, thrust and retreated throughout one long afternoon. They stirred up clouds of dust and attracted the eyes of the servants, who stood at respectful distances completely transfixed by the sight of their mistress spinning through the deadly motions of warcraft. She did her best to work through the exercises with the goddess's calm façade. She voiced no fatigue. She never protested against a challenge. She wiped sweat from her face and stood straight even while her chest heaved and billowed.

In the solitude of her chambers at night she curled on her side and hugged her legs to her chest and cried at her body's torment. She did not recognize her own arms. They were thinner in some places, thicker in others, more angular, cut around the muscle in new ways. Fortunately, she could always recognize herself in the new shapes. The altered contours of her forearms, the shapes of the veins on the back of her hand, the striated cords at the base of her neck: it was always her, Mena. She was not so much changing into something different as she was emerging from beneath a long-held disguise. In the privacy of her inner rooms she stood unclothed, admiring the changes. In public, of course, she did her best to hide them.

If the priests knew anything of her daily routine—and they must have—they did not speak of it. Mena gave them no excuse to find fault with her. She was prompter in her duties than before. She was always on time for the evening ceremonies, for the special displays put on for visiting dignitaries, and she was more easily found inside her compound than previously, when she had spent her free moments in solitary exploration of the harbor floor. She sat through meetings in Maeben's garments without so much as a crack in her resolve. In the space of two weeks she had to twice meet with grieving parents, ones whose children had been taken by the goddess. She found herself speaking through the goddess in ways meant to please the priests. She had never quite done this before, and she did not like to recall some of the things she had intoned before the tearful, penitent parents. "Look not at the sky," she said once, "if you wish Maeben to see your reverence."

How unfair, she thought, to tell people to fear something as ever present as the heavens above them. She herself often searched out the raptor form aloft over the inner mountains. Why had she forbade the people from doing the same? Her words, she realized, would flow from one mouth to another. Soon the whole village, and eventually the entire archipelago, would know Maeben on earth's new proclamation. They would walk through their daily lives with bowed heads. Vaminee, the first priest, must have been pleased with her, though, if so, he did not deign to show it.

Melio, on the other hand, was not shy in voicing his disapproval of her service to the goddess. They still met at night to talk through what they practiced during the day and to plan for the future. They were both Acacians, he reminded her. These island deities were nothing to them. They were petty powers—if powers at all. Worshipping them did nothing to heal the rift between humankind and the Giver. *That* was what was important. *That*, perhaps, could help restore rightful order to the world. If Mena wished to pray, she should do so in Acacian and to the Giver. Aliver would summon her any day now; she had to be ready in every way possible.

"But instead you worship a sea eagle?"

Mena sat across from him in the dim light of a handful of candles, the night air around them still enough that the flames stood straight.

"What of the children? Your Maeben snatches children and carries them screaming to—"

"Don't!" Mena snapped. The word burst from her as forceful as a sword thrust. She could not listen to him speak so flippantly of the taken children. "I've no choice. I am Maeben. She happened to me. She came into me and I became her. I was nobody when—"

"You were a princess of Acacia."

"—I arrived here. I knew nothing. I had nothing. I was nothing but an orphan child! I didn't speak the language. I didn't know a soul. I was alone! Can you understand what that was like?"

"So the goddess snatched you up as well. And you are thankful for it?" When Mena did not answer, Melio shook his head, turned away, and took in the night sky. "No, I don't understand any of it. You're a young woman, Mena. That child you speak of is no longer. You're no goddess and you know it. The priests know it. The poor fools who revere you know it. You're all playacting some shared delusion. Maeben taking children to serve her in her palace? How absurd. Your goddess is nothing but a voracious bird. It lives on the isle north of here, and not in a palace either. Instead of worshipping it, somebody should shoot it from the sky. I have seen her aloft myself. If I had had a bow I would not have hesitated to use it."

Mena was silent for some time and then said, "You're right. You don't understand."

Whatever differences they had during the evening, they were forgotten as they carried on with their martial sessions during the day. Mena learned the Fourth Form—that of Gethack the Hateful—with ease. By the Fifth, however, she found herself struggling. It was not that her ability was any less—just the opposite. Her skills, she felt, were increasingly hampered by the Form. What did it matter how the Priest of Adaval went to work on the twenty wolf-headed guards of the rebellious cult of Andar? Learning the Sixth Form just made her doubts even clearer. She came to feel that there was a difference between the strokes she made during fencing and the way she would attack if her goal was actually to kill the person she faced. Having distinguished this difference, she wondered why one would ever waste time attacking in a manner that the partner already expected. Yes, the motions of dueling back and forth through the preordained motions of the Form strengthened the body and honed the reflexes, but such practice seemed beside the point.

She broke off in the middle of the Sixth Form one afternoon, exasperated. "This is too much dancing. No wonder our army fell so easily." Melio started to protest, but Mena gestured that she meant no offense. She wiped sweat from her brow and thought for a moment how best to express herself. "Why should we learn the steps of myth? The Early One casting back the gods of Ithem? What has that to do with anything? We won't be fighting the gods of Ithem. Why pretend that we will?"

Melio had an answer for this, but Mena did not pause to hear it.

"These things you are teaching me are all very well," she said, "but it seems to me that they constrict the sword instead of freeing it. You've taught me that the Forms are the basis of our military system?"

Melio nodded.

"Then you see the problem."

Melio was not sure that he did.

"I know I'm holding in my hand a wooden sword. But I'm supposed to think of it as a real blade, one that was conceived, fired, pounded, and honed to an edge all for one reason, yes? What is that reason?"

The tutor's answer had about it the tones of memorized maxims. "It's the link between the swordsman and his opponent," he said. "Properly used, the blade is an extension of the body, of the mind. A sharp blade is the tool of a sharp mind—"

"No." Mena shook her head, impatient. "To cut! That is the reason. I don't know anything about 'an extension of the mind.' Whenever it comes unsheathed, the intent should be to cut. Not to parry, not to dance, not to aim a blow that your opponent already knows is coming. A sword is a weapon. I want to learn to use it as one."

"True swordplay is not like the fencing we do here," Melio answered, "especially against opponents ignorant of the Forms. But having a host of known responses makes one quick when speed is needed."

Mena's head bowed slightly; her eyes canted upward to study Melio as he spoke on, his voice heavy with a tutor's authority. She lowered her gaze to the ground, pursed her lips as if the gesture was necessary to clip words that wished to escape her.

Eventually she broke in. "Raise your sword. Try to cut me—if you can do so before I cut you."

"This is a race to the cut, then?"

"Yes," Mena said, "you could say that."

They both stood in ready position. Mena nodded; Melio did likewise. A moment passed and then, they both knew, the duel could commence. One of them was more prepared for it than the other. Mena's strike was simple. Direct and executed without hesitation. She stooped low and sliced hard at Melio's left leg just below the knee. He did not have a chance to parry, and as the leg came out from under him, he twisted over the pain of it. He dropped to the hard-packed soil. Mena stood above him, the tip of her sword nudging his abdomen.

"I'm sorry, but here's my point: why dance through fifty moves when a single one will suffice?"

Melio stared at her with a look of alarm in his eyes. She reached out a hand and pulled him to his feet, smiling as if all she had just said had been some sort of joke.

From then on their fencing was never as it had been. Mena learned the rest of the Forms, memorizing and mastering the moves quickly. She did so in a perfunctory way, as if she was simply appeasing him. She focused her full attention on fencing, convincing Melio to fight again and again "to the cut." Initially, Mena scored more strikes. Melio seemed reluctant to commit to the stated rules, which were that from the moment they began each of them tried to immediately strike their blade into the other's flesh. Smarting from blow after blow, he quickened to match her. Soon their quick bouts of three or four moves had stretched to seven or eight. Before long their matches went into double digits.

Mena writhed at night, sleepless, her body like a weed twisting with rapid growth. She was raw with bruises, with abrasions, with stressed bones and muscles daily shredding and knitting anew. But she knew she was improving. She began to think of techniques Melio had not taught her, as when she pressed her body close to his and stuck like glue against him so that for some time neither of them could strike effectively against the other. Another time she abruptly dashed him with her shoulder, using it as if it were a weapon also, springing away from the impact with a vigor that caught him by surprise. She learned how to smack his blade with a collision that several times knocked it from his hands, and how to touch blades in a manner that made the two stick together instead of bounce apart. At times she slowed the rate of her movements unexpectedly, feeling that the center of her timing was in her abdomen. With a deep internal contraction she changed her rhythm so completely it left Melio stumbling to adjust.

Mena could not be sure how skilled her tutor actually was, but on a morning toward the end of the last month of spring the two fenced their way to a standstill. She stunned him by striking at several different points on his body with a single cut. Though Melio parried her, the shock on his face registered. He realized as well as she that with a single downward blow she had nearly cut him at the neck, on the side, and at the back of the knee, without losing any of her initial momentum.

After this, Melio stood some time, panting, watching her from behind the dark locks of his hair that stuck to the sweat of his forehead. "Who would have thought that Princess Mena Akaran would be the first to challenge me with the true use of the sword?"

"Don't look so surprised about it," Mena said. "All I've proved is that we are equals."

"Easily enough said, but perhaps you don't know what it means."

"Of course I do. It means I'll have to find someone else to fight. You know of the stick fighters?"

Melio voiced his opposition to the idea over and over again. He explained things she already knew but which he could not help but voice, as they seemed too important for her to ignore. She had not been trained to stick fight. The art and technique of it was vastly different from the swordplay they had been practicing. The sticks didn't cut, but this didn't mean they weren't dangerous, even deadly. Stick fighters came from the hill villages of the islands. They were the poorest of men. They claimed warriors' blood but could do nothing with it but test themselves against one another, trying to earn quick bounty from betting. They danced as if they were entertainers, strutting and preening and catering to the betting crowd, but when they attacked they did so with all the force they could muster. They dislocated shoulders with downward blows, broke forearms with twirls, thrust into abdomens so hard that the bodies bled on the inside. He had seen a man's skull cracked open, watched another man blinded in one eye, another with his collarbone smashed to pieces so that it would never heal properly. And yet another fighter, a master of the craft, had managed such force in his whirling strike to a man's back that the victim was unable to walk thereafter. He crumpled to the ground, devastated by what had just happened to him, and never again rose to stand on his legs.

"These are men you want to test yourself against?"

If she entered the circle with one of them, she risked a hundred injuries and would gain nothing for it. Why do that? It simply did not make sense. She was vain beyond all reason if she believed a month of sword training had prepared her for such a test. And, anyway, if found out, the wrath of the priests would fall upon her, endangering everything.

Thus was Melio's rant. It did not do the least bit of good. Mena chose the day she appeared in the rough ring of the stick fighters. She dyed her skin with blackberry juice, leaving it a strange tint but not entirely unnatural. She wrapped her torso in a binding cloth that flattened her small breasts, dressed as a laborer, and bound her hair as Vumu men did. She held her open eyes above a smoky fire long enough to redden them, like those of a mist smoker. No doubt she looked unusual, but none who saw her imagined her to be the priestess of Maeben.

With Melio as a guide, she found the stick fighting gathering at the far side of Ruinat. Discovering it was the easy part. Getting into the ring, she thought, might be more difficult. She shouldered her way into the throng of men. They were young and old, laborers and dockworkers, hill farmers and urchins of the town, the smell of them rank and thick, the air clouded with sweat and mist smoke. She knew these people. She recognized faces from ceremonies. But she was not Maeben now. There was no distance separating them now. She was not arrayed in the guise of a goddess.

The ring man approached her, taking her in from head to toe, grinning. She thought he might ask her to explain herself, to justify being there. But he had no interest in her credentials. He was all business. He informed her that all new fighters had to earn the right to compete. Their first match was always with the one who held the ring's title. The new fighter had to put up the entry fee. The sum, of course, was essentially forfeit. She would lose, but afterward she would be able to compete with lesser fighters.

"If I win," Mena said, keeping her voice clipped and low, "am I then the title holder?"

The man laughed. "If you win, you've earned a place at the bottom, that's all. Do you still wish to fight?"

"Of course."

"Then you fight Teto," the ring man said.

Teto, the said champion of the ring, was happy to oblige. He pushed through the sweaty bodies and stepped into the circle of cleared sand, where Mena awaited him. His stick, which he held toward the point and carried pressed up against the back of his arm, slid through his loosened fingers until his fist tightened around the hide-wrapped hilt. He moved with a demeanor quite different from Melio's. His bare feet were careful in their placement but playful. He was light upon the toes, his legs rubbery bands of muscles that supported a floating, tranquil torso. His head seemed the weightiest portion of his body, eyes deep set in the skull and hard on her.

Mena did not have time to think much. Teto opened the duel; she responded. Within a few seconds she decided to fight him with the deadening defense. It was not something she had practiced before or named in advance. But from the first moments she knew that his strength was his greatest attribute and his pride in this was likely his greatest flaw. Instead of exerting extra energy in the impact of their sticks, she let her own force give when she parried. She stopped his strike but without the normal impact he was used to. He struck again harder and harder, his anger showing on his face and in the quickening pace of his strikes. But each time he touched her stick, it gave against his with a limpness he clearly found disturbing, as if he had struck a heavy rope that somehow diffused his force.

The end of the match came so quickly that the onlookers stood stunned afterward. Teto rushed her, his stick straight before him, intent on impaling her with his blade or flattening her with the rush of his body. Mena simply touched his stick with hers, slipped to the side, kept his weapon in place with the pressure of hers sliding over it. She lifted to clear his hilt and then snapped her stick across the base of his exposed neck with all the force her body could muster. And that was it.

Teto dropped to the sand, his hands clasped to his throat, writhing in agony, his cries of angry pain the only sound within the hushed arena of bodies. For some moments the spectators stared about confused, looking from one another to the two fighters and then around again, trying from the scene before them to understand the blinding motion that had preceded it, each of them blinking as if in so doing the world would snap into the rightful order, the outcome of the match reversed. Mena let them study this for a few moments, and then she turned on her heel in the sand and pushed through the crowd.

"Where was your fear?" Melio asked, jogging to keep up with her as they wove the back alley trail toward the temple compound.

"I don't know," Mena said. And it was true. She had forgotten there even was such a thing as fear. She'd felt only exhilaration and purpose as she faced Teto. Now she jogged with a positively giddy energy. "I just knew I could beat him. I had to be careful, yes. But I did not fear."

"He would have liked to have hurt you."

"Yes, I'm sure."

They carried on in silence for a time. As they came out of the shrubs near the compound wall, Melio said, "Can I convince you not to do that again?"

Mena stopped and turned toward him. Looking at his brown eyes and crooked lips and disheveled hair she realized that she felt very different in his presence now from the way she had when he first arrived. She was more at home within herself, more at peace, especially so when in his company. Strange that all the hours fighting could bring them closer. All the time with their bodies pressed close together in physical contest, moist with sweat, each trying to best the other, pain and humiliation only a mistake away. Part of her wanted to acknowledge that there was something special in what they had become to each other. But she was not sure just what to say or how to say it.

She spoke simply. "Thank you for the things you've taught me."

He shrugged. "I'm not sure that I taught you anything, Mena. It feels more like I just reminded you of things you already knew. You may have been born to wield a sword. Do not laugh. I'm not joking. . . ."

He hesitated a moment. The deepening furrows in his forehead suggested he might have something more to say. He did have something more to say! The same sort of thoughts she herself had. She read it all on his face in an instant. Though it sent a trilling of excitement through her body, Mena moved before he could speak. She patted his arm and turned and jogged the last stretch to the compound.

Arriving back at the gate, she found Vandi waiting for her. The summons he bore was the one she had come to most dread. She was needed in the anteroom of the temple in little more than two hours. It could only mean that Maeben had taken another child. It was the fourth in less than two months.

She parted from Melio without a word, shutting him out of the com-

pound. Inside, Vandi waited to one side as she stripped naked and stepped
into her bath, scrubbing her skin furiously to remove the berry tint from her
skin. Vandi watched her with his greenish eyes, his lips tightly clamped. He
offered neither comment nor question, though he must have noted every detail of her disguise. He had even seen her hand her stick to Melio.

Mena scrubbed her face raw without actually getting all the stain off.
But when she could take it no more she gave up. She and Vandi walked
briskly to the temple, where he dressed her as the goddess. The makeup ap-
pliers lathered unguents on liberally. By the time they set her headdress in
place she looked firmly within her role. Only then did she remember to slow
her breathing and cool her body and think away the beads of sweat that
threatened to smear her façade. She thought back to her claim that she had
not been afraid to fight Teto. It had been true at the time, she was sure. She
tried to summon such courage again. Looking into the faces of grieving parents, however, was not something she would ever grow comfortable with.

She seated herself on the large chair in the anteroom of the temple.
Vaminee stood in his usual place beside her. He tugged his robes snug and
showed Mena his chin in profile, nothing unusual in that. Tanin, the second
priest, took up a position at her left hand. He was not usually a part of these
interviews. He watched her with an intense consideration that made her
skin itch.

"Priestess, you may be interested to learn," Tanin said, "that a delegation of foreign warriors arrived in Galat yesterday."

Mena felt a need to reach out and steady herself, but she knew she was
already seated, already steadied. Being careful to keep her voice neutral,
blandly uninterested, she asked, "What do they want?"

"We thought you might have an opinion on them," Vaminee said.

"How could I know anything about them?"

Neither priest responded.

"I—I've heard rumors that war may be coming to the foreign lands. If
that's true, perhaps these soldiers want our aid."

"That may be true," Vaminee said, "and it may not be true. They claim
to seek a lost child and believe she may be living on Vumu. In any event, it's
none of our affair. I've told the foreigners nothing as yet. The goddess is dis-
pleased with the islanders. That's all we need concern ourselves with. We
must first appease Maeben. Then we will decide on a course for dealing
with the delegation."

This was meant to end the subject, but Mena had to know at least a
little more. "The foreigners . . . what nation are they from?"

"How should I know?" Vaminee asked.

"They are pale," Tanin said. "They have skin like pig flesh."

An ugly description, but coming from Tanin it was hard to know its accuracy. "I should meet with them," Mena said. "As Maeben, I mean . . . Perhaps it is Maeben's wish that Vumu play a role in the world. If I see them while in the goddess's garb I might understand what she would wish."

"You've done poorly at that lately. The fourth child taken since—"

"That's no fault of mine! I hate that the goddess takes children. I'd do anything to make her stop."

Vaminee closed his eyes, head tilted slightly, the muscles of his jaw rigid with anger. "You forget yourself entirely, girl. I didn't want to believe it, but it's whispered that you've been playing about with wooden swords. Is this true?"

"Within the walls of my compound I'm free to—"

"So it's true." Vaminee exchanged glances with the other priest. "You must stop this at once. People talk, Priestess. You may do as you wish in your compound up to a point. You cannot dishonor Maeben."

The curtain at the far side of the room parted, indicating that the grieving parents were about to enter.

Vaminee noted it but continued. "You will stop immediately. And your friend—yes, I know of him—will leave next week when the floating merchants embark. If he remains, he will suffer for it. And you will suffer for it."

The procession stepped through the entrance. The two parents, flanked by lesser priests, moved forward slowly, with grief-drenched reverence. From the instant Mena saw the couple she felt her heart accelerate. It took her a moment to truly understand why. They stepped forward slowly, faces tilted toward the floor, hands held before them beseechingly. They seemed so very familiar. Their shapes and movements . . . she'd seen them before! It was the same couple she'd seen weeks before when they'd lost their baby girl. If her eyes weren't lying . . . if it was really them . . .

"No," Mena said. "Not them . . . I promised them the goddess wouldn't take their second child."

Vaminee snapped his head toward her. "Foolish girl! That promise was not yours to make. Look these two in the face and see the results of your false pride."

CHAPTER

FORTY-EIGHT

The cliffside resorts of Manil were amazing to behold. As black as the night sky, the basalt walls rose more than two thousand feet into the air from the sea swells, vertical all the way to their heights. Residences had been wedged into fissures up and down the expanse of stone. Some actually hung from protrusions, slung in place by intricacies of architecture Corinn could only marvel at. They were painted pale blues and violets, hung with banners that danced in the air's tumultuous currents.

As the homes were playgrounds in which rich merchants mingled with nobility, the Akarans had never deigned to buy a property here, but others among the extended royal family had. A girlhood friend whose family had a holiday home at Manil had bragged that the lower floors were made of thick glass panes that provided views of the waves hundreds of feet below. She claimed she could step out of bed and walk across her room, all the time watching the paths winged by gulls beneath her feet. Corinn had never visited that particular villa. She had been wary of believing the girl; but the memory had lingered, enough so that she recalled it from the moment she set eyes on Manil.

To reach the estates from the sea, one docked within the protection of a gated port, hemmed in by great blocks that had been lowered to serve as breakwaters. One morning well into the Acacian spring, Corinn stepped from a pleasure vessel onto this stone pier, Hanish Mein at her side. The two climbed into an open-top carriage and began the switchback ascent up a series of ramps. Though she still tried, it was getting more and more difficult to hold to her aloofness. Hanish was constant in his attentions, more so recently than ever. In the weeks since Calfa Ven he had requested her company on every journey. And there had been several. He had somehow managed to get her to serve as a guide to the high circles of Bocoum. With carefully placed questions—during what must have been orchestrated moments of solitude—Hanish again and again got her to open her mouth and speak civilly to him. She still planted barbs in him when she could, but he proved more consistent with his courteousness than she could be at rebutting him.

The villa they were to stay in was lavish in the way only vacation homes ever were, designed to attest to the owner's wealth, to pamper guests for short periods. It would have belonged to an Acacian family, perhaps one known to her. She did not ask. Such things failed to trouble Corinn as they once had. Everything, it seemed, had once belonged to Acacians. Now it belonged to Meins. She knew she should consider this a personal affront, but indignation was hard to hold on to year after year. She had been fluent in the Meinish language for some time. Aspects of their culture that had once seemed foreign to her now blended—in courtly circles, at least—so intricately with Acacian ways that it was hard to know where one ended and the other began.

The villa had been anchored to the plains above the cliffs. It draped over the upper rim and stretched down several stories. One room flowed into the next with a sensation almost like sliding, as if the rooms moved to adjust to your progress. One reached a room simply by initiating a motion toward it. Corinn found it all somewhat disconcerting, yet pleasurably so. All the walls facing the sea made full use of the vistas, with building-length patios or windows set low on the walls to reveal the heaving sea far below. The mosaic pattern on the floor simulated ocean waves, whitecapped and frothy. Porpoises leaped into and out of the swells. Fishermen clung to tiny boats, tilted at precarious angles that would have overturned actual vessels. Left alone in her room, Corinn spent a portion of the afternoon on her knees, studying the details, dragging her fingertips across the tumultuous motion. It was so well done. She loved the way the fishermen seemed always on the verge of destruction, loved that their smiling faces suggested they thought it all a great game.

The first evening, she and Hanish attended a banquet hosted by a newly rich Meinish family. In times past Hanish would have entertained the gathering at her expense, finding something to needle her about. But the usual entourage had not come on this trip. Hanish was cordial enough with his hosts, but he never truly engaged with them, despite their repeated efforts to bring him to the center of things. He simply did not seem that interested, neither in them nor in the music; nor in the food and drink so abundant around them; nor in the fawning gestures of men and women alike, all of them so eager to praise Hanish Mein, their hero, the only Mein to ever ascend to the throne of an empire, the one who might yet lift the old curse. He was the greatest chieftain in the history of their people, and folk such as these never tired of praising him for it.

Instead of paying them any mind, he blocked out a space for himself and Corinn to share privately. She could no longer deny—at least not to herself—that she enjoyed speaking as he listened. She enjoyed answering queries, liked to have his gray eyes upon her, liked knowing that the rest of the room watched from outside the pull of his gravity. The confidence which she had once thought of only as arrogance actually had an allure to it.

And Hanish relaxed in her presence, even as troubling affairs of state crowded his mind. He told her of the league's ongoing campaign against the Outer Isles raiders. It had not gone as easily as the league had predicted, he said. Not at all. One captain of the bandits called himself "Spratling"—an ironic play on words, no doubt, as there was a tiny, inconsequential fish that went by that name. This Spratling was not at all inconsequential. In addition to hobbling a warship and actually killing a leagueman, he had exploded a portion of the league platforms. The initial blast tore the warehouses to pieces and threw up a spray of flaming pitch that set the entire structure ablaze. Even the stuff that fell into the sea continued to burn. It floated on the surface and came riding the swells toward the other platforms with each shift in the tides. The fires, his sources said, burned for a week before they were contained or dissipated. The raiders had done so much damage that the league postponed the spring shipment of mist. They would be months working to recover, backlogged in every province.

"All because of a little spratling." Hanish dismissed it all with a wave of his hand. "Anyway, it's only a temporary setback. The league has a thousand weapons to bring to bear. That's what they're saying; I'd like to believe them. When they're crippled, we're crippled as well."

"Have you considered doing away with them?"

"With the league?" Hanish asked.

Corinn hesitated a moment. "I know the league has been around for ages, but if they cannot even defend themselves against a band of raiders . . . why not handle the trade directly?"

"No chance of that. You cannot imagine how entrenched the league is. They have steel hooks planted in every aspect of the world's affairs. They are efficient at what they do usually. Perhaps most to the point, they've made many powerful persons rich beyond their dreams. This was true in your father's time; so it is true in ours."

"You never miss a chance to point out that my people began the world's injustices," Corinn said, feeling a flare of her old anger. "We were the villains who created the Quota, who brought mist to the Known World, who conscripted slave labor to work the mines. You want me to know that this foulness was inside me all along. You act as if you had a righteous mandate to overthrow it, but how have you made the world better? You've killed the slave master, but instead of freeing the slaves you've stepped into his place—"

Hanish interrupted, speaking in a flippant tone that ignored the import of her argument altogether. "Will you dance with me?"

Corinn showed her annoyance with a cold stare. "Meinish music isn't fit for dancing." This was not just an insult. Their tunes were still strange to her ears. Compared to the lush, all-encompassing fullness of Acacian ensemble groups, the plucked notes of the Meinish instruments were discordant, the melodies spare and unpredictable. She could not imagine how to dance to it. Nobody else was.

"So you would dance, had we the proper music?"

When she did not answer immediately, Hanish took her by the wrist. He squeezed her fine bones between his thumb and forefinger and tugged her toward the center of the room. "In all the many centuries that musicians have played Meinish tunes, I'm sure that someone has danced to this one. Someone has felt within the sounds a rhythm suited to the movement of two bodies. That's how I like to think of it. One must find rhythms others' ears don't hear."

The hand at her wrist slid somehow into the grip of her palm. The other swept around her back. He pulled her close. She yanked her arm to loose it from his and stepped back, but instead of breaking free she found Hanish swept forward, the movement of her arm a gesture in what was suddenly choreography. Her backward step had been so perfectly timed to his forward motion that she almost believed she had initiated the intimacy. Try as she might she could not manage to break the flow of their movements. Before long she stopped trying. It was amazing, really, how well he moved and how much her body enjoyed the swirling pattern they cut across the floor.

"Corinn," Hanish said, "I cannot pretend to have a noble answer to your question. I have not made the world better. I know that. But I've made it better for my people. Believe me, we deserve it. No other people has suffered like mine has."

"I suppose that's my fault also."

Hanish waited a few moments after this, moving through the dance, his eyes furtive in a way Corinn had never seen them, canted off to the side. "Not you, but your people, yes. Your people gave birth to the Tunishnevre. They created it. On winning the throne through all manner of deceit—and if you think I'm treacherous, you should know your own blood, Corinn—Tinhadin turned on my ancestors and cursed them. He was a sorcerer. He had but to speak a thing to make it happen."

"Santoth," Corinn said. "You're talking about the Santoth."

Hanish nodded. "Tinhadin had a gift that perhaps you have as well, if you knew how to use it. He cursed the line of Mein with everlasting purgatory. No man of my family has found peace in death since—not one in over twenty generations. Our bodies don't rot. Our dead flesh doesn't burn. Our souls remain trapped within. We're not alive, but we linger. Just linger."

Several other couples had joined them in the open space. They twirled about in imitation of Hanish's dance, their faces eager for the eye contact he denied them. Corinn thought he might change the subject for fear of being overheard, but he carried on without even lowering his voice.

"There is no greater curse than being forever trapped between life and death," he said, "allowed neither one nor the other. Can you imagine what it means to be a spirit contained within a corpse for year after year, no end of it in sight? Death comes for all things. All things—humans and beasts, trees and fish—everything is promised release except my ancestors. Except me. This is what the Tunishnevre is. This is why it grows greater with each passing year. This is why your people make sure their own corpses are made into dust and cast out into the wind. Your customs remember the curse and fear it, even if you don't. I find that's often the way of things. Collective memory has a wisdom individuals cannot match. I'd like to find a way to free them so that they could truly find the peace and rest of death. Perhaps—should you ever find it in your heart—you could help me do this."

"Me?"

Hanish nodded. "You may have an importance you have not yet imagined."

"Is it true that you speak with them?"

"In a manner, yes."

"What do they tell you?"

They bumped against a couple that had gotten too close. Hanish stopped moving, dropped his arms, and spoke quietly in a way that made his voice an intimacy. "They tell me a great many things, Corinn. Right now

they are telling me it's getting too crowded here, Princess. They suggest that
we retire."

They spent the entirety of the next day together. Hanish seemed to
have nothing to do except entertain her. On horseback they rode the coast
road to the north, flowing over the contours of the plateau, sea to one side,
manicured farmland stretching off to the west. His escort of Punisari guards
kept a good distance behind them, well out of earshot of their conversation.
For the first time they truly spoke without the possibility of anybody over-
hearing them. They did not, however, use the solitude to speak of anything
of any significance.

At a famous spot they stood above a fissure in the rock face that channeled the power of the swells into a foaming eruption of spray. It came
rhythmically, like blasts blown up from some undersea bellows. And after
lunch they shot quail released one by one for their pleasure. The birds took
to flight in a frenzy, the flapping of their wings audible even from a distance.
By no means were they easy targets with a bow and arrow. Hanish made
only one grazing contact with a bird; Corinn pinned five. There was something satisfying about making a hit: the way the bird's wings stopped instantly, its course altered, the way it dropped from the sky, a dead weight
that twirled with the awkward appendage of the shaft imbedded in it. Once
her arrow passed directly through a bird, so smoothly it carried on into the
distance and sank into the ground long after the bird had thudded down.
Hanish applauded, and she found ready occasions to tease him, which
clearly gave him pleasure.

When he proposed that they refuse the evening's invitation to dinner
Corinn did not object. They ate together at the far ends of a too-long table.
The main course was scallops simmered in a chili sauce, topped with fragrant herbs. It was wonderful on the palate, a play of sweet and fierce that
sent Corinn's body temperature soaring. They drank a dry, pale wine that
made Corinn suck her cheeks absently. Hanish imitated her; Corinn ac-
cused him of selecting the fare just to make her look a fool. He did not
deny it.

Later, they shared a sweet liqueur on the villa's main balcony. Below
them the sea darkened as the sun passed from view. Before long the moon
appeared and shone behind a lacy weave of thin clouds. The breeze carried
a chill with it, but not uncomfortably so. Just enough to pimple the skin.
Corinn stood near enough to Hanish to smell the scented oils that had been
rubbed into his skin. She brushed her shoulder against his absently. Once

she felt the electric shock of her breast grazing his arm. Did she intend such moments? Did she orchestrate them or had wine and liqueur—which had pleasantly blurred the edges of the world—made her so clumsy with her body as that? She was not sure.

Holding her small glass out to accept Hanish's offer of a refill, Corinn asked, "What next? Will you offer me a draw on a mist pipe?"

The question was posed playfully, but Hanish rubbed the grain of the weathered balcony abutment nervously, looking for a moment like a child trying to leave an indentation with just the pressure of his fingers. "Never."

"Did you bring me here to seduce me? Is that what this is all about?"

Blood rose to Hanish's cheeks. Even his forehead reddened. She had never seen such an involuntary display register on his features before. "I brought you here to offer you a gift. I fear you'll throw it back in my face."

"I strike fear in you, then?"

"You fill me with trepidation, Corinn, in a way that nobody has before."

Corinn looked at him, her face giving nothing away, waiting. Hanish motioned for her to sit beside him on a nearby bench, from which they leaned forward and gazed over the railing. They sat side by side, near enough that their legs touched at the knee.

"What if I said that this was all yours?" Hanish asked. "This villa, I mean. There is no reason you shouldn't have the best of everything. You were a princess; you are still a princess. It confounds me that you won't take me at my word on this. I imagine a day when you and your siblings will gather here and enjoy—"

"You need not buy me, lord. I'm your slave anyway."

"Please, Corinn," Hanish said. "This home belonged to a family called Anthalar. You knew them, yes?"

Corinn nodded.

Hanish admitted that he had met one of them himself. It was during the war, before a battle. He had given the young man death, he said. He had always regretted that death. He saw strength in him, pride. He reminded him of his brother Thasren. So angry, so intent on doing right for his people. But it could not have been any other way. Being where he was that day, the young man simply had to die. A life lived truly created regrets such as this. There was no way around it. He regretted the things done to Corinn also.

"I know you cannot be bought," he said, "but if you have any kindness within you, you'll understand this gift is one I must try and give. If I've kept you penned up in the palace for too long I apologize. I used to fear to let you out of my sight."

"Why?"

He shook his head, just enough to indicate he was not going to answer that question just now. "But you're not a slave. You know that, don't you?"

"Yes, actually I do know that." Corinn drew her knees in, breaking the contact between them. She no longer felt giddy or elated from the drink. "I saw real slaves once. I was staying with a noble's family in a village near Bocoum. I knew I was wrong to do it, but my friend and I stole out late at night and climbed onto the roof. We did this sometimes back then to look at the stars and tell stories. But this night we found a spot from which to watch the street below and there we saw a strange . . . Well, at first I thought it was a parade. But who has a parade in the middle of the night? In complete silence? And in what parade are the marchers all connected by chains? They were the same age as I was then. Ten, eleven, just on the verge of starting the change. They were chained at the necks, one to another to another, hundreds of them. Men drove them with drawn swords. They made not a sound over the shuffling of their feet and the tinkle of chains and . . . I never forgot that silence. It was dreadfully loud."

"This sounds like a dream to me," Hanish offered.

Corinn shook her head. "Don't even allow me that much. It was no dream. Some part of me knew it, even back then. I did not know details, but I knew not to ask any adult what that procession had been. It was the Quota, of course. The Quota, upon which everything depends." She stared at Hanish for a long moment. The small scar on his nostril was more pronounced than usual, his nose flushed from the liqueur, perhaps. "Why do the foreigners want our children so badly? What do they do with them?"

"Some questions are best left unanswered. But listen, you've confessed to me. Let me do the same. I want you to understand me and my people. We suffered so terribly during the Retribution. Do you understand that level of suffering? Twenty-two generations—as many in my line as in yours. But yours reigned supreme; mine struggled just to survive. And eventually we began to dream that old wrongs could be set right. All of that disruption we caused over the years—the petty squabbles and hijackings, the raids on Aushenia—none of that was true to our character. That was all just noise we made with drums and horns, behind which we hid our true objectives. We wanted Acacians to believe they knew us. I know our success gives you no joy. I'm just trying to explain myself. It is your right to judge us, but it is mine to want you to judge us fairly."

"And so you killed my father," Corinn said. She intended her voice to sound cold, angry, but instead she heard something pitiful in it, a desire to be comforted.

"I wish every day that there could have been an alternative. You do not know how much I wish I could have come to know you in some other way. But what I did against the beast that was the Acacian Empire I did not do against you. I'm no monster. Sometimes I wish the world to believe me so, but in truth my only distortion is that I feel the sorrow of an entire people. I must think of them first, understand that? I don't love that I now send thousands of children into bondage. I hate it. But my own people have to come first. Understand that and you understand me."

It was not that Corinn was untouched by what he said. It was not that she did not believe him or that she did not warm at the thought of this softness in his heart. She felt all these things, but habit had so sharpened her tongue that she responded with a meaner thought, one meant to defend herself even now.

"This is a strange method of seduction," she said.

Hanish lifted his face to hers, his eyes brimming with moisture. The weight of his tears shifted as he moved and broke free from both eyes, spilling down his cheeks. It was so achingly pathetic a transformation that Corinn reached out to him. She touched him at the shoulder blade. She slid her fingers in line with the bone, across the fabric of his shirt, and onto the bare skin of his neck. She had wanted to touch him there for so long. His flesh was warm, soft as she imagined few parts of him were. She thought she could feel his pulse through his skin, but it may have been her own throbbing at her fingertips.

It was tiring being faithful to her father, she thought, exhausting to hope that her siblings would appear and have some influence on her life. Her stomach churned with the acids she daily nurtured. Why not just give herself to Hanish? Who better than he? She wished that Hanish actually had the power to make her whatever he wanted. She wished that she had the temperament to accept whatever role he shaped for her. He did have a capacity for cruelty. That would remain, no matter this show of intimate vulnerability. In the morning he would be Hanish Mein again, and the world would never know of the cracks beneath his façade of complete control. But for some reason—and despite everything she knew to be right and true—she wanted to learn this very trait from him. She wanted to eat it piece by piece from his mouth and take it inside her and be a partner to it.

She did not retreat when he looked into her face. There was, in fact, an expression on her face like defiance. "How did you know to bring me to *this* villa?"

"I've made it my business to know. Tell me it pleases you and I'll be happy."

"Are there rooms here with glass floors?" she asked, knowing the answer already.

Hanish nodded. "In the children's bedrooms. They are below us."

"Show me them," Corinn said, in barely more than a whisper.

CHAPTER
FORTY-NINE

Aliver returned to the world of the living. He parted with the San-toth, promises made on both sides, and he walked himself gradually back to an understanding of his corporeal body. At first, his limbs swung unwieldy about him, heavy as if flowing with molten metal. His legs were a chore to lift. Each time he set a foot down he felt guilt for placing the burden of himself onto the earth. Why had he never noticed that before? The flow of time, the progression of the sun, the brutal heat of day, and the sharp cold of night: so many things to remember. It seemed the world's volume was out of all order. What should have been the tiniest of sounds—wind stirring sand grains to tumbling, a grumble of thunder in the far distance, the blast from his chest as he coughed—rocked him right to the center. Again and again he had to stop in his tracks, hold his head, breathe low and shallow. With each step he considered turning around. But this was never really an option. It was like the hunger of a mist smoker for the green cloud. He had no intention of giving in to it. In fact, he had never felt more resolved to face his fate back in the Known World.

He met Kelis just where the man promised he would be. Something about being with another person broke down the last barriers between Aliver and the world. He heard another human voice for the first time in what seemed like ages. He opened his own mouth in response and was relieved to find his speech no longer the discordant clatter it had been. By the time they reached Umae, he and Kelis were running again, the pair of them looking much as they had when they left weeks before.

Umae, however, was not the same as it had been. It had doubled in size, lapping out of the gentle bowl that housed it and reaching out in all directions. Makeshift tents clustered around the main village, satellite settlements that had a fledgling look of permanence to them. As he and Kelis approached, calls went up announcing them. People thronged the lanes between the fields, perched in acacia trees, squatted on every area of available ground. Walking through them, Aliver heard inflections that marked the dialects of neighboring tribes. He saw Balbara headdresses made of ostrich feathers and seashell necklaces from the eastern shore and the skintight leather trousers worn by the hill people of the Teheen Hills. A cluster of high-cheekboned warriors greeted him with a timed shout. He had no idea what people they were. He answered them with a nervous nod, which—judging by their grins in response—sufficed quite nicely.

Thaddeus and Sangae awaited them at the center of the village. Both of them wore similar expressions of fatherly relief, pride, awe. Sequestered safely inside the chieftain's compound, Aliver did the best he could to answer their rapid barrage of questions. It must have been unsatisfying for them. He was vague on every detail. He knew it. His sentences dribbled away half finished. He paused for long intervals, stumped at how to possibly explain his experiences among the Santoth. He could not really. Most of it had happened in a place without words. Some of it—now that he was firmly back amid the tumult of humanity—seemed as hazy as the dream-world.

Both of the older men seemed to understand this. They were thrilled that he had made contact with the Santoth, delighted that the sorcerers recognized Aliver, and overjoyed that he had returned safely. They explained that from the day he left rumor of his mission had escaped the village and flown across the plains. Aliver Akaran was among them! He was a man who had killed a laryx! The prince had gone in search of the banished sorcerers! Neither Thaddeus nor Sangae had planned for the news to escape. It happened spontaneously. People who had kept his identity secret every day for nine years could not hold it any longer. The world, it seemed, was hungry for word of him. In no time at all the pilgrims began arriving.

"The ones gathered here are just the first to join you," Thaddeus said. "We can move north from here at any time, gathering our army as we go. We'll pull together a host like the world has never seen, so grand an army, of so many nations, that Hanish Mein will have to face us." The former chancellor paused, seeming to realize he was getting ahead of himself. "Prince, does this plan please you?"

"We cannot simply amass numbers," Aliver heard himself say. "We have to train them as well. Without discipline and coordination our host will be but a flock for the Mein and the Numrek to slaughter."

Thaddeus glanced at Sangae. He sent him some message with a slight motion of his eyebrows, as if marking a point earned, and then returned his gaze to Aliver. He was glad to hear the prince thought on such scale and looked for details within it. He explained that he had been doing the same thing for some time. He had been in contact with several former Acacian generals over the years. They had all nurtured support among intimate groups. They had sworn themselves to secrecy and waited for his call to arms. One of them, Leeka Alain, formerly of the Northern Guard, had found Aliver's younger brother.

Aliver interrupted. "He found Dariel?"

Thaddeus nodded. "I received correspondence to that effect while you were gone. They should be on the way to us soon. And they're not the only ones. There are people in every corner of the empire who remain loyal to the Akarans."

His brother was alive! The news that one of his siblings had actually been found and won over to this effort filled Aliver with relief, followed fast by a flare of worry. Little Dariel! How could he survive amid the coming turmoil? He almost said that Dariel should stay in hiding, but he caught himself. He was picturing the small boy Dariel had been. That child was no more. The years would have changed him as much as they had changed Aliver. Even more, for he was so young when the exile began. He wanted to grasp the old chancellor and ask him question after question. Where was his brother? What sort of life had he lived? What had he become?

He would pose all the queries later, he decided. Before that he had to ask something else. "You say people in every corner of the empire remain loyal to my family. Are you sure of this? We did so little for them."

"Because they remember your family's nobility," Sangae answered. He said this solemnly, his wrinkled chin jutting forward. No doubt he believed it completely, somehow feeling some ownership of that nobility himself.

"They believe in you, Aliver," Thaddeus said, "just as they loved your father. They likely love your father in death more so than they did when he lived."

Neither answer surprised Aliver, but neither seemed satisfactory either. He turned to Kelis. "How do you see it?"

The Talayan cleared his throat and answered with complete honesty, as Aliver knew he would. "Because the entire world suffered from Hanish's war. Life is worse for them now, under the Mein's new tyranny. But you . . . you're a symbol of a lesser evil. That's about all people can believe in and hope for. So it feels right to them."

"That's not good enough," Aliver said. The answer came crisply. Hearing the words he felt a confidence in them that surprised him. It *wasn't* good enough to be a lesser evil. If he was going to do this at all, he had to aim higher. "I don't want them to fight just to return to the old position of bondage. If I win this war, Thaddeus, it must be with the promise of changing everything for the better. Tell people that if they fight with me, they fight for themselves so that they and their children will always be free. This is a promise I make them."

Thaddeus gazed at him for a long moment, his face unreadable. So unreadable, in fact, that he must have worked hard to render it so. Eventually he asked, "Are you sure?"

"Yes," Aliver said.

"You speak an ideal that may prove hard to put into practice. The world is corrupt from top to bottom. Perhaps more than you know."

The prince looked hard at Thaddeus. "I'm more sure about this than anything else. This war must be a fight for a better world. Anything less is failure."

"I understand," Thaddeus said. "I will make sure that message is known. Your father would be proud to hear you speak."

Aliver stood and moved over to one of the windows. He lifted the shutter and, squinting against the sliver of brilliant light on his face, studied the scene outside. "All these people," he said, "they came of their own accord? They've been told the truth. Nothing more?"

"Yes," Sangae said. "We've heard from all the southern tribes, Prince. They know the mission you're set on. Most want to aid you. That's why they've sent emissaries here, to attest to their faith in you. They may spin tales of their own about your greatness, about how you found the Santoth. They may even pass stories of feats you accomplished in your childhood. The kind of prodigious feats, Aliver, that may surprise you to hear of. But Thaddeus and I, all we did was admit that you lived and that you were ready to retake the throne of Acacia. That was all they needed to hear to flock to you."

"You say most want to aid me. Not all?"

Sangae shook his head regretfully. The Halaly, he explained, were the only powerful tribe not to respond enthusiastically. They had sent not a single soldier or pilgrim or representative bearing gifts and praise. They did send a messenger saying that they were aware of the claims being made in the Akaran name. They would, they said, hold council on them. With the

Halalys' haughty nature it seemed unlikely they would move without prompting of some sort. They were but one tribe out of many, but after the Talayans they were the second most numerous.

"We would do well to win them to our side," Kelis said. "They are good fighters. Not as good as they think, but still . . ."

"Fine, then," Aliver said, once again surprised at how quickly the decision came to him. "I'll call on them."

⁂

The kingdom of Halaly lay rimmed on three sides by hills. It centered around one great basin out of which a river flowed. The shallow lake there so teemed with aquatic and avian life that Halaly people never went hungry, even during periods of consistent drought. It was this bounty that made them the powerful nation that they were. They depended on the tiny silver fish that thrived in the lake—a protein source that was fried or put in soups, dried or pickled or crushed into a paste and fermented in earthen jars buried in the ground. As their totem, however, they picked an animal more in keeping with what they believed their nature to be. It was a less than original choice.

"Does every man in this land believe he was fathered by a lion?" Aliver asked, as he and Kelis approached the mud walls of Halaly. The stronghold stood three times a man's height, lined across the top with twisting barbs of sharpened iron. It was formidable in appearance, but the wall served mostly to impress visitors, to seal the inhabitants safely away from the creatures that hunted in the night, and it stood as a backdrop upon which lion hides were pinned.

"Not all," Kelis said, studying the skins. "On occasion a leopard did the deed."

They had left Umae secretly, just the two of them. Aliver wanted to catch Oubadal by surprise, to honor him with a visit, and to hear whatever he had to say privately. He had been warned the Halaly chieftain would expect some sort of reward in return for his support. Just what he might want Aliver was not sure.

Since little surprised the chieftain of the Halaly, he was waiting for Aliver under a large shelter, a cone-shaped structure supported by a weave of gnarled shrub wood trunks, opened at the sides and thatched up above. Oubadal sat at the center, flanked by a few attendants. A group of aged men sat at the edge of the enclosure, just inside the line cut by the shadow. They followed Aliver's approach with yellowed eyes and a belligerence at odds with their twisted, aged bodies, as if each of them were capable of leaping to his feet and throttling the newcomers should they pose any threat or cause any insult to their monarch.

Oubadal wore his royal status with a composure modeled on his totem, with the wide swell of a bare chest and a thick neck. His gestures were slow, eyes heavy and languid in their movements, his features rounded and prominent. Oubadal wore a gold nose ring on the flare of his nostril, brilliant against the charred blackness of his skin. The chieftain studied Aliver's features with undisguised interest, intrigued by the thin blade of the Acacian's nose and slight lips and by the dilute color of his skin.

"I wondered when you would come to me," the chieftain said. "I heard of your triumph over the laryx. Congratulations. You should be proud; I was in my time. I am too rich now to chase after animals. Others do this for me. Nor have I ever spoken with the fabled Santoth. You are a prodigy, Prince Aliver." He bared an impressive set of teeth, not exactly a smile but with some measure of mirth in it.

"I see there is not much Oubadal does not know," Aliver said. "Then you will know why I have come to council with you also?"

The chieftain thrummed his thick fingers on his thighs a few times, a sign that Aliver was being too hasty. He moved the conversation back to pleasantries, asking about the health of the Talay, testing Aliver's knowledge of that nation's aristocratic families. Aliver answered as best he could, while silently chastising himself for launching into the point of his visit too quickly. As comfortable as he was in this country, he still too often forgot the traditional formalities in his haste.

When Oubadal fell silent a half an hour later the two men passed a few moments listening to the whir of insects outside and the calls of children in the distance. They each sipped a palm beverage, cool and refreshing in the languid heat. Aliver glanced at Kelis, who confirmed that the moment had come.

"Noble Oubadal," Aliver began, "you may know already what I wish to speak with you about. Soon the world will be thrown into another great war, a struggle that will set right the wrong done when Hanish Mein led his people and a foreign army against Acacia. It may seem that the Mein prevailed, but in truth my nation was caught by surprise and only temporarily vanquished. My father had already begun a plan to unite the great powers of the world against the Mein. I am before you to ask for your support in this struggle. In return for your wisdom and for the strong arms of your fighting men Acacia will reward you greatly."

Oubadal held a fetish stick in his left hand, a cross-shaped staff dipped in gold, wrapped in leather bands, and adorned with certain bird feathers. Before he answered he used the butt of it to scratch his neck. "Why should my people shed blood for you? You are a prince without a nation, whereas Hanish Mein has both fists clenched around a sword and each capable of slaughter."

"I am not without an army," Aliver said. "Have you not heard how soldiers flock to me? And this fight is not just for my benefit. Does not Hanish Mein reach his arm down here and grasp at your wealth, taking this and that as he wishes? They steal the very children of your land and sell them to some unknown master on the other side of the world. That sounds to me like the work of your enemy. You don't call them friends, do you?"

"No, of course not." The chieftain looked around him as if he would spit at the thought of this. "But why should I care which race of pale men robs us? These Mein are no different from the Acacians who came before them. Don't look insulted, Prince! There can be no offense taken at the truth. The Mein have doubled the quota in slaves, true, but they don't ask where we get slaves from, you see? This is a difference that robs our enemies more than ourselves. You understand me?"

Aliver felt keenly the insult of being classed as pale, but he let it pass without comment. "My father had no wish to rob anyone; neither do I."

"Many in his name crept down into our lands and stole from us. You are either a skilled deceiver or you are ignorant of the workings of the world. You lived in a beautiful palace, did you not? An entire island you called your own. Horses and jewels and fine food, servants to attend you. How do you think all that was paid for? I will tell you something. Come close."

Oubadal beckoned with his staff. Aliver leaned forward and supported himself, somewhat awkwardly, on his hands and knees. The chieftain slanted toward him, fragrant with sandalwood and the sharp tang of sweat. "Men such as you and I are not blessed by the Giver. This is the lie the people eat. In truth, we rule because we know better than our people that the Giver has left us. There is no world but the one we make, and the world your father presided over was one that made a few very rich and kept many very poor."

A few of the old men along the periphery murmured their approval. One smacked his tongue from the roof to the floor of his mouth, making a popping sound.

The chieftain continued. "It was not just gold your people took from us, not just slaves. Your people grasped hold of *my* younger brother, of *my* sister, and *my* father's second wife, to hold them captive. *My* people, understand? My very own blood. Leodan kept them locked away with one hand and grasped my father's heart in the other and made him know that if ever the Halaly spurned him, my father's children would suffer for it. I've never seen them since. Even now I don't know if they are alive. Can you give my siblings back to me? Can you promise that?"

Aliver blinked before he spoke, held his eyes closed for a long moment, and then opened them slowly. "I don't know. A thing like that might have been handled from Alecia. My father may not have known. . . ."

"What king can claim ignorance?"

"A wiser one than claims all knowledge," Aliver snapped. "Acacia was an enormous nation. Much of its running was in the hands of the governors. If you knew my father, you would understand that he valued family above all else. He would not have harmed yours in such a way had he known about it."

Oubadal shook his head at this. "With complete power comes complete responsibility. Our people give us a gift when they hail us; the price we pay is that our souls bear the wounds of their sins. If you cannot accept this, you do not deserve the crown you seek. Crawl back and be a child; seek your mother's teat."

A sparrow darted under the enclosure and flitted around inside, landing on one beam and then another. Aliver looked up and watched it. This was not going as he had planned. He felt like a fool, just like that child the chieftain alluded to.

"Now, enough of this," Oubadal eventually said. He changed the pitch of his voice and stepped down from the high oratory of a moment before. "No man can go back to his mother's teat; let us move on. There is a way for you to get what you want. You know of my enemies, the Balbara? They've plagued my people since the first days of the earth. The Halaly have been their masters for some time now, but in recent years they've grown bold. They thumb their chins at us and encroach upon our lands and sometimes raid our outlying villages. I have had enough of it. I wish to destroy them."

"Destroy them?"

"Yes. I'll kill all their warriors, castrate their boy children, and sell their women as concubines to bear Halaly children. If you help us to wipe them from the earth and recognize my people as equal to Talay and promise us the right to collect tribute in your name—"

"I want no tribute."

"Hah! When your people were in power, Acacia drank tribute like a thirsty man wine. It will be the same again, I'm sure. When we are made equal to Talay, you will agree that our lands should be renamed Halaly: not just on our maps but on yours. Why should the land from one horizon to another all be called Talay? And if they still live, you will return my family to me and take no further captives from our people. Grant me what I ask you, and the Halaly will help you in your war. You will find no stronger fighting men than mine. I can bring ten thousand warriors to your cause in a week's time. You have never seen fighters like mine, Prince. I don't know much about these people who fight for the Mein—the Noom-reek—but we will drive them before us like laughing dogs, their tails between their legs." He flashed his grin again. "I can guarantee that the Bethuni will stay loyal to you as well. If you like, we can exchange a blood drink to bind us, so that the agreement cannot be broken, even if you or I perish."

Aliver stared at Oubadal for a long moment. He no longer felt frightened by the man's heavy eyes and calm air of superiority, nor humbled by his own ignorance, not when this man's version of leadership was so vile. He would just have to find another way. "I will not help you destroy an entire nation. If you are so mighty, why not do it yourself? Why not ask the Bethuni, if you control them also?"

"The Bethuni are bound by older loyalties," Oubadal said. "They have a blood bond with the Balbara. They cannot fight them, but neither do they love them. I won't speak from the side of my mouth to you, Prince. Without your help, the war between us and the Balbara would be uncertain. They aren't without bravery."

Aliver said, "Perhaps I should be speaking to the Balbara. I've come to speak to the wrong nation."

Oubadal seemed amused by this observation. "If, Prince, you were friends to our enemy and came against us, you would find yourself cursed in many ways. Who would be your army? The Balbara and Talayans? We would fight them. And while we did, the Bethuni would attack Talay. The coast tribes would not fight us, as they are bound to us by blood. If the Balbara did not come against us but marched away with you, we would pounce on their women and children or the old ones. And because they know this, they would never do it. And so you would gain nothing, except the defeat of your cause before you had yet begun."

"When I am king of Acacia you will no longer talk to me thus," Aliver said. "You will remember respect."

"If you were the king of Acacia, Prince, I would bow before you and suck your big toe." Oubadal glanced around at his companions, who fell into laughter, the old men especially so. "But you are king of nothing right now. Is that not the truth?"

Aliver barely managed to get through the formal courtesies of leave-taking, so anxious was he to run out into the open air, away from the scent of sandalwood and the lazy, simmering intensity of Oubadal's eyes.

Kelis stopped him a little distance outside the village gates. He grabbed him by the elbow and slowed him to a halt. "Oubadal can bring us ten thousand fighting men. You cannot walk away yet."

"I will not slaughter a blameless people," Aliver said. "This is not what my father intended."

"This is the way things have been done since the beginning, by all races of men," Kelis said. "Do you want to achieve your goal or not? I know what you believe. You have noble intentions, but rarely do noble men shape the world. They talk about it, while men such as Oubadal act. Do not leave here without making this moment yours. It is not yours yet, Aliver. So do not leave."

Aliver sat down on the parched gray earth and cradled his head in his hands. Thaddeus had said that the world was corrupt from top to bottom. Here was his first proof of it. He tried to still his mind and see good in this somewhere, but there was no good in it. He could not begin this war in such a foul way, not if he was to maintain any grip on his humanity. He tried to think of some other terms the chieftain might accept, but the convolutions of tribal alliances were so frustrating that he kicked out at the dirt. It was stupid! It was petty! Too coarse and small. It was one small example of all the practices he wanted to wipe the world clean of. Thinking this, he had an idea.

He said, "What if I told Oubadal that I'm demanding his help, not asking for it? What if I said that I am Prince Aliver Akaran now, but I will be King Aliver Akaran come the fall. What if I remind him that I'm a lion, and say I will not concern myself with the squabbles of the cubs at my feet. What if I tell him the Santoth sorcerers answer to me now and that with them I'll wipe my enemies from the earth. He can join me and be of aid—on my terms—or he can suffer the wrath of powers he cannot imagine."

"You could try that, I suppose," Kelis said. "You will have to look him in the eye as you say it, though, to make sure he doesn't bite your lip. If you call him a cub you'll be insulting him . . . unless, of course, you *are* a lion. There's no insult in the truth."

Aliver rose and looked his friend in the eye. "I am still hesitating, aren't I? You don't think I should."

"I believe that if you speak from your heart each time you open your mouth, you cannot go wrong."

Aliver turned and looked back at the stronghold. From this distance the hides pinned to it looked like tiny things. Like the pelts of alley cats. He started walking. When he heard his friend's footfalls beside his, he asked, "Tell me something, Kelis. All these people who claim they are descended from lions—what proof do they offer?"

Kelis smiled. "There is no proof. They just say it and try to sound convincing."

Mena told no one what she intended, not even Melio, who had inadvertently helped her to form the plan. She took only the Marah sword and the few things that she could carry in a shoulder sack. She crept out of her compound and through the still streets, grayed with the coming day. Part of her was afraid of being discovered. Another part moved with quiet confidence. She could walk silently when she wanted to. Years before, as a girl, she had crept past the Marah guards to discover the horrors of the Kidnaban mines. If she had accomplished that, no Ruinat villager or slumbering priest would wake to question her now. Of course, it was the foreigners that had prompted this, made it urgent. They were Meins, Melio had said, disappointment in his voice. It was only a matter of days before they left Galat and came for her. They must do something, he'd said. So she was doing something. It was not the thing Melio had proposed, but it was something.

She chose a skiff from among those beached on the shore, tossed her sack inside, and shoved the craft into the water. An hour later she swung around the far tip of Vumair and caught sight of Uvumal. The island broke jagged and green out of the sea, like upright shards of broken glass poorly disguised beneath a covering of plant life. It was a short sail away, but she had never made the journey before. Nobody ever did. The island was considered sacred to the goddess. It was her home and sanctuary. Since the rise of Maeben worship it had been left wild. It had not been forested or hunted, no hillside plots cleared for tilling. It seethed with feral density. The undergrowth was a tangle of plant life. Here and there massive trees broke up out of the canopy. They were lopsided giants, with long stretches of trunk that erupted in knots of branches. They were twisted by age, torn at by the

weather, each of them a totem to savage antiquity. Such was Mena's destination.

The beach she dragged the skiff onto was a sublime stretch of bone-
white sand, untouched by human feet. Palms secured to the higher sand
leaned toward the water. Natural debris littered the beach—driftwood, co-
conuts and their husks. Crabs skittered sidelong through fallen fronds
and . . . Something caught her eye, a surprising enough object that it
snagged her attention and took her a moment to believe. The weathered
head and upraised arm and upper portion of the torso of a child's doll jutted up from the sand. It was a creepy, eyeless form, its arm frozen in what
looked like a frantic gesture of greeting.

Nor was it the only man-made object. A length of rope and a fishing
buoy lay a short distance away. Farther on, a piece of fabric draped a stone
like laundry set out to dry. Mena's eyes darted around for a few frantic seconds, until she was assured that she was alone. How strange. People may
not have journeyed here, but their rubbish did. She walked a few steps
toward the items, nervous lest the goddess spot the insults before she could
snatch them up. If the priests knew of this, they would forbid the custom
of dumping refuse into the current off the southern harbor point. She began
to form the words with which she would broach the subject to Vaminee.
There are a thousand ways to defile the goddess, she would begin. One must
remember that a thing dropped in one place does not simply vanish . . .

Catching herself, she drew up and cursed under her breath. It was so
easy to drop back into her prescribed role. She was not here as the domestic servant of the goddess! She was not here as her eyes and mouth. She had
no plans to take any message back to the priests.

She spent the rest of the morning pushing into the forest. She had
imagined the inner island would be silent and brooding, a place she would
have to creep through, fearing every twig beneath her feet. Instead, the leaf-
thick air thronged with a cacophony of birdsong. Monkey calls swept
through the trees in waves. Insects screeched, chirped, whirred with abandon. She stepped on the woven mesh of mangrove roots, squelched through
heavy mud that stank of bad eggs. The sword on her back snagged again and
again. She grew so twisted and jammed within the undergrowth that at
times she simply stopped moving and hung suspended, resting. And then
she carried on.

She took a late breakfast sitting on a pebble wash beside a thin
stream. She thought of the doll on the beach. Whose had it been? There
were a thousand ways to explain how it might have been lost. Perhaps it was

old. It might have been discarded by a child who did not care for it anymore, made a plaything for a dog who was careless with it. Was it a lost treasure swept away with the tide, mourned with small tears? Had it been tossed to the sea by grieving parents? Or had it fallen from the sky? She regretted leaving it. She should have at least dug it from the sand and set it in the skiff and promised it that she'd return and bear it away.

By noon she was scrambling, often on all fours, to ascend the interior hills. For all the difficulties of the terrain, it did not take her long to find what she was looking for. Standing on the trunk of a fallen tree and gazing through the slit its descent had cut in the canopy, Mena spotted the aerie. It perched near the crest of a hill three ridgelines away. The tree that housed it pierced the canopy and rose up to a singular height. It was a giant, ragged beam. Much of it looked dead. It was bone white where long swathes of bark had peeled free. Many of its branches were broken halfway or nubbed close to the trunk. The nest perched near the top. From a distance it looked like a crosshatched confusion of debris, flotsam deposited there by a strange act of nature. She could see no movement in it.

From the moment she started toward it, she lost sight of the nest, so thick was the woodland. Down a ridge and then up, down another and then up, down and up. Cresting each rise she veered intentionally to the right. Once atop the third ridgeline she turned left and progressed along it, hoping this would take her to her goal. It took two hours, during which time she could not see more than a hundred feet. She feared she might walk within a stone's throw of either side of it without noticing.

In the end she found it with her nose. There was a stench. A reek of decay, of rot. She wanted very much to avoid it. It repelled her, and for that reason she turned toward it. Within a few minutes she approached the base of an enormous trunk. It was larger than any near it, wide enough around that it would have taken four or five of her arms' lengths to embrace it. The smell rose from a putrid mixture of bird droppings and flesh and bones that littered the ground: rib cages, femurs cracked open, bits of dried organs, a rodent's skull, a leather sandal, the withered stick of a forearm . . . a child's forearm and a hand.

Mena vomited. It was an instant release, over almost immediately. She wiped her mouth and stared at the arm, transfixed, stunned out of thought for many breaths. This was why she'd come. She had known this deep within her all along. She had strapped the sword to her back for a reason, but she had also journeyed here with a stubborn kernel of hope. Perhaps— some portion of her wished—she would find that Maeben did live in a palace high in the trees. Perhaps she really did snatch children to be her servants. Perhaps she'd find proof of everything she'd been told to believe, everything she'd spent years representing to the people of Vumu.

But no matter what she might have hoped, that arm refuted it. She had devoted her life to a lie. She had stood in judgment of innocent people. She had chastised them for . . . what? For loving their children with all their hearts? For wanting lives with no limit on joy? And all the time her goddess was but a flesh-eating beast.

She moved closer to the limb. There was something about the way the fingers—shriveled and leathery though they were—clenched. Squatting, she could just make out a glint of metal. She reached out, pinched the object in her fingertips, and pulled it free.

It was a silver eel pendant. She had seen such a form before . . . in the water beside the pier months ago. She had loved the shape of it in the rippling clear sea; it was just as fine now. A hole pierced the rounded bulb of the head. The threadlike remains of the string that had once held it dropped away. She imagined the owner wearing it about her neck. It might have been the first thing she reached for when death swooped down from above and sank its talons through her flesh. She felt sick again, this time with the memory that she had warned the villagers not to look up into the sky.

She rose, fastened the pendant to her necklace, and looked up at the tree. It would not be an easy climb. The bark was rough and crevassed enough that she found ample holds for her hands and feet, but it was also crumbly in places, rotten and termite bored. She tore away chunks with her hands. It was amazing, really, that the tree still managed to stand. She found a handhold and a nub for her foot, pulled herself off the ground, and began the slow ascent.

An hour later she broke free of the canopy, having passed through regions of animal and insect life she had never conceived of. She blinked at the brightness of the world and felt the touch of moving air over her sweat-drenched skin and noted how the tree swayed. Despite a strengthening breeze the stink increased. The branches grew more crusted with droppings. They dirtied her hands and made it harder to trust them. She had to dig her fingernails into the stuff. Upon reaching the bare stretch of naked bark just below the nest, she straddled a branch, leaned back against the trunk, and caught her breath.

A flock of yellow parrots skimmed above the treetops to the north, fast flaps and then long glides, flap and glide. Below her, parakeets darted into and out of view, sticking close to shelter. Nothing larger floated on the air, no great raptors, nothing of divine origin. She did note the thickening clouds off to the east, a storm gathering, perhaps the first of the summer downpours.

The nest above her seemed to be empty. It was silent up there, save for the occasional rustle and shift of the nest material. She could get up and into it, look around, decide what she would do next. She hoped this last knowledge would come to her, for she had no clear idea as yet.

Opening the lid of her pouch, she drew out a coil of rope. It was a thin weave made from plant fibers, oily in her fingers. She shook loose the knots. She let one end of the rope fall free and tried to ignore the breathtaking height the dangling coils betrayed beneath her. The near end had been fastened to a three-pronged hook, a tool she had adapted from a deep-sea fishing lure. She flung the hook up and over the nest. It caught on the first attempt. The first few tugs gave slightly. A few twigs snapped before it set firm.

As she gripped the rope and stepped off the branch, the eel pendant fell free from her chest and then banged back against it. She dangled for a moment, her full weight committed to the rope. She caught herself starting to invoke a prayer to Maeben. She clipped the words and swallowed the unspoken portion. Once she stopped swaying, she climbed up, hand over hand. For some reason she thought of Melio, perhaps because her lithe fitness had so much to do with his training. But then she reached the tangle of brittle branches that was the nest and could think about nothing except how to claw her way up over the curve of it.

She was clinging there, panting, trying to find a decent placement for her hands, when an avian head rose up from inside the rim of the nest. It was just more than an arm's length away, a grotesque, hooked visage. It opened its beak and squawked. Something was wrong with it, Mena knew, but she could not stop to think what. She expected the bird to take flight, and she moved more jerkily for fear of it. She scrambled as far back as she could. The nest swayed with the shift of her weight. Branches and twigs snapped. It took an absurdly long time to position herself well enough to let go with her right hand and draw the sword. Once she had the weapon in hand, however, she knew exactly what to do. She swung at it, using all the full, awkward force she could muster. The sword bit the bird on the neck, but the blade angle was off and it did not cut deep. She yanked it out—still surprised that she had the time to do so—and struck again. She got the angle and force right this time. The creature's head sailed up and away from its body, then plopped down next to it.

In the nest a few moments later, staring at the convulsing body of the thing, she realized what had seemed strange about it. The bird was feathered sparsely, ill formed and pathetic, no bigger than a vulture. Fully grown sea eagles were two or three times as large. It was not Maeben at all. It was barely more than an infant of the species. Mena half formed a joking comment about the things only a mother could love, but she did not speak it aloud.

She sat down across from it, thinking how very strange this all was, amazed that she was actually here, in a sea eagle's nest well above the forests of Uvumal, across from a corpse, with a naked sword in her hand, swaying as the wind buffeted the creaking, aged tree from side to side. Who was she? When had she become this person? Perhaps this was all madness, she thought. It was a crisis of her own creation. She could envision two paths for her future now: one of them that ended no farther than this aerie, the other one such a complete leap into the unknown that she could scarcely believe she had conceived of it. And yet in some bizarre way either course was acceptable to her.

She realized that she could just climb down now. She had taken a child from the goddess. Let her see how it feels. Mena could grasp the rope and swing into the air and be down from these heights before the storm—which was even more palpable now—dumped rain on the canopy. She could go home feeling she had accomplished something, an act of retribution, sealed in blood.

She could, she thought, but no, she wouldn't. She was not finished yet.

By the time she distinguished the flapping of wings from the sounds of the strengthening wind, she had repositioned herself. She lay back against the nest with the dead infant in her lap, propped against her chest. It was headless, of course, but she held the severed part roughly in place with one hand. Thus situated, she watched the mother return, hoping the disguise would help her get close enough to strike.

The raptor appeared in silhouette against the clouds. Her wings flared just before she landed, massive, like a gesture meant to hide the entire sky. The nest shifted as the bird's weight came to rest, talons squeezing the brittle branches near to snapping. She was enormous. She must have stood as tall as Mena did. Maeben. There was no doubt this was Maeben. Her beak could close around Mena's face; her talons were each a vicious dagger capable of disemboweling her with a single tearing motion. Mena did not doubt any of this; yet she was glad, glad to finally face her. She was filled with an emotion, but it was not fear. She had never hated harder than she did at that moment. To be a child snatched by this monster . . . just a child . . .

Wait, she thought. Wait until she is closer.

There was a short stillness, and then the eagle cried out. The call was sharp, piercing in a way her offspring's had not been. Maeben nudged her chick, pulled back, and then thrust forward again, knowing now that something was wrong.

Mena shoved the infant away and swung for the bird's head. She might have ended it there, but the sword caught a branch, shifted, and only grazed the creature's beak.

Maeben rose screeching into the air, her visage one of carnivorous indignation. She screeched again, a cry so fierce Mena's eyes shut against it. She had the momentary sensation that the sound had shredded the skin of her face just as the talons would. But then her eyes were open again.

The eagle plunged, talons first, with all her power and weight. Mena stumbled backward. Her heel caught, and she fell over the edge of the nest. Trying to grasp something, she let go of the sword. As she fell free of the lip, the fingers of her left hand grabbed for the fiber rope. The fibers tore through her palm, slick and abrasive at the same time. She somersaulted around and got her other hand on the rope. This yanked her to a halt. Then whatever had held the fishhook anchor snapped. Mena dropped through the air a few frantic seconds. She smashed into a branch. It broke almost instantly, but it had slowed her enough that, falling again, she looked down and grasped for the next lower branch. She hit it with her chest, swung around it, and dropped, horizontal now, to the network of branches just below it. That stopped her. The rope cascaded around her. The hooks fell just beside her and one of them pierced her leg.

She would have cried out, but events were crowding so fast upon her she did not have the luxury of that time to waste. Smacked by a furious gust of wind and a splattering of rain like icy stones, the tree leaned farther than it had yet. Tremors ripped down through the rotten trunk. She felt it give and knew it had cracked somewhere below the canopy of the other trees. It was going to topple.

Maeben was aloft again, beating the air as she tried to get at Mena, lashing with her beak, her talons reaching. Mena yanked the hook from her leg and hurled it at the eagle's face. Her aim was off. It sailed past the raptor, over her shoulder. It hung there for a moment, a still line having missed its mark. The great bird kept flapping her wings, intent on her prey, gauging the moment of attack, ignoring the import of the tree's slow motion. It seemed an endless moment.

Then the pull of the falling tree sped up so rapidly it broke the pause. Mena felt herself recede from the bird. She was descending with the tree, but she did not take her eyes off the eagle. She saw the rope tighten, saw how the far end, which had started to fall on the other side of the eagle, began to be pulled down with the tree. The line snapped taut. The rope cut into the wing, dragged over the feathers and bone until the hooks caught in the bird's flesh at the shoulder joint. The rope—the far end of which was knotted in the limbs of the falling giant—yanked Maeben downward with a force the bird clearly could not fathom. Her beak opened in disbelief, wings flattened behind her body, eyes, for once, filled with terror.

Mena had seen enough. She pushed herself away from the toppling tree, turned in midair and, with her arms outstretched as if she too could fly, faced the canopy rushing toward her.

End of Book Two

Book Three

Living
Myth

CHAPTER

FIFTY-ONE

Hanish lay a long time without moving, aware every second of the body pressed against his. He did not want to wake her, to have to talk and smile and begin the day with a lover's platitudes. At least that was how he explained it to himself. Better to minimize how good it was to feel her naked contours in the places they touched. Better not to fully admit how right it felt to have the curls of her hair entwined in his fingers. He knew that traces of her would cling to him in many ways. This pleased him, but it was better not to acknowledge that at some level he held still so that he could absorb more and more of her into his skin. He would taste her all day on his tongue, in the corners of his mouth, as a scent off his own body that he would catch in the air as he turned his head. He would have liked *not* to have thought about all these things, but he could think of nothing else.

No woman before Corinn Akaran had thrust herself so deeply into every conscious moment of his existence. Since that night at Calfa Ven she was never truly out of his mind. He refused to put a word to the emotion he felt for her, but this did not mean he didn't sense the word—vague and sentimental as it was—lurking in the air between them. She had been shy that first night, unsure of herself, coy with her body and all the more attractive for it. Her reticence was short-lived, though. It seemed that if she was going to give herself, she wanted to do so completely, with abandon. Her mouth in kissing him was driven by a hunger that stunned him, her lips and tongue and teeth all devouring him at once. It almost felt like she had conquered him, instead of the other way around. A disquieting thought.

It was remarkable how much it elated him to have her near. When she was not near, he either actively thought of her or moved around nagged by a feeling of unease. He was neglecting his companions. He knew that they felt slighted. Considering their fragile egos, he should not go long without finding ways to praise and acknowledge them, but the very thought of it seemed tiresome. Nobody else seemed as interesting as Corinn. No other face gave him such a feeling of well-being to look upon. No one listened to him as she did. With nobody else did such mundane pastimes as archery, which they spent hours at, become sure pleasures. She was so much better at it than he was. For some reason this fact tickled him like a joke of his own devising.

What had he been thinking when he began this? He'd said he would keep the princess close, to watch over her and make sure she was there if the Tunishnevre needed her. So when did that effort become this swirl of emotion? It was dangerous; he knew that. His thoughts were not focused and clear as they had always been before. Just the day previous, he had been stunned to realize he'd been asked a question that he had not heard at all. A circle of faces stared at him, concern and surprise on their features. He was not fully himself, right down to the fact that he would not and could not do away with the thing that weakened him. He should shove her back into her place. He should cut the affection between them with public, bladed wit. Corinn was, after all, easy to insult. She was quick to rile. A few comments poking fun at her now would send her into flaming anger, which would be a better thing than the situation he now found himself in.

But he simply could not. Why should he have to? Consider all the things he'd accomplished in his life. All the gains he'd won for his people. He'd conquered the Known World! Even now the Tunishnevre wound down from the Methalian Rim, only weeks away from their deliverance. It was his successes that made it possible for Maeander to push his search for the other Akaran girl out to Vumu. If he found her, they'd have the blood they needed from a second source. Corinn need not bleed, need not die. Considering all these things, why should he deny himself love?

Oh. There was that word! The very fact that he formed such a sentence in his head prompted him to rise. He peeled himself away from the princess, really not wanting to wake her now, not wishing to have to speak. It took ages to pull his arm, clammy with their mingled moisture, from under her neck.

Dressed a little later, straight backed in a thalba and looking perfectly at home within his icy composure, Hanish read the letters his secretaries brought him in his office. The first was from the log Haleeven kept. He was meticulous in his entries, detailed and rigorous and honest. Because he received such correspondence at least twice a week, Hanish had followed every step of the Tunishnevre transport. Not one of those steps had been easy. Just getting them out of their burial slots had been an ordeal. The chamber had been built to house them indefinitely. The original architects had not considered that the ancestors might someday be removed. They were crammed in close together, stacked high in honeycombed alcoves.

Haleeven had all manner of ramps and pulleys set up. It was an awkward business in the small space. It would not have been easy in the best of circumstances to wring from the workers the necessary level of care and precision, but it was especially hard with the lot of them nervous about the seething, incorporeal presence all around them. One night nearly fifty of the conscripted laborers fled from their makeshift camp outside the gates of Tahalian. Each and every one of them had to be hunted down. They were then punished in ways that served as considerable deterrents to any others with similar notions.

Keeping the workers in line; wrapping, housing, and transporting the ancestors; flattering the priests; maintaining roads softened to mush by the spring thaw; driving forward through swarms of ravenous insects; negotiating the steep descent from the Rim down to the Eilavan Woodlands: each task provided myriad challenges to Haleeven's abilities. Now, at last, they were making their way through the woodlands and into the farmlands that would lead them to the coast. The hardest portion was behind them, although in his dispatch Haleeven cautioned that the going would be slow. They were on paved roads now, but they could hardly move any faster for fear of the jarring effects on the ancestors. Their frailty required gentle handling, as much so now as ever.

There were several other pieces of correspondence as well. One was from the warden who looked after the island land outside the palace and lower town. He claimed that the acacia trees, which he had faithfully sawed close to the roots, were managing to sprout anew. They were hardier trees than they'd thought. They'd never really died, apparently, and it would be an ongoing effort on his part if he was to keep the trees from returning.

Another missive was marked with Sire Dagon's seal. He requested an audience. *Request,* was how it was written, and yet the leagueman named the time later that day with such an air of finality that it was more like a demand. Fine, Hanish thought. It was about time the League of Vessels reported to him. Whether that was Sire Dagon's intention for the meeting or not, Hanish decided he would make it the focus.

Hanish was always surprised by the look of leaguemen. The fact that they were so thin and fragile looking sat uneasily beside their demeanor of complete calm, unchallengeable control. Sire Dagon wore a head cap ringed with bands of gold. His gaunt features were as pallid as ever. His neck seemed longer than it had been the last time they met, but Hanish assumed this was a trick of his own eyes.

They bowed to each other, and Sire Dagon took a seat. He collapsed his body into it and exhaled a fatigued breath. He slipped a hand inside his robe and drew it out, holding a short length of a mist pipe. It looked to be of blue glass, with a small bowl and the thinnest tendril of a mouthpiece. He flipped the lid from the bowl with one of his long fingernails and checked the packed material. It smoldered instantly, as if it had either been lit already or had sparked to life as the latch opened. He said, "I would offer you a smoke, but I doubt you could handle this purity."

Hanish cocked his head and straightened it, mouth wrinkling enough to convey his respectful disdain for the drug. "I know too little of how the league is responding to the attack on the platforms. You must fill me in."

The leagueman waited long enough before speaking to demonstrate that he did so at his leisure, not at Hanish's command. He began by reiterating in vague terms that the losses on the platforms were manifold, creating problems both now and for well into the future. Those further problems the league would deal with as appropriate. For today there was the immediate issue that they had been made late in delivering a shipment of quota to the Lothan Aklun. It was not just time that was at issue, however. The blasts and subsequent fires on the platforms had burned the warehouses in which the quota was stored before transport. The area for this was quite a large complex of buildings, a miniature metropolis, really. During the resulting chaos, the product—as he referred to the slave children—rioted. They swarmed to other sections of the platforms. They began spreading the fires with them, running through the lanes with torches smeared in pitch. The Ishtat Inspectorate squelched the uprising, but not before the entire platform verged on destruction. In the end they had to cut loose the warehouse unit and drag it away to burn itself out. All the product was destroyed. An entire shipment.

"You should have told me this before," Hanish said.

Sire Dagon drew on the pipe. He exhaled a cloud of powdery-blue smoke and said with a detached air, "We don't consider league affairs to be your concern."

"It's all my concern. When have our interests not been aligned?"

The leagueman fixed a stare on Hanish that might have been angry, though it was hard to read emotion on the emaciated configuration of his features. "The league is a commercial venture. To us, everyone is an adversary, no one more so than our rich clients. I am surprised you haven't realized this by now."

Hanish had realized such things long ago. The league had weathered the war on calm waters and emerged at the far end of it in a better position than ever, with little apparent concern about the fate of the Akarans, with whom they had dealt for twenty-two generations. This had once seemed a clever boon for his own interests. Now their lack of loyalty troubled him. Better not to show it, though. Instead, he mused, "I don't suppose the raiders intended such an outcome. The common lore is that they're fighting against organized tyranny. They wish to free slaves, not incinerate them."

"Such are the unconsidered consequences of violent action masked by ideology. The innocent take the brunt of it. It's always been that way and always will be that way." He scowled at the nuisance of such things. "We will deal with the raiders soon enough. No force is better suited to deal with this than the Ishtat Inspectorate. When we find the raiders, we'll squash them for good."

Hanish motioned with his finger that he wished to pose a question. "*When* you find them? I thought you had spies on every rock rising out of the Gray Slopes."

"We do, but since their attack on the platforms the group led by Spratling has vanished."

"Is that so?"

Sire Dagon glanced at Hanish, checking the tone of the question against his facial expression. He placed his thin lips on his pipe, inhaled, and held the vapors in his chest a moment. "What the league needs now is to immediately replenish what we've lost. To that end we have devised a plan to take the units from the coastal city of Luana, north of Candovia. We'll recoup the loss in a single action."

"What do you mean?"

"I mean we'll take the units from Luana. We'll arrive under cover of night, subdue the place, and leave with the product we need."

"The children you need," Hanish clarified. "Which is how many?"

Sire Dagon answered flatly, "Two thousand." Before Hanish could respond, he continued, explaining that there was a festival in the region that brought the population together. Children, in particular, gathered in the city to celebrate the return of spring. It pulled them in from all the neighboring villages and towns. It would not be a perfect venture. It would be hard to find children up to their normal standards. Perhaps they would have to accept some out of the optimal age range. But they believed it was the preferred remedy to the problem.

When he was finished, Hanish sat staring at him. Two thousand? Among those people such a number would mean almost every child in the region. He felt like bridging the space between them and smacking Dagon's bony face for such a number. Two thousand? It went against everything the established quota system guaranteed. It unmasked the barbarity of the whole thing in a way they might not recover from.

For a time he sat massaging his temples. He thought of Corinn. He would tell her all about this later. He would look in her face and listen to her response and gain some measure by which to weigh his own feelings. That would be good. It grew harder and harder to gauge the effect his decisions had on the world. She would help.

"You know," he said, speaking through an exhaled breath, "some have argued that the league has outlived its usefulness. Some say you take too much and give too little."

Sire Dagon sneered. "What learned adviser whispered that in your ear?"

Hanish ignored the question. "You expect me to allow you to take an entire generation from those people? I cannot. I will not. The provinces are tense enough already. What nation in the Known World won't see such an action as a threat to them? They'd be outraged. It could be the spark that ignites all manner of unrest. No, you must find some other way. The world still needs to be repopulated, not harvested."

Sire Dagon flipped his pipe closed and stuffed it away. After contemplating the chieftain for a moment, he said, "I've not been clear on something, Hanish. The orders have already been given. The raid, in all likelihood, occurred yesterday. I am here as a courtesy, so that you need not be surprised when the news reaches you. Scowl at me all you like, Hanish. Threaten me. Fume at me. Reach across the space between us and throttle my neck if you want to. Stab me with the blade at your waist. I'm entirely at your mercy. Just know that if you do so you're like the ant that bites a man's little toe. You bite one moment, the next you're squashed. You rule the Known World at the pleasure of the League of Vessels. Haven't you realized that yet? And the revolt you fear has already begun. It didn't take our actions to start it. Look to the provinces, Hanish. Look to Talay and put your ear to the ground and hear the name those people are murmuring with more and more urgency. You'll see you have enough problems to attend to. Leave us to our business. And know that whatever revolt is coming is nothing compared to the risk of angering the Other Lands."

"So you do fear someone," Hanish said. "You insult me, put me in the place you believe I should occupy, but the Lothan Aklun you fear."

Sire Dagon had risen to his feet, ready to depart, but something in what Hanish said softened him. The look he fixed on the chieftain was almost kind. "You understand so little of the way the world works. It's not the Lothan Aklun we fear. The Lothan Aklun are not so different from us of the league except that their wealth surpasses ours. The ones we have reason to fear live just beyond the Lothan Aklun. It's they that the Lothan trade with, just as you trade with us."

The last few moments had introduced too much information for Hanish to grasp at once. He was not sure which thing to question first, and he felt an almost adolescent need not to show his surprise. He cast his voice with a tone of disinterest, as if the question were not particularly important to him. "What are these people called?"

"The Auldek," Sire Dagon said, after weighing for a moment whether he should answer. "You've never set eyes on one of them and you never need to. Knowing too much about them would only keep you awake at night. Yes, even you, Chieftain. But believe me, Hanish, on the day that *they* decide it's worth their effort to set their sights on us—to punish, to reap the products themselves, even out of simple curiosity—on that day the world you love ends forever. Only the League of Vessels keeps the world in balance."

Hanish stopped the leagueman from departing. "Don't go," he said. He bit down his pride. "I . . . thank you for telling me about Luana. I understand that the league must act decisively in these tumultuous times. I won't fault you for it. It would be easier, though, if you sat with me a little longer and told me more about the things I don't know. Better that you share with me than that I work against you. Don't you agree?"

Sire Dagon considered this. He said nothing, but he did lower himself back into his seat and pat his pocket to locate his pipe.

Chapter Fifty-two

The seas below the southern coast of Talay were blacker and more violent than any the raiders of the Outer Isles had ever seen. Currents
converged from two sides of the continent, mixing with the waters chilled
from being in the shadow of the earth's curve. For five days running, mountainous waves lifted and dipped the *Ballan*. The ship tilted on each rise,
crested like a bird taking flight, and then crashed down the other side in a
momentary rush toward the depths. Sailors who had never been sick in
their lives went weak-kneed, turned yellow, gave up all pretense and swagger. They spit up everything they had eaten. After that, they produced
things they could not recognize and still later tried to loosen their internal
organs and offer them to the sea as well.

Off to the north the coastline of Talay stretched in featureless desolation, nothing but a distant smudge of sand-duned shore, no trees or mountains or human settlements to break the monotony. Forlorn as it was,
Spratling longed to drag himself onto its shores, to sit sodden and snot
nosed on his backside and wave the *Ballan* into the distance. If nothing else,
such improbable fantasies helped pass the hours.

They witnessed things they had previously heard only tales of. Lights
rippled across the heavens at night, multihued flapping ribbons. Spratling
tried to hear the sound of them, sure that such massive contortions of color
must tear the air like thunder. The silence of them never seemed right. Once
a family of whales performed an aerial ballet off to starboard: leaping one after another into the air, canting to the side, and crashing down in a foam of
spray. Another time they sailed past an enormous island of floating ice. The
lookout who spotted it cried an alarm in a rising adolescent voice. He later
admitted that he feared they had come upon a land of ghosts, a thing people of the Known World should not see, a trespass for which they would be

punished. Spratling had tousled the young man's hair. Inside, however, he tingled with the same thought himself. What a venture they were on! He scarcely believed it was happening, and it still amazed him to recall how easy his crew had actually made it for him.

It had happened just a couple of days after the attack on the platforms. Gathered together on the deck of the *Ballan* as the sun set, he'd looked up from his tea and said, "I've things to say. You may think some of them are mad, but here it goes anyway."

He began by swearing that he had loved every minute of his time among them. It had been wonderful the way they moved from place to place throughout the Outer Isles, living dangerous and free, by no laws except the ones they held to mutually. He considered each of them his brother or sister, aunt or uncle. He cited individuals by name. He recalled moments shared in the past. They had been a nation unto themselves, hadn't they? They'd had a true enemy in the League of Vessels, and they'd bested them on more than their fair share of occasions. He was proud of that.

The trouble was, he had said, he could not go on like this forever. He had come from the Inner Sea, from the heart of workings of the Known World. He had fled a great turmoil and tried to forget it. He had tried to put it behind him and to pretend he owned no part of it. It had almost worked. But not quite. He had never really forgotten. He could not pretend not to have to answer to his native country, his blood, and his destiny. The time had come for him to reckon with the fate he had delayed for some years now. So that was what he was going to do.

Almost apologetically, he noted that with Dovian gone the *Ballan* was his. He would not command anyone who did not want to join him, but he was going to take the ship down around Talay, back up its eastern coastline, and into the Inner Sea. If Leeka Alain was right, a war was brewing. He had reason to hate Hanish Mein, and if it was in his power, he was going to help bring his rule to an end. He hoped at least a few of those listening to him would come with him. But everyone had to make up his own mind. It would be dangerous and the chances of victory were slim and the rewards at the end of it uncertain, but . . .

"Well, that's about all I can say about it."

He had sat a moment in a silence. Truth was, there was more to say. Truth was, the only part of this that was really hard for him was the part still left to say. Dovian had prompted him toward it—made him promise he would do it, actually—and he had come to believe in it himself. He had to say it. He needed to claim his identity.

"Before you make up your minds, there's something else . . ."

He hesitated again. A man cannot become a boy again, and yet that was what this felt like, like stepping back into a child's fearful existence, an act of faith in a world that offered little proof that faith was merited. If he said what he wanted to, he would be admitting to being the child who had been left shivering and tearful and alone in a broken-down hut in the mountains. Powerless. Abandoned. Staring through the cracks at a massive world that didn't give a damn about him. And who would save him this time?

"Spratling, we're not inside your head, man," Nineas said, cantankerous as usual. "Whatever you're thinking, spit it out so we can hear it."

"What I'm asking is that you not call me Spratling anymore." There, he'd said the first part. It wasn't so bad. The faces watching him did not seem surprised or judgmental or disdainful. He saw no mirth in their eyes. "That was a name for a boy in hiding. I'm thankful for it, but I'm not in hiding anymore. If you call me anything from now on, call me Dariel. Dariel Akaran. That's who I am."

He hated the moments of silence this was met with. Where was his confidence? Where the surety he felt when in command of battle? Something about the simple act of being asked to be called by his true name humbled him so completely that he wanted to fold back into himself. But he did not regret it. His leadership of these fighting men and women meant nothing if they did not acknowledge who he was. The battle against Hanish Mein wasn't theirs to take on if they did not want it, and the least he could do was level with them.

A voice said, "If you are a prince, then all of us around you are members of your court. That right?"

"I always knew I had nobility in my blood," Geena piped, wrinkling her eyes in what passed for her expression of mirth.

Clytus stood up, smiling, and stepped toward Dariel. "Don't look so surprised, Prince Dariel Akaran. You'll get no argument from any of us. Most of us have always known who you were. We always believed it. Dovian made sure of it."

The mention of Dovian—of Val, now that he was Dariel again—nearly brought him to tears. He hid it by taking on a swagger. He asked which of them, then, had the balls to take war to Hanish Mein. Wren's was the first voice to answer, followed by many others.

That was how this journey had started, with glib enthusiasm and camaraderie. Dariel was thankful for the memory of it. He did not for one moment take his crew's loyalty for granted. Nor did he hold himself apart from them. He was their captain, right enough. They all knew that. But this "prince" business did not change a thing between them. He took on no airs, and they offered no new degree of reverence. So things were exactly the way he wished.

Coming around the curve of Talay and finally heading north again, the *Ballan* passed right by a league trader heading south. The vessel racked its crossbowmen and showed every sign that they would welcome a skirmish. But the raiders had the wind behind them, and they blew past without so much as a nod of acknowledgment. Dariel had the ship's flag hoisted. Let them know who we are and wonder what we're up to, he thought.

They were a week ripping north into the warming seas. For another few days they nosed along the coastline south of Teh, debating where to dock. On Leeka's council, Dariel did not sail around the cape. Teh itself was populated by hordes of sun-loving Numreks. And beyond it the Inner Sea bustled with far too many ships. So the *Ballan* came to dock at a trading town called Falik, a Balbara port that served as a conduit from eastern Talay into the interior.

From the moment he stepped onto the pier and began negotiating docking fees, there was no doubt he was at the edge of a great, populous, and distinctly different culture. Dariel felt the palpable foreignness of the place all around him. He was no stranger to cultures other than his Acacian ancestry. His crew was a mixed-raced bunch, with origins and customs they held to with a sort of immigrant pride. But he had mostly faced diversity on a small scale, among a handful of people bound by common inclinations. In Falik a wall of dark faces punched him in the eye no matter where he looked. Scents of foods strange to him followed his nose, competing one against the other to distract him, confuse him. He could not quite be sure if the speech that bombarded his ears was of a single tongue or many languages thrown together. Either way, he had never heard such an unintelligible confusion of human speech.

As wide-eyed and staring as he was, the Balbara showed little interest in him. They went about their business as if he were but a vapor of a man, meriting no more attention than their brief exchange required. He felt sadly pale in comparison, a glass of weak tea floating in a sea of black coffee. It was not even that the population was entirely Balbara or even homogeneously Talayan. There were many other races among the throng. Perhaps four out of ten persons showed their distant origins in some way. But the Balbara were so forceful in their presence—with the solid impact of their skin color and the breadth of their features and the muscular bulk of their bodies—that they always seemed more populous than their actual numbers.

Dariel left most of the crew with the *Ballan*. With a small company, including Leeka and Wren and Clytus, he set out for the village his brother was supposed to have called home all these years. On the first day of his arrival at Palishdock, Leeka had named the village of Umae as Aliver's hiding place. Thaddeus, the old soldier claimed, had known all along where Aliver was. He had ordered Leeka to bring Dariel to him when the young man was ready. Now, it seemed, Dariel was ready, though he did not entirely feel like it.

Leaving Falik, they fell into the flow of caravans heading inland, dusty travelers who likewise covered the miles on foot, some tugging camels and horses and mules laden with all manner of goods. For the sake of anonymity, it felt good to move within the traffic of people, just one of many beating the hard-packed path across a coppered landscape of shrub and acacia. Dariel expected the numbers to dissipate once away from the port, individuals turning toward their differing destinations. Three, four days in, there was no sign of this happening. He had no way of gauging what the normal flow of pilgrims and merchants might have been in the region, but he soon realized that the migration in which he flowed was not a normal thing. Their numbers were increasing. On waking each morning he found more tents had sprouted around him during the night. People, he came to understand, were speaking of revolt, of change, of war. They were heading toward the same conflagration Dariel was.

Leeka walked beside him at greater ease than ever before. Now that they were in motion, the man seemed to relax. His long work of convincing Dariel to confront his fate was behind him. This, it appeared, was something of a pleasure jaunt. His stern features mellowed. For the first time Dariel wondered if the man had been a father. Had he been married? He could be a grandfather now, and he might, from the look of him, have been a pleasant one.

He once said, "You look rather pleased with yourself."

"I am pleased with the world," was Leeka's response.

Late on the fifth day Dariel asked him if they were approaching a great city or trading outpost. He thought there would be only small villages all the way to Umae, which was a small village itself. Leeka answered that this route connected the dots from village to village. But no, he said, there was no great city on the horizon.

Dariel studied the distance as if he doubted this, as if through looking hard enough he would see buildings rising from between the spaced acacia crowns. "Maybe we should cut away from the main route and travel alone," he said. He did not offer a reason for this. He was not sure he had one. He felt safe enough. It was just that throughout his life as a raider Dariel had always been among small bands of people. They had lived scattered throughout the island chains. It was beginning to unnerve him to have so much humanity around him, especially when they were supposed to be navigating the wilds of the Talayan bush country.

"We cannot cut away from them and yet still reach our destination," Leeka said, humor in his eyes. "Even if we did, we'd find others walking beside us."

That evening their small group built a fire. Wren went off to buy meat and returned with an entourage of several adolescent Balbara boys. They were obviously enamored of her, clamoring over each other to be useful. Dariel offered no greeting to them, but they settled in and the others seemed happy enough to jest with them. The boys spoke Acacian proficiently, except when reverting to their native tongue to share peals of laughter at the foreigners' expense. Before long a flutist joined them, offering music in exchange for food. By dusk they hosted a festive gathering, from which people came and went as they wished.

Dariel sat at the edge of it, feeling strangely deflated. He could not put a finger on why. Nobody else seemed to feel the same melancholy. Clytus—mildly intoxicated at this point—led the boys in a raunchy song about an old peasant who loved one of his hens in an inappropriate way and got into all manner of trouble for it. Leeka sat in quiet conversation with a honey-pale man whose origins Dariel could not place. Even Wren seemed at home among these people, laughing with them. She looked up at him and smiled every so often, but she took no notice of his mood. And that was part of his problem. Nobody noticed him. Nobody looked at his features and read his identity on his forehead. He had wanted to remain anonymous until finding his brother, but now that it was clear he *was* anonymous, he began to doubt this whole venture. How could he be central to the workings of the world when nobody even knew who he was?

Still, listening to the roundabout flow of the conversation he did hear a few things that interested him. Several people claimed to have just recently come off the mist. They did not know how it happened. They had not planned it, and each of them admitted they had committed their lives to the opiate. They would have worked all day forever just so long as they could dream their nights through in mist trance. But something had changed.

Each of them had a different story, but all amounted to the same thing. The mist, instead of providing them joy, became a nightmare. Instead of losing themselves in their most cherished fantasies, they were thrown into the most vivid versions of their greatest fears. This happened night after night, getting worse each time. Within a week the nightmares were so bad that every one of them stopped the drug and chose instead to suffer through the near-death experience of withdrawal. It was an ordeal they would never forget, but they did not die because of it. And now, clear headed and free from the hunger, they had found joys in living they had forgotten about entirely. It was a miracle of sorts, and it seemed to be spreading across the world just like a contagion.

At some point an Acacian joined them. He offered to tell a tale of the Snow King in exchange for a few strips of goat meat. In between pauses in which he chewed or drank, the man told of how the Snow King decided that only the ancient, banished magicians could bring balance back into the world. He went in search of them, ranging all through Talay, fighting back packs of laryx, going days without food or water, stumbling through regions that would have withered most men. He told of how he eventually found them, rocklike giants that they were, and how he had to use tricks and cunning to convince them to join in the coming war.

Dariel sat listening, fascinated by what seemed like a distant legend. But he had never heard it before. He could recall no mention of this Snow King, which surprised him. The epic tales he had learned in childhood were clearer to him now than most things from those times. Besides that, the title the storyteller had given this king made no sense at all. There was nothing in the dry, sun-ripened landscape that had anything to do with snow. Why would such a land produce someone called by that name?

Eventually, during a lull, he asked as much. "The Snow King? Who do you mean by that?"

The Acacian set his eyes on Dariel. His face showed the disdain for what he observed: the loose-fitting shirt of a sea brigand, open down to the navel, longish hair caught up loosely in a ponytail. But he was eating their food and could not give offense.

The Snow King, he explained, was Aliver Akaran himself, the heir to the throne of Acacia. He took that name on the night his father was stabbed by the assassin's blade. "That night it snowed in Acacia. Snowed, understand? When white balls of ice fall from the sky. It hadn't done so in a hundred years, but the royal children were so fearless they wished to play in the snow, to toss it at one another and test themselves, yes? Well, Aliver—the oldest—said that by the end of that night he'd be crowned Snow King. It was a prophecy, see? A prophecy because his father was killed that very night. That is why we call him the Snow King. It's a name he gave himself. I'm surprised you haven't heard it. Most of us here are on our way to join the Snow King. He pledges that if we fight for him, we can make the world a more just place. I believe him."

"We all do," said one of the boys, a sentiment that several others echoed.

"He says it doesn't matter that we are each small compared to the might of the Mein. He reminds us to think of the ants that live in the acacia tree. They bore holes into the thorns and live inside them, and they defend the trees against any who would harm it. To them the tree is life. It's their world. They live their entire lives high up in the branches. The Snow King says to think of those ants and the power they have when they all remember their purpose and answer the call. That's what we're doing. That's why we're here, to defend the tree that gives us all life."

Dariel did not sleep a wink that evening. He walked through the next day with an uncertain hold on reality. He was not troubled by thoughts or memories, nor was he elated and anticipatory. He simply felt a blankness at his center. He realized this space had been there within him for years. It had inflated inside him as he lay trembling in the mountain hut, and he had lived with it ever since. He knew that he was approaching the place and the moment when this void would be filled in one way or another. This nearness awed him. Whatever came, he would accept it. Perhaps that was why he stopped imagining, hoping, or dreading what was to come.

Leeka promised that they were near their goal, so they walked on through the dusk and for an hour or so after dark. The land took on a rolling, pastoral quality. They must have gained some altitude, for the evening was cool and pleasantly breezy. And then came the moment when, with Leeka at his elbow, Dariel crested a hillock and gazed out over Umae. The sight that opened up before them caused him to stop in his tracks. The land was filled with as many points of light as the sky. Hundreds of them, dotting everything in his wide view.

"They are just fires, Dariel," Leeka said. "Campfires and lamps."

"But so many of them! It's like a city."

"No, not a city. It's just a village, but around it is the beginning of your brother's army. And yours, as well."

Together they walked down toward the sea of lights, the individual points bobbing and rising with each step. Their entry into the camp and progress farther into the town was a blur. Leeka handled it entirely. Dariel could not have said how long it took, but at some point he found himself approaching a particular compound. Leeka whispered that this was the place they were searching for.

A Talayan squatted on his heels a little distance from the door. He did not move anything except his eyes as Dariel approached, following him each step of the way forward. The man's expression did not change in any overt way, but there was something in the quality of how he stared that altered. By the time Dariel stopped before the man, he was sure that there was something like a glimmer of humor behind the stillness of his handsome, dark-skinned façade. Dariel opened his mouth to speak, but the Talayan beat him to it.

He said something in his native language. Dariel started to say he did not understand him, but the man smiled and motioned for him to enter. In accented Acacian, he said, "Welcome, Prince. Inside. Please, go inside."

The tent stretched off a considerable distance, supported here and there by gnarled beams of wood that lifted the fabric. Lit by oil lamps, it was crowded with stools and couches, tables and charts that made walking into the space feel like entering a maze. Dariel stopped and stood, looking around.

At about the same time that he spotted a human shape bent over a small desk, the man raised his head and saw him as well. His hair was close-cropped like a Talayan's, but his skin was a lighter shade of brown, a sort of tanned richness. His face conveyed intelligence, and for a moment Dariel imagined him to be an adviser of some sort, perhaps a scholar with a specialty useful to the war planning.

Then the man was moving toward him. In motion he was fluid and strong, like a Talayan runner. A warrior after all, then. He wore a sword at his side, a gently curved blade unlike anything Dariel had yet seen in Talay. But there was nothing aggressive in the man's motions. He walked with his chest exposed, arms held out to either side. His hands were empty and his legs pushed carelessly through the footstools that clogged the space between them. It almost seemed like he was rushing forward to embrace him. This was such an unlikely possibility that Dariel just watched as the man's face got closer. It was smiling and pained at the same time, and terribly, terribly familiar.

And then he understood.

CHAPTER

FIFTY-THREE

Corinn began to believe that she could recover joy. It was not easy. There would always be memories to weigh her down during quiet moments. The specter of death would ever lurk in the dark regions of her thoughts, but the ache of loss did dull with passing years. Old sorrows lost their urgency, especially in the shadow of new affection, which could be so delightful. It was possible to live with some measure of joy, to forget anything but happiness for short periods of time. Her father had always wanted her to be happy. He would welcome her contentment, no matter what vessel bore it to her.

Hanish Mein, of course, was responsible for spurring these thoughts. Corinn's submission to him was not first and foremost a sexual matter. It was not about the lovemaking that night at Manil or the physical intimacies they had shared since. It was something more frightening. It was the act of allowing herself to want him to see her, admitting to him that she wanted him to know her, to understand her, to care for her. She had been so long bottled up in defense against the world that allowing her barriers down was the greatest act of faith in a person she'd made since childhood. She had to remind herself of the many secrets Hanish had confided in her. They were both giving, both trusting. They were both vulnerable. She would not have let down her defenses in any other circumstance.

But she was pleased that she had. Nine years after the tragedies of the war, she had found an order to life, a position that made sense, and a partner to share it with. Their liaison was fresh and newly created, and yet it was so much a part of her that she could not imagine any other way of being. They were together as much as the circumstances of Hanish's office would allow. They shared the same bed each night. She was so absolutely hungry for him, insatiably and embarrassingly so.

One evening she made him wait for her in bed. When she entered the room she did so from the far side. She wore only a diaphanous shift, so short it was really just a shirt. Walking toward him, feeling his eyes on her, knowing the candlelight would highlight the contours of her hips and abdomen and breasts, she hummed with nervous excitement. It was the strangest of feelings. She felt tawdry and jaded, her lips moistened with oil, eyes shadowed like a courtesan's. But she also tingled with innocence, as if she were a child again, girlish, walking in the glow of an appraising eye that seemed somehow fatherly. Very strange, she thought, but also decidedly to her liking.

She continued to accompany Hanish on state trips, and in the space of just a few weeks she made herself indispensable in social matters. She stood at his side when Hanish met Candovian tribal leaders at a summit near Elos. At Alyth she tutored the taciturn leagueman Sire Dagon in archery. She won compliments from him by the end of the day, both on her skill with a bow and on her entrancing character. She served as hostess on a pleasure barge that embarked from Alecia and traced a large circle back to port hours later. She was perfectly suited, it seemed, to serve as an intermediary between the rich merchants—many of whom were Acacian—and the ruling Meinish aristocracy.

All of this was much to the chagrin of the ambitious hangers-on that made up the chieftain's court. They had been happy enough to have Corinn around when she was a pincushion to receive Hanish's barbed witticisms, but now that she was elevated it was another matter. She never heard any of them speak a word against her, but she could imagine their thoughts well enough. They hated her. She knew it. She could feel it. Sometimes she even thought she could see physical manifestations of their loathing wriggling beneath their skin. She was, after all, a lowly Acacian, of a conquered race. Her beauty was of a rich-toned ideal that was not supposed to win Meinish men. In their minds she should never be anything more than an entertaining mascot. Even Rhrenna, who had once seemed the truest friend she was likely to make, spoke to her no more than she had to, with no particular kindness when she did.

There were more somber moments in their relationship as well, as when she and Hanish stood side by side on the viewing platforms of the Kidnaban mines. They looked down on a crater whose scale denied plausibility. Hanish pointed out the Akaran flags that still flew from the platforms. "Akarans created this," he'd said. "How did your people ever conceive of such things? Where did they get the gall to imagine they could harness the labor of millions?"

She had felt just enough insult in these questions to consider one or two sarcastic responses, but she said nothing. They would not have been true on her tongue. He was right. The scale of the injustice was incredible. He might be the driving force behind it now, but he had not been the one to conceive of it in the first place. She wondered how she had lived so many years at the heart of an empire without knowing by whose labor her prosperity had been assured.

At the mines she decided she would never be so ignorant again. It was a simple enough thought, but thinking it changed something in her. From that day on she seemed to more readily remember specific details of things. It felt like she learned more each day, more of history and lore and political wrangling, more about the dispersion of power and the strings that hummed and shifted behind the visible workings of the world. She even felt an increasing capacity to tap records held in remote portions of her consciousness. She could recall things she could not remember that she had ever learned. She felt the gears of her understanding interlocking and an order to the workings of the world settling into place. This, too, buoyed her spirits and fed her feeling of well-being.

How she hated it, then, when she began to hear sour notes. It was a small thing, barely consequential, but it really quite annoyed her to learn that Hanish had received a serious proposal of marriage. The woman was a third cousin of Hanish's, of the familial line that claimed ownership of Hauchmeinish's relics. Whatever those were, Corinn thought. A bag of bones and rags, undoubtedly. But this woman—barely more than a girl, really— had the type of pedigree the Meins favored. She was reported to be the ideal of Meinish beauty, pale and thin, straw haired, with features sharpened to crystalline points. She had never been down from the plateau and thus had not felt strong sun on her skin. Corinn never saw her likeness except in her own mind, where the girl lived, breathed, and threatened.

As the summer heated up, she sensed a murmuring tension growing in the palace, something being discussed just out of earshot. She tried to believe that it was only excitement at the approach of the Tunishnevre, but she could not help wondering if she was not somehow at the center of the talk. What if Hanish did marry somebody else? What if it was all being planned behind her back? What if she was thrust once again into the role of mascot? That was what all of the Meinish aristocracy hoped and prayed for. Her only comfort came from the fact that Hanish himself had told her about the mar-riage offer. He had laughed at it. He had no need for marriage as long as he had her, he said. He did not take such proposals—and this was far from the first—seriously. Why, he asked, should she? If he was aware of the insult buried in his declaration, he did not betray it in the slightest. Why, Corinn almost asked, did it not occur to him to consider her as a bride? But she could not bear to hear the answer.

One morning she rose late from bed. It was her second rising that morning. Earlier, Hanish had crept over to her in the predawn light and whispered in her ear, blown the hair from her face, and nibbled at her jaw-line. She had felt the firmness of his body. She loved his body, so lean and smooth. It did not take much for him to convince her to make love, even though she feared her breath was not fresh. If he noticed this, Hanish did not seem to mind.

Afterward she had fallen asleep in his arms. By the time she roused again, Hanish was gone. The sun cast golden geometries of light through the windows. She did not like rising late, hated that the servants might think her indolent. She spoke to her maids with a crispness that suggested they were somehow responsible for her tardy start. She could not help it. She felt uneasy at her center, off balance and queasy in a way that reminded her of being at sea on a small vessel.

She got up and dressed. Once this was complete, however, she was not sure just what to do. She had nothing planned. Before long she found her-self wandering the palace. There was a hush about the place, corridors and courtyards empty, doors to occupied rooms shut, while those that were ajar opened onto hollow spaces. It was unnerving, both because such stillness was unusual and because she was quite sure there was a bustling motion oc-curring just out of view. It seemed that something was going on, but what-ever it was happened in places where Corinn was not.

Whether she intended to arrive at Hanish's council room she would not have been able to say. At some point it was just there before her. A ser-vant had entered recently bearing a tray of lime water. He left the door open behind him and was working his way around the table, refilling glasses. Corinn moved forward slowly, watching Hanish lecture the others, all of whom sat around a massive table. She could not see the ends of it or every-one in the room, but she recognized several senior generals by the backs of their heads and profiles. Whatever was happening it was an unusually large gathering of officers.

A guard stood to one side of the council room door. He was burly, Meinish, wrapped in bands of stained leather, with a battle-ax propped on the floor, his hands atop the curved blades of it. His gaze was set on a point directly in front of him, but he let his eyes slip over to Corinn long enough to express his disdain. She should not be here, he was indicating, although he did not have the power to say as much. Corinn ignored him.

She did not walk through the doorway, but she stood where she could see Hanish. She was not sure what she wanted, but if she caught his eye she would motion to him in the hopes that he would smile at her or blush or look away to hide his memories of their recent passion from the roomful of officers. As she watched him, she began to make out what he was saying.

". . . he should get no farther than that. If we face him, it must be far from here." He leaned over the chart spread on the table and pinned a spot with his finger. "We must keep this contained within Talay. Your generals can handle the repositioning of the troops. Have them see to it until Maeander returns. When he does I'll—" He broke off for a moment. As he raised his head, his eyes touched on Corinn's. He chewed a thought a moment and then began to round the table toward the door. He moved slowly and resumed speaking. "When Maeander returns he'll oversee the entire operation. You and your officers can all report to him directly."

"Will you eventually join us?" one of the men asked.

Hanish had cleared the table now and moved away from it. Several of the generals' heads turned to follow him. He said, "I don't foresee doing so. Maeander can handle it. I have the Tunishnevre to resettle."

He reached the door. As he set his fingers on the handle, Corinn took a step into the corridor. She smiled, head to the side in a gesture meant as a playful apology for disturbing him. He stared right into her eyes and, without a word, swung the door shut in her face.

Corinn, standing there in shock, heard his voice on the other side. She could not make out his words anymore, but he carried on with his sonorous discourse. It took considerable effort for her to turn beneath the guard's nose and move away with dignity.

An hour later she intercepted Rhrenna as she walked across one of the upper courtyards. The Meinish woman came on toward her without seeing her, her view obstructed by the wide, hanging rim of a hat meant to shade her from the sun. She did her best to maintain a winter pallor. Corinn did not think it particularly suited her. Her imperfect features and streaked blond hair would likely have been more attractive if her skin had some color to it, but such was not the Meinish ideal. Corinn had come to suspect that few Meins sincerely preferred their own ideal above the beauty of other races, but that was hardly what she had searched out Rhrenna to discuss.

The young woman resisted stopping for a chat, but Corinn convinced her to sit on a nearby bench. They were in the open air and plainly visible if anyone should take an interest in them, but they were out of earshot as well. The bench stood next to a stone balustrade that overhung a drop of a hundred feet down to the next terraced level. Rhrenna sat with her back to the view, preferring instead to flit her eyes around the courtyard. She was clearly anxious about being seen with the princess.

Corinn came straight to the point. "What is going on?" she asked. "There is something strange in the air. Something is happening. Do you know what it is?"

Rhrenna's blue eyes looked everywhere but at Corinn. "You don't know?"

"No, I don't."

"Hanish didn't tell you?"

"No."

Rhrenna considered this for a moment. Her voice did not soften. "Why should I tell you, then?"

"Because I've asked you." When this got no response, Corinn said, "Hanish doesn't tell me everything. He keeps a great many secrets from me." She did not like having to say this. She was not even sure if it was true, but she imagined hearing it might soften Rhrenna. It was what they all wished for, wasn't it? To be reassured that Corinn had not truly won their beloved chieftain's confidence. She was but a plaything for him, nothing more. Part of her wanted to slap Rhrenna across the face that very moment, to spit at her and declare at the top of her lungs that Hanish loved her above all else, more than he had ever love a weak-skinned, goat-faced Meinish girl. But that would get her nowhere.

"I know what the court thinks of me," she said, her voice weighted with apparent umbrage. "I know you all hate me because you think Hanish favors me too much. You don't really know, though, what it's like between us. He doesn't feel for me the way you think he does. Please, Rhrenna, tell me what you know. We were friends once, weren't we?"

Something in Rhrenna gave. It happened on the inside and spread up through her features. "But if Hanish doesn't want you to know . . ."

"Rhrenna, you know something that I do not. Perhaps everybody knows. I could find the answer a thousand different ways, but I am asking you. Whatever you tell me, nobody will know that I learned it from you." Then she added, "I will be in your debt."

Rhrenna lifted her blue eyes a moment, questioning what power Corinn had left with which to repay a debt. "It is not true that you could find the answer a thousand different ways. What is happening isn't public knowledge yet. It will be soon, I suppose, but I only know because my father—who is on Hanish's council—told my brother. And he never keeps secrets from me." She looked around. Annoyance flashed across her face, although whether this was directed at Corinn or at herself was not clear. "It's your brother."

"What?"

"Your brother Aliver. They say he's been living in Talay. He's just come out of hiding and he's gathering an army to attack us. He has no chance of winning, but—" Rhrenna paused, alarmed at the expression on Corinn's face "—he is going to start a war."

Corinn, who had stood throughout their conversation, now sat down. She touched her knee against Rhrenna's and let the woman clasp her hands. Of all the things that Rhrenna might have said, she would never have imagined news of her brother to be a possibility. It hit her like a blow to the abdomen that thrust up toward her heart. She felt the oncoming rush of a great weight of thoughts, but she knew that she was not ready to confront them yet.

Throughout the hours leading up to the evening meal, through the meal, and on into the early evening, the weight of the news perched on the crown of her head like an inverted pyramid, the point touching her, the vastness of it stretching up from there. Her brother was alive! That much echoed in her ears. He was trying to start another war. That part of it was spelled out as well. But she did not take her thoughts the further step toward formulating what her response to this news was. She actually moved through the evening with the erect posture and slow bearing of a person balancing an object on her head. Hanish acted normal all evening, not discussing the earlier incident or even mentioning that he'd had a council meeting.

Later, she prepared to spend the evening with Hanish in the private baths. Steam baths had never been an Acacian custom, but the Meins had managed to channel heat from the subterranean ovens for the purpose. Corinn had been slow to enjoy lounging around naked, sweating and breathless in the heat, but she had come to accept it as part of the day, a time spent with Hanish in a manner no other woman did.

Alone in Hanish's bedroom, they had both taken off their clothes and slipped on their robes before Corinn asked, "Why did you treat me so rudely?" She had not planned to call him on this. It just came out, perhaps because she had a whole host of other things to keep from him now. This thing seemed small by comparison.

Hanish spun to face her, incredulous. "What do you mean? When was I rude?"

"Today, when you slammed a door in my face. Don't tell me you've forgotten."

"Oh," the chieftain said, nodding in a way that indicated he recalled the incident but somehow also conveyed that Corinn had misunderstood it. He came back to her and took her hands in his. "I meant no insult by that. None at all. You must understand, though, that what passes between my generals and me is for our ears only. I share everything with you, but that does not mean my officers should have to as well. They must hear me without distraction, and they must speak without censoring themselves. They would do that in front of you. Men of the Mein—"

"They hadn't even noticed me."

"Who can know what another sees? Men of the Mein don't discuss serious matters in the company of women. This is just the way my people are. And there's the issue of who this particular woman is." He invited Corinn to smile. She did not. "Think of it this way: you did me a great favor. I am in your debt for it. You know, of course, that many say I'm too close to you. Many wish we weren't so enamored of each other. With that small action of demonstrating where I draw the line, I have assured my generals' confidence. They'll happily wag their tongues to others. They'll say, *True enough, Hanish may dote on the princess, but he knows how to keep her in her place.* Let them think that, Corinn. If they do, you and I can enjoy each other all the more."

"What were you talking about, anyway? Something with Maeander . . ."

Hanish dismissed it with a flick of his hand. "Don't worry about it. Unrest in Talay. It's nothing, though. Rumors, grumblings. Honestly, Corinn, if it becomes anything of importance I'll tell you all about it. But, now . . ." He stepped closer, changing the pitch of his voice in a way that suggested carnal intimacy. He slipped an arm down the small of her back and tugged her close. "Let's make our way to the baths, yes? We'll soak, and then we'll lie side by side as the kneaders do their work, hot oil and all. And then, once they're finished . . . we'll send them all away and think of something more to do as we steam."

As he walked away, Corinn had the uncomfortable sensation that he had slammed a door in her face again. Hanish paused at the far side of the room. He let his robe slip from his shoulders and crumple on the floor. Naked, he dipped his hands in the basin of oil and herb-scented water there, massaging the moisture onto his shoulders, rubbing the muscles of his neck. The lamp to his side highlighted the contours of his body. His back muscles reminded her of slender wings, folded and hidden beneath his skin. He glanced at her and said, "Come."

He walked through the portal and out of view. Corinn—twisting and heaving on the inside, still expressionless on the outside—followed him, loosening the knot that held her robe as she progressed.

And so despite the things unsaid by her lover she might have allowed herself not to determine her allegiances based more on desire than on blood kinship. She did not think this through in so many words. She did not say, "No matter what is to come I choose Hanish. He is the one I love, need, want most in the world. He is the one I can believe in because he's here beside me now. I hunger for him; he feeds me. Nothing else is as real." But had she been forced to say this, she might have. And even if she wasn't forced to, she might have lived by such a creed without ever having uttered it.

Might have, that is, up until the middle of that night, when she was pulled out of a dreamless sleep. She waited a moment in the stillness, sure that her name had just been spoken. She turned her head enough to see Hanish. He lay on his back beside her. He was awake. She almost lifted her head and asked if something was troubling him. His eyes were open. They stared straight up at the ceiling, but his expression was vague, unfocused, his cheeks flaccid and mouth gaping. He might have been asleep, except that his gray eyes were open, blinking every so often. And then she heard him say, *Of course. I have not forgotten.*

She heard him say this? No, she hadn't heard anything. He did not actually speak. His lips had not moved. The room was dead quiet and had not been disturbed by anything louder than their breathing. But somehow he had formed that thought and sent it out and she had picked it up.

Again, she nearly sat up and spoke, but she was stopped by something issuing from another source. It was a force that she felt in the air, which she pinpointed as being beyond the foot of the bed. It was not a single person; it was a chorus of separate, intertwined entities. She could not actually hear their words. It was something more amorphous than that. She knew, somehow, that they were not even in the room. She simply understood the con-

426 | Acacia

tent of their message. She knew what they were saying. They were accusing Hanish of weakness. They were testing his devotion, prodding him with accusations that he was betraying them.

Ancestors, he answered, *you are all that matters to me.*

Corinn lay without moving a muscle, staring at Hanish's open eyes, listening to it all, chilled to the center, breathing shallowly. She took in the back-and-forth between them, the accusations and denials. At first it just seemed a bizarre thing, an incredible curiosity. She was so perplexed by what was happening that it took her a while to realize that they were circling around and around one particular issue—herself. When they brought it up directly, she felt her breath catch in her throat. They asked Hanish if he would kill her. If it came to it and was necessary, would he drain the Akaran bitch's blood?

Hanish did not hesitate in answering. *She is nothing to me,* he said. *I hold her close only to make sure she's safely here for you.*

They did not believe him. They asked again. This time he answered directly, so clearly Corinn had no difficulty understanding him. Clearly enough that she would hear the words over and over again in her mind ever after.

I would kill her without remorse, ancestors, Hanish said, *at the very moment you wish her dead. . . .*

CHAPTER

FIFTY-FOUR

The note lay on the pallet beside him. The corner of it was warm from where his forearm had rested on top of it. It was impossible for Melio to believe that anyone could have placed it there. He was a light sleeper, likely to wake at no more than the sound of another person's breathing. As part of his Marah training, he had learned how to be watchful of the world even while he walked through dreams. Yet there it was. A square of paper that could have been placed there only by someone's stealthy hand. He would have grabbed the missive up quickly, except that he dreaded its mysterious placement was a harbinger of news he could not face. When he noticed Mena's Marah sword leaning against the wall he was even more worried.

He lay propped on his elbow for a time, staring at the letter, at the weapon, hearing the sounds of the waking world outside the open windows and through the thin walls, the drip, drip caused by the night's heavy rains. Since Mena had disappeared a week earlier, he had been staying inside the priestess's compound. The servants, fearful and superstitious, had accepted his presence. They even took comfort from it. They had grown more dependent on him than any of them would have predicted. They had been taking orders from Mena for so long, they were at a loss for how to act without direction. They needed the focus he provided as he organized a search effort. Even as he lay there, Melio knew they were but a word away. He almost called to ask how the letter might have gotten there beside him and to have their company as he read it.

Eventually though, he unfolded the paper and read it in solitude. As soon as he had digested the words, he bolted from the pallet. He sprinted from building to building, room to room, calling Mena's name. His voice alternated between rising and choked, desperate and sternly controlled. The servants followed him. They fanned out to every corner of the priestess's compound.

Within a few minutes it was clear Mena was nowhere on the premises. None of the servants had seen or heard anything of her, and they were most distressed that Melio had a piece of physical evidence that she had been among them. He did not divulge the contents of the letter. He crumpled it tight in his fist and sat down on the wet dirt of the courtyard. To the horror of the servants, he cried into his clenched hands. He knew it was unfair not to tell them what drew the tears. He knew that they could only misinterpret his emotion in the ways most frightening to them. But he could not help himself.

His breakdown was short-lived. The man who regularly made the first morning trip to the markets returned, shaken by something he had seen outside the temple. On looking at the man's face, which was a pale, ashen shade of his natural reddish brown, Melio found a way to act again.

By the time he and the servants arrived at the main entrance to Maeben's temple, a small crowd had gathered and was growing moment by moment. The gates were closed, but it was not entry to the sacred grounds that the people wished for. They all stared—silent and slope shouldered, some with hands to their mouths, a few on their knees, one with an arm raised and pointing, as if he doubted that the others could possibly see what he did—the corpse of a large sea eagle.

The rope attached to the corpse had been flung over one of the carved figures of Maeben's head. The dead eagle half hung beneath this, leaning awkwardly against the wooden pillar, its head crooked at an angle only the deceased could manage. It was sodden from the night's rains and bloody and mud stained. Its open eyes were crusted with filth, immobile, staring. As a once-live predator it had been massive, impressive, and frightening, but Melio knew that was not what drew the slack-jawed wonder out of these people.

"Look at your goddess," Melio whispered.

The woman just next to him turned. She had heard him. Her greenish, gold-flecked eyes half hid behind a crosshatch of black hair, but they were intense, probing. He could not help but answer them.

"That's what you fear, isn't it? That this bird is the one you call Maeben. I think she is. You are right." He turned back to the corpse, feeling pieces of the cryptic missive falling into place. "Your Maeben is dead, and I know who killed her."

The villagers had begun to back from him as if a dangerous animal had materialized in their midst. Their eyes shifted between him and the corpse, unsure which was a greater threat.

Melio tried to gentle his voice. He wanted them to understand, not to fear. He needed them to trust him, although he was not sure why yet. "Mena—the priestess you called Maeben on earth. She did this—"

"Silence!" a voice bellowed. The first priest, Vaminee, arrived, shrouded in the trappings of his office. The peasants parted for the priest, bowing and deferential. Tanin stood just behind his shoulder. Melio had never seen either of them, but he knew them without introduction. In vulnerable moments Mena had described them with words that suited the figures before him exactly. Temple guards flanked them. Instead of metal blades their swords were wooden, with edges only as sharp as the material would bear. They were skilled, Melio knew, at their own style of swordsmanship, a technique something like stick fighting.

"But it's true," Melio said, forcing his voice to steady. "This is her doing. This is a message to—"

Tanin answered. "You are not a prophet of Maeben! You've no right to speak for the priestess. Nor for the goddess. First Priest, I charge that this man is defiling Maeben through some trickery. He has killed . . . one of Maeben's warriors."

The expression on Vaminee's face never wavered. His features were rigid, anger trapped in stone. He said, "Find the priestess. Bring her to me. The rest of you, crawl from here on your knees. Pray forgiveness for having witnessed this vileness." The peasants began to drop into the mud as instructed. Vaminee turned and locked eyes with one of the temple guards.

Melio understood enough what message passed between them. He would be seized and bound in a few moments, perhaps beaten or ceremonially killed. He knew that it would look criminal to the villagers around him, but he could not let himself be captured. These priests would twist everything. Even Mena would not be able to stop them.

Just to his left stood another guard, a young man who had forgotten the sternness of his office on seeing the dangling raptor. Melio rounded on him with an open expression on his face, as if he were about to offer a word of apology or explanation. He drove the flat of his left hand up into his nose with force enough to shatter it. His other hand found the man's stick hilt and drew the weapon as the youth fell, howling and spraying blood.

"Kill him!" Tanin said.

His words carried enough authority that the rest of the guards swarmed. They drew their weapons and created a circle around Melio and steadily closed the perimeter. By design their weapons were meant to inflict punishment and demand obedience, but they had been trained to use them to lethal effect also. Melio kept up a constant motion, spinning this way and that on sure feet. He tried to recall his lessons on fighting multiple opponents, but nothing in his recollection addressed fighting out of a circle of fourteen foes.

"You're making a mistake!" he cried, both for the guards to hear and for the priests and the crowd. "Harm me and the priestess will rage at you. Don't you see what's happened here?"

The guards faltered, slowed.

"I said kill him," Tanin repeated.

Melio took one hand from the stick hilt long enough to point at the corpse. "This Maeben is no more. This Maeben will never take your children again. The priestess did this for you."

"Kill him this instant!"

One of the guards leaped forward behind a downward strike. Melio twisted his torso to avoid the blow. He snapped his stick hard and fast, hitting the man with the blade flat across his cheek. The force of it spun the man into the air—head first and body following—and dropped him limply to the ground.

The others had not moved. "I don't wish to fight with you," Melio said, addressing them. "I don't even wish to fight with the priests. If Maeben was a goddess, then the priestess is a god slayer. It's the truth. The priestess will tell you so herself."

Tanin had had enough. He pushed through the crowd to the space left open by the fallen guard. He snatched up the man's stick, holding it in a manner that showed he knew how to use it. With him inspiring them, the circle began to close again.

Talking was over. Melio picked out one stick at random and smacked it so hard he almost knocked it from the hand that grasped it. He felt another attack coming from behind and he spun to face it. He took one man out at the knee and hit another with a downward strike that audibly snapped his collarbone. Tanin yelled for his death over and over. Melio tried to find him in the seething crowd of bodies and weapons, but it was too much of a blur. He ceased to think of his actions. He just let his body whirl and leap, duck and thrust and slash. His movements arose directly from a quick place in his instinctual mind, faster than the plodding engine of his consciousness. He heard the crack of wood on wood. He knew that his stick often touched flesh, snapped bone, but the attackers came on and he could see no end to it.

This may have gone on for many minutes, or may have been no more than a few seconds. He lost track of time until the barrage of weapons began to fall off one by one. Soon he was spinning and slashing, spinning and blocking in a dance with no actual attackers.

He stopped moving. He stood panting, drenched in sweat, eyes darting, stick held in a ready position. The guards had drawn back. Most of them weren't even looking at him anymore. They gazed at something beyond him. Only Tanin stared fixedly at him, his face twisted with rage and disbelief, his mouth an oval hungry for oxygen. Melio understood the look. They had not touched him. Not one of them had gotten through his defenses and touched wood to flesh. He had left men on the ground all around him without ever suffering a single injury. This obviously mystified Tanin. But it was not the reason they'd stopped.

A Vumuan woman pressed forward through the crowd, a shock wave of confusion preceding her. People shouted as she passed, grabbed at her, questioned her. She ranted as she pushed through them. Whatever she said whipped the frenzy higher, but she did not stop until she reached Vaminee.

She knelt before the priest and began an impassioned speech. Melio had to concentrate hard to understand her. There were others behind her, running from the same direction she'd come, likely bearing the same news.

Just an hour ago, the woman reported, Maeben on earth had arrived at the magistrate's home. She'd walked through the gates in all her finery. She'd strode past the stunned guards and demanded to see the foreigners who were staying there as his guests. They'd spoken to her in their strange tongue for a few minutes, and then the foreigners seized her. One of them, the tall one with hair like gold thread, actually placed his hand on her divine person. They left immediately for their vessel and were already sailing away on the receding tide.

Melio heard the whole of this in one inhalation and did not understand it until the woman finished. Then it hit him in the chest, the first blow to land on him that morning.

"They have the priestess?" Tanin asked, still breathing heavily.

"Yes," a man, a new arrival, said. "She tried to speak. I heard her. I was closer than this one." He motioned toward the woman dismissively. Then, remembering himself, he dropped to his knees facing Vaminee. "Honorable Priest, she turned her eyes to me and she said, 'People of Vumu . . .'" He stopped without finishing the sentence.

"People of Vumu?" the first priest demanded. He finally lost his menacing calm. "What more did she say?"

"That's all. They pulled her away. They did not let her speak any more."

Melio only half listened to the chaotic discourse that followed, but he knew they were tossing about a version of events that escalated minute by minute. The foreigners had grabbed her, abducted her, dragged her away to their strange nation. Somebody began a moan that spread from person to person. Another shrieked that the foreigners had killed Maeben. The goddess was dead to them and the priestess was a prisoner of evildoers.

Melio sensed dawning possibility. There was something in this. Something he could do with these events, perhaps something Mena had only half envisioned when she'd set out on it. He steered away from the sorrow he knew hovered just behind his shoulder. He could give in to that later. But now—right here—he had to seize the moment before it was gone forever.

He pushed between two of the guards who had just been out to kill him and closed on the eagle's corpse. He smacked it with his palm, clenched, and tore away a handful of feathers. He tossed them in the air above the crowd. Eyes turned toward him. Voices died down. Even the two priests fixed on him, waiting for what he might say. He was not sure himself until he opened his mouth.

"The goddess lives in the one called Mena," he said. "Do you hear me? The goddess lives in Mena! She went to fight the foreigners and to challenge the people of Vumu to prove themselves." He paused, only now understanding the question to which his oration was leading him. "People of Vumu, the priestess is in danger. She's in the hands of an enemy. People of Vumu . . . what will you do to save her?"

CHAPTER

FIFTY-FIVE

Mena always knew when they were coming down to her. She heard the impact of their hard-soled boots on the narrow wooden stairs. Maeander always stepped in first, followed by his shadow, the Acacian traitor named Larken. They always stood on the far side of the room, rocking with the motion of the boat, staring at her with bemused expressions. They could not come to terms with how she had been delivered to them. They asked her several times why she had come to the magistrate's house that morning. Each time she answered the same. She had heard they were looking for her, she said. This simple statement never failed to make Maeander grin and look back at his friend.

There was a great deal more to it than that, of course, but she felt no need to tell them anything more. They were carrying her back toward the center of the world, toward Acacia. That was what she wanted. Despite themselves, they were doing her bidding, not the other way around. Better to keep quiet about it, though. She told them nothing of the events directly prior to her showing up at the magistrate's. If they had not left so promptly they could have learned a great deal more about her than they knew, but this suited her as well. They saw before them a young woman of small, almost petite stature. She sat demurely, with an upright posture, dressed as a bird, feathered and adorned, a priestess who had lived a cloistered life. No doubt they knew her to be a virgin and took amusement from discussing it.

They could never have imagined that she had returned from Uvumal in the middle of the night. She had trudged up from the shore through the shadows of a wood-shaded lane. She limped on her battered right leg, bruised so deeply that the whole of the thigh was blue and purple and black. She wheezed from an injury done to her chest. The damage might have happened during the fall through the canopy, bouncing as she had from branch to branch, poked and jabbed and snapped about like a dead thing until she had finally come to rest tangled in a crosshatch of branches. Or she might have caught the lung sickness from a chill she had taken as she worked her slow way back through the forest, dragging a heavy burden behind her and then sailing a rainy sea toward Vumair. She would never know.

Ruinat had been hushed and sodden, pressed beneath the black blanket of a cloud-heavy night. Water collected in wagon ruts and footprints and depressions of every sort. She walked without care for the puddles. She just cut through them, halfway up to her ankles in the muck. She wore her sword strapped to her back, and behind her she pulled a burden great enough to cause her strain. She had twined the rope around her waist several times, tied it off, and run the rope up over her shoulder. The far end had been wound tight around the trussed bird, pinching its wings into its body. She was bringing it home, an offering to the people of Vumu, one they would have to decide themselves what to do with.

Climbing the temple steps took considerable effort. The corpse caught on each corner. She had to lean forward to ascend. Once on the top step, she loosened the rope from around her waist and flung it over the stone carving of Maeben. She tugged with all her weight, which was only enough to drag the bird into a semiupright position. There she left it. She simply dropped the rope and turned away without considering it further.

Inside her compound she moved with greater ease. She knew where every servant slept and that they would not vary their routine in her absence. That was how she noticed an extra person sleeping in one of the rooms. Melio. She had only to hear his breathing and to smell his scent in the slumbering air to know it was him. She hadn't expected this. Hadn't accounted for it in her planning of the evening's events. But she knew she had to communicate with him in some way. It would be incomplete, she knew. It would drive him mad. But she had to give him something in return for all he had done for her.

It took her a few moments to pen a note to him. She held it to her chest as she entered his room. She sipped shallow breaths and moved with the silent stealth that had always come to her at moments of need. She propped her sword against the wall, where he was sure to see it on waking, and then she approached his sleeping form. She knew she would not wake him, so she placed the folded square of paper close to his face, safe within the shelter described by his bare arm. She risked extra moments gazing at him. She took in the generosity of his sleeping features, and for the first time she did not question why her eyes so loved to linger on his features.

They were perfectly imperfect. She had never seen a face that pleased her so. Not, at least, since she had last looked up into her father's face as he told the myths of the old times.

Though what she felt for Melio was different from what she had felt for her father, she still knew that people named the emotion love. She had known this was what she felt before she entered the room. She loved him so much that if she woke him she would never have carried through her plan. That was why she had let him sleep and instead wrote in crabbed, rusty Acacian letters . . .

> M,
> *You were right about everything, of course.*
> *I was slow to learn, but I know it now,*
> M.

Below this, not an afterthought but a postscript that it took her a few minutes to pen, she wrote two more lines.

> *I love you.*
> *If ever the world allows it, I'll prove it to you.*

It took a few hours of hushed preparation to move her plan forward. There was only one last deception necessary to open the path toward the heart of things. She moved stealthily to her dressing chambers, stripped naked, and washed in the basin of flower-scented water. She dressed in the goddess's robes. She slipped into the garments in the closed space of her dressing chambers. She applied her makeup by feel. When she felt she was passable in appearance and when she sensed the coming day, Mena left her compound and went to the magistrate's house, wherein lay the sleeping Meinish party.

The rest happened quickly. Maeander asked her only a few questions before being satisfied as to her identity. She was on their vessel within half an hour, and the ship was unmoored and in motion only minutes later. She felt it when they cleared the shallow harbor waters and began to ride the heaving ridges that rolled south to north this time of the year.

Maeander seemed to enjoy his time questioning her, despite the fact that she could not tell him anything he did not know already. She knew only as much about her brothers and her sister as Melio had been able to tell her, and none of that was particularly concrete intelligence. Actually, Maeander informed her of much more than she told him. From him she learned that Aliver was, in fact, alive and well in Talay. He was amassing an army in the center of that nation, gradually moving northward as his numbers grew.

"They say he's become quite the speaker," Maeander said. "He's been touched by a sorcerer's hand and now he's rousing the masses with his oratory. He speaks of freeing the Known World from suppression, from forced labor, from harsh taxes, even from the Quota. Strange that he seems to have forgotten who created that world order in the first place."

There was a rumor, unconfirmed as yet but credible, that Dariel had joined him. Until recently this youngest of the Akarans had been but a raiding thief of the Gray Slopes. And Corinn, Maeander said, had been converted to the Meinish cause by the pleasures of his brother's bed. "Many called her the chieftain's whore behind her back. I'd never do so myself, of course."

"No," Larken added, as if on cue, "if you were to call her anything, you'd do it to her face."

Listening to all this, Mena managed to control the emotion that swelled in her. She had dealt with much of it already, in her own way. As she dragged Maeben's corpse through the forest she had been bombarded by memories from her childhood. They jabbed at her as much as the tree limbs and gnarled root networks and bloodsucking insects. She even spoke to her siblings as she walked, trying to explain herself to them, asking what they had become, trying to see if they could unite again and be the same again. Of course not, she knew. Nothing could be the same. Nobody could have imagined she'd become what she now was, nor could she imagine what they were. But she decided that there was no doubt in her—she loved them no matter what. Nothing Maeander said changed that in the slightest.

Maeander disembarked at Aos. He had something to attend to there but would likely arrive in Acacia about the same time as they would. Mena was left in Larken's care. Out of Maeander's shadow, the Acacian was a different man. He swaggered the same way, smiled with the same arrogance, held his body with the same self-adoration. But these things were natural to his character. What was different was that he conveyed himself as a free man, not just a hanger-on. He spoke with a casualness that almost suggested disdain for Maeander's authority, although Mena was not entirely sure why it felt this way. It was nothing he actually said, just something in his attitude.

The evening after they sailed from Aos, Larken entered with several Acacian servants trailing behind him. Mena had noticed that all of the servants were Acacian and most of the crew was made up of Talayans. Only the captain himself, his first mate, and the Punisari guards were of Meinish blood. The servants set out trays of cheeses and olives, small broiled fish, a carafe of lemon wine. He thought he would share this last meal with her, he said. The next day they would sail into Acacia and she would no longer be exclusively his.

Mena found no reason to object. It was not that she liked Larken or wished for his company. He felt Mena's fate was in his hands now and would soon be in Hanish's hands. Mena herself had no say in the situation. But speaking from this assumption, Larken was somewhat careless in the things he said.

"Is it true?" Mena asked. "The things he said about my siblings, I mean."

"Oh yes," Larken said, running his fingers over his cheekbone, down and under his lips, a gesture he often made while talking. He sat on a stool, near enough that he could reach out and touch Mena if he leaned forward. "Maeander never lies. What he says is always true. It's when he is silent that you have reason to fear things aren't well."

Mena lifted a glass of wine to her nose and inhaled it. The scent was familiar, but she was not sure why; she had never drunk wine before. "I look forward to seeing my sister. I will see her, won't I? Hanish won't keep me from her."

Larken considered the question, seeming to weigh not the answer itself but to turn over how much of it he should give her. "Let's just say that Hanish has a purpose for you and Hanish has a purpose for Corinn. But they are different purposes, separate destinies."

Mena set the wineglass down, having consumed none of it. She realized the reason the wine scent had smelled familiar. It had often been on her father's breath at night, when he told her and Dariel stories. He always had a glass of the wine nearby. He would sip it and talk, sip and talk, and when he kissed her good night she had tasted it on the warm air exhaled from inside him. "What makes you think my brother won't have wiped Hanish Mein from the Known World before we get too far into these separate destinies?"

"It will not take that long." Larken grinned and looked down in a manner that indicated he was leaving things unsaid. "And beyond that it's a matter of simple logic. I hate to tell you this, Mena, but we're ready for him. We welcome it, really. Meins are fighters. They are not happy when the peace lingers too long. They never stop training, preparing, hungering for the next battle. The boys not old enough to fight last time are young men now. Oh,

how they want to prove themselves! We still have the Numrek. I've been surprised at how well they take to a life of leisure, but they will be happy
enough to pick up their spears and axes again. And we have other weapons
as well. Not the same sort that Hanish unleashed the first time. One can do
such things only once. But we've other weapons, believe me. The type of
things that will wake you screaming in the night. But they are no nightmare. When Hanish releases them, they'll roam through the bright daylight.
Believe me, Hanish is quite ready to face Aliver Akaran and an untrained,
polyglot horde, no matter how large it is or how much Aliver whips them
into a frenzy."

Mena stared at him for a long time, fingering the eel pendant at her
neck as she did. "Larken, tell me something. . . . You are an Acacian. You always will be. Don't you have some wish to redeem your honor? Is that not in
you somewhere? You could do so even now. You could join me and my
brother and help take back the things you betrayed earlier. With your
knowledge you would be an immense aid to my brother. You could null your
crime."

"Hardly," Larken said. "I hear you, though. I would not be the first to
have a change of heart like that. But it's not . . . a way of being that suits me.
I've cast my lot with the Meins, and I'm quite happy with it. You should see
my villa in Manil. I have servants for every purpose, Mena. Every purpose. I
live a life I would never have achieved as a Marah guard. When Hanish or
Maeander calls for me, I come and serve, but most days I am no different
from the richest of nobles."

"You care only about yourself, then?"

"Who else is there to care about? I am only myself. . . ."

"Change yourself to something better, then! You have only to do it, and
it will be done. This is something I've discovered for myself."

Instead of answering directly, Larken asked her if she had ever heard
the Meinish legend of the bear giant Thallach. This Thallach was an enormous northern bear, he said, against whom the first men of the Mein tested
their valor. They went one after another into the mouth of his den and did
single combat with him. They died one after another, such a steady feast
that Thallach never even had to leave his den. His food came to him instead.
This went on for many years. Many men died. One day a holy man convinced the people to try another way. Why send their best and strongest and
most beloved to their deaths time and again? Why not make peace with the
bear? The people, weakened and fearful, believed there was wisdom in this.
The holy man went at the head of a delegation, offering Thallach a feather

of peace, promising him that they would feed and care for him and worship him as a god from that day forward. "Do you know what Thallach said to them in answer?"

Larken had moved his stool up close to Mena's bench. He let the question hang a moment, although from his pleased expression he obviously did not mean for her to answer. "Thallach said—" he leaned forward, bared his teeth, and growled, a long, low rumble of sound and vibration and the heat of his breath on her ear. "Then he devoured them, one and all, just as he had done all the others. What else, really, would you expect a bear to say or to do? Thallach could not be anything but what he was. Nor can I. Nor do I wish to be! So don't try to make me something that I am not. I'll tell you something you don't know about me. I'll ask you afterward if you still think I can be redeemed."

He explained his role in handing Corinn over to Hanish. He wanted her to understand that he had not just switched sides from the standpoint of a defeated soldier. He had not just sworn loyalty to a new master. He had lived his life in preparation for just such a betrayal. He had behaved in such a way as to gain the highest degree of trust within the Marah hierarchy. He had been a perfect soldier, without a blemish on his record. He had honed his sword skills with a drive his teachers always commented on. He had withstood anything training threw at him without so much as a whimper of protest, and he had willingly put himself forward as a candidate for special assignments. But he had done all of this so that if the opportunity ever came to grasp for something grander, he would.

He had watched Hanish Mein rampage into the world, and he knew fighting against him was a losing proposition. He got his hands on Corinn with joy in his heart. She had been so easy to trap. *You can believe in me. I live only to protect you*, was all he had to say. When he turned her over, he felt not the slightest remorse. He would have done the same with any of the rest of them, even with Mena herself, if she'd had the misfortune of falling into his hands.

"I have had that misfortune," Mena said, a joke spoken without mirth.

She spent the night examining a thought that she had not considered before. What if Larken had captured her all those years before? What if she had grown up in the palace just as Corinn had? Would she be the same person she now was? Impossible. Might it be a better thing to have grown into something different? Of course not. She could not imagine that to be true. She could not conceive of not having grown to maturity on Vumu, with the villagers around her. She could not imagine never having become Maeben on earth. It was so much a part of her. Even though she had to break with the goddess, even though she had found her out as a fraud and cast her down to her death, she still would not want to be anybody but who she was now: the Mena who emerged from Maeben's shadow.

The destiny their father had intended for Corinn had been curtailed and warped even more than Mena's had. Larken had robbed her of the challenge to become herself in a world away from Acacia. That was the gift their father had given them, but only now—an adult inside herself, just beginning to learn what her siblings had become in their respective exiles—did she begin to understand the gift for what it was. Because of Larken, Corinn had been denied it. Mena, who had not felt an emotion she could name for the man throughout their discussions, named one now. She hated him. She spent the night deciding what she would do about it.

The next morning four Punisari guards gathered her. Larken stood waiting for her near the bow. He was in full military dress, his torso wrapped in a thalba, two swords of differing length at his waist, a small dagger sheathed horizontally across his flat abdomen. Her eyes were quick in studying him. If he noticed, it was only with a certain amount of vanity. "So, you've had the night to consider it," he said. "Do you still think I'm redeemable?"

"Yes," Mena said, continuing toward him, "in a manner of speaking, you are."

"What manner is that?"

Her strides were steady, unhurried. It took great effort to keep her eyes on his in the brilliance of the morning light and to block out the bombardment of motion and sound of a ship at sail. "It would not do to explain it to you now," she said. "You may understand when it happens or you may not. It doesn't really matter."

"You've become resigned. That's almost sad, Princess. Almost sad—"

Mena arrived before him. She stepped so close one might have thought she was about to kiss him. Instead, she reached forward and grasped the hilt of his long sword. The fingers of Larken's sword hand twitched, but he did not reach to wrest her hand away. Even this he found amusing. "That's an intimate touch, Mena. You should take care what you grasp hold of."

The blade sang free in one smooth pull.

Larken held his arms up in a gesture of mock alarm. "Impressive, Mena. Do you know that drawing another man's sword isn't an easy thing? It's the type of move one often botches: angle of pull wrong, the motion hasty or jerky—you know, that sort of thing. . . ."

Mena backed a few steps, testing the feel of the blade, weighing it. She knew guards rimmed the deck behind her, but Larken had stopped any attack with a motion of his fingers. She had calculated he would. She could feel their eyes pinned to her, but she also knew that the Talayan crewmen and Acacian servants watched her.

"What now?" Larken said. "What do you mean to do with that?"

"To kill you."

"I'm affronted, but that's very unlikely. You have guts, Mena. I would never say otherwise. Your problem is that swordsmen don't get much better than me. I don't think a girl raised as a Vumu priestess has much of a chance. I'm just being honest with you. I could have stopped your hand before you ever drew. You know that, don't you? And as you can see, you are surrounded by my guards and by an entire ship's crew."

She said, "I'll take care of them after."

Larken could not help but grin. "I wonder if your brothers are equally bold." Motioning toward his companion sword, a blade shorter than the other but just as deadly in its own right, he said, "I also have another weapon."

Mena positioned herself as if to begin the First Form. "That's why I took but one."

Larken drew his sword as Mena began toward him. Slack wristed, he swept his sword low, from right to left in the motion to counter Edifus's unusually low opening attack. It was a disdainful gesture on Larken's part, and it was the last motion he was ever entirely in easy control of.

Mena's attack bore no resemblance to the Form. Her very first move broke out of it, a whipping motion of her blade. The tip drew a quick circle that caused Larken a moment of hesitation. Her sword bit into his wrist at an angle. The honed blade sliced up along the bones and cut free a sizable amount of flesh and muscle like it was soft cheese. His sword hand died, dropping the weapon.

Despite the shock and pain of the cut, Larken was quick enough to extend his left hand for the hilt. He would have caught hold of it, too, except that Mena circled her sword back and sliced the grasping hand. His four fingers twirled into the air, each of them dragging thin loops of blood with them. Mena would never forget the look on his face just then, nor in the following moment, when she carved a smile into his abdomen.

Before Larken had even crumpled to the deck, Mena severed the sword arm of the Punisari nearest her. A moment later she took a second one out with a jab that cut the neck artery and drained the man's head of blood. There were two more to kill, she knew, but she had never felt more in control of her destiny. She circled away from the remaining guards, leaped up onto the railing, tiptoed along it, and came down on the other side of several crates. The move gave her enough time to speak a few words to the sailors and the servants, who all watched her with expressions of awe. She named herself and demanded—in the name of her father and in the cause of her brother who would be king—that they rise up at that moment and take the ship with her.

When a beige-skinned man from Teh shouted her name joyously from the crow's nest in which he watched the scene, Mena knew that the ship would be hers.

CHAPTER

FIFTY-SIX

Hanish's secretary returned to the chieftain's offices in a whirl of motion, a sheaf of papers pressed to his chest, the royal stamp and wax sticks prickling from the fingers of his hand. He did not even acknowledge the man waiting for his return until this person cleared his throat. He paused, set the papers down, and sighed, as if Rialus Neptos had sorely tested his patience just by semivocalizing his presence.

"He cannot see you now," the secretary said. "You arrived a day too late, Neptos. He sent a message, though. He departs today for the Mainland on business that cannot be postponed. He will be happy to meet with you, or with Calrach himself, on his return. A week's time, perhaps. Maybe a fortnight. In the meantime he counts on Numrek support through the coming conflict. The Numrek are his strong right arm, his battle-ax, and he won't forget to reward them once Aliver is squashed. Calrach should answer to Maeander, as he will be in charge of the Meinish forces. All other details he'll specify in due course. That's the message."

The ambassador knew that he would regret anything he said in answer to this, but he could not help himself. "But Calrach himself asked me to put a proposal—"

The young Mein partitioned the air with a motion of his fingers, as if he were spreading out a fan between himself and the ambassador. "I said everything Hanish asked me to. You may leave now."

The arrogant twit, Rialus thought. The twit! Don't direct me out with a raised arm! Don't you lay a hand on me and don't you dare shut the door when I've not yet agreed to leave! He said none of this, of course, and the man *did* direct him out with a raised arm, *did* touch him at the elbow, and *did* shut the door firmly behind him.

A moment later he stood in the hallway outside the office in the company of a brutish guard who looked down on him from beneath a cornice of golden eyebrows. The man unnerved him slightly, but Rialus did not move away. Besides the guard the hall was deserted, nothing but a few life-sized statues that somehow made the space seem that much more desolate. Rialus, not knowing what else to do, just stood there.

Well, Rialus thought, that was a complete failure, one that was sure to cause him grief. Calrach had not just sent him to Hanish on a mundane assignment, or to clarify the details of how and where the Numrek would fight. He had charged the ambassador with broaching the subject of the Numrek receiving Quota payments. As far as Rialus was concerned, this was an absurd idea. The Numrek lived as freely as they wished. They regularly hunted the hill people who lived in the Teh Mountains. They used the captured peasants for the same purposes they would use Quota slaves. So what was the use of demanding yet more from Hanish, who had already been, to Rialus's mind, quite generous to them?

But there was no reasoning with Calrach. He had gotten the idea into his head and none of Rialus's subtle attempts to dissuade him from it had worked. Now, however, the relief he might have felt about not having to speak to Hanish about this filled him with dread. He'd have to return with nothing for Calrach. Maybe he could pretend that he had spoken to Hanish. The chieftain was thinking it over, he could say. He'd have an answer when he returned, something like that. But that was a dangerous deception. For all he knew Hanish would summon Calrach personally, instead of going through Rialus. He'd done so before. They would meet and in the first few seconds the Numrek chieftain would know he'd lied. If that happened, he would not put much value on his own skin. Why did it seem that every situation in his life sat squarely at a convergence of several dilemmas? Always had, he thought, and perhaps always would.

He stood there for a few minutes more—trying to remember a time when this had not been his fate—before he realized he was being watched. One of the shapes standing down the hall was not one of the life-sized statues he had assumed it was. It was a woman's form. When she peeled away from the wall and motioned to him, he knew exactly who it was.

"Princess Corinn?" he asked, walking toward her.

She did not answer. She turned and led him down the hall, off into a side corridor, and through a small door. It all happened quickly, and it took Rialus a moment to recognize the large, jumbled chamber they had entered. It was the library, rank with book smell, lit by floor-to-ceiling windows. Judging by the silence and stillness of the air, it was empty.

Corinn led him across the room to one of the window bays. There she turned and faced him. "Nobody comes here at this time of day. The other doors are locked, so we're quite safe. If anybody starts to enter we'll hear them and can slip away." She said all of this with cool assurance, but as he began to question her she stepped toward him. "Rialus," she asked, her body close to his, "will you be truthful with me?"

Rialus inhaled the citrus scent of her breath. He had not actually spent very much time in her presence. He could not even have said for certain that she knew his name. The fact that she did and the perfection of her features stunned him. Each shape and proportion and shading was flawless, just as it was supposed to be. He stammered that of course he would be truthful.

"Then tell me," Corinn asked, "do you ever look back with longing?"

"With longing, Princess?"

She studied him a moment. He had the feeling she was sizing him up, measuring whether or not she could say what she wished to. Despite himself, he hoped she would find him to her liking. "I mean," she said, "do you regret the fall of the Acacian Empire? You turned on your own people, Rialus."

"I had reason to," he said defensively. "You have no idea what—"

Corinn stopped his words by brushing her fingertips over his lips. "Don't be harsh with me. I know, Rialus, that you felt slighted. I know you aspired to greater things than living up in that Meinish wasteland. I believe, though, that you blamed my father wrongly. Do you know that he spoke of you once that I remember? He did. He was saddened by one of your letters to him. He said that of course this Rialus Neptos was a good man; it was the council that exiled you to Cathgergen, not my father. He said he'd have to force the council to relieve you of your post and bring you back to a worthy position in Alecia. He would have done that, Ambassador, except you did not give him enough time."

Words failed Rialus, but he managed to shake his head. He did not understand what she was trying to do, but what she was saying could not— could not—be true.

"You don't believe me?" she asked. "How would I know of the letters you sent him? How would I know you were unhappy in the north? I was close to my father, Rialus. I loved him very much and he loved me. He often spoke to me of the things that troubled him, including you. And I'll tell you this—there is a reason I remembered your name. It is because just a few weeks later you were decried as a traitor. I thought, *No, that cannot be. Not the*

Rialus my father spoke so highly of. But it was you. You did betray him, and here you stand because of it. What I want to understand is whether you feel you chose well. Is your life now all you dreamed it would be?"

Rialus could not figure out just how to respond. Her words were insulting. He should lash out at her for them. He certainly had more than enough to say about how he had been slighted. But there was no condemnation in her tone or in her gestures or in her face, which seemed all openness and curiosity. He had expected her rancor, but he felt none coming from her. What he did feel was . . . well, it was something he had not felt from another person in a very long time. He was not even sure he remembered the word for it. At least not until Corinn reminded him of it.

"I'm not asking because I wish to judge you. Truthfully, I empathize with you. I've betrayed ones I love also. I understand what it's like to make honest mistakes, ones that you regret and wish, wish, wish you could make amends for. I thought perhaps you were the same, Rialus."

Empathy. That was the word. She *empathized* with him. It was too much to comprehend—both the emotion itself and the possibilities it suggested. In defense, he fell back to an old refrain. "We are hardly the same, Princess. I'm an ambassador. It's a position of authority and importance—"

Corinn indicated that she had heard enough. "Fine. Life is exactly as you'd wish it to be. I don't believe that, of course, but I'll not argue the point with you. Tell me this, then—what do you think of my brother's return?"

Tell her about Aliver? He almost asked her why she wanted to know. The reasons were obvious—although they were also contradictory. He's my brother and I love him, she could say. But that was not what he wanted to hear for a variety of reasons. He was a threat to Hanish, she could say. But that, despite the safety it suggested in respect to his current allegiances, wasn't quite what he wanted to hear either. So he tried to keep his answer neutral. "He remains a mystery, Princess. I cannot—"

"Don't lie to me. You don't have to and I wouldn't lie to you. The truth is, Rialus, that I don't have a single friend in this palace. Not a single person cares what becomes of me. Hanish is not my friend, understand? He can never know that we've spoken or learn even a word that passes between us. Swear to me that you understand that."

He nodded, though he did so in a hesitant way that was meant to indicate he was not agreeing to the entirety of whatever deception she might be proposing.

If Corinn noticed the vague caveat he intended she gave no sign of it.

"Rialus," she said, "I very dearly need a friend—a powerful friend. That's why I'm speaking to you now. Do you, Rialus, also want a friend?"

He answered before he had time to censor himself. "Yes, very much."

"Then I will be your friend. We will give each other things, as friends do. First, tell me of my brother. Hanish tries to keep me ignorant, but he's just cruel. It does you no damage to tell me things everybody else knows already. Just help me understand what's happening in the world."

He could do that, he thought. She needed him. She had said so herself. What would it hurt to tell her things that everybody else knew anyway? He was not ready to accept her empathy, but he could do this.

He spent the next half hour filling her in on everything he knew. He found his voice surprisingly nimble as he detailed Aliver's movements, his troop strength and makeup. He told of the myths swirling around him, rumors of sorcery and such. Little of this impressed Hanish, however. The chieftain was annoyed by the timing of Aliver's return. He would have much preferred to see the Tunishnevre's move completed. Hanish had drawn in all the troops he could from the provinces and concentrated them around Bocoum. The Numrek had not joined them yet, but they were ready to march and planned to do so the moment he returned. The war, he said, was only days away from beginning.

He was surprised by the manner in which Corinn questioned him. Again and again she asked for details, specifics, and explanations. He gave them as best he could. When she asked him what posed the greatest threat to Aliver's army, Rialus answered, "Why, the Numrek, of course. The very ones to whom I'm ambassador."

"Yes, the undefeatable Numrek . . . Are they truly so fierce?"

Rialus spent a few moments singing their praises as regards martial matters. He was aware of the irony of this—considering how much he hated them—but the more Corinn asked of him, the more he was compelled to offer.

"If the entire world turned against them, of course they'd be defeated," he concluded, "but not without doing a great deal of damage. I'm sure Hanish Mein considered moving against them. But that was before. Now he's quite happy to call them allies again."

"So he needs them?"

"Very much so. Hanish may have tricks up his sleeve, but he most definitely needs and relies upon my wards."

Corinn's face went troubled, hesitant, and unsure. She seemed to forget Rialus for a moment. She placed a hand upon the windowsill in a way that highlighted the curve of her breast. Reaching out seemed almost a measure to keep her from fainting. Her eyes stared through the window in a way that suggested she was thinking hard enough that she was not actually seeing. She chewed the corner of her lower lip.

"Rialus, what do you want most in the world?" She turned toward him. The resolve on her face and in her voice indicated that she had settled whatever had been bothering her and was ready to move forward. "I think I know. You want to be respected. You want to be rewarded. You want Hanish to acknowledge that you helped him and Maeander triumph against my father. You want the sort of spoils men like Larken received. You want to never have to wake without a beauty beside you, one who'll do exactly your bidding. These are some of the things you want. Why wouldn't you? Why wouldn't any ambitious man crave such things? I'm right, aren't I?"

Rialus opened his mouth, but Corinn did not wait for his answer.

"Hanish will never give you any of those things. He laughs at you. He thinks you're a fool, a coward, an idiot. He once joked that if he didn't make you ambassador to the Numrek—a job he considers most foul—he'd have made you a court comedian. You wouldn't even have to practice your act, he said. You'd only have to be yourself. That's what he thinks of you."

"I—"

"You know I'm telling you the truth. You've always known it, and you hate Hanish for it, don't you?"

"Ha-ha-hate is not the word I'd use," Rialus said. "Princess, I was under the—the impression that you quite loved Hanish. That you—"

Corinn threw back her head and laughed. She opened her mouth so widely he saw straight to the back of her throat. Most disconcerting.

"You are a funny man," she said, once she had gotten control of herself again. "I don't love Hanish. Do you?"

Rialus was relieved that she did not pause for him to answer that question.

"Of course you don't. You're like me." She pressed the wedge of her hand between her breasts, somehow a belligerent, not sensuous, gesture. "You and I are done with love. I'll never give this heart to a man again. Not even to you, Rialus, charmer though you are. You may think whatever thoughts of me you like. I cannot get them out of your head and I don't care what you fantasize. But you'll never have my love; nor do you want it, do you? You'd like the shell of me, but not what's inside. Anyway, there will be others for you, many others. Others more beautiful and vacuous than I. Understand?"

He nodded. He did understand. She was not, as she pointed out, the empty beauty that he had imagined her to be. There was much behind her face that he'd not been aware of before. She was, he realized, something he'd never considered her to be. Dangerous. That's what she was. He did not know exactly how, could not imagine what power she wielded, and yet he now believed she was not a woman to be crossed.

As if answering this thought, Corinn said, "Hanish betrayed me in ways that I can never forgive. In ways I won't forget. Not this time. Rialus, I hope you'll be truer than he. I have a message for you to take to Calrach. I have an offer to make him. I've looked into getting off the island myself, but I can see no way to do it. I'm a prisoner here, Rialus. But with your help . . . If we succeed in pulling off what I have in mind, you'll be a very lucky man. You'll be rewarded after the war with everything you've ever felt you deserved. I, and my brother, will make sure you have it."

CHAPTER

FIFTY-SEVEN

Thaddeus Clegg could not have been happier with the man Aliver Akaran had become. Perhaps nobody but the former chancellor recognized how much the prince resembled his father in his features and timbre of voice, in the intensity and intelligence of his brown eyes, and the upright carriage of his torso. He was very much like Leodan had been in his youth. But Aliver had taken all these traits and honed them to a greater level of sharpness. Leodan had dreamed of and cogitated on action, reform, justice, but never truly acted; Aliver now lived and breathed all of these things and strove to shape the world accordingly. Thaddeus had been concerned over Aliver's initial reticence to fully take up his mantle of responsibility, but that seemed ancient history now. Since returning from his search for the Santoth, the prince had not faltered. When he asked to again wear the King's Trust, Sangae did not hesitate to retrieve it for him. With it hanging from his side Aliver Akaran looked every bit a hero in the making.

Aliver's first task—that of winning the Halaly to his cause—had not been an easy one. He refused to join them in a petty war to exterminate their neighbors. Instead, he convinced them to put provincial squabbles behind them. They shared a common enemy far worse than any threat one Talayan tribe posed another. Defeating Hanish Mein, he argued, would be the single greatest thing any of them could do to change their fortunes. He promised that when he was king he would remember every deed done for him and every deed done against him. He would reward them all in manifold ways. The Halaly, he had said, could be leaders among Talayans, or they could be the sole people left without a say in the coming world. They'd be laughed at by future generations who would look back with ridicule on a people so blind to the changes at hand, who had been rendered inconsequential because of it. It could not have been easy to look Oubadal in the face and say such things, but Aliver managed it.

The chancellor had first heard reports of all of this from others. When the prince returned from Halaly and began to march north, he witnessed it himself. Aliver held forth to the ever-increasing throng flocking to him. People gathered to hear him each afternoon, when he issued rambling discourses to whomever sought him out. He spoke with a prophet's fervor and made greater and greater leaps of vision each day. He detailed beliefs and intentions that Thaddeus had not expected, had not planted in him, or imagined himself. Yet they were ideas of such nobility that he could not fault the young man in the slightest.

When Aliver said he would reward those who aided him, he did not mean to do so in the old ways: with riches, by bestowing power on one tribe instead of another, by elevating one upon the shoulders of another. He wanted to break the old way along its twisted spine and throw the pieces out. He asked tribes—whether in Talay or Candovia, Aushenia or Senival or anyplace else—to think of one another as members of extended families. They did not have to love one another unquestioningly or agree upon everything or give without the expectation of receiving. But he would have them sit down at council together and seek out ways that they could mutually gain from policies meant to benefit them all. Each of them could find prosperity themselves, and smile upon their neighbors' boons as well. Why should it be any other way?

"Edifus was wrong," Aliver said one afternoon, in words that played again and again in Thaddeus's mind afterward. "Tinhadin was wrong. Too many generations following them accepted the same inequities. My father, Leodan Akaran, even he could not see how to break free from the tyranny of his own stature in the world. He *knew* it to be wrong. I felt this to be so; I knew it without knowing it; I fought not to see it because I knew nobody wished me to see it. But then came Hanish Mein. Then came the greater evil that burned through the land and left it charred and damaged in so many ways. I abhor Hanish Mein for the suffering he inflicted upon the world. I hate that even now I must ask for thousands to give their lives in fighting him. But for one thing I thank him. When Hanish Mein broke the chain of Akaran rule he set the stage for a shift in the fortunes of the world. Hanish himself is not the beginning of a new age. He is only the pause between two sentences. The earlier Akarans spoke the first sentence and it was a disappointment; I and those who come after me will speak the second sentence and it will be one of justice."

Hanish Mein nothing but the pause between two sentences . . . Thaddeus had never imagined laying the situation out so boldly. Nor did Aliver stop there. He promised to do away with conscripted labor in the mines. He'd cancel the Quota and never trade for the mist again. He swore his ultimate responsibility would be to rule in a manner that benefited as many as possible. He did not accept the belief that the natural order of humanity was that of a few benefiting from the work and suffering of the masses. He loved his ancestors—let no one say otherwise. They were wrong to have structured the world like this, but they also made him possible. In his name—and in theirs—he would shape a better future.

Whatever hesitancy Aliver may have had as a youth had vanished. He had burned it away like baby fat from his lean body, and during the daylight hours he moved with unflagging vigor. Sometimes, at night, in close company, his face and body showed fatigue, worry. But that, Thaddeus thought, was to be expected.

By the time they reached the open plains that stretched all the way north to Bocoum many were calling Aliver more than just the Snow King. He was proclaimed a prophet of the Giver. Nobody, people said, had ever spoken such noble truths to so many ears. The Giver worked through him. With this war the Giver was testing the world for righteousness. Perhaps when they triumphed, the Giver would return to the world and walk among people again.

Aliver never made such proclamations himself, but the ideas caught like flames touching the dry Talayan grasslands. It flowed from person to person, village to village, into and out of different languages. It leaped mountain ranges and sailed across seas. The people were hungry for a message such as this one. They ate it with ravenous mouths and received it with clear eyes, especially as person after person shook off their mist dependence. Thaddeus sometimes woke in the night, fearing that events were rolling forward too rapidly, but there was no going back now.

The old man still counseled the emergent king, but increasingly he found himself carrying out Aliver's wishes instead of the other way around. Thaddeus handled communications with the wider world through all the channels he could. He alerted the hushed resistance in every corner of the Known World that Aliver Akaran had announced himself. They need not be hushed any longer. He imagined the scenes being played out as the news spread. Quick guerrilla strikes against Meinish interests. Trade convoys attacked. Outposts torched. Miners rising in rebellion. Soldiers picked off by ones and twos. Aliver wanted life made hard for the Meins in every way possible and in every place possible. But these acts of resistance should be kept small, he said. He wanted to sow clear-headed discord in every distant corner, while at the same time building his army and pushing up from the heart of Talay. He would arrange it so that his force was such a massive wave, Hanish Mein would have no choice but to meet him in what promised to be as great a battle as anything fought in the first war.

Aliver's new army spoke different languages, had different customs, made war in differing ways. They were young and old, men and women, experienced soldiers and rank novices. They were fishermen and laborers and mine workers, herders and farmers; they were of all professions imaginable. Unifying such diverse groups into a fighting force posed an incredibly complex set of problems. Hanish did not contest their northern progress, but he drew his provincial guards in toward a central point. They received reports that he was massing troops along the Talayan coast. The time when the two forces would clash was very near.

Fortunately, Leeka Alain was itching to be in military command again. The legend of the rhinoceros-riding general had not been forgotten. Leeka was, after all, the first man to separate a Numrek head from the neck that supported it. He had outlived an entire army and fought in battle after battle throughout the first war. Though a few years older now, he was still a general whom others would follow into the fray. He threw himself into ordering and training Aliver's growing army.

He broke them into units meant to use their diverse talents. He instructed the officers beneath him to think creatively about how each person could be used to strengthen the whole. He simplified the battle commands, selecting the best words from a variety of languages so that the calls were crisp and understandable and so that each people heard at least one of their words spoken on their officers' lips. He trained them through drills that got them used to functioning as units. By staging mock battles in which newer troops faced an onslaught of veterans, he accustomed them to the close-up tumult of two armies smashing together. He worked them hard but always left them just enough energy so that they could march the day's allotment as they moved north. New troops were accepted the very moment they offered themselves and were thrown into the routine without delay. He might not get them completely ready to face units of Punisari or hordes of Numrek warriors—who could be truly ready for such things?—but he would have them as prepared as humanly possible, even if he had to throw out much of Acacian military tradition and rethink the entire endeavor.

More than any other thing, though, Dariel's arrival had done a great deal for Aliver. It bolstered him like no other single thing had. The night of Dariel's arrival, Thaddeus had rushed to the council tent and found the two brothers locked in an embrace. They must have been holding each other for some time. They sat on stools, arms entwined, speaking to each other in whispers. Shyly, Thaddeus drew up close to them. He was not sure what to do until Aliver's eyes touched on him. The prince reached out with one hand and pulled the old chancellor in to hug. Dariel—his face that of a man now, though the child was still there in the shape of his eyes—welcomed him with a sad smile. Thaddeus managed to whisper a greeting to the young prince before emotion choked his words away.

In the days that followed, the brothers got reacquainted amid the flow of daily events. They were together often during the day, touching at elbows, listening to the same councils, making decisions together, weaving the years they had spent apart into the fabric of their daily, busy existence. Thaddeus had wondered if there would be any friction between them. Would they be strangers to each other? Would they size each other up, men now and perhaps competitive, considering the possibility that one of them might soon be king? Would the years apart have damaged their relationship in ways not easily remedied? But Thaddeus saw nothing like this. There was a great deal of catching up to do, yes, but neither of them seemed at all awkward with the other. Perhaps Leodan had shaped them, in those early years, to be better siblings than most.

Pausing in the entranceway to Aliver's tent one evening, Thaddeus could not keep himself from eavesdropping on the two. He had not meant to do so, and he certainly had no ill intent. But hearing Aliver's low voice on the other side of the flap stopped him in his tracks. It was not the same voice the prince usually spoke with. There was an open frankness to it, an undisguised sincerity. It was the voice of a man speaking to his brother, to one of the few people in the world from whom he did not need to hide anything.

Aliver was talking about how hard it had been for him to be thrust into Talayan culture. It was overwhelming. Early on, he had hated his pale skin and straight hair and thin lips. For a time he had shaved his head and spent too many hours in the sun and even pouted his lips to make them seem fuller when talking with young women. Fortunately, this was years ago. He had grown more comfortable in his skin the last few years. He knew who he was now, knew what he had to do, and, finally, he could look at Dariel and see his family reflected back at him. That was a wonderful gift.

Speaking through a laugh, he said, "So I thank you for living this long. Please, continue to do so."

Dariel shared just as much with Aliver, detailing how strangely lonely he had felt growing up among the raiders. There had been people around him all the time, coming and going in the swirl of adventure and cama- raderie, and yet he had been lonely. He loved them all, he said, especially Val. The giant of a man had been all the father he could. He had given his life for Dariel, in more ways than one. Things like that could not be repaid. Such gifts could not even be earned, he said. "I've no idea what I ever did to deserve it."

"Val had a life to live, too, right?" Aliver asked. "Maybe doing what he did was his way of living with honor, his way of finding meaning. Often, I think, the men who do the most with their lives are the most afraid of . . . not being worthy of the faith of those that love them. Of course, it makes our lives harder as well. You and I, we have to be better than we might have been otherwise. We are links in a chain, aren't we?"

Hearing this, Thaddeus felt sure that to some extent the prince was talking about him. It embarrassed him, and furthermore he knew that no matter what he did for them he could never be as close to these Akaran chil- dren as they were to each other. He loved them absurdly, with an intensity that had increased over the years. It felt like he had taken Leodan's feelings for his children and added them to his own and mixed them within the great hollowness left by the death of his wife and son. He was father and uncle, mourner and penitent for past crimes all at once; the combination was almost too much to bear. A fitting punishment, he thought.

As the younger Akaran heir needed to be brought into the fold, to know everything, to have a hand in all that was happening, Thaddeus took over from Leeka Alain and carried on the young man's education. One evening, while encamped about a hundred miles from Bocoum and the Ta- layan coastline, he shared a tent with Dariel and Aliver and Kelis, who in many ways seemed a third brother now. Dariel asked about the Numrek, be- ings that he had not yet laid eyes on. He asked if the tales told about them were true.

"Depends which tales you mean," Thaddeus said. "Some are decidedly true. Others are decidedly not."

"Is it true that they were *forced* out of their land?" Dariel asked. "I've heard that was why they came across the Ice Fields and joined with Hanish."

Thaddeus nodded. "Those whom the Acacians never defeated on the field of battle came to this land as a vanquished people, fleeing forces they feared enough to trudge into the unknown." He let the significance of this sit for a moment. "This world is larger than we know, with more in it to fear than we have yet imagined. Don't let this cloud your thoughts, though. For the moment Hanish Mein is the enemy. If we don't defeat him first, we'll never have to worry about what might come after."

"Well," Dariel said, "if they were never defeated during the first war, how do we plan to defeat them now?"

He had asked Thaddeus the question, but the chancellor deferred to Aliver for the answer. The prince sat on a three-legged stool, his legs planted widely, leaning forward, an elbow propped on one of his knees as his fingers massaged his forehead. He indicated that he heard the question only by balling his hand into a fist and pressing his knuckles flat against his skull. Studying him, Thaddeus realized something was weighing on him more heavily than usual.

"I'm not sure," Aliver finally said. "I hate that answer, but it's the truth. I wish I could have all the pieces in place before putting any lives in danger. . . ."

"But you cannot," Kelis said, speaking Acacian for the others' benefit. "If you waited to have everything in place, you'd be forever waiting. There are many things we have only partial knowledge of. Some speak of creatures the Meins received as presents from the Lothan Aklun. Antoks, they call them. But nobody can tell us what these are. We cannot know, but neither can we wait forever."

Aliver let the interruption sit for a moment, showing neither agreement nor disagreement with it. "There are the Santoth. They are why I've not fought against how rapidly things are moving. I know their power. I believe they will help us. I don't know exactly how, but if anybody can defeat the Numrek, they can. If they join us on the battlefield, they will find a way."

Again, Dariel found something to question. "You said *if* the Santoth join the battle. Is it possible they won't?"

"They promised they would, but there's a condition attached. I told them that I'd give them *The Song of Elenet*. They need it, they say, in order to get the impurities out of their magic. They won't leave the south until I tell them I have the book."

"But we move farther north each day," Dariel said.

"The distance doesn't matter. I'm never out of contact with them. My bond with them is stretched by the miles, but it's not broken. Believe me—

they can hear my thoughts when I send them, and I can receive theirs when they wish. If the book dropped in my lap tomorrow I could summon them immediately. The problem is that the book isn't going to drop into my lap. I've no idea where it is, and nobody has stepped forward to tell me. I've been too lax about this. I did not let everyone know how unequivocal they were. . . . I used to think I would simply summon them whether I found the book or not. Once they joined us, they'd have no choice but to help. Afterward—once we won—I'd find *The Song of Elenet* and give it to them. I'd honor the promise, just change the order of the events to get there. But I'm not sure of this anymore."

"What is different now?" Thaddeus asked, feeling this might be the core of what troubled him, wishing that he himself had given all of this more thought. When he was younger, and his mind sharper, he would have probed everything. Waiting for the prince's answer, he knew he had not done so as completely as he should.

Aliver looked up, straightened, and seemed to take in the room anew. He wiped under his eyes with his fingertips. "The way people have been coming off the mist . . . it's because the Santoth are aiding them. I told them that I could not fight with an army drugged and groggy every night. In answer they whispered out a spell. I heard it inside my head and felt the way it slipped out across the sleeping land each night. It moved like a thousand serpents, each seeking a user."

"That's incredible," Dariel murmured. "I heard how people were breaking free of the mist, but . . ."

"Yes, it is incredible," Aliver said. Having agreed, though, he struggled a moment with how to express the further things he had to say. He illustrated his thoughts with his fingers a moment, but then gave up on the effort and let his hands rest on his knees. "I could sense that there was corruption in the spell. It's what they always told me. I don't know how to explain it. I could not actually understand the language. It barely even seemed a language at all. It's a sort of music, as if voices plucked tunes from millions of different notes. The notes were like words. And they weren't like words. . . ."

He glanced around from face to face, searching them, hoping that they understood him better than his capacity to put it into words. He seemed disappointed by the incomprehension he saw looking back at him. Thaddeus felt he should say something, but he had already understood Aliver's point. Instead of refuting it, he sat, feeling its import grow on him.

"I cannot explain it," Aliver continued, "but the Santoth were right, of course. The spell was garbled at the edges. They didn't *intend* to make the mist dream into a horror, but that's what happened. They made the mist state a living nightmare that preyed on each person's greatest fears and weaknesses. They made it such a torment that the users feared the drug more than the torture of withdrawal, more than losing forever the dreams that they always sought the mist for. Understand me? It may have worked, but that was not the song they wanted to sing. They would have gentled them off with a loving pressure. Instead, by the time the spell took hold, it had twisted into something malevolent. If that's what happens when they're reaching out to our allies to help them, what might they unleash when they strike out to slay our enemies, when the song they intend is one of death and destruction?"

What a question, Thaddeus thought. Exactly as he would have put it himself. He had no answer to it, and sat in silence with the others.

"You know," Dariel eventually said, a tinge of humor in his voice, "if this all ends well for us, we'll have a most amazing story to tell. A most amazing story. One to sit on the shelf beside *The Tale of Bashar and Cashen*, as father used to say. Remember how he said that? '*The most amazing tale is yet to be written*,' he said. '*But it will be, and it will deserve the space beside Bashar and Cashen*.'"

Aliver said that he understood that tale differently now. He began to explain what the Santoth had taught him, but Thaddeus could not listen to him. He knew the instant the words were out of Dariel's mouth that something crucial had been said. It sent a shiver up from his lower back that fanned out across his musculature. He'd heard Leodan use just those words, but in a different context.

Somebody approached the tent door. The guard posted there gruffly asked the person's business. A woman's voice piped up in answer. Thaddeus could not hear her words, but there was a confident tone to them. Thaddeus assumed he understood the situation. The princes were young men, handsome and powerful. There were certainly women who vied for their attention. It surprised him neither brother had paid much attention to—

The woman shouted something. Thaddeus did not catch it, but Aliver and Dariel both shot to their feet and rushed toward the tent flap. They were out past it before Thaddeus could make sense of it. He sat forward in his seat, listening to the excited sounds that followed, but it wasn't until Dariel called for him that he actually rose. Pushing through the tent flap into the torch- and star-lit night, he saw the two princes sharing a multilimbed embrace with a young woman. She was as sun-burnished as they, as lithe and strong. She wore the dual swords of the Punisari at her waist. The fact that she went thus armed drew so much of his attention that he failed to realize a far more important thing.

"Thaddeus," Aliver said on noticing him, "look, it's Mena."

By the Giver—when had he become so dim-witted? So slow? When had his eyes lost their ability to see what mattered? Mena. It was Mena. She disentangled herself from her brothers and walked toward him. Her strides were so determined and the swords so prominent at her side that he half believed she was about to cut him down. Mena, who had always been so smart. Who'd always understood people intuitively, even as a child. Mena, whom he'd feared he'd lost, whom he'd spoken to sometimes in his dreams, who'd named his crimes in those nightmares by counting them off one by one on her small fingers . . . For that Mena he would stand still and accept whatever havoc she would wreak upon him.

But if this young woman remembered all the ways that Thaddeus had betrayed her, she gave no sign of it. She closed on him with open arms. She smashed against his chest, arms thrown around him, her head nestled beneath his chin. Thaddeus's eyes moistened immediately. It took a great deal of effort to balance his head in such a way that the tears did not break over the rims of his eyes. She could have squeezed the air out of him and he'd not have moved until he lost consciousness and crumpled to the ground.

Drawing back from him, Mena slipped her hands up his neck and clamped them around his head. Her grip was surprisingly strong. She tilted his head forward, spilling the tears onto his cheeks. "You are exactly the same," she said. Her voice had a foreign accent to it, a bit of the thickness of Vumu that she somehow transformed to music. "Not a new wrinkle on your face. Not a blemish or freckle I don't remember."

Thaddeus gave up all pretense at controlling his emotion. He let it flow, more completely even than he had on reuniting with Aliver or on embracing Dariel. Three of Leodan's children were together now; all of them— all of them—were alive! It was simply too much joy, too much relief and sorrow to contain. He let it flow.

What he did later that night was not the rash action it might have seemed. Or so he told himself. At some level he had known for a while that he had done all he could to help Aliver onto the path of his destiny. That job was complete. Aliver would either fail or succeed, but he would not turn away from either result. He had everything he needed to win this war except for one thing. He needed the book that would help his sorcerers sing his cause to victory. Though others had been asked to hunt for the book, there was nobody more likely to actually find it than he himself.

In the early hours of the next morning, before the sun had risen, Thaddeus Clegg set out to find this book, marching north ahead of the army, toward Acacia and the palace in which he hoped the volume might still lie hidden.

CHAPTER

FIFTY-EIGHT

Hanish had not enjoyed his last parting with Corinn. He'd looked her square in the face as he took his leave, unsure of how she would respond, prepared for a petulant show of emotion. Perhaps he even craved some such outpouring. Instead, she had been strangely reserved. She had not protested his leaving to meet Haleeven and the caravan transporting the Tunishnevre. Nor had she asked to come with him, which he'd anticipated. Though she wished him success and speed, her lips had no vigor during their final kisses. She had not pressed her body to his as she usually did. She gave him nothing but polite indifference. He half wondered if she'd started to tire of him already, but it was a silly thought that he brushed aside. The truth, he thought, was simply that she'd grown more adept at hiding her feelings, more like a Meinish woman.

As he sailed from the island toward Aos he convinced himself of this. She had been full of emotion she wished to hide, he decided: a trembling at the edges of her lips, an intensity in her eyes, something betrayed by the annoyed way she flicked at a lock of hair that fell over her forehead. Yes, it was all there. He could not pin it down in exact terms, but she was not so different from the fragile girl who'd experienced the loss of her family. She'd been abandoned and the shadow of it hung over her still. She did not like parting, though she'd tried stoically not to betray this. Ironic, he thought, considering that it was his *return* she needed to fear.

He also suspected she had heard about Aliver's emergence in Talay. Perhaps she'd even heard rumors that Mena and Dariel were alive as well. He wasn't sure how that would affect her. In truth, he struggled with the news himself. How was it possible that all the search parties over the years had not found them? Why had nobody betrayed them for the riches he would have gladly paid them? It had been a lasting frustration, and now it was an untimely annoyance. At least he had Maeander to rely upon. He and his love of mayhem, with his weapons of war and those warped creatures he was so enthusiastic about: he would take care of the Akarans.

Having ordered this in his mind, he did his best to box away any emotions he had for Corinn. He had ordered the Punisari to shadow her closely. He drew out clear boundaries beyond which she was not allowed to pass. The guards were not to make this obvious to her, of course. Let her feel as free as she pleased, but keep her caged within the safety of the palace. That was all she needed to do to be in place to fulfill her role. If none of the other Akarans could be made to stand in her place, Corinn would have to die upon the altar to release his ancestors. This would grieve him, yes, but he would reckon with that later. He was strong enough, full enough of purpose, that he could and would do what was necessary.

That was the purpose of this trip, after all. He was going to help Haleeven bear the Tunishnevre on the last leg of their journey to Acacia, to the chamber he had built especially for them. There was no greater responsibility now. There never had been and never would be after this work was complete. Even the pending war with Aliver and his growing hordes did not compare. Maeander was more than capable of handling that. He trusted his brother's martial skills completely. Success in defeating Aliver was of crucial importance, certainly. That was why he had given Maeander leave to use all the resources he needed, including unveiling the antoks, creatures never used in battle in the Known World. But still, a poor outcome on the fields of Talay would not decide this contest. Releasing the Tunishnevre would.

He disembarked at Aos and walked up from the docks without pausing to take in the resplendent grandeur of the place. Under Acacian rule, the port town had been developed as a prosperous settlement. But that was before the war. Now a handful of Meinish nobles and quite a few elite Punisari resided here, ensconced in wealth and beauty unimagined back when they had huddled against the cold in Tahalian. Perhaps the memory of that was what kept Hanish moving without raising his eyes. His people had come so far, but they'd yet to transform themselves into a true imperial nation. They were still, in many ways, occupiers parading in the skins of those they'd conquered, adorned with their trappings. He hoped to change that soon with the aid of his liberated ancestors.

Fresh horses awaited him and his contingent of Punisari. They mounted and rode away from the city without pause, ignoring the magistrates waiting to greet them. For two days they rode through the patchwork of farmland that provided the empire so much of its food resources. They camped simply each night, not even erecting tents, as the summer weather was so fair, the skies so very blue and cloudless. On the third and fourth days they cut through the rolling grass country, riding past flocks of sheep and cattle tended by young men and women who stared at the Meins as if they were wolves in disguise.

It amazed Hanish—as it still always did—to ramble across the great expanse of riches he now controlled. It was all his, he reminded himself. All rightfully his and his people's. The world belonged to those bold enough to take it, and who had ever been bolder than he?

That night, camped at the edge of the Eilavan Woodlands, Hanish pondered this question at some length. He searched in the generations of Meinish warriors for any whom he considered his equal. He had once viewed them all with awe, but now, as he ticked them off one by one, he found each of them lacking in one way or another. Only Hauchmeinish seemed a man of undeniable greatness. The times had been so tumultuous that Hauchmeinish was born into war and lived his entire life in the center of a whirlwind. He had certainly been a fierce fighter, a gifted leader upon whom fell great trials to test his mettle. Who else could have led the Meins as they had marched, desolate and beaten, into a frigid exile meant to destroy them? Hauchmeinish had made sure they persevered, but in the end his was a story of defeat. What would Hanish say to him when he looked him in the face? Should he bow before such an ancestor? Or should he bend his knee before him?

Hanish knew what they would expect: him with head bowed to them, humble, grateful. They had always spoken to him in whispers that said he was nothing without them. He was simply the product of their labors. All his achievements were owned by the collective. No single man mattered compared to the force they embodied together. He had lived his life by just this credo, and it had not failed him. So why did his mind seem to buck against his old certainties now, when he was so close to finishing his work?

It troubled him to realize that it was Acacian heroes he most respected. Edifus might have been his equal. Tinhadin surely was. Had he warred with them, he was not at all sure that he would have prevailed. Edifus had fought so doggedly, without flagging, scrapping with any and all who stood against him. He had not been a man of guile or cunning, but he had fought in the front ranks of every major battle of his career. Tinhadin had been a different sort, all treachery and betrayal, a model for cutthroat duplicity, a man willing to embrace the horrors of a vision so broad few others would even have conceived it. It struck Hanish that he had learned from these founders of Acacia. In a way, he revered them, even though they had been his people's greatest foes. He fell asleep wrapped around the comforting—and disappointing—thought that there were no men such as those two to face him now.

Later, his eyes snapped open on the creamy splash of stars painted on the night sky. He cast around a moment, his senses screaming alertness throughout his body. He spotted the guards standing at eight points around him and others sleeping on the ground, the horses nearby. Everything quiet, just as peaceful as when he had drifted off, the air filled with cricket calls. It was not anything happening around him that had woken him. He had been dreaming of an Akaran female, a woman who looked exactly like Corinn. But she was not Corinn, and it had not been an amorous encounter. It had to have been . . . Mena. Sword-wielding Mena. A wrathful goddess: that was how she had described herself in the dream. She had raised her weapon to show it to him. The blade was drenched in blood. It dripped the stuff as if the metal were a spring of red liquid. It was the sight of that weapon and her woman's hands on the hilt that had thrust him up from slumber. But why dream of her? Wasn't Aliver the one leading the rebellion? Why awake fearing someone who in daylight hours he still considered a girl?

He knew little of Mena except that she had killed Larken with his own sword, slain several Punisari afterward, and stirred the crew into revolt. The last part was probably the easiest. It was an unfortunate reality of imperial life that each Mein had to depend upon a host of conquered peoples to keep the world functioning, to man ships and cook meals and build roads. Still, it should not have been possible for petite Mena to so completely elude them.

Hanish decided that if the opportunity presented itself, he would sacrifice Mena during the ceremony. Better to have her out of the way. Perhaps Corinn would even manage to forgive him. Perhaps at the end of it all they could have a life together. Hanish rolled to one side, feeling the contours of the ground beneath him. He shut his eyes and tried to sleep and tried not to think of Corinn. He achieved neither.

The next day, sitting on a rise that provided a view of the winding path of the road through the Eilavan Woodlands, Hanish caught sight of the approaching caravan. Cavalry rode in the fore and off through the woods along the flanks. Then followed units of Punisari, marching in tight formation, hemmed in by the narrow lane. Beyond them stretched a snaking length of wagons and laborers and priests, ox-drawn contraptions loaded with hundreds of sarcophagi. In each, Hanish knew, resided one of his ancestors. He heard the crack of the drivers' whips carried to him on the breeze. It was actually happening, he thought. It was really going to happen.

Riding closer, through the cavalry and foot soldiers and on toward the body of the procession, he could not imagine how they had managed to traverse the rutted, abused, and sodden tundra of the Mein Plateau. In summer it would have been a jolting journey through a fetid landscape of bog land spread thinly over a rocky underlayer, with so many opportunities to tip to either side and spill their loads, such mires to get stuck in. Perhaps they would not have been able to do it at all without the aid of Numrek technology. It was they who had taught the Meins how to make wagons of such size, with those enormous wheels and with flexible undercarriages that did not snap under pressure. Still, the thought of these great contraptions negotiating the steep, switchback trail down from the Rim set tingles of trepidation through him. He would have to question Haleeven about it later, after thanking him, congratulating him. It was a feat he would have a poet write a ballad about.

Hanish's uncle grinned like a madman when he saw his nephew. The two men greeted each other by crashing their heads together. Forehead impacted against forehead. They pressed skin to skin, each with their hands wrapped around the other's skull. It was an old greeting, reserved for close relatives and for times of great emotion. It was meant to hurt. But the pain of it was nothing compared to the impact of Haleeven's appearance. Hanish had never seen a man so haggard, save the beggars that roamed the back alleys of Alecia: unkempt of clothes, speckled with grime, lips chapped from his tongue that darted, darted, darted out to moisten them. His eyes hid behind low-hanging brows, and the skin of his face sagged, as if the tissue itself had been fatigued by the recent weeks' work. His hair was shockingly white. Hanish tried to remember if it had been so before, even a little. He did not think so. It stood up from his scalp as if each hair were a tendril of silver thread frozen by an icy breeze.

Pulling back from him, Hanish said, "You look well."

The lie was out of his mouth before he realized it. Haleeven let him know what he thought of it with a frown but was merry again the next moment. "No, *you* look well. I—I'm not so well. This is some mission you sent me on, Nephew. Some task . . ."

"But you've done it."

Haleeven studied him a moment, then nodded. "Come, let me show you everything."

At Haleeven's side, Hanish visited each of the ancestors. He climbed upon the great wagons, touching the sarcophagi with his hands, whispering his greetings, invoking old prayers of praise. He felt the life within the containers palpably. They pulsed with an undeniable, ferocious energy. It lashed at the world in muted silence, as if each of them were screaming bloody murder inside a sound- and motion-proof chamber. Hanish noted the fatigue and unease in the laborers' every gesture. They were hollow eyed with fear, wrung more by the emotional toll of their duties than by the physical labor. Even the oxen, usually calm creatures, were skittish and needed to be tightly controlled.

Haleeven's description of the journey was a long tale of hardship and setbacks, told through the afternoon and continued that evening over supper in camp. When he was finished, the two men sat in silence, the night settling around them. Hanish could not see the stars for the trees blocking them, the undersides of the foliage glowing with firelight. Haleeven lit a pipe full of hemp leaf and drew on it, a habit Hanish had not known he had taken to. He almost said something disparaging. But it wasn't as if Haleeven were smoking mist. Perhaps he'd earned a vice. Hanish had just begun to think of Corinn again, when his uncle broke the silence.

"They are so impatient," Haleeven said.

Hanish didn't need to ask whom he meant. "I know."

"They are angry."

"I know. I've made—"

The uncle snapped forward from his reclined position, shot out a hand, and grabbed his nephew by the wrist. He waited until Hanish met his eyes and then pegged them to his with a burning intensity. "You don't know! You haven't felt them like I have these many days. They're fully awake now. They seethe with animus. They want revenge so badly they tremble with the nearness of it. I fear them, Hanish. I fear them like I've never feared anything on earth."

Hanish pulled his wrist away, slowly but with a twist that broke the man's grip. He spoke with the conviction he knew he should feel, trying to believe his own words. "Their anger is not directed at you, Uncle. We have nothing to fear from our own."

"That's what they have always told us," Haleeven said. "What have you told the princess?"

"About what will happen to the Tunishnevre? I told her that she could help me release them. A drop of her blood, I said, and her blessing was all we needed to break the curse. She has not offered to give it, though. And I haven't pressed her. She thinks I can do it without her blessing."

"You can," Haleeven said. "And did you tell her what breaking the curse means? Or that there are two different ways to do it, each with a very different outcome?"

"I said that it would free the ancestors so that they could escape to true death and finally rest. I said they just wanted peace and release."

"That's all you told her?"

Hanish nodded.

Haleeven was quiet a moment, and then he said, "So by omission you lied to her."

"Yes, I did. She believes the ancestors want peace, when in fact what they truly want is to walk the earth again—"

"With swords drawn—"

"Wreaking bloody vengeance."

The two sat for a time after this, nothing more to say now that they had shared what they both knew and had known all along. Hanish extended his hand and motioned for the pipe. Haleeven turned it and slipped it into his hands.

CHAPTER

FIFTY-NINE

Maeander had thought it before, but he knew now that it was true beyond a doubt: nothing stirred his blood as much as the promise of warfare. Carnal conquests, games of physical prowess, acquisition of riches, hunts of animal and/or human quarry, and skirmishes: all of these paled to insignificance compared to the promise of carnage on a massive scale. He had thrived on the bloodshed of the first war and had largely been bored since. On several occasions he had tried to convince Hanish to let him make war on one people or another, but his brother always dismissed him as a joker. Now, finally, after nine years of peace, he felt his heart quicken again. Aliver Akaran had returned, and he had brought enough friends with him to make it interesting.

As Maeander disembarked his troops at points along the central Ta-layan coast and marched them a short distance inland, he thought of the coming conflict as a grand diversion. He could not spot within himself any tendril of fear or concern or worry that fate might have some unpleasant outcome in store for him. He could not lose. He knew that much. He had never met another person with a mind as suited to slaughter as his. Perhaps the fabled Tinhadin might have rivaled him, but few others could. His troops were honed and ready. Hanish had made sure they did not luxuriate in their military victory too much and grow soft, like the Acacians had. It had not been easy to manage this, as most of them had become wealthy men overnight. But Hanish had sworn them to a strict level of discipline. With a few exceptions, they'd lived up to it.

They were a more formidable force than they had been in the first war: fitter, better provisioned, broader of outlook and training, and just as proud. They were not hungry the way they'd been in that earlier conflict, but they were determined to preserve what they had won. The younger men craved glory similar to their father's, uncle's, and older brother's. They had obtained weapons that Aliver would be entirely unprepared for, surprises that might prove more dramatic than even the Numrek had been.

In addition to the faith he had in himself and his troops, the Tunish-nevre had promised him that he would triumph over the Akaran. Aliver's blood would spill at his hand; they had assured him of this. They had given him permission to kill the young man himself, if need be. Corinn would suffice in the ceremony to free them of their curse, but Aliver could not be allowed to live on as a danger to them.

Watching the upstart prince's thronging army from atop a ridgeline overlooking what would be the battlefield, Maeander was as excited as a boy who imagines such scenes inside his head. He spent a few days arranging his troops into camps from which they could be deployed. If Aliver believed the revolts throughout the empire would leave the Meins with scant allies, he would be disappointed. Hanish had called upon the entrenched leadership in each province, those who had grown rich by supporting Mein-ish causes, those who so enjoyed being elevated above their peers that they would fight to preserve their status. These groups had worked to put down the rebellions at home and answered Maeander's call for troops. The Numrek had yet to arrive. Word was that they were but a couple of days away. They would miss out only on a little of the action. He wasn't sure he would need them anyway.

Talay might be largely out of his hands, but he did hold Bocoum and most of the coastline, with infinite resources for seaborne resupply. League vessels dotted the sea in the thousands, waiting to fulfill whatever need might arise. His forces numbered a solid thirty thousand. Each of this number was a fighting man, trained and selected for this battle. His army, he believed, was a steel blade that would cut through Aliver's bloated forces. It would have been nice to still have Larken as his right hand, but that was not possible thanks to Mena, a strange, deceitful creature.

Because of this, he hoped that Aliver would accept his invitation to parlay. He would like to look Mena in the face again and search for signs of her martial skills that he had missed during their first meeting. He wondered what Aliver might look like in person. He worried that his appearance would be disappointing—it was better to imagine a gallant, skilled foe—but still he was curious and knew that Aliver would likely be deceased before another opportunity presented itself.

The Akarans, however, declined. They sent a message to remind him that during the last war the Meins had used the honored tradition of parlay only to unleash a foul weapon. This would not, Aliver said, be allowed to happen again. If Maeander wished to surrender himself, his brother, and every Mein who had fought against or profited from the fall of the Akaran Empire, then they might have something to talk about. Otherwise, they should decide the matter on the field.

Maeander answered that this was fine with him. He had nothing much to say to the prince either. This was not exactly true, as became clear from the further message he sent back. At this point, he said, he would not even have accepted Aliver's unconditional surrender. Maeander believed the prince had cast his lot on the day he chose to come out of hiding. From that day to this, his life was ticking down toward its conclusion. Considering this, there was no possibility that talking would do either of them any good, and this simple exchange of messages served the purposes of parlay reasonably well. He would never have sent such a wordy message before the first war, but it felt natural enough now. Perhaps the cultured life available on Acacia was having an effect on him, making him more verbose.

Before dawn the next morning he sent conscripted laborers far out onto the plains to clear the field of debris. He had the catapults wheeled into place. The sun rose on the assembling troops. Between the two armies stretched a wide, flat expanse of open ground, dotted here and there by shrubs and a few acacia trees. Aliver's troops outnumbered his nearly two to one. They formed up into ordered rows, divided into units that must have had autonomous leaders, but this did not hide the polyglot diversity of them. Maeander called them Acacians, but in truth they were mostly Talayans, with all manner of other peoples mixed in among them. A great many of them wore Akaran orange. Some had shirts or trousers in the color; others tied strips of cloth around their foreheads or on their arms or made belts from material of that hue. The Balbara troops—who went about nearly naked—marked their chests with ochre paint. All in all, they made for a most colorful display. Maeander had particular reason to be pleased by this. They would be crippled, he believed, by language barriers, by differing customs, by such a range of skill and bravery and battle preparedness that all he needed to do was stir chaos into their midst and slaughter them as they imploded.

He opened with two simultaneous maneuvers intended to deny Aliver any opportunity to grasp the initiative. He set his troops marching, and he had the catapults begin to lob boulders of flaming pitch at either wing of Aliver's forces. His army was tightly formed, disciplined. They progressed forward with a steady pace that could not be ignored. The front lines of the

Acacians would have heard their chants and the rhythmic tromping of their feet and the bursts of sound as different clans shouted in answer to prompts of their family names. All frightening enough.

Add to it the tremendous snapping motions of the catapults as they shot searing paths into the sky, arcing, arcing, falling before a tail of black smoke. They had modified the weapons from the ones the Numrek had first brought into the Known World. These were larger, improved versions of the originals, with massive gear works and the capacity to hurl missiles twice as far as before. With help from league engineers, they had managed to make the pitch into stable spheres that they could roll onto the cocked catapult arm before lighting them. Once airborne, they held their shape and burned undiminished until they smashed back to earth. Embedded within them were small, pronged iron tripods. On impact they dispersed across the ground, their sharpened, barbed points almost always ended sticking straight up. They were small weapons, but he was sure they would lame men and horses by the hundreds. Aliver had no weapon like this, nor would he be prepared for its devastating power. In response, his troops offered up timed barrages of arrows that—though they inflicted some damage—seemed of little more consequence than a swarm of gnats.

The first orbs exploded before the armies ever met. The blasts fanned out in all directions, incinerating everything within a fifty-yard radius and throwing globs of molten matter even farther. The soldiers ran away from the impacts in a frenzy, clambering over one another, pressing bodies in toward the center. Confusion already sown. Maeander had several of the catapults repositioned and recalibrated. Within a few minutes the first of them dropped an orb on the rear of Aliver's forces. It took out a unit that might have expected to see no action the entire day.

Let them feel surrounded, Maeander thought, hemmed in by fire and destruction on three sides, facing their executioners on the other. Watching the billowing smoke and the waves of confused motion within the enemy ranks, he turned to offer a grin and jest to the man beside him. That man was not Larken, however. The thought of this soured his mood. Only for a moment, though.

The two armies met as the rain of fire from the sky continued. Watching what happened next, Maeander could not have been happier with how he had planned this action. He'd placed a wedge of cavalry in the center of his line. Aliver could not match them even if he wanted to; he had no cavalry unit at all, just a splattering of mounted men here and there. Hanish's horsemen were heavily armored, bearing lances with which they darted foot soldiers, puncturing breasts and necks and faces before yanking the weapons out. They were top-heavy, muscled men who had trained and trained and trained for a moment like this. They could repeat their over-hand thrusts hundreds of times without fatigue. Their horses were the largest in the empire, unshakable, belligerent mounts trained to smash men beneath their hooves.

Within a half hour they had carved a gash right toward the center of the Acacian troops. This might have seemed a risky maneuver, as they were soon deep within the enemy, hemmed in on three sides. But behind the horsemen poured a river of infantrymen, swinging swords and axes. The weapons were of such quality and honed to such sharpness that they cut through flesh and muscle and bone, leather and light mail. Aliver's lightly armored troops fell in bloody pieces before them. Maeander's foot soldiers ate into the center, leaving the bulk of the enemy army as largely immobile targets for the catapults.

In many ways Maeander felt that he controlled the ensuing slaughter with his own hands. It went on for hours, through the morning and into the afternoon. It was fatiguing just watching this bloody work. By the time he signaled for his troops to pull back he was drenched in sweat, muscles sore as if he had been in the thick of it all day himself. Nothing had transpired the entire day that he had not planned and pulled the strings of. He had lost few men and slaughtered a great many, it seemed. It was only because of the sheer numbers of Aliver's troops that any of them were left.

His generals, when they debriefed later that evening, were not as san-guine. They'd killed many, yes, but not as many as Maeander seemed to think. The battle that they described bore a resemblance to what Maeander had witnessed, but it differed in some particulars as well. Numbers, for one. The Acacians had been trampled, hacked, battered. Some of them had fallen to grave wounds. Many, however, managed to back away despite injuries that should have lamed them. Others, whom the infantrymen believed they had dispatched and stepped over, rose sometime later and attacked them from behind. To their eyes the catapults had not been as destructive as Maeander thought. They had hit, yes, but only the immediately incinerated died. The others were blown from their feet, sent hurtling. They were aflame one mo-ment and then out, steaming and largely unharmed the next.

"They're hard to kill," one officer said. "That's the disconcerting thing. They are just hard to kill."

All the generals who had viewed it up close agreed. None of them could make much sense of it. Again, Maeander wished he had Larken to consult with or his brother or uncle . . . but he doubted any of them would have advised him in any way he could not manage himself. Regardless of the details, the day had been theirs. If the Acacians came out to meet him on the morrow, it would be the end of them. His generals did not dispute this much, at least.

✳

The next morning Maeander joined the front ranks of his soldiers. He wanted to see the enemy up close, to take his bloody part in the victory he anticipated. But from the first moment the two armies met, nothing transpired with the inevitability he had imagined. The enemy did prove hard to kill. Wounded, they fell back when they should rightfully have fallen dead. Those he thought killed often crawled away or rolled back up to their feet, not so badly hurt as he imagined. It almost seemed like he had to separate a head from its body to be sure of a kill.

And they fought improbably well also, despite their inferior weapons and training, regardless of their thin or partial or nonexistent armor. In one instance, clashing hand to hand with a boy in his early teens, Maeander found himself having a hell of a time killing him. It should have been easy. The boy was a slender-shouldered Bethuni, fighting with only a spear, his legs and arms and chest all bare, easy targets. He was terrified, Maeander could see. He was trembling, eyes wide and frantic. He managed to move just fast enough, blocking, defending, occasionally lashing out. Maeander could not help but laugh at him, at the strange combination of the boy's fear with Maeander's inability to strike him. It was comical, until the whelp nicked his shoulder. Angry at this, Maeander dove to press his attack. But, pushed by a sudden surge of motion from one side, he lost sight of the boy. He was left fuming and spitting, watching him slip away, something like mirth in the lad's brown eyes. This incident was just one of many of the morning's frustrations.

Back on the ridge that served as his command center later that afternoon, Maeander concluded that Aliver's separate units were functioning with a rapidity he had not noticed at first. Communications passed quickly from one part of the mass of troops to the next. Too quickly, really, to be explained. Maeander had the catapults focus on destroying the handful of moving viewing towers interspersed throughout the Acacian army. He could not know for sure, but presumably these towers housed generals, tacticians, perhaps even the Akarans themselves. It struck him as foolish to draw attention to oneself that way, but the towers were there. They were being used for something. Twice he saw projectiles explode directly atop the mobile towers. That was satisfying. Whether an Akaran was in one or not, each explosion had certainly taken officers with it.

By the close of the day he was feeling better again. He would open the next day by destroying the rest of the towers. He'd switch tactics, sending the cavalry around to flank the Acacians while concentrating the catapults in the center. The orbs of pitch were running low, but he would use them anyway. That was what they were for. He would finish them and finish Aliver off in a massive hail of fire. Two days of slaughter and injury would have left them crippled, depleted. His men were still strong, still numerous. The third day would end the entire thing.

But overnight it seemed Aliver's army replenished its numbers. New recruits must have poured in to replace the fallen. The army the Acacians fielded the third day looked little diminished from what it had been on the first. It didn't make sense that they could so swiftly incorporate the new additions, but they placed them on the battlefield the very day of their arrival. Somehow, they fought with the discipline and grace of veterans.

And his downpour of fire? It poured down, rightly enough, but it had even less impact than in the days before. One tower, directly hit, buckled beneath the impact, flared into flame, and then . . . well, then the blaze went out, as if a breath of wind had extinguished it. Even as Maeander stared, the structure seemed to regain its footing, to rise back into shape. It smoldered, blackened, but it survived. By the time he called the day closed he felt he was fighting at a standstill. Instead of reveling in victory he felt himself floundering. He was not winning at all. And if the trend continued, the following day would see his troops driven backward.

The first day had confused him slightly. The second confounded him. The third worried him. He entertained the thought for the first time that perhaps Aliver had been blessed by some form of sorcery. He had thought all such things long dead, but what other explanation could there be? Nothing else made any more sense. With this realization came the first tingling of doubt. It appeared like an itch at his elbow, a nagging sensation that he just could not get rid of. If he scratched it with reason, it vanished, but only until he pulled his fingernails away. Then the itch crept across his skin again. He didn't like it at all.

The Numrek had not arrived. Where were they? What game were they playing? The league was still readily available, but it would be four days before they could resupply the pitch orbs. His men were starting to look worried around the eyes. A messenger from Hanish arrived, demanding news. He had the man sequestered in a tent, guarded.

That evening he came to a decision. He was going to try something Hanish had cautioned should be used only as a last resort. They had a weapon they had not yet revealed to anybody. It had been a gift from their allies across the Gray Slopes. Not a disease this time but another thing unheard-of in the Known World. He did not like revealing their secrets if it was at all possible not to. But the situation they faced, Maeander's gut told him, was just that sort of dire circumstance.

He sent a messenger to Aliver, proposing a two-day break in the fighting. Let the morrow be a day spent clearing the field, tending the wounded, and let another follow to honor the dead. Aliver agreed. With the delay in place, Maeander next contacted the vessels that carried the secret cargo, docked, as they were, in the harbor of Bocoum. He needed the antoks, he said. Bring them to shore and ready them.

CHAPTER

SIXTY

Corinn knew she had only one chance to speak to the leagueman. He had arrived in Acacia secretly the night before. She learned of this because she had coerced several of her servants—none of whom were Meins, of course—into feeding her bits of intelligence. Before her shocking discovery that Hanish would offer her as a blood sacrifice to his ancestors, she would never have looked to servants for such information. It would have seemed inappropriate, like lowering herself, demonstrating weakness. But she had decided that there was no weaker outcome than her ending up dead on some altar, nothing more pathetic than being led to her own slaughter in the throes of doe-eyed love. She had no intention of exiting life quietly. Indeed, she had no intention of exiting at all.

After learning what she had that strange night, all her old assumptions had to be revised. Her servants had once been faceless, nameless beings at the periphery of her vision. But from that first morning she saw them differently. She could not help but study their faces, wondering what they knew that she didn't. What did they think of her? To whom did they owe loyalty? She took to watching them, observing their demeanor in various situations. She tried to gauge which of them were more disposed to her than others, which wore resentment barely disguised, and which looked like they could be manipulated. And then she had begun to cultivate them accordingly.

It had paid off. The servants were not as loyal to the Meins as she had assumed. It almost seemed as if they had been waiting for her to wake up and conspire with them. She learned that many of them believed Aliver's return was fated. A male servant had told her that Rialus Neptos was in the palace. Another had informed her of Larken's death. When a girl named

Gillian brought her word of Sire Dagon's arrival on the island, Corinn thanked her with an embrace and a peck on her cheek. Apparently the leagueman had asked to have a messenger bird readied for dispatch as soon as possible. He himself was scheduled to depart first thing in the morning, so Corinn wasted no time.

She left her quarters in the gray light of predawn, working her way through the palace silently, by memory, carrying no torch or candle. She had dressed carefully even earlier. She wore a light blue dress of a silken material, one that framed her collarbones and neck to flattering effect. Leaguemen were men, after all.

She had come to understand that the palace was a sort of prison for her now. Neither Hanish nor anybody had ever said this, but she had not been off the island for several weeks. The few times she had mentioned possible trips, Hanish had brushed her off. Recently, Meinish guards' eyes followed her with a different sort of attentiveness than before. She watched their demeanor as she approached the edges of the royal grounds or when she ventured near the council chambers. She never pushed it far enough that any guard had impeded her, but she became quite sure Hanish had put her under surveillance. There was an invisible boundary thrown up around her. Her skin crawled with awareness of it.

The area of the lower palace reserved for the league, however, was largely a privately run compound. She passed into it without drawing attention to herself. Presumably, Hanish had never considered that she would have any desire to communicate with the league. Once through its gates, she did not have to contend with Meinish guards at all. She did, however, have some difficulty convincing the Ishtat officers to send her request for an audience to Sire Dagon. In the end she managed it only by threatening them with Hanish's anger, pointedly suggesting that it was the chieftain himself who had sent her to see the leagueman. This won her a meeting, although only a few minutes were promised.

Entering Sire Dagon's office, she found him already shuffling through papers with his long fingers. He glanced at her with a distracted air, as yet giving her only half his attention. "My dear princess," he said, "what can I do for you? Please be brief with me, as my time is regretfully short. You have some . . . communication from Hanish?"

The princess was not as nervous as she had imagined she would be at this moment. She knew that the grip of her dilemma should be enough to paralyze her with fear. At times she had found herself standing still, staring off into nothing. She often thought back to the past, to her father, to her mother, to her short-lived exile on Kidnaban. But she was not the same now as she had been as a child. She felt increasingly disconnected from her old way of being. She could affect the world, she believed. She could have a say in her fate. Perhaps the thought of Aliver still living and breathing gave her strength. If this were true, though, it was an irony. The agenda she worked for was only partially in line with what she imagined Aliver's to be.

"You can tell me why you have returned," Corinn said. "What news do you have?"

The leagueman's eyes rolled up and fixed on her. "Am I to believe that Hanish requests this information?"

"If you wish. But you are not Hanish's pawn. I know that, even if he doesn't. If possible, let this be between you and me. You would not have stopped in here and requested a messenger bird without news of some import. I have reason to be curious."

"That I can believe. You may not like what I have to tell, however. Why ask about things you cannot change?"

Corinn shrugged. She wanted to know, she said, for the sake of the knowledge itself.

Sire Dagon mimicked her shrug. He pressed his thin lips together derisively but relaxed them the next moment. "If you must . . . I returned to dispatch a message to the Inspectorate. It seems one of our patrols spotted a . . . well, a *fleet*, I guess you could say, of fishing and merchant and trading vessels sailing into the Inner Sea. They're Vumuans. For a number of reasons, we've concluded that they are on a mission to rescue your sister."

"My sister?"

"They've come to join the battle, which invariably means they are not on the Meinish side. It is my intent to send a messenger bird to the Inspectorate, who will then crush the fleet before they ever reach Talay. They'll be like a child's toy boats bobbing on a pond compared to our warships."

Corinn heard him, but she had not yet fully swallowed the mention of . . . "Did you say that Mena is alive?"

Sire Dagon chuckled. "I thought that would interest you. Your sister is a goddess." He said the last word with feigned reverence. "A goddess . . . Tribal peoples always amaze me. It may be that she's not a goddess at all but is actually a goddess slayer. I'm not sure which it is, really. My information on this is vague as to the particulars. I can tell you, however, that she was captured by Maeander and Larken. She didn't stay captured long, though.

She stabbed Larken in the heart with his own sword. She killed two Punisari and injured several others, and then commandeered the vessel and convinced the crew to sail her to Talay. By the end of the voyage, it seems, she had convinced most of the sailors to join your brother's cause. Hard to imagine, isn't it? Little Mena, a sword-wielding deity slayer, a match for one of the craftiest Marahs I have ever set eyes on."

The leagueman had been shuffling through his papers as he relayed most of this. He paused, looked up, and studied Corinn a moment. "My dear, this does tug at your allegiances, doesn't it? Perhaps I shouldn't have told you. I always heard you were of fragile temperament. It must be very strange to be Princess Corinn Akaran. It might surprise you, but I find these developments with your siblings quite interesting. Consider what they have become: one of them leads an army that is loyal to him; one is called a deity by people who are fanatically devoted to her; another is a raider, a sea captain who also has followers that would die for—or at least *with*—him. Not what your father would have planned, I'm sure, but at least they have made something interesting of their lives. Pity that you weren't allowed to become anything but your conqueror's mistress."

Corinn had been about to express shock and confusion at the strange news of her sister. She had pursed her lips, about to ask for a chair to sit in. She might even have looked to Sire Dagon for guidance, for help. But all these possibilities vanished the moment he expressed pity for her. She did not want pity. She would not accept pity. Nor would she allow the suggestion that her life added up to nothing of interest or worth to stand.

"You are mistaken," she said. She stepped around his desk and drew close to him. She felt the invisible barrier between them, the point that marked the perimeter of what Sire Dagon considered to be his private domain. She pressed against it and felt it resist, felt it bow back against her. The leagueman's face showed no outward sign of consternation, and yet she could tell that he was fighting the desire to step back. Something about this pleased her, gave her confidence. "You, as a member of the league, know that appearances are one thing. The substance beneath is another. Isn't that right?"

"You have already answered your own question."

"So it may be that you don't know yet what lies beneath this façade. You think nothing does, but you should know better. The league, after all, claims to have no hidden interests. But that's absurd. It's not just wealth you want, is it?"

"We want only to continue as we have," Sire Dagon said. "We serve the world's powers. We bring nations together to nurture trade and mutual prosperity—"

"Please, Dagon," Corinn said. "Don't insult me. You have a different objective. I can feel it behind your mask."

"I wear no mask, lady."

"Of course you do." She moved a half step closer, cocked her head as if she were searching for something minute along his hairline. "As a child they sewed it to your face with hair-thin thread. Perhaps you have gotten so used to it that even you don't recognize your own deceit. But the stitch is still visible, Sire Dagon. It is right here. . . ." She lifted a hand, fingers pinched as if to tweeze the thread in question.

The leagueman batted at her hand. He twirled away, the fabric of his gown brushing her hip, stiff, heavy fabric that felt almost like a plate of pliable armor. "Your arrogance knows no bounds."

"I hope not, but I don't as yet know. I have only just discovered arrogance and taken it to heart. You, however, thrive on it. You want to control the workings of the world. You want to know that you are godlike, that you pull the strings that make nations dance. Isn't that what you want?"

"As I said, we want only to preserve what we already have."

"And what is it that you have?"

Standing at a distance again, Sire Dagon regained his composure. He grinned. The question pleased him. "Now you ask something of substance. What do we have already? What do we want to preserve? Consider this . . . If we don't transport water to the Kidnaban mines, the workers die of thirst. There is little water on the island, and they cannot get off because we control the seas. So if we say that they die by drought, they die by drought. Consider that only the league makes pitch now. Even the Numrek cannot be bothered to produce it. Why should they when we do the work and give it to them? So we—the league—hold the secret of how to toss down flaming meteors from the heavens. Only we do business with the Lothan Aklun. Only we know the full extent of the power they serve. We are the ones that keep the Other Lands at bay so that the Known World can continue to believe itself a complete world. Do you understand what I'm telling you? Add these things up and add more things than I can even begin to detail to you, and what is the result? I will tell you. We don't want to become like gods. We already *are* gods. We don't *want* to pull the strings attached to every soul in the Known World. We already *do*. Had you the eyes to see them, you would realize a million tiny threads stretch out from each of my fingers.

This is the truth. The Giver left the world to us, and the Known World has felt the hand of no deity but us ever since. Not Akarans. Not Meins."

"Not the Lothan Aklun?"

"They are a separate matter."

"I know they are," Corinn said, again drawing nearer to him as she spoke. "They are not the power you have always led people to believe, are they? Hanish told me what you told him. You do business with them because doing so is a lesser evil than being without the trade they facilitate. They are rich. Richer than you, and you covet their wealth, don't you? You call them a great power because of their riches, because that is all that matters to you. But you hate it that you must share the trade with them, as an unequal partner. Sometimes at night you dream of having their palaces as your own. That is what arouses you more than anything else in the world. Am I right?"

Sire Dagon backed away, his face soured. "First I lecture you; then you attempt to lecture me. I've no time for this. I'll give you one last opportunity to tell me what brought you here."

Corinn, feeling strangely at ease with being prompted and with the lie she was about to utter, said, "I come with a message from my brother. He wants you to stop aiding Hanish. If you do, he'll make it greatly worth your while."

"He wants us to stop aiding Hanish?" he repeated, his eyebrows wrinkled and dismissive. "Did I not just explain that neither Meins nor Akarans control the world?"

"But neither do you, not alone, at least. Not without winning the consent of the masses. That's what my brother can bring you, even more completely than Hanish."

"Your brother! He angers me as much as he amuses me. Do you know that he's somehow convinced people to come off mist? It's most disruptive."

Corinn had not known anything about people coming off mist, but she took it in without showing surprise on her face. "That is exactly why you should wish him victory. He frees them to help him win this war. Once won, however, the situation afterward will be very different. We can make it one that will please us both. Aliver isn't my father, nor am I. Tell me that in truth you don't think a new Akaran dynasty would benefit us both. Think of all we accomplished together before. Hanish Mein was but a necessary awakening for us. But, believe me, we are now fully alert."

Sire Dagon focused his narrow-set eyes on her and stared with an intensity that would have withered Corinn only a few days ago. Even now, it was hard to meet. "Let us say that I take you at your word," he said. "I've heard nothing that would merit such a change of policy. Your brother is not going to win this contest, Corinn. Trust me. I have access to information you do not. As that is so, why would I align myself with a losing cause, especially one that espouses a desire to hurt my interests? Answer that question convincingly and we will talk further. Fail to, and I will take my leave, Princess."

Struggling not to look away, Corinn tried to prepare the entirety of what she had to say. There was a great deal to sort through, and it all swirled in her head as she met the leagueman's gaze. Part of her wanted to release a whole litany of confessions, to lay it all before him and be judged, understood, sentenced. But she was not here for that. She would not tell him how she had loved Hanish and how it twisted her with misery to find their relationship all false. She was not going to admit that she hated her own weaknesses, that she realized she had been a fool all her life, a lamb being led to slaughter. Nor did she intend to tell him how much pain she carried within her; that she still ached from longing for the life she might have had with her siblings; that she sometimes thought of Igguldan, the prince who had fallen to his knees loving her; and that she still raged against having her father taken from her and against losing her mother while she was but a girl. She held all these things eddying in her mind, but she plucked her message from among them.

Soon the words she would speak fell into place. She would repeat that the league must—for their own preservation—distance themselves from Hanish. They must pull back the navy supporting Maeander, disregard that fleet of Vumuan ships. They must wait. That was all they need do, for now. Not act against Hanish—just not act for him either. Just as they had not aided or hindered either side in the first war. If Hanish prevailed, the league's inactions would not have caused him that much harm. They would be chided but forgiven. What else could Hanish do? Really, they would lose nothing by drawing back. But if the league continued to aid the Meins and they lost . . . then Aliver would be without mercy upon them. He would abolish the trade completely. He would turn the rage of the world squarely on them and fight with all his power to destroy them. And if none of that convinced him, she had yet another promise to make, one that she doubted he would easily ignore.

It was a lot to ask, but on the tenth flare of the leagueman's nostrils she opened her mouth. "Sire Dagon, I can tell you on my brother's behalf that he has no desire to hurt your interests. Just the opposite, he—and I—believe that a partnership between the league and the Akarans can be even more profitable than ever before."

With this opening, she had the leagueman's interest. Sire Dagon nodded that she should continue, that his attention was hers, for one last time, at least.

CHAPTER

SIXTY-ONE

There was nothing of the familiar, natural order of the world to be heard in the dawning day. None of his usual awareness that creatures of the night were bedding down as the day laborers took their place. No morning birdsongs. No cockerels with their heads lifted to announce their ownership of the brightening world. No barking of village dogs. He heard no children with their instant enthusiasm, their shouts and laughter. Nowhere did he hear the lilting of women's voices as they greeted each other in ways and with words that were themselves ancient Talayan customs. Nor was the air brushed with the sound of threshing, that rhythm that over the years had become a gentle enticement to awake, as constant as the rising sun and just as welcome.

On the morning that his contest with Maeander Mein was to resume, Aliver lay awake on his pallet in his war tent, missing all these things. Such moments felt as far gone now as memories from his childhood. They were glimpses of an innocent world that he could scarcely believe in anymore. Back then, he had thought of himself as suffering through an exile, but now every day of his years in Talay seemed idyllic. Remembering that he had once lived like any other person in a normal world pained him physically, a bodily ache that had plagued him through the night, even during his short bouts of sleep. All the troubles and worries and fears that had seemed to matter back then were inconsequential compared to what he now faced.

He rolled himself upright and pressed the fatigue from his eyes with the knuckles of his fists. A few minutes later he pushed through his tent flap. Around him spread the throng of humanity that had rallied to his cause. Hundreds of tents and shelters, thousands of men, women, and children rising for another day of his war. The Halaly guards, who by their own initiative shadowed his every motion, nodded greetings to him. He saw faces all around lift toward him, smiling and hopeful. They all believed that this war was as good as won. They trusted him completely now, felt he was like Edifus returned, like Tinhadin. Though he explained that it was not so, they seemed to think *he* was the power protecting them, not the unseen Santoth.

He kept his eyes moving, afraid lest his gaze rest too long on any one of his faithful followers. He could show them no uncertainty. *You can feel it,* Thaddeus had said shortly before he disappeared, *but never show it.* Aliver had not realized how he had come to lean on the old chancellor until he departed. In a way it felt like his father had spoken through his betrayer's mouth, strange as that seemed. He had said that all people were fumblers at life, even kings. But an effective king moves as if he were a hero of old. Such heroes never doubted themselves. *Not as far as the world could tell, at least.* Aliver missed the man greatly. Thaddeus had not said a word of parting, but the prince knew what he searched for. He prayed him speed in finding it.

He found Mena and Dariel conversing over breakfast. They sat side by side, touching at the knee, both of them cupping their wooden bowls in one hand and spooning porridge with the other. Mena so petite, yet honed to a keen-edged strength her scant clothing did not hide, dangerous even though she presented to the world a kind, wise face, sword at her side within easy grasping range; Dariel with his ready smile and energy, a devious twinkle always close behind his eyes, his shirt open right down to his flat abdomen. They leaned in close together and spoke as they ate. They looked like . . . well, like two unlikely siblings at ease with each other. The years they had spent apart seemed to have faded into insignificance.

A seizure of emotion racked Aliver. He wanted to leap the space between them and tackle them both in an embrace. If he did so, he'd end up rolling on the ground with them. He'd pour tears all over them. He'd blubber and cry, and he was not sure that he'd be able to rise from such an embrace and do the things he had to do. He, or they, might die in the hours to come. He knew it. Part of him wanted to say a whole host of things to them in preparation. He should crack open whatever part of him was most fragile and share it with them, so that they would understand and remember him. He yearned to spend days and days with them, learning everything about the lives they had lived, probing them to help him understand the life *he* had lived, seeking in their memories a more complete picture of everything they'd each been through.

He had opened up some of his vision of the future to them. When they prevailed, he had said, he would not rule over them. He would not be a tyrant who left them no say in the running of the empire. They would share all decisions among the four of them. They would reach decisions by consensus, by compromise. They would find within long conversations with one another a wisdom greater than what they could come up with singly. They would take greater responsibility for the workings of the empire at the same time as they provided for increased representation from its diverse regions. Everyone would have more say in shaping the future.

All of this he meant and believed, but it was the prince, Aliver Akaran, speaking, not the brother. The brother still had a great many things he hungered to share with his siblings. As he proceeded to walk toward them he acknowledged that nothing in his life had ever fallen in line with his imaginings; whatever was to happen, that fact would stay a constant. The very fact of the day awaiting them made it impossible for him to launch that embrace or let flow those tears. Such emotion was for later, for quiet times when thousands of lives did not hang in the balance. Instead, he spoke wryly, as any older brother to his younger siblings.

"How is it that you two are always up before me?" he asked.

Mena rose, smiling, and squeezed his elbow.

Dariel said, "The question is how you manage to sleep at all."

"Lightly, brother," Aliver said, using an old Talayan saying. "I sleep lightly and tread to keep my head out of the sea of dreams."

Within the hour the three of them were armed and dressed for their roles. Previously, they had each headed portions of the army. Mena and Dariel were new to massed warfare, but they were quick and seemed to see with far-reaching eyes. Mena had fought in the front lines of the battle, amazing everyone with her skills as a swordswoman and with her ability to kill without remorse and yet maintain a humble, human character. Dariel had a flair about him that inspired almost comical glee among the troops. The tales his raiders had spun about him had the masses believing he was impervious to injury, untouchable, blessed. They were symbols the people were keen to rally around. Aliver's instructions—passed through them and voiced to the masses—had an uplifting effect that not even veteran generals like Leeka Alain could duplicate.

That was part of what the towers had been for. From them the three siblings sent messages to one another with mirrors and by raising different colored flags. They also allowed Aliver to communicate with the Santoth, the elevation making it easier for his consciousness to reach out to theirs. But after the last day of battle, when Maeander had focused his catapults on them systematically, the towers had to be abandoned. They had turned into deadly targets. The second day Mena had just escaped being trapped in one by chance. She had been held up as she approached the tower. Instead of being up in it, she watched it being destroyed from just outside the catapult's explosive range.

Aliver himself had been in the last one hit on the third day. He had only just climbed to the top and opened his mind to the Santoth and felt the connection between them uncoil and snap fast. The next moment the soldiers about him all dove for the floor. And then it felt as if the sun had fallen to earth. The roof buckled and slammed down upon him. Flames hurtled in from each opening, buffeting him about like plumes of molten liquid. The world viewed through his eyes went from golden flame to charred blackness and past that to nothing. For a few elongated seconds he swam in the baffling pain of his flesh being scorched from his body. He remembered that he had had a dying thought, but as with something that happens in a dream, he could not recall what it had been. Perhaps he had not even completed the thought before the change happened.

It was quick, the recovery. One moment he was in an incinerator; the next the flames peeled back from his body and seemed to evaporate. The structure, which had been twisting to the ground beneath the weight of impact, found legs. The wood flexed like muscle just awakened. The whole tower groaned with exertion. A second later it was upright. The heat vanished. Aliver's flesh was intact. The men and women all around him rose back to their feet, bewildered.

He had answered their silent questions with what he knew to be the truth. As surprised as he was himself, he projected his words with confidence, as if he was stating something any tutored child would know. Theirs was a blessed cause, he'd said. The Santoth, though they were unseen, protected them. He had already given a speech arguing that they were all part of a mythic present. He reminded them of this and asked them to imagine the song future generations would sing about this army. They been drawn from all the reaches of the Known World and were protected by ancient sorcerers who wanted nothing more than to return to the world of the living and right old wrongs. This was too magnificent an endeavor to fail, he said.

He did not mention that the sorcerers had likely protected him personally—saving others because of their proximity to the prince. Nor did he reveal that they had only managed to do it so dramatically because the connection between them was fresh and new, the moment fortuitously timed. But a partial truth, he had learned, sometimes reached farther than the whole of the thing. He knew that the entire army would know of what happened within a few hours of the event. They would spin another tale of magic and prophecy around him. To them *he* was the magician. It was all his doing, they believed. Though he knew this to be false, he saw that it emboldened them. That, at least, was a worthy thing.

With the towers abandoned, the three siblings walked toward the front ranks of the army. The troops were still forming up, tightening their ranks and marching over the rise and down onto the long slope that led to the field of battle. As they walked a messenger sent by Oubadal found the siblings and uttered a message that Aliver could make no sense of. It had to do with the enemy's deployment, something about them not taking the field. They were close enough to a vantage point that Aliver just brushed past him and strode forward to see for himself. What he saw stunned him.

Before him stretched row after row of his own soldiers, progressing down toward the established point of deployment. But beyond them the field was empty. Bare. A pale and dry expanse, dotted only with occasional shrubs and acacia trees. There was no massed army. Aliver yanked his spyglass from his chest pocket. In the distance the enemy camp sat quietly, dense with shapes and shadows he knew to be people. Fires sent plumes of smoke up here and there, straight lines that only gradually angled to the east. They were there, but they showed not the slightest sign that they intended to fight this day. Had there been a misunderstanding? Was the truce meant to last for more than two days?

"What are those?" Mena asked.

The moment she posed the question Aliver saw them. There *were* a few objects on the field, but at first they barely drew the eye. Compared to the host he had expected to see, these objects required a new focus, so much smaller were they in scale. At least, so they seemed until he studied them more carefully. There were four crates lined across where would have been the front ranks of the enemy army. They were built of wood and reinforced with an outward skeleton of thick metal beams. They stood as tall as two or three men and stretched about a hundred strides in length.

Within a moment or two of study Aliver felt his pulse ramping up toward higher speeds. There were things inside the crates. He could not see what, but he could feel them. He sensed motion inside, felt the bulk of some hidden life-form pressed tight against the cages—yes, they were cages—that held them. He worked his jaw as if in preparation to deliver an order. Nothing came yet.

Dariel said, "How kind of Maeander to leave us presents. A peace offering, perhaps?"

Aliver did not answer.

A half hour later they stood before the front ranks of their army, Oubadal's Halaly warriors closest to them. They were always the first to muster for battle, proud race that they were. Behind them the entirety of their force stood at the ready. They were all in position now, looking like the same colorful array of diverse persons and garish garments that had presented themselves the first day. The crates stood but a hundred strides away. From this distance Aliver could see that a handful of men clustered around each container. Judging by the look of them they were not warriors. They wore simple leather garments of brown from head to toe, drab uniforms that blended with the sandy landscape. Some of them carried pikes with barbs at the ends. These were long, unwieldy weapons, not the type of thing intended for use on humans. Not one of them looked like a person of authority, nor was there any sign even of a Meinish officer, much less Maeander himself.

"Have we a plan?" Dariel asked.

As ever, there was a twist of ironic mirth in the question. Aliver liked this about his brother, but he did not get a chance to answer him. The near side of the four crates opened at the top corner and tilted forward. The handlers tugged them open with ropes. They jumped away as the sides slammed down to the ground, stirring up clouds of dust that billowed around the openings, hiding whatever shadowed inside. The handlers circled around to the sides of the structures. They snatched up their pikes and held them defensively before them.

Aliver swallowed, waited. He could think of nothing else to do, not until he knew what he faced. The clouds drifted away, and there was nothing but the dark geometry of square openings. He felt the held breath of his entire army.

"There," Mena said, "the one at the eastern edge!"

Yes. There was movement. Just a highlight back in the shadows at first, but then a muzzle pressed out into the daylight. A flat snout with two flexing nostrils, it had a swinish character to it, with such a crosshatched confusion of barbed tusks that it was hard to say which belonged to the upper or lower jaw, just that these mouth parts hung higher than a man's head and were longer than an entire boar's body. It came forward slowly, as did the others, Aliver knew, though his eyes stayed fixed on the first.

The creature was massive. The distance did nothing to hide this fact. Its eyes sat close together above its snout, a hunter's gaze, telescoping vision. Its forelegs were swinelike, shoulders joints of muscle and bone like nothing he had seen before. Its upper spine jutted up as if to push through its flesh. Ridges ran down its back toward a rear that sat much lower, with short, stout hind legs, bunched with fibrous bulges. They were a sprinter's legs. It wore a natural armor plated across much of its torso, calloused lumps that looked like enormous warts that been sanded into calcified plates.

Aliver knew what he was looking at. The rumored beast. The weapon a few had named but nobody had reasonably described. An unnatural, garbled form of life, worse, by far, than any laryx. A creature of foul sorcery. He gave orders for the troops to back away. Perhaps there was no need to fight the beasts. They were hundreds of paces away. If the army just backed up and over the rise, quietly, slowly . . .

One of the creatures, the first to emerge, bellowed. The other three answered him. All four of them raised their heads, scented the air. They focused their eyes on the mass of humanity stacked before them on the slope, row after row. The sight excited them. The dun-colored keepers stood to the side and behind them, their pikes at the ready, but the creatures ignored them.

Aliver reissued the order to back away. Such a maneuver was not easily accomplished, though, not with so many people to coordinate. They had barely moved at all when the creatures—the antoks—began to approach them at a trot. The sight of them was enough to panic the army. Soldiers who had fought bravely the days before turned and ran. Some dropped their weapons and tried to climb over others to get away. All three of the Akarans shouted for calm. Aliver reversed the order to retreat and tried to get them to form up, turn around, and face these things with weapons ready. Some took up his call, but not all.

Thus the antoks arrived amid a grand confusion. They barreled right into and through the tight-packed humanity, their cloven feet beat the earth as if it were a skin drum, vibrating with each staccato impact. They squashed people underfoot, knocked them back, raked their jaws from side to side. They snapped people up from the ground and hurled them, bloody and screaming, into the air. The four each cut a different path of destruction. At times they went to their slaughter with such frenzy that they simply followed their nose on a course that could only be random, looking, strangely, like puppies in their boundless enthusiasm. On other occasions they worked together, with focused cunning, schooling their quarry like swordfish slicing through anchovies. They moved in bursts of speed entirely beyond the soldiers' capacity to match or escape. They left scarred paths behind them, jumbled with the shattered bodies of the dead. The soldiers brave enough to face them with weapons drawn could do nothing. Arrows and spears skittered off their armor. Swordsmen could scarcely get within striking range without being trampled.

One of them passed so close to Aliver that spit from its muzzle splattered his face. By the time he had wiped the blood-tainted liquid from his eyes the creature was far away, raging. The prince's gaze fell on a woman just a few strides away from him. She sat upright in a strange, broken-backed position. Her body had been smashed at her pelvis and pressed down into the ground. Tears rimmed her eyes and her lips moved, saying something he could not hear. Her arms tried to make sense of things, the lay of the land and her position in relation to it. The flat of her hands swept across the ground as if smoothing the wrinkles from a sheet. He had seen injuries in the previous days' fighting, but the complete, pathetic frailty betrayed in her smashed form gripped him.

He scanned the field again. Dariel was nowhere in sight. Mena he caught a glimpse of in the distance. She was running, sprinting after one of the creatures, hunting it, though it paid her no mind at all, there being so many bodies to rip apart. In the space of a few minutes the antoks had killed hundreds. They showed no fatigue. No interest in pausing over the dead. No desire to eat, even. They simply wanted to kill. He watched one of the antoks pin a soldier's lower body beneath its hoof. It contemplated the thrashing for a moment and then bit down. It ripped the man in half, shook the torso about as if it were a plaything, and flung it in the air.

Aliver knew he had to do something. The entire throng was gathered here in his name. He could not let them die. He pushed a steadying chant up and tried to hold the thought on his forehead. The Santoth. If he could reach them, they could provide protection. He could explain to them what was happening and they could work their sorcery to shrivel the beasts where they stood. He tried to contact them. Twice he felt his call unfurl from his body like great coils of rope tossed into the air, but both times the connection snapped. It was so hard to focus with shouts of horror buffeting him in waves.

He had just started to try a third time when Kelis shouted for him. "Look," he said, pointing with his chin at something off to the northeast. "Others come."

"What others?"

Following the Talayan's direction, Aliver spotted a company of men nearing the northern edge of the battlefield. His first thought was that it was the enemy coming, though the direction of their approach was not from Maeander's camp nor were they very numerous. In the half second it took him to lift the spyglass to his eye, he considered the tremulous possibility that it was the Santoth already answering their desperate need. He searched the enlarged, jittery view of the world through the spyglass and realized it was neither of those two possibilities.

What approached was a force of perhaps a hundred soldiers. They jogged across the plain directly toward the carnage. They were nearly naked, most of them brown-skinned and short of stature and slight. They carried no banner and wore no colors and were lightly armed with what looked like wooden training swords.

One of the antoks had spotted the arriving soldiers. It peeled away from the swathe of destruction it had been carving and ran at them with a burst of joyous speed. Aliver tried to steady his spyglass. The soldiers, seeing the beast coming, stopped. They spoke among themselves, frantic, debating, their eyes never leaving the antok for long. One of them, taller than the rest, touched something in Aliver. He was familiar in some way, but he could not pause to consider it.

For most of its sprint it looked like the antok would barrel right into the newcomers. But as it neared it slowed, slowed, and then broke its forward motion completely. It slid across the dry soil and skidded to a halt just before them. The soldiers held their wooden swords before them. Each stood still, unflinching, their torsos naked and brown and utterly defenseless. They were absurdly brave, and Aliver twisted with shame at what was about to happen to them.

But it did not happen. The antok did not attack at all. It moved in close to them, sniffed, tilted its head this way and that. It walked some distance along the line of them. It pawed the earth in what looked like confusion, studied them from several angles, found none of them satisfactory. Then it turned and began to trot back toward the main army.

Aliver—thankful, amazed, grateful—could not pull his eyes away from these newcomers. The antok had not touched them. Hadn't harmed a hair on any of them! It had stood inches from their naked chests, before weapons that could not possibly have harmed it, and . . . and . . . what? There was a thought pressing against the back of his consciousness. It was almost painful knowing it was there, feeling the ridge of it trying to break through, something so very important. Something about the newcomers . . .

and also about the handlers still standing beside the cages. . . . It was the reason they were not being attacked.

He jerked his spyglass from the newcomers back to his army. The visual impact of this was all it took. He realized what it was. He only mulled it a moment. That was how long it took for him to become as sure of it as if he had trained the beasts himself. He whispered it to Kelis, and then lifted his voice to shout it to the others.

CHAPTER

SIXTY-TWO

Mena had been pursuing the same antok for what already seemed like hours. There should have been guards beside her every step of the way, but she had bolted so quickly they lost her from the start. She had run across a field with the dead, slipping in their blood, at times tangled in entrails. She'd jumped over bodies and slammed through the screams and pleas of the injured. Drenched in sweat, her legs burning and chest heaving with the effort, she refused to stop. She tried not to hear or see anything but the creature she hunted, knowing that if she did, the horror of it all would be too much.

No matter how she chose her course she never managed to close on her prey. Nor did she know what she would do if she did, except that it involved channeling her anger through the steel edge of her sword. She felt no fear of the creature at all. Her hatred was too complete. Maeben lashed at her from the inside, trying to burst through and rip the beast apart with furious talons, cursing Mena's feeble body: wingless, short legged, slight as it was. This made the princess even more angry.

She stopped long enough only to hear her brother's instructions because a hand clamped on her shoulder. The pincer grip locked the joint to that particular spot in the world. The rest of her body had no choice but to snap to a halt. She spun, ready to lash whomever it was with her tongue. The face that met her was such a mask of creviced and fatigued stoicism—firm, soldierly, entreating, and irrefutable all at once—that her words evaporated.

"Princess," Leeka Alain said, "stop all your running about." A handful of guards clustered behind him, panting and sweat drenched. To her surprise, they used the pause to begin unbuckling their armor vests, tilting off helmets, cutting the orange bicep bands from their arms. The general said,

"Tell me, what people go to war nearly naked, with wooden swords? A brown-skinned, black-haired people?"

The answer was out of her mouth before she had any grasp of why he would ask such a thing. "My people—Vumuans, I mean."

Leeka grunted. "Yes, well, your people have come after you, Princess. Good thing, too, because they've shown Aliver the way."

"The way to what?" Mena asked, distracted. Her eyes lifted and searched out the antok, its ridged back cutting through the masses like a shark's fin jutting out of the sea.

"The way to calm the bloody hogs and then, perhaps, to kill them. To begin with you must strip."

Her attention snapped back to him. "What?"

"Down to the skin."

"Are you serious?"

The old soldier frowned. "It's not that my eyes won't welcome it, Princess, but the order comes from your brother. Strip and follow me. It's a mad idea, but it may be the only way to survive the day. You won't be alone in nakedness."

He took off at a trot, ripping off his mail vest as he went. Mena followed, sheltered within the corps of disrobing soldiers protecting him, watching as the man yanked his undershirt over his head and tossed it away. He undid his sword belt, drew the blade, and let the scabbard fall. She was about to ask him what he could be thinking when he glanced back at her. He explained what had happened while she had been bent on her hunt. As she listened she took in the changing scene around her.

The antoks still rampaged, still sent soldiers fleeing, still tossed shattered bodies into the air, but everyone not directly facing the beasts had found a singular purpose. They were all shedding their clothing. They tore off garments, stamped themselves out of trousers and cut armbands free with daggers. People tossed the fabric from their bodies as if it scorched them with its touch. Only when they stood naked to the world did the army begin to regroup, not as the units they had been sectioned into. Instead they formed large, seething islands of humanity, standing shoulder to shoulder.

If Mena understood what Leeka was saying correctly, Aliver believed that bright colors attracted the animals. The handlers, the Vumuans: neither had been attacked because they wore a color—brown—that the antoks considered neutral. Perhaps it was natural to them, Leeka was saying. Maybe they'd been tamed by brown-skinned people. Or perhaps they had been trained this way so that their handlers did not come under attack. Acacian armies—even this one filled with so many Talayans—had always worn the bright orange of Akaran royalty, making them easy, flaming targets. Whatever the explanation, it was worth trying. Their clothing and armor did not protect them from those tusks and hooves and that fury anyway.

Mena, who had never been ashamed of her body on Vumu, was down to her skin in a few quick motions. As she rebuckled her scabbard she looked at herself. She was brown on the chest, arms, and legs, tanned a rich tone. Her upper thighs and pelvis were lighter. It made her wonder.

"I'm thinking the same thing," Leeka said, studying her. His own naked chest and pelvis were pale from having long been covered. "What I wouldn't give to have been born with Talayan skin right now. But come, let's join the others. They'll shield us."

She understood what he meant a few moments later, when they joined with that amorphous body of humanity, sliding in, skin against skin, sweat lubricating the process. The Talayans of all tribes formed the outer wall. They pulled in the lighter-skinned Acacians and Candovians and Senivalians and Aushenians—anyone whose complexion was not dark brown. These they passed in from hand to hand, shoving them toward the center, shielding them. Mena had to fight to keep herself near the edge so that she could be involved in whatever was to happen. She lost contact with Leeka and his guards. She shouted to identify herself as the princess, smacked soldiers in the back of the head, elbowed, and jabbed.

Soon she had about her a guard of Bethuni soldiers. This helped, but for a frustratingly long period she could not see anything except the towering men around her. Eventually, she stepped upon a rock outcropping that provided her a vantage of the scene all around. The Bethuni pressed against her from all sides to hold her secure. She placed her hands on their shoulders, thanking them with her touch. The rest of her being focused on the scene before her.

The sea of humanity around them had taken on a collective uniformity of coloration. Not one of them bore any of the bright garments that had distinguished them before. Instead, they trod their clothes into the soil beneath their feet. The antoks were all contained within this ocean of people. They still ripped through the crowds, but not in the same way as before. They moved in fits and starts, hesitating, casting around for their next targets. Each time they spotted a swatch of color they surged forward again, as if desperate to pin somebody as the owner of it and punish him accordingly. They ignored persons they could have smashed as they ran down lanes of bodies that peeled open before them. They surged past naked breasts without the slightest interest. It was color that mattered.

One of them scooped up bodies from the ground and whirled them into the air. Another tore into a mound of discarded clothing and shredded the fabric. It spun inside a multicolored whirlwind of its own creation, stamping and fuming. And then it abruptly halted. Swatches of cloth floated down around it, draping its flanks and back and even falling around over its head and snout, snagging on its tusks. It panted, looked about, snuffed, and grunted. It was, Mena could see, confused. It was the lead antok and it bellowed to the others. Each of them answered in turn, a call that echoed the first's frustration and unease. They did not draw any closer together, though. Each had become encircled by brownish, moving walls of humanity whose frailty they did not seem to recognize.

In the hush after the leader's call, Mena realized how quiet the plain was. Thousands of soldiers stood all around the creatures, but nobody talked. Nobody shouted orders. No horns blew. There was a background noise of sorrow in the air, muffled sobs and occasional bursts of agony from the injured, but the silence was such that Mena could hear the antok's footfalls and breathing. She even heard the closest one's joints creak as it walked, slowly now, before the wall of people facing it. The humans were like children beside the huge beast. If it straightened its legs, it could have stepped over them and walked with ample clearance beneath its belly.

Watching it, Mena's eyes found Aliver for the first time. He was not far away, just a way down in the wall of bodies facing her across the space left open for the creatures. He stood only a few strides away from the stiff-jointed antok. He was so like the Talayans in his carriage and musculature that her eyes must have passed over him several times before picking him out. He held the outer line, shoulder to shoulder with the Talayans around him. He was a shade lighter than they, but she could not deny that he, too, was brown. And she could not pretend that he was not in danger.

The beast was but a few of its strides from him. Its gaze focused on one man and then another and then another as it moved along the line, getting nearer to Aliver, searching for any excuse to kill. Its tusks were like the naked blades of so many curved swords. Mena placed a hand on her sword hilt and felt her pulse thrumming in her grip around the leather. She watched the antok step closer to her brother. She wanted to break free and dash toward him. Every muscle and fiber in her cried to leap the distance between them with her sword slicing the air before her. She was near enough that if she launched herself from the shoulders of the man in front of her she would land in the clear, pull her blade free and . . .

Aliver looked at her. His head did not move. His body did not change position in the slightest. But his eyes shifted and focused on her. He drilled his gaze into her, his look heavy with import, telling her something. But she did not know what. She shook her head just slightly. He rolled his eyes back to the antok, stared a moment, and then looked back at her. He repeated this three times. That was all the time he had.

The antok broke the visual contact between them as it moved past Aliver. Mena's eyes bumped along the animal's coarse-haired hide, over its plates and dried skin and wrinkled rump. When it cleared her brother and came into view again, Aliver's attention was only on the beast. By the motion of his body, Mena knew a sound came from his throat. She did not hear it, but she saw his neck flex, his mouth in an oval, as if he had exhaled sharply. The swine swung its mighty head, causing the nearest group of soldiers to billow away, leaning back one on another on another. It doubled back. It closed the space between itself and its taunter, finding renewed interest in the prince. It studied him with a single, bulbous, veined eye, so close to Aliver's face that it could have licked him. It looked up and down Aliver's body.

Aliver gazed right back into the eye. He must have felt the creature's breath on his face. Moisture—sweat and blood and foulness—sprayed him with each exhalation. Aliver stared at it, his visage stony, no emotion on it that she could read. It was just his face as it might look captured in stone. His lips moved again. Whatever he said registered on the faces of the Talayans around her. They all, in single motion, let their eyes drift upward.

What was he doing? Mena wondered. What did he want her to see? He must know something, she thought. How else could he look so calm? So perfectly in control, as if he owned the beast already? As much as she wanted to fly through the air propelled by Maeben's rage, she also felt a lump at her center that housed her love for her brother and her pride and confidence in him, a faith that at that moment verged on hero worship. She knew he could prevail. Could, except that there was something he was trying to tell her that *she* did not understand. She looked all the harder to figure out what it was.

Aliver held the King's Trust in his right hand and his dagger in the other. He must be planning to attack, Mena thought. And if he was planning to attack, he must have found a weakness. She looked at his face and gauged what his eyes were looking at on the far side of the antok. She searched out the same point on the side of the animal facing her. And then she saw it.

Between the plates on the creature's shoulder, an area of hide rose and fell rhythmically. It throbbed. Throbbed. Throbbed. It bulged in a manner that could only mean an artery lay beneath the thick skin. She would never have noticed the spot if the animal had not been standing still. Without taking her eyes away, she leaned close to the nearest Bethuni and spoke into his ear. It took him only a moment to see it also.

She whispered, "Tell the others to watch and do as my brother does."

A moment later she saw Leeka Alain's head jut up above the crowd. He studied the antok for a long moment, then looked at her, nodded, and disappeared back into the crowd. Whispers fanned out from hushed mouth to hushed mouth.

She was not sure how much time passed between that and what happened next. It seemed no more than a few seconds. The animal, losing interest in the prince, began to turn away. Mena watched as Aliver dashed at the antok. He ran two strides and then leaped. He slammed the dagger to the hilt in the tissue of the foreleg and used it as an anchor to swing upward from. The next move was almost delicate, rendered in slowed motion. Aliver, straight armed above the planted dagger, touched the tip of the King's Trust against the artery, and sank half its length home. He released the dagger, grasped the sword blade, and yanked downward. He dropped his full body weight onto the blade. It sliced through the flesh in a descending tear that severed the artery.

The antok snapped around in the direction of the wound, but Aliver kicked away from it, pulling the sword free as he did. He landed on his feet some distance away, out beyond the shower of blood. The pulsing fount sprayed out over the nearest soldiers. They shaded their eyes from the stuff, which looked black and thick as oil. It was a geyser that the beast spun and spun into, getting drenched, seemingly in search of its source.

Aliver stood away from the others, alone and nearest the monster, sword up and drawing circles in the air. The King's Trust looked so very light in his hands, so slim that at times the blade all but disappeared. Aliver talked softly in words that Mena could not make out, waiting for the creature to remember him. Eventually the antok stopped its circular dance and spotted him. It squared off, staring, wobbling and drunken. It blinked rapidly, as if it were trying to clear its head. That was where it was hurt—in the decreased flow of blood to the brain. It blinked and blinked; it seemed to have trouble focusing. It shook its head and snuffed.

Aliver stooped down and peeled a piece of fabric away from the ground. He held it in one hand, snapped it until it flapped loose, spun it so that the unsoiled orange caught the sun. He said something else to the antok. He let the fabric drape over his chest.

This was an invitation the vile thing understood. It roared and ran forward, limping but intent now, looking as fierce as ever. Aliver waited until it was only strides away, and then he flung the fabric up into the air. The antok lifted its head to follow, jaws open, body rearing up. Aliver ducked beneath it. He jabbed his sword into the creature's underbelly and sliced it open from chest to abdomen. He was out from under it by the time it began to collapse, spilling its insides around it in a flood of viscera.

CHAPTER

SIXTY-THREE

It had not been particularly hard to get into the palace, although—as with the clue about *The Song of Elenet* that drove him here—Thaddeus had learned how only because of something Dariel had casually uttered. One evening shortly after he had joined Aliver in Talay, the younger prince had spoken about how he had come to meet Val of the Verspines, the raider who became his surrogate father. He had detailed what he could remember of the subterranean regions of the palace. Much of what he described was rendered in vague terms. Where he did have details, they sounded skewed by childish imaginative flourishes, filled with eccentric characters who inhabited labyrinthine tunnels that, by the sound of it, looped out through miles unimagined by the palace dwellers above.

But Dariel was both specific and credible about the time he had almost been swept out to sea. It was a memory not blurred by the passage of time. There was a platform just above the water level, he said, at the northern edge of the island near the Temple of Vada. It was a small flat area cut into the rock for some long-ago purpose. Just above it, set at an angle into the stone that probably made it hard to see from the water, was an entry point. The passageway it opened into led upward through hidden regions that wormed all the way into the palace, even as far as the nursery chambers.

Thaddeus committed the description of the entry point to memory. After departing without ceremony from Aliver's camp he marched his old man's body north a few days. Then he angled off to the west to avoid Maeander's massing army. Arriving at a port town on the coast, he bought the smallest sloop he could imagine risking the seas in. He sailed at sunset that very same day. The wind was with him for most of the night journey, and the graying light of predawn found him bobbing in the waves near the temple, just out from the rocks that marked Acacia's northern coastline.

He searched for as long as he dared in the coming light. Eventually, he committed himself to making landfall. Knowing he could not leave the boat to be discovered, he set its sail to angle out to sea, jumped overboard, and watched it slip away on the breeze. He swam for the rocks and clawed his way back, for the first time in many years, onto the island of Acacia.

It still took him longer than he wished to locate the entry point. By the time he did he was awash with sweat, breathing heavily, and fearful lest he be in the midst of yet another great folly. He thanked the Giver profusely when he found the slit in the stone. He slipped out of the light into environs that were, in fact, every bit as forlorn and eerie as Dariel had described.

For all the risky faith of the journey he was amazed at the ease with which he climbed up into the palace. He was slipping through the halls so suddenly that he was not actually prepared for it. It was hard not to step out into the center of the familiar corridors and walk as if he still belonged within them. He stopped himself. He had to be careful, especially now. He withdrew and kept to the shadows throughout the daylight hours. He could not always tell the abandoned corridors from the passageways still used by servants, but he placed himself at cracks in the walls through which he could see and hear the goings-on of the palace. It amazed him to think somebody could navigate unseen this way. He wondered if anybody had during his tenure here.

He knew the answer as soon as he formed the question. His skin crawled with the certainty of it; of course he had been spied on before. The leaguemen: if anybody used these corridors it would have been them. Weren't they known for their nearly clairvoyant anticipation of coming events, decrees, opinions? Perhaps they still used these regions to observe Hanish as well. Thaddeus redoubled his efforts at secrecy, only moving at all so as to place himself where he could observe the pattern of Meinish palace life.

What struck him was that there was no pattern to it. The place hummed with disarray. There was a bustling energy in the staff and servants, an undercurrent of excited confusion that had a singular quality, as if it marked the approach of an unprecedented event. His command of the Meinish language was tolerable. From snatches of conversation, he pieced together that Hanish had been away from the island but was soon returning. As night settled down on the palace, he decided that this accounted for the level of excitement. It did not feel quite complete, but he wasn't here as a spy.

His mission was a singular one. If what he had finally figured out from clues that had lived within him for nine years was correct, *The Song of Elenet* had resided in Leodan's library all along. It had, in a way, never been lost. And *if* the room had not been disturbed, the volume would still be sitting in the same place it likely had for decades. All he had to do was get to the library unseen, find the book, and then extricate himself from the palace and the island, still unseen.

In the still hours of that night, Thaddeus crept toward the library, half focused on his stealth, half reliving the distant moments that had planted the clues that had led him here. It pained him now to recall that last exchange with Leodan. It had pained him every day and night since, but now he understood it differently from the way he had before. When he remembered Leodan's face gazing at him, he was no longer sure that the dying man was recalling the life they had shared together. He was not even sure if Leodan had been looking at him with love or with mistrust or hatred. He wasn't sure of any of this because Leodan had spoken to him in code. He had specifically *not* told him where the book was. He had not entrusted it entirely to him or to the children, who would have been too young to know what to do with it. Instead, he had placed the clues to its location between them. Clearly there for them to see once they were ready to see it, once they really needed to see it.

Leodan had written: *Tell the children their story is only half written. Tell them to write the rest and place it beside the greatest story. Tell them. Their story stands beside the greatest tale ever told.* It was as simple as that. He had told Thaddeus that the children's story should be beside "the greatest story," and he had told the children that the greatest story was that of the Two Brothers. Put them together and the answer was obvious. *Their* story was not just the story of their lives. It was not even just the history of the Akaran line. It was a longer narrative of human folly. It was the tale of how humans had learned to become gods, to control language, how they had angered the divine, enslaved the Giver's creatures, and secured their dominion over the world. It was the story of Elenet's betrayal.

The library door made far too much noise in opening. The hinges creaked from disuse. The smell was just as he remembered, dusty and heavy with mildew, oily with the scent of sandalwood. The moon cast its white light through the large windows, several of which were open enough to let in a breath of night air. Thaddeus navigated beneath the moonlight. He knew his way through the tall stacks of books by heart, and he found the book exactly where he thought he would. The ease of it amazed him. The book *The Two Brothers* was just where it was supposed to be, and beside it was the plain spine of an ancient volume. He knew the instant he cracked it open that it was the book he sought.

It was *The Song of Elenet*, the dictionary written in the first sorcerer's own hand. His eyes, drifting over the cover, found nothing on it that named it explicitly. Its cover was plain worn leather. It had a utilitarian look to it, as if it might be a record book for a minor government official. Flipping it open, nothing in the appearance of the lettering or the opening headings suggested the import of the contents. It seemed crucial that he read enough to prove he was not mistaken. Just enough to confirm that he had the right book. He sat down with it in one of the window bays and leafed through it, feeling a breath of stale air brush his face with each passing leaf.

Each page prompted him to turn to the next, but not because of what he read. He turned pages because he *could not*, in any real sense, read it. He found his mind could not hold the words for any longer than the second his eyes took to pass over them. He was reading, and yet he wasn't. There before him was a page full of script, and then another, and another. Plain letters and words, written in an innocuous hand on paper that showed its age in its coarseness. It was a page like any other, filled with words he almost recognized. But try as he might he could not comprehend even a single sentence of what he read. He could not hold a phrase, a thought, an impression even, of what was right there before him. He lost himself in the effort of it, flipping page after page, always feeling he was on the verge of cracking its meaning. He lost himself in the attempt, without realizing how much time was passing.

Eventually, infuriated, he hissed, "What good is such a thing?"

The sound of his voice jolted him. He looked around the library, watched dust float in the air, listened to the silence, and searched for any sign that he might have been heard or seen. The chamber was still and empty, but he realized that it was not night anymore. It wasn't even early morning. The full light of a clear day cascaded through the windows. Hours had passed while he sat with his head in the book. He had been so preoccupied someone could have walked in and tapped him on the shoulder. He could hear voices in the courtyard outside, the click of shoes passing in the hallway, a grinding sound as somebody moved a heavy piece of furniture in a nearby room.

And then he felt the weight of the book, as if it consciously pressed against his thighs, taunting him to try again. He snapped it closed. He was not, of course, meant to read it. He had not intended to try. It could only be understood with close study, and should only ever be examined by one who would commit his life to learning it, to accepting the magnitude of what such knowledge entailed. Thaddeus was not that person. He jammed the volume under his arm and moved for the door. He was very tired, dull with hunger. It would take all his strength to get out of this place alive.

As he approached the door, a voice flew through the opened window just to his left. A woman's voice, calling to someone. He did not hear the spoken words clearly, but something about them hooked him with a curiosity to see who had spoken and to whom. He stepped closer, craned his neck to see. The view spread out before him slowly, each portion of it taking his breath away with its grandeur.

A group of three women stood with their backs to him. One of them motioned across the courtyard at another young woman. This one seemed to have been stopped in her progress. She hesitated a moment, then turned and proceeded toward the others. Watching her draw nearer, Thaddeus realized who she was. Corinn. It was Corinn. Bits and pieces of Leodan and Aleera were there on display, as were various shadings of resemblance to Aliver and Mena and Dariel. She carried all their traits with a grace beyond any of them. Her posture was upright in a courtly manner, her waist slim, breasts and shoulders snug within a sky-blue dress. She was a part of Acacia's splendor, he saw, in a way he no longer imagined the other siblings could be.

Having thought this, though, he knew it was only partly right. She belonged here but not like this. Not as a prisoner; not as mistress to Hanish Mein; not as a living, forced betrayal of all that she held dear. He could see all of this on her face as she spoke with the other women. She was stunning, but that did not hide the misery residing just below the surface. Her face had about it a brittle aura, a crystalline fragility. She looked as if she could explode into a thousand pieces at any moment.

Thaddeus surveyed her for as long as she stayed in the courtyard. It was the second time he forgot his need for stealth. He viewed her and her surroundings from various windows, learning all he could from what he observed. It did not take long to confirm that she was under close surveillance. People spying on one person may hide their actions well from that person, but they are often as obvious as the sun to others. Guards watched her covertly. Passing officials viewed her with sidelong glances. A servant walked into and out of view several times, holding a basket that she neither dropped off nor added to. In all of this Thaddeus observed hidden signs of her captivity. Because of it, he decided to rescue her.

This thought had already crossed Thaddeus's mind. He had rolled it over as he marched across northern Talay. He had dismissed it, though. Everything depended on his retrieving the book, and rescuing the princess added layer upon layer of complexity to the mission. It provided many more opportunities to fail. And he could not fail. He had even gone so far as to imagine conversations with Hanish in which the still-captive Corinn was used as a bargaining point. He doubted Hanish would hurt her. Not after having kept her alive and in health for so long, not after lying night after night in the same bed with her. She'd be safe enough, he had thought, until the conflict reached its conclusion.

But that was before, when Corinn had been but a notion, a phantom he thought of daily but had not laid eyes on in nine years. How different he felt now that he saw her. If he managed to escape this island with both *The Song of Elenet* and with Princess Corinn, he would have made great strides toward redeeming his earlier sins. All the children would be safe. The future of the world would lie in their capable hands. The fact that he might be able to make this happen meant that he had to try. Of course he did.

CHAPTER

SIXTY-FOUR

Maeander had watched it all from a platform set up beside his tent back in the Meinish camp. He had his own seeing aid, two spy-glasses strapped together to bring the distant scenes into binocular view. He had hummed as the Acacians marched down the slope in battle formation. He had smiled at their hesitation as they spotted the antok cages. He had imagined the bewildered expressions on their faces and laughed out loud in occasional, quick guffaws that startled the men around him.

Still, the destruction the beasts caused when unleashed stunned him. He thought he knew what to expect. Over the years since the league had brought antok pups as gifts from the Lothan Aklun, he personally checked on the training the creatures received. He watched them grow from the size of suckling pigs. He had instructed the trainers to prepare them for some moment like this. They taught them to hate all color, infused them with fear of visual variation. Through long months of work they forced them to equate orange and red, purple and green and blue with pain, with suffering. And they had taught them that the only way to answer such things was through fury. For the most part this had not been difficult. Fury was in their nature from the moment they kicked their belligerent ways out of their mothers' wombs.

But what he watched during those first few hours went beyond his imaginings. With a view of the entire field, he saw the way the four mon-sters worked in loose coordination. They plowed through the dense concen-trations of troops, but not with the random abandon the Acacians must have perceived. They also looped out to the edges, pulling in the fleeing, herding them back, controlling the entirety of the frenzy. Amazed, Maeander real-ized that the trainers hadn't lied about their potential; the Lothan Aklun tales about these creatures were true. He was, he believed, going to watch them slaughter every last one of the Acacians and their allies. They would not stop until every scrap of moving color was squashed or shredded. He had felt, mixed in with the euphoria, a pulsing dread of the foreigners from across the Gray Slopes. If they gave weapons such as these away, what sort of powers did they keep for themselves?

This thought was cut short before it went too far. The small band of strangers arrived, Vumuans he soon learned. He knew exactly why the antok did not destroy them, but he did not anticipate that in all the confusion of battle the Acacians would be able to put together the clues themselves. He cursed when he saw them stripping off their clothes. He wanted to shout for them to stop. That won't save you! Die with bravery, not with back-sides exposed to the world! And yet he watched as they slowly brought the beasts under control, surrounded them, hemmed them in with walls made of their very flesh. Each and every one of them stood naked and vulnerable, their hearts exposed. By no other means than that they calmed the antoks' savagery. He would never have imagined such a thing.

Nor could he believe his eyes as he watched Aliver find a way to kill the antoks. There he was, naked as the day he was born and looking much like the Talayans around him, wielding only two lengths of steel in a show of bravery that would have made Maeander himself proud. He could not see every detail precisely, but he saw Aliver leap on the beast's side. He saw it charge Aliver a few moments later and could tell that when the creature collapsed whatever wound had dropped it had been fatal. The others of Aliver's army simply followed his example, with variations. Within a half hour all four of the antoks lay dead. Triumphant Talayans climbed on them and danced their jubilation.

The generals who sat in council with him that evening sought to highlight the gains they had made. The Acacians would not be able to field an army the following day. The officers estimated the enemy had lost more than fifteen thousand souls to the antoks in the short space of time they had rampaged. It was a phenomenal number. About a quarter of their entire force. Also, there had been no sign of sorcery on the field. No outside force aided them. Perhaps the one who had been working magic for them had perished before the antoks. Or perhaps he had had only so much of the witchcraft at his disposal. It may have been used up, just as anything else can be used up.

"Aliver has delayed his defeat," one general said, "but we'll be ready to finish this now. We should march on them in full force in the morning.

Overrun them. Even if they don't take the field. Let us slaughter them in their camps and lay them beside their unburied dead."

Several murmured agreement. Another, filling the silence where Maeander's response should have been, said, "Remember, we lost not a single soldier today. Not one. Not even Hanish could have done better."

But such things were cold comfort to Maeander. This time it was he, not his advisers, who saw the gains the enemy had made despite what looked like defeat. The tale of Aliver killing the first antok himself would course across the land with the speed of a contagion. It would make the prince a legend of gigantic proportions and stir the land into an even greater frenzy.

He got word of two other disturbing developments that night. The league-controlled vessels all along the coast had withdrawn. They gave no explanation and refused all efforts at dialogue offered by the few Meinish captains in control of their own boats. There was treachery in this, but it went as yet unexplained. It meant, of course, that Maeander could not evacuate his forces if they were driven up against the sea. Though he did not voice it aloud to anyone, he wondered if this was not his brother's doing, a chastisement, a challenge. It did not make any sense, but that did not stop the thought from spinning about inside his head like a wheel in perpetual motion.

Even later that evening, sitting alone in his tent, his gaze fixed on the motionless flame of the oil lamp on his table, a messenger brought him another piece of correspondence. It was a letter from his brother, sent across the sea pinned to a messenger bird. It mentioned nothing about the league—perhaps Hanish had not yet heard what happened. Instead, he wrote with enthusiasm, reporting that he had already sailed from the Mainland. The Tunishnevre were with him. All of them. They were undamaged by the journey and writhing with life. They were bursting to be free. He would have them safely within the new chamber on Acacia within a few days' time. And then he'd free them.

And then, Maeander thought, you'll have completed your life's work. And I—I'll have done nothing more than helped secure your fame.

The thought filled him with despondency. Fast behind this came an old memory from when he was eleven years old and Hanish had just turned thirteen. Their father was still alive then, vocally proud of them both. In honor of Hanish's birthday, Heberen had arranged for them to dance a Maseret before a revered group of veterans in the Calathrock. It was to be one of Hanish's last duels as a novice—the last time it would not be a fight to the death. They used real knives, but they wore their thalbas over chainmail vests. Spots on their chests marked their heart points. This was the target they were each to aim for to end the contest.

They were both lithe and strong, their bodies growing in exuberant bursts. Maeander was nearly Hanish's height and strength and had suspected for some time that his skills at the dance surpassed his brother's. On this occasion, before the roomful of elders, he could not help but push Hanish to the edge. He had not planned to do it. It just happened. Pride billowed in him and drove his actions. He moved faster than he had previously, with unexpected shifts in tempo. He marveled at how composed his brother's face remained; even more impressive and annoying because Maeander felt the strain he was causing him. He did not attempt to win the duel. That would have been too overt an insult. But he did want to make sure the elders saw him, and so he drew Hanish's blood. He nicked his left nostril with a backhanded maneuver, looking up at the crowd as he did so. A few moves later he let Hanish touch his heart point. He left the arena satisfied with himself. A face cut was not considered important in the rules of the dance nor was it a serious injury. But it would leave a lasting scar. He was pleased about this.

That night, however, he was yanked from his dreams. He awoke to instant fear. He felt a living weight pressed down against his back. Someone clenched his hair and wrenched back his head. The flat edge of a knife blade touched his skin, angled just enough that he could sense the edge of it tasting his flesh.

And then Hanish's voice spoke from close to his ear, cold and precise. One way or another, he said, Maeander would never humiliate him again. "Don't deny that you didn't mean to! Everybody with eyes saw it. I felt it. You would have me know that you are my better. You wish me to fear you, don't you? But I don't fear you. It's my knife at your neck, brother. It always has been and always will be. I could kill you right here, right now, if I wished to."

Maeander did not doubt him. His brother might have spoken with the Giver's voice, so complete was his assurance. Hanish told him that he had a choice to make. He could die right there—with no accomplishments to his name—or he could agree to help him change the world. "Swear to the ancestors that you'll never work against me. Swear that you'll always obey me. Swear it to them and I'll let you live. Otherwise you die right here, right now. Nobody will question me for it. You know that."

The answer poured out of Maeander to his lasting shame. Perhaps the one thing that had kept him true to the oath he swore that night *was* how much it shamed him. Faced with death, he balked. He lay there paralyzed with fear, horrified that he might miss out on the life of glory he so vividly imagined. It was, he knew, a moment of unforgivable weakness. Hanish had pressed him up against the only real thing a Meinish male could be made to fear—a death before having achieved greatness. Ironically, by the Meinish code, he should still have hissed defiance back at Hanish. He should have accepted that worst of fates with smiling indifference. He did not.

That fact would have been an unbearable disgrace, except for what Hanish did next. Having heard the pledge muttered, Hanish's weight went limp on top of him. His breathing came in gasps. After a few mystified moments, Maeander realized his older brother was crying, bawling from someplace so deep within him that each sob wrenched upward from his gut. Maeander did not move, did not even mention that Hanish still held the blade to his throat. They had never spoken of that night since, though Maeander remembered it almost every day.

And now . . . now Hanish was on the verge of his greatest triumph. Maeander, by comparison, had failed. That was what it amounted to. He had failed. It did not mean defeat for his people. Nothing Aliver could do would stop Hanish from completing the ceremony to release the Tunishnevre. When the ancestors walked the earth again, they would be an invincible force. All the tricks and ploys and strategies he and his brother had devised would be nothing compared to the fury they would unleash. So by holding Aliver's army in northern Talay he had aided his brother's complete victory. That was fine enough. But that was not the point. The point was that Maeander Mein would have no true place of glory in the story anymore. Who would remember him? Who would sing of Maeander after Hanish accomplished the one thing his people had yearned for for more than twenty-two generations? It felt as if Hanish had never removed the blade from his throat.

Facing this, Maeander decided that there was only one honorable way left for him to redeem himself. He sent messengers to his generals, informing them that they would be launching a delayed assault in the morning. He had something in mind to open the day. He would not live through it, but that did not matter. If he joined the Tunishnevre now he would be unleashed with them in the days to come. He would be one of the Tunishnevre, one of the ancestors his brother must revere. Anyway, he had been too long without looking the enemy in the face. Even Hanish had never done that. And if he accomplished what he hoped to, Hanish would never be able to take it from him.

None of what he thought or planned was even remotely evident on his face or in his demeanor the next morning. He set out from camp at the vanguard of his personal force, just a handful of Punisari striding through the slant of the rising sun, all of them taller than the norm, their burned faces like stonework chiseled to match their musculature and bearing. Each of them had straw-blond hair down below their shoulders; a few wore the traditional knotted locks to remind them of the years their ancestors roamed the wilds in exile; all knew to what work they went and none showed the slightest sign of hesitation. Maeander had drawn together each of the three braids that, with their weave of colored ribbons, numbered the men he had killed with his own blade. His torso was wrapped in a gray thalba. The only weapon on his person was the Ilhach dagger secured horizontally across his abdomen.

So accompanied and armed, Maeander approached the Acacian camp across the scarred desolation that was the previous days' battlefield. He carried a banner that indicated the desire to parlay, and he wore a façade of composed, smiling humility.

CHAPTER

SIXTY-FIVE

The paper swan was waiting just inside the portal. Somebody must have shoved it underneath the door. Just how this was accomplished was not clear, considering the object's placement, the way it stood upright several inches from the crack beneath the door, a space not as tall as the stylized, geometric creature that must have passed beneath it. Also, there was a note beside it. Just a ribbon of paper so thin it was hard to pick up. Corinn did so carefully, pinching it between two fingernails. *Accept this gift*, she read, *in the event that you need it*.

It was unsigned, but Corinn knew who had sent it. How Sire Dagon's agents had gotten past the outer guards she could not guess, and the feeling that perhaps they had actually been inside her room while she slept made her skin tingle. She held the swan to her nose and sniffed, carefully. No scent at all. Squeezing the paper between her fingers, she could feel the coarse texture of crystals inside it. She knew that the grains were distilled from the roots of a wildflower by a process known only to the league. They made from it a lethal poison, one that could not be tasted or smelled or detected afterward. She thought to look at the note again, but it had crumbled and flaked away. Nothing remained of it but a residue on her fingers and a few traces on the floor. The breath of air underneath the door was dispersing these already.

She was in her old room, where she sometimes spent the night when Hanish was away. It provided her greater privacy, and she had begun to need solitude more and more of late as she sought to master the swirl of thoughts inside her. She had awoken that morning believing that the next few days were going to change the course of her life completely. This swan message reinforced this belief. It was a small, silent, potent confirmation that forces at play in the world were moving in league with her. Knowing better than to handle it too much, she pressed the bird's wings flat and slipped it under her belt.

She turned and walked back toward her dressing area, where she had been before noticing the swan. She sat on the stool at her makeup table, an array of mirrors reflecting variations of her image back at her. She intended to plan out the events to come, but she paused for a moment, looking into the mirrors. As she did often lately, she felt queasy. Each of the views of her face showed a different character. Depending on the angle, she looked miserable or stunning, delicate or agitated or self-assured or . . . wicked. Yes, viewed in near profile, from the left, she could not help but acknowledge a previously unnoticed cruelness in the tilt of her eyes and her mouth and in the manner with which she held her chin, as if it were a weapon protruding in warning. She hated what she saw there. Or sometimes she did. At other times she hated what she saw from the other angles instead. Which of these faces should she present to Hanish on his return?

Hanish was scheduled to arrive the next day. He would be sailing at the vanguard of a fleet of vessels bringing his fabled ancestors to the island. He had sent her a letter just the day before, filled with his enthusiasm, alluding to his plans for getting the ancestors into the newly constructed chamber as quickly as possible. He spoke of his joy at seeing ships loaded with the sarcophagi. What a wondrous sight, he had written. As if she would feel the same! He reminded her how much he hoped she would stay true to her promise to help him free them to their eternal rest. Once she did so, the rift that had scarred the Known World for centuries would finally be mended. Meins and Acacians would have a new chance to assuage their old animosities. The land, he promised, could finally start to heal. This was what his war had always been about. It was a long battle, an epic journey, but the end was near. He wrote: *You, Corinn, will help to make it all possible. My people and yours will both revere you for it. And I will revere you for it.*

"He knows nothing of what's inside me," Corinn said to the silent room around her. There was a time when the truth of this statement would have pained her. Now, however, everything she had planned hinged on it. Hanish thought he could play her for the world's greatest fool; she, however, was resolved never to let that happen. "He knows nothing of what's inside me."

"No," a voice said gently in answer, "no man does. No man ever could."

Corinn snapped to her feet, spun around, and searched for the source of the voice. She saw nothing at first. The room was empty, crowded only with her family objects, safe beneath the pastoral murals on the ceiling, the

walls softened by hangings dyed various colors. A man split the border between two wall tapestries and stepped into view. He was but a few strides
away. His nearness, the concreteness of his presence was so shocking, her
breath caught in her throat.

"Have no fear," the man said. "Please, Princess, don't call out. I'm here
to help you. I serve your brother, and I serve you."

She recognized him after only a few words. Thaddeus, the chancellor.
Her father's closest friend. His betrayer. By the Giver, he was old! His face
was creviced, his cheeks sunken, his frame stooped. He looked so very fatigued, bags beneath his eyes, unsteady on his feet, swaying slightly, carrying a book cradled against his chest. Somehow she managed to speak
through her surprise, asking the first thing that came to mind. "How did
you get in here?"

Thaddeus asked if he could sit. He spoke softly, casting his words
with a deadened lack of inflection. "I will happily tell you everything,
Princess Cor—"

"You are in my room?" Corinn asked, growing more incredulous as the
impossibility of it took hold of her. "How can you possibly be in my room?"

"Please, may I sit? If I don't, I may well collapse. And . . . please, can you
make sure we will not be disturbed? I cannot be discovered. I'll explain
why."

Corinn stared at him. She knew she had to think quickly. Visitations
such as this had an import she could not mistake. She could not stumble,
for whatever brought this man out of the past and into her room simply
could not be ignored or squandered. And he certainly did not look to be any
physical threat to her. However he got here and whatever brought him and
no matter how she was going to deal with it, she should listen to him, and
she should do so alone. She whispered, "Wait here."

She stepped into the hall and informed her servants that she did not
wish to be disturbed for any reason. She had guards placed at the outer
doors to her chambers, and she moved Thaddeus into the sheltered alcove
just inside the balcony. There she had him sit in a high-backed chair as she
paced in front of him. He told her everything. He explained how he had gotten into the palace and how he navigated the secret passages inside the
walls. It took him hours upon hours to get into her room, but he had eventually found a low tunnel that opened in the corner behind her bed. She
would be amazed to know that it was there all along, hidden by a simple
trick in the architecture. But he was not starting at the beginning. . . .

Aliver had sent him, he said, and then he launched into a breathless, earnest description of the man her brother had matured into. How he'd grown to fulfill, to exceed, anything Leodan might have imagined for him! He had a grand vision. He had a gift for moving masses. He was fired with urgency and purpose. He spoke of Mena and Dariel also, the sword-wielding priestess and the daring sea raider. Together they were engaged in a battle they could not lose. Aliver had inflamed the people with a belief that their fates were in their hands. He, when victorious, would not rule *over* them. He'd rule *for* them. By their permission and only in their interests. He'd wipe away all the hidden foulness that drove the Known World and find new ways to prosper. He'd build trust among nations, ennoble the downtrodden, break the spine of the league, do away with the Quota, abolish conscripted labor.

The old chancellor went on and on. Corinn listened, realizing that she was supposed to be suffused with relief, with joy, with anticipation. She tried to feel these things. The more he spoke, though, the more it all seemed to Corinn like mad ranting. Pure fancy. The stuff of children's tales. A fantasy in which she did not feel she had any part. How could he believe any of these things could come to pass? She had heard some of this story before, from Rhrenna and Rialus. She had gleaned still more from overheard conversations. But it seemed less believable than ever now that this man actually sat before her in his aging flesh. He spoke like a newly converted disciple, worshipping a prophet of—of what? Equality? Liberation? It sounded like Aliver planned on building an empire in the sky, some idyllic kingdom that would float on clouds. Such a thing would vanish like the clouds, she wanted to say, blown away by the first strong breeze. She flared inside with a surprising degree of bitterness, but she made sure not to show it.

A golden monkey appeared on the balcony. It must have jumped from someplace high above, and it seemed startled to find them in the shaded alcove. It called out in a high, birdlike chirp. It was brilliantly colored against the blue background of the sky. Corinn turned her back to it.

"Hanish is returning tomorrow. He is bringing the Tunishnevre with him. He wants me to help him perform the ceremony that will end the curse. He says when this is done, much of the rift between Meins and Acacians will be healed. It will be history, he says. Not the present or the future anymore. What do you think of that?"

"He is bringing the Tunishnevre here?" Thaddeus asked. He sat in silence for a time, mouth hanging open, eyes glazed. "I should have known that. Of course he is. . . . He's had the time to prepare a chamber here. He sent his brother to fight Aliver, not because he did not take the threat seriously, but because he had a greater purpose for himself. He has had you safely here all along. . . . I should have foreseen this. We have looked back into our own myths for allies; why would Hanish not do the same?"

He looked up at Corinn, his old, veined eyes fixed on her face. "You asked me what I think of it? I think Hanish is lying. The lore says that there are two ways to end the curse on the Tunishnevre. He could free them with a gift of your blood, a forgiveness offering. But that is not what he intends. If he takes your life from you unwillingly and slays you on the altar, then he will wake his ancestors, not free them to death. He will bring them back to life. They will get their bodies back and walk the earth again, Corinn. They will be incredibly powerful and vengeful in a way that has no bounds. If that happens, we have lost for good. This is why you must come with me."

"Is that why you came here," Corinn asked, "to rescue me?"

"I came for another reason," the former chancellor said. He told her about the Santoth and the corruption of their knowledge and about the great, great need for *The Song of Elenet*. He had found it, he explained, because he finally put together the clues that Leodan had left for them. Aliver did not yet know of his success. He did not even know he had come here. He needed to get the book to him as quickly as possible, but now it was just as important that she flee the island with him. It would be risky, but if they escaped via the route he had come into the palace, they would emerge not far from the Temple of Vada. He could cross to the temple and, he was sure, he could convince the priests to give him some small vessel. He would return and pick her up and then they would fly with the wind. Perhaps he could even send word to Aliver from the temple, so that he could act accordingly.

Corinn kept her face blank. She did not want to address this notion of flight yet. "Is that book *The Song of Elenet*?" she asked, pointing to the volume sitting on the man's thighs. It did not look like much, really, but she noticed that he had never taken his hand from atop its cover, as if he feared something might befall it even here, with just the two of them in the alcove.

Guardedly, he nodded.

She stretched out her hands toward it.

"Princess, we don't have much time," Thaddeus said. "I gather Hanish is to return tomorrow. We must—"

"Let me see the book," she said, keeping her eyes focused on the chancellor's and making sure her words had the ring of command to them. She was sure that if she had not been looking at him so intently he might have refused, delayed somehow, thought of an excuse, or changed the subject. He opened his mouth to say something, but before he could she pulled the book from his grasp and moved away a few steps.

The book was much lighter than it looked. It opened with the slightest pull of her fingers. From the moment she looked upon its contents she knew for a certainty that nothing in her life would ever be the same. The page was full of script, curling, looping, dancing words. They moved before her eyes, growing and changing as she watched, becoming one word and then another, written in a foreign, beautiful language. The words she read struck her like notes ringing in her soul. She did not know what they meant, but as her eyes touched them, they rose off the page and filled her with song. They welcomed her. They praised her. They danced in the air around her like exotic birds. They assured her that they had been waiting for her. Waiting for her. Now everything would be all right. She, she, she could make it all all right. They rubbed the entirety of her being with the sensuous, humming intensity of a hungry housecat. She could not explain how she knew or heard or understood any of these sensations or declarations or promises at that moment. But the messages and the sublime radiance of the voices that spoke them were undeniable. This book was, without doubt, the very gift she had waited her entire life to receive.

When she folded it closed and the room returned to normal and she could again focus on Thaddeus, she already understood things she had not before. She already saw with clarity what had to be done. "This is wonderful," she said, meaning it completely. "Tell me the truth—does anybody know of this book? That you have it and that it is here, with me?"

"No, you need not fear that. Only you and I know. By the look on your face . . . You—you saw something in it?"

She smiled warmly but did not answer him. "You have done a great thing. My father was right to love you."

Whatever his doubts, this assertion brushed them away. His old eyes instantly brimmed with moisture. "Thank you," Thaddeus said. "Thank you for saying so. You can forgive me, then?" Corinn said she did not know what he meant. What had she to forgive? She could only thank him. This caused a tear to drop from one of his eyes, which he wiped off his cheek. He fell into another discourse. A stream of words tumbled from his tongue, a whole explanation of what and why he had done it, how he had regretted and prayed and worked to see things put right.

Corinn did not listen to much of it, but she did look at him, nodding, her eyes open and large. Before he finished, his fatigue started to overcome him. His gestures grew sloppier. His words blurred at the edges. When he blinked, his eyelids fought his efforts to reopen them. She sat there only long enough to decide what she was about to do, and then she interrupted him.

"Enough, Thaddeus," she said. "I see no stain on you. Understand?" She reached forward and touched her hand gently to his chin. "You are unblemished. We need say no more about it. I'll get you something to eat and drink. Rest here. When I return we'll figure out what to do and how to do it."

Sensing that he might protest, she pressed *The Song of Elenet* back against his chest. This seemed to ease him. A moment later, after having stepped out of her barred door and sent a servant for tea and light fare, Corinn stood alone, trembling and hushed. The memory of the song was already bittersweet. She so loved it. It had made life seem a blessed thing, right and good. With the song anything would be possible. She already hungered to go back and open the book again. She knew that learning the language it spoke would not be easy. It would require months or years of focused study. The book had somehow conveyed this to her. It would give her so much, but only if she created the opportunity to study it quietly, perhaps secretly. Why had her father—and the generations before him—ignored the *Song*, hidden it away? Such folly. She would not make that mistake.

If she was to do what she was coming to believe she must, there were so many things to see to and so little time to complete them in. The challenges still before her had to be met with her wits alone, with the cunning she already possessed, building on things she had already set in motion. She would have to think every step of it through, cleaning every possible mistake away ahead of time. She had to turn over everything Thaddeus had said about Aliver's intentions in her mind so that she understood it all and knew how best to face it. She would have to pen a note to Rialus and find a way to send it via messenger bird. That would not be easy, but she had to manage it only once. She would need to explore these passageways in the walls. And she'd have to take care of Thaddeus first.

When the servant returned, Corinn took the tray from her and said she still did not wish to be disturbed for any reason. She watched the young woman, an Acacian, depart, closing the door behind her. Corinn set the tray down. She slipped her fingers into her belt and pulled out the folded paper bird. With a tap of her finger it took on its swanlike shape. She squeezed the ends of it between her fingers, tilted, and watched as a fine powder fell sparkling into the tea. She hoped it was as odorless and tasteless as the league chemists claimed. She realized that in some portion of her consciousness she had already planned on using this poison on Hanish. As she watched the tiny grains dissolve, she put that from her mind. She would find another way to deal with him. How fortuitous that the package arrived today, just before the chancellor stepped out of the wall. Another sign this was meant to be, meant to happen this way.

She picked up a silver spoon and stirred the liquid in slow circles. She felt no anger at him. The betrayal that he seemed so troubled by did not even register in her thoughts. No, it was not an emotional decision at all. It was simple. Thaddeus had brought her the very thing she had been searching for, without her ever knowing that she had been searching for it. She knew, as if from some ancestral memory newly discovered and stirred to life, that she was meant to have that book. She was *meant* to. That was why Thaddeus had brought it to her instead of taking it to Aliver. He did not know this, but it was clear to her. She was the one—not Aliver—who would come to understand the way the world worked. Aliver was a dreamer, naïve and idealistic; the world, she believed, would always play such men for fools. She was the one who knew how to use power. She was the one who understood beyond any doubt that she could rely on nobody but herself. And the *Song*. The knowledge in that book was for her to use. Perhaps she would allow Aliver to use it also, she told herself. Yes, she would. When the time came, once she had come to know him and made sure he was not a fool driven by philosophical fervor.

When she walked back into the room she carried nothing but the mug of steaming tea. The former chancellor was sleeping. He sat upright in the chair, but his head canted over at an unpleasant angle, his mouth agape and his breathing a nasal rasp. She watched him a moment, struck with a feeling of nostalgia that never quite congealed into a specific memory. She told herself that what she was about to do was a good thing. Some would die; some would suffer. But when all of this was over, she would help create a world different from anything that had come before. She would do so because she loved her family, because she wanted to assure their success, wanted to make sure they did not fall prey to the fatal errors their rhetoric suggested they were prone to. What she was about to do was not done against them; it was done for them.

She moved forward slowly. She approached with the stealth of an angel, carrying the mug of tea before her, the heat of it like molten lead cradled in her palms.

CHAPTER
SIXTY-SIX

The horror of massed warfare was beyond anything Dariel had experienced in his years as a raider. Fortunately, he held a serenity at his center that helped him through it all. Ever since reuniting with Aliver and Mena he had become a younger, happier, more buoyant version of himself. He knew they were engaged in a life-and-death struggle, but he was not alone in it. He had seen his sister lead an army into battle with her sword stretching from her hand as if it were part of her. He had watched his brother stand naked before a nightmare of a beast without blinking and then watched him cut it down like a hero out of legend. Incredible that these two were *his* siblings. He was not an orphan after all. He had a family. Soon they would have control and then everything—all the death and suffering, all the years in exile, all the injustice that made the world foul—would be set right.

Such conviction helped him function in the aftermath of the battle with the antoks. He was up before dawn the following morning, having slept just over two hours. He strode from his tent still caked in blood, grit beneath his fingernails and in the creases of his forehead and neck. He was eager to do what he could for the injured, the dying, and the dead. He took just a moment to splash water on his face and to scrub some of the filth from his arms, and he paused this long only because Mena ordered him to. She had checked him for injuries, queried him about how much he had rested and if he had eaten or drank. She was his older sister, after all. She was one of the few in the world who could demand that he do such things; he loved her for it. When this was all over he would sit with her in tranquillity and explain everything he felt for her. He would give her gifts and admit that he had always remembered how kind she had been to him when he was a child.

Thinking such things helped him deal with the pain and suffering the beasts had inflicted on so many good people. He wrapped that feeling of familial connection around him like a cloak. It helped him through the morning, as he checked and bandaged wounds, spoke words of praise and encouragement, lifted water gourds to parched lips. He whispered in the ears of the departing. He told them how much they were loved and how well they would be remembered and honored by future generations.

He passed a couple of hours at this before the news reached him. The shouted words blew past him at first, as quick as a gust of wind that snatched away his protective cloak. It took him a moment to understand what he had just heard. He did not believe it entirely until he stood beside his brother and sister, stunned and staring at the small company of the enemy in their midst.

There were just ten of them, tall and blond, long-haired and fierce, armed only with daggers. They projected complete ease, assurance with themselves and indifference to the thousands of hate-filled eyes fixed on them. Maeander Mein. Dariel could not imagine what he wanted, but from the moment he saw him, a knot tightened at his center.

While one of the Meinish officers formally announced him to Aliver, Maeander looked around with a thin-lipped grin on his face, studying Aliver and others as if he had never seen a company quite as amusing before. He had a loose-limbed power to him. He was perfectly proportioned, muscled but not overbulky, his torso tight and slim, as if he carried much of his strength at his core and down in his thighs. Dariel imagined him to be fast and found it easy enough to believe his reputation as a skilled killer. But his arrogance heated Dariel's blood.

"Prince Aliver Akaran," Maeander began, once the formalities were concluded. "Or do you prefer to be called the Snow King? I must say that's a strange appellation. I see no sign of snow. Should a flake fall on this scorched earth, it would sizzle and be gone just like that."

Aliver responded calmly. "We don't choose what others call us or decide how history will know us."

"That is very true," Maeander said. "We can strive for greatness, but who can know? I am sure your father never imagined that one of his offspring would lead a ragtag army up from the deserts of Talay. Or that another would be mistress to his conqueror, another the symbol of a Vumu religious sect, and the last a common raider of the seas. No matter how hard we try to make it otherwise, our lives are always surprises, aren't they?"

As he spoke his gaze left Aliver and settled on Mena. It lingered on her face, then slid down her body as if he were sizing up a courtesan. Before he looked away, though, he nodded to her. It was a deferential, almost respectful gesture that seemed distinctly different in character from what Dariel had expected. Finding Maeander's gaze on him the next moment, Dariel felt like smacking the smirk off his face. But he was not at all sure that he would be able to if he tried, such was Maeander's dangerous ease.

"What do you want to say to me?" Aliver asked.

Maeander held his hands out like a merchant attesting to his honesty. "I want to make you an offer. A simple offer. Dance a duel with me, Aliver. Just you and me, fairly matched, to the death. Nobody will interfere; all can see which of us is the greater."

"A duel?" Aliver asked. "What will this solve? You do not ask me to believe that your army will admit defeat upon your death, do you? Hanish will pack his things and leave Acacia, return to the wilds of the Mein? That would tempt me, but it is not a possibility. We both know that."

Maeander laughed. He acknowledged that he promised no such thing. Neither did he ask Aliver to swear to a similar oath. But why not face each other like men? There was a time when leaders stood before their armies and let their own blood sanctify the contest. It was they who had the most to gain or lose; so why should they not risk their lives as willingly as they put the lives of others in danger? It was a noble ideal that Meins and Acacians had both subscribed to once. It had been forgotten over the generations since Tinhadin's rule, when nobility was squashed, reviled, and—

"You're mad," Dariel interrupted. He could not help himself. Aliver seemed to be considering the offer. Nothing in his tone or demeanor suggested the disdain Dariel thought appropriate. He wanted to make sure his brother understood how he felt about this absurd proposition. "We have an army that fights for its own reasons. Every man and woman here is free. And they war for even greater freedom. Not one soldier in this company would risk Aliver's life before his own."

Voices affirmed this from all sides. They clapped, shouted, cursed. A few tossed quick insults.

Maeander deigned to look at Dariel long enough to ask, "You are the raider, yes? I would not expect you to know anything of honor. I am proposing only that Aliver do his part, that he face an equal and be tested."

Dariel spat on the ground. He felt Mena's hand touch his elbow, but he yanked away. "An equal? You are not a king. You are not Hanish. Why would Aliver Akaran risk your treachery when this isn't even about you? You must be truly desperate." Turning to shout to the crowd, he said, "That's the only reason he's here. The Mein are desperate! We have them beat, friends. That's what this is about."

Eyes back on Aliver, Maeander spoke through the tumult that answered Dariel. "Nothing rallies an army like a symbol. If—or should I say *when*—you kill me, Prince Aliver, you have my permission to saw my head from my shoulders. Go and mount it on the tip of a tall pole and hold it up for the world to see. Maeander Mein killed! Aliver Akaran triumphant! Your army would double overnight. The downtrodden masses—most of whom have forgotten whose heel ground them into the dirt before my brother's did—would rise in one great wave. Prophecies fulfilled! Destiny! Retribution!"

Aliver seemed at ease with this discussion. He did not seem surprised by the situation, did not seem at all troubled by looking into the face of the man who had orchestrated so many days of death. He leaned forward slightly, engaged, one hand raised to gesture, quieting the troops. "And if I perish?"

"That is the beauty of it," Maeander said. "Your death would spark some similar effect. Anger! Rage! What a hero you would be, having sacrificed yourself for your nation. Sometimes a martyr inspires a curious kind of devotion. . . ."

"You speak well," Aliver said, "but all the same things could be said of you. Should you triumph, you would have the same rewards. So isn't this duel ultimately without effect?"

"No, not at all. I am feared but not loved. I am powerful but not the supreme chieftain, as your brother pointed out. No, you would gain more from my death than I from yours."

"So why do you offer this duel?"

"Because he's a fool," Dariel said.

Maeander dropped his smile, replaced it with an instant mask of gravity. "He is right. Just think me a fool, Aliver. But fight me. I challenge you by the Old Codes, those that were in place before Tinhadin's time. As a man of honor, you have no choice but to accept. You know this, even if your brother does not."

During the private council that followed, Dariel tried to speak reason to Aliver. He reiterated his belief that it was madness to concede to a duel. It was a ploy, a trick of some sort, a last-ditch treachery. Nothing good could come of it. Maeander should be repulsed or seized or killed on the spot. He did not deserve the protection of parlay. Dariel said these things numerous times in varying ways, growing frustrated that Aliver heard him with equa-

nimity and yet still seemed resolved to accept the challenge. It was clear
from the moment the small group gathered in his tent that he had made up
his mind. He did not sit as he motioned for the others to do so. Instead, he
stood stretching, moving about, keeping his body limber.

In his quiet, measured voice, accented by his Talayan origins, Kelis
asked, "What are these Old Codes Maeander spoke of?"

Aliver explained that they were the unwritten standards of conduct
from the far past, when the Known World was made up of self-governing,
tribal powers. Each had his own customs, even more varied than what exists now. But when dealing outside a particular tribal group they relied on
established rules of conduct that everyone understood. He named several of
the customs, and might have gone on if Leeka Alain had not finished
for him.

"Some of the Old Codes are best forgotten," the general said, "but Maeander did evoke a known precedent. Bastard that he is. In those times kings
met before their respective armies and tried to settle their disputes before
putting their armies at risk. Sometimes they fought to the death. The First
Form—Edifus at Carni—was such a duel."

"And Tinhadin did away with these codes, didn't he?"

Leeka sighed, chewed his answer a moment. "To our lasting shame. He
rewrote everything, though, not just these codes. He brought the entire
Known World under his control, and much that had been could no longer
persist."

Melio Sharratt, who had led the Vumuan force the day before, sat beside Mena. He was the one who had taught her how to use a sword. He had
also helped save them from the antoks, and because of it nobody questioned
when Mena pulled him into the council. Indeed, Aliver remembered him
well and had commented last night on how fortuitous his arrival was. Melio asked if anyone ever stood in and fought in the king's place.

Aliver jumped in before anybody could answer, firm but smiling. "Nobody will stand in for me. Not you, Kelis—I see you thinking it. And certainly not you, Melio. Still think you're my superior—as you were when we
were boys?"

"Not at all, my lord," Melio said deferentially. "You surpassed me
long ago."

Aliver paused in his exercises and looked one after the other of them
in the eye, his face sun burnished, lean, handsome. His brown eyes showed
touches of gray in them, flecked with stony veins of silver. He had never
looked more like the ideal of a young king. "Maeander is right. I cannot ig-

nore the Old Codes. They are part of what we're fighting for. I believe in the notion of a leader's responsibility that he cites. If I believe it, what choice do I have but to accept what he offers? I'd be betraying everything that I want to be if I did. I didn't wake up this morning expecting this, but here it is. Better that I welcome it than run from it."

Nobody offered a rebuttal to this. Even Dariel could not think how to argue anymore. "If all this is decided," he said, his voice bitter, "why are we here talking?"

Humor curled up the corners of Aliver's mouth. "I'm here for the pleasure of your company and to keep those men out there guessing."

"Can you promise me you won't die?" Dariel knew he sounded childish, but he thought the question and could not help but ask it. "Can you promise that?"

No, Aliver admitted. Of course he could not make that promise. He stepped close to Dariel, grasped him with a palm set along his jawline. He called him Brother and reminded him that he had been beside their father when Thasren Mein stuck a poisoned blade in his chest. He was an arm's length away, he said. He saw the blade as it thrust forward. He saw the face of the assassin, and he had seen it a million times since. He could carve it out of stone and have the visage accurate to the last detail. This duel was not really offered this morning. It had begun the day he let Thasren kill their father.

"We fight for noble ideals," he said, "but also blood is blood. Fathers must be avenged. That, also, is an Old Code. Maeander may have forgotten it. But not I."

As he unfastened the King's Trust and set it on the field table before him, Aliver explained to a messenger that he was accepting the challenge. They would fight with daggers. No other weapons. No armor. It would be only the two of them, and whatever happened Maeander and/or his men would be allowed to safely depart when it was over. Such were the specifics Aliver swore to.

Outside again a few minutes later, the sun seemed to have bleached the world. It was too bright. Dariel stood squinting as he watched the space for the contest marked out. It would be a small oval, hemmed in by a wall of bodies, all of them unarmed, sworn not to aid or hinder the two. He stood watching as Aliver and Maeander walked the space, stripped down to the few articles they would fight in. They received instructions and had their weapons examined, washed clean of poisons, checked for secret devices.

Mena came up behind Dariel, grasped him by the shoulder, and whispered. "Didn't Aliver slay the antok? Hasn't he communed with the Santoth? Before that he hunted a laryx. Perhaps sorcery has been at work in his life all along. Have faith in him, Dariel."

And then it was time. Aliver stood before the other man shirtless, wearing just the knee-length skirt of a Talayan runner, his knife like a sliver of ice in his hand. Maeander wore a thalba so thin the contours of his muscular chest and abdomen showed through. His knife was shorter than Aliver's, with a slight curve to the tip, a dark tint to the blade. Aliver said something. Maeander looked puzzled a moment and then seemed to understand and respond.

Dariel did not hear the exchange. He watched what followed from a strange, muted place, not aware of his body at all, hearing nothing and taking in only what the harsh glare of the sun highlighted. He watched the two men circle each other. They measured each other's strengths and weaknesses with cursory thrusts and parries. He saw Maeander's thin lips smiling and joking, keeping up a steady stream of commentary that Dariel could not hear a word of. He watched Maeander dive into an attack, so fast he was like a hooded snake. Aliver flew up from the strike, a leap that took him over Maeander's head, slashing as he did. Maeander, still snakelike, leaned backward. He flattened himself to the ground, his shoulders touching the dirt even as his legs moved him under Aliver and away.

At any other time that series of moves would have dumbfounded Dariel, but the two did not so much as pause to acknowledge what had passed between. They circled more, jabbed more. Their knives clashed. As they pulled apart, Aliver cut the skin of one of Maeander's knuckles. The tempo increased. The two men became blurs of motion, slipping around each other, attacking and retreating, spinning so quickly it was hard to keep track of who was who. Somebody drew blood from the other's shoulder. One of them fell and had to scramble sideways on all fours. Dariel thought it was Aliver, but the next moment Aliver was in the air above the cloud of dust, spinning around like a deadly acrobat, his blade at the tip of his orbit, slicing the air.

Watching him, Dariel felt the first inklings of hope. Aliver was blessed. How else could he dance ahead of every assault Maeander made, faster than him, more perfect in execution, deadly artistry in motion, pressing his own attacks with flourishes that made Dariel imagine the Form that this would one day become. Yes, that's what this was! He was watching a Form being created. . . . Mena was right; sorcery had to be at work here.

And Aliver was right; he would win this in his father's name. He would conclude the duel begun years before.

And then Dariel saw it happen. For a few seconds all his mind registered were the physical details, the scene itself in vivid colors, one second passing into the next without understanding the significance of what he saw. Aliver, having ducked beneath Maeander's punching dagger thrust, pulled on his chest and shoulder muscles to create the slicing arc that would tear through Maeander's abdomen, just as he had disemboweled the antok. This, at least, was what should have happened. What did happen was different.

Maeander jumped, a quick concussion of power shot from his thighs, through his balled calf muscles, and down to his toes. He floated up into the air. Aliver straightened as his blade skimmed across Maeander's abdomen, so close Dariel believed the point split the fabric of his thalba. Aliver lifted as the other man did, wanting this motion to end the contest, wanting it so badly that he focused his everything on carving into flesh. What he forgot was the knife still in his opponent's outstretched hand, behind his head as Maeander's arm came to rest on his shoulder. He was still focused on his attack as Maeander drew the point of the blade into the back of his neck.

The shock of realization showed then, but it was too late. Maeander carved a crescent from the back of Aliver's neck, around the side of it, through the artery there, and all the way beneath his chin. He caught Aliver's spinning form almost gently, lowering the bloody mess of him down to the ground. A second later he spun upright and away, Aliver's knife in his hand, upraised, triumphant, oblivious to the nature of frantic tumult he had just created. It was as if Maeander had orchestrated the entire thing.

Dariel dashed in with the swarm of people rushing toward Aliver. He had to shove and yank others out of the way, yelling, although he could not hear anything, not even himself. He got his arms under his brother, felt the warm wetness of him, the dreadful limpness of his weight. Fearful lest he cause some further injury, he tried to be gentle, to soothe, to reassure. He spoke close to Aliver's temple. He hated the way his head flopped about. He cursed himself for being so clumsy. He thought perhaps he should lower him down so that he did not make anything worse, but then he realized Mena was across from him, holding Aliver just as he was, her face as white as death, contorted with grief. With grief, not with fear. Not with worry or anxiousness . . . with grief.

Looking down again, Dariel saw what was right there before him. He understood the enormity of what had just happened. He would never again be able to look at another man's neck without seeing the injury that had killed Aliver Akaran. It was too much. Too much. Whatever emotion was in him was full beyond his capacity to contain.

He stood. His eyes shot out in the direction Maeander's group had departed in. It took him a moment, but he spotted them, a small cluster progressing through the throng that cleared the way for them reluctantly. He felt thousands of eyes beating on him. He knew what they were waiting for, and he wanted what they wanted. He felt the emotion they did, and with their gazes fixed on him he became the center of it. An uncontainable rage, a pure abhorrence that poured from his eyes as if a star were exploding inside his head. He wanted to commit a crime of honor. Wanted to right here and now, before thousands of witnesses. He knew he would be ashamed of it eventually and that he would have to reckon, not with the act itself but with knowing ever after that Aliver would not have approved. But there was no stopping it. When he opened his mouth he did the worst possible thing. He asked for a thousand accomplices. Eyes still fixed on the receding backs of the Meins, he bit down on the virtues that his brother would have demanded of him. He whispered, "Kill him."

When nobody responded, he raised his voice and shouted the command as loudly as he could. This time, they—and he himself—heard his voice clearly.

CHAPTER

SIXTY-SEVEN

Hanish used transport vessels from his personal fleet and others lent to him by Meinish nobles eager to take part in carrying the Tunishnevre the final waterborne leg to Acacia. They made the journey from the Mainland without incident. On arriving, they took over the docks. They swarmed the area, occupying every mooring, driving away the fishermen and merchants, bullying the populace back into the lower town. They would have cleared the place no matter what, but the work was made easier because the port was not as busy as it normally was. League ships, in particular, were conspicuously absent. Hanish noted this and considered having it explained before he proceeded any farther, but the area appeared to be secure. Also, his Punisari were armed to the teeth and ready to repel any treachery. He ordered his ships to begin disgorging their cargo.

Within an hour rows of sarcophagi were threading through the docks and ascending toward the palace via the sloping system of ramps. Before leaving the seaside, Hanish watched the first of the ancestors enter a gate in the palace walls. The shadowed mouth swallowed them one by one, each a relief, each finally safe and sliding home into the special chamber constructed to house them. Their long journey was finally at an end; a new one scheduled to commence soon, the next day, if possible.

Even as he made his way up toward the palace, with Haleeven beside him, Hanish's secretaries and assistants rushed down to meet him. They bombarded him with news, with dispatches, reports, with a host of matters that had been waiting for his attention. The docks were not crowded, they explained, because league ships normally stationed there had departed. Some that had been scheduled to arrive had not. Sire Dagon had evacuated his compound without explanation the day previous, taking all his staff with him. There was something amiss with them, though nobody knew what. They were not even sure if the league still provided Maeander naval support.

This prompted him to ask what news they had of Maeander and the battle. The latest letter from his brother appeared in his hands a moment later. It had also arrived that morning. As he began to read it, he was reminded of his annoyance at not being able to communicate with Maeander through dream travel. He had long suspected Maeander of intentionally blocking him out, unwilling to allow him the access to his consciousness that such communicating made possible. Thus, striding up across the cobbled stones, he first got word of the antoks' failure, via a message that had traveled strapped to a bird's leg and was at least a day old.

The antoks had inflicted damage, Maeander claimed, but they had not decided the matter. They were not the invincible beings he had hoped they would prove to be, and Aliver seemed to have some form of sorcery aiding his side. But this was all right, Maeander wrote, because he had something else planned. He said no more than that. Hanish would not know what he planned or how it turned out until another of these birds flew across the sea.

"He is too cryptic," Hanish said, showing the note to his uncle.

Haleeven read it without comment, setting his chin in such a way as to remind his nephew to focus only on the details at hand, the things ahead of them, waiting in the palace.

Though he thought of her constantly, Hanish had no plan to see Corinn until that evening. He did not tell her this; she would know it already. Anytime he returned there were a million things to see to, now more than ever. He spent the rest of the morning and early afternoon in his office, dealing with everything piled upon his desk during his absence. Military advisers gave him event-by-event details of the war in Talay and of the outbreaks of troubles all around the empire. They had concentrated so many of their forces with Maeander that the provinces were thinly controlled. Too many of the troops holding them were of foreign blood, their loyalties suspect. They warned that should Maeander suffer a real defeat, Aushenia and Candovia and Senival would all likely burst into outright rebellion. And the Numreks had not joined Maeander. They were simply absent from the proceedings and had not responded to any of the orders dispatched to them. This might be an ill thing, Hanish thought, but he could not imagine what the Numrek were up to and still imagined they would appear belatedly, once they had made some point or another.

What he found more troubling than anything was Aliver's emergence as a skilled leader and as a figure around whom myth could be spun, one who might walk with magic. The fact that he personally killed the first antok was a great nuisance. Minstrels would be telling grandiose tales of Aliver's victory over them for years to come, no matter what Maeander managed to accomplish against him. It would be best, he thought, if they could capture all of the Akarans alive. Parade them through the streets of every city in the empire. Let the populace see them in chains. That, perhaps, would kill the myths. The truth usually could, if one faced it honestly.

The one comfort Hanish had was that he did not believe he was yet in danger. The Acacians might think they were gaining ground, but their small victories meant little. Nothing would stand up against Meinish power after the ceremony. Aliver might have some meager sorcery working on his behalf, but Hanish would soon tap the accumulated rage of generations. This fact, likely, was why the league had withdrawn. They had reason to fear the power they knew was going to be awakened. Good, Hanish thought. Let them tremble for a while. Perhaps the ancestors would take the reins of the world in their newly animated hands. He wished they would. Let them rage through the provinces, winning them back; let Sire Dagon stand before them and try to flex his muscles. Hanish would happily rest and attempt to forget the things he would need to forget.

As the day began to fade, his thoughts more and more returned to Corinn. Enough so that he eventually pushed himself upright and dismissed the advisers and his staff, saying he would continue with them in the morning. He asked Haleeven to join him in inspecting the ceremonial site. After that, he knew, he could finally go to Corinn and spend a last night with her.

The chamber had been under construction since the end of his first year in control of Acacia. It was a monumental project, conducted in semisecrecy. It was one long, slow exercise in excavation. Diggers went at the bedrock beneath the eastern base of the island, just below the palace. It was never too obvious a project, never worked by more than a modest stream of laborers. All the stone quarried inside exited through one access point. They used it to extend the docks and create an artificial island out at sea, making it easier for the league's large ships to moor there. There were many uses for the material and nothing was officially said about why it was being mined.

Hanish knew the lower town was alive with rumors about what he was constructing deep in the earth. An unassailable keep. Torture chambers. Cages in which he would raise unnatural beasts. A chamber like the Calathrock for conducting games and military drills. It did not matter what they speculated; they would never quite get at the truth.

Inside the cavern, looking about as workers positioned the last of the sarcophagi in place, priests overseeing all with the stern visages rendered stark by the white light of clean-burning oil lamps, Hanish marveled at the structure. It had been carved to the specifications conveyed to him by the undead themselves. In many ways it resembled the chamber back at Tahalian, with ancestors stacked row upon row. It had needed to be built here, of course, on Acacia. It was here that the curse against them had been created and here was the only place from which it could be reversed. The slots that housed each sarcophagi had been carved directly into the granite itself, smoothed and polished, like an enormous beehive cut from stone. When his ancestors breathed again and reached out and touched their corporeal fingers to the world for the first time in years or decades or centuries, they would be able to caress the very stone that the early Akarans had stood upon when they set out to bind the world.

At the center point of all this was the Scatevith stone, the single great block of it so dark and dense it seemed to suck life into its murky depths. It was the very piece that had been carved from the basalt at the base of the Black Mountains, high up on the Mein Plateau. His ancestors had been forced to offer it as a gift to help the Akarans build the great wall outside Alecia. After his victory, Hanish had it cut out of that wall and brought here to serve as the platform on which an Akaran would die. Everything was in place.

He tried to remind himself of this, to say it like a prayer that would clear away all else. But he could not help but imagine Corinn as she would be tomorrow. She would walk in halfway through the ceremony, when Hanish had already invoked the ancient words as whispered to him by the ancestors. She would come toward him in all her grace, believing she was to offer healing drops of blood. He would look her in the face, assuring her, moving her as close as he could to the moment of death without her seeing it coming. At some point she would figure out what was happening. He might have gotten her into position upon the stone and stood her over the bowl waiting to gather her blood. He might be holding the knife in his hand, might even be preparing her to receive its cut. But . . .

At some point she would realize that he was not just there for her blood but for her life as well. She would likely see it in his eyes or his gestures or hear it in the quavering of his voice if he did not control himself perfectly. She would not, he was sure, go quietly to her death. He imagined her fighting against him as he dragged her up onto the stone. She'd be cursing him, tearing at his face with her fingers, bucking against him, gouging at his eyes. What would she say to him? He could think of a thousand insults, and they'd all be true.

Haleeven, standing beside him, intuited his thoughts. "I wish there was another way," he said. "But there isn't. Things have come to this in just this way. I, at least, know how hard you tried to find the others and how much you give up for the Tunishnevre. It is for this that you were chosen. Because you have the strength to do it."

Hanish felt a pressure surge up from his gut and threaten to pour out of him. He knew his uncle was trying to help, but he could not listen to such things now. "Leave me," he said. He raised his voice and ordered the workers to depart the chamber for a few moments. He wished to be alone.

He sat until they drained out, ignoring the dour looks on the priests' faces. When the place fell silent, when he could just faintly sense the satisfied pulse that was the Tunishnevre's heartbeat, his eyes clouded. His face reddened. He blinked and blinked rapidly, embarrassed by the flood of tears he could not stop from streaking down his cheeks. He wiped them away with the hard edge of his hand, anxious lest somebody—one of the priests perhaps—stick his head in and see him. But the tears came with their own strength. The emotion began with thoughts of Corinn, but it was not just about her. His grief at knowing what he had planned for her intertwined with dread of the forces he was about to unleash. The Tunishnevre. A spiteful pantheon of his hallowed ancestors. How he feared them. How he loathed them. He had lived, bowing to their animus, all his life, and now he would soon meet them all face-to-face, flesh and blood, as men before him, animated by a warped version of the Giver's tongue.

When he was a boy his father had often taken him into the chamber at Tahalian. Heberen would press Hanish's forehead to the cold floor and make him remain prostrate like that for hours. He left him alone, saying that he must learn to hear the voices of his ancestors. Only if he heard them would he be able to serve them. And serving them was all his life was really about. How frightened he'd been! Alone in the dark, the angry cries of spirits in the air, hundreds of corpses surrounding him, living and dead at the same time. He had barely allowed himself to breathe, so aware was he that he sucked them in with each inhalation. He had heard them all right. Every day of his life he'd heard them in some way or another.

He had wanted to ask, even as a boy, why the ancestors so craved life again. If living was only a prelude to death—and if the living were but servants of the deceased—why then did the old ones want so very badly to walk the earth again? He had the question formed and solid in his mind since his eighth or ninth year. But he never asked it. He feared that to ask it was to reveal a lie that would shame his ancestors and embarrass him in some irreversible way. Now, decades later, what choice did he have other than to carry the lie through? It was what he had worked for all along. If he failed at the awakening, he failed at the main thing he had striven for throughout his life. So he reaffirmed that he would not fail. Haleeven was right. In choosing him, the Tunishnevre had chosen correctly.

By the time he left the chamber he had drained the well of his tears, though, as he discovered, he would soon need to replenish them. His secretary collided with him in the hallway just outside. He had been progressing at a dead run. The moment he had recovered himself he thrust a curled piece of paper at him. It had just come by a messenger bird from Bocoum, he said.

"From my brother?"

"No," the man said, his blue eyes round and nervous. "It's not from him, but it's about him. It tells of two deaths." He stretched out his hand, trembling, to offer the note. "Please, lord, you will want to read it yourself."

Some time later, when he stepped into his quarters and saw Corinn look up at him, watched her stand and begin to walk toward him, beautiful as ever, her gown kind to her contours, the train of it trailing the stones, tiny bells tinkling to mark her progress, Hanish knew himself to be every bit the impostor, the coward, the villain that Corinn would name him if she knew him truly. He knew it, but he rushed toward her embrace. He heard himself utter the news to her, and he luxuriated in the solace of the moments to come. They would each comfort the other. They would both share their losses. She wouldn't hate him just yet, because only the two of them in all the world split equal measures of exactly the same kind of suffering at that moment.

So he thought of that, and he tried to forget that on the morrow he would kill her.

CHAPTER

SIXTY-EIGHT

"How can you be dead?" Mena asked for the hundredth time. She sat on her camp blanket late in the evening of the day after Aliver's duel. Her tent stood limp around her, the night still, no breath in the warm air outside to blow against it. She clasped her eel pendant in one hand, tugging at the string around her neck, unsure whether to use the necklace as an amulet or to tear it free and toss it away. Beside her Melio slumbered restlessly. He lay facedown with one hand tight around her ankle, his grip firm and constant, as if his fingers and thumbs, at least, were still awake.

"How can you be dead?"

She spoke softly, not wanting to disturb Melio. They had been through it enough times already: she asking that same question, he whispering answers for her, finding new words of solace, pushing her away from the well of grief she wanted to fall into. The last two days had been a strange, chaotic courtship of sorts. They had not spoken of the letter she had written him. When would they have? But it was there between them, as was the fact that he had chased her across the sea with an army he managed to spin out of nothing. If ever they saw the calm of a peaceful world, she would look no farther than Melio for love; that love, however, hung on the other side of a yawning, unpredictable *if*.

The time that had passed since Aliver's death at Maeander's hands had been the longest ordeal of Mena's life. Nothing even slightly compared. She had not really had a chance to reckon with her brother's killing. The world did not pause to grant her the moments she needed, and things had happened too fast following it. As Dariel had ordered, Maeander and his entire entourage were pounced upon. Mena stayed with Aliver, cradling him, trying to focus only on him, but she heard what happened. The Meins fought bravely. They formed a pronged-star formation, each of them facing out at the innumerable sea of Acacians and Talayans and Aushenians, as representatives from every corner of the Known World all turned against them. Maeander had ranted and laughed the entire time, calling them honorless bastards and whores, belittling them with a verbal dexterity that matched his martial prowess. They killed a great many before they were all cut down. Their dead bodies were abused, stabbed and stabbed again and again. Everyone, it seemed, wanted to wash their blades in Maeander's blood, to punish him for what he had done and to try to forget the things he had said. Mena hated to hear of it, hated knowing that Dariel had been there among them, venting his misery and confusion on a corpse.

This was not all the day had in store for them, though. Scarcely had the fervor died down before new shouts sprayed out through the masses. The Meinish army, using the distraction, had marched all the way across the field unnoticed. The Meins were emboldened, whipped into a frenzy by their leader's death. They rushed in, shouting vengeance. They knew of his fate and of the treachery by which it was achieved before news could possibly have reached them. It had happened just moments before! Maeander must have told his generals exactly what would transpire before he set out that morning. Because of this, his army fought with a level of fury and indignation beyond anything they had shown previously. Maeander had made himself an instant hero, a leader of greater stature than he was in life. He had become a martyr. And, just as he had said, a martyr inspired devotion. A curious kind, he had said. What he meant was a ferocious kind.

As soon as she had given orders to protect Aliver's body, Mena grabbed up her weapons and ran to face the enemy. Try as they might, Mena, Dariel, Leeka, and the other generals could not muster their forces into order to meet the attack. The army had lost itself in grief and uncertainty. Even as they tried to respond to orders they seemed dazed, made tentative by the realization that Aliver would not be leading them to the victory. The Snow King was dead. He would not give to them all the myriad things he had promised. He would not sweep into Acacia with a righteous sword, victorious. And if he would not, how could they?

The battle raged right among their tents, over cook fires and around latrines and amid stacks of supplies and foodstuffs. At some point Mena stopped trying to rally others and focused on her own deadly desires. She led by example, and quite an example she became. She ran deep into the Meinish ranks, filled with a hunger to kill and a rage of such humming intensity and heat that it felt like she would combust if she stopped moving even for a second. The sword that Melio had returned to her whirled around

her with its own mind and deadly purpose. She but followed it, pushing farther and farther into the enemy, knowing that she had to stay away from her
own. She was killing too fast to pick out friend from foe.

And though it was rage that propelled her she felt no joy as she
achieved this slaughter. Just the opposite. It was a nightmare battle. In
everything around her she saw signs and sights of Aliver. As she hacked and
sliced, severed limbs and peeled skin from faces and sent ears spiraling up
from her blade and spilled bellies onto the dirt, she saw Aliver in all of it.
She knew that she was slaying an enemy—his enemy—but he was there in
every Mein killed, in the shape of limbs and the expressions in glazed eyes
and in the voices crying out in anguish. It was maddening. It made her a
whirlwind of violence, as if she could butcher her way through this notion
of her brother's violent death. The bodies she left around her in hacked piles
numbered in the many dozens. If her blade had not been the finest of steel,
she would have dulled and bent it before the day was out. Instead, however,
even at the close of the day it had edge enough to slice through the crowns
of skulls and cut clean through muscle and bone.

Eventually, the Meins withdrew. They had not been defeated, not even
beaten back. By the look of the camp and the heaps of Acacian dead the
Meins could be assured of closing this business on the morrow. Oubadal's
Halaly had been the first to face the Meinish attack; word now was that
they were no more, gone completely, killed to the last. This was a great
blow. Even the tribes that had begun the war fearing or loathing them had
learned to respect them these last few days. Now they were gone.

Kelis, Aliver's great friend, was grazed by a spear across the abdomen,
a serious enough injury that he was bed bound and in great pain. How many
more would die during the night? How many would slink away defeated,
fleeing to their homes, wishing they had taken no part in this war?

As she walked amid the carnage, her limbs trembling, every inch of
her crusted in gore, Mena felt the eyes of her troops on her. Even Dariel, who
had earlier ordered an honorless murder, stared at her in awe. Perhaps they
were all seeing for the first time what a monster she actually was. She
wanted to shout at them. What were they looking at? Of course she was a
killer. She was Maeben. She would always be Maeben. Always better at rage
than anything else. It was hard not to feel she had personally killed every
corpse in sight herself.

In the tent later that night, with Melio's arms around her, his words
close in her ears, his body rocking hers . . . then she found stillness enough
to believe that she had not been killing Aliver over and over again on the

field. She remembered holding his blood-slick body in her hands. He had been so hot, heat pouring from him like a furnace. She had tasted rust on her tongue and in her nostrils. There had been a terrible moment, she recalled, when her fingers—while trying to find the wound and measure its damage—actually slipped inside the fissure. It was the strangest of memories, for each time it came to her she remembered the incredible softness in the warmth of his tissues. Nothing she had ever felt before had been so soft, so delicate. And yet at the same time she felt a gut-wrenching revulsion rooted in the thought that her fingers had caused the wound, that they could cut just as easily as her blade.

But all this was before. Now Melio lay in his fitful slumber, grasping her with one hand, protecting her. What a strange thought, that. What could she need protection from? Her body wanted desperately to sleep, but she would not let it. She feared that her unconscious mind would conjure something horrible with that slip of her fingers.

"How can you be dead?" she asked again.

In the silence after this she returned to something else she'd been spinning around in her mind, an exchange she had had with Aliver before the duel. He had pulled her aside as they were exiting the council tent. He waited for the others to move away slightly and then he fixed his eyes on hers. "If I die," he said, "hold the King's Trust for a time. When you think he is ready, give it to Dariel. I want him to have it. You don't need it, right, Mena? You've created a mythic sword of your own."

He smiled. "Another thing, and this is important. You must be prepared to summon the Santoth." She had started to protest, but Aliver silenced her. She had to accept this responsibility. If he died, he explained, everything fell upon her and Dariel. Dariel had great strength within him, but he was still too emotional. He was the youngest of them and would be too emotional until it was tempered out of him. Only she would have the focus to see above the turmoil and send a call out to the Santoth. She protested that she didn't know how, but he told her she would learn how when the time came.

He said, "I don't plan to leave you today, Mena, but if I do—and if our cause seems on the verge of failure—call the Santoth. Speak to Nualo. He is one of the Santoth, a very good man, Mena."

"What about *The Song of Elenet*?" she had asked.

Aliver had looked at her sadly. "I don't know. You think I know how to do all of this, Mena? I don't. I wish we had that book, but call them even if you don't have it. And then . . . see what happens."

After that he had walked to the arena of his death.

Had he really said that? *See what happens?* It did not seem possible that such massive challenges could be overcome with vague, hopeful sentiments like that. Aliver had spoken of communicating with them but never clearly enough that Mena had imagined trying it herself. It required opening the mind. It involved reaching a quiet, meditative state, his consciousness empty of everything except thoughts of those he wanted to communicate with. He let his call uncoil from his body, he had said, and find direction on its own accord. It might take a long time, but eventually he would hear them within him, answering. Then he would speak to them directly from his being. They had read his mind to some extent, but he could also focus particular thoughts and transmit them. It required patience, faith. . . .

Yes, he had said that, too. It required *faith*, the same word she had whispered into Dariel's ear. But Aliver's death seemed to refute faith as powerless. Maybe it was, or maybe it counted only when it went in the face of adversity so great nothing else could be called upon. That was what she faced. By all reason she knew that in the morning the Meins would slaughter everyone gathered to face them. It would be but the mopping up of a victory already achieved. Knowing this, she resolved to try faith one more time. She had promised to, so she would.

She looked about as if she might find some tools to aid her or should rearrange the objects in the tent or pull her ankle from Melio's grasp. But there were no tools for something like this. Her surroundings were what they were, and she did not want to break the connection with Melio. She settled herself, pressed her thumbs against the spine of the eel pendant, and closed her eyes.

She tried to still her thoughts. For some time she fought a barrage of violent images from the day's fighting and of Aliver in death and in the duel moments just before, when anything was still possible. . . . Distractions like these seemed to have lain in wait to ambush her. Get past these things, she thought. Clear the mind. Think only of the Santoth. She could not visualize them since she had never seen them. Instead, she tried to locate the energy of them. She thought of it as a point of light in the empty heavens, and then as a hint of warmth in surrounding cold, and then as the beating of life in a silent eternity: all of these things she searched for inside her mind. It felt like no more than a mental exercise, all within her instead of out in the world. But she kept at it.

At some point, she realized, she found that point of warm, beating light. No, she did not find it; she created it. She focused on it and brought it closer and closer and closer, until it was the palpable center of her. It was right there within her. She tried to formulate a thought to push into this, but there were too many different things to say. She could not narrow it down to one thing. Instead, she took in all of it: all her fears, hopes, and desires, wishes and dreams; all the horrors of the recent days, the scenes of bloodshed, the antoks, the duel; all the death and all the suffering promised on the morn. She spun them like a ball before her and pushed them into that light. If the Santoth were to understand anything, they might as well understand all of it.

Once she was sure she had done the best she could with sending the message, she listened. Waited. Searched the answering silence. It seemed to have no end, but she waited, not knowing what else to do. She simply waited for a response.

It did not come.

She awoke as dawn's light suffused her tent. Surprised that she had slept, she drew up from her crumpled position. Melio stirred beside her. Outside she heard the sounds of the camp awaking. Somebody walked by, feet crunching the dry earth. She realized that Melio was not gripping her ankle anymore, and this saddened her.

With that, yesterday poured into her, memories of all of it, including what she had attempted to do. She had tried to summon the Santoth, just as Aliver had asked her to. But there had been no response. She had listened so hard and long that the act had finally lulled her into sleep. That was all that had happened. She was not even sure that the whole exercise had ever left the confines of her own skull. That light was just something she had imagined, that she had fantasized in her tent, sitting beside Melio in the early hours of what would be a terrible day. That, she thought, was the best she had managed to do. It would not be enough. Aliver had made two mistakes, then, not just the one of dueling Maeander.

The reality of what the day offered crept back upon her. The coming day was completely unavoidable, already upon her. The only thing good about it was that at last this would all be concluded. At least she knew how she would die. Maeander had known how he would. That was where his calm had come from, his assurance. He had nodded to her, indicating as much, though she only now realized that was what he had been saying. He had been predicting his future. She should have cut his head from his shoulders right then. She should not have let him control their world as he had. That was where she had made her first mistake.

Or was it? She had made mistakes earlier than that. And it wasn't just her mistakes that mattered. There were so, so many things that should have been different, going back years. No, not years—decades and centuries. Back to the early ages, to when the Giver still walked the newly created earth. Somebody back then should have cut down Elenet before he stole that which he should never have stolen. But if that was true, then wasn't the Giver truly to blame? This was all his creation. He was the one she wanted one day to stand before and take to task. Why did he let it all go foul so quickly? Barely was the dew of creation dry before he let his children betray him. And why didn't he care that some now strived for right in the world, that some fought so that there could be a greater peace afterward? She feared the question. He might turn it all around on her and assault her claim at righteousness—she being the killer that she was, so easily enraged, so skilled at murder. Perhaps Hanish was no more a villain than she was. Perhaps there was no difference between good and bad . . .

A hand yanked the flap open, a shaft of light blinding her for a second. And then she heard the voice of Leeka Alain, awed in a way unusual to it. "Princess, come. You should see this. Something is happening."

CHAPTER

SIXTY-NINE

Rialus Neptos was a pathetic runt of a man. Never was this more obvious than when he stood flanked by Numrek warriors, tall men, shoulders wide, with balled knots of muscle at the joints, like grapefruits beneath their burgundy-tinted skin. He was a weasel in the company of wolves. Stooped to fit beneath the low ceiling of the palace's hidden passageways, any of the Numreks could have grabbed the ambassador by the neck and shaken the life out of him with one of their hard-knuckled fists. Had Corinn not needed him to translate the instructions she was about to give, she might well have asked them to do just that. Strange, she thought, that her fortunes relied on such dubious allies.

She'd rarely had occasion to stand so close to Numreks. She had sat near them at a few banquets over the nine years since the war, but what she remembered most vividly was the image of them in their former pallor. She had seen a party of them for the first time just after her capture and return to Acacia. Their complexions had been pale and blue-tinted, just starting to burn beneath the sun. They were like creatures from a subterranean cave abruptly shoved into the light of day. They had been so different from the smooth, dark-featured beings that she looked at now. She would almost have thought them different creatures, save that she recalled the stature and shape of them, their full heads of dark hair and their features, gaunt and muscular at the same time. She hated them with undiluted spite back then. She did not feel that different now. But her feelings were not the point; the work at hand was.

A few hours before that she had lain in bed beside Hanish, her fingertips touching his, listening to him sleep. Before that she had been entwined with him in the bedsheets, their naked bodies slick with sweat, with tears and passion. She had panted in his ear, and he had said her name over and over. And before that they had just held each other, both of them reeling from the news of their respective brother's deaths. The irony of it all took her breath away. Aliver and Maeander, mutual victims; Corinn and Hanish, lovers who pretended their affair had nothing to do with the struggle between them.

But that was earlier, before the light of day. In truth it had everything to do with them, and she knew Hanish believed so as much as she did. When she parted with him a few minutes ago, she kissed him full on the mouth and wished him success at beginning the releasing ceremony. It was time, she said, to begin to heal, to stop the insanity of the war, to put to rest the old hatred between their people. It was time to honor the dead. She had promised to prepare herself and join him. Instead, she went to her room, closed the door behind her, and slipped into the hidden entrance Thaddeus had described to her. She found Rialus and the Numrek just where she had instructed them to be—inside the walls of the palace.

They were actually here. Actually standing about in armor, weapons hanging on them, their breath fouling the enclosed air. She felt a momentary spasm of panic at what she was doing. She overcame it by thinking about the betrayal Hanish planned for her, by reminding herself of her vow never again to act like a lamb, by affirming that she had to avenge her brother, and by recalling the beautiful promises in the *Song*.

Serving as translator, Rialus introduced her to their leader. Calrach looked her up and down, studying her shape, bemused. He said something that piqued the interest of those around him. Even Rialus looked at her with surprise. "Princess," he said, "is it true that you're carrying a child? I can hardly tell, but Numrek . . . have a nose for such things."

Corinn had no interest in beginning the conversation this way. She had to control the urge to slide her hand across her belly. "Calrach," she said, "how many men do you have with you?"

Rialus answered without translating the question. "Two hundred."

"Two hundred?" Corinn asked. "When I wrote you, I told you to bring a force to take the entire palace, parts of the lower town, as well. You bring me two hundred?"

"Princess, this was as many as we could manage," Rialus said. "It's amazing we weren't spotted as is. You know how hard it was to ferry two hundred of these men in a few small boats at night? Any more and we would have betrayed your plans. Although I don't mind saying this passageway is incredible! To think that generations of enemies could have slipped inside the heart of Acacia, if only they'd known the way . . ." Noting Corinn's thin-lipped look of impatience, Rialus clipped his digression. "Anyway, two hundred Numrek are more than enough to take the palace from the inside. They are hard to kill."

"Hanish has an entire army here. Punisari among them: they're hard to kill too."

Calrach, annoyed at being kept out of the conversation, nudged Rialus. The small man spoke to him in the Numrek tongue, fluent and animated. Calrach found what he said amusing. Looking at Corinn, he spoke his discordant answer.

Rialus translated. "Punisari aren't a problem. He says he'll capture the palace for you within a few hours. The cleanup, he says, will take longer than the deed itself."

Corinn stared at the Numrek's wide-spaced eyes, the irises the color of amber. She had never noticed that before. They were almost attractive to gaze into. Strange to stand here quietly talking with Calrach about the things they were discussing. These Numrek did not have to hate to kill. It did not matter that they had no deep-seated grievance with Hanish and his people. They had gripes, yes, but they were not truly wedded to this generational struggle. She knew it did not really matter to them who won, so long as they benefited from it. This suited Corinn. There was no ideology to twist their motives or to cloud their thinking. There was a simple honesty to their avarice, an understandable reason to the things they asked from her in return for their aid. With such a people she would always know where they stood and where she stood.

"You can accomplish this attack?" she asked. "You are certain?"

Calrach said that in war nothing is certain. But then he grinned and said, "Nothing except Numrek victory." He looked around to bring in his fellows, who began to grumble their affirmation. It took a few moments for them all to answer, even the dim shapes hulking far down the corridor wanting to make themselves heard.

"Don't speak in contradictions," Corinn said, once they had quieted enough. "It will foul everything if—"

The Numrek interrupted her. He spoke for a few moments, and then Rialus translated. "He says they'll kill them all."

"That's all he said?"

Rialus smirked. "It's the substance of it. He described their methods as well, but I didn't think that would interest you."

Turning back to Calrach, Corinn said, "Then do it. Kill everyone. Everyone, without hesitation. Show them no mercy, listen to no plea. Kill all of them except Hanish himself. Keep him alive for me."

On hearing this last instruction, Calrach shrugged. That was fine with him, he said. Hanish was of no interest to him anymore. Before he left, though, he asked her to confirm the terms of their agreement. When she did, he grinned, his teeth prominent and glistening in the torchlight. "We will happily accept that. But how do I know you will keep this promise?"

"You can know it," Corinn said, "because what you want is exactly what I want as well. I don't promise it as a gift to you. It is in both our interests."

Calrach studied her for a long time after hearing the translation of this. His gaze was appraising, invasive, and yet indifferent as well. Eventually, he pronounced, "I much prefer working with you to dealing with Hanish. Because of it, you will have your palace back. And, as you wish, we will tell nobody what you've promised us. It will be our secret, yes? Between Princess Corinn and the Numrek. Nobody else need know—until the day that we reveal it to the world."

Corinn stood to the side as the procession of burly soldiers marched past her. They were absurdly large and loud. Their leather trousers squeaked as they trod. Their weapons and random bits of armor clanked and grated. Many of them talked in their discordant language. Behind their screens of wiry hair, some grinned as they passed her. A few even laughed at jokes she had no inkling of, as casual as if they were simply proceeding to an exercise. Two hundred had seemed a small number when Rialus pronounced it, but midway through the line of them they seemed innumerable.

And then they were gone. Quiet settled in, a living presence in its own right that occupied the space as if disgruntled by the previous intrusion. Rialus, who was to have no part in the fighting, stood near at hand, shifting, nervous, clearing his throat often as if about to speak. Corinn ignored him. Another seizure of doubt gripped her. It wrapped around her torso and squeezed the breath out of her and set her insides churning. The implausibility of what was happening and the fact that she, Corinn, was making it happen: it was almost too much to fathom. She felt the ceiling pressing down on her. She kept checking it with her eyes, suspecting, despite herself, that it was sliding downward. For the first time she noticed the bizarre carvings that lined the nearby space, forms half human and half animal. Was that what her people had once looked like? Were those her ancestors?

Rialus interrupted her thoughts. "May I ask, Princess, how you learned of these secret passageways?"

"Thaddeus Clegg," she heard herself answer.

"Clegg?" Rialus asked, alarm in his voice. "Truly? That old traitor? He's here, in the palace? He's not to be trusted, you know. What is he—"

"He is dead, Rialus. Not a threat to you in any way." He is gone, Corinn thought, but the gift he left me remains. One day, when she learned to use it, she would do many things. Good things. Benevolent things. She would not need to kill then. Would not need to make allies of—

"Well, may I ask how do you plan to proceed now? You're not exactly working toward the same goal that your brother was. He is done for now, I'm sorry to say, but Mena and Dariel remain. What happens when—"

Corinn turned on the ambassador and stepped up close to him, enough so that he backed away a step, unnerved by the suddenness of her movement. Something about directing her agitation at him helped her get a grip on herself. "No, Rialus, you may not ask me anything. When we speak, it's because I've asked you something. That's all there is between us, understand? I need you, but I don't have any delusions about the nature of your loyalty. It is the same as with the Numrek. Like them, you will be loyal for one reason—because only I will give you all the things you want. The Meins would flay you alive. My brother or sister would imprison you as the traitor you are. Only with me have you any chance of happiness. Do you doubt it?"

Rialus did not.

"Good. I will deal with my siblings when I have to. I love them, of course. They love me. Do not concern yourself with it."

She stopped talking and motioned that Rialus should keep quiet as well. Faintly, she heard shouts of alarm and then the clash of weapons. They came to her muffled and warped by distance, almost ghostly. They were the type of sounds she might not have even noticed if she had not been listening for them. She had heard enough tales about how the Numrek fought so that she could envision the scenes now spreading through the palace. Right at that moment, she imagined, the Numrek were pouring through the halls. They were appearing at the very heart of the palace, completely without warning, igniting utter confusion. They were dashing from room to room, swinging those battle-axes, severing arms and splitting skulls, pinning breasts to the walls with their spears, driving the points of their swords into bellies, showing no mercy to anyone.

She pressed her palm against her abdomen, hit by a quick montage of the people she had sentenced to such deaths. Men like Haleeven, Hanish's uncle, whom she had actually liked. Women like Rhrenna, who had been her friend and Halren, who had laughed at her at dinner that night at Calfa Ven. Guards and soldiers, maids and servants, officials, noblewomen and their children. The quick barrage of faces and names struck her like so many punches in the gut. What a nightmare she had unleashed! She stepped back and reached for the wall for support. She had to remember that they were her enemies. They always had been. Every one of them. If they seemed genteel and harmless, it was only because men had killed effectively enough in their name to assure it.

The ambassador stepped toward her, inquiring if she were well.

Corinn spoke coldly. "You said earlier that you did not think I'd be interested in all that Calrach said. In future, Rialus, when you are translating for me, translate exactly. It is not for you to edit what I—or they—hear."

Rialus nodded, meekly accepting the reproach. A moment later, looking askance at him, she watched a smile of satisfaction draw across his face. She almost snapped at him, asking why he smiled. But then she understood why. She had just promised him a future. Such things, it seemed, were now hers to bestow. Or to take away.

This would take some getting used to.

CHAPTER

SEVENTY

When he stepped out of his tent in the predawn that morning, Leeka Alain had already decided that this day was to be his last. He had fought so much in his life, in so many varying terrains, from these arid fields to the mountains of Senival and the marshes of Candovia, right up to the high tundra of the Mein and through the woodlands of Aushenia. He had squabbled with Maeander Mein's troops; fought outright against Hanish's; clashed with Senivalian mountain tribesmen; and battled Numreks, a race he had discovered before anyone else in the Known World. He had even tamed one of those foreigners' rhinoceros mounts. He had stood shouting into snow squalls and through storms of catapulted fireballs. He had triumphed a few times but also been defeated more than once. He'd even sunk to the level of a belly-crawling mist addict. Yet he'd been resurrected and given another chance.

That made him one of the luckiest men alive. Thanks to Thaddeus Clegg's hard discipline, he had been given a second opportunity at life. With it he found the young prince Dariel. He had a hand in teaching him his name and in turning him from a raider into a man worthy of the nobility to which he was heir. He had seen Mena, lithe and small of stature, become an artist of martial craft the likes of which he'd never witnessed before. What she did the day before with her sword was incredible. It made no sense, looking at her slim frame and intelligent face, that she could be such a tornado of rage. And he'd seen King Leodan's eldest become a prophet of change, a noble man who spoke of a better world and was willing to fight—and die—in the struggle to bring it into existence. What, he wondered, could ever best watching his prince in all his perfectly formed glory cutting down the antok, a beast right out of the caves of hell? That would stand as the high point of his life, just as Aliver's death the next day was undeniably the lowest moment he'd ever known. What a shifting, chaotic tide their fortunes followed.

Leeka did not regret the life he had led. He certainly would not alter a moment of the years he put in laboring for his king and country. It was possible, though, that his journey through life was not going to end as he would have written it himself. This truth, he decided, he would face with as much composure as he could muster. At least he would lose with dignity and die in a manner befitting the code by which he had lived. That, he believed, was what the coming day's last stand against the Meins was to be about. He walked into it with his armor on, sword at his side, his face as creviced and venerable as he could muster as an example to those under him.

Such, at least, was his intention when he split the flap of his tent and stepped through the portal. But what he saw on the southern horizon was so bizarre and unexpected that he lost his composure immediately. His jaw hung loose. His mouth formed an amazed oval. His eyes became two copper coins that widened more and more with each passing moment.

What he saw was this: a sky roiling with clouds of red and orange, combusting with plumes of yellow and purple, with great mountains of movement stretching up into the heavens. All of this was a background upon which a company of giants approached. The sight of them was bizarre and surreal, their shapes incorporeal enough that on occasion the last stars of the dawn sky, seen between gaps in the seething clouds, twinkled right through them as well. Their shapes were in black silhouette, enormous figures of elongated vastness, their bodies rocking with their strides. Their arms waved in the air to either side as if they were moving across shifting ground, searching for balance. Their legs must have spanned miles with each step. Behind the first giants he saw the indications of others and felt the pressure of still more beyond that, coming up from around the curve of the world. He scanned his memories for anything to explain such a sight. He recalled only one thing.

"Could these be God Talkers?" he asked Mena, once she had emerged to answer his gruff command. "When Tinhadin exiled them, did they not rampage down toward the south like enraged giants? That's what I recall from my childhood studies." From his childhood studies? The very idea sounded absurd enough that Leeka doubted his own sanity. He might be dreaming or hallucinating. Mena might look at him and name him a madman. He asked, without his usual command of voice, "You see them, too, I hope?"

Mena did not respond, but she stared in a way that was answer enough.

Dariel joined them a moment later, just as speechless. Within a few minutes what remained of the entire army stood gazing to the south at the scene playing out across the heavens. It was hard to gauge how far away the figures were. Each of their strides appeared massive. Their legs seemed to stretch out as if the foot would plant itself beyond the onlookers. But the next step after that was just the same, and again after that. For all the strangeness of this Leeka knew they were, in fact, getting closer. But the territory they traversed was beyond his ken.

Leeka sensed alarm building around him. Personally, it had not occurred to him to be fearful. Something was happening here, yes. Something unexpected. Even without knowing what it was, he welcomed it. But considering the things they had witnessed recently, it made sense that others would be afraid. They were not all old men, like him. They were not all resolved to die as he was. Of course, they would conclude that whatever was coming came *against* them.

Somebody began mumbling a prayer in Bethuni. Another uttered the word that named Meinish ancestors, saying that they were coming to avenge Maeander. Still another yelled that it was Maeander himself returning. He had been killed in contradiction to honor, and they were all to be punished for it.

"Calm! Let us be calm," Leeka said.

Nobody seemed to hear him. People began to back away, tripping over things, their eyes dilated with growing fright.

"All of you stand!" Leeka bellowed. "Hear me! Whatever comes, be brave with us and welcome it. We still fight for Princess Mena and Prince Dariel. Our cause is just—"

Mena grabbed the general's arm. "I know what they are," she said. "You're right. They're God Talkers. I called them back." She piped up, her voice sharper than Leeka's, higher pitched. It got attention. They had nothing to fear, she yelled. The giants coming were Santoth sorcerers. She had called them. They came to answer her, and they were friends of her brother's, friends to them all. "There is nothing to fear."

The tone with which she pronounced this last statement did not really contain enough certainty to match her words, but just hearing her speak had a calming effect on the soldiers. Instead of fleeing, the troops drew closer together. They tightened up, flanking the royals and the general. Even those who had not been near them and who probably had not heard Mena's words gravitated toward her, perhaps remembering her feats from the previous days and taking some comfort from them. Together in one mass, they waited.

Leeka, standing just behind the Akarans, saw Dariel turn his head and heard him whisper in his sister's ear, "I hope you're right about this, Mena."

"Me, too," she said, once more staring at the sky. "Me, too."

When the shapes changed, they did so quickly, all of them going through it in the space of a few compressed seconds. One moment they were the towering figures they had been since Leeka first laid eyes on them. The next they were smaller. And then smaller again. Then smaller. It was so fast that Leeka's eyes were still in the sky when there was no longer anything to see up there. The billowing clouds consumed themselves in a silent implosion. Behind it the morning sky emerged, its normal pale shade of Talayan blue.

Leeka wondered if that was the end of it. A light show in the heavens, without substance, hard to read or understand, finally disappointing. But that was not all of it. He heard inhaled breaths all around him, felt Mena's arm brush his unintentionally. He lowered his gaze.

There on the earth, just yards away, walked a group of men. They were of normal stature, of flesh and blood, moving at an easy pace, about a hundred of them. They swayed slightly, as the giants had, but in most ways they were everything those shapes had not been: small, corporeal, tangible. They had the stooped postures and the thin limbs of old men, with gaunt, hungry faces. They should not have been frightening. Yet Leeka could not help but step back, pressing against the barricade of bodies just behind him.

The first of the men stopped just a few strides away. The others bunched up behind them. Leeka stared at their faces. They were not right. They were not normal. He saw them in concrete detail: the individual shapes of their noses, the jagged ridges of their hairlines, the shape of their eyes, and their slow manner of blinking. But he could sense stitches at the edges of their foreheads, or just under the chin, as if they had taken on the skins of others and wore them sewn onto their own skins. At times tremors rippled across their flesh, leaving them different from before. The longer he looked, the more he thought he saw bits and pieces of familiar persons in their features. He even saw himself in the scowl on one, in the eyebrows of another, the jawline of that one. . . .

Who called us?

The question appeared in his mind. He heard it, even though it had not been spoken. The figures had not moved their mouths, but the words sounded within him with a choric timbre of blended voices. Glancing around, he knew he was not alone in having received the question.

Who called us?

"I did," Mena said. Her voice sounded as brittle as a twig. She seemed to think so herself. She tried again. Without opening her mouth, she spoke, *I did. Are you Santoth? Nualo? Is one of you Nualo?*

The figures drew in. They seemed to slide toward Mena on rollers. One of them stepped forward. He managed to convey that he was Nualo, without overtly affirming it. Leeka just knew, and he knew that everyone nearby knew also. They were all part of this.

Why was it not the firstborn? Nualo asked.

Mena glanced at her brother, at Leeka. She swallowed. *Aliver—the firstborn of us—has died. . . .*

Flushed, her lips trembling, Mena carried on. *He was killed by our enemy. That's why I called you. Before he died, he told me only you could—*

The Santoth did not let her finish. They asked for proof of the firstborn's death. Mena told them that his body was nearby. Instantly, the sorcerers drifted toward it. They knew how to find Aliver's corpse without needing to be directed.

Unable to speak, not knowing how to begin, Leeka did not move. Nobody else did either, except to look into one another's faces. Dariel eventually broke the silence, saying, with a strained hint of his usual humor, "I've asked this before, and I'll try it again in this situation . . . Do we have a plan?"

Mena did not have time to answer. The Santoth were already returning, sliding into the same positions they had been in previously. Leeka barely managed to follow the exchange Mena fell into with them. So much passed between them, not just words but other thoughts that did not take verbal form. While Leeka got tangled in it, Mena managed to sort through the weight of information floating between them. The Santoth admitted that they had felt Aliver's death when it happened. They had known the moment the connection between them was cut, but they had hoped it was not so. They had believed him when he promised to free them. Only he could do so because he was the first of his generation and a direct descendant from Tinhadin. They wanted to know how he could have allowed himself to die with his promise to them unfulfilled.

Mena could not answer that; it just was. She asked if he could not live again, though. Could they not bring him back to life? Did they not have the power to heal him? But Nualo, speaking now for the others, said no, no, no. They could not restore life. Elenet had never learned how to achieve that.

The Giver had protected this knowledge above all else, and he had departed without ever having spoken the words. There may not even be words for restoring life, not to a person who was truly dead, with no sorcery involved.

Then do what you can do, Mena said. *Help us defeat the Meins. They come for us even now. Look, if you don't believe. They come.*

Nualo and the others turned in the direction she pointed. It was true. The Meinish army approached, looking more numerous than the day before, marching in to finish what they had started. Looking at them, Leeka realized how completely they were defeated. He might have hoped the giant shapes in the sky would have unnerved them, but they marched forward as if they had not seen anything unusual. He felt the collective heart of the troops sink. The end trudged toward them. It was but minutes away.

We cannot, Nualo said. *We would only cause harm.*

"As if they are not planning on just that?" Dariel said, but there was no humor in it, especially as spoken words sounded so discordant in the company of the Santoth.

In one shared capsule of thought, Nualo explained that the Giver's tongue was ever deceiving. Men were not meant to possess it. They should never have studied it. The power they wielded was a dangerous thing even at the best of times, even when they had *The Song of Elenet* to read from. No matter what good they tried to do, it always became corrupted somehow. Tinhadin had not banished them without reason. No Santoth wished to tempt the dangers of using their knowledge for violence now. If they began it, they could not say where it would end.

Nualo said, *The prince knew that we could do nothing without first studying The Song of Elenet. . . .*

Dariel cut in. "Why are we having this discussion?" He lifted his gaze and took in the northern view, thronging now with Meins, loud with their singing and their taunts. Snapping back to the Santoth, he held his words with a clamped mouth and communicated with them as Mena was. *Aliver is dead! That army is coming to destroy us. You see them, don't you? Explain to me how you have any hope of coming in from banishment if we die? You've no hope at all, and you know it.*

Nualo turned his complete attention on the younger Akaran. A crease formed on the Santoth's forehead and slithered down across his eyeball and changed the shape of his nose and bent one corner of his lips before he swallowed it. Leeka knew that that crease was an expression of anger, of desperation, and a sign of how hard it was for these banished ones to inhabit this physical world. He heard Nualo say, *You do not know what you are asking.* Watching him, Leeka believed that to be a true statement.

Exasperated, Dariel turned and set off toward the Meins, calling for others to do the same. He gathered up his things when he passed his tent. A few answered him, but Mena stayed focused on Nualo. *Maybe he doesn't,* she said, *but you do. I called and you came. You didn't come here to do nothing, did you? Do what you can now. Later, when the world is at peace, we'll find The Song of Elenet. You'll be able to speak pure again. Then you can undo any wrong.*

Nualo and the others sat with this for some time. Their faces changing ever more quickly now—creasing, morphing, becoming pocked, peeling, and then healing, their features impermanent and shifting. They were agitated, angry, hungry. Yes, they were hungry, too. They spoke among themselves.

Leeka heard the clash of the battle just beginning. He felt the pull toward it. He could not let Dariel die without him. He had turned and begun to move away when he heard Nualo say, *Others have made the mistake of believing that good comes from evil. It is not so. Nothing today will be any different.*

Leeka kept walking. He put his hand on his sword and felt the contours of the grip in his hand. He knew there was more coming from the Santoth, though. He knew how to sense anger, knew how it drove people to action, and he felt it pulsing behind him with a growing intensity. They were going to do it. No matter their wisdom and wish for peace, beneath it all, they were human. They raged against their fate. They mourned their savior's death. They wanted revenge. And they wanted to do the one thing that had been denied them for generations. They wanted to open their mouths and speak.

Whatever happens, Nualo said, *stay behind us. Do not follow and do not look. It will be better for you if you do not look.*

Leeka was still moving forward when the Santoth strode past him. One of them gestured with his hand in a way that pushed the old general back, almost knocking him from his feet. They did this to others also and to those in front of them. With motions of their fingers and hands they grabbed soldiers from right in the fray and yanked them back from the Meins. Leeka saw Dariel seemingly get pinched up by the head and moved across the ground, ending up dropped on his bottom beside where his sister stood. Mena helped him rise, and then she turned him away from the battle. She cried for others to do the same.

"Nualo said not to look!" she said. "Do as he said. Whatever happens, do not look."

Leeka had to consider what he was about to do for only a few seconds. He did not truly weigh the decision. Nor did he intend even the slightest disrespect with his act of disobedience. But he had woken that morning intent on death, sure that he was stepping into the sunlight for the last time. Now, presented with what was to be a sight for the ages, he could not turn his back on it. Let it be the last thing he ever witnessed, if it had to be. He turned from Mena and Dariel and from the huddled back of the Acacian forces. He followed the sorcerers into battle.

He was among them as they fanned out across the field, close enough to see that they worked with their eyes closed. Their lips moved. They spoke. No, they sang. They filled the air with a twisting, twining, melodious confusion of words and sounds. Their song had a physical density to it. Musical tones brushed past Leeka with an audible slither, with a texture like the spiny contours on a serpent's back. Every now and then, one of the sorcerers moved a hand through the air, a slow gesture as if he wished to feel the substance of the ether with his fingertips.

The Meins backed away, bewildered, hesitating. A few of their generals tried to restore order and press the assault, but they did not get a chance to. The Santoth all attacked at the same moment. They strode forward without breaking their composed gaits, but they covered distance in leaps and jerks hard to measure. They shouted out their strange, incomprehensible words as they went. They waved their arms and swatted the air like madmen plagued by invisible demons.

Leeka ran to stay with them. He was behind a Santoth as he approached a group of blond-haired soldiers. They were ready to meet him, feet set wide, their swords in their two-handed grip, elbows cocked. But with one swipe of his arm the Santoth stripped the armor, the clothing, and even the skin from two soldiers. They dropped their swords and stood uncomprehending, the striations of their facial muscles and tendons and cartilage raw to the air, their abdomens so completely opened that their inner organs slipped out of them in a tangle. The Santoth was past them before they fell, and he did the same to others beyond.

Another sorcerer punched at the air, a strange motion with no immediate opponent. A second later a whole cluster of soldiers a hundred yards before him liquefied. They each became thousands of pea-sized balls of fluid clustered in human form. The drops fell to the ground, each bursting on impact, leaving the earth pooled from a red-tainted rain. Another wizard blew his fury straight from the back of his throat with a force that warped the air in front of him and tore a bloody path as straight and limb-snapping as a rolling boulder's.

In the space of a few seconds everything had changed. The Meins fled in chaos. Many of them dropped their weapons and tore free their helmets. They clawed at their fellow soldiers. They trampled others in their hysteria. They pushed and shoved, fear in complete control of their actions. It was clear that they were utterly defeated. Whatever they saw in the faces of the sorcerers shot them through with terror. And the Santoth followed, pursuing. As they did so, their fury grew. They moved faster, made grander gestures, roared out more powerfully. They stamped their feet, making the ground buck and shift around them. Slabs of earth tilted up, as if the earth's crust were made of cheap board and axes were smashing up from underneath it, throwing soldiers somersaulting in the air.

Leeka muttered to himself that this was not possible. It could not be. He refuted it over and over again. It was not possible, even if it all felt intimately familiar to him. It was akin to his fever time, when he had burned with nightmares in that pile of dead bodies high up on the Mein Plateau. The images that had raged in his mind then were much like the ones around him now. But those dreams had not been real. They were delusions. He wanted to believe that these visions were also tricks of his mind. He should not accept them, could not trust them. If his eyes were to be believed, the world was a mural painted on a flimsy canvas. It could be ripped to shreds. According to his eyes, rents could tear through the sky and into the earth and sometimes shred through the flesh of those caught with it. These scars mended just as quickly as they began, but the sight and sound of them was an amazing horror. And, if his eyes did not lie, the sky poured down a deluge of serpentine horrors. Snakes, worms, centipedes the size of ancient pine trees, eel-like creatures pulled up from the black depths of some great ocean: all of these thudded down to the ground. They twisted and writhed, batting the Mein legions about, flattening men. The beasts rolled and came up with soldiers smashed paper thin against their sides. And he knew that his eyes were not seeing the worst of it. The real horrors, he was sure, were just at the edges of his vision, just outside his capacity to focus. No matter that he snapped his head from side to side, eyes darting, frantic. Still, he never saw the complete ghastliness he felt was there just beyond.

He spotted one of the Santoth, standing still, his mouth opened in song. It was Nualo. Leeka moved toward him. He drew as near as he dared and stood panting, fatigued as he had never been in life before, exhausted by something more than just the exertion. *It is hard on the living to be near magic*, he thought. *Such force is—*

Nualo turned around. It was not a sudden move, just a slow rotation that seemed initiated by his eyes, the head and the rest of his body following. He scanned the battlefield behind him. He had never imagined such fury. His eyes contained a raging intensity that trembled as if all this chaos was mirrored inside them. They roared without sound.

Corrupted. Such force is corrupted. He heard these words in his head and knew that Nualo had placed them there to complete his unfinished thought. *How do you live?*

Looking into Nualo's eyes and knowing what writhed and ripped and screamed all around him, Leeka could not answer the question. It felt as if he had been tugged out of the normal order of the world and observed all this from a space within and without it at the same time. He was being allowed to witness this, to live through it, but he could not even begin to explain how and why this could be.

He would later be unsure just what he had seen. So much of his memory of the day would be a shattered collage of the impossible. But there was one thing he knew with certainty. The power he observed was frightening not just for the destruction it caused but because it was so completely and utterly evil. Its intent may not have been conceived with wickedness. Nualo and the other Santoth were not themselves malignant. Even the rage that propelled them was rooted in a love of the world, in a longing to be able to rejoin it. But the power they unleashed had its own seething animus. If the language of the Giver all those years before had been one of creation, and if that act of creation had been a love hymn that sang the world into being on music that was the fabric of existence itself and that was, as the legends held, most wondrously good to behold . . . if that was so, then what the Santoth released was its opposite. Their song was a fire that consumed the world, a hunger that ate creation, not fed it.

Corruption, Leeka thought, *doesn't even begin to explain it.*

Nualo must have heard this, but he did not respond. He turned away, disgusted and impatient. He again unleashed air-rending shouts from the cavern of his mouth. He moved forward, arms flailing the world before him into shredded ribbons.

Leeka did what he now believed he was meant to do. He ran to keep up. He ran so that he could be a witness, so that somebody would know, so that if ever the time came, somebody would be able to testify as to why the created should never appropriate the powers of the creator.

CHAPTER

SEVENTY-ONE

It took all of Corinn's concentration to keep her gaze elevated above the gore that littered the palace. She tried to keep her eyes vacant, uninterested, letting the bodies on the floor; the blood-splattered walls; and the strewn, shattered debris remain vague, only defined enough so that she could navigate through them. She focused on mundane objects in the distance, murals at the ends of hallways, doorframes, particular bricks singled out on the walls. Soon she planned to lock herself in her room until the cleanup was complete, until every sign and sight of the carnage she had orchestrated was scrubbed from the floors and walls and washed out of fabrics. She would send Rialus to the lower town to conscript the Acacian peasants huddled there for the task. She would pay them with freedom, with privilege, with her love and thanks. She would infuse them with pride in the Acacian Empire again. There would be a great deal to do, but these things would all come later. First, she had to walk these halls and complete one more task.

She found Rialus waiting for her. Earlier, when a Numrek soldier returned to inform her that the palace was controlled, Rialus had gone before her to assess the situation. Now he looked queasy. His tongue was quick enough, though, and he began talking before she had even reached him, expressing his amazement at how easily the palace had fallen. Her plan had worked perfectly. The palace was under her power already. The lower town was shut tight and trembling. There might be a few Meins hiding in the servants' areas and in the town, but the Numrek were hunting them down door to door. The priests protecting the Tunishnevre had proven quite stubborn. They had clung to the sarcophagi until they were ripped from them and killed on the spot. Several noble families were caught trying to sail from the ports, their yachts piled high with all they could carry. A few boats had managed to get away. The Numrek, not being a seafaring people, did not—

Corinn cut him off. "Where is he?"

Rialus did not need to ask whom she meant. "In the ceremonial chamber, as you ordered."

As the two walked, Rialus rattled on, detailing what he had learned about the battle. Much of it had gone just as the Numreks imagined. Their surprise appearance had created instant chaos. The first killed had been two Meinish women whose heads had twirled in the air before they had so much as voiced their alarm. Most of what had followed was pure butchery. Meinish guards fought bravely enough, he supposed, but they were cut down in ones and twos. Few of them had managed to organize a cohesive response. There had been a large skirmish in the main upper courtyard, where the palace battalion had focused their efforts. The Numrek had welcomed the sport of it.

Hanish had been in the ceremonial chamber when the attack began, but he had rushed out to respond. He and a band of Punisari held the lower courtyard right to the last, trying to block the entrance to the chamber. The Numrek had surrounded them, pushed in on them with their greater numbers, working at them like so many butchers slaughtering ornery beasts. The Punisari had not made it easy. They were Hanish's best men, lean and muscled, capable of lopping free even a Numrek's meaty arm. Each of them had blocked and struck at peak speed, blurs of motion that betrayed no fatigue, many wielding two swords. They had fought in a circle formation, drawing closer together as they fell. None of them had made even the slightest overture of surrender. Hanish himself spoke to his men the entire time. Few Numrek, however, know any but their own language. None could tell Rialus what the chieftain had said to his men as they, and everything they had ever fought for, died.

"Pity," Rialus said. "I'd have liked to have heard what he made of the situation. Bit of a surprise, I imagine. Not what he had planned when he woke up . . ."

The last two remaining with Hanish had been the hardest to get rid of. They had reached a pitch of fighting that made it almost impossible to land a strike. One was eventually taken down after his leg was sliced off at the knee. He fell and, trying to right himself with the use of his blood-spurting stump, he became easy prey. The other got stabbed through the back of the head with a Numrek lance, an injury that, by the look of it, cut his spine and rendered his body instantly immobile.

Hanish, after this, had done his best to fight to the death. At some point he had realized that the Numrek were not trying to kill him. He had stopped fighting, let his blade droop and rotated it in slow circles, waiting. When none attacked, he pulled his Ilhach dagger and would have slit his belly, had the Numrek not grappled with him first. This also must have been a strange sight, a horde of the burly-armed soldiers dropping their weapons and struggling to pummel into submission a man who was intent on ending his own life—this when they were covered in gore from a few hours of blood work themselves. Rialus admitted that the Numrek had ill treated Hanish, but he left them little choice. He still lived. He was bound as she ordered and awaited her in the chamber.

When Rialus seemed to have exhausted his knowledge of the day, he turned and studied Corinn's profile. "Princess, this is a work of genius, of simplicity. Once it is cleaned up, the world will bow to you and your beauty. They'll forget the bloodshed here." He hesitated a moment, his tongue flicking out to moisten his lips. "Of all the surprises you've devised, none is more of a revelation than you yourself are. I pray you never find reason to disfavor me."

Something about this praise touched her. She felt a flush around her eyes, an itch that suggested tears were not far behind. She spoke quickly. "Thank you, Rialus. You have been a great help to me. I will not forget."

Corinn left the ambassador standing in the open air outside the passageway into the chamber that now housed the Tunishnevre. She steadied herself a moment and drew out the one weapon she now carried. She walked past the Numrek, milling about the entrance, and into the dark corridor with a crisp step unconsciously modeled on Maeander's stone-chipping gait. As the chamber opened up around her, she felt the seething incorporeal life in the air. She tried to ignore it, moving through the huge space of the place with no outward sign of discomfort. It took great effort. If air could scratch like claws, the air in this room would have shredded her. If silent screams could consume flesh, she would have been eaten alive. All her instincts told her to turn and run. She did not. She cut her progress with the point of her chin. Pride, even in the face of the undead, now seemed of greatest importance to her.

Hanish hung suspended over the Scatevith stone. His arms were bound above him, secured at the wrists, and his head slumped forward as limp as a corpse's. He was naked from the waist up, his chest ribboned with bruises and abrasions. A gash under his armpit dripped a stain of blood, like rust, stretching all the way down into his trousers. He was bound at the ankles also, in such a way that if he tried to move he would be able only to writhe in the air but not kick out. One of his feet jutted out at a strange angle, broken. Perhaps most horrible, though, was his hair. It had been hacked away by Numrek swords, leaving his pate uneven, mangy, his scalp exposed in some places.

Part of Corinn wanted to fly to him, to grasp him around the torso and lift his weight and find some way to get him down and to beg forgiveness. She wanted to search about on the ground for clumps of his straw-colored locks and stick them back in place. It seemed unfathomable that Hanish, the chieftain of the Known World, could be reduced to this state within the space of a few hours. Is this the way the world worked? The way she had the power to affect it?

As she approached, she tried not to let any of these questions or emotions show. This man would have killed her. Pride, she thought, despises uncertainty. She began speaking as soon as his head lifted and his eyes found her. "I had thought to enter here with a bow and a quiver of arrows," she said. "I thought I might have you nailed to the wall, splayed out as a target. You recall how good a shot I am, don't you? I would have had you name the spots you wished me to place each arrow in."

Blinking, Hanish seemed to have trouble seeing her. Drops of blood from his wrists speckled his forehead. He looked dazed, as if he might not be entirely conscious. But then he said, "One in my heart would have been enough."

Corinn crooked her mouth, making it a knot that kept her emotions hidden.

"I never thought it before," Hanish continued, "but I see now why you were so apt at archery. You kill best from a distance. You can shoot an arrow from hiding, from a safe place. I can see now why that sport suited you."

A safe place? Corinn had never in her life found a safe place. She planned to, though. She planned to. She lifted the dagger and held it high enough for him to see. "And yet here I am with your blade. You are going to die on it."

Hanish smiled, his teeth brown with blood. "So this is all your personal revenge? You were scorned, and because of it you ordered thousands killed. Do you know what that makes you? It makes you just like me, or perhaps worse than me."

I am not like you, Corinn wanted to say. But she feared her voice might quaver around the words, suggesting things she did not wish suggested. She stayed to her planned script. "Before you die you should know all the ways in which you've failed. For one, you have lost everything to me, your concubine. Everything. I've cut out the heart of your empire. Even if your dead brother's army defeats my dead brother's army, they cannot change what I've done here."

She felt herself warming to her words. Saying them to him made her feel better than she had in many years. She climbed the granite steps up onto the Scatevith stone, feeling the ceremonial import of the platform, the honeycombed ranks of the Tunishnevre all around her, their energy as palpable in the air as electricity. It was hard not to feel that the sarcophagi were going to begin opening one by one, the dried corpses in them animated by their own hatred.

As she spoke she studied the bowl carved in the stone that Hanish had planned to drench with her blood. "Already there are boats sailing the sea in all directions, each of them a herald of the change. Messengers will fly from here within the hour. They will tell the entire Known World that Hanish Mein is dead and that Acacia is once again in Akaran hands. Also, your Tunishnevre will never walk the earth again. If that was what you lived your life for, know now that you failed at it."

Hanish sucked his teeth and then spat, a halfhearted gesture that left a stain of saliva on his chin. "I should have chained you the moment I heard what your sister did to Larken. I should have realized Akaran women were deadlier than the men."

She moved closer, the dagger held high enough, near enough, that it was a threat to his bruised skin, no more than a quick slash away from his ribs and muscles stretched taut by his bondage. "Is that why you Meins don't let your women fight?" she asked. "Are you afraid of them?"

"I should have chained you," Hanish repeated, fixing his gray eyes on hers. "But I loved you too much. That thing—love—is what I should have feared. Now we both see why."

"You cannot win me over now," Corinn said, though the words did not come out with the clipped tone she wished for. Her hands were sweating. The dagger grip was slick against her palm. She wanted to put it down, just for a second, so that she could wipe the moisture from her skin. She thought, How can I even now feel something for this man?

The life seemed to be draining out of Hanish with each breath. He let his head drop forward again, a low, ruminative moan reverberating in his throat. He asked slowly, with pauses so that he could inhale or exhale, "Would you kill me now? Do that for me. My ancestors have things they wish to say to me . . . directly. Never let the past enslave you, Corinn. The dead seek to burden us . . . to twist our lives as badly as they twisted theirs. Don't let them." With that he fell silent. His breathing came regular but labored, his lungs struggling against the pressure his hanging body put on them. It was not clear if he was conscious anymore.

The knife, held high, shone with the light from the few unbroken oil lamps. She raised it and looked beyond it at her former lover's chest, at his neck, at his muscled abdomen. Where does one stick a knife? No place seemed right. Each and every portion of him was too familiar. She had held that chest close to her too often, brushed her lips over that skin, and listened to that heart beating within that cage of ribs. In a way, she knew, a piece of that heart beat inside her, small, quiet, growing. There was no place on him into which she could thrust this blade. Instead, she did something else, something she had not been aware she'd even considered an option.

She pressed the honed edge of the dagger into the palm of her other hand. It cut the flesh easily down to the bone, without any real pain. Removing the blade, she clenched the wounded hand into a fist, held it up for a moment. Crimson oozed between her fingertips, inching tentatively over her hand. "Do you know what?" she whispered. She wanted Hanish to hear her, but hoped he would not look up, hoped that the words would enter his unconscious mind, unsure that she could say them into his eyes. "I am carrying your baby. Can you believe that? You've fathered the future of Acacia." She bent and pressed her bloody palm into the receiving basin, leaving a blurred handprint that the stone sucked up like a sponge. "I will raise this one well, as an Acacian. Whether that is a joy or a punishment is up to you. But neither you, nor your ancestors, will have any say in this child's fate."

She could not be sure if she heard Hanish call to her as she turned and descended from the stone. She might have, but the air was too filled with other sounds. Who knew if she was supposed to have intoned certain words in a certain way? Perhaps she should have spoken the language written in *The Song of Elenet*, the hidden volume that she would begin to study soon. Surely, she did not do it quite right. But she did the thing that mattered. She offered her blood, willingly, in forgiveness. In the first moments afterward, the air filled with a thousand cries that she might or might not have heard, protests from those ancient undead at being denied their second chance at life. But it did not last long. In their coffins, she sensed, those ancient bodies of Hanish's ancestors finally gave up their long purgatory. They became dust, and the spirits within them rejoined the natural order of the world. They joined the mystery, no longer trapped outside it, no longer a threat to the living in any way.

When she stepped back into the sunlight, she found Rialus staring toward the south, transfixed enough that he did not note her approach. She followed his gaze. As her eyes adjusted to the glare of the late afternoon, she made out the seething clouds that fascinated him. There was a storm of some sort on the horizon. The heavens shuddered with the power of it, alive with color, flashing with what must have been bolts of lightning, though they were like nothing she had ever seen. It might have been an ominous sight, but the longer she stared, the more she resolved that whatever was happening out there was at a great, great distance. It was not going to affect them.

Reassured of this, she reached out and touched Rialus on the shoulder. He turned toward her, his face letting go of one set of questions and adopting another. Seeing the blood dripping from her hand, he asked, "Are you hurt?"

She said that she was not.

"It is done, Princess?"

"No," she answered. "How could I kill the father of my child? If I do that, he will have brought me down to his level. He'll have debased me. I just looked at him and knew that if I drew this blade through his flesh, I'd relive the moment over and over again for the rest of my life. I'd never be free of it. I'd see him in my child's face. Do you understand? He would rule me, even in his death. So I could not do it." She turned her eyes away from the small man's, not liking the familiarity taking shape in them, surprised at how readily that confession had poured out of her. Enough of weakness. She said, "So instead, Rialus, you will do it. Here, use his own blade against him. I give this as a gift to you."

Rialus took the weapon and stared at it, incredulous, the sliver of metal curved like a lean moon. He looked from it to her and then back to the blade again. He could have been a dealer in Meinish artifacts, so intently did his gaze drift over the lettering engraved in the collar and across the twisted metalwork of the guard and down the ridged contours of the handle. But Corinn, studying the slow evolution of thought behind his features, knew that his mind was not on the details of the weapon at all. He was rushing back through his long list of grievances against Hanish. He was recalling the ways he had been belittled, mocked, shunned over the years. He was thinking how powerless he had been and how much he yearned for revenge.

"Can you do it?" she asked.

"Is he . . . secured?" Rialus asked.

Corinn said that he would give him no trouble. He was secured. He was waiting. Nodding, Rialus turned and moved toward the passageway. "Yes," he said, just barely audible, "this I can do, Princess, if it is what you wish." He walked with short, hesitant steps, a man dazed by an act of fortune so complete he had never imagined it and doubted it yet.

Once he was swallowed by the shadows, Corinn turned back to the churning chaos at play in the southern heavens. She had never seen anything like it. There was fury in it, but it was muted by distance. Of more note was the beauty of it: the way the high reaches seemed aflame with liquid fire, dancing with colors she could not even recall the names of. With colors that she was not sure she had ever seen before. She could not help feeling the display was meant for her, that it somehow marked the change in the world that she had just arranged. She wished that she felt more joy than she did, more relief, more solace, but something about the sight touched her with melancholy. She could not put her finger on it. She did make sure to refute what Hanish had said, though. He was wrong. She was not like him at all.

"I am better than you." Corinn said this aloud, although there was nobody around her, nobody but herself to convince.

End of Book Three

Epilogue

It was a chill afternoon, windblown and low clouded, the sea all around Acacia whitecapped and desolate. The memorial procession left the palace via the western gate and followed the high road toward Haven's Rock. They walked the winding ridges, a long, thin line of mourners. The hills around them dropped down into valleys that tumbled headlong into the gray waters of late autumn. Mena strode near the front, with her remaining siblings and the small, cobbled-together remnants that passed now for the Acacian aristocracy. She followed an ornate cart that carried two urns of ashes. In one were those of Leodan Akaran. Thaddeus Clegg had secretly kept them hidden all these years. In the other urn were the remains of Aliver Akaran, a boy who became a leader the ages would remember, a prince who never quite became a king.

It had been nearly ten years since Mena last traversed this route. She still remembered that earlier occasion, riding horseback with her father and all her siblings. At the time she could not have imagined her father's death or Aliver's or the strange, diverse lives they had lived between those two terrible events. Progressing in silence, she could not help recalling the child that she had once been. Looking at the plumage dotting the landscape, she remembered that she'd once been afraid of acacia trees. It would have seemed a silly thought—a tree is but a tree—except that she knew she had replaced those childish fears with new ones.

Now she feared her dreams. Too often in them she faced Larken again, her first kill. Each time the experience was much like the event had been in reality: she full of certainty, moving with purpose, able to slice the flesh of him without any inkling of remorse. It was the same with her reveries of the battles in Talay, especially the afternoon after Aliver's death three months ago, when she had killed with such abandon that it had seemed she had been designed for no other purpose. On waking, the details of all the deaths she had caused hung before her like hundreds of individual portraits, floating between her and the world. She knew such things would haunt her for years to come. It was not exactly this that she feared, though. The frightening thing was knowing that in an instant she could and would slay again. She really had taken a bit of Maeben into her. It would always be there beneath the skin. Her gift of rage.

She was not the only one to emerge scarred from the war. Dariel trudged just behind her, Wren at his side. The young woman seemed ill at ease in the formal dress the occasion required. She had been a raider all her life and she looked it still, her joints loose and her posture casual in a manner that was slightly aggressive. But Mena liked her and hoped that she would bring her brother happiness for a long time to come. Dariel needed joy. He was still quick to laugh, nimble with jokes. He had a mischievous beauty when he grinned, but he seemed to think himself solely responsible for Aliver's death. When he thought nobody was looking at him, he wore the burden of it like a cloak of lead. Mena had yet to present the King's Trust to him. He was not ready, but he would be someday.

Others had not emerged from the conflict at all. Thaddeus Clegg had been inside the palace when the Numrek had attacked. He apparently died in the slaughter that Corinn ordered. Why he was there and whether or not he had come close to finding *The Song of Elenet* might never be known. There was no sign of it. Corinn even questioned whether the volume existed at all. There had been a note in a pocket next to his chest that told where he had hidden King Leodan's ashes, which he had kept safe all these years. He was the only reason they had the king's remains now.

Leeka Alain's fate was shrouded in still more mystery. A few swore that they had seen him trailing behind the Santoth when they turned from their destruction and retreated into exile again. If these ones could be believed, the old general ran behind the sorcerers, wrapped in the great confusion surrounding them. Perhaps he had become one of them. Or maybe he had just been vaporized by their fury. Either way, no trace of him remained in the Known World, except the high regard he would always be held in, rhinoceros rider that he was.

And the world itself had not been the same since the Santoth were unleashed. Mena could not pinpoint exactly what was different or how it might affect the future, but she knew the ramifications of that dreadful day in Talay were not completely behind them. At times she could feel the rents they had torn in the fabric of creation. At other times it felt like the seams holding the world together threatened to burst. The passing days eased some of the confusion in the air, but it was not gone completely. The Santoth had let spell after spell out on the battlefield that day. They had only spent a few hours weaving magic, but who could say how the remnants of the Giver's twisted tongue would change the world?

When they climbed to the rolling plateau that stretched to the cliffs, Mena saw Corinn, who was ahead of her, look over her shoulder. She seemed to decide to slow so that Mena could catch up with her. What a revelation her sister was. Nothing at all like the girl Mena remembered. In truth, she felt little easy affection for her. There was an innate connection between them, a bond in the very blood essence of them, but it seemed an ever-prickly thing to navigate. It had been an incredible surprise to learn that Corinn had taken Acacia back from Hanish Mein. The fact that she had done so with the aid of the Numrek, and that she had forged some sort of agreement with the league, further stunned the younger siblings. The two of them had felt themselves in command just behind Aliver. They had been fighting the war, they thought. They had been at the center of all the struggle, or so they had believed. To discover that Corinn awaited them on a liberated Acacia, and that she was undeniably in power, with her own Numrek army and with a fleet of ships at her disposal . . . Mena had yet to come to terms with it all.

She still thought of their reunion with unease. An event that should have been joyous in so many ways was . . . well, she was not sure exactly how to categorize the experience, but it was not what she would have imagined. It was a week after the Santoth had cleared the field of every Meinish soldier in sight. She and Dariel sailed into Acacia's harbor, the two of them standing at the prow of the sloop she'd taken from Larken, gazing up at the terraced city that had once been their home. It was all as she remembered, really, but that still felt strange because she had spent so many years doubting the details she had recalled from her past.

Behind them came a ragtag fleet bearing the remains of the great army. Though she knew they were weary, she felt propelled by the weight of them at her back, as if they were the wind that billowed the boat toward the docks. They were triumph. And relief. And fatigue. They bore grief with them as well, but this had already become inexorably commingled with victory. Mena doubted she would ever feel unadulterated joy. Thus far, life had not provided her this, not as Mena the girl princess, not as Maeben on earth, not as the sword-wielding warrior of the Talayan plains. Still, she watched the island approach with anticipation. She was finally going home.

They docked and disembarked amid a reveling throng. The air rang with the music of flutes and cymbals, sweet with incense and fragrant with roasting meat, simmering stews, and frying fish. Corinn, they were told by the officials that met them, awaited them nearby. Indeed, after leaving the docks and cutting through crowds gathered in the lower town and up to the second terrace, there was no missing Corinn. She stood at the first landing of the granite stairway, the central one that led up toward the palace. An entourage flanked her. It was a mixed company that appeared to be made up of advisers and officials, with a contingent of Numrek officers conspicuously close to her, like personal guards. Though they did not wear particular uniforms, they were all clothed in sanguine colors, shades of crimson and brown and auburn. Mena knew a little of how Corinn had recaptured the palace and defeated Hanish, but it surprised her that her sister seemed to already have some sort of government in place.

Corinn was the centerpiece of this arrangement. How marvelous she looked! Mena remembered that she had always thought her sister a beauty, but the sight of her was more astonishing than she had expected. She wore a long-sleeved gown of a light, shimmering fabric, a creamy color touched with a hint of orange. Her hair was intricately made up, ribbons woven into a tight bun, pierced through with a spray of quills and the white plume of some bird. Her features were perfectly formed, delicate, her bosom and the flare of her hips highlighted by the shapely gown. Her arms were sensuously formed—shapely but not overly lean or muscled, like Mena's—her wrists and fingers as expressive as a dancer's when she extended them in a gesture of greeting.

Clearly, she was waiting for them to climb the steps. As they did so, Mena had an unforgivable thought. She did not know where it came from and thought it a coarseness of her war-weary mind. She imagined Corinn snatching one of those hairpins out and snapping it forward, a weapon, a poisoned dart. How frustrating and foul, she thought, that such an image would come to her at what should be a happy moment. What was wrong with her?

With that question in mind, looking up at Corinn's splendor, Mena realized what she herself looked like in comparison: half naked in a short skirt and sleeveless tunic, small and wiry, leather brown, her arms and legs scripted with all manner of cuts and abrasions, her hair an unkempt cascade. She suddenly felt the salt crusting her cheeks and the grime in the creases of her elbows and the film of dirt and sweat on her sandaled feet. She glanced at Dariel. Dashing as he was with his open raider's shirt and sun-burnished skin, he too looked more a ruffian than a prince of Acacia. Why had they not thought to make themselves more presentable?

Corinn finally began to descend toward them to close the last few steps. She stretched out both her arms, palms upward, her head listing to one side, her eyes gone kind. "Welcome home," she said, "my sister, my brother. Welcome, Acacian warriors."

She carried on speaking, words that seemed strangely formal, as if they were part of a scripted greeting, meant more for the onlookers than for Mena and Dariel. Corinn brought them into a short embrace and then pulled them back and studied each of their faces in turn. Her eyes brimmed as she did so, her full lips trembling slightly. In everything she was courteous and loving and generous, and yet it also seemed wrong somehow. Even when she raised her voice and asked the crowd to welcome this "daughter and son of Acacia" home, and as she smiled down on them through the answering cacophony, Mena could not help feeling that behind the loving façade Corinn was not actually pleased with what she saw in them.

That was how it had been between them ever since. Mena could not point to any specific slight on Corinn's part. Her words were never cruel, never less than appropriate. They spent evenings together over fine food and wine, talking of the past, all of them coming to know one another again. They rode horseback as they had done as children, and they sat together as a unit facing the myriad challenges of putting the empire back together again. Dariel seemed completely trusting of her, enough so that Mena never voiced her uneasiness to him. But through it all Mena feared that there would never be the easy, natural warmth between them that there had been with Aliver and that she still felt with Dariel. Corinn went through the motions of such a relationship but did not quite allow it in substance. If they were a triangle now—as Corinn herself said—three points of a family core, Corinn seemed to want them to understand that she was the apex; Mena and Dariel were the base that supported her.

None of these things was far from her mind during the wind-buffeted funeral procession. Corinn smiled as she fell in step beside Mena. She lifted her arm from the now-obvious swelling of her pregnant belly and rested her fingers on Mena's arm a moment. "Sister," she said, "the day has finally come. We will make our father very happy today. You know that, don't you? I'm sure he always hungered for the day that he would be released into the air like mother was years ago. He'll blend with her and become part of the very soil of this island. He'll be in every acacia tree. Remember that."

That, apparently, was all she meant to say. As she began to move away,

Mena asked, "Are we going to make a better world?" Corinn looked at her, quizzical, and she fumbled for the right way to explain the question. "You didn't know Aliver—at the end, I mean. If you had heard the things he said . . . He had so many ideas of what we should do with power. He talked of a different order to the world. He believed we could eliminate things like the Quota—"

"I don't have quite as much time to ruminate on such things as you do," Corinn said. "Are we going to make a better world? Of course. We rule it instead of Hanish. Who doubts that is an improvement already?"

In her recent conversations with Corinn, Mena had grown wary of disputing her sister. It was not that Corinn grew angry or touchy, as she had done when she was younger. It just seemed that she had usually decided matters in her own way. Once decided, she was unassailable. "Of course it's an improvement," Mena conceded. And then gently added, "It's just that we've not abolished the Quota. We haven't closed the mines or—"

"I don't lack ideals," Corinn said, "if that is what you're suggesting. But speaking of ruling is a very different thing from *actually* ruling. There is no rest from my work. I will get to all the issues you have mentioned in time. For now, we are still hunting down fugitive Meins, those that fled Alecia and Manil with all the treasure they could pile on their yachts. And the provinces . . . you'd be amazed, Mena, how they turn against us, throw up barriers, insist on conditions, lay claim to things that are not theirs to claim. If they would just accept the order of things, we could get on with making the world—what did you say—'better'? And the Lothan Aklun, whom none of us have ever seen, they are a worry hanging over all of this. The irony is that I find myself relying most heavily on two forces I had most loathed before: the league and my Numrek. In the end they made everything possible for me."

Mena almost said that an army fought and thousands upon thousands died for the cause as well. She almost invoked Aliver's sacrifice, almost reminded her sister that the Santoth had a great deal to do with their victory as well. But Corinn had not mentioned *their* victory. She had claimed the Numrek as her own and used the word *me* instead of *our*. Mena could have challenged her on all these things, but instead she said, "I will help in any way I can. Just ask me."

"You are already helping. Carry on with organizing the army and training a new class of Elite. We will need superb warriors, ones with nobility and skill. Who better than you to instruct them?" Corinn smiled, thin lipped and curt. "I hear the storytellers are already spinning a legend about you.

They talk of how you did battle with a goddess and tossed her down from her mountain perch. Those who wish to reopen the academy come to me promising that they will teach your swordsmanship methods as their highest Form. You, my little sister, are as much a legend as Aliver."

"It was just a tree, actually," Mena said, "that the eagle nested in—not a mountain. And I did nothing more than manage to survive against it."

Corinn studied her a moment, amused, her eyebrows ridged like two identical peaks. "The storytellers never get it right, do they? In any event, I am glad that your gallantry was not the death of you."

Suspecting Corinn was about to break away, Mena asked another thing that had been troubling her. "Sister, what did you offer the Numrek for their allegiance? I still don't understand it."

"They may govern a large portion of Talay as they see fit."

Mena thought a moment. "Yes, but that doesn't seem like enough."

"So you say." Corinn looked away, seeming to have lost interest. "Enough speaking, though. We are here to honor two men. Let us do so without distraction."

In many ways it was wonderful to look upon the polyglot diversity of the company that gathered beside the cliffs. They all stood rooted to the earth, trying not to grimace at the bird stink that roared up on the wind ascending the cliff, cold and damp from the sea below. Candovians stood touching shoulders with Senivalians, who, in turn, stood next to Aushenians, brilliant in their white garments. Outer Isles raiders mixed among Acacian aristocrats. Sangae, Aliver's surrogate father, stood among a group of Talayans, beside a band of Halaly, and another of Balbara. Vumuans had tied eagle feathers into their hair. The Bethunis wore pale paint on their faces.

In keeping with tradition, two honored persons not family members lifted the urns from the wagon. Dark-skinned Kelis, healed from the wound that almost took his life on the same day as his friend's, carried Aliver's urn; Melio, with his long brown hair whipped about by the wind, held Leodan's remains: the two of them beautiful in the manner distinctive to their peoples. So young, Mena thought, youthful and strong, full of life. This was all as Aliver would have had it.

She wondered, though, what he would have made of the more dubious guests, like Rialus Neptos, who hovered at the edges of the company, red faced and sniffling, the collar of his cloak pulled up around his ears. Sire Dagon and several other leaguemen also attended, each of them seated on stools carried out for them by servants. What place had those men here— men who had abandoned Leodan, who had for years hunted and tried to destroy Dariel? They watched the proceedings with their chins tilted, their eyes often drifting up into the cloud-heavy sky, as if their minds were already elsewhere.

And Calrach and his Numrek contingent stood in a place of honor. Mena found it hard not to stare at them, almost more so because of the gentility of their demeanor, the neat clothing they wore, and the way each of them had his hair swept back from his face and fastened in a braided tail that hung down his back. Their faces were not actually that different than those of other races. Mena was not sure, however, if she thought they now looked more like other humans than before, or if she had come to feel that other humans resembled the Numrek more than she had acknowledged before.

The ceremony was a simple one. They were gathered together as witnesses. There was no eulogy. No last rites. No words spoken in commemoration of the deceased. No music to play on the watchers' emotions. All of these things had been dealt with previously, in the days leading up to this one. Here, at Haven's Rock, the two dead men were to be released as had all Acacian kings. Corinn made it clear that she considered her brother to have been a king, even if the crown had never officially been placed upon his head.

Once everyone was in place and watching, Corinn took the urn from Melio's hands. She spoke her father's name and wished him peace in returning to the substance of the earth and joy in finding his wife again and becoming one with her. From the moment the stopper was pulled free of the urn, fleeting streams of ashes escaped. When she tipped it down the plume sped away on the wind like smoke, flowing back over the assembled group, back over the island. A moment later, she released Aliver's ashes the same way, thanking him for the feats of heroism he would always be remembered for. Corinn bowed her head and, in so doing, asked them all to hold to silence in remembrance of the dead.

Mena tilted her head but did not close her eyes. She watched her sister, standing with one arm cradling her belly, fingers moving back and forth in small motions to a rhythm kept inside her head. She held still against the wind, as if better to cut through it with the sharp lines of her features. She looked untroubled by emotion. Impatient, yes, but detached in some fundamental way.

The questions that had plagued Mena since Aliver's death came to her again, disturbing what should have been a tranquil moment. She wondered if Aliver had made a mistake that morning when he had agreed to duel Mae-ander. Had he known that he would lose, or had he been so twisted with the desire for revenge that his judgment suffered? She hoped the latter was not true. She wanted to believe that somehow he had done just what he wished to, and that even this was all as he would have wanted it to be. She wanted to believe that her father, all those years before, had set in motion exactly the chain of events he chose to. She wanted to believe that this was all his doing. But, unlike her sister, Mena found it impossible to find solace in absolutes.

Once the ashes were dispersed, Corinn turned and studied the dole-ful faces watching her. She seemed to have little patience for the emotions she read on them. "You here," she said, having to speak loudly to be heard over the wind, "represent all the peoples of the Known World. Do so with pride, with hope for what is to come. These kings of Acacia . . . they are free, as is our nation. We have now the possibility of creating the world these two dreamers wished for." Her gaze fell on Mena for a moment and then passed on. "So, my people, wipe the mourning from your faces and let us turn into the coming days as Leodan and Aliver would have wanted us to. Let us meet them together, with strength in our hearts, with confidence in everything we do."

A few moments later, Corinn stepped away from the cliff. She stopped beside Mena, leaned in close, and asked, "Do you really want to know what I offered the Numrek? There is one thing they want above all else—to re-turn to their homeland and revenge themselves on the Lothan Aklun, who chased them up into the ice years before. This is a war I believe we must par-ticipate in, for our own reasons. When the time is right we will begin to pre-pare. We and the Numrek and the league will launch a fleet into the Gray Slopes against the Lothan Aklun. Once we defeat them, we will control the trade with the Other Lands. *Then* I will have enough power to change the world for the better." Corinn drew back so that she could see her sister's eyes. "Our battles are not over, Mena. We will not be safe until the whole world bows to us. Now you know what I intend."

With that she moved away, leaving Mena standing as the procession is-sued around her. She felt a person beside her and knew it to be Melio when he slipped his hand into hers and asked if she was well. Mena was not sure how to respond. Watching Corinn's back as she receded, she realized that she had not fully acknowledged the world as it was now to be and who was to rule it. She understood for the first time just who her sister really was.

She had heard the title before, but now it came to her like words engraved in the air before her. It stunned her. There before her, receding down the hill through the windswept light of dusk, went the Queen of Acacia, with her forearms cupped around her heir and her entourage close behind her, the future hers to shape.

The End